KEROSENE
COWBOYS

Lorraine,
You have been such a special
friend to me and I love you for it.
you are incredibly beautiful and
stunningly intelligent.

Randy Arrington

July 15, 2007

KEROSENE COWBOYS

MANNING THE SPARE

A NOVEL

RANDY ARRINGTON

iUniverse, Inc.
New York Lincoln Shanghai

KEROSENE COWBOYS
MANNING THE SPARE

Copyright © 2007 by Randall Steven Arrington

iUniverse books may be ordered through booksellers or by contacting:

iUniverse
2021 Pine Lake Road, Suite 100
Lincoln, NE 68512
www.iuniverse.com
1-800-Authors (1-800-288-4677)

This is a work of fiction. All of the characters, names, incidents, organizations, and dialogue in this novel are either the products of the author's imagination or are used fictitiously.

ISBN: 978-0-595-43240-0 (pbk)
ISBN: 978-0-595-87701-0 (cloth)
ISBN: 978-0-595-87581-8 (ebk)

Printed in the United States of America

This novel is dedicated to Stephen "Butch" Freeman (Captain USMC, Ret.) whose zeal for living and for Naval Aviation was as contagious as his brilliant smile. His life was cut short in a tragic aircraft accident on January 25, 2006 in Ketchikan, Alaska.

Butch Freeman was a modern-day *Kerosene Cowboy*, riding a bucking bronco in the rodeo of his two chosen professions. But his bronc wasn't made of hair and hoof it was made of metal and wires, carbon fiber and glass, bombs and bullets. And Butch always rode for the full 8 seconds, every time out of the chute, strapped to his saddle inside the cockpit. From the first day you met Butch, you knew you were in the presence of greatness. You quickly realized that his contagious smile could immediately light up any room, rendering even the most stubborn people helpless to defend against his cheerful demeanor and positive attitude.

Stephen Freeman died on January 25, 2006 displaying his exemplary courage and genuine heroism to the very end. Eyewitness accounts confirm that Butch was maneuvering his L-39 Aircraft until the last possible moment, attempting to steer it away from populated areas on the ground, before finally initiating ejection at tree top level.

Stephen "Butch" Freeman is a true American Hero, who served his country with honor and great distinction. His life was filled with the kind of things that screenwriters extol in their scripts, but movie directors can never adequately capture on the big screen, precisely because it was reality not fantasy. Every one of us should be so lucky.

I'm not exactly sure who first said this but I once heard that courage and honor are the true measures of men. This story is a tribute to a cadre of courageous and honorable men who wear the coveted "wings of gold" proudly on their chest. I was allowed to be one of them for an all too short period of my life. I thank them for molding me into a Tactical Naval Aviator and for occasionally insulating me from my own ineptness.

CHAPTER 1

▼

NO SLACK IN LIGHT ATTACK

0422 is a lonesome, tranquil time of day onboard the Naval Air Station in Belle Chasse, Louisiana. On this dark December morning the only sound was the faint, guttural noise of forlorn frogs advertising desperately for mates. In his BOQ room Lieutenant Brad Ackerman was sprawled comfortably naked, face down in the serenity of a pile of sheets, a Navy issue wool blanket and three feather pillows. For some strange reason he was proud that he had slept in the buff for the past ten years or so. Soon, too soon, his peaceful slumber would be rudely interrupted. That contraption will perform its duty in eight minutes. In just eight short minutes the alarm on that cheap clock radio will spring into action, and the young jet jock will be shocked into relinquishing his deep sleep; awakened by a vulgar apparatus strategically placed on the particle board night stand with only one function, to startle and disturb.

In about an hour Teen Angel, as he was affectionately referred to by his squadron mates, would be conducting a briefing for a group of A-7E Corsair pilots about to fly a War-at-Sea training strike against the battleship USS *Missouri* (BB-63). The huge warship was patiently awaiting their arrival deep in the blue waters of the Gulf of Mexico. This would be the first line period for the *Missouri* since its participation in Operation Desert Storm, some eight months ago. She had been in a dry dock facility in Pascagoula, Mississippi for the past two hundred days undergoing repairs and upgrade modifications. After completion of hostilities in Desert Storm, several key members of the Senate Armed Services Committee had argued for de-commissioning of the *Missouri*, sometime during the second quarter of Fiscal Year 1992. But the Pentagon desired at least three more years of service from the historic battleship, and Navy brass had successfully lobbied Congress to appropriate the necessary funding for the old gray girl. Her initial sea trials began fifteen days ago.

Brad Ackerman's call sign was Teen Angel perhaps because he was cursed with a baby face and looked more like a big kid instead of a single-seat attack pilot. A more likely explanation was all the young women who routinely flocked to him in his white uniform whenever he gave a presentation at "career day" events in the New Orleans area. Undoubtedly this augmented his ego and he thoroughly enjoyed provoking the envy of his squadron mates. This was to be Ackerman's first flight lead since being designated a Strike Leader by the TAR Commanding Officer of VA-204, Commander John "Duke" O'Grady. The CO had earned his call sign "Duke" fourteen years ago primarily because he walked with a John Wayne-like swagger after consuming only a couple of beers. The acronym TAR denoted he was an active duty reservist not a "weekend warrior" like Brad. Nobody else in the squadron knew this but when they were alone, Teen Angel would call the skipper "Puke" because five years ago he had witnessed O'Grady vomit from a moving taxi onto the streets of Perth, Australia. Brad had kept this knowledge to himself revealing the incident to no one, but he never hesitated to gently remind the skipper of their little shared secret. Embarrassment can be a truly humbling experience even for a tactical naval aviator. After several years apart, the two light attack pilots had been reunited as members of the VA-204 *River Rattlers*, a Navy Reserve A-7E squadron home based in southern Louisiana.

At 0530, or *oh dark thirty*, the arrogant yet humble Lieutenant Ackerman would most certainly be confronted by a group of unmerciful, heckling, professional Navy fliers as he attempted to choreograph their movements for the War-at-Sea mission. He would have to be at the top of his game to survive the guaranteed barrage of verbal abuse about to be leveled at him. These men would surely keep him on his toes if only *because* of his new designation as Strike Leader. He would indeed have to earn that title again and again over the next several months, or at least until another fledgling Corsair driver earned the label and replaced him as the latest human target of the old salts.

BUZZZZZZZZZZZZZZZZZZZZZZZZ! "I'm up Mom," was the first response as a dazed half asleep Brad fumbled in the dark for the sleep button on the radio. After locating it he clumsily knocked the plastic box to the deck, but not before he was able to silence its intruding clamor, thus ensuring himself another ten minutes of relaxation in the twin bed. After a few moments, the euphoria of being a flight lead about to direct a division of Corsairs in mock battle against a formidable opponent forced him to rise from the small rack. As he staggered toward the head, his six foot two inch frame stumbled briefly over an empty beer bottle carelessly strewn on the floor. Walking into the bathroom Teen Angel snatched a tennis shoe from the floor, nimbly squashed a good-sized Louisiana cockroach then retrieved the dead insect with five Kleenex tissues. He flushed the lifeless protein carcass down the commode, watching as it swirled around counterclockwise in the water before disappearing into the aperture. Subconsciously, his head gyrated to the motion of the pest until it vanished. The maid would undoubtedly see the remaining bug residue on the wall and clean it up later today, he thought as he tossed the Nike shoe back towards the vicinity of the bedroom.

In the shower, as the stream of warm water was cascading over his body, Teen Angel was already preparing his mind for the sortie he was about to lead. With his eyes closed, he rehearsed in his head the discipline that had become second nature to him over these past seven years as a SLUF driver. Back at Cecil Field, the Corsair instructor pilots had methodically drilled these procedures deep into his brain. At that moment he recalled how the fear of failure always motivated him to over prepare for flights as a student in the A-7E RAG or replacement air group, fleet training squadron. Fear, properly channeled, can be a great motivator.

"No slack in light attack," he whispered to himself through the water and shampoo bubbles dripping over his mouth. This behavioral dynamic had stuck with him in all aspects of life not just flying. A sly smile crossed his lips as he thought how proud his father would be to know this fact if he were still alive to witness it today. Brad's father, a career submariner, was Chief of the Boat for the USS *Scorpion* (SSN-589) when it was tragically lost at sea near the Canary Islands. The disaster had left all 99 of the submarine's crewmen on the ocean floor in May of 1968. He had always considered his dad to be a true American hero and often drew inspiration from his example. Today his demeanor as flight leader would be scrutinized from the first moment of the Ready Room brief until he shut down his jet's turbofan engine to conclude the hop. Although his stomach contained a few butterflies, he was nonetheless confident of his capacity to command the attack jets during this critical training evolution. As he stepped from the refreshing shower, Brad snatched a towel from the rack hanging on the wall then buried his head deep into the caressing white material. As he dried his face with the large cotton cloth he let out an *Indian war yell* to ensure his body was fully awake, and to break the tension. This blood-curdling scream had been a part of his morning regimen ever since his days at Stanford University. It was a scary sound but it always calmed his pent up stress.

Standing in front of a cracked hazy mirror, feet planted casually on the cold linoleum floor, Lieutenant Ackerman began inching a razor across the left side of his face. After each stroke he would turn the faucet back on to dispose of the used lather, unconsciously conserving water like he had been taught while on carrier deployment. On the fourth pass with the double bladed device, he sliced into his skin, surprised by the shrill sound of the alarm clock once again. Briefly, and without warning, humility invaded his thoughts as he realized he had forgotten to reset the switch when he jumped out of the bunk. By the time he reached the radio to retrieve it from the carpeted floor, the phone started to ring and the bath towel began to turn red.

"Ackerman Winter chateau," blurted out Angel in an artificial tone of conceit as he simultaneously silenced the alarm.

"Shut up you skin dick, I'm just calling to make sure you aren't late for your first brief as strike lead," retorted Lieutenant Commander "Rocky" Stone, Brad's very best friend in the squadron. And so it begins Ackerman thought as he wiped away shaving cream sediment from the telephone receiver.

"I'm awake and raring to go Rock, thanks. Do you need a ride to the squadron or did you bring your *porter* with you this time?" Porter was short for air porter, the term Naval Reserve pilots used for the vehicles they left in the employee's parking lot at the New Orleans International airport. Some were more like junk heaps that barely ran instead of dependable automobiles. Rocky's porter was an old Ford *Pinto* that had been painted haze gray and adorned with aircraft lights, radio antennae, a vertical fin and tail numbers so that it looked just like an A-7 Corsair. The car had been handed down within the squadron for the past fifteen years like a pair of old Levi's in a West Virginia coal miner's family. Lieutenant Commander Stone was its latest owner in a long line of distinguished title-holders.

"I managed to get the *gray ghost* cranked up last night, so it's here. I'll see you at the brief in about 40 minutes," Stone replied in a brusque manner, sensing their early morning conversation was far from over.

"Where were you last night Rock? Did you forget we were going to meet at the O' Club for a beer?" A twinge of animosity echoed in Brad's tone.

"I was flying non-rev and got bumped twice. I barely caught the last flight out of Minneapolis." Rocky knew this explanation would solicit sarcasm but he said it anyway.

"How about those airline pass privileges," scoffed Teen Angel. Suddenly he was quite pleased that he had chosen to work as a stunt pilot for Paramount Studios in Hollywood as his civilian occupation, instead of pursuing an airline career like most reserve aviators. The old saying that "fighter pilots make movies, attack pilots make history" held special meaning for Brad because he was an attack pilot that made both history and movies!

"Put an egg in your boot and beat it ass wipe! And save the pompous attitude, you'll need it later." Stone abruptly hung up the phone.

Standing in the cramped bathroom, Brad was in front of the mirror again, this time to double-check his look. He felt a slight sting as he quickly peeled off the tiny section of toilet paper covering his razor nick. Instinctively he began the self-inspection regimen. Main zipper on the green zoom bag properly situated, level with the bottom of his bright orange Velcro nametag. Sleeves rolled up to mid biceps, representing the cool position. Khaki piss cutter cap tilted slightly forward on his scalp, with the proper "rudder up" crease in the rear to further indicate he was a tactical naval aviator. He hated wearing hats but was going to bite the bullet and make an exception this morning. Light brown hair tucked neatly behind the ears to provide that "fresh cut" military facade. Zippers on leg cuffs full open. Black flight boots appropriately dull. "It's time to rock and roll," he proudly announced to himself. Brad grabbed his cherished green flight jacket, quietly slammed the door to the BOQ room, then headed in the direction of his cherry red Porsche; one of two that he owned. The other was in Los Angeles. Driving alone in the hollow blackness the huge pair of gold wings on his front license plate were barely visible. Unexpectedly, Brad recalled the week he had driven this Porsche from Los Angeles to New Orleans. How he had, at first, dreaded even the thought but then how totally enjoyable the actual experience had been traveling along *Route 66*. He impatiently switched the radio station attempting to locate a suitable song for this God-awful time of day in the *Big Easy*.

As Teen Angel sauntered from his 911S toward the squadron building he immediately recognized a familiar figure standing in the shadowy luminescence of an amber nightlight mounted five feet above the side entrance door. The man was clutching an unlit and unfiltered Camel cigarette in his hand, hair slightly in disarray. It was Chief Martin, the *night check* maintenance control supervisor.

Robby Martin was young for a Chief Petty Officer just 29, two years younger than Brad. Despite his youth, Martin had proven to be a damn good Chief.

"Good morning Chief, isn't it a bit early for you to be up?"

"Mornin' Mister Ackerman." Martin rolled his eyes and cleverly avoided responding because it was clearly too early to counter the young officer's taunt.

"Chief, I thought you were trying to quit *again?*" Brad quipped, noticing the unlit cigarette held gently in the chief's hand.

"You don't see any fire at the end do you Lieutenant?"

"So you just have to feed your oral fixation by holding it in your hand, is that it?"

"Something like that sir." Martin was obviously not amused with the early morning levity, especially since he had been working 12-hour shifts for the past three weeks, while Ackerman had been off playing cowboy stunt pilot in LALA land.

Brad hastily slipped past him into the lower deck spaces of the hangar, sensing the Chief's displeasure but knowing he would recover in a few minutes. As he strolled into the squadron Ready Room on the second deck, Teen Angel caught a glimpse of Commander Jack "Juice" Mayhew and Lieutenant Ed "Cookie" Cline huddled near the Bunn coffee maker exchanging one-liners. In the background was the squadron coffee mug board that had rungs for twenty-five personalized, triple-thick mugs. In order of seniority, each pilot had his tactical call sign embossed under his rung with a customized squadron coffee mug dangling down from the brass hanger. Teen Angel's cup was closer to the bottom than to the top, but he didn't mind because he never drank coffee. The wooden piece was a source of tremendous pride amongst the River Rattler aviators because it had an exquisite carving of an A-7 chiseled into the top of the board. As he continued further into the room Teen Angel noticed Rocky in his peripheral vision already comfortably seated in the front row rearranging kneeboard cards.

The Ready Room was basically a trophy area for the squadron. The walls were covered with pictures of past triumphs and numerous plaques and awards the squadron had earned over the past twenty years or so. Three F. Trubee Davison awards were hung in one corner symbolizing that Attack Squadron 204 was the finest Navy Reserve A-7 squadron during those particular years. The *limpus dickus* plaque also adorned an adjacent wall. This plaque bore the name of the aviator who had been the biggest buffoon during the previous month, for any number of reasons. It was truly an honor to receive this type of stigma from your shipmates.

The River Rattler Ready Room was also the main briefing space for missions, but it likewise doubled as a sanctuary where pilots congregated to relax and socialize with each other. Strategically placed on the *We Love Us* wall were framed and matted photographs of past squadron members and some old black and white shots of the A-4 Sky Hawk, the squadron's previous aircraft. The back wall also had an autographed *Blue Angels* lithograph from the 1990 New Orleans Air Show. That year, one of Teen Angel's former LSO students was the opposing solo on the team. Finally, in the rear of the room was an Ace-Deuce board complete with a Plexiglas dice-rolling device. Ace-Deuce was the Navy's term for a shorter version of Backgammon.

"Good morning men. You too Juice!" said Teen Angel with his characteristic sarcasm.

"What are you a stand-up comic? Did you bring any donuts with you Angel?" inquired Commander Mayhew in a cynical tone of voice, as if Brad was only good for one purpose.

"Not this morning sir. I remembered your annual flight physical is scheduled for tomorrow, so we can't have you eating any more fat pills until after your weigh in," taunted Angel.

"Asshole," replied a suddenly sedate Juice as he lowered his head back to the coffee mug. The statement was just a defense mechanism. He really liked Brad.

"He's been on the *Juice Plan* for the last five weeks, and is four pounds under his maximum weight," smiled Cookie.

The "Juice Plan" was how Commander Mayhew prepared for his Navy flight physical, and he had been doing it for the last ten years. A month before his annual trek to the flight surgeon, Mayhew would resort to drinking only diet cranberry juice and eating two *Lean Quisine* diet meals a day in order to drop the twenty extra pounds he routinely sported during the remainder of the year. Juice was overweight because of his affinity for eating big "hunks" of French fries and huge bowls of ice cream at least three times a week. His favorite ice cream was Blue Bell, a brand available only in Texas. In fact, Juice would sometimes take cross-country flights to NAS Dallas just to buy a case of Blue Bell Homemade Vanilla, and to rekindle an old flame or two in the Fort Worth area.

Obviously pleased with how he handled the morning's first encounter, Teen Angel moved over to the dry erase whiteboard. Holding a copy of the VA-204 'River Rattler Briefing Guide' he began to write the intricate details of the hop on the board. In ten minutes he was finished.

"Let's get started gents," said Brad as he placed a War-at-Sea kneeboard card on two chairs for Juice and Cookie. He observed them casually walk to their seats, pick up the cards and sit down. He winked as he handed one to Rocky.

"Attention to brief," stated Angel in an official sounding tone of voice. The three men straightened up and directed their eyes to Brad standing behind the oak podium in the front of the Ready Room. For the next twenty-five minutes, as Ackerman deftly verbalized the particulars for this training mission, each man was busy personalizing his own kneeboard card with radio frequencies, INS positions, rendezvous points, bingo fuel figures, emergency field locations, air defense system capabilities, hard deck altitudes, weapons data and strike profiles. The usual wealth of information contained in a briefing of this magnitude covered most of the front and back of the card. As he was nearing completion of the brief Teen Angel boldly stated what he expected for plane-to-plane communications between the Corsairs.

"All I want to hear out of you guys on the radio is 2, 3, 4, Mayday, or lead you're on fire!" Although his intention was to inject a little satirical humor into the briefing, this sentiment actually portrayed the radio discipline of tactical naval aviators. They were extremely short and to the point whenever they spoke over an open microphone. Air Force pilots on the other hand, were not known for brevity in their communications. In fact they were notorious for being embarrassingly long winded on the radio. Naval Aviators hated this and winced whenever they had to listen to some Air Force pilot broadcast his thoughts over the airways.

"Great line you egotistical Angel," laughed Cookie. "And just where did you learn it from, those movie fags in Hollywood?"

"No, Juice taught it to me seven years ago at NAS Cecil Field in Jacksonville, Florida," replied Brad. Anymore questions before we head to the paraloft?"

"I agree with using HARM, the SAMSON Decoy and the mirror pop-up attack, but why are we simulating delayed fusing on our Snake Eye MK-84 bombs for this mission?" queried Commander Mayhew.

"In the real world sir, I would want the bombs to penetrate deep into the hull before exploding in order to have an increased probability of sinking the warship," responded Ackerman.

"Good answer," said Juice as if he were proud to have been one of Teen Angel's mentors, despite the occasional jesting he had to endure at the hands of the younger aviator in front of their squadron mates.

"ANYMORE questions?" asked Brad in a stern tone of voice. The three pilots shook their heads no in unison and then all four aviators headed down the hallway toward the parachute loft where their flight gear was stored.

As they walked, Rocky and Juice ducked quickly into the men's bathroom for a last head call prior to the hop. But Juice was not really in need of a piss break. He was up to something. Mayhew was going to keep a close eye on these three knuckleheads. Positioned strategically behind the bathroom door as it closed he could hear Teen Angel and Cookie as they passed by chatting unsuspectingly. For the past year and a half, the squadron had been plagued by a merciless practical joker that struck about twice each month. Coincidentally, this timeframe corresponded to the date when Teen Angel, Rocky and Cookie had become members of VA-204. Juice had been the victim of several of these pranks and he was now in close proximity of his three prime suspects. Four months ago Commander Mayhew had privately resolved himself to catch and appropriately reprimand this squadron buffoon, at least to salvage some of the dignity he had lost at the hands of the clown. He listened intently to ensure that Angel and Cookie were indeed heading for the paraloft. He likewise kept an ear out for Rocky standing behind him going about his business at the urinal.

The paraloft was a drab windowless room that housed the squadron's flight gear and all the various paraphernalia associated with that equipment. Three large straps, equipped with parachute Koch fittings, drooped down from the ceiling in one corner. This apparatus was used to make vital adjustments to a torso harness as the pilot would dangle from the sling, suspended about twelve inches above the deck. Most aviators did not look forward to this type of torture because it usually squeezed their balls *blue* during the entire excruciating ordeal. On the opposite side of the room, two ancient-looking sewing machines were situated caddy-corner to each other. The name Singer was so worn on them you had to get your eyes to within a few inches of the contraptions to make out the letters. The tan colored walls of the paraloft were lined everywhere with tall green lockers for storage. In fact the only empty piece of wall had been covered with a picture of Vanna White, that blonde babe from the TV show *Wheel of Fortune*. Vanna had graciously autographed the poster for ultimate personal effect.

The enlisted men known as parachute riggers were responsible for this squadron space and VA-204 was extremely lucky to have one of the very best in the business, Petty Officer First Class Mark Joseph. Joseph was a career sailor. In fact he had been in the Navy for almost twenty-two years now, the last fifteen as a pararigger. Although he had come close on two separate occasions, Joseph had never quite made enough points on his Chief's exam to be promoted to E-7. Brad's father used to always say that when you promoted a First Class to Chief, you just lost a good sailor. In his thinking, it was the First and Second Class Petty Officers who were the true backbone of the Navy. As a young Division Officer

Ackerman had verified this maxim many times over, although the A-7 community did have a cadre of outstanding enlisted men that wore khakis as well.

As Teen Angel and Cookie entered the paraloft together, Petty Officer Joseph was sitting in the corner busily sewing a squadron patch onto the left sleeve of a green nomex flight jacket. He stopped briefly to acknowledge their presence then continued about his business without saying a word. The VA-204 squadron patch depicted a huge open-mouth rattlesnake, its sharp fangs dripping with venom, and the length of its body wrapped several times around a green MK-84 bomb. This entire scene was set against a radiant orange background. The patch was supposed to be rather ominous looking to convey that the squadron was an effective weapons delivery system, a force to be reckoned with; a killing machine just waiting for a target folder. The River Rattler squadron motto *Get in quick, get your load off, get out quicker* was likewise conceived to articulate this menacing attitude. The squadron motto also had a dual meaning when you read between the lines, and the double entendre was somewhat demeaning to the female of the species.

Standing in front of his locker Cookie positioned the top portion of a G-suit around his waist with the zipper directly below his navel. The deep green color of his G-suit was tarnished in several areas with the dull white stains of salty sweat. This discoloration was evidence that the pilot had been working hard pulling many G's while dropping bombs, or in dogfights with other aircraft during Air Combat Maneuvering (ACM) scenarios. Most pieces of flight gear were tinged with these blemishes and they had a slightly offensive odor that permeated them as well. It was something you *expected* and accepted as a tactical naval aviator. A good analogy would be the scuffmarks that a football player might have on his helmet after a hard fought game of knocking heads against a worthy opponent. The scuffmarks like the sweat stains were tantamount to badges of honor. With a quick tug of the slider Cookie zipped the G-suit snug around his mid-section then rotated it ninety degrees to the right.

As he bent down to engage the slider on the leg sections of his G-suit, Cookie looked up at Teen Angel and chuckled as he said, "You remember the last hop we flew with Juice?"

"Yea, we kicked his ass all over the Eagle Golf Warning Area during those dogfights," Brad said with a devious smile on his face. "He never did figure out that we had conspired to team up against him on every ACM engagement."

"Remember in the brief how he had called us 'target A and target B' in that conceited tone of voice, and informed us that we were merely *grapes* ripe for his picking?" added Cookie.

"Uh huh, then how utterly demure he was during the debriefing after we waxed his ass." As they chatted, both men were unaware that Juice was listening to their conversation a mere twenty feet from them.

"So you two *little pups* ganged up against me on that ACM hop last week huh," blurted out an enraged Juice as he broke up their dialogue and marched straight towards them. Only then did Teen Angel and Cookie realize that Commander Mayhew had been standing just outside the paraloft door eavesdropping on their entire conversation. "Well boys, I have ways of getting even with young bucks like you, and you both just made my shit list!"

"Throttle back Juice," said Rocky as he sauntered nonchalantly into the paraloft, just in time to save the two Lieutenants from one of Commander Mayhew's infamous tirades. "Let's finish suiting up and get to our jets shipmates, we got a hop to take and a battleship waiting for us in Whiskey-91," Rocky adamantly reminded them. Grabbing their helmet bags, Cookie and Teen Angel quickly departed the paraloft then ambled slowly in the direction of Maintenance Control.

"Are you about through with my flight jacket Petty Officer Joseph?" queried a suddenly calmer Commander Mayhew as he meandered over to his locker.

"Yes sir, I am just finishing it up now. It'll be waiting for you when you return from your hop," answered Joseph.

Nodding approval, Juice opened his locker. As the door swung out, a huge and very realistic looking rubber snake fell onto Jack Mayhew's head, settling near his feet.

"Oh shit!" screamed the Commander as he leaped away from the falling snake. "I am gonna castrate that guy when I catch him" shouted Juice in disgust, simultaneously hoping his fear had not shown too clearly. Petty Officer Joseph and Lieutenant Commander Stone couldn't help but snicker, even if it was in suppressed silence. At the entrance to the stairwell, Teen Angel and Cookie could hear Mayhew's outburst. They briefly scanned each others face, wondering who was the practical joker, then with a quick wink of the eye decided it was time to get to Maintenance Control.

CHAPTER 2

▼

TIME TO ROCK & ROLL

Sitting atop a large countertop were four green discrepancy books containing all the maintenance, QA, fuel and ordnance data for the jets assigned to each pilot on this training mission. Standing patiently behind the counter was Chief Martin ready to respond to any questions the aviators might pose regarding the status of an aircraft or its systems. It was Martin's job to have all the correct answers at his fingertips, to resolve any maintenance problems that might arise and to ensure the sortie was launched without any unnecessary delay. Plopping both helmets down near their feet, Teen Angel and Cookie grabbed the aircraft books and began to scan through the maze of paperwork contained within. Pilots routinely reviewed the last ten or fifteen discrepancies or *gripes* that had been logged after previous flights, to get a better feel for what they might expect from their jets during this hop. Five minutes later Rocky and Juice entered Maintenance Control and joined in the ritual.

"Did you comb your hair with a shoe this morning Chief Martin?" teased Rocky looking up from his discrepancy book. A few giggles could be heard in the background from several enlisted men working in the shop. Undoubtedly, the chief would make them pay for their insolence in the near future.

"No sir, my crew has been slugging it out for the past eleven hours and I didn't have a chance to spruce up this morning. We're still making last minute preparations for the annual corrosion inspection scheduled to begin tomorrow at 0800," said an obviously exhausted Martin.

"Port and starboard for three weeks huh?" quizzed Lieutenant Commander Stone.

"Yes, I've been working them hard, but they will pass with flying colors," piped in Commander Mayhew.

"Thanks MO, I believe we're ready for yet another opportunity to excel," added the Chief, acknowledging Mayhew's status as the squadron's TAR Maintenance Officer.

"I am counting on you to take care of CAG Sullivan this weekend on the golf course Angel, when he's not flying," said Juice reminding Brad that it was his responsibility to keep the Carrier Air Wing Commander busy and out of the skipper's hair for the next two days.

"I'm up to the task sir. I'll hand "Squid" Sullivan his lunch on the golf course," replied Ackerman with his characteristic assured demeanor.

"That's Captain Sullivan to you Lieutenant," said Juice briefly slipping into his formal military tenor for the benefit of the enlisted men present.

"Duty, honor, country and eighteen holes on the links, is that your creed Angel?" asked Cookie Cline sarcastically.

"If ordered to go into harm's way, that's where I'll go boys. Just steer me into the wind and launch me," cracked Brad. The officers all chuckled, signed for their aircraft then headed for the jets parked on the flight line. Judging by the stoic look on his face, for the second time this morning Chief Martin was not amused.

"See you in a couple of hours Chief, I'm gonna take this jet out for a spin," remarked Commander Mayhew as he politely handed his discrepancy book to Martin.

As the four pilots departed the hangar bay and walked into the crisp dawn air of the ramp area, brilliant rays of orange sunlight were now visible emanating from the East. These beams of early morning radiance cast long, sinister shadows over the aircraft and every piece of ground support equipment positioned on the tarmac. The cool stiff breeze from the Southwest whipped around the men's faces blowing their hair as they strode confidently toward the airplanes. A dull whirring sound was audible as the wind flurried about their ears. It was indeed an eerie yet familiar scene for the men of naval aviation. As he arrived at Corsair number 411, Brad's eyes quickly found his name stenciled in black ink on the side of the haze gray aircraft just below the cockpit. It read: Lt. Brad Ackerman, *Teen Angel*. His call sign, like all of them, was italicized for added effect. Every time he saw his name printed on the cheek of 411, a sudden flash of self-esteem would tickle down his spine like a shiver during a chilly evening. It was another reminder that he had the honor of wearing the wings of gold.

As if transplanted into a surreal daydream, Brad suddenly found himself wandering through the memory banks of his brain. He thought of his last flight in the Training Command, eight years ago in Beeville, Texas and how the Commanding Officer of VT-25, his advanced jet training squadron, had met him at the ladder of the TA-4 Sky Hawk as he climbed down from the cockpit. When Brad's flight boots hit the ground, the skipper popped the cork on a bottle of Moet champagne to be the first to congratulate a new Naval Aviator and to help Brad celebrate the achievement. When Ackerman turned to face the CO, the skipper promptly planted a shiny new pair of gold aviator's wings onto Brad's nametag over the left side of his chest. This was his *informal* winging ceremony right there on the ramp, standing in the leaked oil and hydraulic fluid. Brad recalled the absolute rush of pride and satisfaction he felt as he strolled into the squadron spaces, walking amongst the instructor pilots and his student naval aviator colleagues. He was now wearing the much-coveted wings of gold.

He recollected how three days later at the *formal* winging ceremony his mother, with a little assistance from the Commodore, had pinned fourteen karat gold wings onto the left side of his dress white uniform. A small tear trickled down her cheek, tugging at the strings of Brad's heart and causing him to miss his father even more. Surely Chief William Ackerman would be proud of his only son's accomplishment on this day. Brad recalled that two hours later Nancy O'Donnell had invited him to her house after the ensuing party to continue the celebration. Ackerman had been flirting with Nancy, the assistant manager of the Officer's Club, for the better part of a year without one shred of success. But the Texas-bred, blonde beauty had routinely given him the cold shoulder, much to the dismay of the usually confident Ackerman.

Nancy's rebuffs would knock Brad down a peg or two but he was always more than willing to take another shot at her. Later that night, after he left his mother at her hotel room, Brad shared a bottle of Chardonnay with Nancy at her ranch style home in the suburbs of Beeville. The two laughed, chatted and flirted into the wee hours of the morning. He chuckled to himself as he abruptly remembered his precious gold wings as they lay on her bedroom carpet. In the haste to remove his dress white uniform, he had crumpled the shirt and tossed it aside without a second thought. He had finally gotten to have sex with one of the most desired single women onboard NAS Beeville and he did so for hours. He was indeed a Naval Aviator. His boyhood dream had come true.

As his mind slowly departed this brief interlude of self-gratification, Brad spotted Airman Bobby Boone. The young plane captain was eagerly awaiting his arrival at the nose cone of the jet. Corsair 411 was Boone's airplane as well and the jet displayed his name in black ink on the nose wheel door. It read: Airman Bobby Boone from Tulsa, Oklahoma. Surely the young enlisted man felt a similar sense of pride from this sight, probably bragging to old High School buddies and his parents. Boone was a good sailor and well deserving of respect. He had always cared for this jet as if it were his prize automobile just waiting for the proper time to cruise the French Quarter in search of a nineteen-year-old honey to neck with in the back seat.

The young plane captain was lingering at the nosecone in anticipation of receiving Brad's signal to dive the duct, a ritual required before every flight in the A-7E. The lip of the intake duct was approximately nineteen feet from the jet's huge turbofan engine. Over the years several Corsairs had suffered severe engine damage due to unseen foreign objects (FOD) being sucked into the turbine blades during the starting procedure. To prevent this calamity a plane captain or the pilot would crawl down the entire length of the intake to ensure that nothing was lurking in the duct or in the vicinity of the turbine blades. Missing tools, forgotten rags, stray bolts, or even a loose quarter had the potential to chew up a million-dollar jet engine. With a quick nod, Brad signaled his consent and Boone leaped down the intake to perform the inspection, his faded dungarees and work boots disappearing in a flash.

Using his peripheral vision, Teen Angel shot a casual cursory glance in the direction of his wingmen. He could see all of them standing in front of their jets waiting for plane captains to back out of the duct, prior to beginning their own extensive preflight checks. Behind him, Brad recognized the muffled groan of a *huffer*, or air start machine, as it cranked up in preparation for the jet engine starting sequence. The machine was used to send a continuous blast of compressed air into the turbine blades in order to assist the pilot in cranking up the turbofan engine. It was sort of a jumpstart for the Corsairs.

All around the flight line dozens of trouble-shooters were in their assigned positions. There were ordnance men, electricians, hydraulics technicians, engine mechanics, liquid oxygen men, avionics specialists and airframes experts all waiting in the wings looking forward to their cue in this familiar choreography. A Line Chief was monitoring the entire show. Senior Chief Esposito was a crusty old man of fifty-three with a beer belly and a shaved head. He had been in the Navy since Christ was a corporal and had seen and done just about everything a sailor could. Right now he was standing in the middle of his personal congregation, two-way radio in hand, barking out orders. All that was needed was a director's chair, a few motion picture cameras, accompanied by several hanging spotlights and this could indeed be mistaken for a Hollywood production on a sound stage thought Angel. In three minutes, Airman Boone pushed himself out of the intake duct and reported that all was clear to Lieutenant Ackerman. After signaling his thumbs up endorsement, Brad immediately began to preflight the attack jet.

"Let's kick a tire then light the fire," exclaimed a jubilant Angel as he began his walk around inspection, with Airman Boone in tow close behind.

Ackerman's circular route around the attack jet allowed him to check the condition of the tires, wheel brake assemblies, struts, angle-of-attack probe, hydraulics reservoirs, oil gauges, bombs and bomb racks, AIM-9M Sidewinder missile, 20MM gattling gun, engine tail cone, vertical fin, wings, literally every system or moving part on the aircraft. But, for a moment he lost focus again. His mind was wandering, and he was now merely going through the motions. Teen Angel looked like a man nonchalantly deciding whether or not to purchase the jet, and Boone was his salesman. Brad was thinking about women and it wasn't even 7AM.

Lieutenant Ackerman had a woman in every airport and they were all five to seven years younger than him. He had a blonde in Dallas, a redhead in Denver, a brunette in Atlanta. There was the preacher's daughter in Phoenix, the Jazzercise instructor in Manhattan, the news reporter in Seattle, the surfer chic in Maui and the starlet in Hollywood. Of course at this moment he was absorbed by the prospects of the Southern Belles here in New Orleans. They were his personal love garden and he watered them as often as possible. A late night phone call, a long gushy letter, a cute Hallmark card, or a dozen roses were just a few of the techniques Brad used to keep them happy until his next visit to their city. Like Brian Wilson of the Beach Boys, Brad wished they could all be *California Girls*, even though there seemed to be a higher threshold of excitement and intrigue in his love life because he only saw these women a few times during the year.

… Concentrate on the mission you idiot, he thought to himself as he shook off the daydream. In ten minutes he was finished with his pre-flight and ready to strap on this 42,000 pound workhorse of Naval Aviation. Brad climbed up the wobbly ladder on the port side of the Corsair. He gently tossed his helmet, chart bag and kneeboard into the cockpit, then straddled the canopy railing. Positioning his head near the top portion of the McDonnel Douglas ejection seat, Angel checked to make certain that the head knocker on the face curtain handle was *safe*. He then repeated the inspection on the lower ejection handle prior to plopping his butt squarely into the hardness of the seat pan. After placing a foul smelling skullcap onto his head, to protect his precious blonde locks, Ackerman donned his gray helmet then waited for Airman Boone to ascend the ladder.

As if to kill time, Angel began to arrange the cockpit of the attack jet, giving it a personalized touch. He placed his pocket NATOPS in the port side of the windscreen underneath the bulletproof glass, in close proximity to the head-up display (HUD). The pages of the checklist were noticeably tattered from use and stained with red hydraulic fluid. Brad then strapped the black kneeboard onto his left thigh making sure he had two government-issue pens available in the side receptacles. Teen Angel was the only A-7 pilot in VA-204 who wore his kneeboard on the left thigh. For him this seemed more natural even though he wrote with his right hand and the kneeboard tended to crowd the throttle quadrant and catapult grip.

Flight gloves were tossed casually into the lower left side of the cockpit underneath the G-suit connection hose. The size nine gloves appeared to be brand new, but in fact they had never been worn. Most tactical carrier aviators did not wear the green nomex protection because of their tendency to get slippery in salt water. Burned hands always seemed preferable to the thought of drowning in a parachute being dragged down beneath a massive flat top boat steaming at twenty knots. Ackerman secured his navigational chart bag into its position on the starboard side of the cockpit adjacent to the INS and weapons computer. This cozy little nest would be his for the next couple of hours.

When the plane captain reached the side railing of the cockpit he immediately began to strap his pilot into the jet. Boone assisted Brad with both Koch fittings on his parachute, plugged in the pilot's G suit hose then connected Ackerman's oxygen line and communications cables. This was a form of royal treatment that all tactical naval aviators received from their plane captains before each hop. After flaunting a toothy smile and flashing an enthusiastic thumbs up sign to his pilot, Boone patted Brad on the left shoulder then descended to the black tarmac. Teen Angel gave him an appreciative wink as he climbed down. Once on the deck, Boone stowed the ladder, buttoned up the left side of the fuselage then situated himself directly in front of the aircraft to prepare for Lieutenant Ackerman's command to begin the start sequence on the Corsair's TF-41 turbofan engine.

Scanning the flight line once more, Ackerman was literally amazed at what he saw. The first movements of this aviation symphony were unfolding before his eyes and it made him feel so proud. Men and machines were in constant motion, sometimes crisscrossing each other's paths. Rocky, in airplane 401, had already completed his engine start and was conducting the post-start checklist. His jet's ailerons, rudder and elevator were being tested to the limits of their travel. Juice was also cranked up, raising one finger high into the air even as he was entering latitude and longitude coordinates into his inertial navigation system (INS) and weapons computer. One finger in the air was the HEFOE signal indicating that a pilot needed a hydraulics trouble-shooter. Brad spotted the hydraulics *bowser* already on its way to the left wheel well of Commander Mayhew's aircraft. Cookie Cline was just beginning his engine start and Brad witnessed the huffer hose snap swiftly into its full shape as compressed air inflated the sixteen-foot long fabric tube.

Two seconds after receiving a nod of approval from Lieutenant Ackerman, Airman Boone signaled for the NC-8 to be plugged into its receptacle on the left side of the plane's fuselage. Suddenly Teen Angel's instrument panel sprang to life as twenty-eight volts of electricity streamed into the Corsair cockpit giving it electronic life. As he made a quick peek at his instrument panel, Brad felt the attack jet shake as the steel nozzle head of the huffer hose was twisted and locked into its position on the rear of the fuselage. Ackerman next gave the signal to apply the huffer air to his jet's engine. With a dull roar, compressed air began to turn the jet's huge turbine blades. At 15% fan speed, Brad introduced fuel and ignition into the progression as the powerful engine slowly wound up to its idle speed. Now turning on its own power, Ackerman signaled for Airman Boone to remove the huffer nozzle and NC-8 from the aircraft. Brad could hear the familiar whine of the TF-41 engine despite the heavy ear protection padding of his helmet. That sound always managed to take his breath away, every time he heard it. It made him feel simultaneously humble and arrogant.

"I may have to catch up with you guys Angel," said Juice on the #2 UHF, or *back* radio, as it was called in the Corsair community. "PC-1 is acting up. I'll keep you informed."

"Roger that Juice, if you don't make the hop Teen Angel flight will revert to attack plan Bravo," stated Ackerman knowing that all the pilots were listening on the squadron's tactical frequency dialed into their back radio.

"Two," replied Rocky.

"Three," answered Juice.

"Four," said Cookie. All three aviators understood the situation and had given the flight leader their short replies of acquiescence.

"411, maintenance control," called Chief Martin on the tactical frequency.

"Go ahead Chief," responded Lieutenant Ackerman.

"402 is the back up jet for this sortie, I am having the discrepancy book brought out to the flight line now just in case the MO's aircraft goes down," advised Chief Martin.

"Roger that Chief, thanks," said Brad abruptly. This episode represented yet another example of the "can do" attitude exhibited by every man in a carrier squadron. Chief Martin was on the ball as usual, despite the amount of sleep he had lost over the last three weeks.

While conducting his post-start checklist, Angel noticed the oxygen gauge on the instrument panel was registering 1100 psi, about seven hundred psi less than the minimum required for this training mission. He held up 4 fingers indicating that he needed the lox man, or liquid oxygen trouble-shooter. As Airman Boone relayed the signal to the Line Chief holding the walkie-talkie, Brad recollected the first time he saw the movie "Lox Man" as a Student Naval Aviator back at Pensacola Naval Air Station. The videotape was similar to all those overly dramatic VD flicks routinely shown to high school students in a futile attempt to scare them into temporary celibacy.

The "Lox Man" depicted a nineteen-year old airman that had mishandled an oxygen bottle during a refilling cycle. The youngster had been critically burned during the accident by the liquid oxygen. The film showed him laying on a gurney in obvious agony from the third degree burns he had suffered to most of his body during the lox explosion. Unlike the VD flicks from his high school days, this film had indeed made a life-long impression on Brad and he was always extra careful with liquid oxygen.

As he was completing his post-start checks, Teen Angel watched in his peripheral vision as Cookie in aircraft 415 was undergoing the final check inspection. Lieutenant Cline's hands dangled loosely over the canopy railing, well outside of the cockpit, to ensure he didn't accidentally activate something while several men were busily scouring all around his airplane in search of anything out of order. Rocky had already been through the final checker and was now taxiing his jet into the marshal or holding area on the far side of the VA-204 flight line. There the two aviators would patiently await Ackerman's arrival. Brad noticed how the bright sun sparkled off the reflective tape pasted to their helmets. In another five minutes he would pick them up in marshal and assume the flight lead for the short taxi to the arming area. Angel felt a sudden shudder as the oxygen trouble-shooter installed a new lox bottle into an access panel on the side of his warplane. The oxygen gauge now registered 1800 psi. The jet was good to go.

The commotion around Corsair 404, Commander Mayhew's plane, had assumed an almost hectic pace as Senior Chief Esposito was personally supervising the maintenance effort on the aircraft's PC-1 hydraulics system. In tactical naval aviation, missing a sortie was an almost unforgivable sin and the Line Chief would not allow it to happen on his watch. Senior Chief Esposito's face was perceptibly red and the veins in his neck distended from the stress-induced blood flow. As he snarled out his commands, a fine mist of saliva was emitted from his mouth and his baldhead rocked back and forth. Most of the enlisted men of VA-204 were afraid of the Senior Chief. So were most of the officers. Teen Angel *respected* Chief Esposito, which was his euphemism for fear.

As the final checker gave Lieutenant Ackerman his thumbs up of approval, Brad taxied 411 slowly toward Cookie and Rocky parked in the marshal area.

"Teen Angel," said Brad over the #1 UHF radio, prompting his flight members to check in on the primary frequency.

"Two," snapped Rocky after hearing the prompt from his flight leader.

"Four," said Cookie, out of order.

"Three will be along in five minutes Angel," Juice sighed as if relieved to have his PC problem almost solved by the maintenance crew. Brad said nothing in reply to the other aviator's comments. This was expected behavior on the primary frequency. Other people would be listening, not just VA-204 personnel, as was the case with the back radio.

"Navy Ground, River 10, taxi three with the numbers and clearance," said Angel in a low husky tone of voice. Some of the female controllers nagged that he sounded mean on the radio. Brad knew it was just his no-nonsense tone of voice, nothing more.

"River 10, taxi to runway twenty-two, altimeter 29.98," replied a squeaky, unsure female voice from the air traffic control tower situated high above the Base Operations building, about 400 yards to the Southwest of the River Rattler flight line. Yep, she was one of the women who complained about Brad's tone of voice on the radio. Slimy split tail, thought Angel with a smirk.

With permission given, Lieutenant Ackerman slowly maneuvered his gray jet near the marshal area toward taxiway Alpha, which led to the arming area and runway twenty-two. He could see Rocky sitting patiently with his oxygen mask dangling off to the right side of his helmet. This was the *cool* position for the mask. As Angel passed Lieutenant Commander Stone's aircraft, Rocky gunned his engine and quickly moved into position about twenty feet behind and slightly to the right of Brad's jet. Cookie did the same a few seconds later, taxiing his Corsair so that it was approximately 40 feet behind Teen Angel and just to the left of the centerline on the taxiway. From a distance they resembled a mother duck with two ducklings in trail. As they arrived and parked in the arming area, six ordnance men, or *ordies*, met them eager to perform their roles in this dance routine. They also wanted to get back to the squadron so they could have a bite of breakfast in the squadron's enlisted mess. It is funny how a person can actually look forward to a small carton of milk, a glazed donut and some Doritos chips at 7:00 in the morning.

The sun now fully illuminated the city of New Orleans and its suburbs with yellow-orange rays of light. The sky was a cloudless beautiful blue, bluer than Julia Roberts' eyes thought Angel. Of course Julia had dark brown eyes, but that didn't really matter to Brad, it was his thought that counted. Nonetheless, it was a great day to be flying and the Navy was even going to pay them to do it. After each pilot brought his jet to a complete stop, both hands again came well out of the cockpit, resting lazily on the canopy rails. Helmets nodded approval almost in unison as the ordies began to perform their jobs.

The ordnance men checked the MK-84 practice bombs, ensuring they would drop when the pilot pressed the pickle switch in the cockpit and that the Snake Eye fins would deploy during his attack run. The one-ton, blue practice bombs were duds and could not explode. The *ordies* charged and armed the 20MM gattling guns with live ammunition, and conducted their heat checks on the seeker heads of the AIM-9M Sidewinder Missiles. As a heat light was passed over the slate gray, sensitive head of the big blue missile, each pilot would hear the characteristic *growl* of the Sidewinder. This growl meant that the *heater* missile was indeed responsive to a thermal lamp and was more than capable of locking up a hot target for acquisition and destruction. Next the ordies checked the condition of the TACS pods on each aircraft. These devices would record the entire mission for playback in the air combat debriefing facility that the Louisiana Air National Guard (LAANG) had built the previous year onboard NAS New Orleans. The Air Force pukes were good enough to let VA-204 use the building, if they were appropriately humble when asking for permission.

"404, leaving the final checker headed your way Teen Angel," said Juice on the back radio.

"Looks like we're a flight of four again boys so its attack plan Alpha. Teen Angel flight, switch to button three," instructed Brad.

"Two, three, four," was the response from his wingmen. Ackerman would hear this same comeback each time he changed radio frequencies during the mission. It let him know they were listening to the proper *freak*. Seven minutes later the division was ready for takeoff.

"Navy tower, River 10 ready for departure," called Brad on button three of the #1 UHF radio.

"River 10 is cleared for takeoff, wind is 240 degrees at 6 knots, contact New Orleans departure on 256.9 when airborne, have a safe flight," said the controller.

"River 10 is cleared," responded Brad to the controller's radio communication. Ackerman lowered and locked his canopy, then fastened his oxygen mask tightly to his helmet. He was now breathing 100% pure oxygen. As Teen Angel taxied across the hold short line, he checked the orange windsock to verify the wind call of the tower controller. The breeze was indeed coming from 240 degrees at about 6 or 8 knots. Brad maneuvered his jet onto the left quarter of the runway leaving enough room for the other three warplanes to get into an echelon right formation on the concrete. With the prevailing wind coming from their right, Ackerman positioned his aircraft on the left so that any residual vortices, or disturbed airflow created during the takeoff run would be blown away from each successive airplane as it rolled down the runway. Out of the corner of his right eye, Brad saw that his wingmen were now in a right echelon formation awaiting his next command.

"Its time to rock and roll boys," affirmed Teen Angel on the back radio.

CHAPTER 3

▼

KEROSENE COWBOYS

Brad raised his right hand so that it was visible to his wingmen through the Corsair's canopy glass. He held out two fingers moving in a quick back and forth motion, meaning he wanted all the jets to come up to full military power for one final engine and systems check prior to the takeoff roll. The roar of the four TF-41 engines was deafening to the unguarded ear. 15,000 pounds of thrust on each airplane was now being held at bay only by the powerful anti-skid disc brakes of the jets. The tremendous power of the turbine engine created a visible little tornado starting at the tip of each intake duct and leading down to the black concrete. This phenomenon was unique to the Corsair. It was so powerful that it could suck up *anything* within a fifteen-foot radius, without mercy or discrimination.

After making a satisfactory final assessment of his own aircraft's condition, Brad turned to his wingmen and immediately received three thumbs up. I was indeed *time to rock and roll*. Raising his hand straight up from the right canopy rail, palm facing towards his helmet, Teen Angel paused for a second then plunged his hand smartly forward. At that moment he dropped both boot heels to the floorboard, releasing his brakes, then reduced power on the throttle by about two percent as the jet lurched forward. This minor thrust reduction gave Rocky a slight power advantage as the two Corsairs began their "section go" takeoff roll. Racing down the runway, Lieutenant Commander Stone stayed in perfect parade position on Teen Angel's starboard side. The small power cushion allowed Rocky to maneuver slightly forward or aft to keep the proper sight picture during the takeoff and climb out. Eight seconds later, Juice and Cookie began their takeoff roll in tandem. As Juice made the same minute power reduction for his wingman, Angel and Rocky had already broken ground and were airborne now climbing to the Southwest, airspeed 170 knots and increasing rapidly.

As his jet passed 40 feet above the ground (AGL), Lieutenant Ackerman nudged his head conspicuously forward, hesitating briefly, then shifted it straight back into the headrest of the ESCAPAC ejection seat. Teen Angel then reached down and raised the gear handle with his left hand. Rocky followed suit perfectly, his wheel well doors closing just a millisecond before Brad's, locking the landing gear safely inside the belly of the plane. Two seconds later, with another familiar head bob, both pilots raised their flaps in order to accelerate to 300 knots for the division rendezvous.

"Departure, River 10 airborne proceeding to Tibby," Brad informed the ATC controller who monitored traffic in the Terminal Control Airspace (TCA) surrounding New Orleans.

"River 10, flight of four, climb and maintain ten thousand feet, cleared direct to the Tibby Military Operating Area (MOA)," answered a familiar voice.

"River 10," responded Ackerman. Now at a comfy speed of 300 knots and climbing at a rate of 3500 feet per minute, Brad anticipated the join up of the second section of Corsairs led by Commander Mayhew. A moment later, after adjusting his side view mirror, he saw Juice and Cookie slide into perfect starboard echelon. Lieutenant Commander Stone had already completed a "cross under" maneuver and was now comfortably situated on Teen Angel's left wing. Turning his head toward 401, Ackerman immediately observed Rocky flipping him the bird. This was the traditional form of greeting between Naval Aviators while they were plying their chosen profession. Angel took a deep breath of pure oxygen, grinned inside his polyurethane mask and returned the salutation with an aggressive middle finger pressed tight against the canopy glass. Now that his division was joined, Brad smoothly leveled off at 10,000 feet and accelerated the Corsairs to 480 knots airspeed for the short flight into the Warning Area and the War-at-Sea training strike.

Leaving the township of Thibbodoux, Louisiana behind the formation, Teen Angel reported "feet wet" to the ARTCC controller in Houston. The Corsairs were now over the choppy blue waters of the Northern Gulf of Mexico ready to begin their search for "Big Shot," which was the tactical call sign of the battleship *Missouri* on the "card of the day" for December 5, 1991.

"River 10, Houston Center, roger feet wet, cleared to operate in Tibby MOA and the Whiskey-91 Warning Area, surface to 40,000 feet, change to tactical frequency, report back up on this freak for your RTB," instructed the center controller.

"River 10 switch to button eleven," was Brad's concise reply. With a motion of Lieutenant Ackerman's hand, his wingmen kicked out into a loose tactical formation and fine-tuned their radar equipment for a surface search. The hunt for the massive target had begun. A day earlier the skipper of *Missouri*, Captain Barney Kelley, had sent a message to VA-204 informing the squadron exactly where his warship would be positioned for the training exercise. But part of the drill was to test the airplane's search capabilities, so Captain Kelley did not have his boat in the exact spot where he said it would be. It was gamesmanship and the aviators expected it. Nine minutes into the search the battleship was located.

"Ten O'clock, 42 miles Angel," reported Cookie over the back radio.

"Roger that, proceed to your initial positions (IP's)," ordered Ackerman. With that said, Lieutenant Cline pulled his jet straight up at 5 G's, banked suddenly to the right then flipped the Corsair onto its back pulling violently for the water's surface. Two seconds later, Commander Mayhew performed one and a half aileron rolls his aircraft ending up inverted. He too yanked hard toward the water in a split S maneuver, but in a different direction than Lieutenant Cline. Brad began a slow but steady descent for the attack section's IP. Lieutenant Commander Stone added a handful of power raised his nose forty degrees above the horizon then performed a slow barrel-roll over Ackerman's jet finishing in perfect Tac-Form position on Teen Angel's right wing. In ten minutes the Corsairs were in a holding pattern, in position and ready for the strike games to begin.

"Big Shot, Big Shot, River 10 is ready for our attack run," said Brad on the pre-briefed UHF frequency.

"River flight this is Big Shot, you are cleared hot on the spar, one half mile astern," was the retort.

"River 10 roger. Teen Angel time hack, begin attack in 60 seconds, ready, hack," declared Brad on the #2 UHF radio. At that moment, each pilot started the sweep movement on the second hand on their aircraft's eight-day clock. The mock war would begin in one minute and each pilot was responsible to have his jet at the pre-determined inbound location, at the correct airspeed and altitude for push time.

Of course this was only a minimal simulation. If this were a real War-at-Sea strike by an entire Air Wing and Battle Group there would be twenty or more airplanes involved. F-14 Tomcats, or *turkeys*, would be flying top cover for the strike package, defending it and the mother ship from enemy fighter aircraft and missiles. An E-2 Hawkeye, or *hummer*, would be providing airborne early warning information about the activity of those adversary airplanes and missile launches. The E-2 would supply vectoring data to the Tomcats for their intercepts of any inbound bandits, while controlling a three hundred nautical mile diameter of airspace around the carrier. The EA-6 Prowler, or *double ugly*, would be actively jamming enemy radar sites and disrupting their radio communications. The S-3 Viking, or *hoover*, would be delivering over-the-horizon targeting info via the data link system, while dissecting the ocean in search of rival submarines. The A-6 Intruder, or *ugly*, would be an integral part of the strike group, launching HARM missiles, conducting laser designation of targets and carrying about two times as much ordnance as the SLUF A-7 Corsair. Finally, two types of helicopters would provide a search and rescue (SAR) capability to the strikers, behind enemy lines and in the vicinity of the aircraft carrier. Not to mention the various friendly surface ships and submarines that would undoubtedly be included into the mixed bag of good guys.

Exactly 60 seconds from the time hack, Cookie commenced his simulated SAMSON run at the battleship. SAMSON was a type of airborne distraction used by most Strike Leaders and it always preceded the main package. Brad had first learned about the advantages of using this decoy device while he was a student in the Strike Leader Attack Training Syllabus (SLATS) at NAS Fallon, Nevada. *Strike U* as it was called, was the *Top Gun* school for Navy attack pilots and the instructors there were big proponents of using airborne diversionary tactics during Alpha Strikes. Basically, the awkward looking mechanism replicated the flight characteristics of an inbound aircraft that would inevitably be detected and tracked by an enemy's acquisition radar. In turn, this inbound bogey would hopefully stimulate the fire control radar to light off and launch surface to air missiles in its defense. If the enemy's Surface-to-Air-Missile (SAM) site did launch its arsenal at the false target, the Strike Leader would have several HARM (High Speed Anti-Radiation) missiles already in the air and these weapons would then home in on that fire control radar location and ultimately destroy the SAM facility. This is what was known as a *hard kill*.

If the enemy radar was shut down to protect its position from the HARM missiles, this was known as a *soft kill*. Either way, the main strike package would have a safe window of opportunity, or refuge within which they could release their bombs on target. Maybe thirty-five to forty-five seconds of time would be sufficient sanctuary for the attackers to get in safely and drop their loads. In fact the Israelis had informed the Pentagon that during all of their previous armed conflicts, the SAMSON decoy flying at 250 knots or more had never failed to stimulate the fire control radar of a single enemy SAM site. It had worked to perfection each time it was used. Reliability had been battle-tested.

Lieutenant Cline was now flying a SAMSON profile of 300 knots at 500 feet over the water on a course of 180 degrees. His radar lock on the USS *Missouri* indicated the huge ship was steaming Westbound at 12 knots, about one third of the speed capability of the boat. Cookie Cline had started his run from exactly seventeen and a half miles away from the battleship. This flight pattern would situate his airplane on top of the target at three minutes and thirty seconds after the push time (3 + 30). Radar detection equipment inside the Corsair cockpit already sensed the sweeps of acquisition radio wave energy being transmitted in his direction. He knew the jet would be locked up by fire control radar in less than two minutes and that his *fuzz buster* would be squawking relentlessly inside his helmet. An unexpected quiver flowed through his body, even though this was merely a training exercise. Cookie's eyes instinctively focused on the chaff and flares release switch. Chaff and flare bundles were the decoy devices tactical jets used to fool radar or heat seeking surface-to-air missiles.

Jack Mayhew had pushed eight seconds late from a point 32 nautical miles away from the strike objective. He was now dashing towards the USS *Missouri* at 480 knots ground speed, level at 400 feet AGL on a heading of 030 degrees. This simulation would put his aircraft in a HARM attack profile overhead the warship exactly four minutes from the push time. Commander Mayhew would not be late. He would make up the eight seconds during the inbound leg. His fuzz buster was currently displaying only faint traces of radar energy. This situation would change radically after he closed to within twenty-five miles. Unlike Lieutenant Cline, Juice was almost complacent in his approach to the War-at-Sea Strike. He had ice water in his veins and was indeed a cool customer during every mission in an A-7E except for one; night carrier landings. Fortunately, reserve Corsair pilots only hit the boat twice each year and it was during the light of day.

Teen Angel and Rocky, the main strike package, had begun their attack run four seconds early. Ackerman was somewhat anxious but still possessed extreme confidence in his abilities and in the strike plan he had developed for this particular mission. Their initial position was 40 and ½ half miles from the USS *Missouri* and the attack section was now in pursuit of its prey flying 520 knots at 80 feet above the water's surface on a course of 270 degrees. The jets actually dipped to 60 feet AGL but would venture no lower during a peacetime training hop. In four minutes and thirty seconds they would be in a thirty-degree dive angle coming off of their mirror pop-up maneuver, delivering a pair of 2000 pound Snake Eye bombs apiece into the sled being dragged by the vessel.

As each mile clicked down, the anxiety and anticipation increased in everyone except Jack Mayhew. Beads of sweat began to seep into Teen Angel's skullcap, but at least they didn't drip into his eyes. He quietly hummed the Del Shannon song *Runaway* to himself as he led the section's ingress into the target area. Lieutenant Cline felt as if several butterflies had been released into his lower abdomen causing his right leg to twitch in a jittery fashion. Cookie jokingly referred to this phenomenon as his stress spasm. Lieutenant Commander Stone's jaw clenched in a rhythmic pattern as he grinded his teeth with ever increasing intensity the closer his jet got to the drop zone. Naval Aviators were always taught that an effective training program caused each mission to be as realistic as was possible in a controlled environment. The goal was to prepare aviators for combat. Actual warfare of course was far more stressful than any training scenario, and the level of exhilaration was tenfold when compared to a contrived setting.

During the attack section's ingress, Jim Stone spotted something on the water in the Whiskey-91 Warning Area and he wasted no time in calling it to Brad's attention. The A-7's were 30 nautical miles from the *Missouri*.

"Sailboat, eleven o'clock, five miles Angel," reported Rocky.

"Visual," replied Brad in a laid-back tone. Lieutenant Ackerman temporarily adjusted the section's inbound course so that the Corsairs would fly almost directly over the vessel. Thirty-eight seconds later Angel and Rocky sandwiched the forty-foot white boat in between their jets screaming overhead at nine miles per minute.

"That red-headed woman standing on the bow wasn't wearing a top Brad," said Rocky with an animated voice, unable to conceal his level of excitement.

"Focus on the mission Rock not that pair of tits, we're less than two and a half minutes from our target," chided Ackerman as he quickly recorded the location of the sailboat in his inertial navigation system for their return flight to New Orleans.

"Eat me skin dick, you saw her too," responded Rocky to Angel's taunt.

"Two minutes to target," was Brad's only response. On the bow of the sailboat stood a tall shapely woman with auburn hair, wearing only a bikini bottom and she was apparently not the shy reserved type. The female was waving her hands wildly as the Corsairs zipped past. Angel scanned his instruments and suddenly realized he had slipped down to 40 feet AGL. He quickly eased his jet back up to 80 feet and re-adjusted course for the battleship. The radio altimeter warning tone, set to go off at 60 feet above the water's surface, either had not sounded off or Brad had missed the aural alarm. He made a mental note to write up that gripe after the flight.

Onboard *Missouri*, the flurry of activity was being controlled by the Combat Information Center (CIC) located in the very heart of the massive warship. The space was dimly lit with red background lighting and it gave the room an eerie feel. Standing in the center of the darkened room was an older looking Lieutenant Commander gently stroking his handle bar moustache as he patiently monitored the situation. He had his finger on the pulse and gave routine updates to the skipper of the ship via the red phone hotline to the bridge.

"Bridge, Combat," said the CIC Officer.

"Combat, this is the Captain, speak to me," came the reply.

"Skipper we are currently tracking two inbound bogeys. Bogey alpha is bearing 360 degrees at 10 miles on a course of 180, speed 305 knots. Bogey bravo is bearing 210 at 20 miles on a course of 030, speed 490 knots. I estimate merge plot in about 2 minutes, but we'll have a fire control solution in less than 30 seconds," was the report.

"With a fire control solution, you are cleared to simulate engagement of the bogeys," ordered Captain Kelley.

"Aye Aye skipper," said the CIC Officer, who immediately turned to the Weapons supervisor, a young Lieutenant Junior Grade, and shot him an inquiring gaze. Apparently the ship's radar was already providing a firing solution on both targets. The Vulcan cannon would be used to simulate the shot down of Cookie's airplane while the Sea Sparrow would be utilized to engage Juice's jet. After receiving a nod from the CIC Officer, the young Lieutenant Junior Grade gave shoot down orders to two second class seamen sitting behind a long console filled with buzzers, buttons and lights. Of course the Master Armament Switch was in the safe position.

Cookie was fully aware that his jet had been locked up by fire control radar; his ears were being assaulted by the incessant warning sounds of the fuzz buster. He was now being engaged by the Vulcan cannon, which in real life would spew out a continuous stream of lead bullets at approximately 8000 rounds per minute. Juice was thirty seconds away from a simulated Sea Sparrow joining him in the cockpit. He was enjoying the strike scenario but thinking about his flight physical scheduled for the next morning at the clinic. He hated flight surgeons with a passion. Their job was to take his job away. Juice calmly dispensed several rounds of chaff and flares into the sky below his jet. Teen Angel and Rocky continued inbound towards the *Missouri*. They were still only receiving faint traces of acquisition radar energy being emanated in search of their aircraft. Perhaps the ruse had worked and the attack section would get into the target area unscathed.

Cookie and Juice passed overhead the battleship in a textbook thirty-second split and were now flying outbound in preparation for their assault on the spar. Precisely thirty seconds after Commander Mayhew had departed the scene Angel and Rocky performed a flawless, mirror pop-up attack on the sled trailing the battleship. Their jets had successfully evaded radar detection. With the precision of Fred Astaire and Ginger Rogers on the ball room floor, both pilots yanked their noses in tandem, thirty degrees above the horizon. Rocky pulled hard to his right while Angel tugged with equal intensity to his left to get the proper separation needed for their bomb drops. As they banked back towards each other, leveling at 2500 feet AGL, both pilots spotted the spar. In a perfect precision tactic, Brad Ackerman and Jim Stone wrenched their jets into an inverted position, placed their bulls eye pipper onto the target then rolled upright to begin simultaneous twenty degree dive-bomb attacks. Their separation from each other was a little more than a quarter of a mile. Surely, even the Russian judge would be compelled to award Teen Angel and Rocky a perfect 10 score for their synchronized, fluid motion. Neither aviator had uttered a single syllable over the radio during the entire attack phase they merely anticipated and reacted to the movement of each other's aircraft.

Angel methodically selected stations three and six on his armament panel then carefully flipped the red-guarded Master Arm switch up and into the armed position. Undoubtedly, Lieutenant Commander Stone was hastily going through a similar sequence inside of his cockpit. Next, at the proper moment, Ackerman pressed the stores release (pickle) button on his control stick. Thirteen seconds after release, two MK-84 Snake Eye bombs smashed directly into the sled. Three seconds later, Rocky pitched one bomb into the spar but the other weapon missed and splashed harmlessly into the water about 500 feet long. He probably scared a whale or porpoise with the errant, unretarded piece of ordnance. Rocky wasn't aware of this at the time, but the Snake Eye fins on his second bomb had failed to deploy. He would analyze and regret this mistake during the mission de-brief but not nearly as much as he would later that evening at the O' Club bar while sharing a beer with his intolerant squadron mates.

Teen Angel and Rocky held overhead at 3000 feet AGL in a left-hand orbit while the second section dropped their bombs onto the target. As Juice and Cookie pulled off their individual attack runs they instinctively looked up to locate the strike leader and his wingman in order to slide into proper position and sequence on the circle. It was time to strafe the spar. After making one more turn in holding and verifying his division was joined in the circular chain, Brad lowered his nose 20 degrees below the horizon, accelerated the Corsair to 480 knots then aimed his internal gattling gun at the metal spar. He selected the *gun low* position, meaning the A-7 would discharge only 4000 rounds of 20mm ammunition per minute. There was a reduced risk of jamming the feeding mechanism at that setting and less likelihood of overheating the titanium barrels as well. This would also assure Angel of having enough bullets to make two complete strafing runs.

"Lead in hot," reported Lieutenant Ackerman to the other pilots. As his pipper meticulously settled onto the middle of the target Brad's right index finger squeezed the trigger for a solid three seconds, unleashing several hundred projectiles into the spar. The machine gun made a subdued buzzing noise as it spit out the bullets. Apparently the ordies had loaded high explosive incendiary (HEI) ammunition for this hop and some of the bullets actually caused parts of the sled to catch on fire after being hit.

"Two's in hot, lead in sight," said Rocky as he armed his gun and began to track the spar.

"Lead off safe," blurted out Brad in a strained voice as he pulled 5 G's rapidly climbing his aircraft to get back into the circular pattern overhead. Lieutenant Commander Stone was now cleared to fire his gun at the target. Rocky started his spray of bullets just short of the target then walked the pattern slowly upward until it filled the center of the spar. Every fifth bullet was a tracer to help guide the line of fire. This, of course, was not the preferred tactic for the 20mm cannon, but Rocky always enjoyed pretending he was in a western movie.

"What do we have here, Robert Redford as The Sun Dance Kid?" teased Cookie as he spotted Rocky's shower of bullets stroll casually up to the target. All four aviators got a kick out of the comment. So did Captain Kelley who was listening in on the activity from his chair on the bridge of *Missouri*. During the strafing attacks the only gun that jammed was Commander Mayhew's, and Juice cussed like a disgusted sailor because he was unable to fire any bullets from his jet.

On the second strafing run, Teen Angel looked back over his left shoulder and thought he saw Lieutenant Cline pulling out a tad low on his pass over the spar. White disturbed airflow streamed slightly up and rearward off Cookie's wings as he pulled off target. I hope Cookie didn't get *target fixated* and overstress another jet thought Angel, quickly darting his eyes back to the strafing circle to ensure he had proper interval in the daisy chain.

After the second strafe run was completed, the pilots quickly maneuvered into a tight echelon formation on Brad's right wing as he circled overhead the spar in a left-hand orbit for the division rendezvous.

"Big Shot, River 10 request fly by," asked Ackerman on the #1 UHF radio. After a brief pause the ship responded to Angel's appeal.

"Rivers are cleared for a low fly by." Permission granted, Ackerman lined the A-7's up at about four miles behind the warship. He accelerated the division to 480 knots before settling to 100 feet above the water. Teen Angel would fly up the starboard side of the vessel and slowly bank the formation to the left as he crossed in front of the bow. Several hundred sailors were busy getting into a good position on the deck of the ship. A precision fly by always seemed to pump up the men stuck on a ship at sea, and most carrier pilots were more than willing to oblige. As he guided his flight to within 50 feet of the bridge, Brad could see sailors holding their cameras snapping away while leaning over the side railing of the battleship. This type of picture was good PR and an eighteen-year old seaman could use it to his advantage back home, whenever he got back home. It was indeed a picture perfect maneuver.

"Big Shot, River 10," said Brad. Jack Mayhew raised his eyebrows and shook in his head, wondering what Teen Angel was up to now. Juice knew the Corsairs would only have enough fuel for perhaps one air combat (ACM) engagement before it would be time to Bingo back to NAS New Orleans.

"Go ahead River flight," replied the enlisted man in CIC sitting at the radio console.

"Is the *old man* available?" inquired Ackerman.

"Wait one." Dropping a pair of binoculars into his chest Captain Kelley picked up the UHF transceiver on the bridge then spoke to Lieutenant Ackerman in his characteristic, deep southern drawl. The skipper, seated comfortably in his cushy leather Captain's chair, was a native of Augusta, Georgia.

"River 10 this *is* Big Shot, go ahead," said Barney Kelley as he squeezed the talk button on the gray telephone.

"Skipper, I just want to thank you for the work today and let you know that anytime the River Rattlers can support you please don't hesitate to call on us again," stated Brad in an extremely deferential tone. His wingmen were impressed by the comment but flabbergasted by Angel's tone of voice. Cookie actually had to remove his oxygen mask to laugh out loud, and to avoid spitting on himself in the process. This was somewhat uncharacteristic of Ackerman who was usually an unmerciful wise ass even with senior officers. Juice and Rocky were too stunned to do anything but hang onto Ackerman's wing.

"Shucks, you kerosene cowboys can come back any old time," declared Captain Kelley. "Have a safe flight home and we'll see you next time, Big Shot out."

"*Wee doggies*, is it just me or does he sound a lot like Jed Clampett?" mocked Rocky, in a genial fashion. The comment quickly elicited four grins.

"Teen Angel flight, switch to button eleven," instructed Brad as the Corsairs banked toward the ACM engagement zone (Tibby MOA) of the Whiskey-91 Warning Area, leaving that grand old lady *Missouri* behind in their side view mirrors.

CHAPTER 4

▼

KNIFE FIGHT IN A PHONE BOOTH

On the short trip back to the ACM area, Lieutenant Ackerman steered the division of A-7's to the latitude and longitude coordinates he had stored in his INS during the ingress of the attack section. When he realized where the formation was flying, Rocky shook his head as he clung to Brad's wing. He knew Teen Angel could not resist a good-looking woman, clothed or otherwise. Lieutenant Commander Stone knew Teen Angel would return to take another peek at the topless woman. Ackerman was indeed a flaming heterosexual. Flying at 80 feet AGL, the four aviators discovered the red headed female still standing on the bow of the sailboat and still waving her hands wildly in the air as the jets flew by. But this time she was completely nude. Brad noticed that the carpet did indeed match the drapes. After passing the sailboat he initiated a shallow climb.

Turning to Corsair 401 flying on the port side, Brad tilted his head back while making a drinking motion with his left hand. Angel's left thumb was stretched out in front of his dark visor as his oxygen mask dangled down on the right side of his helmet. Rocky Stone replied to Brad's fuel check signal by flashing an outstretched palm with five fingers clearly visible, followed shortly by three fingers held out sideways. This meant that Stone had five thousand eight hundred pounds of JP-5 remaining in his tank. Looking to the right Ackerman repeated the fuel check signal to the second section. Juice reported fifty five hundred pounds of gas left and Cookie was at fifty six hundred. Glancing down, Teen Angel saw his fuel gauge registering 5.9. This meant that Commander Mayhew, in 404, was low man of the flight. All Navy pilots were extra cognizant of their fuel state because you can never have too much jet fuel, except when your aircraft was engulfed in flames. The old adage 'gas is good, more is better' was usually a true sentiment in Naval Aviation, especially during Blue Water Ops on the aircraft carrier.

Arriving in the very center of the Tibby MOA on a Northerly course, Brad gave a kiss off gesture to Juice and Cookie who immediately made a 180 degree turn to the right and accelerated to 500 knots. Not a word was spoken. Brad's left hand gently pushed his throttle forward as he tugged smoothly on the control stick to initiate a shallow climb. His pre-flight briefing called for a twenty-mile split between the sections prior to the beginning of the 2 v 2 engagement. Leveling at fifteen thousand feet Ackerman veered to the left to begin the dogfight. If his timing calculation was correct, there was now 20-22 miles distance between the jets.

"Juice we're turning back inbound," called Teen Angel.

"We are coming at you too Angel," reported Jack Mayhew.

"Fight's on boys!" said Brad, in a somewhat excited twang, to formally initiate the ACM engagement. Their separation was just over twenty-one miles. The four Corsairs would merge plot at 15,000 feet on a reciprocal heading in about one minute and ten seconds. Their closing velocity (V_c) was well over eleven hundred miles per hour.

"Rocky" Stone was flying in a modified *stinger* position, well below and slightly less than two nautical miles directly behind Ackerman's aircraft. From this vantage point he would witness the beginning stages of the dogfight unfold and be able to attack the rival section with the advantage of stealth and surprise. But, if he screwed things up he would be relegated to high-speed cheerleader status. Stone and Ackerman had secretly decided to use this tactic today just before the hop began. Rocky momentarily scanned his airspeed indicator noticing that Brad had increased their speed to 520 knots. In less than a minute Brad's eyes locked onto the rival Corsairs.

"Tally ho," blurted out Angel. A few seconds later, Juice and Cookie, flying one mile abreast, located Ackerman's airplane in the blue sky and maneuvered to take him right through the middle of their speeding jets. But, they did not immediately spot Rocky. The ploy had worked to perfection.

As the first three Corsairs crossed paths Angel instinctively pushed his throttle to the firewall, quickly achieving the maximum rate of thrust (MRT) on the A-7.

The Stanford graduation ring on his left hand momentarily scraped up against the metal catapult grip inside the cockpit, causing blood to trickle down his finger. Brad's body stiffened with anticipation as he suddenly yanked his jet upward at 5 G's simultaneously rolling left toward the tail section of the aircraft zooming past him on the port side. As the G forces increased beyond three, a valve opened on Teen Angel's G-suit allowing engine bleed air to fill the bladder inside the suit. The compressed air squeezed the lower half of Ackerman's body from the top of his flight boots to the middle of his abdomen. Brad grunted out loud as he sensed the first assault of pressurized air being exerted on his torso. This action prevented blood from pooling in his stomach region while ensuring a continuous supply of blood and oxygen to the brain.

"Oh God how I love this," gasped a breathless Teen Angel.

Cookie saw Brad's jet climb and begin to turn toward his so he mirrored this maneuver by pulling 6 G's and initiating his ascent a half second before Brad. Lieutenant Cline groaned inside his oxygen mask as he convulsed his midsection to struggle against the effects of the G forces. This little trick provided extra protection against the possibility of G loss of consciousness (GLOC) above and beyond the security provided by the anti-G suit. Cookie's oxygen mask strained and pulled in reaction to the forces of acceleration. The microphone inside the mask pressed up against his lips and teeth, while the metal bayonet clips that secured the breathing apparatus to his helmet dug into the sides of his face leaving deep compression marks. Despite the tremendous strain being exerted on his body, Cookie smiled because he perceived that he had apparently beaten Angel to the first punch in their dogfight. Juice watched this action out of the corner of his eye, but at the same time he was still scanning in an attempt to locate Rocky. He knew he was out there somewhere.

Angel and Cookie began to run out of energy at about 28,000 feet, but both aviators kept banking hard in an attempt to get behind the wing line of each other's airplane. Now their noses pointed straight down at the water as they desperately tried to regain lost airspeed. Angel was manipulating his jet with rough aggressive movements, while Cookie was using much smoother, assertive control inputs. Cookie had indeed gained a slight altitude advantage over Angel and the vertical separation would work to his benefit very soon. After three turns in their engagement the two became intertwined in a quasi-rolling scissors fight, separated by about four thousand feet at the top and bottom of their fur ball in the sky. They would be flying at 100 knots or less over the top then accelerate to over 450 knots at the bottom of their huge little beehive. As they converged to within 100 feet of one another, both pilots wrestled to keep sight of the opposing aircraft, flailing away in their ejection seats. Their heads appeared to be on a swivel and they could clearly see each other inside the cockpit as they passed canopy to canopy, one climbing up the other sliding down. Sweat saturated Angel's skullcap so that it was now permeated with the sweet stench of his perspiration. For some strange reason, the Tasmanian Devil cartoon flashed inside Angel's thought pattern for just a moment during the heated action.

"Oh Juicey, I see you," giggled Rocky as he began to maneuver behind Commander Mayhew's Corsair. Rocky was close to being in a good position for a *heater* or Sidewinder shot. But he didn't want a *Fox Two*. He was after a much bigger prize. Rocky wanted a gunshot on Juice.

"Oh shit," muttered Jack Mayhew to himself. Juice was still at 15,000 feet just turning in a lazy circle around the skirmish already in progress. He was sort of a high-speed cheerleader for his wingman Cookie, who was actively tangled up slicing through the skies fighting Brad. This momentary loss of situational awareness would cost him. After hearing that he had been located by Rocky, Mayhew immediately leveled his wings and jerked the Corsair straight up as hard as he could, hoping to force Stone into an overshoot situation. As his fight ensued, Juice began to talk to himself inside the cockpit. He became his own slow-speed cheerleader.

"Come on Jack, don't let this punk get the better of you," he mumbled quietly. "Force him to make a fatal error then pounce on him." Twisting his head back and to the left, Mayhew could now plainly see the jet behind his wing line at about the seven o'clock position. Rocky, coming off of a high yo yo maneuver was gradually closing to within about 2000 feet. But Juice already knew how he would win this engagement and earn bragging rights at the O' Club bar tonight. He would lure Rocky closer and into a low-speed dogfight. Jack's flight boots would do a toe dance on the rudder pedals and then he would simply swoop down on Rocky's jet with his patented "rudder over the top" departure maneuver. This somewhat dangerous tactic had worked every time for Commander Mayhew when he found himself on the defensive in a dogfight. He had used the strategy hundreds of times in his career. As Juice and Rocky fought on, Angel and Cookie continued their rolling scissors clash separated by 6,000 feet, their airspeed slowly diminishing with each pass over the top.

"This looks like a knife fight in a phone booth," cracked Cookie as the A-7's stabbed at one another in the confined airspace of their dogfight. His 20 x 10 vision allowed him to clearly see all four jets aggressively thrashing about in the small corner of the Tibby MOA. Cookie almost never lost situational awareness in combat scenarios. How poignant thought Angel as he moaned silently then yanked his nose back down through the horizon and towards the water. He was still attempting to drag his lift vector behind the tail section of Cookie Cline's Corsair while at the same time extending to salvage some precious energy. Cookie simply straightened out his wings and heaved directly for Ackerman, one mile above him and closing rapidly. The two aviators slithered to within 60 feet of each other on this, their sixth pass. Cline was almost positive that Brad had given him the finger as they traded places in the fur ball yet again.

"Guns, Guns, Guns," shouted a jubilant Jim Stone. His voice noticeably strained against labored breathing inside the oxygen mask. He was now less than 1500 feet behind Juice and still approaching. Rocky had placed his aircraft's snout well out in front of Commander Mayhew's airplane to compensate for the *bullet lag* induced by those extreme G forces. In real life, the Corsair's 20mm shells would spit out the muzzle of the gattling gun then bend back toward the earth as they pursued an airborne target. The bulls-eye reticule of the A-7 gun was not designed with a built in lead angle like fifth generation combat aircraft had. So Corsair pilots had to create a lead vector in order to successfully engage an enemy airplane with their machine gun.

Hearing that Rocky had achieved a guns solution on him, Jack Mayhew suddenly raised the aircraft's nose even higher then stuffed his right rudder antagonistically to the floorboard. But Juice Mayhew had grossly miscalculated his jet's airspeed. The nose of the Corsair quickly began a violent dance, bucking and yawing first to the right then to the left. If you have ever seen a rodeo cowboy clutching a Brahma bull for less than the full eight seconds, this was a very similar ride. Juice had a sinking feeling deep in the pit of his belly just as the airplane violently departed from controlled flight, causing him to strike his head on the left side of the canopy glass. He blacked out for just a few seconds then recovered.

Although a bit blurry, Jack Mayhew's vision was slowly returning to his eyeballs. In the powerful collision with the canopy glass, Juice's helmet had been forced well down over his brow. Commander Mayhew gently pushed his gray form-fit helmet back into its proper position on his head then hurriedly assessed his jet's condition. He soon realized the A-7 was in an upright spin. Spin recovery procedures instinctively rushed to the front of his brain. He knew what to do and his demeanor was surprisingly calm considering the difficulty that an A-7 has in recovering from a fully developed spin. Juice first neutralized all of his control surfaces. He then made a swift scan of his instrument panel. The turn-and-slip indicator showed a severe yawing and rotation. The turn needle was pegged out to the right and the ball was stuck in the opposite direction. Jack's altimeter read 19,280 feet, and he was now screaming out of the sky at 8,000 feet per minute.

Airspeed was steady at 70-80 knots. He would most assuredly bust the 5,000 foot hard deck before he could successfully recover from this upright spin. Sorry strike leader! After two complete un-commanded rotations of the jet, Juice placed the control stick slightly forward of the neutral position with full lateral deflection to match the right hand rotation of the Corsair. Then in unison he stepped vigorously on the left rudder pedal. Now all he could do was to wait and ride it out.

During this commotion, Rocky had rapidly overshot Mayhew's airplane and had gotten spit out of the fight. As he dashed by, he was abruptly aware that Juice was in real trouble.

"I'm ballistic," barked Juice over the radio, "y'all get out of my way."

"Knock it off," instructed Brad without delay after hearing the last radio call and sensing the perilous situation of Commander Mayhew. The dogfight was unexpectedly terminated. Immediately, all wings were leveled and three pairs of eyes focused on Juice in 404. Everything was now running in slow motion for Jack Mayhew and he remained quite composed throughout the entire ordeal. His squadron mates however, did not. The three of them started to coach Juice by blurting out spin recovery procedures, clumsily stepping on each other's radio transmissions like Air Force pilots.

"Would you amateurs please shut up while I get out of this here predicament," commanded Juice using his serious pitch. Brad nervously watched the drama unfold from his lofty 12,000 foot perch. A fear chill coursed through his veins. How would he explain to "Duke" O'Grady that he had lost an aviator and a Corsair during his first flight as strike leader? 404 kept falling right through Brad's altitude and within a few hundred feet of his jet. Mayhew stubbornly kept the spin recovery controls in place, but the idea of pulling the face curtain ejection handle suddenly loomed large in his thought process. But as he descended below 4,800 feet Juice could sense that the aircraft wanted to return to controlled flight.

"Come on baby, you can do it," said Juice. "Easy does it sweetheart." Then, just as quickly as the jet had left controlled flight it returned to a stable condition. Without any further delay, Juice flipped the Corsair back onto its stomach as he bottomed out at 2,200 feet above the blue-green swells beckoning below. Davey Jones' locker would not claim another victim this day thought Commander Mayhew. He meekly began a climb to join his wingmen.

"Can we go home now Angel?" I'm really hungry and I need to clean the shit out of my skivvies," Mayhew joked.

"You betcha baby," responded Ackerman. "Y'all join on me at 8,000 feet for the return to base (RTB) and a carrier fan break." As the division left the Whiskey-91 Warning area and headed for NAS New Orleans, none of the aviators had any idea of the monumental decision that had already been made last week at the Pentagon. The magnitude of that decision would affect their lives and that of their family for the next ten months.

CHAPTER 5

▼

THIRD LAW OF THERMODYNAMICS

John O'Grady parked his baby blue 1957 T-Bird, with a gaudy Fly Navy sticker plastered onto the rear bumper, in the space marked *Commander John "Duke" O'Grady, VA-204 Commanding Officer*. This was Duke's first day back in New Orleans after a brief six day TDY to Norfolk, Virginia. The block lettering spray painted onto the soiled concrete was a bold orange, the official squadron color. The skipper's carelessly parked vehicle intruded by about a foot or so into the parking spot reserved for his Executive Officer (XO), Commander Don "Slug" Levitan, a Selected Air Reservist (SAR) from St Louis. The XO had lost his job as a 727 Captain for Eastern Airlines when the company folded up its tents several years ago. Slug was now a 747 First Officer for Federal Express, and was currently delivering packages in the orient. He would not make this month's Drill Weekend due to the twelve-day trip. This of course didn't really matter to Duke who was in the habit of parking any way he pleased. Outside of the cockpit Duke was fairly sloppy, but once he strapped himself into a jet he was a flawless professional. Around the ship he was impeccable and his men would follow him into the most precarious situations because they trusted his leadership. Ironically, as a young junior officer (JO) constantly in hot water with his CO's and Department Heads, O'Grady never dreamed that he would one day command a tactical squadron himself.

Commander O'Grady was a hard drinking, hard charging aviator whose passion was flying jets in the Navy. He also loved women, fast cars and classical music. Blondes, vintage Thunderbirds and Beethoven were his favorites. He spent many a night running around with his curly black hair on fire until about four in the morning, only to fall asleep in the arms of a strange woman while listening to Beethoven's Fifth. Most females found O'Grady to be fairly irresistible, especially whenever he turned on his New York City charm. This morning he arrived at the squadron at 0815, forty-five minutes late.

Duke had spent the last hour at the NAS Dental Clinic getting his biannual teeth cleaning. He wasn't a huge fan of dentists but two years ago the clinic had a new dental hygienist transfer in from Jacksonville, Florida. She was a nubile twenty-four year old Second Class Petty Officer with long legs, platinum blonde hair, and a pair of major league knockers. He simply could not resist, because the young hygienist routinely wore one of those short, tight fitting smocks while cleaning teeth. Duke was almost sure she was naked underneath the white uniform and he had even fantasized about having sex with her in a dental chair. Her name was Tanya Billings and she was ever so gentle with those sharp torture devices known as dentist tools. O'Grady referred to her as "eye candy" whenever he mentioned Petty Officer Billings to his *most* trusted squadron mates. Of course Teen Angel was included in this group. Growing up in Jacksonville, Tanya had developed a remarkably friendly nature. But during her brief four-year stint in the Navy she had learned to be particularly flirtatious with officers and Commander O'Grady was the latest target of her enticing demeanor. After placing a vinyl car cover over his precious baby blue, Duke headed for the side door entrance to the squadron.

As Duke walked casually into Maintenance Control, Chief Martin was the first to spot the skipper. The chief was now working on some serious overtime, but fourteen-hour days weren't all that unusual for the men of Naval Aviation. Martin had been scheduled to go home over an hour ago but had stayed to conduct a thorough turnover briefing with the oncoming shift of maintenance men. Today the skipper was wearing his khaki uniform and his hat was a bit cockeyed to the right side of his head. It appeared as though his Rowenta iron had been broken for the entire month because his uniform was saturated with wrinkles. Perhaps he had changed dry cleaners or perhaps he had passed out and slept in his uniform last night. Occasionally, O'Grady resembled a UPS deliveryman rather than a professional naval officer.

Underneath the gold wings, on the left side of his uniform shirt, were five rows of medals and ribbons, which Duke had earned during his twenty-year tenure as a Naval Aviator. He had one Distinguished Flying Cross, three Air Medals and various other individual and group decorations. "Fruit salad" described this array quite nicely.

"Attention on deck," snapped Robby Martin. All seven men in the shop became rigid, standing with their eyes fixed straight ahead, staring at lifeless walls.

"At ease men," said O'Grady coolly. "Good morning to you Chief. Is the squadron ready for CAG's team of inspectors?" inquired Duke.

"Piece of cake, skipper," stated a self-assured Martin. "I'm just about to go home and sleep for a few hours. I'll be back at quarter to seven tomorrow morning for Drill Weekend. The MO gave us the night off."

"Then hit the bricks Chief, I'll see you and your night check crew on Saturday." You deserve some time off based on what I hear." Even as he said this, the skipper thought to himself, chiefs don't really sleep! As Martin nodded and headed for the exit, Lieutenant Ackerman's voice was heard calling on the squadron radio frequency.

"Maintenance, 411 will be on deck in five minutes. All aircraft are up except 411, which will be down for the Radar Altimeter. I also need some Lox," informed Ackerman.

"Angel, I may have pulled 8 G's on 415," confessed Cookie, breaking into the conversation on button twenty.

"Okay, then we'll also need to check the G meter on 415 guys," said Brad to correct his initial status report to Maintenance Control.

"Roger that sir, we'll be waiting," replied a young Airman sitting adjacent to the radio transceiver. He then flipped up a red-guarded switch to announce the flight's arrival to the entire maintenance crew over the PA system. Immediately several troubleshooters emerged from various shops, donned their cranial helmets and protective gear then headed for the tarmac. Hearing that Teen Angel's flight was about to land the skipper decided to amble on out to the flight line to watch the jets in the break.

After informing the tower of his intentions, Teen Angel maneuvered the division of warplanes to a point about eight miles on the extended centerline for runway 04, directly over the Lafitte Bridge. This was known as the *initial position*. The wind had apparently changed in the last ninety minutes and was now coming out of the Northeast. Angel could see long reeds of brown-green marsh grass and fields of sugar cane plants leaning in the breeze below him as he passed overhead. The creepy black water in the bayou was also swirling about as the wind howled. Brad leveled the flight at 800 feet then smoothly accelerated to 500 knots indicated. Even though the maximum airspeed below ten thousand feet was 250 knots, armed forces jets operating at military airports routinely disregarded FAA rules and procedures. Bending regulations was also firmly ensconced as part of the enduring tradition of flying as a tactical naval aviator.

"River 10 the pattern is empty, at the approach end numbers you are cleared for the carrier break," advised the tower chief on button three.

"River 10 roger," replied Ackerman as he instinctively inched his throttle up a bit further, yet ever conscious of leaving his wingmen a little excess thrust to play with as they maneuvered to remain in textbook echelon position. Looking down for a last check of his flight instruments, Angel noticed the airspeed needle was now pointing to 520 knots. His division of Corsairs would be over the numbers in less than 50 seconds.

The formation of A-7's was close and tight. Angel's heart rate quickened just a bit and over in 401, Rocky's jawbone tensed in preparation for the carrier fan break. Naval Aviators would rather crash, burn and die than look bad around the ship or the airfield. Crossing the runway end identifier lights Lieutenant Ackerman took a quick peek at Rocky, patted his right shoulder with his left hand then nodded twice toward the port side of his aircraft. This was the non-verbal signal for the wingmen to hang tight with their leader and perform the fan break. Two seconds later, Teen Angel slowly rolled his jet into a sixty-five degree angle of bank then pulled three G's. Rocky, Juice and Cookie followed his lead to perfection as the four airplanes tilted and swayed in unison, level at 800 feet above the airfield.

In this part of the choreography, achieving proper separation for the full-stop landing was tricky business. But each pilot knew his procedures cold. After a momentary delay, Lieutenant Cline in the number four slot of the formation immediately reduced his throttle to idle and commanded the massive speed brake (or *board*) to fully extend out of the bottom of his jet's gray fuselage. Cookie Cline hung in his proper position for about a "one potato two" before he began to slowly slide out of the echelon. Commander Mayhew, in the number three position, retarded his throttle so that he had only a handful of power above the idle stop and after forty-five degrees of turn he reduced his pull to about 2 and ½ G's, then extended his board about half way. Gradually, his jet inched out of the formation. Lieutenant Commander Stone, number two in the formation, hung in with Angel twice as long as Juice did. After about ninety degrees of turn he started to methodically separate from his flight leader with power adjustments and use of the fifteen-foot barn door (speed brake) lodged in the belly of the Corsair. Brad kept his power at MRT until he had turned a full one hundred thirty-five degrees from the initial heading. Only then did he reduce his power to idle and punch out his speed brake to slow the jet to landing speed.

From above, the division of A-7 jets resembled a Japanese fan opening on a hot summer day in Osaka. As the carrier fan break maneuver was completed each aircraft ended up with about twenty-five hundred feet of lateral separation at exactly 800 feet altitude, and flying at a comfortable airspeed of about 142 knots. They were indeed flawless in the break that morning and ready for their full-stop landings.

"Shit hot," shouted Commander O'Grady as he was standing behind, but in close proximity to Senior Chief Esposito. The Senior Chief was somewhat startled, not by the comment, but by the fact that he had allowed the Commanding Officer to sneak up on him without his sensing it. Perhaps he *was* getting old Esposito thought to himself. At least he hadn't dropped his walkie-talkie. As the jets landed in sequence, separated by approximately eight seconds, the skipper spun around quickly and headed toward his office on the second deck of the squadron building.

"Senior Chief would you tell Lieutenant Ackerman that I would like to see him and his entire flight crew in my office in thirty minutes," said O'Grady as he brushed past.

"Aye aye skipper," replied a suddenly stiff Esposito. Duke O'Grady mumbled to himself as he continued walking without even slowing his pace.

Lieutenant Ackerman patiently waited for all members of his flight to finish being de-armed at the end of runway 4. Then as the division of *war chariots* progressed along taxiway Alpha back toward the River Rattler flight line, four Corsair canopies opened simultaneously on cue. Just like *the Blues* thought Teen Angel with a smile of self-satisfaction that he believed was well earned. As they continued to taxi, black and orange New Orleans "love bugs" swarmed all around the jets. The insects were glued together in their familiar mating ritual, flying aimlessly as they were breeding. Ungloved hands could be seen brushing away the careless yet annoying pests. Several landed inside the cockpits while some of the little creatures, oblivious to the imminent danger they faced, flew straight down the intake duct and suffered a sadistic demise. After only 14 days, life was violently terminated before they could even procreate their chromosomes and bug DNA.

Brad completed his post-flight checklist then gave Airman Boone the cut signal as he shut down the turbo-fan engine. The hop was over. Four planes and four pilots had returned safely after completing their War-at-Sea training strike. Mission accomplished.

Standing at the counter inside Maintenance Control once again, the four avia-tors removed black government pens, the kind that actually worked, from their flight suits and began to fill out aircraft yellow sheets and discrepancy forms. Sweaty helmets and skullcaps lay on the deck near their feet. Chief David Carter, on the other side of the partition, was close at hand for any discrepancies that needed to be resolved. Carter was Chief Martin's *day check* replacement and he smelled like a bottle of Old Spice aftershave lotion had been broken over his head that morning.

"Chief can I have an *attaboy* sheet please," requested Ackerman as he deliber-ately drew in a big whiff of air and turned his head from side to side with flared nostrils.

"Its underneath your discrepancy book sir," responded Chief Carter, deliber-ately disregarding Teen Angel's blatant head movements. "I took the liberty of anticipating that you would give Airman Boone yet another *attaboy* sir."

"What is that horrible smell?" asked Rocky Stone in his acerbic tone of voice.

"Do we have a rodent problem in this space Chief?" teased Cookie Cline. Sev-eral subdued chuckles erupted like a subtle volcano from the men seated at their desks in the shop.

"No, it's Chief Carter's cologne," answered Commander Mayhew in his typi-cal brusque manner. Carter's face began to blush even before the MO finished his sarcastic, but true remark. The chief, retaining his composure, remained silent and professional in his demeanor. He would not take the bait and almost as quickly as it had arisen, the restrained laughter subsided. The period of silence that followed lasted only for a few seconds.

"I need an *attaboy* form too Chief," chimed in Cookie before realizing the document was waiting for him under his green book as well. The squadron had several outstanding young enlisted men serving as plane captains and these *atta-boy* certificates were a small way of recognizing their dedication and superior per-formance. After receiving ten *attaboys*, plane captains got a day off from work. Airman Boone had earned thirty-two *attaboys* in just the past three months alone; fifteen of these had been awarded by Lieutenant Ackerman.

As he was about to complete his paperwork, Lieutenant Commander Stone, the squadron's Assistant Maintenance Officer (AMO), had a somewhat uneasy feeling snake down the back of his neck. He knows that the embarrassing and potentially deadly spin episode with Juice was played out over the River Rattler tactical frequency on button 20. But he was almost certain that none of the radio transmissions were picked up here at the squadron because the jets were 120 miles away from home plate; a distance that is well beyond UHF range. But

Rocky wants to be damn sure in order to protect Juice from any possible recrimination. So he decided to discretely check to see if anything was overheard on the radio.

"Hey Airman Howard, we tried to call you about five times from the Warning Area to report our aircraft status, but you didn't answer. Did you not hear any of those transmissions or what?" inquired Rocky.

"Sir I have been sitting here since 0715 and the only radio call I received in the last hour was the status report that took place about 20 minutes ago, the one where Mr. Ackerman told me you'd be on deck in five minutes," stated Howard with an expressionless face.

"I see. Is your radio working properly?"

"I think so, but I'll have *ski* from avionics take a look at it just in case. Maybe it needs to have the receiver tubes changed or something."

Satisfied, Rocky returned to his yellow sheet and completed the details of the hop for his aircraft; he fat-fingered an extra .2 flight time for himself. In two minutes all the pilots finished up their gripes then headed for the paraloft to hang up their flight gear. As they departed Maintenance Control, Angel headed toward the jelly donut waiting for him in the enlisted mess. As he walked down the corridor he reminded them all to meet in the skipper's office in five minutes.

Commander O'Grady's office was not plush by any measurement of that standard. In fact, Duke's workspace was a messy little cubbyhole located in the most innocuous corner on the second deck of the squadron building. It was of an office without windows and had very little taste injected into its decor by the current occupant. Teen Angel would often tease the skipper by inquiring when his decorator had died. On the front right edge of Duke's desk sat a rather gaudy looking A-7 model carved from the wood of a eucalyptus tree. It had been painstakingly painted in royal blue and haze gray, the colors of O'Grady's first fleet squadron the VA-46 *Clansmen*. A red and black checkerboard kilt highlighted the top of the vertical fin. Duke had the model made in Olongopo City in the Philippine Islands when he was a mere pup on his first cruise. The carving also featured an assortment of weaponry hanging from miniature bomb racks.

On the dingy tan wall behind his desk Duke had mounted his naval officer's sword, crooked of course. Hanging on the right wall was a framed picture of Commander O'Grady shaking hands with Robert Livingston, the celebrated Congressman from the 1st District of Louisiana. The Honorable Mr. Livingston, an ex Navy enlisted man, had only thrown up once that afternoon during his familiarization ride with Duke in a TA-7. Finally, a large set of Brass Naval Aviator's wings had been mounted with extra care on the remaining wall. Underneath the wings was a squadron group photo taken while skiing in Lake Tahoe and another group shot taken onboard the USS *Eisenhower*. This was Duke's personal sanctuary on drill weekends.

Wiping the last remnants of donut powder from his chin and lower lip, Lieutenant Ackerman strolled casually into the CO's office only to discover his wingmen already comfortably assembled. Angel thoughtlessly transferred some of the sugary white substance from his right hand onto the right thigh portion of his green flight suit. Nomex, although fire retardant, was apparently not resistant to the stains caused by donut dust residue. Neither was the skipper's blue cut pile carpeting.

Quickly surveying the situation, Brad noticed that Juice and Cookie had settled onto a red corduroy loveseat with threadbare in all the important places, while Rocky was comfortably parked in a brown, scuffed leather chair. Duke O' Grady, wearing his wire-rimmed reading glasses, was slumped in a swivel chair with his feet plopped up on the edge of his desk gnawing on a Delta Airlines ink pen, courtesy of his Admin Officer Mike Morley. Dozens of important and not so important papers were strewn neatly and liberally across the oak desktop. The skipper's desk was a professional mess. Teen Angel soon realized he was last again and would have to stand during Duke's remarks, whatever they were going to be.

"Nice of you to join us Lieutenant Ackerman," chided the skipper, making doubly certain to use extra modulation on the word lieutenant. "First off gents, I called you all here to tell you how *shit hot* you were in the break today." With those two words all four pilots felt that narcissistic sense of self-pride which had the dangerous capacity to consume one's very soul, blocking out any semblance of humility. Juice would always say that God must surely be a naval aviator. Why else would it be that much fun to hurl your body to and from the deck of an aircraft carrier. Additionally, Uncle Sam, the guy with the beard, paid you rather handsomely and the chicks were free to boot! *Dire Straits* would most assuredly be envious of *us* Juice would remark.

"I also want to remind you of your individual responsibilities for tomorrow's CAG corrosion inspection which by the way is the most significant task to be accomplished during this month's drill weekend."

"Skipper, we are ready," reassured Commander Mayhew. "Rocky and I will be in the hangar bay at 0700 monitoring the inspection, and Teen Angel will rendezvous with CAG at the driving range at 0715 for their golf match. CAG Sullivan should be out of your hair for at least the first four hours sir." Mayhew also informed the skipper that the squadron Operations Officer, Commander "Klutz" Fitzgerald, had scheduled Commander Sullivan for a bombing hop between

1300 and 1600. Finally he advised Duke that Commander Mike "Shroud" Morley and Lieutenant Mark "Fantasy" Love would supervise the practice recall using the *calling tree* to ensure all the phone numbers were still accurate for VA-204's reservists, even though most of them would be at the squadron bright and early tomorrow morning. This personnel recall exercise was merely a ritual performed during any type of CAG or Chief of Naval Reserve (CNAVRES) inspection.

"Angel, I don't want you to piss off Squid Sullivan," barked the skipper.

"Do you want me to let him win *again* Duke?" asked Teen Angel in an incredulous voice.

"No, I am not saying that. Just don't piss him off by pulling his chain for the entire four hours you are together, okay." Brad nodded in compliance with the commanding officer's request.

"Okay, *youz three guys* can leave now, I need a moment alone with Cookie," said Duke in a half-hearted somber tone, utilizing his best New York City accent. Just then the skipper's phone began to ring. Picking up the receiver Duke cupped his hand over the mouthpiece and issued one final decree. "And uh, close the door on your way out Angel," ordered the skipper. With that, Juice, Rocky and Teen Angel made a quick beat for the exit. As Angel walked gradually toward the door, he and Cookie quickly exchanged winks of support. But then Angel quietly began to snort the closer he got to Cookie because he knew his wingman was gonna get his ass royally chewed for overstressing yet another jet. In fact, this would be Lieutenant Cline's second overstress in the last twenty days.

"What are you laughing at dick head?" asked Cookie under his breath.

"I am just reminding myself of Kepler's *Third Law of Thermodynamics*," Angel shot back.

"Oh yeah smart guy, and what is that," inquired Cookie.

"If the heats on somebody else it can't be on you," Brad said pompously and looking like a cat that just ate a two-pound canary.

"Kepler was an astronomer you moron!" Cookie turned to face the skipper as Brad walked through the doorway.

Teen Angel, ever so gently, closed the door behind him but then remained just outside the skipper's office well within earshot of the imminent tongue-lashing. He desperately wanted to listen to the verbal spanking about to be administered to Cookie. At that moment Commander "Shroud" Morley emerged from his office, catching Brad eavesdropping on the skipper and Cookie.

Way back in 1984, as a second tour Lieutenant coming off the carrier USS *Midway*, Shroud had been selected as an *alternate* for the Blue Angels Flight Demonstration Team. Of course, this was tantamount to being first runner-up in a Miss America beauty pageant. Meaning you only get to wear the crown and move into the coveted top spot if the real winner could not perform her duties for any reason during the year long reign. Missing out on his tiara, Commander Morley was reassigned as an A-4 instructor pilot in VT-24 located in Kingsville, Texas. Suffice it to say he was somewhat embittered by that little chapter in his career path, having never really gotten over it. Of course his squadron mates wouldn't let him fully recover from the episode either, taunting the "almost" Blue Angel at every appropriate opportunity. It is a well-known fact that in the Corsair community they eat their young, so you should never bleed in those shark infested waters. Shroud was a hemophiliac. He bled often.

"Take a hike skin dick!" said Commander Morley, intentionally clearing his throat several times before beginning to speak.

"Come on Shroud, this is gonna be a priceless ass chewing," retorted Angel with a devious smirk covering his face.

"Beat it bub!" ordered Commander Morley.

"Aye aye sir," responded Brad. After offering a lackadaisical and highly patronizing salute, he promptly sauntered toward the direction of the officer's head.

The G meter of 415 had clicked to the eight setting meaning Cookie had pulled at least 8 G's and perhaps as much as 8.9 G's during the hop. This little "tattle tale" black box had only recently been installed fleet wide into the left side panel of the A-7, and only after the incessant urgings of the LTV Corporation in Dallas, Texas. After the modification, reported overstressing of airframes had doubled.

In the skipper's office Cookie was standing rigidly at attention, eyes fixed but not dilated, receiving his latest spanking. He nervously swallowed and licked his lips at every opportunity. He was suddenly aware of the chap stick he had deposited into the upper right pocket of his flight suit. The verbal diatribe would probably last about two to three minutes. It would only take that length of time for Duke to grow weary of meting out discipline to a fellow aviator for something as trivial as an overstressed jet.

The skipper knew full well that the maintenance crew would merely have to jack up the Corsair, check a few components then return the A-7 to an *up* status. It would take less than thirty minutes and the jet would surely make the next launch. Besides, Duke would quickly remember how he used to feel when he got yelled at as a Lieutenant standing tall before the CO or his Department Head. It happened too frequently as he recalled. But he *was* the VA-204 squadron commanding officer and had to occasionally set a leadership example, even with men who wore the legendary wings of gold.

"I understand the concept, of training like you fight Cookie, but you gotta remember that the LTV engineers only saw fit to allow us Corsair drivers seven G's of acceleration forces on this hunk of metal. And this is your second over-stress episode this week." The skipper was mistaken of course it was two in the last three weeks. Cookie didn't know if Duke wanted him to reply or not, so he avoided direct eye contact and kept his mouth shut, except to lick his lips yet again. Frustrated by this obvious lack of remorse Duke summarily kicked Lieutenant Cline out of the office space with some sort of a disgusted but unintelligible final comment. In reality, the commanding officer would forget about the incident seconds after Cookie shut the door behind him. Lieutenant Cline, however, would not. Cookie always remembered *Murphy's Law*. 'If something can go wrong it will go wrong.' And Murphy was an optimist!

CHAPTER 6

▼

PIDDLE PACK

Sauntering into the officer's bathroom Cookie was immediately overwhelmed by the unique aroma of human excrement combined with Escada cologne. The assault on his nostrils quickly made him realize that Teen Angel was in one of the stalls taking his morning dump. At first he ignored Brad's presence and positioned himself directly in front of one of the three urinals hanging on the wall. Propped up on the commode, Teen Angel angled his head ever so slightly to the right so that he could peer through the door crack to see who was disturbing his quality time alone on the throne. Both men remained silent.

As Cookie unzipped his flight suit he immediately recognized the face of Saddam Hussein pasted inside the bottom of the porcelain fixture. A red bull's eye was situated directly over the Iraqi dictator's open mouth on the flimsy portrait. The urinal on Cookie's left featured a picture of the Ayatollah Khomeinie. The one on his right had the face of Mohammar Khaddafy strategically in place. Lieutenant Cline's flow of urine hit the tyrant Hussein just above his scraggily moustache. Cookie laughed quietly to himself.

The new Aviation Intelligence (AI) Officer, Lieutenant Junior Grade William Pack, was responsible for this insolent yet pertinent homage to Hussein and the other two *rag heads*. None of the reserve aviators had met the new AI yet. Undoubtedly, for the next several months, LTJG Pack would be like an injured fish desperately swimming in the middle of a frenzy of feeding sharks. He would learn to endure the inevitable invectives or die a tragic death in the process thought Cookie. In Naval Aviation, *Darwinism* ruled the order of battle.

"The skipper wants to have a little chat with you before we head out to our War-at-Sea debriefing at the RTVD (Real Time Visual Display)," said Cookie breaking the awkward silence. He was of course being deceitful with Brad.

"Okay then, I'll meet y'all down at the Air Guard auditorium at 1000." In fact, several surface warfare (*black shoe*) officers and enlisted men had already gathered at the amphitheater of the Louisiana Air National Guard (LAANG) Air Combat Center. They were juggling papers trying to look professionally busy, even though the formal debriefing of the War-at-Sea training exercise was still thirty-five minutes away. Lieutenant Commander Ken Randall, the Operations Officer from the USS *Missouri* and the black shoe team leader for the debriefing, was particularly looking forward to meeting Lieutenant Ackerman in person. He had spoken to Brad over the phone numerous times in the past two weeks in preparation for this strike, and had wanted to finally meet the face that was associated with the arrogance. This particular RTVD facility was somewhat larger than the RTVD amphitheater at the Navy Fighter Weapons School at NAS Miramar, and the one depicted in the 1986 blockbuster movie *Top Gun.*

"That sounds good to me Angel." With that said, Lieutenant Cline quietly slipped out of the officer's head, passing Commander Steve Fitzgerald who was coming in. Brad was unaware that Cookie had departed.

"Teen Angel, is that you liberally scattering your scent all around?" ragged Commander Fitzgerald as he washed some grease off his left index finger down into the sink.

"Yeah, it's me Klutz," responded Angel, recognizing the voice. "But my shit don't stink. So how did you know it was me?"

"I saw that old Hershey bar shine on your flight boots under the stall door and thought Tom Cruise never looked this good taking a crap. So, it's just gotta be Brad Ackerman from Hollywood USA!" remarked Klutz.

"Is *Cook* still out there pissing on a rag head?" asked Brad while pulling some Charmin toilet paper off the roll.

"No he's gone," replied Fitzgerald as he finished drying his hands with about five tan colored paper towels, then hastily departed back to his desk in the squadron operations office. Again, the door made almost no audible sound as it closed. Unknowingly, Brad continued to talk to Klutz even though he received no further responses. As he chatted on, Teen Angel didn't hear the door open when Lieutenant Junior Grade Pack entered the bathroom. Hearing what appeared to be a full-blown, yet distinctly one-sided, conversation in full swing, a funny smirk came across Bill Pack's face. The young officer appeared to be a bit nervous as he began to open the fly on his khaki pants to relieve himself into the urinal housing the picture of the Ayatollah Khomeinie.

Lieutenant Junior Grade Pack remained uncomfortably silent, not really knowing what to say to the unseen voice emanating from behind the middle stall door. Lieutenant Ackerman, peering through the door crack yet again, began to get somewhat irritated because he could still see the shape of Commander Fitzgerald standing at the urinal in his khaki uniform, wearing his brown aviator shoes. Brad also recognized the trademark crew cut hairstyle that had been extinct since the middle 60's except for two other notable exceptions, Johnny Unitas and Howie Long. Unitas and Long had the mettle to be trendsetters. Klutz Fitzgerald was just hopelessly stuck in the 60's. Could it be that the OPSO is purposely *flemming* (phlegm, ignore) me thought Teen Angel. Nobody ignores Teen Angel!

Flinging the metal stall door open with a tremendous bang, Teen Angel rushed what he assumed was the figure of Commander Fitzgerald standing just eight feet in front of him. Playfully, he pinned the khaki clad officer directly up against the urinal. The cold feel of the porcelain made both men cringe slightly. In the first few seconds of their struggle, LTJG Pack's squadron nametag was ripped from his shirt, falling into the piss and blue colored water at the bottom of the urinal. Just as he was about to exact an appropriate amount of revenge from Fitzgerald, the startled LTJG began to speak with a voice that was unfamiliar to Brad. As an obviously embarrassed Ackerman backed off to a safe distance in order to assess the situation, Bill Pack turned around and proceeded to piss all over his newly purchased brown aviator shoes. The cuff of his right pant leg was soon drenched with the unpleasant smell and the warm wetness of his own urine. The mistaken identity was now complete. Pack was so stunned that he couldn't even speak.

"Oh my God, I am sorry pal. I thought you were somebody else. Your crew cut and body build fooled me. Who are you anyway?" giggled Brad as his eyes instinctively searched the right side of the man's khaki shirt for a nametag.

"I'm the new squadron Aviation Intelligence Officer, Bill Pack," he answered with a fair amount of hesitation in his voice.

"Damn happy to make your acquaintance Bill, I'm Brad Ackerman, call sign Teen Angel." Brad quickly decided there would be a better time to shake the new guy's hand. "So sorry for this little incident, I'll make it up to you somehow," promised Ackerman as he swiftly left the restroom and walked toward Duke's office. Bill Pack remained in the officer's head for several extra moments, collecting himself as much as was possible considering the discomforting ordeal he had just been subjected to at the hands of Ackerman. Pack spotted his nametag in the urinal and after a quick flush he reached down to retrieve the piece of plastic. He washed the orange colored ornament off in the sink and replaced it on his uniform shirt. Teen Angel couldn't wait to tell the skipper about how he had just welcomed the new AI into the *River Rattler* clan.

Still seated comfortably at his desk Duke casually raised his eyes, removed his spectacles then watched incredulously as Teen Angel simply strolled into his office, invading his privacy without so much as a head nod of permission.

"Skipper your not gonna believe what just happened," stated an unduly proud Brad. Duke listened intently as Ackerman boldly recounted the story that had just unfolded a few moments ago. A sly smile slowly filled the skipper's face as each word of the incident came out of Teen Angel's mouth.

"That's funny stuff. We will have to give Mister Pack the name 'Piddle' as his call sign during the next AOM," laughed Duke.

"Perfect skipper," agreed Brad. Just then the STU-III (Secure Telephone Unit) phone, situated on a wall panel in the back corner of Duke's windowless workplace, began to ring. Without any hesitation Brad immediately picked up the receiver, even as Duke's smile turned to a bewildered look of astonishment.

"This is Commander O'Grady's office. How may I be of service?" stated Teen Angel in his best deadpan character.

"Hello, I would like to speak to Commander O'Grady. This is Hank Andrews, the Secretary of the Navy," said the official sounding voice on the other end of the fiber optics line.

"It's for you skipper!" said a somewhat stunned Ackerman, as if at a temporary loss for words, a truly unusual condition for Teen Angel to find himself in.

"No shit, give me that phone, and get the fuck out of here," declared Duke as he roughly grabbed the black receiver from Brad's hand, trying extra hard to hide his slight grin. Ackerman headed for the door, closing it as he exited the skipper's office space. Commander O' Grady and H. Lawrence Andrews III (SECNAV) briefly exchanged pleasantries then settled into a serious ten-minute conversation, a relatively long duration for the secretary to speak with someone who was not *flag rank* or who wasn't his superior in the grand scheme of political appointees.

The Secretary of the Navy was a native of New Orleans. He was born at Tulane Medical Center and had graduated from Tulane University before going on to Yale Law School, despite his aversion for cold weather. His father and mother, both possessing the same pedigree, were career diplomats in their second professions, serving in various posts and countries over these last twenty years or so. Even though he was supremely educated, Hank Andrews spoke with a characteristic N'awlins drawl, which can best be described as a combination of French, Southern and New York all rolled into one annoying dialect. In fact, most of the highly educated New Orleanians tried to hide this betraying evidence of their New Orleans roots, but not Hank Andrews. He was overtly proud of his heritage and didn't care that his N'awlins brogue made him lose fifty IQ points in the eyes of non-southerners. Non-natives who reside in the *Crescent City* never quite get acclimated to the intonation or the unique vernacular. Commander O'Grady's facial features grimaced noticeably as the conversation unfolded. Duke was from New York City.

As their discussion continued, and in excruciating detail, Andrews explained that a small problem had surfaced at the Pentagon about seven months ago in May of 1991, shortly after the signing of the treaty which officially ended the Gulf War. Then in September, the conundrum had assumed a whole new meaning and sense of urgency for several of the more liberal-minded political types *inside the beltway*. Andrews forged ahead with his story as Duke removed his left shoe and sock, placed his bare foot on top of the desk and robustly scratched his instep. It seems that the timetable for active duty squadrons to phase out of the A-7E Corsair and transition into the new FA-18A Hornet was running way ahead of schedule, probably due to and *in spite of* Desert Storm. In fact the Chief of Naval Education and Training (CNET), Admiral Sheridan Cosgrove, had informed the Secretary of the Navy that the entire fleet transition evolution would beat the original timeframe estimates by ten to twelve months; a truly seminal accomplishment for the United States Navy.

After two weeks of intense arguments in the *puzzle palace* (the Pentagon) over the possible alternatives created by this accelerated timetable for FA-18 transition, one of SECNAV'S Deputy Assistant Secretaries (DASN), a Naval Reservist one weekend each month, had formulated a rather innovative plan to address the situation. Secretary Andrews had in fact initially approved of his deputy's idea during an informal briefing, while wolfing down a twelve-ounce medium-rare tenderloin at Sam and Harry's in Washington, D.C. But later that same week, when the deputy formally presented his strategy to some of the Navy's top admirals, he had basically been laughed out of the meeting on the fifth floor at the Pentagon. Tail between his legs, the DASN meandered back to the sanctuary of his fourth floor office space. Duke closed his eyes tightly, wondering how long this was going to take before the politician got to his point.

But all vehement opposition to the young deputy's proposal evaporated in September of 1991 when the Tailhook scandal erupted like a small volcano, spewing its allegedly immoral lava all over the streets on *the hill*. O' Grady squirmed a bit during this portion of Secretary Andrew's comments because he and several of his VA-204 pilots had been at Tailhook in September of 1991, maintaining their usual *low profile*. Duke replaced the tan sock over his foot but left the brown shoe on the floor beside his desk.

The Tailhook Association, a private organization that advocates and lobbies Congress on behalf of carrier aviation, holds its annual convention every September in Nevada at the Las Vegas Hilton. Each year throngs of active duty, reserve and retired Naval Aviators congregate with unrivaled passion in the city that Bugsy Siegel invented. During the 1991 Tailhook event several females, some military and some civilian, had complained to the Navy of being sexually harassed at that hands of hundreds of drunken Naval Aviators. The purported sexual harassment occurred on the third floor of the Las Vegas Hilton, in a corridor commonly referred to as the *gauntlet* to convention goers. News of the supposed sexual harassment spread throughout the country faster than gonorrhea at the Mustang Ranch whorehouse. The liberal media was eager to fan the flames of the scandal whether the allegations were true or not.

Then, like a bum on a bologna sandwich, several female members of Congress promptly pounced upon the Tailhook scandal for the obvious political leverage it could confer. Surely the lengthy public investigation of the Tailhook disgrace, hyped through the vehicle of media sensationalism, could serve them well in their political futures if they espoused politically correct positions for their constituents. Fearing the repercussions, most of the Navy's top brass scrambled for the nearest camouflaged location, hidden or out in the open, hoping the furor would soon dissipate. At this point in their phone conversation, Commander O'Grady suddenly had visions of democratic Congresswoman Trish Schneider of Colorado and Vice Admiral Steve Evans dance through his brain for some reason. A progressive bitch and a gutless coward thought Duke as he changed positions in his chair to prevent his left leg from falling asleep.

During the ensuing investigation, numerous Navy pilots had their careers placed in limbo while the public scrutiny played itself out. Sensing a second chance for his proposal, the Deputy Assistant Secretary had buried himself for three days inside his office to revamp the original sales pitch, explained Andrews. On the second evening he discovered something that, for some unknown reason, seemed to elude the admirals. The USS *Enterprise's* (CVN-65) forward deployment, scheduled for April 10th through October 9th of 1992 would be the last ever carrier cruise for the Navy's A-7E Corsair aircraft. The light attack jet would be formally retired when the *Enterprise* and her Carrier Air Wing (CAG-2) completed that next extended at sea period. Both of the carrier's Corsair squadrons would then transition to the FA-18 Hornet upon their return to the mainland, separated by approximately six months in the training cycle. The SLUF (A-7E Corsair) would never make another cruise for the United States Navy; even reserve squadrons would phase out of the Corsair soon thereafter. This final cruise of course could serve as an enduring tribute to the Corsair. An episode to be remembered in the annals of United States naval history elaborated Andrews, continuing his story without skipping a beat or waiting for any response from Commander O' Grady, his captive audience.

Andrew's deputy assistant secretary had continued his research well past midnight of that second night, finally discovering that VA-113 was one of the two A-7E squadrons scheduled to make the final Corsair cruise as members of CAG-2 onboard the *Enterprise*. VA-113 was also the next squadron scheduled to be transitioned to the FA-18 Hornet. Additionally, several VA-113 pilots, including their CO and XO had been directly implicated in the Tailhook scandal. Since numerous hypocritical Congresswomen were seething at the mouth to see a few heads roll as soon as possible, with some form of disciplinary action being meted out to the guilty parties, the deputy believed he had found a way to appease everybody involved, at least temporarily. It was at that moment, after guzzling his last sip of lukewarm coffee, that the Deputy Assistant Secretary of the Navy for Reserve Affairs knew he had found a suitable resolution to the dilemma.

The solution he formulated was that a reserve A-7E squadron would be activated for a six month period to replace the VA-113 Stingers in the *Enterprise's* active duty Carrier Air Wing for the last A-7E Corsair carrier deployment. VA-113 would then transition early to the FA-18, ensuring that fleet modernization continued at a brisk pace, while a capable reserve Corsair squadron would fill their void as members of CAG-2. The Reserves, after all, had made a significant contribution to the Gulf War effort. This would be just another appropriate way of recognizing that contribution to the egotistical active duty military cadre, especially those pompous admirals. This alternative to the dilemma would effectively kill three birds with one stone. The DASN gave a last lethargic gaze at his yellow legal pad full of scrawled notes, vigorously rubbing the exhaustion from his blurry and bloodshot eyes one final time before heading to the Metro station and the fifty-five minute train ride home to Bowie, Maryland.

1. Transition VA-113 early to the FA-18, (keep moving forward).

2. Give some (much deserved) acclaim to the Navy Reserves for their valuable contributions during Operation Desert Storm (fuck those admirals).

3. Remove two pilots from leadership positions as a result of their involvement in the Tailhook scandal to appease those hypocritical female members of Congress (get 'em off SECNAV's back).

4. This could work!

"So my deputy's plan involves VA-113 being taken out of CAG-2, transitioning them early to the FA-18, while a Navy Reserve A-7E squadron would be activated and inserted into CAG-2 for the last Corsair cruise. Skipper, I have chosen your squadron, VA-204 for this assignment and I have already gotten approval from Secretary of Defense Cheney and President Bush. Both of them think it's a great idea, with tremendous political potential for the upcoming election year," said Hank Andrews. Duke O'Grady, a staunch Republican, silently agreed as he clumsily wedged his left foot back into the brown shoe.

"Mister Secretary, the *River Rattlers* would be honored to perform this mission sir," replied Duke, "but I anticipate that we will need your personal help during the next several months of preparation." Subtly perceiving that the underlying message of that last comment conveyed more than a concern over training and operational readiness, Secretary Andrews sought to minimize the skipper's anxiety.

"No problem Commander. I will personally monitor your progress and y'awl can count on me for anything you may need to prepare. I won't let those active duty pukes give you too much shit either, I promise. Oh, and other thing, keep this under your hat for now Commander. I am flying down later tonight and will inform your men tomorrow at an all hands muster on the first day of your Drill Weekend," informed Andrews.

"I understand sir. What time do you want to address the squadron Mister Secretary?" inquired Duke, duly impressed that the SECNAV was aware his squadron would hold its December Drill Weekend starting tomorrow.

"At 1500 in your hangar bay, just after I play a round of golf with Admiral Tommy Thompson and take all his cash," laughed Andrews.

"That will work out perfect sir. Our CAG-20 corrosion inspection will be completed by then and we will be boiling up some Louisiana crawfish at that time to celebrate the results," said O' Grady.

"I hope they are *Bell River* crawfish skipper. Oh and one more thing. Have you got anybody who can join Admiral Thompson and myself in our golf match tomorrow? Unfortunately, Tommy isn't a very talented golfer and I enjoy competition." Admiral Thompson of course was the Chief of the Naval Reserves and was stationed across the Mississippi River in New Orleans.

"I think I know a couple of good partners to round out your foursome Mister Secretary," answered Duke. Knowing exactly whom he would be coerced into assigning to this sensitive and politically important task, O' Grady tightened his jaw just a bit as he continued with this casual segment of their long distance conversation. Duke had now slipped out of his other shoe and sock and was busily clipping the toenails from his right foot as it rested somewhat uncomfortably up on his desktop. As the telephone chat wound down to its conclusion, Commander O' Grady held the phone receiver tightly in between his ear and shoulder as he scrunched over clipping away, toenails flying carelessly all over the carpet, desktop and important personnel papers. After completion, Duke scooped up the nail residue, all that he could see, and tossed it into his trashcan as he waited impatiently for Secretary Andrews to wrap up his comments.

"By the way skipper, thanks for that Mardi Gras party invitation you sent me the last two years running. Very innovative card design I must say. Perhaps I will be able to make your carnival shindig this February." With that Andrews abruptly hung up the telephone on his end. Duke replaced the phone receiver back into its cradle then put his shoes and socks back on.

CHAPTER 7

▼

WORK HARD, PLAY HARD

Standing just a few feet outside the open doorway of the *River Rattler* line shack, strategically situated adjacent to the flight line, Senior Chief John Esposito almost growled as he preached to a cadre of fifty-two active duty enlisted men during the day-shift maintenance meeting. The daily gathering was two hours later than usual on this Friday morning because of the four-plane War-at-Sea strike sortie that had just been completed. After recovering the division of attack jets and dutifully attending to their post-flight requirements, all of the airmen had been *milling around smartly*, laughing and scratching with each other in the cool Louisiana breeze. They had been standing and acting rather casually on the black tarmac waiting for the meeting to begin; casually that is, until the Senior Chief began to rumble. When he spoke people stiffened up instinctively, as if a three-foot steel rod had been shoved up their spine. When Esposito bellowed, sailors paid attention.

John Esposito had only nine more months to serve in *this man's* Navy before he would retire after forty years of continuous and *usually* distinguished active duty service to his country. Senior Chief Esposito was indeed an exceptional sailor with two fists full of various ribbons, medals and commendations as proof of that claim. But he also had quite a few disciplinary episodes recorded in his service jacket; the worst being the time he had knocked out the Executive Officer of a Marine F-4 squadron while on liberty during a West Pac cruise. One punch from Esposito's gigantic southpaw fist and the *jarhead* light Colonel was laid out, face down in a puddle of muddy water next to Club Jolo in Olongopo City in the Philippines.

Chief Esposito of course had retrieved the XO, dusted him off and then threw him into the back of a jeepney, an extremely gaudy Philippine taxicab. He even shelled out fifty Pesos and instructed the little Filipino driver to take the Lieutenant Colonel back to the Main Gate of the Subic Bay Naval Base. The multi-colored jeepney soon sped off down the street toward the front gate of the base as a small crowd began to assemble to see what all the commotion was about. Unfortunately for Esposito, the Shore Patrol arrived on the scene and quickly arrested him, even though the exact details of the fight were somewhat sketchy. John Esposito spent the next twenty-four uncomfortable hours in the brig, deep in the bowels of the USS *Constellation* (CV-64).

That drunken skirmish cost him a promotion because his skipper at the time, Commander John "Long Horn" Angus of the VF-1 *Wolf Pack*, busted him back to E-6 and even fined him a cool thousand bucks at the ensuing Captain's Mast. It took Esposito five long years to re-earn his khakis and once again be promoted to Chief Petty Officer (E-7) after that little altercation in the PI. But in reality, Commander Angus had never enforced the $1000.00 fine. In fact, he ordered his Personnel Officer to bury the fine in the paperwork. Additionally, "Long Horn" Angus was instrumental in Esposito being promoted to Senior Chief (E-8) just sixteen months after reacquiring his E-7 rank.

Esposito would be fifty-four years old at his retirement. If anybody had the guts to do the math, they might figure out that he had joined the Navy illegally at the tender age of fourteen. But the ruse had worked because even at fourteen John Esposito appeared to be much older. In 1952, the Navy recruiter in downtown Chicago never even questioned the phony birth certificate that the young Esposito had presented to him at their first meeting. The official looking document, complete with the embossed raised seal of the great state of California, confirmed that John was born at the Corona Naval Hospital in 1934 (instead of 1938). Thus, in the recruiter's mind, Esposito was eighteen years old, and a Navy brat to boot, from the get go.

After he enlisted the following week, Esposito and his recruiter went out to Cubby Bears directly across the street from Wrigley Field. There the two drank eight pitchers of German lager beer and munched on Chicago-style hot dogs and whole Jalapeno peppers well into the wee hours of the morning, to celebrate his enlistment. Coincidentally, the recruiter had also signed-up more new enlistees than anybody else in the Great Lakes Naval Recruiting District that quarter, so their drinking exploits had double meaning. Shortly after the recruiter projectile vomited into a garbage can behind Cubby Bears, Esposito made sure that the drunken sailor made it safely home before he rode the "L" train back to the two-room dilapidated flat on the South side of Chicago that he shared with his waitress mother. John's dad had abandoned the two some 12 years ago. This type of all-night drinking and good-guy heroics would be repeated numerous times during Esposito's naval career. Esposito had a stomach made of iron. He was like-wise as mean as the *junk-yard-dog* character made so famous by Jim Croce, and undoubtedly could whip *Bad Bad Leroy Brown's* ass on any given day.

"The reserve sailors will be here tomorrow, all one hundred eight of them. As you know our CAG-20 'end of the year' Corrosion inspection begins promptly at 0700," shouted Esposito so even those men in the back could hear him speak. Actually, the mechanics of the Marine helicopter squadron that shared the other side of the hangar space with VA-204 could easily make out what the Senior Chief was verbalizing that morning, loud and clear.

"I have been hearing you men say for the last month that you all want to do good during that corrosion inspection. And I have seen the hard work you've put in to that end. But don't let me catch any of you guys playing *Jose Fuck Around* this weekend or there'll be hell to pay, I shit you not!" admonished Esposito. Many of the enlisted men in attendance that day had personally witnessed the Senior Chief make good on that unsympathetic pledge before. And all of them were terrified to incur the blunt end of his indignant wrath. Suddenly that cool gentle breeze felt as frigid as the Wicked Witch of the West's tit in a Colorado snowstorm, evoking shivers down several backsides.

"Treat this corrosion inspection as just another opportunity to excel," the Senior Chief continued. "I had better be seeing a bunch of squared-away sailors scampering around the hangar bay tomorrow. I don't want any of you to sud-denly become infected with incompetence or laziness. Remember this ain't the Water Company, this is the United States Navy," reminded the Senior Chief in a mocking tone. A wave of subdued laughter began to spread through the relaxed formation of men because this last comment was a direct, although good-natured, shot at the Maintenance Officer, Commander Mayhew.

Juice Mayhew was fond of using quite a few different comic annotations when talking to the enlisted men. His two personal favorites were: 'We didn't get much done today, but we're gonna give it hell tomorrow, and 'The best job I ever had was working for the Water Company, because it was five guys leaning up on a shovel watching one guy dig a ditch.' Esposito despised this mentality, sarcastic or otherwise, and had fought hard his entire career to keep *his* sailors from ever acquiring this type of attitude or demeanor in their naval profession.

Jack Mayhew was also legendary for his rather slipshod behavior in the Navy, especially since he transferred into the TAR ranks of the reserves. He probably deserves most of the credit for coining the phrase 'It is easier to beg for forgiveness than to ask for permission,' because of two fairly well known events that occurred only two years ago in October of 1989 when he was the Squadron's Administrative Officer. Similar to Duke O' Grady, Juice was a stellar Naval Aviator within the close confines of the cockpit. But once he *un-assed* his jet aircraft he literally detested administrative chores, and his threshold of disgust often drove him to innovation.

Every six months the squadron was required to perform a total recall of the entire cadre of reservists assigned to VA-204, in order to practice for the real thing should it ever be needed during preparation for war. And eighty-five percent was the minimum acceptable success rate for the recall drill. When the call came in that October morning from the CVWR-20 staff to initiate the biannual Reserve Recall Drill, Juice quickly decided to innovate just a little with CAG'S preferred procedures for this function. Mayhew, then a Lieutenant Commander, made only one telephone call that day sitting at his desk. He simply waited for a three-hour period then phoned the CAG Admin Officer at NAS Cecil Field in Jacksonville, Florida to report that he had achieved a ninety-two percent success rate with the recall drill.

On Friday of that same week, Lieutenant Commander Mayhew was obliged to monitor the Quarterly Physical Fitness Test (PFT) for his men in the Administration Department. Juice, who disliked strenuous physical activity quite a bit more than his administrative tasks, again decided on utilizing a novel approach with regard to established Navy procedures. After all, 'the good Lord only gives you so many heartbeats in a lifetime.' At noon Juice had his entire administrative department, decked out in Nike running apparel jog on down to the Baskin-Robbins ice cream store located onboard the Naval Air Station New Orleans. Once there he proceeded to buy a round of milkshakes for them all. Not surprisingly, every one of his men passed their PFT that day. Somehow the travesty of these two charades had eluded the attention of the Commander Selection Board and Juice was promoted to O-5 (full Commander) just ninety days later.

For the past fourteen months, Senior Chief Esposito had to go behind Commander Mayhew's back to ensure that the enlisted men of VA-204 didn't adopt a lethargic attitude based on the MO's teasing commentary and relatively lax behavior in front of them. He wanted to make certain that on his watch they were hard working, disciplined men at all times. Esposito had even asked Duke O' Grady to support him in this endeavor, which he did the moment he became the squadron's Commanding Officer. *Work hard, play hard* was officially incorporated as a part of the *River Rattler* motto six months ago at Commander O' Grady's Change of Command ceremony. Esposito heaved in another deep breath to wrap-up his lecture.

"And I don't want the CAG staff to see any gear adrift in your workspaces. I will not allow this inspection to become a goat rope," harangued Esposito. Whether he realized it or not, the Senior Chief's discourse and mannerisms were very reminiscent of Knute Rocke's famous let's *win one for the gipper* speech at Notre Dame. And, in just under twelve minutes he had used about every invective he had learned over the past thirty-nine years in the Navy.

"Now get out there and make it happen!" Finally, out of energy and out of ideas, Esposito released the men to their duties but he reached in and grabbed Airman Earl Hamilton by the arm as the crowd gradually dispersed. "Can I see you in my office for a minute Airman Hamilton," said the Senior Chief. It was a statement, not a question. Several of his colleagues saw the anxiety in Hamilton's eyes but doubted it was anything more than an act for their benefit. They all knew that the Senior Chief had a soft spot in his hardened heart for ADAN Hamilton, probably because he was from Aurora, Illinois the birthplace of Esposito's late mother. In fact, John Esposito saw a lot of himself in the youth, thirty-nine years removed of course.

As the two men, actually one man and one teenager, walked into Esposito's small cluttered office space, the Senior Chief suddenly spun around and plopped his large muscular behind squarely on the edge of his desk. His extremely, solid belly jutted out a couple of feet from his torso, straining the buttons on his khaki uniform shirt so much so that Hamilton could see his white undershirt through the gaps. The fit and trim Airman Hamilton wore crisp new dungarees freshly ironed so they were without wrinkles. At that moment, Hamilton wondered when was the last time Esposito had passed the Physical Fitness Test (PFT). The Senior Chief was soon leering at the youthful airman who stood rigidly with his eyes fixed on nothing in particular in the back of the room.

"What is this shit on your mug?" said Esposito as he roughly pawed the young man's nineteen-year old face.

"It's, a beard Senior Chief," muttered the somewhat insecure Hamilton.

"Horse shit! A baby's behind has more hair on it than you got on those smooth cheeks of yours Airman Hamilton," chided the Senior Chief. Hamilton shifted his body trying not to let his level of discomfort show. He was not successful.

"Have you ever seen me unshaved son?" quizzed Esposito.

"No senior chief, but then you get a little carried away with your razor," responded a semi-brazen Hamilton obviously referring to Esposito's shaved skull.

"I don't want to ever catch you with those piddly ass whiskers growing on your chops again. When you show up for work at my squadron, you will have a fresh shave on your baby face. Understand sailor?" Hamilton just shook his head, glassy eyed.

"So how was your time at the AD "A" School in Florida?" asked Esposito in a more relaxed tenor. Maybe the Senior Chief actually missed Hamilton. After all, he hadn't seen the kid for more than 6 weeks because of the training course. AD "A" School was the basic aircraft engine mechanics training which enlisted men must attend prior to going on to specializing in a particular type of engine. Hamilton would continue his training next month in the A-7 Corsair engine, after which he probably would be promoted to E-4 or Third Class Petty Officer. The Senior Chief had personally recommended Hamilton to the skipper for both of these assignments about three months ago. And Commander O' Grady had even pulled a few strings to get the kid in earlier than usual after an initial request.

"It was good training Senior Chief, but I didn't get laid if that's what you really want to know," answered Hamilton.

"That's too bad. We may have to work on that in the near future," grumbled Esposito. Handing the kid a *Bic* disposable razor Esposito said, "Now trot on down to the head and shave that crap off. If I had some tweezers I'd do it for you. Then get back to work and remember it's lefty-loosey, righty-tighty with those wrenches son. Make it happen!"

As Hamilton departed the line shack, the Senior Chief flipped on the Sony stereo receiver located on a TV stand behind his desk. *Sweet dreams are made of this, who am I to disagree* sang Annie Lennox of the British rock group The Eurythmics, at about fifty-five blaring decibels. This was strange because Esposito only listened to Country Music, like Waylon and Willie and the rest of the good old boys from Nashville. As he turned the volume down to a more palatable level, he tried punching the station set switches on the front of the receiver. He quickly discovered that some joker had changed all the memory buttons to 94.7 WFNG, a New Orleans station that played contemporary and 80's rock and roll, twenty-four hours a day.

"Its only rock and roll but I *don't* like it. Sorry Mick Jagger," chided Esposito in a hushed voice so nobody would hear his comments. Well at least it wasn't Walton and Johnson or that smart ass Grease Man from Jacksonville thought Esposito. He turned the radio off then headed out to the flight line to kick a few butts.

CHAPTER 8

▼

EARNING YOUR FLIGHT JACKET

Even though one fourth of total flight time must be flown at night, for most Tactical Naval Aviators when the sun goes down its time to shed their *speed slacks*, splash on a little cologne and head for the O' Club bar. Undoubtedly, there would be a bevy of beauties adorning the barstools this Friday evening at the Jack Black Memorial Officer's Club. After all, it was the day before a huge Drill Weekend for the air station with Navy, Marine Corps, Air Force and Air Guard units all scheduled to be in town for their last drill of 1991. Indeed, the *Jackson's* ($20 bills) would be flying across the bar tonight.

Without question many of the single, and not so single, women in Southeastern Louisiana were aware of this fact and would be out in search of a pilot for a little rest and relaxation before the hectic pace of the holiday season took its annual toll. It wasn't close to the spectacle that occurs each Wednesday evening at the Officer's Club at Miramar Naval Air Station in San Diego. It couldn't even compare to Thursday nights at the Spin Drifter Tavern in Jacksonville. But for Belle Chasse, Louisiana it was the only game in town on a Drill Weekend. Besides, Bourbon Street could always serve as a logical follow on to the antics at the Jack Black.

The O' Club bar and restaurant, which had been cleverly attached to the BOQ onboard the Naval Air Station New Orleans, was named in honor of a

River Rattler A-4E Sky Hawk pilot. The reserve aviator had been killed when his engine suddenly flamed out over the Gulf of Mexico some fifteen years ago. The squadron was in New Orleans, visiting their future home station, on a short weapons detachment. Unfortunately for Lieutenant Jack Black, when he pulled the face curtain handle to initiate the eject sequence the rocket motor on the ejection seat did not discharge. The jet's canopy failed to leave the fuselage as well when he ran through his 'ditching checklist' procedures. After countless futile attempts to shed his canopy, Jack realized he was trapped in the jet.

Because he was unable to escape from the cockpit Jack rode the *scooter* into the salty waves, within eyesight of the Chandelier Islands, to his ultimate demise. Lieutenant Black's last words over the UHF radio that steamy summer afternoon were 'Tell my wife and children that I love them dearly. A-4 Sky Hawks forever.' Black's wingman watched in total disbelief as the scenario unfolded before his eyes. Even the Houston ARTCC traffic controller felt utterly helpless as he recorded the distressing final words of the pilot. The NAS New Orleans Commanding Officer dedicated the O' Club in memory of Lieutenant Black in March 1978, when the VA-204 *River Rattlers* officially transferred to New Orleans from Memphis.

As if on cue, Lieutenant Brad Ackerman and Lieutenant Ed Cline met in the hallway just outside of their adjoining BOQ rooms. Teen Angel was dressed in the royal blue, long-sleeve pullover by Ralph Lauren that he had purchased just two days earlier at Nordstrom's on Rodeo Drive. The cotton shirt had the red silhouette of a man on horseback wielding a polo mallet high into the sky. Brad also wore the usual pair of faded Guess blue jeans. The stone in his Stanford class ring, encircling his left ring finger, contained the royal blue Star Sapphire that he had purchased while in Thailand during his *nugget* cruise five years ago. Cookie was clad in tan Dockers and a red knit shirt from Macy's Clubroom collection. The shirt's color was dulled from a few too many washings. He also sported his U.S. Naval Academy ring, which was quite a bit larger than any ring should be. But then *ring knockers* were notorious for buying extra large jewelry upon their graduation from *Boat School*. Both pilots, of course, wore flight jackets. The two men made eye contact, smiled briefly then turned toward the saloon without speaking. Their eye gestures conveyed all that needed to be said.

Brad Ackerman was 6 foot 2 inches tall with smooth, fair skin. His ID card stated that he weighed in at 195 pounds. But he actually tipped the scales at 205, which was 11 pounds under his maximum weight according to Navy standards. Ed Cline was a tad bit shorter than Teen Angel, but was much leaner than his squadron mate. He also had facial features that were slightly more rugged. Both were more handsome than any male deserved to be and they often used this to their advantage in life.

Teen Angel and Cookie literally pranced into the O' Club bar wearing their trophy flight jackets, their brown leather fight jackets complete with an abundance of commemorative patches earned over these past nine years in the Navy. The surplus of patches, like sweat stains on a G-suit, was equivalent to badges of honor in the lore of Naval Aviation. Each jacket was liberally adorned with various cruise badges, centurion and double centurion emblems from different aircraft carriers, top hook awards, an array of squadron insignia and air wing crests, an A-7 Echo Driver patch, an A-4 Sky Hawk logo, and miscellaneous school patches including SERE, SLATS, and Top Gun. These precious jackets were revered like the crown jewels and emblematic of one's experience and expertise. Even though most refuse to admit it, jacket envy, similar to penis envy, is a substantial part of Naval Aviation.

The aviators quickly located two empty barstools in the middle of the right side of the L-shaped bar. Sitting down Cookie ordered a Budweiser while Brad requested a Coors Light. Holly Carter, the petite, raven-haired beauty who would serve as their personal barkeep for the remainder of the evening at the Jack Black, winked while coyly placing a pencil between her crimson lips. She couldn't be more than five feet tall, all 102 pounds of her. This was Holly's first night on the job and she was wearing a tight fitting, bright red tank top with no bra. Anyone could plainly see it was a bit chilly in the club that evening as the outline of her pert nipples strained against the taut spandex blouse. She turned slowly in a beguiling manner to fetch the round of beers.

Angel and Cookie's eyes were glued to Holly's mesmerizing rear end while she sashayed in a plaid miniskirt to the beer cooler behind the bar. Her extra-long locks swayed over her back as she walked. The red-green color of her skirt was a nice touch for the Christmas season. Holly's firm behind had been superbly sculpted by years of aerobics regimen, and it resembled a pear half sliced in two equal portions by her thong underwear. As they waited for her to bring the liquid refreshment Teen Angel was suddenly overwhelmed by a daydream.

Ackerman unexpectedly recalled the morning he received his first leather flight jacket, about nine years ago at the Pensacola Naval Air Station. It was during the third week of Aviation Indoctrination (AI), the training course that all Student Naval Aviators must successfully endure before the final academic *weed out* cut was made and actual flying could commence. Back then that first flight jacket was nothing but a cured piece of empty brown goatskin, even though it was still a prized possession for the twenty-something, would-be aviators.

Brad had been fitted for his size 42 Long jacket just three hours before a rather large enlisted aircrew man (AW) callously chucked him out of a YP (Yard Patrol) Boat into Pensacola Bay. The AW-2's tattooed arms were larger than Brad's thighs. In the cold water Ackerman and his classmates would remain until they were snatched up into a hunk of warm gyrating metal commonly referred to as a Navy SH-3 helicopter; but only after spending a couple of excruciating hours in a one-man life raft. This of course simulated rescue of a downed aviator at sea. Teen Angel unconsciously shivered as he recalled the frigid temperatures in the bay that morning. His location in the water was less than two miles from where National Airlines had crash-landed a Boeing 727 into that blue-green inlet several years earlier.

A month before his first carrier deployment Brad had received the most prized possession of all, next to those Navy wings of gold (*the golden leg splitters*). That's when he acquired his *fleet* Naval Aviator flight jacket. Of course, the green Nomex jacket had the same patch scheme as his leather replica, repeated right down to the last infinite detail. In addition to providing warmth, flight jackets were truly *I Love Me Walls* that you could wear around in public to flaunt before your fellow Naval Aviators, Air Force pukes and, not surprisingly, women. Holly delivered the beers and placed them on cardboard coasters in front of Cookie and Teen Angel. They each took long swigs of the refreshing brew that cooled their throats as it gushed down. Cookie took the opportunity to strike up a little pleasant conversation with Holly. He was, of course, trolling.

In a truly bizarre episode of daydreaming, Teen Angel's mind flashed back to Hollywood and the wrap party for the motion picture *Always* in May of 1989. It was Brad's very first movie credit as a stunt pilot for Paramount Studios and the first time he had worked with the acclaimed film director Stephen Spielberg. Shortly after Brad had gotten off active duty on June 15, 1988 Ackerman was hired as a corporate pilot by Tom Singer, a member of the Board of Directors of Paramount Studios. Singer, an old submarine buddy of Chief William Ackerman, had hired Brad as a favor to kid's late father. A month later, when one of the stunt pilots had an accident while working on a particularly hazardous scene in the movie *Always*, Singer had suggested Brad as a replacement to Spielberg, while the two gorged themselves on Caesar Salads at the Paramount Commissary. Spielberg hired Brad that very afternoon.

At the party on the back lot of Paramount, Spielberg publicly praised Brad's courage and daring piloting skills, which he displayed during a variety of scenes in *Always*. Many of the film's aviation stunts required flying into staged forest fires and performing hazardous low-level antics for the camera. Spielberg's public praise only served to enhance Brad's already arrogant demeanor at the motion picture studio. Ackerman recalled how he had stood silent, wearing his green flight jacket, humbled by the movie mogul's kind words. But Brad had quickly become known as a stunt pilot who could also deliver the goods during filmmaking, usually on the first take. Directors and producers liked this about Ackerman because it saved them production costs.

Toward the end of the wrap party, after several hours of mixed drinks and caviar, a young and coming female starlet had asked Teen Angel to *give* his green flight jacket to her. Brad, of course, initially scoffed at her request. How dare her even broach this subject.

"Do you know what you have to do to earn this flight jacket honey?" teased Brad.

"No, but just tell me what it is baby and I'll do it for you here and now!" replied the blonde starlet without any hesitation or purpose of evasion evident in her soft sensual voice. Her beauty was indeed breathtaking and her green eyes hypnotic. Brad negotiated a quick trade agreement with the woman for his spare green flight jacket, the one that he had back at his condominium in Westwood. They would consummate the transaction the following evening at her Malibu beach house.

Unknown to Brad, Spielberg had been loitering just around the corner and heard every word, drinking up their conversation with a spoon for the comic effect. From that moment on Spielberg had taken an immense liking to Brad and decided to use him for aviation stunt scenes in all of his movie productions that required them. He also teased that he would have to keep Brad away from his wife, actress Amy Irving. Ackerman laughed to himself while still in the midst of his daydream because Spielberg and Irving divorced just four months after that wrap party for *Always*. In fact, two months ago, Teen Angel had attended Spielberg's second wedding to actress Kate Capshaw, the femme fatale from *Indiana Jones and the Temple of Doom*. Shortly after the wrap party for *Always*, Spielberg contracted with Tom Singer to allow Brad to work on his next project which was tentatively titled *Jurassic Park*, a film adaptation of a Michael Crichton novel about dinosaurs that come back to life after a series of DNA experiments. The shooting schedule would kick off at a remote island location in the Caribbean in January 1992.

Spielberg would later introduce Teen Angel to the celebrated film director, and decorated former WW II Marine pilot, George Roy Hill during a cast party at his home in Beverly Hills. Hill had retired from directing and left Hollywood to pursue a teaching career at his alma mater Yale in 1988. The two, despite their age difference, became fast friends and had flown together on several occasions when Hill was back in Southern California. Teen Angel found both multi-millionaires to be surprisingly down-to-earth. Brad had even taught Spielberg the aerobatic intricacies of the loop, barrel roll, and half Cuban eight in the director's spanking new Grumman Tiger.

Displaying the same precision that Rocky and Teen Angel had exhibited during their section pop-up attack on the *Missouri*, Cookie and Teen Angel simultaneously spun around in their seats. It was time to make a quick *fighter sweep* of the female talent in the room. Both pilots nonchalantly took another sustained pull of beer from their long necks. Angel removed the empty bottle from his quenched lips a mere second before Cookie did the same.

"Another round Holly," shouted Cookie, while turning his head in her direction behind the bar. Straining his neck he glanced at her inviting ass one more time, even as he wiped away beer residue from his mouth with the back of his wrist.

"I'll get right on it boys," was Holly's quick condescending response. She didn't turn around to face them as she spoke.

Just then something caught Brad's attention on the terrace. He spotted about twenty guys and one butt ugly woman sitting and standing around a large table on the patio deck just beyond the side entrance to the club. They were drinking, smoking and generally having a grand old time. All of the men were wearing green flight jackets with a single patch on the right breast. The emblem was a depiction of the cartoon character *Yosemite Sam* firing a couple of pistols at a small airplane that had crashed into an open ocean. *Bayou Bushwackers* was apparently the name of their organization as it was embroidered underneath Sam's feet on the logo. Additionally, each man's jacket had a nametag with a goofy looking pair of gold wings on it. Seeing that the wings were gold in color, Teen Angel was now extra curious. Leaving Cookie alone at the bar for just a few minutes, he maneuvered a little closer to their table and all the commotion.

As he approached, Brad saw a couple of the men were busy attending to three large pots of boiling crabs. He could also see a massive cloud of cigarette smoke lingering near their table. Brad wondered what the interior lining of their lungs must look like. As he drew closer he could see that the group of men at the table had a dice cup and they were busy rolling for drinks at their secluded location on the veranda. But Ackerman noticed that they were doing it all wrong. He immediately decided to stroll over to their table and teach them the proper mechanics of rolling for drinks in a Navy Officer's Club. He also wanted to know more about them.

"Hi guys," were Angel's opening remarks. "My name is Lieutenant Brad Ackerman and I don't want to be rude but you're playing that game all wrong. May I show you the correct way to roll for drinks?" asked an appropriately deferential Teen Angel. As his comments hit their ears, the group's clamor was promptly hushed. One of the older men, apparently their leader, looked Brad squarely in the eyes then spoke up without any hesitation.

"Sure kid, give us the *gauge* on the game," he said using some Navy lingo in an apparent attempt to impress Brad. His nametag read: *Jeff Carlyle, Aviation Branch Chief.* As the ten men huddled closer to hear Ackerman speak the unattractive woman excused herself to the ladies room. Teen Angel quickly thought 'there isn't enough powder on earth for that nose.'

Over the next five minutes, dice cup in hand, Lieutenant Ackerman explained in great detail the mechanics of the dice cup game. The group listened intently to his explanation and conversed quietly with each other during portions of Brad's impromptu lecture. Satisfied that he had imparted the requisite knowledge, Teen Angel then embarked on an effort to ease his curiosity.

"So who are you guys anyway?" inquired Ackerman.

"We work for the United States Customs Service," replied Jeff Carlyle as his colleagues cackled, then continued to smoke their Marlboros and drink their round of Jack Daniels. One short little man stirred the crabs as they continued to bubble and boil.

"You mean those guys who check the underwear in your luggage at New Orleans International Airport?" asked Ackerman. As soon as he spoke the words he knew how stupid they sounded.

"No, no we fly airplanes right here at the Naval Air Station. We *drive* those blue and white business jets with the long snouts and all the antennae hanging off the fuselage. And we fly specially equipped Black Hawk helicopters," replied Carlyle.

"Oh I get it. You are those guys with the *Omaha* call sign I hear on the radio every now and then. You chase those drug cartels who try to smuggle cocaine into the country," responded Brad, obviously happy with himself for knowing this information.

"That's right. Say, you wouldn't consider coming to work for us would you Lieutenant Ackerman? We are currently looking for a few good pilots. I think you would naturally fit right in with our people," solicited Carlyle. Brad proceeded to explain that he was very happy flying Corsairs for the Navy Reserves. Besides, he already had a fabulous civilian job in Hollywood flying for the motion picture studios. Ackerman politely thanked Carlyle for the offer and then promised to pass the job information on. You never know, maybe someday one of his squadron mates will be looking for a job thought Teen Angel.

"Hey, do you guys need some help picking up women in here? I've noticed that you only got one woman hanging around your table, and she looks like five miles of bad road," chuckled Brad, regrettably not knowing the full story.

"Well unfortunately, that unpleasant looking woman is my wife," replied Jeff Carlyle. Open mouth insert foot, thought Brad. While he spoke Jeff placed his right hand on the back of Ackerman's suddenly pouting shoulders. As he stretched out his arm Brad could plainly see that Jeff was wearing a .45 caliber semi-automatic pistol holstered to his hip. It was only then that Teen Angel became fully aware of all the bulges under the flight jackets of the ten men. Brad's body language became increasingly uneasy.

"Its okay, its okay, I know she's a dog. But she has many other ways to keep me happy," smiled Jeff Carlyle. With that said Ackerman gave a farewell handshake to Carlyle then walked his embarrassed, red face toward the barstool. As he walked away in Cookie's direction the song *if you want to be happy for the rest of your life, never make a pretty woman your wife*, was ringing in his brain. That woman is not a wife, thought Teen Angel. She's a life sentence!

CHAPTER 9

▼

LET'S BLOW THIS POP STAND

While he waited for Teen Angel to return, Cookie politely asked Holly to bring him the cordless telephone as she delivered a fresh round of suds. Cookie wanted to find out what the hold up was for Rocky, who was late again as usual. From eight feet away, Holly slid the phone down the smooth bar top to Lieutenant Cline so that it stopped directly in front of his Budweiser bottle.

"Nice lag," said Cline, complimenting her shuffleboard skill. Clutching the receiver he dialed Rocky's BOQ room.

Cookie allowed the phone to ring eleven times. Just as he was about to hang up out of frustration, Rocky answered. He was down on one knee by the twin-size bed as he snatched the receiver into his wet soapy palm. He clenched his teeth as his other hand was busy rubbing the impending bruise he had suffered to his left thigh from the fall. Apparently his drenched feet had slipped on the slick linoleum floor sending him tumbling *ass over teakettle* into the corner of the room. Rocky at first had wanted to ignore the incoming call. But then he had bolted from his hot shower in the middle of the eighth ring thinking it could be the skipper or the MO with some sort of maintenance request. After all, the corrosion inspection was looming and, as the Assistant MO, Rocky wanted his department to have all their ducks in a row. Water and soap bubbles dripped down onto the faded green bedspread.

"Lieutenant Commander Stone," said an out of breath Rocky into the black phone's mouthpiece.

"Hey dick head, you're late again!" said Lieutenant Cline as if to reprimand the senior officer.

"I just got out of the shower and I am standing here dripping wet and naked," informed Rocky, trying to sound as cool as possible under the unnerving set of circumstances. He was relieved nobody had witnessed the just concluded, embarrassing tumbling event. The Russian judge would have probably given me a three point five he thought to himself, his sense of humor abruptly returning.

"Thanks for the visual," said Cookie. "Now throw on some duds, splash on some Old Spice and get your butt down here ASAP," ordered Cline in his best commanding resonance. Rocky, of course, was in no particular hurry to get to the O' Club this evening, especially after his lackluster performance on the bombing spar. He knew that his errant MK-84 bomb drop during the War-at-Sea strike against the USS *Missouri* would undoubtedly be a major topic of the barroom banter; at least until his squadron mates began to focus their attention on more important matters, namely women.

"Order me a Heineken Cookie. I'll be there in ten minutes," said Rocky as he plopped the receiver down to end the annoying conversation. But he missed the phone's cradle. Like a third string fullback inserted into the lineup during the last two minutes of a blowout, Rocky ineptly fumbled the telephone's handset sending it sprawling to the floor. The dull pain in his left thigh throbbed as he yanked the phone receiver back up by its twisted cord. It twirled counterclockwise as he pulled it up and then slipped it into its normal resting spot on the telephone base unit. Cookie punched the 'end button' on the cordless phone and laid it on the bar in front of him, just as Teen Angel arrived dutifully back by his side. The two leaned in over the bar railing and sucked down another healthy amount of fermented barley and malt nectar. Standing somewhat awkwardly at the jukebox, an Air Force A-10 Warthog pilot pumped a five spot into the machine's paper money receptacle then patiently studied the available music selections.

Just then, Teen Angel felt a tremendous slap on his back and both he and Cookie heard the dull thud of coarse flesh on Nomex. Brad reeled around to see Juice's smiling jovial face, capped teeth and all, standing behind him looking like the proverbial Humpty Dumpty surrounded by all the king's horses and all the king's men. Jack Mayhew's entourage that evening included Commanders "Klutz" Fitzgerald and "Shroud" Morley, and Lieutenants "Comatose" Gross, and "Sugar[2]" Cane. The four were laughing and scratching, and basically demonstrating the customary demeanor in the opening five minutes of any social gathering of aviators. Hearing the amplified uproar, Holly hustled her steel buns and stretched tank top over to their end of the bar. Making first eye contact with the fresh new female face approaching, Commander Mayhew decided he needed to freshen up just a bit more to make her acquaintance.

"Wait a sec, let me spruce up just a tad before I meet this girl, said Juice to his squadron mates. As he usually does Juice pretended to spit into his palms then ran both hands brusquely back through his hairline as if to slick down his scruffy hair, apparently trying for that polished, Coach Pat Riley look. The pilots howled at Mayhew's time-honored routine.

"What'll it be fly boys?" said Holly to direct their attention to her.

"We're not fly boys, we are carrier attack pilots honey," said Juice as if to inform Holly of her reprehensible error. Brad quickly shook hands with Juice, squeezing harder than their normal cordial greeting, to distract him from attacking Holly any further at this juncture.

"The first round is on me," said Comatose Gross. This was a good thing since he usually conked out at about nine or nine thirty. Holly pulled out her pad and pencil to jot down the large order of assorted beers and mixed cocktails requested by the six aviators. She twirled her black hair and chewed her Trident sugarless gum in an exaggerated fashion, even while flaunting those coy brown eyes, as each man stated his request. Where was Van Morrison when you needed him thought Teen Angel?

Holly's flirtatious mannerisms were an immediate hit with the five late arrivals. Men, especially pilots, always think there is a chance no matter the obstacles in their paths she thought to herself. They are so cute and so very naïve. Holly giggled as she finished documenting their alcoholic desires and one order of chili-cheese fries with her #2 pencil. No need to wonder who had requested the fries; it was Juice of course, who was apparently engaging in a little culinary celebration because he was four pounds under his maximum weight for tomorrow's annual flight physical.

Mayhew would have to stop eating and drinking at around 2000 to start the required twelve hour fasting cycle, however, so that his blood work would give an accurate reading on the condition of his hemoglobin and cholesterol. As Holly walked away seven pairs of hungry eyes followed her every move, at least for the first eight or nine seconds. At that moment the jukebox was blaring the words written by Don Henley and Glen Frey of the Eagles: *Raven hair and ruby lips, sparks fly from her fingertips, echoed voices in the night, she's a restless spirit on an endless flight.* 'Witchy Woman' indeed thought Teen Angel, as his baby blues remained riveted to her provocative, feminine figure moving behind the bar.

"The skipper said to start the shenanigans without him. He'll be here around 1730 or so," said Juice to update everyone. Unknown to them all was that Duke O' Grady was going to be late because he was meeting SECNAV'S Gulf Stream-Five (G-5) aircraft that was due to arrive at the Naval Air Station New Orleans around 1700. Secretary Andrews was going to spend a little quality time in the *Crescent City* the night before his momentous announcement at VA-204, and his big golf match with the Chief of the Naval Reserve Forces. In fact, the Secretary already had an 8:00PM dinner meeting arranged with Congressman Bob Livingston at Commander's Palace. The two politicians would undoubtedly discuss duck hunting and military appropriations over some of the finest French cuisine in the world. At that moment, Duke was eating a melting Snickers candy bar while awaiting Hank Andrews' arrival at the Passenger Terminal along with the NAS Commanding Officer, CAG Sullivan and Admiral Tommy Thompson.

Squid Sullivan had flown an F-14 Tomcat over from Cecil Filed, and the Admiral had ridden in his motorcade across the Crescent City Connection Bridge from his office on Dauphine Street. Both men had arrived just forty-five minutes prior to the anticipated ETA for the SECNAV. As he sat there patiently, munching away on the chocolate bar, Duke O' Grady remembered when the Secretary of the Navy was carted around the country in a souped up A-3 Whale. And even though the interior had been reconfigured so that it was luxurious, the SECNAV'S A-3 was still a flying hunk of junk. The G-5 was quite a step up from that bucket of bolts thought Duke.

Lieutenant Commander Jim Stone strolled confidently into the O' Club looking more like a college linebacker than a Naval Aviator. Five more VA-204 pilots trailed closely behind him into the bar. Rocky was just over six feet tall with a chiseled jaw, and built out of solid muscle and granite. If he could locate a cowboy hat and a set of spurs, Rocky could double for the Marlboro Man on billboards without any problem. Too bad he was afraid of horses. Cookie sometimes called Jim Stone 'muscle head' to mock his stalwart physical appearance because, although he was highly intelligent, Rocky often succumbed to his inherent ignorance. In jest, Teen Angel called Rocky the stupidest smart-guy he'd ever met.

Cookie Cline would also pester Jim Stone about punching sides of beef at the meat packing plant just like the Rocky Balboa character did to prepare for his big boxing match against Apollo Creed. Rocky tolerated but basically ignored this treatment because he adhered to the age-old adage never bleed in shark infested waters. Cookie gave Rocky an energetic high-five then handed him the bottle of Heineken he had ordered five minutes ago, just after their phone conversation had concluded.

"Nice shooting this morning at the spar," said Cookie in an attempt to provoke Rocky. Jim Stone didn't take the bait. He simply grabbed the beer, summarily ignored the insult then continued to stride deeper into the barroom. Rocky was strategically not wearing his wedding band that chilly winter evening and his chin was raised high, exuding condescension. Like Warren Zevon's *Werewolf of London*, his black hair was perfect and his clothing immaculate. Too bad he didn't have a Pina Colada in his hand.

At age eighteen, Rocky had longed for a coveted appointment to the U.S. Naval Academy at Annapolis, Maryland. He had even dreamed of playing linebacker for the Midshipman football team ever since he was twelve years of age. But unfortunately, *Canoe U* had turned him down flat. So, Jim Stone had to settle for a college education at Temple University in his hometown of Philadelphia, and an NROTC ticket into the commissioned officer ranks of the Navy. Football went by the wayside as well, after his freshman year.

"Is that Aqua Velva I smell on your neck Juice?" cracked Rocky as he approached the burgeoning cluster of squadron mates loitering at the end of the bar. He vigorously shook Jack Mayhew's outstretched hand to reaffirm their dynamic friendship.

"Very amusing wisecrack," retorted Juice. "Didn't they have any men's clothes where you bought that shirt Rocky?" Mayhew was obviously pleased with his comeback.

"This shirt costs more than your whole wardrobe Juice, including your fifty pairs of Sansabelt slacks," taunted Jim Stone. He was of course, borrowing one of Teen Angel's patented barbs.

"Are you ready for a little action tonight Rock?" "Things are shaping up rather nicely, if you get my drift." As he spoke, Juice made a gesturing motion with his head toward Holly, accompanied by Tom Selleck's classic *Magnum P.I.* flirting motion with his eyebrows, all while holding a 'seven and seven' gingerly in his callused right hand.

"Well unfortunately my extremely jealous and overtly suspicious wife has my dick back in Minneapolis," said Rocky with a slight twinge of irony evident in his discourse.

"Didn't you bring your spare dick," chimed in Comatose Gross eavesdropping on the ongoing conversation, but knowing exactly where Rocky intended to steer the repartee. He had seen this act before.

"Hang on a second and I'll check," said Rocky, pulling out the waistband on his Tommy Hilfiger slacks a good two inches from his stomach. He gazed down into his crotch area with a serious face. "Yep, looks like I brought the spare!"

exclaimed Rocky with a big shit-eating grin on his robust face. The gleam in his eyes was quite apparent as he signaled for Holly to fetch another round of whisky and wine for his squadron mates.

As the fresh round of drinks was being dispensed by the nubile bar maid, Rocky decided this would be a good opportunity to formally address the group of attack pilots. It might also be his only chance while they were all still coherent. Clearing his throat and hoisting a slightly warmed Heineken over his head, Lieutenant Commander Stone commenced his short, impromptu sermon on Romance and the Naval Aviator.

"Gentlemen if you please, a point of Parliamentary procedure, I have the floor," said Jim Stone in his finest dramatized intonation. Without any delay, all of his squadron buddies twisted around to face him drinks in hand and devious expressions smeared across their faces. They quieted down for the moment at least. After a brief, but highly exaggerated pause, Rocky continued. He had even aroused Holly's attention. She gazed attentively at Rocky as she plunged dirty glasses into a sink full of hot soapy liquid and then rinsed them off in the adjoining basin of cold water. Teen Angel just rolled his eyes and sneered. Like Comatose Gross, he had seen this act before as well.

"First off, how *does* my hair look tonight?" inquired Rocky as he pretended to flaunt his fresh haircut for the boys, moving like fashion model Christy Brinkley on a Paris runway.

"Thin, very thin" shouted Teen Angel.

"Perfect," hollered Lieutenant Gross with a hand cupped to his mouth simulating a cheerleader's bullhorn. Intense laughter consumed the collection of men even as they watched Rocky's every move.

"I give you two things to remember this fair night," began Lieutenant Commander Stone, his right hand placed reverently over his heart, his left hand still hoisting the green Heineken bottle high into the air. "We are looking for maximum return for minimum effort. As such, the dynamic for the evening is this. If they are married, we are married. If they are single, we are single. If they are divorced, it can't be half as bad as the one that we just went through," instructed Rocky. His squadron mates snorted wildly.

"And always remember the Naval Aviator's Creed with regard to women." Rocky placed a clenched fist over his mouth in yet another dramatic pause for effect, briefly collecting his thoughts for a more flamboyant dissemination. He was also giving his audience another *staged* opportunity to interact with him verbally.

"Oh yeah, and what's that skin dick," heckled Klutz Fitzgerald from the back of the pack. The light attack aviators at the end of the bar hooted and howled at this remark, playing the game as if they had all read the script. At this point, a table full of Air Guard F-15 Eagle drivers over in the far corner of the room started to pay attention to the hubbub. Even the group of Customs pilots glanced up from munching on their boiled crabs to see what all the fuss was about inside the club. Several of the women now congregated in the bar, although not admitting it with their body language, were straining to hear Jim Stone's spontaneous oratory. Rocky resumed the word play; his audience was now somewhat silent with expectation.

"Number one, look for a woman who is five to ten pounds overweight; they will have low self-esteem. "Number two, go ugly early. Number three, if she doesn't come up to your standards, lower your standards. And number four, no woman is ugly with your balls under her chin." Rocky took a long, pronounced guzzle from his beer bottle at this point as if to savor the moment. After each rule had been dictated, the laughter amongst his brethren became more boisterous and widespread. In the end the clamor from the rowdy bunch of aviators was almost deafening at their end of the bar. Rocky had just the ticket to suffocate the uproar, at least temporarily.

"Now I would like to end my brief dialogue with the A-7 pilot's prayer," advised Lieutenant Commander Stone as he respectfully bowed his head. His squadron buddies deferentially followed his lead but likewise they all knew the insolence that was forthcoming. "Dear God, please don't let me fuck this up!" The pilots let out a huge belly laugh the moment this remark hit their ears, even though they knew it was coming. After listening to every word of Rocky's rhetoric, Holly's face turned bright red from embarrassment, but she got a kick out of the comments as well. With the sermon now officially completed, Lieutenant Cline decided to walk over and initiate some trivial chitchat with the Air Force A-10 puke still deciding on his musical selections. He must not have been equal to the task because had only chosen the one Eagles tune after five minutes, and *Witchy Woman* was just finishing its play. After a couple of moments Cookie broke the silence at the jukebox.

"Say you might want to take Bruce Springsteen's advice," was Cookie's affable opening statement to the Warthog driver. Cookie considered the A-10 nothing more than a lumbering 30mm canon that somehow fooled the laws of aerodynamics by getting airborne.

"And just what do you mean by that comment?" responded the Air Force Captain.

"Go check your look in the mirror," replied Cookie.

"And why should I do that pal?" said the Warthog pilot, his face contorted by a disgusted frown, as if he could sense Cookie's impending insult.

"Well because you have several nose hairs that constitute the bulk of that cheesy moustache of yours." The Air Force pilot wasn't sure if Cookie was joking with him or not, but he quickly left to find the mirror in the Men's head. Cookie took that opportunity to select some of his favorite music from the jukebox, using up what remained from the A-10 pilots five bucks in the contraption. The music machine was filled with mostly oldies; songs that ranged from the late 50s to the early 80s. Pilots relished nostalgia, thought Lieutenant Cline as his first pick began to play. It was *That'll be the Day* by Buddy Holly and the Crickets in honor of the fresh new face behind the bar.

Women and pilots continued to trickle into the O' Club at a brisk pace as the barroom calmly settled back into its usual Friday night rhythm, now that the tumult caused by Lieutenant Commander Stone's enlightening oration had slowly dissipated. The room smelled of alcohol and designer fragrances. Rocky had skillfully grabbed an empty seat next to Shroud Morley and the two were soon engaged in a deep semi-private discussion. Teen Angel sat on the last bar-stool in the corner of the saloon surveying the room like a male lion in the long grass of the Serengeti Plain. His cunning and stealth while in pursuit of the female species was legendary. Brad's *Montana* blue eyes moved deliberately in their search pattern, memorizing each detail of his prey before undertaking the final mad dash to inflict the killing bite. Predatory behavior was in Brad's blood and right now he was looking to cut one from the herd, especially since his regular New Orleans squeeze was out of town recruiting nurses for Baptist Medical Center. As he scrutinized the female patrons, Angel *nursed* his second bottle of beer. Ackerman never drank more than one and a half alcoholic beverages in an evening. Never!

After only a few minutes of surveillance, Brad established a radar lock on a long-legged red headed wench standing alone at the opposite side of the L shaped bar, the long-end side, sipping a vodka martini. The woman had to be almost six feet tall. She was likewise stealing a glance at him from across the barroom expanse. When they made eye contact and she realized that Teen Angel had caught her looking directly at him, she quickly averted her gaze but not before a coquettish grin spread across her burgundy lips. Her smile was warm and engaging. Suddenly there was no other person in the O' Club in Lieutenant Ackerman's mind. All distractions ceased as he methodically focused his attention solely on her.

She had large brown, bedroom eyes; powerful yet soft. One look from this *heavenly* Medusa and any man would instantly turn to jelly and go weak in the knees. Merely contemplating being allowed into her close proximity could drive lesser men senseless from the anticipation. Even from across the room, her demeanor was intoxicating and her body language literally beckoned Brad. He had no alternative. Teen Angel calmly rose from his seat, Coors Light in hand, and meandered over to her location. The two quickly began to talk and flirt as though they had been lovers in a previous lifetime. She smelled delicious thought Brad as the two embarked on that pleasant journey of getting acquainted with an attractive person of the opposite sex. Her name was Danielle Le Claire, and she was an Assistant DA working for New Orleans District Attorney Harry Connick. As they talked both of them got that giddy feeling inside induced by covert flirtation. Somehow Brad knew instinctively that paradise would be their final destination that evening. He could feel it in the pit of his stomach. He just knew!

Sitting next to Rocky, Shroud Morley stopped his half of the conversation to observe Brad and the stunning, but slightly mysterious red head. She was dressed fashionably in a Donna Karan white silk blouse, the top two buttons unfastened, and a pleated Navy Blue skirt that extended to about an inch and a half above her knees. Some Italian guy named Versace had apparently designed the skirt, whoever he was. Ample cleavage protruded from her Victoria Secret under wire brassiere. Shroud wondered briefly, if her breasts were store-bought but then dismissed the question as not relevant. Her cognac colored purse was Gucci eel skin, the genuine article. Tan pantyhose and three-inch, dark blue high heels made her slender toned legs look exquisite. She wore just a hint of eyeliner and mascara. She didn't even need that.

"Do those two know each other?" inquired Shroud, nodding his head toward Teen Angel and Danielle Le Claire.

"No I don't think so," responded Rocky, shaking his noggin momentarily from side to side as he continued to peel off the label from his Heineken bottle. Perceiving the romantic potential apparent in the first few moments of their encounter stimulated Shroud to go further with his line of questioning. After all, nobody knew Teen Angel any better, with the possible exception of Duke O' Grady. Commander Morley was curious to know where all Brad's charm, confidence and charisma emanated from.

"How can Teen Angel be so lucky with so many women, while I have to suffer with my wife, the psycho bitch from hell? Is it chemical or something Rock?" asked Shroud Morley, deliberately brazen in his tone. His face adopted a sinister expression of displeasure as he chugged what remained of his Tanqueray gin and tonic. Shroud's throat heaved as he swallowed the last extra large gulp of harsh liquid, leaving only a few ice cubes to rattle around as he slammed the glass back down to the countertop. Rocky couldn't help but laugh upon hearing his last profound comments.

"There's a lot about Brad that you don't know Shroud. What you see on the outside is hiding a terrible pain on the inside that I believe he never fully recovered from," answered Rocky, nonchalantly tossing his empty Heineken bottle into the trash receptacle behind the bar.

"Tell me more Rocky," requested Commander Morley. No longer having a beer bottle to distract him and seeing Holly hustling a tray full of tequila shooters over to some Marine helicopter pilots, Lieutenant Commander Stone seemed ready to oblige Shroud's request. So he proceeded to tell all the pertinent details he knew about Ackerman's past. Brad had apparently opened up to Rocky one evening onboard the USS *Lexington*, when the two Landing Signal Officers (LSO) had shared a stateroom during a particularly arduous Carrier Qualifications (CQ) detachment last year. Scratching the side of his head, as if to dredge up what he grasped of Teen Angel's past, Rocky began telling the story in greater detail.

It seems that when Brad was a 19 year old sophomore at Stanford University he was head over heals in love with a statuesque blonde cheerleader named Tara Thomason. She was a senior about to graduate and embark on a career as a high fashion model in New York City. In fact, Tara had already graced the runaways of Paris, Milan, London, and New York during her last two summer breaks from school. She could have left college two years earlier but had promised her parents that she would earn her Bachelor's Degree in English Literature from Stanford before commencing her modeling profession.

She was an incredibly good-looking woman, with stunning, symmetrical facial features highlighted by elevated cheekbones and a dazzling smile. I mean breathtaking. Teen Angel told Rocky that it hurt just to look at her because all your breath would involuntarily depart your body for a few seconds. Imagine that, brilliant and beautiful. Not a bad combination for a cheerleader or a model thought Shroud as Rocky continued his tale. She absolutely adored Brad. Or so he thought at the time.

Brad Ackerman was a scratch golfer during his sophomore year at Stanford, almost certainly headed for the PGA Tour one day. But then it happened. Disaster reared its ugly head. That first August after she had graduated, Tara was modeling in New York and Brad had flown into JFK as a surprise for her 22nd birthday. He was only 20 and had just finished second in the 1980 U.S. Amateur

Golf Championship. Bribing the doorman at the entrance to Tara's high-rise building, Brad quickly took the elevator to the sixth floor and found her front door unlocked. Unknowingly and unannounced he just strolled into her 5th Avenue apartment. He was lugging a duffel bag, a bottle of Dom Perignon champagne, a huge bouquet of red roses and three heart shaped balloons full of helium. He looked like an incompetent juggler at a cheap circus; the one that isn't Ringling Brothers and Barnum & Bailey.

To his utter and total dismay Brad discovered Tara down on her knees giving a blow job to some clothing designer big shot with a pencil dick and a huge wad of cash in his wallet. Suffice it to say Brad's heart was crushed like a watermelon in Gallagher's *sledg-o-matic*. So were the roses. That next fall at Stanford Ackerman enrolled in the NROTC program and his golf game suffered so much that year he almost lost his athletic scholarship. Brad was severely depressed his entire junior year, carrying a *Statue of Liberty* sized torch for Tara. He quit the golf team outright at the start of his senior year then didn't pick up a club for the next five years.

When he finally regained his emotional stability he literally went overboard with women and it has been that way ever since. Even now he is hurting from that emotional sting and uses his world famous exploits with women as a salve for his still shattered spirit, explained Rocky. His heart has never been fully repaired. It is still broken into little pieces, yet beating away inside his chest cavity. But I guess it's a good thing because if this had not happened Brad probably would have never become a Naval Aviator, reasoned Rocky. Lieutenant Commander Stone, still not able to grab Holly's attention, persisted with his narrative.

Brad's father used to always tell him that when you fall in love with a woman you are taking a gigantic risk. And that when you tell a woman that you love her, you are saying here is my precious heart. Hold it in your hands. Fondle it, caress it, take extra good care of it, and please never break it. It's a big gamble, but it is worth it if you find the *right* woman. If you want to grab the gold ring on the merry-go-round of life you have to climb onto the horse and go around a few times, was Brad's father's motto. Genuine love is the greatest gift any human can experience. While love's fire rages there isn't any finer feeling to experience anywhere else in the universe. Similar to that *new drug* that Huey Lewis sang about, the emotion and passion of true love consumes your soul. But when love fades, and it will, there isn't any more abysmal feeling to suffer through anywhere else in the universe. Unfortunately, like poker, to win the pot you gotta be in the game.

"Chief Ackerman, Teen Angel's submariner father, was sort of a quasi prophet and had taught Brad a great deal at an early age, as if he knew he wouldn't be around much longer to nurture his only son. I often think he passed on some sort of prophetic aptitude to Teen Angel. It's a bit scary, but I'll get into that another time," said Rocky. Without being asked, Holly slid two more drinks in front of Shroud and Rocky. She was a blessing. Maybe she was a psychic as well thought Shroud as he sipped his perfectly prepared gin and tonic. Rocky took a swig of beer, anxiously eyed the Heineken label then went ahead with his story line of Brad Ackerman's history.

This woman is still haunting Brad and he can't seem to flush her from his brain cells. A logical assumption thought Morley. Despite this obstacle, Ackerman had graduated with honors, *Suma cum laude*, from Stanford. It was a full six months earlier than expected after that little debacle with his model girlfriend. It only took him 3 and ½ years to earn his Bachelor's Degree. Rocky had to pause and laugh at this reality because he had been on the five-year plan at Temple. But then Teen Angel does have an IQ of 160 rationalized Rocky to himself without revealing this fact to Shroud. Brad was real Mensa material.

After receiving his commission in December of 1981, Ackerman had started Navy flight school in March 1982, earning his wings on November 10, 1983. He had his wings of gold pinned on that morning by the Commanding Officer of VT-25, right there on the tarmac in Beeville, Texas. It was at the conclusion of an ACM hop. From there of course, he got orders to the Corsair RAG, and then eventually joined his first fleet A-7E squadron, the VA-105 *Gunslingers*, at Cecil Field. Lieutenant Ackerman left active duty in June of 1988.

"Teen Angel, Cookie and myself all met during a CQ detachment onboard Lady Lex and the three of us ended up here at VA-204 a year or so later. Now you know all that I know about Teen Angel," said Rocky to finish up. He of course knew much more but was thirsty and exhausted from his long day. Both pilots took a hefty mouthful of liquid refreshment. Momentarily contented, their thoughts and actions moved on to other more imminent distractions in the rau-cous Friday night confines of the Jack Black O' Club.

By this time, Teen Angel and Danielle Le Claire were so deeply engaged in their *get acquainted* conversation that Brad didn't even realize Commander May-hew had parked his butt into the barstool next to his. Ackerman's capacity for sit-uational awareness, both in and out of the cockpit, was usually more intuitive. But he was supremely preoccupied at that moment by the lovely Danielle. Juice was actively badgering Holly behind the bar, but using his soft genial approach in hopes of tangible results.

As they talked, Brad subtly absorbed Danielle's very presence. He immediately recognized that she had an admirable quality of innocence about her, as if she wasn't fully aware of her tremendous beauty or the mesmerizing effect she had on men. This enticed Teen Angel even further because he sensed it was genuine and not a selfish facade. Juice persisted with Holly his antics semi-controlled yet bursting at the seams.

Miss Le Claire might be a Harvard trained lawyer but she didn't flaunt it. For a moment Brad suddenly recollected what his father use to teach him about educated men and women. He would say that the mark of a truly educated man was that he was embarrassed to speak to nobody and made nobody embarrassed to speak to him. But, he also said women are like trolley cars. There will be another one along in half an hour, all you gotta do is wait. Danielle pulled a pair of reading glasses out of her purse and placed them on the bridge of her nose tantalizingly slow as their conversation resumed.

Danielle wore modest but chic jewelry. A delicate gold chain cunningly decorated her right ankle, barely visible but attracting attention nonetheless. A Swiss made Movado sports watch with gold and silver trim adorned her left wrist, while plain yet elegant gold hoops dangled gracefully from her earlobes. Somehow during their chat, the topic of Mardi Gras had popped up even though Fat Tuesday was still two months down the road. Teen Angel had already reached into his flight jacket pocket and produced the VA-204 Mardi Gras Party invitation for her to peruse and hopefully enjoy. Brad thought that she looked highly intellectual in her designer glasses as she surveyed the exterior of the oversized card. Danielle discerned that Brad was inviting her to the festivities by presenting her with the card, although he made no verbal comment to that effect. Body language was in high gear that evening as well as oral communication skills. Without warning, she almost fell off her barstool from intense, convulsive laughter as she opened the card to read what was on the inside. Brad deftly caught her as she slipped, expertly playing the knight in shining armor role. Touching her hand and forearm generated a warm feeling in his heart, one that he hadn't experienced in quite some time.

On the other side of Teen Angel Jack Mayhew was slowly yet methodically proceeding to get tanked up, despite his looming flight physical scheduled to begin at 0730 tomorrow morning at the NAS medical clinic. After downing his fourth seven and seven in about an hour he ordered yet another round of drinks for his friends then started hitting on Holly with increased fervor. Apparently Juice was now enlightening the nubile young bartender about the laborious training process involved in becoming an A-7E carrier aviator. Instinctively, Teen

Angel turned one ear to hear Jack Mayhew's rhetoric while he continued to engage Danielle in modestly suggestive dialogue. Brad's Coors Light was now lukewarm in the palm of his right hand, and he hadn't touched a drop for the past twenty minutes.

"A tactical naval aviator is trained to be a courageous, independent thinking warrior at all times in his life," bellowed Juice, speaking louder than he needed to. The jukebox music was audible yet toned down several decibels to allow easy conversation in the bar. As she popped open and delivered beer bottles, Holly maintained continuous eye contact with Jack Mayhew as she listened to him speak. She was talented as well as courteous. Jack rattled his mixed drink slowly, fished out an ice cube and tossed it into his mouth. He crunched the square of frozen water between his teeth then continued his relentless attack on Holly. The extreme cold of the now crushed ice caused some temporary pain in Juice's back molars. He was tough and did not let on.

"In fact the A-7E graduation hop is an evolution during which the student pilot plans and wages nuclear war against an entire enemy country single-handedly. And he has to avoid all the air defenses systems and put his bombs on the target within 10 seconds of the time he planned to deliver the weapons. Undeniably, tactical naval aviators have a tremendous sense of camaraderie and teamwork, but in combat if the team breaks down they can get the job done by themselves," informed Jack. He peered deeper into Holly's eyes wondering if it was indeed time to go for the quick kill. Leaning back on his chair, Juice swiftly knocked back a healthy amount of his cocktail as if this was the final dose of liquid encouragement he needed. After twisting his head to the left Juice distorted his lips to let out a brief, whiskey scented belch. He resembled Sheriff Buford T. Justice in the 'choke and puke' scene of the movie *Smokey and the Bandit*.

"Hey baby, how's about you and me blow this pop stand and go some place to slam crotches?" said Juice going for broke. Even though she was not offended, Holly's cheeks blushed and turned crimson as she peeked all around to see if anybody else had heard the come on. One person had indeed heard Juice's insensitive remark and he was now doubled over clinging to his barstool. Brad gasped for a breath of air like a high school cornerback thumped in the vulnerable part of his abdomen by a 250 pound fullback on a humid Friday night. Apparently his last small taste of warm Coors Light had slithered down the wrong pipe as listened to the uncouth suggestion posed by Commander Mayhew. Danielle patted Angel vigorously on the back as he slowly convulsed to a normal breathing pattern then turned toward Holly in a veiled rescue attempt. He was trying desperately to hide his intense desire to laugh out loud.

"You'll have to pardon my squadron mate sweetheart," said Teen Angel in his best Humphrey Bogart twang, unwittingly mocking Duke who was the squadron's impressionist. Grabbing Mayhew around the shoulders Teen Angel continued, "You see my friend Juice here is a direct descendant of the gorillas in the mist of Tanganyika, Africa. Dian Fossey actually studied Jack's grandfather and he is only the fourth generation of his family that is walking upright!" Holly winked at Teen Angel, smiled broadly then ambled over to a group of older women to take their order. Commander Mayhew could only manage a faint smirk in Brad's general direction after the junior officer released the tight grip on his shoulders and turned back to work on Danielle.

As Duke O' Grady marched confidently into the room, the entire cadre of VA-204 pilots stopped their juvenile exploits to receive the beloved skipper into their little congregation at the O' Club bar. Like Moses, his presence parted the waters and they enthusiastically welcomed him in to their squadron Red Sea. Cookie cleverly noticed that Tanya Billings was following close behind the skipper, but not so close as to blow their cover. Her thick mane was pulled back tightly into a luxurious, platinum ponytail. It started from the middle of the back of her head and was pinched firmly in place by a deep purple scrunchy. Her taut, squeaky clean hair jutted out about two inches before gravity finally took effect. The color looked exquisite against the backdrop of her deep black wool sweater. The stock commodities price for peroxide must be rising through the roof, thought Cookie to himself. He made a metal note to invest in peroxide futures when he returned home to Atlanta. Tanya also had that freshly scrubbed smell, almost like she had just eaten two shower-sized bars of Zest soap, and the aroma was now wafting generously from her pores.

"Giddy up" said Cookie under his breath, as he laid eyes on Tanya, the skipper's little enlisted *chippee*.

"How does a guy get a drink around this clip joint?" asked Duke forcing his way into the horde of *River Rattler* pilots crowded together at the bar. Tanya kept walking but slowed her pace. Holly casually tossed a cardboard coaster in front of the skipper and stood at his beck and call, at least temporarily.

"A six pack of those would be fine babe," said Duke pointing to the Michelob logo on the coaster, "but I'll start off with just two." He was of course ordering for Tanya as well.

"Where have you been skipper?" asked Klutz Fitzgerald as if it was any of his business.

"I had to see a man about a horse!" responded Duke in his tone of voice specifically designed to dissuade any further discussion on the topic in question.

After politely excusing himself from Danielle's presence, Teen Angel approached O' Grady giving him a brief head nod of welcome. Duke grabbed him roughly by the neck, spun him around and the two men walked out into the center of the room. O' Grady had spotted an evolving scene in one corner of the bar that sparked his interest.

"Teen Angel I am going to teach you something right here and now," said the skipper with his right hand clenched firmly around the back of Brad's neck. It was no secret amongst the squadron mates that Duke had enormous feelings for Brad Ackerman. Those feelings had been nurtured over the last six years of their professional and personal relationship.

"Okay, what is it Puke," teased Ackerman after confirming nobody was in range of his insolent remark to the skipper.

"Look over at that table and tell me what you see," instructed Duke craning his head toward that remote and darkened corner of the room. Brad focused his 20/10 vision eyes at that location. He squinted to improve his reduced light capacity.

"I see Lieutenant Eli "Pops" Petibone sitting intimately in the shadows drinking Kamikaze shooters with two sixty year-old broads," answered Brad.

"And I always thought his tactical call sign was "Pops" because the little hair he had remaining on his scalp had turned a milky gray," concluded Duke.

"Me too," said Teen Angel shrugging his shoulders in confusion. "Why, do you know something that I don't know skipper," inquired Ackerman like a mischievous child about to play doctor with the girl next door. Slowly but surely the two pilots grinned then turned back towards the bar.

"Another piece of the puzzle," concluded Teen Angel as he headed in Danielle's direction, happy to see her still seated and likewise unaccompanied. Their eyes lured each other into a magnetic stare as Brad approached her location.

CHAPTER 10

▼

FULL CONTACT CRUD

The O' Club was now jam packed to the brim with women and aviators of all persuasions. With more people continuing to stream in, the club was beginning to push its envelope toward the outer edges. The thrust of human activity near the bar resembled afternoon, rush hour commuters pressing toward a Metro car on a *federal* Friday in Washington, D.C. About half the pilots were in civilian clothes while the other fifty percent were clad in their sweaty zoom bags; sporting that smell of success in tactical aviation. Non-aviators wore uniforms. Behind the bar, Holly was busier than a one-legged man in an ass-kicking contest. She had been joined by Miss Melinda, a stout middle-aged woman with that 'sag of success' hanging over the belt loops of her stretched denim jeans, and by the O' Club manager Mr. Fontenot. Both now assisted Holly Carter in rationing out the booze, popcorn and beer nuts. Coin and currency were changing hands at a rapid pace.

Melinda James was a divorcee who worked as the assistant payroll officer at the Personnel Support Detachment (PSD) over at the Naval Support Activity in Algiers, Louisiana. She had divorced her fireman husband several years ago due to adultery and physical abuse, and hadn't heard from him since the final decree was granted by a Jefferson Parish judge. Miss Melinda, as the pilots habitually called her, moonlighted as a bartender on the heavy nights at the O' Club to make ends meet. The forty-something, African-American woman was now a single mother raising two teenagers on her own; a daunting task for even two parents to endure. This evening the rather ordinary looking mother of two was wearing her blue-gray Adidas running shoes. Too bad she didn't do more actual running in them. Thankfully, she wasn't wearing a belly-shirt behind the bar.

Curly haired Larry Fontenot had been the Officer's Club manager for the past fifteen years, assuming that auspicious title on the day of its grand opening. The sixty-three year old Fontenot, a retired Navy Master Chief, was a man of good humor who was routinely badgered for using hair color products. His shade this month was a rich, lustrous looking chestnut. At least it was his own wavy locks, slightly enhanced by a *natural enough* looking weave purchased from those hair club people who advertised at three in the morning on TV. For some reason Larry was overly proud that he didn't have to resort to wearing a phony-looking toupee, or *wig hat* as it was called in the colloquial vernacular of N'awlins.

Larry Fontenot had seen and heard just about everything you could see or hear when aviators gathered together to blow off a little steam. And he had consistently and successfully nurtured the club through good and bad economies in Southeast Louisiana. When the oil bust of late 1981 hit New Orleans hard, Larry had innovated to keep the coffers full at the Jack Black. Early in 1982, Fontenot had been responsible for bringing in Bourbon Street strippers each Friday night to properly kick off Drill Weekend for the reservists in attendance. He had also cooked up the lingerie lunch show every Saturday from 1100-1300. These ideas had proven to be a boon to the club's revenue and success for over six years, and he had never even contemplated laying off any of his employees.

That all changed in 1988 when the Navy Wives' Club began to complain vociferously to the CO about the appearance of immorality given off by these events. The NAS Commanding Officer that year, a weak-kneed P-3 Orion pilot, was apparently sympathetic to the wives' concerns. He summarily terminated the two short-lived traditions thus incurring the wrath of the drilling reserve pilots. It seems that the P-3 puke's wife was president of the Navy Wives Club in 1988, so he caved after only two months of pressure from the spouses. The Catholic Archdiocese of New Orleans had even sent the NAS skipper a formal letter of praise after his Jesuit Priest had informed them of his highly commendable decision. Normally, tactical naval aviators don't have much use for P-3 pilots and this gesture only served to strengthen their disdain for that breed of aviator. Duke would always harass P-3 guys by claiming that they were in a *different* Navy, not his!

Behind the L-shaped bar at the Jack Black Officer's Club were two more of Larry Fontenot's novelties. On the long side of the bar was a huge rectangular mirror, which had the effect of making the entire room appear much larger than it actually was. Dozens of unique shaped and colorful booze bottles were placed just in front of the looking glass as well as a theater-style popcorn maker. The iron kettle of the popcorn maker was pumping out its hot commodity about every five minutes that night at the O' Club. On the short side Larry had installed a huge fresh water aquarium. It was sunk back into the wall about three feet and was furnished with a wide variety of exotic-looking fish. At the bottom of the tank lay a size 36C ladies brassiere and a pair of pink lacey panties. Nobody had ever claimed responsibility for this prank and Fontenot had decided to leave the ladies undergarments in the tank for the fish to play with as they pleased. It was a conversation piece to say the least and the longer customers remained in the bar the more they spent.

The bar also featured two dingy-looking, antique cash registers; the kind that had large keys which resembled an oversized Smith-Corona typewriter. When you punched in the price paid by the customer on those keys, the cash drawer would plunge out towards your belly, and a bell would ring sharply as little round dollars and cents tabs popped up behind a clouded glass window situated at the top of the device. The mechanisms waxed poetic from the nostalgia alone. It would be right at home as a prop in any western movie being filmed in Hollywood.

"Say skipper, did you put in your application for Clown College yet? You're gonna need a job after you retire next year you know," chided Comatose Gross attempting to engage Commander O' Grady in a little competitive mockery. Unfortunately Lieutenant Gross had brain-farted, forgetting that he was not even in the same league to try and match wits with Duke.

"Son, I have more flight time on the ball at the ship than you have flight time," responded Duke, giving the junior officer a break by not ripping into him more vehemently in front of the squadron pilots.

"Yeah, but the majority of your time at the ship was spent looking at a red ball, low on the glide slope skipper," chimed in Teen Angel to augment Comatose Gross in the verbal exchange with the Commanding Officer.

"Now boys, you don't want to mess with your old skipper this evening. I have better things to occupy my time tonight than a couple of rookie grapes like you two," said Duke as he laughed and walked over to sit next to Tanya Billings. The enlisted dental hygienist was patiently waiting for Duke about eight seats down the bar, daintily sipping her Michelob while munching on beer nuts.

At that moment a thin, wiry woman staggered skillfully into the O' Club leading a small enclave of rather rough-looking chicks. Her auburn mop was too closely cropped for a woman's hairstyle. It wasn't *butch* but it *was* a little boy's cut. Almost immediately, her focus narrowed like a quarter horse wearing blinders on a Saturday afternoon at the race track. Her eyes contracted with increasing intensity as she adroitly guided the women swiftly past the *River Rattlers'* modest, yet raucous assembly at the bar. There would be no small talk at this locale, if she could help it.

Apparently she had witnessed VA-204's saloon antics in the recent past and wasn't amused in the least. She certainly didn't want to subject her girlfriends to any more audacious pilot behavior than was absolutely necessary for a successful evening. The tough looking babe walking out in front of the group resembled the *alpha* female leading a pack of wild Australian Dingos, thought Rocky as he gave her flock a quick once over. She walked as if a small peach tree limb had been jammed up her ass. It was sort of a tight-cheeked shuffle. And the signals she emanated were similar to the warning signs a lighthouse radiates out to mariners on the high seas. Just like the robot on the television show *Lost in Space*, her whole appearance was saying 'WARNING WILL ROBINSON, DANGER' loud and clear. The dominant female was moderately attractive and her tits pointed towards Philadelphia, up and ever so slightly to the right.

As it turns out Rocky had met this particular alpha female last month right here at the Jack Black, although he couldn't recall her name. From their brief conversation while sharing a glass of Chardonnay that soft November night, Rocky had discovered that she was a Woman's Studies Professor at Tulane University, whatever that meant. He also ascertained that she wasn't yet persuaded which side of the romance batter's box to stand, so she had dabbled with a little *switch-hitting*. Apparently, tonight she was batting from the *right* side of home plate once again, thought Jim Stone.

Following closely on the alpha female's heels was a woman wearing a black, tight fitting dress. It was especially low cut in the front revealing ample skin and just a hint of her soft appendages. She had a 'bob' style haircut that made her look like that little Dutch boy on a gallon-sized can of flat, latex house paint. The lady also had a rather large derriere and smelled like a hundred dollar French whore. As she walked energetically away from Rocky's position, he could see that she was carrying a cashmere topcoat across her arm. Lieutenant Commander Stone tapped Shroud Morley's forearm and with a brief head dip he directed both their eyes to her figure moving away from them toward a table on the other side of the room. There seemed to be an excess of residual movement in her gait.

"You know, walking away like she is, that woman's ass resembles two bulldogs wrestling up under a sheet, ridiculed Rocky. Shroud took a slug from his drink and silently agreed as the chilled elixir hit his belly.

Over in the adjacent game room of the bar, a small storm was brewing in a china teacup. Several of the Louisiana Air National Guard (LAANG) F-15 pilots had gathered around the O' Club billiard table, another Larry Fontenot innovation. Apparently the Eagle drivers were looking for some worthy competition to engage in a friendly game of full contact *crud*. The Marine rotor heads were too busy arm wrestling for tequila shooters at their table, so they were out. The P-3 boys couldn't find four guys who were competitive enough to even attempt a game of crud. While the Warthog drivers wouldn't tear away from their philosophical discussions and martinis long enough to play. Hearing the hubbub, Cookie strolled up to the pool table solo, palming a fresh Budweiser in his right hand. After exchanging a few sociable insults with the F-15 pilots, Cookie soon convinced them to play *coed*, full contact crud. He likewise counseled them to stop spilling their beers on the felt tabletop.

"Put together your *interceptor* team and I'll be right back with a *light attack* lineup," advised Cookie. "By the way, nice ascots," teased Lieutenant Cline referring to the charming but slightly effeminate neckwear worn by all Air Force pilots under their zoom bags. He departed the room and walked back to the bar to recruit his four-person team.

Coed, full contact crud is traditional aviator's game played at a billiard table with four-man teams consisting of two boy players and two girl players on each squad. After the team members are chosen, an unfortunate and hopefully inebriated individual must then be selected to function as the game's official arbitrator. Naturally, this referee receives an undue amount of crap from competitors and spectators alike during the ensuing competition because of the many difficult judgment calls he is required to make during the course of the action. As usual, all decisions made by the ref are cast in *Jell-o* so he can easily be coerced into reversing his pronouncements with an appropriate bribe of beer or hot wings.

The white cue ball and the black eight ball are positioned at opposite ends on the pool tabletop by the referee, and a coin toss is then completed to determine the order of play. The winner of the coin toss is designated Team A and they are first up in the rotation followed by Team B; the loser of the coin toss. To initiate the game, the first competitor on Team A rolls the cue ball by hand so that it strikes the eight ball, causing it to roll as well on the tabletop. Next, the first contestant from Team B does the same, but now the pasty colored cue ball must collide with the ebony colored eight ball before the eight ball stops its spinning motion. This rotation continues as each opposing team member takes his or her turn in the proper order. One rule of the game is that participants may only roll the cue ball from one of the long-ends of the pool table, not from the sides or corners. The player's hips, in the judgment of the referee, must be squarely behind the long-end side of the pool table for a turn to be judged legal. Opponents are allowed to maneuver about the table any way they please, and may grab the cue ball from any position around the table. But legal rolls can only be initiated from one of the two long-end sides.

Each contender starts the game with three lives to his credit. As the game progresses, players lose one life for each error committed. Yield three lives and you are expelled from the contest by the referee. This normal rotation dynamic persists until somebody doesn't hit the eight ball before it stops its motion or a player commences a roll improperly positioned on the pool table. Each mistake will cost a player one life. Likewise, if the cue ball is accidentally driven into a pocket a life is forfeited. But if a competitor knocks the eight ball into a pocket, the next opposing player must surrender a life. When you start losing team members it gets more difficult to win the contest. Of course, the game proceeds until one contestant remains and still has a life to spare from the three he or she started out with.

All players are required to keep both hands touching the sides of the pool table except for the one whose turn it is to roll the cue ball. It is 'full contact' crud because the opposing team members try to block the other players with their bodies as they attempt to seize the cue ball and properly position themselves to hit the eight ball. As you might suspect, with women playing there is inevitably some good male-female contact with crotches, asses and tits coming into close proximity. This is undoubtedly why tactical naval aviators prefer to play coed, full contact crud. They cracked the code on this angle of the dangle long ago.

Gathered together in a quasi-football huddle to discuss crud tactics, the *River Rattlers* started to devise their team strategy. After all, the honor of the squadron was now at stake here in this trivial contest of supreme skill on a billiard table. Without question, the most gifted crud players in VA-204 were Cookie Cline and "Slug" Levitan, the Executive Officer. Unfortunately, the XO was currently flying a FedEx 747 loaded with several tons of purple and orange boxes into Tokyo's Narita airport, so he wasn't available. The last VA-204 CO, Commander Steve "Jerk" Martin, would have been the next logical choice but he was now growing potatoes in a Boise suburb; languishing as an Idaho farmer after twenty-two years of dedicated naval service. The strategists hastily settled on

Teen Angel as the best available alternative to complete the male quota of the *River Rattler* starting lineup.

Selection of the female component to represent VA-204 in the crud game had slightly different determining factors. Skill, cunning and physical prowess were not significant elements in this choice, as was the case with their male counterparts. Incredible beauty combined with the obvious potential for the most T & A was the essential ingredient that swayed the judge's final decision for female team members. In short, crud aptitude was not essential, in fact the less talented the girls were the more likely they would show a fair amount of T & A during the hectic pace of the very physical game. *Something*, some vital body part might accidentally fall out of its secure resting place. Danielle Le Claire and Holly Carter were the most unambiguous choices to fulfill those stringent requirements. But they might need coaxing and there could be a small dilemma with Holly because she was working behind the bar. Hearing the tactical discussion progressing, Duke left Tanya's side once more and interjected himself into the mix.

"Leave Holly to me boys," said a reassuring Commander O' Grady. "Teen Angel you go over and prevail upon Miss Le Claire that she has to play."

"Aye aye skipper," answered Brad as he crisply saluted in the skipper's general direction then walked towards Danielle to complete his assigned tasking.

Larry Fontenot and Duke O' Grady spoke semi-privately for about five minutes. The two men were hinged directly over the tattered wood, swinging door that separates bar patrons from bartenders. The polite discussion with the O' Club manager seemed more like thirty minutes to Duke because he was unaccustomed to hearing the word no. Undoubtedly, Larry could see the large crowd in the bar and he needed Holly to concentrate her efforts on bartending duties. Larry Fontenot's frowning face shook vigorously back and forth for about four and a half minutes before it abruptly stopped. Whatever argument O' Grady utilized on Fontenot must have worked. Larry finally smiled, although somewhat reluctantly, then issued his personal approval for Holly to play in the crud match. Duke O' Grady's legendary charm was equally effective with men and women. When he wanted something he usually got it. It was only a matter of time.

Comfortably seated next to Danielle Le Claire, Teen Angel had much less trouble arranging for the second female team member to volunteer for duty. After hearing Brad's explanation of the game and its rules, a coy smile slowly embraced the thirty-two year old woman's full lips. Danielle rose from her barstool and displaying highly provocative etiquette, she gracefully raised one leg at a time to remove her dark blue, Salvatore Ferragamo pumps. She tossed them playfully to

Brad for safekeeping. Brad juggled for a moment but was able to catch both shoes, the second one by its three-inch stem.

Danielle rolled up her blouse sleeves, delicately groped for her purse then yanked out a tiny perfume bottle. She seductively refreshed her wrists with a supple dab of its three hundred dollar an ounce contents, and then politely grabbed Brad's arm as he escorted her to crud destiny. In her stocking feet, Ackerman towered over Danielle who was now a full three inches shorter. Brad also noticed that she had petite feet with extremely high arches, similar to a prima ballerina. Her toenails were freshly manicured and polished with a fire engine red color, Brad's favorite shade on a woman. As they walked, Juice brusquely relieved Teen Angel of Miss Le Claire's high heels, partly because he knew Ackerman was going to be way too busy playing crud to properly baby sit them. But Commander Mayhew also had some devious plans for the elegant looking footwear flashing through his brain.

At the end of the bar, the *River Rattler* pilots huddled together again. One by one they squeezed the *official* VA-204 coed crud team into the middle of their scrum. Here the squad would receive final strategic instructions, and a little low-speed cheerleading, before making their way to the game room pool table. As this scene was unfolding, Duke O' Grady pushed behind the bar through the swinging door, strapped a slightly soiled white apron around his waist then began to take drink orders from customers. Apparently this was the deal maker for the club manager. With a wink and a nod, Larry Fontenot directed Holly over to the *River Rattler* pilots to receive her crud tactics briefing. The look on Tanya Billings face could choke a thoroughbred horse as she twirled the end of her ponytail with increasing vigor. The young enlisted girl wanted to spend some quality, clandestine time with Duke but was now confronted with the proposition of having to share the object of her romantic desire with the entire bar; at least until the crud game was finished.

Breaking their huddle, the entire VA-204 contingent methodically made its way over to the pool table. As the herd hoofed along, Juice ordered a bottle of cheap Moet champagne from Melinda James. Bending down in front of a small refrigerator situated just below the fish tank, Miss Melinda visually located the sparkling wine on the bottom shelf toward the rear. As she arched over reaching into the icebox her shirt busted loose in the back and the crack of her ass rudely emerged. *Plumbers crack*, thought Juice as he unsuccessfully tried to pry his eyes away from her rear cleavage. Melinda crammed her hand and arm deeper into the cold recess of the refrigerator, removed the bottle then stood and placed it in front of Juice. Digging in a drawer full of various utensils Melinda finally produced a small corkscrew as she skillfully tucked the shirt tail back into her Levis 501's with her free hand. She plopped the shiny metal device next to the bottle of champagne on the bar then sought eye contact with Juice.

"Put it on our tab honey," instructed Commander Mayhew as he snatched the green bottle and corkscrew off the bar top with his left hand, firmly grasped Danielle's high heels in his right, then maneuvered to the front of the horde moving toward the game room. Lifting the shoes rudely to his nose, Juice sniffed the velvety soft interior lining. This he did to the anxious delight of his squadron mates and to the utter dismay of all the women watching the spontaneous show in the Jack Black O' Club. The high heels had the distinct odor of baby powder.

"Oh, how sweet the stench!" declared Commander Mayhew to a backdrop of nervous laughter. As the group reached the pool table, Juice uncorked the champagne then proceeded to pour some of the bubbly liquid into one of Danielle's high heel. After a short winded, perverse toast he drank the cool effervescent liquor from *Cinderella* Le Claire's leather slipper. Although not many people were paying close attention to Jack Mayhew's antics, silent laughter immediately permeated the game room underneath the competitive chatter.

"Good evening interceptor pilots," jeered Rocky to open the crud festivities. "I am Lieutenant Commander Jim Stone and it will be my distinct privilege to be your humble referee this fine soft evening." Subdued laughter evolved quickly into roars of amusement from the *River Rattler* clan, even as the LAANG bunch shouted their disapproval in raised harmony.

"We want somebody neutral and totally impartial. We don't want no *sluf* driver to be the judge. No offense intended," shouted a short bony Major with a bad moustache and silver colored command pilot wings on his flight suit. His nametag said his call sign was *Toe Joe*. He, like most of the capacity crowd of F-15 Eagle pilots, was just about half-way to being fully inebriated on this Friday night. Teen Angel momentarily slipped out of the billiard cubbyhole as the good-natured ruckus lingered and the mutual derision grew rowdier. Rocky left as well, in search of alternate entertainment. Apparently his feelings had been trampled somewhat by the verbose rejection of his refereeing services, so he wandered toward the alpha female's pack of wild dogs seated at a medium-sized table flanking the juke box.

After meticulously explaining the game of crud, and humbly stuffing two chunks of boiled crab meat into his salivating mouth, Ackerman shrewdly persuaded Jeff Carlyle, the U.S. Customs Aviation Branch Chief, to mediate the competition. The lively discussion in the game room was still proceeding as Ackerman reappeared five minutes later with Jeff close at his side. Three of Jeff's pilots accompanied Carlyle, curious to discover the source of the burgeoning bedlam. Recognizing Jeff Carlyle from past NORAD (North American Aerospace Defense Command) flight operations briefings, Major "Toe Joe" Palooka agreed to the selection. The fight was on!

Brad took his position on the pool table next to Danielle and the rest of the crud competitors. The LAANG team consisted of two youthful captains, with equally scruffy facial hair above their top lips, and two large-breasted *significant others*. The Air Guard captains wore green flight suits and checkerboard ascots around their necks, while the barefoot ladies had on long skirts and plain solid-colored blouses. One of their females had naked flat feet while the other was clad in bleached white socks with tiny portraits of *Pooh Bear* embroidered on the elastic tops. Brad assumed the women were spouses since they each sported an over-sized rock wedged onto their wedding ring finger. Surely their hubbies must be wealthy airline pilots to be wearing diamond jewelry of that magnitude.

Klutz Fitzgerald and Shroud Morley spoke briefly with Jeff Carlyle, placating their own minds that he was adequately prepared to function as a competent crud game official. After placing an arm around Carlyle's shoulders, Shroud cleverly slipped a twenty dollar bill into the palm of Jeff's right hand without anybody in the overstuffed game room detecting his deceptive deed. Shroud also noticed Carlyle's left hand was curiously empty.

"Somebody trot on over to the bar and bring this man a brewski," hollered Cookie, barely audible above the clamor in the semi-secluded space. Jeff grinned as he sensed the familiar feel of paper currency. He swiftly stuffed the bill into the right front pocket of his flight jacket as he prepared to deliver a short discourse to the spectators and participants.

"Kind ladies and good gentlemen, I want a good clean fight here," he coached as the room settled down a bit out of feigned respect for the designated ref. Carlyle lowered his head, purposely took a sagacious ten second pause then proceeded. "Of course the *Marquis of Queensbury* rules must be observed at all times," advised Carlyle, playing his role perfectly. "Now go to your corners and come out fighting at the sound of the bell." With that said, Carlyle took an exaggerated bow. Always an astute judge of talent, Brad puffed up a bit. He had made the correct choice. Carlyle's role playing was impeccable and he was an ideal fit for the crud festivities. The onlookers from both camps howled their approval. Most everyone in the room had apparently seen Barry Fitzgerald deliver these famous lines in the fight scene of the motion picture *The Quiet Man*.

Before he hung up the phone in his BOQ room, Lieutenant Mark Sugar[2] Cane showered his wife with passionate kissing noises, while she did the same for him on the other end of the fiber optics cable in Utah. Cane's darling bride, a church secretary at one of the local Mormon congregations and a distant relative of the Osmond family, was deeply in love with, and over-dependent upon Mark. She was exceedingly vulnerable to be precise. Lieutenant Cane had earned the call sign "Sugar Sugar" while a RAG student in VA-122 at NAS Lemoore because he was *double* sweet. His character display back then was far too placid for an attack pilot that was being trained to be an airborne killing machine. Duke had shortened the call sign to Sugar^2 about three months ago during a particularly lively AOM (all officers meeting).

In his exuberance, Mark actually slobbered some spit into the tiny holes of the telephone mouthpiece during the *kiss ass* routine with his spouse. Actually, he had just finished informing his wife about every minute detail of the immoral activities he had seen thus far that evening at the O' Club. As usual, he offered names and indictments to his marital companion quicker than a hooker offered her services to a *John* in a Cadillac on Airline Highway in New Orleans.

As usual, Mr. Cane reassured Mrs. Cane that he was not participating in the unscrupulous behavior in any way. He was loyal to her and deserving of complete trust at all times. Mark reiterated that he had never violated the vows spoken to her before God and some four hundred guests seven years ago at the sacred Mormon Temple in Salt Lake City. What was it that Shakespeare would say: *Me thinks he doth protest too much!* Both spouses pursed and smacked their lips in a disgusting fashion then ended their long-distance conversation. Did Alexander Graham Bell have any idea that his seminal invention would be abused in this manner way back in 1875? Probably not!

Despite his meek exterior facade, Mark Cane was a terrific naval aviator; above average at the ship and exceptional on a bombing range. But he was sort of a kiss ass with his wife. *Pussy whipped* according to Commander Mayhew and just about all the rest of the *River Rattler* pilot cadre. After all, they had witnessed him and his decidedly obsequious behavior towards his spouse way too many times in the past on Drill Weekends, and during numerous squadron detachments to a variety of venues. He literally fawned over Trish Cane and she was absolutely clueless with regard to his unbridled infidelity. Of course she would never hear about Mark's extramarital trysts from any of his squadron mates. There was an unwritten code amongst tactical naval aviators, no sexual gossip. Ever! All but Mark Cane strictly adhered to this staple of respect at VA-204. Duke O'Grady had suspected Lieutenant Cane of violating that trust, almost immediately but he lacked hard evidence.

Sugar^2 Cane drifted back into the bar, spotted Duke hustling drinks then parked his can on an empty barstool in a flash. Slightly embarrassed, he was still visibly stimulated from his phone conversation. But it was dark in the bar so nobody gave a second look at his crotch. Instinctively, he did a fighter sweep of the bar room scanning for more familiar faces. He found Rocky Stone gabbing away with the wild dogs near the juke box. Rocky had assumed his characteristic *birddog* posture with the ladies. He was obviously hunting wild game. Next Mark's eyes settled on Pops Petibone still seated and sharing an intense dialogue with the two *blue hairs*. What was that all about, thought Cane? Apparently satisfied for the moment, Lieutenant Cane squirmed back around in his chair to face the bar.

"Can I get another Diet Pepsi when you get a chance skipper?" requested Mark Cane. O' Grady looked up, gave a furtive wink, popped open an aluminum can then handed it to Cane. Duke didn't speak a single word. He jotted down the soda selection on the VA-204 running bar tab.

"Where did everybody go skipper? Are they on their way to 'Brain Child' Bracken's house for our Annual Christmas Party so soon?" asked Lieutenant Cane. It was twenty minutes until seven o'clock and the *River Rattler* Officer's Christmas Party wasn't scheduled to begin until eight.

"No there's a big crud match up in the pool room. Some F-15 jockeys challenged us," answered O' Grady as he poured the seventh of nine tequila shooters for the Marines. At that moment, into the club marched three more VA-204 latecomers, Lieutenants "T-Ben" Hebert, "Plato" Themopolis and LTJG Bill Pack, the squadron's new AI. Before Cane could ask the next obvious question, T-Ben (little Ben in Cajun speak) beat him to the punch.

"What are you doing skipper, if I may be so bold as to inquire sir?" Duke held up his right index finger in T-Ben's direction, as if to buy some time for an explanation. He shouldered a tray of tequila shooters and an extra large order of Buffalo wings that had just been delivered from the kitchen then swaggered toward the Marines' table. Larry Fontenot couldn't stop grinning. He was amazed at what he was seeing from Duke O' Grady. The Commanding Officer of a Navy tactical squadron was serving as a bartender, facilitating his junior officer's entertainment session in the adjacent room. That was true unselfish leadership.

"Talk to your wife *again* today Sugar squared?" badgered T-Ben. Hebert knew that Cane called his wife about five times each day. He knew it, but couldn't fathom it.

"You guys can rag me all you want *little* Ben. But I stick by my love philosophy," responded Cane in a cocksure fashion.

"Thrill us with your philosophical insight," said Plato as he joined T-Ben's verbal joisting match against Mark Cane.

"A man's outlook on life is directly dependent upon how much pussy he is getting. It's not quality, its quantity. I plan to keep my flow continuous, so I speak with my wife often when I am away," advised Sugar[2] in a contemptuous tone of voice.

Less than intellectually satiated, T-Ben and Plato decided it was time to change the subject. There was an FNG (fucking new guy) in their midst and they needed to get to know and to trust him a little better. LTJG Pack looked antsy and uncomfortable as he stood wide-eyed at the bar; as if he was on the outside looking into a Roman menagerie. He made brief eye contact with Duke O' Grady but had no idea who he was. Pack had reported for duty less than a week ago and Duke had been out of town in Norfolk, Virginia for the past six days. LTJG Pack had checked into the squadron by presenting his orders and Officer's Training Jacket to Commander Randy Bracken, the active duty Safety Officer who was the senior man and acting CO in O'Grady's absence. Leaping out of the undercurrent of constant chatter, muffled roars still percolated from the game room.

Since there seemed to be a slight lull in the action, T-Ben decided it was a perfect opportunity to launch into his *targets of opportunity* satire. He quickly summoned up his accentuated *coonass* dialect for the spoof. Mostly for the benefit of Bill Pack, Hebert began to train his eyes on the women in the bar to analyze the talent in the room that night. Lieutenant Glen Hebert was a native of Cocodrie, Louisiana. With a 3.24 GPA, Glen was valedictorian of his graduating class of seventeen seniors at Justin Wilson High School. Seeking fame and fortune he relocated to the metropolis of New Orleans, calling the *Big Easy* his home of record since graduating from Loyola University in May of 1984. T-Ben was one of the funniest human beings on the planet and there was almost nothing that this Cajun boy wouldn't eat. Teen Angel had personally seen him suck the marrow out of fried chicken bones at a local *Popeye's* restaurant. T-Ben's mother even had a gourmet recipe for 'Nutria Gumbo' that had become a delicacy in the Hebert household. Nutria being those overgrown rats that infest Southern Louisiana swamps. Glen Hebert was often unmercifully teased by squadron mates for eating 'Road Kill Jambalaya' while growing up destitute in the marshlands of Cocodrie.

Glen's father was a fisherman by trade and his mother a stay-at-home Mom who was charged with raising T-Ben and his seven younger siblings. Momma Hebert did almost everything by hand in the early days of their marriage, including canning, laundry, sewing and good old fashioned ass-whippings. When Glen's father was not out on his boat *Ti Croissant* fishing in the warm waters of the Gulf of Mexico or chasing down alligator in the swamps, he was busy running a small family-owned seafood store in Cocodrie. The dilapidated wood sign drooping down over the hinged screen door to the seafood market read: *If it swum, I got it!* And they *did* have the widest variety of seafood for sale there, from fresh gulf shrimp to swamp alligator filets; from crawfish and oysters to alligator gar. You name it, they had it! People routinely came from miles around to stock up on their favorite Louisiana seafood delicacies at Hebert's. Neighbors would come just to sit a spell, to kick off their shoes and leisurely rock in the hand-made rocking chairs. Or they would come to enjoy a hot plate of red beans, rice and sausage on lazy Monday afternoon. You could always find someone willing to play a competitive game of checkers on the front porch of the Hebert's Family Store or to discuss the latest corruption scandal in Louisiana politics. This was tradition built on years of habit. Relaxation was not for sale at Hebert's, it was freely distributed by the entire clan.

"Well let's see what kind of talent we got in here tonight gentlemen," said T-Ben as he donned his aviator's sunglasses with an arrogant swagger apparent in his gestures. He then systematically stroked both sides of his chin with his right hand to lampoon an overly-intense mental process. For the next several minutes Glen Hebert used his astute New Orleans acumen to scrutinize and report what he observed that evening in the Jack Black. In one barstool he saw a girl obviously from Chalmette; a *Chalmettian* from just across the Mississippi River bend, wearing one of the three dresses that she owned. It was probably the only clean dress she had that night, so there had been no choice. She was clearly divorced, receiving no alimony from her two dead-beat ex-husbands and living in a trailer park on the outskirts of town. Tonight she was actively searching for hubby number three, but trying not to look the part. She drank her JAX beer like a sailor on liberty after a long line period at sea.

Just arriving back from the ladies room was a couple of *uptown* girls who had gone to the bathroom together to giggle and discuss the male prospects in the O' Club. They were clearly sisters in pursuit of a couple of scoundrel pilots to take back to the two-story cottage they shared in Lakeshore Estates overlooking Lake Pontchartrain. The over-sized antique home had been handed down in their family for generations. Daddy probably still deposited cash into his girls' checking accounts while they postponed finding a full-time career after their graduation from Tulane's Newman College for women. Since the birth-control pill made them gain weight, they undoubtedly carried their designer diaphragms with them in their stylish Longaberger purses.

On the opposite flank of the juke box, not the side where Rocky and the wild dingos had gathered, there was a table filled with Delta Airlines stewardesses on layover from Dallas, Texas. Their *shit-kicker* twang gave them away almost immediately. They were stopping off for a few drinks prior to heading out to *Mudbug's*, the huge 30,000 square foot honky trunk on the West Bank of New Orleans. Undoubtedly these girls would be two-stepping with ignorant, rough looking guys wearing clean cowboy hats later that night; mail-order cowboy hats they only wore on Friday and Saturday evenings. They weren't *real* cowboys, just pretenders!

Sprinkled amongst the aviators in the room were several secretaries, some female lawyers, a few college seniors and of course the ever-present typical housewives whose husbands worked on the oil rigs off shore for 60 days at a time. Most of the ladies were looking to get lucky with a pilot. Bill Pack's eyes caught a glimpse of Duke during a brief reprieve from his bartending duties. He was leaning over conversing with Tanya Billings. Her body language betrayed her true feelings for O' Grady.

"Hey, I recognize that blonde seated at the bar talking to the bartender in khakis. She is the hygienist from the base Dental Clinic," said LTJG Pack. "I met her when I checked in, but who is that officer she's talking to?" laughed Pack wanting T-Ben to articulate Tanya's personal storyline for the group. Plato Themopolis tugged at Glen Hebert's jacket sleeve, offering an unnecessary reminder. It was too soon to bring Pack completely into the fold of squadron dirty laundry. After all, Pack was of unknown moral character and couldn't be fully trusted with sensitive information like this just yet. The skipper would have the ultimate discretion in this regard. T-Ben deftly directed the group's attentions away from Duke and Tanya.

Over in the game room the coed, full-contact crud game was now building to its inevitable crescendo. Planned or not, Teen Angel and Cookie had lost all three of their lives early on during the stiff competition around the pool table. Cookie had even sustained a twisted ankle after being cross-body blocked by one of the Air Guard captains while he attempted to snatch the cue ball. Cookie could not feel the pain, as it had been temporarily alleviated by numerous bottles of Budweiser. Lieutenant's Cline and Ackerman were now relegated to mere spectator status, and they cheered for Holly and Danielle like sophomores at a cross town rivals homecoming game.

The LAANG team had been decimated as well by the action and was down to a single residual female, the one in Pooh Bear socks. The white anklets were now soiled from running around on the dirty game room floor for the past fifteen minutes. All the remaining contestants had but one crud life to spare. The final Air Guard girl had just rolled the cue ball and missed. She was now frantically maneuvering to the other side of the billiard table to grab the white ball for a second attempt. Her breasts bounced and jiggled to the delight of the crowd. Jeff Carlyle's view was slightly hindered on the other side of the table from Brad, so he didn't witness Ackerman sticking his foot out in a not so veiled effort to snag one of the Disney logo socks and disrupt the Air Guard team member. It didn't matter. She saw Brad's foot and stomped on it for good measure, stuck her tongue out then confidently rolled the cue ball at an angle into the eight ball. After the collision, the black sphere rapidly disappeared into one of the side pockets. The Air Guard pilots cheered wildly. With that shot Holly was forced to relinquish her last remaining life and was promptly removed from the competition by Carlyle. Jeff was munching down another free Buffalo wing, courtesy of Major Toe Joe. The game was almost over now, as only Miss Pooh Bear and Danielle Le Claire remained alive. Both women breathed heavily and had visible sweat stains in vital areas of interest to the male dominated audience.

At the bar, Tanya was hinting to Duke that she really wanted to have dinner that night at Chez Paul, the French/Cajun restaurant owned by the culinary artist Paul Prudhomme. She was in the mood for a little Blackened Redfish. In the background you could hear the song *Man Eater* by Hall and Oates wailing away. Duke O' Grady knew there would be no time for such nonsense that evening because he and Tanya would be attending the Annual VA-204 Officers Christmas Party at Randy Bracken's house. In fact they would be departing the O' Club in about thirty minutes or so. With a twinkle of legendary charm in his eyes and in a hushed voice Duke boldly suggested a breakfast at *Camellia Grill*, the renowned New Orleans eatery, tomorrow morning as a suitable alterative. The sexual innuendo was subtle yet evident. With a coy smile and a squirming torso, Tanya acquiesced to Duke's offer. She was in love with Commander O' Grady but he wasn't aware of it just yet.

Cookie was the first to depart the game room. He flashed a quick double thumbs up to Duke indicating the *River Rattler* triumph then he made his way back to the bar. The rest of the spectators filed out in short order to resume their saloon activities. Danielle Le Claire and Teen Angel were the last two people to leave the game room. She wore the enthusiastic smile of victory proudly on her face, but didn't exactly know why. The final ovation for Danielle in the game room was humbling to say the least. Feigned indignation and insult began to diminish as the crowd dispersed to their separate locations in the Jack Black. Money had calmly changed hands and competitive banter ceased temporarily. As Danielle eased back into her high heels she could feel the cool moisture in the lining and smell the acrid bouquet of the champagne and baby powder mixture. The chill of the slowly evaporating liquor made her feet and toes tingle. Her whole body followed in turn and a shiver consumed her momentarily. She flashed an odd look in Brad's direction.

As the VA-204 pilots were making their final departure preparations, working out the logistics of the car ride to Brain Child Bracken's house for the annual Christmas party, Danielle excused herself to find the ladies room. Sensing the crowded conditions, Brad offered his BOQ room to Danielle. She would have more privacy there and they could get on the road quicker.

"It's room 103 Danielle, and the door is not locked," advised Brad. "If you see any dirty underwear just kick them aside." He wondered if there was anything, an article of clothes, a photograph, a love note, anything embarrassing left lying haphazardly on the floor of the room. He would have to take a chance. Brad gave Danielle cursory directions to his room as she headed off towards the officer's living quarters.

"Thanks, I'll be right back," she said politely. Clutching her purse Danielle departed the bar area to relieve herself. Teen Angel watched her as she left. Her body gently swayed with a sophistication that was unprompted.

Room 103 was on the bottom floor about thirty yards from the front entranceway to the club. To get there Danielle had to traverse through the foyer that housed the administrative offices and reception area of the Bachelor Officer's Quarters. One lonely looking third class petty officer sat at a desk behind the welcome counter, ready to receive newly arriving weekend guests. Partially hidden by a speckled gray partition, she was trying to look professional but was actually preoccupied with her game of solitaire, anxiously awaiting the end of her shift. Five hours would seem like ten to the twenty year old, especially when she would be forced to deal with drunken reservists and their myriad of requests. Adjacent to the main door of the BOQ vestibule, a tacky throw rug rested underneath two cloth-covered easy chairs and a leather loveseat. The three articles of furniture had a large glass coffee table and its collection of magazines and newspapers surrounded. The chairs appeared as though nobody had ever sat in them but the loveseat showed obvious signs of wear. The tedious tan walls of the small atrium were filled with oil paintings of navy ships and aircraft portraying famous battles in U.S. naval history.

As she eased past a colorful portrait depicting the battle of Midway, the long line snaking out from the ladies room made Danielle appreciate Brad's courtesy all the more. She really had to go bad after the physical activity she had just endured at the pool table. Danielle walked briskly down the west hallway and noticed the even-numbered rooms were on the right and the odd-numbered rooms on the left. The hallway carpeting was a dingy light green. After only thirty seconds of searching she spotted the door bearing the black numerals 103; the number three hung just a tad lower than the one and the zero. Grasping the handle she pushed the metal door wide open with one continuous fluid motion. Relief was imminent.

As the room sprung into full view, Danielle's eyes and ears were immediately assaulted by the unexpected, yet steamy sights and sounds of a naked man and woman, locked in a missionary embrace on the twin bed nearest to the door. From the look of things the hefty woman was extremely flexible; pretzel-like. Two feather pillows had been advantageously positioned under the woman's head and gyrating behind, not that she needed any extra padding down there. A third pillow had been cast down to the floor near the chest of drawers. The mattress was askew on top of the bedspring as the two lovers were energetically engaged deep within the throws of their passion. Garments must have been literally ripped away from their bodies because clothing was scattered all over the room. A man's pair of underwear was in the vanity sink next to a black sock turned inside out. A huge lace bra decorated a lampshade. An extra jumbo size pair of pink panties covered the phone and hung low over half of the night stand. Shoes were rudely strewn about the room. This was indeed intended to be a *quickie*.

The woman at the bottom of the clinch sensed the open door, swiftly straightened her legs then tried in vain to cover up the exposed body parts with the bedspread remnants. But there was not enough unfettered material to adequately get the job done. The sheet, securely wedged under their writhing bodies, was no help either. The man on top, still wearing a lone black sock on his left foot, didn't miss a stroke; his hearing blunted by the sensory overload of an impending orgasm. Danielle closed the door in utter embarrassment and positioned her left hand over her mouth as if to suppress the emergent laughter. She backtracked in search of Lieutenant Ackerman.

"Back so soon? That was quick," said Brad as Danielle slid next to him in between barstools; her close proximity indicative of someone who wanted to whisper a piece of sensitive information into a willing ear. She lowered her eyes, gathering herself then revealed the newsflash to Teen Angel.

"No, I didn't get a chance to go. A man and a woman were in 103 having sexual intercourse on your bed Brad," responded Danielle, apprising Ackerman of the lewd activity transpiring just down the hall in his BOQ room. Her voice quivered a bit as she recalled the stunning visual. Teen Angel laughed out loud briefly then suddenly switched gears. In Danielle's mind, Brad wasn't supposed to find the situation funny, even though it was hilarious. For a moment, their minds became one. Ackerman arched his head slightly back then twisted his cranium to unconsciously crack his neck bones. He did this whenever he was in an uncomfortable situation, which wasn't all that often.

"Why were you in 103? That's Rocky's room number. I told you 108," informed Brad. As soon as he spoke the words, their earlier conversation came flooding back to his short term memory. Brad had been assigned room 103 last month when he was in town for a ten day stretch. Danielle had been the victim of his understandably easy mistake.

"Oh shit! I told you the wrong room number babe. I am so sorry." Teen Angel's complexion quickly turned to blush as he methodically and sincerely explained the reason behind his error. She was in a forgiving mood; the elation of the evening's activities still fresh and uplifting on her spirit. She urgently needed this type of reprieve from her duties in the DA's office. On a weekly basis, Danielle Le Claire prosecuted some of New Orleans' most despicable criminals. Murderers, rapists, she dealt with all the scum of the earth.

"No problem. Are you sure its room number 108?" Danielle asked in a semi-skeptical tenor.

"Yes, yes. Would you like me to escort you down this time around sweetie?" offered Brad, realizing the answer was negative. Danielle bashfully declined and again departed the club in search of the tranquility of a private toilet. This time there were no slip ups. She locked the BOQ and bathroom doors behind her then took care of business. Deliverance at last!

Three minutes after Danielle Le Claire disappeared Rocky strutted back into the bar and made a beeline for Teen Angel who was now chatting with Cookie and Duke. Tanya Billings was nagging close aboard. Duke O' Grady had finished up his duties, had been properly relieved by Holly Carter behind the bar and was now making final logistical arrangements to hit the bricks for the *River Rattler* Christmas Party. After some last minute tabulation, Holly brought the VA-204 bar tab and placed it in front of Cookie who had asked for it. Cookie Cline nonchalantly reviewed the purchases then signed the charge slip. He padded the $240 dollar total with a cool forty bucks extra for Holly. Cookie expertly signed the name of *Doug Gross* at the bottom of the blue and white carbon document, peeled the three layers apart then stuffed the bottom copy into his flight jacket pocket. Apparently, Comatose Gross had forgotten that he had given Holly his MasterCard for that initial round of drinks, and Cookie had covertly advised Holly to use that charge card to ring up the squadron's bar tab. The shock probably wouldn't hit Lieutenant Gross until he discovered his grievous blunder tomorrow on the first day of Drill Weekend at the AOM.

Teen Angel had a smirk streak across his mug as he scanned Rocky's face for any visible sign of a guilty conscience. None was evident as Rocky drained the last of someone else's beer. The large butted woman with the Dutch boy haircut who smelled like a hundred dollar French whore quickly slid past Rocky and Teen Angel, rejoining her playmates by the juke box. She winked at Rocky Stone as she planted firmly into her seat, spilling a drink in the process. The margarita and ice cubes spread out over the table top in an uneven pattern. Slamming the empty beer bottle down, Rocky consulted his blue and gold Rolex Submariner, the only conspicuous opulence he ever displayed. The watch, worn upside down on his right wrist, read twenty minutes past seven. Making eye contact with the table of Dingos, Rocky flashed an engine start signal with his left hand held high over his head. It was time to go. The wild dog women followed Rocky, their new alpha male, to the parking lot. They were now honored guests invited to the *River Rattler* Christmas party.

"Rock, you always taught me that you can drink girls pretty but you can *never* drink them *thin*," said a perplexed Brad Ackerman. He was searching for a suitable explanation because this woman was quite a bit more than ten pounds overweight.

"Angel baby, she was sudsin' like a Maytag!" said Rocky after a short belch. He pounded a fist into his sternum to help dissipate the gas. "What can I say?"

"Thanks for the visual Rock!" replied Teen Angel shaking his head.

CHAPTER 11

▼

DA BITCH

Commander Randy "Brain Child" Bracken, the VA-204 active duty Safety Officer, shared a spacious two-story home with his heiress wife Dana Rothschild. Luxurious Greek revival mansion was a more suitable description of the residence. Dana, a thoracic surgeon at Baptist Medical Center, and ever the spoiled aristocrat, had kept her maiden name after their marriage. It was her third nuptial and his first. Dana's father, Alexander, used to tell his law firm partners at Rothschild, Falgout and Timmerman that his daughter's first two marriages didn't last the length of a baseball season. He was likewise tired of shelling out two hundred grand to finance repeat weddings just to satisfy his youngest child's latest romantic impulse. To his surprise and gratification, Randy and Dana would celebrate their seventh wedding anniversary on Valentine's Day in February 1992, a scant two months away. He was actively praying for a grandchild from the couple some day in the not to distant future, even the Petri dish variety. Right now the Bracken's were his only hope for grand kids since both of his sons were unmarried; one a confirmed bachelor cavorting around Europe, the other a practicing homosexual in San Francisco.

Bracken had been good for Dana and her dad was grateful for Randy's subtle, yet stable influence in his aloof child's life. She needed his moral strength and simple, unblemished character as a solid foundation to knock her down a notch from that upper-crust perch she customarily occupied. In fact, all three of Alexander Rothschild's children suffered from chronic myopia. The condition affected their attitudes not their eyesight. Long ago, he used to threaten all of his children with a six month forced exile to a Third World country in order to help them more fully appreciate the lavish station in life that they had inadvertently inherited from their family's 200 hundred year history in New Orleans. It would be safe to say that Alexander Rothschild liked Randy Bracken almost immediately due to his unpretentious disposition and because of the many fascinating aviation stories he would reveal to him over a competitive game of chess. The two also enjoyed sharing the occasional Cohiba Esplendidos Cuban cigar, smuggled into the country by Rothschild's wealthy business clients, and a snifter of French brandy. Bracken called it cognac, but it was really Alexander's favorite Marquis de Montesquiou Napolean Armagac, the world's richest brandy. In reality, Brain Child Bracken couldn't discern the difference between Lowenbrau lager and Brew 102, much less brandy that had been aged for forty-five years in a dark oak barrel.

Randy and Dana, the unlikely couple, lived in uptown New Orleans on the 1400 block of Jackson Avenue, an affluent white neighborhood known as the Garden District to New Orleanians. The locale had earned this moniker about twenty-five years after a massive levee break in 1816. The barrier breach had allowed the mighty Mississippi River to inundate the small community with a three-foot coating of nutrient-laden alluvial silt. It was this new layer of fertile soil that caused lush plant life to flourish and give the region its contemporary nick-name. The community was also a throw back to an earlier era of Southern Aristocracy, which was a euphemism for luxury tempered by austere racism. As the crow flies, the Bracken's lived about four miles from Duke O' Grady. The skipper's rented one story dwelling, with a loft, was located at 4139 Prytania Street, just a stone's throw from Tulane University and Audubon Park. Duke's place was exceedingly modest compared to the extravagant mansions prominently featured in the Garden District.

In the master bathroom, Dana Rothschild was just finishing up in the shower, allowing the hot water to surge liberally over her supple body. Six spray nozzles gushed at her from all sides and from top to bottom in the immense shower stall. Teen Angel and Duke always made it a special point to call Dana *Mrs. Bracken* or *Mrs. Brain Child*. She hated them for these insults to her individuality, but loved them even more for the variety of unselfish deeds they performed for her without seeking recognition. Dana stood relaxed under the warm torrent for a solid twenty minutes, letting it saturate her too white skin and almost depleting the upstairs water heater of its scorching contents. Thankfully, Randy Bracken had showered first. The brass water-flow levers made a squeaking sound as she finally twisted them to the closed valve position. *Dr. Rothschild* made a mental note to call the plumber tomorrow and get the handles oiled or greased, or something; anything to stop the infuriating squeal. Randy wouldn't fix them. He was not a handy-man around the house. "I fly 'em, I don't fix 'em" he would say, borrowing one of Teen Angel's infamous and annoying adages.

Stepping out onto the thick ivory-colored rug Dana grabbed the luxurious, shower-sized towel and began to pat her bare skin to dry off. She located a smaller bath towel, also made from Egyptian cotton, and wrapped it around her shoulder-length strawberry blonde curls, now piled high over her head. When blown dry, her hair looked like it had just come straight out of a hot waffle iron, all crinkled and creased. Dana did this on purpose to give her hairstyle more volume. Letting the larger towel slide smoothly away from her torso, she began using one dry corner to wipe away the fog in the framed, oversized tilting mirror. The antique cheval glass fixture was positioned directly in front of a large bay window featuring a collage of superior stained glass. As her reflection gradually materialized, Dana Rothschild stood quietly admiring her naked form reflecting in the polished mirror. Thankfully the surgery scars, although only three weeks old, were not visible around her nipples. The 38D silicone breast implants were perfection; worth the twelve thousand dollars she and Randy Bracken had forked out to her plastic surgeon colleague at Baptist. She loved how they filled out her otherwise anorexic physique.

As an MD, Dana was thoroughly familiar with the well-known risks of silicone but she downplayed them for the visible benefits. The implants had given her a newly discovered self-confidence and her mid-life crisis at age 37 was surely on the down slope. Dana even looked forward to the *River Rattler* annual Christmas Party that she and her husband had agreed to host for the squadron officers this year. Of course, Dana would be proud to show off her new surgically enhanced bosom to all the wives and girlfriends who wanted to view them in the privacy of the upstairs master bathroom. Following the surgical procedure, and after the swelling had subsided, Dana was fitted for her Sak's Fifth Avenue Christmas party dress a full size larger than normal. She was truly happy as she lathered herself up with an abundant amount of Aruban skin lotion, which contained the world's richest Aloe Vera oil extract.

Downstairs in the kitchen Loretta Mayhew was busy assisting with last minute party preparations. This year's Christmas bash was being catered by Emeril Lagasse. Emeril had been head chef at Commander's Palace for ten years, but he now owned his own award-winning restaurant in New Orleans. Loretta was actively helping the catering staff arrange hors d'oeuvres, entrees, desserts and party favors on two tables located in the living room and family room of the Bracken home. The staff hadn't requested her assistance, but they got it anyway. Shrimp Remoulade, Deep Fried Turkey with Oyster Dressing, Turducken (a de-boned chicken jammed into a de-boned duck then stuffed into a de-boned turkey), Sausage Jambalaya and Crawfish Etoufee were displayed on one table. Southern Pecan Pie, Sweet Potato Pie, Pecan Praline Fudge, Bread Pudding with Bourbon Sauce and Bananas Foster were situated on the other table. This standard New Orleans fare made up the bulk of the evening's cuisine. The Mayhew's were best friends with the Brackens, and Loretta could always be counted on to assist.

Mrs. Jack Mayhew was a decidedly slender woman; too slender. In fact without her clothes on she was downright emaciated! Loretta normally weighed a scarce 102 pounds and was fairly flat-chested. Last year she had stopped smoking for health reasons. Her physician was finally able to convince her to abandon the habit shortly after discovering a small black spot on her left lung during a routine physical examination chest x-ray. The spot had turned out to be benign but the episode had apparently scared Loretta straight. She quit smoking cold turkey the next day and hadn't touched a cigarette since. Unfortunately, smoking was a vital component of Loretta's weight control method. One spring night, after realizing that she had gained nineteen pounds, she did it for the first time.

After dinner that evening with Jack and their two children, when the coast was clear, Loretta excused herself from the dining room table and went into the master bathroom. She turned on the shower, lifted the toilet seat then forced an index finger down past her uvula. Loretta's petite body shook violently as she puked up her meatloaf, peas and mashed potatoes into the commode in two quick heaves. This had become her bulimic ritual and she had done it every night for the past seven months. She now weighed in at 97 pounds and was once again moderately comfortable with her appearance in a mirror. Nobody had any idea!

Loretta looked worn out. Exhausted! Withered from the hard life she was forced into by a dead mother and an alcoholic father. But she was tough and had a strong gentle spirit. Loretta's extremely long coarse hair extended just below the top of her buttocks and was showing the superficial signs of turning prematurely gray. Just a hint of muted silver color was growing ever more visible with each passing month in her brunette locks. From an early age Loretta had lived a harsh cruel existence. Her mother, a full blooded Hawaiian, had died as a result of contracting West Nile Virus while on vacation visiting her in-laws in Natchez, Mississippi. The doctors speculated that she had most likely become afflicted with the deadly syndrome after being bitten by an infected mosquito while horseback riding in the woods of the Natchez Trace. The horrific story had made all the papers back in 1962. Loretta Mayhew's father, an Army Colonel from Jasper, Wyoming, suddenly stopped attending his AA meetings and started drinking again six weeks after the disease took his precious wife's life.

Jack Mayhew had first met Loretta Fleming while on shore leave during his nugget cruise with the VA-22 *Fighting Redcocks* onboard USS *Constellation* (CV-64). The two had shared five glorious days and evenings together, soaking up the sun, touring the island of Oahu, gorging on Kobe steaks, even taking hula lessons at a Hawaiian luau. Jack even rented a Cessna 172 to give Loretta her first flying lesson. They soared for hours over Oahu and the island of Kauai with its mini grand canyon. Loretta even cut her classes that whole week at the University of Hawaii. She wanted to spend some quality time with Jack. Biology and political science could wait. Even though Juice Mayhew had never written a single piece of correspondence in his entire life, the two budding lovebirds exchanged letters twice a week during the remainder of that six-month carrier deployment. When they were reunited on the return voyage home to San Diego, Jack asked the nineteen year old to become his bride. Juice was seven years older than Loretta and he had rescued her that day.

In the vanity area Dana Rothschild was fully decked out in her Halston Christmas dress with the rear zipper undone, bending over the counter applying the final touches of mascara and eyeliner to her thick furled lashes. She was still learning how to properly position her torso with the newly augmented breasts and sometimes her movements appeared awkward and contrived. Dana used a concave makeup mirror to complete her expert primping. Tilting her body forward, the small butterfly tattoo was visible in the small of her back. This overt act of rebellion had taken place sixteen years ago on Bourbon Street and it truly pissed her father off when he finally discovered the mark. Alexander Rothschild didn't speak to Dana for a whole week that October.

Dana's life had always been too easy. Her heritage of perverse wealth and extravagance had spoiled her rotten. She wasn't Leona Helmsley but she was leaning in that direction right up until the moment she met Randy Bracken, almost eight years ago to the day. Brain Child had just arrived in New Orleans to work as the assistant VA Programs Officer at the Naval Reserve Center on Dauphine Street. The two had accidentally bumped into each other at the Café Du Monde near the Saint Louis Cathedral; Dana spilling her purse in the process. After retrieving the contents of Dana's handbag and exchanging the typical polite comments, they shared a pot of chicory coffee and an order of beignets for the next two hours. The even had their fortunes told by the tarot card reader in the French Quarter.

For their first real date, Randy and Dana attended the Monster Truck Rally in the Louisiana Superdome. 'Very few neurons' were in the dome that evening according to Dana Rothschild as she sat down in the loge section of the indoor stadium. But when it was over, she admitted to having a great time watching the monster trucks jump and twirl, and crash and tumble all over the dirt floor of the Superdome. The two shared a chocolate freeze at the Camellia Grill around midnight. Then, wrapped up in a thick plaid quilt, they necked like teenagers in Bracken's pickup truck in front of the Audubon Zoo before Randy drove her back home around 2:30 AM. Dana felt like she was on a high school date and the déjà vu was refreshing. She was falling in love with Randy Bracken, but she was fighting it. Fourteen months after that first date, the couple recited their wedding vows on Valentine's Day in 1985. They eloped to Las Vegas, Nevada. Yes, it would be safe to say that Alexander Rothschild liked Randy Bracken almost immediately.

The doorbell was ringing wildly as Randy Bracken switched off the fluorescent lamp and emerged from the empty four-car garage into the hallway that connected the den to the front entranceway of his home. Wearing a new silk tie depicting Santa and his reindeer screaming through the starlit Christmas Eve sky, Brain Child peered through the portal to see who was standing on the front porch. On the Nicole Miller necktie, Santa and his sleigh were being actively targeted by a huge A-7 gun sight reticle. Randy had just added this very personal touch yesterday afternoon, emptying a bottle of 'White Out' in the process. Undoubtedly, Duke would get a hoot out this holiday neckwear. Dana would not because he had ruined a one hundred dollar, designer tie. Looking through the peep hole past the pine wreath decoration on the front of the door, Bracken saw that no less than fifteen revelers had pushed through the metal security gate and were now crowded on the terrace. Several folks spilled out onto the circular driveway, congregating near his Ford pickup and Mrs. Bracken's black Mercedes 450SL convertible. Others stood on the freshly trimmed front lawn near the black jockey statuette and the terracotta birdbath.

As he opened the heavy front door, Dana had just finished descending the stairway to join him in welcoming their party guests. She stood next to the twelve foot Christmas tree, adjacent to the bottom of the spiral staircase, in front of the Van Gogh. The side-railings on the flight of stairs were laced with intertwined strands of white garland and dangling silver icicles. The Noble Fir pine tree had been double-flocked in soft pink and was tastefully decorated with rose-colored ornaments. Dana looked divine in the full-length red gown that was backless down to just below her shoulder blades. She wore no bra and the extra-taut spaghetti straps that draped back over her silky-smooth shoulders were tied into a bow behind her neck. She was truly exquisite indeed. Even though she was a bit over-dressed, Mrs. Bracken was ready to play the role of gracious hostess for this quorum of less than regal reserve naval aviators, wives and pilot groupies.

Before the oak door reached its full aperture, this initial throng of people poured into the foyer, hands shaking and coats flying then the lion's share forged its way on into the center of the Bracken home. Over the next hour or so guests would arrive every three to four minutes, barging into the residence without even offering a courtesy knock. Dana loathed this type of unrefined and uncouth behavior. Randy didn't seem to mind because he himself was somewhat uncivilized and his squadron mates were always considered a welcome part of his extended family. Soon about sixty to seventy partygoers were devouring gourmet Christmas cuisine, gurgling down spiked eggnog, chit-chatting out by the pool and hot tub, or tripping the light fantastic on the Mexican ceramic tile of the back patio. All the squadron officers would be in attendance except for the XO.

Jack Mayhew placed a *Hallmark* Christmas card and a bottle of *Cold Creek* Merlot on top of the mahogany desk inside Randy Bracken's office den. The greeting card depicted *The Three Stooges* all dressed in Santa suits talking to an Arabian Sheik. Juice never arrived at someone's home empty handed; *ass and face* as he would say. He always brought a symbolic gift indicative of his appreciation for the invitation. After chucking his flight jacket toward the leather couch in the den for safekeeping, Commander Mayhew's ears were suddenly assaulted by the voice of Nat King Cole crooning about somebody's chestnuts roasting over an open fire. The jacket skidded off the fine Corinthian leather cushions, landing rudely on the solid-wood floor in front of a bookshelf. The left sleeve nestled up against a copy of Adam Smith's *The Wealth of Nations*. Mayhew's face cringed as he turned around in search of the source of the nauseating seasonal racket. Locating the culprit, he marched straight for the stereo system and the record turntable sitting inside of a large entertainment center in one corner of the family room. As he walked passed the food table, Juice eyed the pecan pie longer than he should have, snatched a handful of cocktail shrimp from the silver serving tray then grabbed a bottle of Coors Light from a Styrofoam cooler. This would be his last alcoholic drink for the night because he realized his flight physical was merely hours away now. 'Shrimp is *seafood*' he rationalized to himself as he approached the entertainment cabinet; it's not fattening.

Scrutinizing the Bracken's collection of record albums in a side cupboard, Jack found the selection he was searching for buried about midway through the stack. Somebody had deliberately attempted to hide this he thought, and he had a pretty good idea who the perpetrator was. Juice delicately pulled the LP out of its worn cover and flipped the disc over to find the song he wanted to play. He then clumsily yanked the diamond stylus needle up off the Christmas compilation; scratching the vinyl soundtrack in the process and sending an irritating screech out through the Bose speakers. Several people covered their ears, while others went on as if nothing had happened. Dana's eyes squinted unconsciously as she cast a frustrated focusing glance in Jack Mayhew's general direction. Juice positioned the LP onto the rubber mat of the phonograph, pressed the 'automatic play' button then popped a shrimp into his mouth to make the short wait more palatable. He chewed with great passion and made an 'umm umm' sound as he swallowed the shellfish down; it needed some Remoulade sauce he thought. The particular song that was about to play, was Mayhew's personal favorite from the 60s and it was tradition in VA-204 to begin every party with this infamous protest anthem. Jack cranked up the volume.

Hearing the voice of Grace Slick bellowing out *Don't You Want Somebody to Love*, Loretta Mayhew instantly knew that her hubby had finally made his grand entrance to the Christmas party. She paused momentarily to preen her hair and naturally tanned, Hawaiian face in the reflection of the microwave glass door, before trotting out of the kitchen area to welcome her husband. Loretta straightened the red and green checkerboard cloth on the family room food table before greeting Jack, still standing by the stereo munching shrimp and slurping beer. Emeril's catering staff just shook their heads. Juice dropped the *Jefferson Airplane* album jacket to the floor then caught his wife in mid-stride as she leaped into his open arms. With a gigantic bear hug he laid a wet slobbery kiss onto her receptive lips, squeezing her slender torso too tightly in the process. The breath was forced out of Loretta's lungs with a whooshing, moaning sound. After five seconds Loretta forcefully broke free from the embrace and pushed herself back to arms length from her husband. Like a tailback in the open field she stiff armed Juice, holding him at bay with her right hand as she lifted the palm of her left hand to her mouth. Loretta then wiped off Jack's slobber, spitting and wincing in mock disgust. It was all part of their feigned greeting ritual.

"How dare you wipe off my kiss woman!" shouted Juice as he raised one eyebrow, pretending to be upset but performing his character to perfection. Jack played this theatrical game with his children all the time as well, and it had evolved into an amusing distraction between loving family members in the May-hew household.

"Now I'll have to give you ten more kisses to replace the one you scrubbed off your mug," said Juice as he puckered up and focused his stare intensely on Loretta's mouth. He used his slithering tongue to simulate moistening up his lips for the next onslaught. "And you can't wipe enough times to remove ten kisses," admonished Jack. Both spouses laughed with gusto then segued into a real conversation between husband and wife.

"Loretta did you call the kids to check on them yet?" inquired Juice, perhaps feeling a tad guilty since he hadn't phoned, but more likely because of his eight years of semi-irresponsible behavior as a father.

"Not yet babe, I've been pretty busy around here all afternoon," answered Loretta, feeling no remorse given that she spent nearly all of her time taking care of their children while Jack was mostly unavailable; an absentee father gallivanting around the world as a navy jet jock.

"You think Ashley figured out that little deception I pulled on her this morning?" queried Juice. An additional twinge of culpability was now evident in Mayhew's expression.

"Why don't you call her and find out for yourself Jack," suggested Loretta. Thinking this was a good idea Commander Mayhew walked back into his best friend Randy Bracken's den, closed the door behind him then snatched the telephone receiver up off the desk. Grace Slick had just finished her tune. Juice summarily punched the wrong numbers into the key pad of the cordless phone, disgustedly hung up after hearing a strange man's voice answer, then tried again with the correct combination. The phone rang seven times on the other end before being picked up, causing some momentary anxiety in Jack. Even though she held the phone in her lap, the Mayhew's teenage babysitter thought it might be her boyfriend calling yet again, so she hesitated to pick up immediately. Loretta removed the Grace Slick disc from the record player, gently reinserted it into its tattered jacket then placed the Christmas music soundtrack back onto the turntable. She twisted the volume knob a few decibels lower to give the party just a nuance of seasonal music. Loretta punched the 'play' switch then hid the *Jefferson Airplane* LP deeper in the stack of albums.

As Danielle Le Claire approached the GNO (Greater New Orleans) Bridge that spans the width of the Mississippi River and connects the West bank of New Orleans with the central business district, she listened fervently to the evening news broadcast on WWL 870. This was the only AM station she had taken the time to store into a memory button on her car's *Alpine* stereo system. Today was a rather hectic and monumental day for Danielle in criminal court as she had delivered her opening argument in a ground-breaking case for the District Attorney's office. Assistant DA Le Claire was lead prosecutor in a trial involving a New Orleans Police Department (NOPD) officer who had allegedly murdered her partner to cover up involvement in a heroin smuggling ring. The illegal narcotics scheme transported hundreds of pounds of the Asian contraband into the gulf coast on a weekly basis. The litigation was highly charged because of the heinous nature of the murder, and because the accused was a relatively inexperienced African-American female. Her dead partner, who had been riddled with eleven 9MM bullets, was a Caucasian male with twenty-two years on the job with NOPD. The cold-blooded cop killing shocked and outraged the residents of New Orleans and was even openly condemned by the black community.

This particular defendant had been hired in 1990 under an innovative program instituted by the *then* recently elected black Mayor of the crescent city. It had been argued that this newly established pioneering policy gave unfair advantage to police officer candidates who never would have been considered, much less actually selected, if the former, stricter employment guidelines had not been preempted by the incoming Mayor. Many people had contended that the Mayor's new *affirmative action* program for officer staffing was simply a fair way to promote 'equality of opportunity' and balanced 'minority diversity' in a city that boasted a population that was 74% black. While still others claimed that the tragic events, which had precipitated today's legal action, were an expected consequence when you place aesthetics and facade above competency and qualifications in the hierarchy of merit. Suffice it to say, that the controversial political issue had been a hot bed of contention for the past two years and Danielle was more than a bit curious to hear how the local news media was reporting the racially-charged events. She didn't pay much attention to the political posturing and brinksmanship that surrounded the contentious recruitment policy; she was just forced to contend with its tragic aftermath. Miss Le Claire maneuvered her vehicle into a 'toll tag only' lane of the westbound traffic for the GNO. She slowed to a crawl, allowing the digital optics machine to read her toll tag then accelerated through the fragile-looking booth to merge with bridge traffic.

Danielle drove her coal black BMW 750IL in the last position of a four-car convoy, directly behind Teen Angel's cherry red Porsche. She had just taken delivery of the *beamer* on Monday, and loved that *new car* aroma and the silky feel of fresh leather upholstery against her body. Her personalized license plate read: DA BITCH just above *Louisiana, Sportsman's Paradise.* This was the nickname that convicted criminals used when referring to Danielle Le Claire from their prison cells in the Angola state penitentiary. Even though she wasn't a bitch to anybody other than felony defendants, or perhaps the public defender's office, she thoroughly enjoyed the irony; as well as the tough portrait it conveyed. Danielle maintained a comfortable five car-length separation at the tail end of the caravan. She couldn't help but notice that Ackerman was steering his sports coupe in a somewhat lazy swerving fashion; as if he wasn't paying all that much attention to his driving. Perhaps he was fiddling with his car radio, or searching for a particular CD. Maybe he had his mind focused elsewhere, thought Miss Le Claire. Ackerman's lackadaisical driving style wasn't dangerous, just aggravating.

Duke O'Grady was leading this procession in his precious baby blue '57 T-Bird with Tanya Billings, driving a white Chevy Bronco, never more than fifteen feet behind him. Unlike when he was leading a bunch of airplanes around the wild blue yonder, Duke didn't waste much time worrying about the other members of his jalopy posse. Either they would keep up or they would not. It wasn't his problem. Tanya was keeping up; apparently glued to the skipper's rear bumper. Her SUV sorely needed a bath and someone had even written the words 'Wash Me Please' on the rear window as a friendly reminder. Tanya's Bronco was so filthy that you couldn't even read the block lettering on her *trusty* set of Firestone SUV whitewall tires. Although they were not aware of it at the time, Rocky Stone was guiding his pack of wild dingo women just three miles up ahead of the skipper's little wagon train. Of course, the destination was Randy Bracken's home and the *River Rattler* Christmas party festivities.

The quasi-motorcade exited the bridge onto the Tchoupitoulas Street off ramp. They quickly negotiated the short distance to Felicity Road then traversed the St. Thomas Housing Project behind the Warehouse District, before crossing over the trolley car tracks. There they made a sharp left onto St. Charles Avenue in *uptown* New Orleans. As the group passed Houston's restaurant, Teen Angel became aware of the flashing blue lights behind his 911S. An NOPD police car was signaling Brad to stop. Apparently they too had been observing Ackerman's laidback driving technique for the last few miles, and wanted to discuss it with him up close and personal. The cruiser wailed its siren momentarily to ensure Brad's attention before he pulled over to the right curb in front of the Pontchartrain Hotel. Teen Angel switched off his ignition then arched his head back several times, twisting to crack his neck as he waited impatiently. He unconsciously began to pick at his fingernails as well.

With the motor still idling, two NOPD cops exited their blue-and-white sedan. Ackerman could make out the words '*To protect and serve*' painted on both doors of the squad car even though they were reflected backwards in his rear-view mirror. The taller or the two had a full head of thick salt and pepper hair while the short cop was obviously deep into the ravages of aggressive male pattern baldness. Each officer squished a dark blue cap onto his head then dropped a baton into the receptacle of his service belt. Gradually, and in tandem they approached Teen Angel's Porsche. Flashlight beams skittered on the road's pavement as they slowly advanced. Brad surveyed their movements in his rear view and side view mirrors with just a hint of anxiety creeping up on him. What the fuck was this all about he wondered as his heart raced a bit. He didn't need protection nor had he asked for any service.

Danielle, temporarily cut off by a horse-drawn carriage hawking Roman taffy, completed her left turn onto St. Charles Avenue. The whole scenario was unfolding before her eyes on the poorly lit street as she eased in behind the police cruiser. She smoothly shoved her transmission into park then killed the BMW's four hundred twenty horse-powered engine. Duke and *tailgating* Tanya continued southbound, fat, dumb and happy; well maybe not that fat. Unaware of the activity taking place just thirty yards behind them, they forged on ahead. Teen Angel pulled out his wallet, popped the glove compartment open to locate his registration certificate then pressed the black switch on the lower console to roll down the driver's side window. Just then he thought, 'oh shit, I don't have a Louisiana brake tag!' How could they know that in the dark? Time dragged as Brad awaited the officer's approach.

"Good evening sir. Would you mind stepping out of the vehicle and walking over to the sidewalk for a moment," instructed the short policeman standing at a forty-five degree angle behind Ackerman's left car door. He was holding a large D-cell flashlight in his right hand, politely shining the focused ray of light on the side of the Porsche and not into Brad's dilated pupils. The officer's much taller partner, standing on the right side of Ackerman's vehicle, was busy checking for any visible sign of passengers or contraband inside the automobile. His right hand lightly gripped his holstered sidearm as he moved in close to the Porsche. Glimmering luminescence from a flashlight danced on the interior of Brad's sports car, emanating from the curbside.

Craning his neck to the left, there was just enough residual illumination bouncing back off the red paint for Ackerman to see the officer's nametag; it read: Sal Picone. The cop wore a sergeant's chevron on the sleeves of his light blue shirt and a 6th District insignia device on both sides of his collar. A green trolley car clanged noisily by as Ackerman gathered himself, deliberately eased the door open then quietly pushed out of the Porsche. Muscles in the lumbar region of his lower back flexed tightly as he thrust his body up from the tan, sheepskin covered seat. Brad marched straight to the curb and stood next to the other police officer whose name was apparently Billy Devine. Teen Angel nodded a nervous greeting to the cop as he came into his close proximity. He quickly noticed that Officer Devine, also from the 6th District, did not have sergeant's stripes. Sal Picone joined them on the damp sidewalk after first closing Brad's door so that it wouldn't interfere with southbound traffic on St. Charles Avenue.

Danielle Le Claire opened the driver's side door, swung her toned legs out to the roadway then slowly rose from an ivory-colored leather seat. She nimbly avoided the leading edge of a small water puddle that hadn't quite filtered down into the curbside drain of the sewer system. As her feet made contact with the black concrete, she could still sense the lingering moisture from the champagne inside her high heels. Despite the engineering prowess of the Bavarian Motor Works, both NOPD officers heard the muffled noise when she gently closed the German automobile's door then began to move toward their location.

"Excuse me lady, but does this matter concern you?" inquired Officer Devine, focusing his flashlight directly at Danielle's face as he skillfully repositioned himself in between his partner and the well-dressed woman moving toward them. Ignoring the question momentarily, Danielle confidently strolled up to Sal Picone without hesitation. Billy Devine didn't intercede because he could sense right away that she wasn't physically threatening. He was less certain about her potential as an emotional menace. Equipped with those long, slender legs she could definitely be a heartbreaker. Danielle had worked on more than a few high-profile court cases with Officer Picone and was semi-acquainted with him. Almost simultaneously, as her face came into better light, the two NOPD police officers recognized her as Assistant DA Danielle Le Claire; one of District Attorney Harry Connick's favorite legal beagles. They also knew her as the lead prosecutor in the racially heated 'cop who gunned down her partner' case, which had been the major topic of *water cooler* conversation for the past five months at the 6th District.

Danielle's identity was instantly recognizable because her picture had been plastered in the Times-Picayune newspaper almost every day for the past week, leading up to the start of the notorious trial. Since they had become partners some eleven months ago, every evening at the conclusion of their duty shift Sal and Billy had shared a late night breakfast at Mother's restaurant on Poydras Street. They drank heaps of black coffee and ate fried eggs sunny-side up. The two cops gobbled down bowls of hominy grits with an ice cream scoop-sized dollop of pure butter plopped into the steaming mixture of hulled corn, and they heartily enjoyed fresh baked Virginia ham. On the house of course! During their midnight breakfasts this past week, with transfixed interest, they read the myriad of newspaper stories that prominently featured Miss Le Claire. The ugly crime, accompanied by yet another promising scandal in Louisiana politics, had even broached into the national papers and network news broadcasts. But Sal Picone likewise evoked memories of her from several murder investigations over the years when he worked as a detective in robbery-homicide division. Danielle was often assigned to witness preparation sessions to help prepare NOPD officers for their critical appearances on the witness stand in court. They had worked together often in this regard, putting numerous felons away, and were conspicuously proud of this admirable law enforcement record.

As she approached Sal standing next to a rather nervous looking Brad, Danielle's mind suddenly flashed back in time. She recalled one specific case where Officer Picone was summoned with his previous partner to an armed robbery in progress at a Danny & Clyde's convenience store on Annunciation Street in the 6th district. Convenience stores are more commonly referred to as a *stop and rob* in New Orleans. During the commission of this caper, two black men, each armed with a .40 caliber Glock semi-automatic handgun, were caught red-handed backing out of the store carrying a brown bag full of loot. It was a mere 360 bucks in small, unmarked bills. During the ensuing gun battle, one of the robbery suspects shot Sal's partner in the abdomen. After returning fire and observing four backup NOPD police officers in hot pursuit of the perpetrators, Sal attended to his partner's immediate medical needs while awaiting the arrival of an ambulance. The wait seemed like an eternity.

A simple man who was remarkably *streetwise*, Sal correctly assessed the situation and made a life-saving choice that hot summer night on the streets of New Orleans. Officer Picone jammed his right index finger, the longer of the two, into his partner's gaping and profusely bleeding wound. They had lain there together on the wet and musty road for almost twenty minutes with Sal continuously encouraging his partner to hang on. Even when the paramedics finally arrived, he refused to remove his hand from his partner's stomach. He rode with him in the ambulance and kept his finger pressed tightly into the cavernous puncture. Sergeant Picone kept his stubby finger inside that bullet hole until an emergency room physician relieved him of his lifesaving responsibility at Charity Hospital. The next morning the ER surgeon publicly praised Sal's actions, claiming that he had without question saved his partner's life the night before. The news media swarmed all over the story like a hive of honeybees attacking a marauding bear. Yes, Danielle remembered these heroic actions by Officer Picone.

The other NOPD cop that had stopped Brad on the way to the Christmas party that evening was likewise memorable to Danielle Le Claire. At 35, Billy Devine was the older of the two; his partner had just made 30. She remembered Officer Devine from court cases as well, and from workouts at the Crescent City Athletic Club. But her memories of him were fundamentally different. Whenever he removed his shirt to lift weights at the athletic club everyone could see that Billy was a living, breathing testament to the prowess of the 20th Century medical profession. He was a walking macramé of surgical scars. A patchwork of scalpel marks were liberally scattered all over his lean muscular body, like doubloons thrown from the King's float on Fat Tuesday; some here, some there. If Danielle's recollection was correct, and it usually was, Billy Devine had been stabbed twice and shot once in the line of duty. He had one bad eye and the vision in his good eye was blurry at best. He had lost his hearing in the right ear and had no cartilage to speak of in his left knee.

Furthermore, Billy had been diagnosed with Hepatitis C a few years back and one arm was shorter than the other. Neither of his thumbs worked properly and his right shoulder had been sliced up with a surgeon's blade more times than a roast beef at Dot Domilise's restaurant. Billy also hated sharks and wouldn't venture more than ankle deep into the ocean. 'A shark would have to run itself aground just to get to him,' Sal Picone used to tease during family vacations in Gulf Shores, Alabama. But Danielle also remembered that Billy Devine was one of the finest law enforcement officers in New Orleans and she had always been pleased to work with him on criminal investigations. He was a superbly talented basketball player as well.

The flashing blue light from the police cruiser illuminated their faces now in a lazy rhythmic pattern. After a few minutes of polite conversation, Danielle convinced Sal and Billy that her date, Lieutenant Brad Ackerman, was not drunk. The two cops let them go about their business, got into their squad car and drove off toward Napoleon Street. After all it was Friday night and that meant Pascal Manales' restaurant and jumbo barbeque shrimp with raw oysters as an appetizer. On the cuff of course!

CHAPTER 12

▼

TGIF

The party was really heating up inside the Bracken home, now almost filled to capacity both inside and out. The skipper and Tanya had just arrived, tactically separate, and were busy placing festive food items onto large, red paper plates. Tanya was downright dainty in her actions at the chow table as she delicately arranged her assortment of food. She gently toyed with the fried turkey, spooned out a bird-sized portion of oyster dressing then dribbled brown gravy gracefully over some mashed potatoes. This she did after diplomatically pressing the gravy ladle into the center of the whipped taters to create a drip hole. To her, and Martha Stewart, presentation was everything in culinary artistry, even if you were on the receiving end. Tanya thoughtfully stuffed a wad of extra napkins inside of her coat for her and Commander O'Grady to share. She knew that Duke was definitely not the dainty type, nor did he even know who Martha Stewart was.

Standing comfortably, a few feet from Tanya, the skipper pitched one food item into his salivating mouth then plopped another onto the plate as he greedily gobbled up his first selection. He did this for a full five minutes, looking up occasionally to see if anybody was paying much attention to his less than Emily Post demeanor. Duke was scarfing down more food loitering around the table setting than he was tossing onto his plate. He was famished because he hadn't eaten since noon the day before and he had worked *two* jobs today; bartender and commanding officer. Duke had also crammed two cans of soft drinks into the pocket of his flight jacket. He didn't know what brand, nor did he really care. He just needed something non-alcoholic to cool his palate. O'Grady had stopped drinking alcohol at 1930 because he had to lead a bombing hop in the morning and the briefing was scheduled for 0730. Discretely, Tanya and Duke gradually moved out toward the crowd to mingle and socialize. Most of the officers weren't fooled by their discretion. Most of the women were.

Of course the vast majority of the men were congregated in one area of the home discussing aviation, war, politics and women. All of the wives and girlfriends were gathered together in a separate *holding facility* gabbing about *chick flicks*, Danielle Steele novels and the latest improvements in PMS medication. Men never entered their conversations, or so the guys thought. Rocky and Cookie, the Delta stewardesses and the gang of wild dog women were all lounging around the hot tub in the back yard, contemplating a skinny dip. The stews were giggling and generally acting coy, the way females perform in public when they don't want men to know they are ripe for a little innocent, immoral behavior. Interestingly enough, very few of the pilots had taken the time to introduce their dates; wives or otherwise, to the party guests. Proper etiquette was in short supply on the male side that evening.

Naval Aviator's social skills and demeanor when in close proximity to their wives is, to put it bluntly, awkward at best. They almost never formally introduce their spouse to other people in a social setting and often look for the first available opportunity to strategically ditch them, consciously or sub-consciously, at a party. Unfortunately, most wives are treated as necessary baggage. They are clumsy to carry but of vital importance to their final objective; passing on those legendary genes to the next generation of tactical naval aviators, their sons. But of course naval aviator's social skills around *other women*, available or not, is the stuff of legend in the tactical aviation community. Even Chuck Yeager was highly envious of the naval aviator's prowess with women, though he never had the audacity to admit it in public. Just then Brain Child Bracken got first wind of what was about to transpire in the Jacuzzi, so he eased on over to give a little friendly advice to his squadron mates who were inciting the event. He yanked Rocky up from his lounge chair and pulled him aside for a private moment between associates.

"Hey Rocky please don't turn my home into a *pump house* tonight. As you and Cookie are aware, my wife can be such a bitch about that," said Bracken, almost begging Jim Stone to desist in order to avoid the inevitable confrontation with Dana.

"Chill out and take a pill bub. Dana is upstairs showing off her store-bought tits to some of the wives at this very moment," advised Rocky. She'll be up there for awhile. You know how fascinated women are with breast augmentation." Bracken was unaware of his wife's activities in the upstairs bathroom. One of the Delta stews had just told Rocky what was transpiring in the master bath.

"Just don't get me into too much hot water with your Jacuzzi antics Rock," pleaded Bracken, not realizing the pun he had imparted by his statement. He left the back yard pool area and walked through sliding glass door into the kitchen to find the beer he had opened and abandoned twenty minutes ago. It was sitting on top of the stove next to his half-eaten plate of food. Rocky resumed his position in the lounge chair and began to prod the ladies to join him in a friendly skinny dip in the 99 degree water of the hot tub. He had at least four takers, one of whom was Cookie. The other three were stews. None of the wild dog women were going to shed a stitch of their clothes, at least in a public viewing.

"Hey do any of you girls know how to conjugate the word stupid?" quizzed Cookie to the group of flight attendants. They all shook their heads in mock ignorance but sensing the playful indignation about to spew out of Cookie's mouth.

"Stupid, stupider and stewardess!" said Cookie, obviously proud of his modest flight attendant humor. He didn't expect a rejoinder.

"Very funny cowboy!" replied the little brown stewardess. "Tell me, what separates a flight attendant from the lowest form of scum on the earth?" Cookie and Rocky were dumbfounded for an answer. "The cockpit door," answered the stew in a scoffing tone. The entire pool area chuckled at this clever retort and full frontal assault upon the pilot profession. "Now you first, off with your clothes and into the hot tub," commanded the petite Hispanic stewardess in an exaggerated Tex-Mex accent. Stripping down to their jockey shorts Cookie and Rocky slipped into the Jacuzzi, removed their briefs under the water then hurled them onto the concrete deck that surrounded the pool area. Cookie's flying undies almost picked off one of the Marine helicopter pilots who had just arrived onto the pool patio, caressing a bottle of cheap tequila. Luckily, the mostly white underwear just missed his head by a couple of inches. The *jarhead* literally leaped out of the way as if he was avoiding an oncoming freight train on a Saturday night in Lufkin, Texas. Streams of jet propelled air shot up from several nozzles strategically situated in the Jacuzzi. Rocky and Cookie beckoned the girls to join them in the tub experience as hot water bubbled up around their necks. Let the fun begin.

"Hello, Mayhew residence," said seventeen year old Cammy Nelson, sitting on the Wal-Mart throw rug in the living room playing Monopoly with Trevor and Ashley, Jack and Loretta's two children.

"Hello Cam, this is Jack. Is everything alright there?" said Juice seeking to assuage his anxiety before proceeding on with the real purpose of the phone call.

"Hi Mister Jack, everything is fine. We're all playing a board game in the living room," responded the teenage babysitter. She didn't want Mayhew to even get a whiff that her boyfriend would routinely call five or six times whenever she had a babysitting job there.

"Great. Watch out for Trevor though, he cheats! Could you please put Ashley on the phone for a second," requested Juice. The truth be known, Trevor didn't cheat at board games but Jack did! He was proud of it. If you ain't cheatin' you ain't tryin, he would rationalize. Juice wedged the phone into his ear with a powerful shoulder as he picked up the bottle of Merlot to read the back label. Cammy Nelson beckoned across the coffee table to Ashley Mayhew and informed her that it was her father on the phone asking to speak with her. She handed the receiver to Ashley as Trevor continued to count out his play money to purchase another hotel for Boardwalk and Park Place. Cammy deftly palmed a five hundred dollar bill from the Monopoly bank when nobody was looking.

"Hi Daddy, when are you coming home," grilled Ashley in her saddest kindergarten voice. Her lower lip protruded out in a pouting gesture as her soft brown hair drooped down over the mouthpiece of the phone. She did miss her father but was likewise torn because she also had more freedom whenever he was out of the house. Ashley was intelligent for a kindergarten kid. Too intelligent!

"Hi boosca boosca," started Jack, using one of the many pet names he had for his five year-old daughter. Mommy and daddy should be home to tuck you into bed later tonight sweetie." He was of course not being entirely truthful; the couple would not be back until well after midnight. Ashley would be fast asleep by that time, snuggled up in her daybed with an array of colorful stuffed animals and Walt Disney storybooks. Undoubtedly her thirteen-inch television screen would be showing old black and white movies or infomercials, but the volume on the TV would not be loud enough to keep her awake. The soft sounds served as a gentle lullaby for Ashley.

"I have a question for you boosca. How much do you love your daddy?" Jack asked. He was baiting his young daughter's standard response to this line of playful inquiry.

"I love you this much," replied Ashley, spreading her thumb and index finger about an inch apart as she played along with another of daddy's trivial games. She tortured her father often in this manner, claiming to love him only a tiny amount. Sensing her father's response a sly, tilted grin enveloped her mouth.

"*What* did you say to me? Maybe you should think real hard and answer that question again boosca baby," recommended Jack to his adolescent teasing child. Ashley's eyes rolled slightly in their sockets. She was extremely good at this amusing pastime invented by her daddy. Too good!

"Oh Daddy, you know I love you all the way behind my back!" admitted Ashley as she repositioned her crossed legs under her bottom. She was sitting *Indian style* at the Monopoly board. Trev and Cam were lying on their tummies, strategizing over properties and counting money again; waiting for Ashley to roll the dice and resume the competitive board game.

"Of course I know that sweetie. Say how was the lunch I fixed for you to eat at school today? Did you like it babe," queried Mayhew who had pulled a small prank on his kindergarten daughter earlier in the day. It seems that Ashley only liked blackberry preserves on her peanut butter and jelly sandwiches. She would never even *try* any other kind of jam despite suggestions to the contrary by her father. But this morning, before he went to work and the war-at-sea strike, Juice made her a sack lunch to bring to school. He made her a PBJ with strawberry preserves and now wanted to see if she had figured out his hoax. Ashley actually heard her daddy moving around in the kitchen early this morning so she got up as well, put on her fluffy pink *Minnie Mouse* slippers then watched as he made the sandwich. But she didn't notice it was strawberry that he used instead of her usual blackberry.

"The lunch was fine daddy. Here is Trevor," said Ashley pawning her father off onto her older brother. Ashley got up and quickly ran off to the bathroom.

Mayhew was always tougher and decidedly more masculine around his eight year-old son Trevor. In fact Juice once accused Loretta of attempting to turn their only male child into a momma's boy. He was furious on Christmas morning two years ago when his wife bought both of the kids *Cabbage Patch* dolls as presents from Santa Claus. When the family approached the Christmas tree at 0500, the look on Jack's face could have frightened a bull moose. As he polished off Santa's plate of chocolate chip cookies that morning, Mayhew watched carefully for his son's reaction. He would not have a *sissy* boy in his family. It took Jack a few days to get over that insulting episode. When he finally saw Trevor fling the doll down to the floor so their Golden Retriever could chew on the toy, he felt utter relief. After some small talk with Trevor, Juice abruptly decided to end the conversation.

"When I get home I'm gonna pounce you and then rough you up boy!" Trevor just giggled at his father's remarks. He knew that when his father was playing rough that he was really just expressing his deep love for him as his only son. With that Juice hung up the phone and ambled back in to the ongoing party.

Upstairs in the master bathroom, Dana Rothschild was indeed giving a semi-private screening of her newly purchased breast implants. She was doing it more for educational purposes than to show herself off to the interested wives and girlfriends. After all she was a practicing doctor. The waiting line from the master bathroom extended out into the hallway as no less than eight women had assembled to view her breast enhancement. It took a full thirty minutes to complete the showing. Undoubtedly, prodding, squeezing and cupping was involved, but in a therapeutic manner. When she concluded her educational presentation, Dana descended the staircase and ran smack into Juice standing at the bottom flicking the rose-colored ornaments and generally admiring the pink flocked Christmas tree. He wasn't exactly sure why, but he was admiring it just the same. Dana looked heavenly, as usual.

"Ah Mrs. Randy Bracken, would you join me in a little Christmas promenade babe?" said a condescending Jack Mayhew, bowing low in deference to her feminine loveliness. Some Greek guy named Yanni was now gently blasting his keyboard harmonies out of the stereo speakers. Juice didn't know who the musician was but his soft rhythm seemed conducive to a slow dance with his best friend's wife. Although initially apprehensive, Dana graciously accepted the invitation and stepped lightly into Jack's outstretched arms. The polished wood floor creaked in spots as they danced across the foyer. The couple moved slowly and a bit awkwardly around the small confines of the entranceway for the better part of three minutes before Dana felt it creep up on her. Pressing tightly against her extra firm 38D augmented breasts, Juice likewise sensed the tingling sensation in his loins as well. At the exact same moment, they both realized what was happening. Juice Mayhew had developed a hard-on and it was jutting into Dana Rothschild's right thigh as they danced together. Dana pushed back, focused her shocked eyes and dropped jaw at Jack's uncouth face then ran into the downstairs bathroom. The door made that ugly crashing noise as it slammed shut with conviction. A few party guests stopped their conversations in mid sentence to ascertain the cause of the commotion, but to no avail. Standing next to the family room food table, chomping on Turducken and Southern Pecan Pie, Randy Bracken witnessed the entire episode in his peripheral vision. He swallowed the last bite of piecrust, deposited his plate into a plastic trash bag then casually strolled up to his best friend Jack Mayhew.

"What was that all about Juice?" queried Brain Child. He sensed his spouse was just a bit pissed off at Jack but then again this reaction was not at all uncommon. He just wasn't aware of the latest reason for her resentment.

"Can I help it if those store-bought tits caused me to get excited Randy? Okay, I admit it. I got a big *woodie* dancing with Dana! I'm sorry buddy. It won't happen again," promised Juice. Bracken just shook his head in mock disgust attempting to please his wife who was now watching from the bathroom door dabbing her puffy eyes with a tissue. She was also gauging the appropriateness of her husband's reaction. Juice patted Randy warmly on the shoulder as he walked into the family room to fill a plate with some food. Bracken made perfunctory eye contact with Dana, threw his hands up into the air as a half-hearted apology for the insult she had just suffered at the hands.... .er uh, penis of his best friend then turned to rejoin the party guests. Mrs. Bracken was not amused to say the least. At that moment, for some strange reason, Randy Bracken thought of the *Church Lady*; the Dana Carvey character from *Saturday Night Live* fame.

Snuggled up to the food table Juice Mayhew was chewing heartily on a carrot wedge as he was piling an extra-large helping of celery sticks, radishes, deviled eggs and cucumber slices onto a Dixie plate. He had also poured about a half cup of low fat *Ranch* dressing into a Styrofoam soup bowl for vegetable dipping and had jammed a bottle of Perrier water into his trouser pocket to help wash it all down. His annual flight physical, scheduled for 0730 tomorrow morning at the NAS clinic, was really beginning to direct his rational thought process at this point of the evening. Jack again stared at the pecan pie longer than he should have.

"Hey, how's that dinner working out for you Juice?" teased Teen Angel as he and Danielle Le Claire emerged from the foyer, making their fashionably late appearance to the Christmas party. With some quick eye contact, Danielle briefly acknowledged Juice then moved toward the kitchen to introduce herself to the women congregated there. The couple was the very last to arrive at the Bracken's home as Duke and Tanya were already happily mingling with the crowd in the back yard by the pool. Tanya sat on the diving board, dangling her naked feet in the warm water watching every move Commander O'Grady made. She pretended to scrutinize the layers of split ends in her long platinum colored hair as she slowly bounced up and down on the springy board, playfully splashing her toes in the water.

"This *rabbit food* is alright I guess, but it sure would taste better if there was a big hunk of French fries sitting right next to it on the plate!" Tomorrow at noon he would be able to resume his usual culinary routine he thought. Brad laughed at the comment then continued on toward the back yard where most of the people were located. He was searching for Rocky.

Near the Jacuzzi the alpha female was sitting in a lounge chair frowning, refusing to have any fun of any kind. The grimace on her kisser was accentuated by the many wrinkles that lined her face and forehead. She had that smoked-turkey face look from decades of sucking on cigarettes. She alternated her attentions between monitoring the party action and plotting some just revenge. Suddenly her frown disappeared as she rose out of the chair, gathered up Rocky and Cookie's momentarily discarded clothes then tossed them over a nearby fence into the neighbor's yard. After making a mad dash, two miniature Dachshund puppies playfully tore into their newly found toys on the other side of the red brick partition. Revenge and leverage was the alpha female's goal in this heinous affront to the two naval aviators now whooping it up in the hot tub with one nearly naked Delta stewardess.

One stew, the Hispanic girl, had her long black locks piled up on top of her head and held in place with one of those plastic clip contraptions. She had brazenly removed her bra but left her panties on as she engaged Rocky and Cookie in their Christmas mischief. Hot water percolated up in between and around her petite breasts. The other three flight attendants had merely slipped off their shoes and were swinging their tanned legs in the bubbly hot liquid.

"Is he married?" asked the Hispanic stewardess in a loud but discreet voice, referring to Rocky.

"No, but his wife is!" replied the alpha female. She had seen this act before and was quite familiar with all the players. The Hispanic flight attendant heard the remark but she didn't care. She was a player as well.

"Love the one your with, I always say honey," was her retort to the alpha female as she daringly removed her silk, lavender-colored panties under the Jacuzzi bubbles then placed them on the side of the deck. The alpha female was further disgusted by this sassy display.

Standing on the covered patio Shroud, Comatose and Klutz were surveying the party scene with great interest. VA-204 parties were the stuff of naval aviation legend. They spotted Teen Angel and beckoned him to join them. Brad pulled a Pepsi-Light from one of the coolers, stuffed a shrimp, dripping with Remoulade sauce, into his mouth then joined them on the patio deck. It was one of those extra-dark New Orleans nights and the stiff Southeast breeze caused the air temperature to feel about ten degrees cooler. It made the hot tub all the more inviting. So did the Delta flight attendants playfully obliging Rocky and Cookie, as if they were reading from a script.

Hey, did you pay for any of those drinks at the O' Club tonight?" asked Comatose to open the conversation as Brad arrived next to them. "That bar tab must have been around 300 bucks or more." His tone of voice was that of a kid who had just gotten away with stealing a few Oreos from grandma's over-sized cookie jar in the kitchen.

"I didn't pay a dime but you did Comatose," said Teen Angel. The delicious irony was apparent in Ackerman's tenor and devious smirk.

"No I didn't shell out a single *Jackson*," said a perplexed Comatose Gross. The controversy even caused Klutz Fitzgerald to listen more intently to his squadron mate's casual conversation.

"Yeah but Cookie signed your name to a MasterCard receipt," informed Ackerman.

"How did he get my card?" Even as he asked the question his faced turned red. Comatose Gross suddenly remembered that he had bought the first round at the O' Club and had forgotten to retrieve his credit card from Holly the bartender.

"I don't know, but he got it somehow." Brad left on that note and walked over toward the hot tub. He made a cursory check for Danielle's location and quickly spotted her still in the kitchen chatting away with Loretta Mayhew and a rejuvenated Dana Rothschild.

As he approached the hot tub Brad was ready to tease Jim Stone unmercifully regarding his poor performance on the bombing spar this morning. He wanted to tell Rocky what Tommy Lasorda of the Los Angeles Dodgers once remarked about Mark McGwire of the Oakland A's just before their 1988 World Series match up. Lasorda, the Dodgers flamboyant manager, told McGwire that 'he couldn't hit water if he fell from a boat!' Teen Angel wanted to tell Rocky that today the only thing he actually *did* hit with those bombs that he pitched off of his wings *was* water! But Ackerman didn't get the chance to throw this insult at his best friend in front their squadron mates and the multitude of women in and around the Jacuzzi. As he walked up to the crowd gathered around the bubbling hot tub, everyone heard a loud scream; a veritable Tarzan yell emanating from the stucco roof covering the patio deck. One of the more inebriated Marine helicopter pilots had apparently stripped down to his skivvies and flight boots, and was in the process of leaping off the roof; hopefully headed for a soft landing in the deep end of the swimming pool.

Everyone in the pool area stopped their various party activities. Forty people looked up simultaneously in response to the *jarhead* 1st Lieutenant screaming at the top of his lungs, pounding his hairless chest. Eighty eyes couldn't believe what they were seeing. After about a six-foot running start the knucklehead pilot flung his taut body, feet first and spread-eagled, toward the pool. His squadron mates below him raised their drinks in a mock salute. Then they belted out the Marine Corps *oooorahhh* yell as he soared toward the warm water in the shallow end of the Bracken's less than Olympic-size swimming pool. It was about an eight foot leap over tables, chairs, party guests, Tanya Billings on the diving board and the Mexican tile lurking below, all just waiting for him to slip up and fall short of his intended goal. It took the drunken Marine aviator less than three seconds to prove Sir Isaac Newton's theory on the law of gravity. As he broke the surface of the water at an angle of about thirty degrees, his head and backside just missed the concrete edge of the swimming pool by less than four inches. This brave and daring feat delighted his Marine buddies all the more and they howled their approval.

Teen Angel, who was accustomed to professional stunt men in Hollywood movie productions performing all sorts of audacious acts, was not impressed. In Hollywood, these types of stunts, or *gags*, were carefully planned and executed with expert, mathematical precision. A few inches shorter and whatever small amount of brain matter that the Marine had in his crushed skull would have been spilt all over the Mexican tile. Brad quickly grabbed a towel from the nearby rack and walked up to assist the dazed Marine out of the water. Neither one of them knew it but in the landing, the Marine had clipped the edge of the pool with his left hand, fracturing his fourth and fifth metacarpal bones. Fortunately, the alcohol in his system acted like an anesthetic, delaying the onset of the numbing pain he would undoubtedly feel when the liquor buzz wore off tomorrow morning. Ackerman handed a fluffy blue towel to the Marine and yanked him out of the water by the right hand.

"Are you okay pal?" asked Teen Angel as the smiling Marine toweled off his high and tight haircut. The soaked and now transparent underwear revealed his pubic region as if he weren't wearing the white cotton briefs at all. He looked like an intoxicated college student at spring break in Daytona Beach, and Brad was the MTV VJ about to interview him on camera for a collector's video.

"I'm fine," he replied, even though he wasn't. Bravado is a dangerous thing in the wrong hands.

"Say do you Marine's still have the letters TGIF stenciled onto the soles of your flight boots in bold white, block letters?" inquired Ackerman.

"What do you mean TGIF?"

"You know, toes go in first!" said Brad to insult the Marine's blatant lack of intelligence.

CHAPTER 13

▼

DANCES NAKED
WITH DOGS

At ten minutes to five the next morning, Saturday, the first day of VA-204's Drill Weekend for December 1991, Teen Angel was cuddled up in a fetal position across the queen-sized bed in the loft of Duke O'Grady's modest uptown home. His clenched feet were rigidly suspended off the right side of the mattress and he wore nothing except one droopy black sock on his left foot. Brad's head was buried deep into a hollow-fill pillow and his arms were wrapped tightly around, clutching at its comforting warmth. He squeezed a second pillow in between his thighs while a third was nuzzled up snug against his exposed back, its full length parallel with the curvature of his spine. The emerald green cotton sheets and goose down comforter, from Duke's first marriage, had been rudely kicked to the floor at some point during Lieutenant Ackerman's scant three hours of slumber in the guest quarters. Miraculously, the skipper's nitpicking ex-wife had somehow missed the plush comforter in the final divorce settlement, some seven years ago.

Brad was sleeping alone, exposed to the frigid night air, and his body showed the initial signs of shivering because his core temperature had dropped a degree and a half around 0200. He had invited Danielle to share his cozy little sack last night as they departed the festivities at Randy Bracken's home, but the Assistant DA had politely asked for a rain check because she had an equestrian lesson scheduled for 0730 this morning. Miss Le Claire did, however, accept Brad's charming request to be his special guest at the *River Rattler* 'all hands' crawfish boil today at 1600 in the picnic grounds onboard the Naval Air Station New Orleans.

Teen Angel was experiencing the effects of deep REM sleep, in the final stages of a particularly satisfying dream sequence. In the night vision Brad was striding up the 18th fairway at the Pebble Beach Golf Links in Carmel, California overlooking the luxurious sailboats spilling out of Monterey Bay. The radiant west coast sun was warming his svelte, tanned body and a soothing Northeasterly breeze tenderly caressed his baby face like the soft touch of a lover's fingertips. Continuing his relentless advance up the center of the manicured fairway, a ten-year old Ping putter was casually slung under his right arm pit as he confidently removed a sweaty Foot Joy golf glove from his left hand. Brad Ackerman was about to receive the well-deserved accolades and thunderous applause from a huge gallery of fans, anxiously awaiting his arrival at the 18th green, the 72nd hole of the PGA tournament. All that remained was for him to gingerly negotiate a slippery little, fifteen-inch birdie putt and he would be crowned the United States Open Champion. With a brilliant final round of 62 on the treacherous links course, Teen Angel had successfully overcome the five-stroke advantage held by Peter Jacobsen, the leader in the clubhouse after the third day of the championship. His life would be complete and he could live out the remainder of his meek existence in royal fashion from the commercial endorsements alone. And, women would flock to him.

Just then a ten-foot Diamondback rattle snake emerged from the rough near a fairway bunker and began to chase Ackerman as he crisscrossed from one side of the short grass to the other. In hot pursuit, the slithering reptile persistently nipped at Brad's black and white Nike golf shoes. NBC caught the whole embarrassing episode on tape and sent it out to an international audience of about forty million highly amused viewers. Teen Angel's dream, unexpectedly transformed into a comic nightmare, abruptly ended and his rapid eye movement simultaneously ceased. His exhausted body involuntarily began to squirm and stretch in preparation for rising.

Through the slightly opened bay window overlooking the skipper's back yard, Lieutenant Ackerman was gently awakened by the high pitched sounds of blackbirds chirping carelessly in the enormous oak trees. Hidden among the shrubbery, crickets ratcheted their hind legs together in unison. It was one of Mother Nature's finest harmonies announcing the dawn of a new day in the heart of the Crescent City. The noise wasn't as bad as locusts hanging in the trees on a steamy summer morning in Tulsa, but it was annoying enough that it began to disrupt Brad's gentle slumber. With his left ear nestled and almost completely absorbed in the fluffy cushion, Brad could hear the muffled clamor of his heart thundering away. He could also feel the reassuring constricting action of his coronary muscle as it pumped life-giving blood throughout the 100,000 miles of arteries, veins and capillaries in his body's circulatory system. Brad's body shook ever so slightly as his heart valves pumped blood at a constant fifty beats per minute rhythm.

With his eyes half open, Ackerman immediately wished the blackbirds would locate the crickets for an early morning insect buffet then maybe all of the infernal racket would cease and he could get another twenty-five minutes of much-needed rest. Teen Angel had set the alarm on his wrist watch for 0515, so he figured he might as well get up now to prepare for the many activities this first day of Drill Weekend held for him. His naked body quivered as he rose off the mattress and looked down from his lofty perch toward Duke's small kitchen and breakfast nook. Brad noticed that some numbskull had left the sliding glass door wide open and it was freezing inside the house. His teeth unconsciously chattered just a bit in reaction to the chilly air permeating the residence. Almost immediately, Teen Angel humbly remembered that *he* had left the sliding glass door open last night after he had taken a well-deserved leak on the skipper's precious long-stem rose garden in the backyard. Duke had just pruned the rose bushes yesterday; Teen Angel was simply watering them.

Perhaps closing the glass door had slipped his mind because of the unsettling encounter he had just experienced at the paws of O' Grady's nine-year old, 120 pound Golden Retriever. The overly exuberant pup had wanted to play with Brad *while* he was relieving his bladder in the rose garden. To avoid pissing on himself, Teen Angel did his best circular jig to ward off the slobbering hound as he finished urinating. Surely if Kevin Costner had witnessed this comic scene he would have been inspired to make a sequel to his Academy Award winning motion picture. It would be entitled *Dances Naked with Dogs!*

Suddenly Brad's skull began to feel quite numb at the realization that *he* was the numbskull. He instantly decided to seek the inviting warmth and rejuvenating effect of a hot shower. Unfortunately he neglected to remove his lone black sock until it was drenched near the drain at the bottom of the stall. He also dropped the slippery bar of Zest soap several times as he was lathering up. Once it slithered beyond the shower curtain and ended up with numerous black hairs stuck to its slimy exterior. He picked them off one at a time before dropping them down into the drain.

Twenty-five minutes later Teen Angel was finished with his morning shower and primping routine in the small cubicle known as the upstairs bathroom. The young attack pilot took a final glance at his baby face in the de-fogged mirror and winked at his smiling reflection, as if to flirt with himself. Brad genuinely admired the fashion statement given off by his newly purchased Greg Norman golf shirt and fine wool trousers. The crisp red color of the *Shark* shirt presented a dazzlingly perfect contrast with the khaki hue of the chino golf slacks. He was ready to face another day, but first he needed to wake Duke O' Grady. Brad momentarily stumbled over his enormous ego as he departed the bathroom for the stairs. The skipper was a notoriously deep sleeper, especially when he was reclined in an actual bed following on the heels of a long night of partying and carousing. Approaching the skipper's bedroom door, in the southwest corner on the first floor of the domicile, Ackerman could plainly hear Duke's freight train level snoring emanating through the drywall. He couldn't help but laugh at the all too familiar reverberation in the narrow hallway. Teen Angel had heard this aggravating sound countless times before and in several countries during numerous, shared naval aviation exploits. Over the years, he had thrown many a shoe attempting to halt that infamous snore, usually to no avail.

With a requisite amount of insolence, Teen Angel rudely flung the skipper's bedroom door wide open in one massive shove from his right hand. It made a loud crashing noise as it proceeded to bang up against the doorstop positioned on the base board at the bottom of the side wall. The rubber and spring device instantly collapsed from the shear force of the accelerating wood doorframe. As the room burst into view, Brad could see that Tanya Billings was already fully awake, unable to sleep due to the skipper's snoring. Strategically covered by a satin sheet and an extra-thick bedspread, she was sitting up on the left side of the king-sized bed, her back pressed gently against the brass headboard. No longer constrained in a ponytail, her long blonde hair had that messy, *fresh-fucked* look that most men adore because of the obvious correlation. Women adore it too, but they won't tell men that. Amazingly, at five in the morning after a grueling night, and with only a few hours of rest Tanya was still a striking young woman. In this assessment, Brad ignored the eyeliner and mascara that smeared the underside of her eye sockets, giving her a sort of raccoon appearance. Ackerman could sense that she was still completely naked under the covers, so he politely averted his attention from her after an initial head nod of acknowledgment for the nubile dental hygienist. Teen Angel's brown eyes hurriedly focused on the outstretched figure of his deep-sleeping commanding officer, Duke O' Grady.

Duke's body was positioned half on and half off the mattress in sort of a slip-shod manner. He wore his usual pair of Calvin Klein designer pajama bottoms that had *The Fertile Turtle* embroidered in Navy blue, just below the front waist-band. Commander O' Grady never slept naked; a deeply ingrained sense of modesty precluded that. Duke's head was resting near the top of a cherry wood nightstand with his nose contorted and pressed firmly up against the front leg of the wooden pedestal. Drool was slowly dripping from his gaping mouth down onto the plush carpet below as he snored ever-more loudly. The short strands of his graying hair, or what remained of them, were pointing in every conceivable direction. His right hand was comfortably squished between his scrunched legs while his left hand and arm were flung back, intertwined in the rails of the brass headboard. Duke always looked fairly untidy at daybreak; sort of like a wolf dog from China. This familiar sight was not a shock to Teen Angel, but it might have been to Tanya. The whole scene was highly reminiscent of the first meeting between the Robert Redford and Paul Newman characters in the motion picture *The Sting*.

"The *great* Duke O' Grady," said Ackerman to good-naturedly mock the skipper's appearance that Saturday morning. Tanya giggled with amusement at the highly appropriate description as Brad threw her a quick wink with his left eye. In less than two hours this same drooling man would be at the VA-204 squadron spaces leading two hundred naval aviation warriors during their numerous events on this Drill Weekend. If his mother could only see him now!

Teen Angel grabbed hold of Duke's left shoulder and, with the gentleness of a clumsy plumber, shook him awake. O' Grady's snoring ceased and he groaned painfully as he opened his eyelids to the unexpected sight of Lieutenant Brad Ackerman hovering over him by his bedside. It was indeed a rude awakening to say the least after his three hour combat nap and sexual liaison with Tanya.

"What time is it Angel," asked Duke, straightening himself up and stretching out his left leg for the reassuring feel of Tanya's muscular thigh under the covers next to him. The cool satin sheets felt extra smooth on his skin as he slid his foot the eighteen inches over to her leg. Duke turned his head away from Tanya's view as he used his left thumb and forefinger to clear away the residual drool from the corners of his mouth. He also swiped away an annoying dog hair from the tip of his tongue that had probably been there for a few hours. O' Grady remembered that he had wrestled with *Beast*, his trusty Golden Retriever, just a few hours ago in the back yard. Beast, his canine best friend, was the only piece of community property that Duke had asked to retain seven years ago in his divorce decree. He wiped the gold-colored strand on the corner of the sheet. This was Duke's way of sprucing up a bit while in bed, although his hairstyle was still flyaway. He looked more like a circus clown than a commanding officer. But he cleaned up nice!

"It's time to get up and go protect the nation for truth, justice and the...." Duke cut him off abruptly by clearing his throat in preparation to speak again. He rolled his eyes as well.

"I know, I know, the Republican way!" I've heard this rhetoric before pal. Now get your butt out of my bedroom so we can get ready in privacy," ordered the skipper with a deep sigh while pointing his limp, right index finger toward the doorway. Apparently his right hand had fallen asleep so he proceeded to open and close his fist then wiggle his fingers around in order to pump some revitalizing blood flow back into the appendages. As Brad departed the room Duke threw off the covers, partially exposing Tanya's naked body. He then headed off to the shower in the master bathroom with Tanya in close pursuit.

After retrieving the broken doorstop and quietly closing the bedroom door, Teen Angel meandered toward the skipper's cluttered garage looking for his second bag of golf clubs that he stored there. He kept the sticks or as Duke liked to call them, the *bag of bats*, in New Orleans so he wouldn't be burdened by carrying them on airline flights back and forth to Drill Weekends or periods of active duty training. Brad, like almost all reserve naval aviators, was not the 'weekend warrior' that civilians conjured up when the term *reservist* was injected into a conversation. Reserve tactical naval aviators actually spent about one hundred days each year working for their squadrons; not just one weekend per month and two weeks per year like the hyped TV ads proclaimed. Any pilot who had that *television dynamic* would be promptly booted from reserve aviation and rapidly replaced by the next aviator waiting in the long line at the squadron door. Behind a plastic trash container full of empty beer cans and a rusting Toro lawnmower, Brad located the black and white Titleist logo golf bag leaning against the rear wall of the garage.

This alternate set of golf clubs, a collection of Ram *Tour Grind* irons, Power Built Persimmon woods and a Ping *Anser* putter, was the same array of sticks Ackerman had used in his three years on the varsity golf team at Stanford University. He had kept them as a memento to remind himself of his best of days and his worst of days, lest he forget. After successfully traversing the intense obstacle course that was Duke's *no-car* garage, Teen Angel counted out fourteen clubs; eleven forged metal irons, two highly buffed woods and a corroding putter. He had a ten degree driver to bang out 280 yard drives from the tee box, and a three-wood for use on those long shots from the short grass in the fairway. The set also contained irons 1-9, a wedge and a sand wedge. All the irons and woods had extra-stiff steel shafts, a swing weight of D-1, and a low kick point on the torque. Only the very finest golfers could successfully handle this professionally fitted set of *bats* on a links course.

Noticing the zipper on the ball pouch was wide open Brad casually jammed his hand into this small pocket at the rear of the bag to search for balls. After a few seconds of anxious digging, his fingers emerged with one solitary golf ball, and that one had an ugly cut in its soft Ballata cover. Severed rubber bands were even visible protruding from the deep fissure in the balls' off-white exterior. Someone, a rank amateur no doubt, had been hacking away with his clubs and had lost an entire supply of brand new, 100 compression Titleists in the process. These were the kind of golf balls that cost a cool thirty-six bucks per dozen, plus sales tax. Ackerman had a pretty good idea who the *wood chopper* was. He also knew that the culprit had probably pumped about twenty-four of his golf balls into various lakes and wooded areas scattered around the track of the NAS New Orleans Aviation Oaks Golf Course. Teen Angel would be compelled to exact an appropriate amount of retribution for this heinous breech of golfing etiquette, soon. Brad made a quick mental note to leave a guest pass at the front security gate for Danielle. He smiled as he thought of the anticipation that would undoubtedly build throughout the day. Indeed, Teen Angel wanted to be reunited with Miss Le Claire ASAP (as soon as possible). Perhaps she could educate him on the latest dressage techniques.

Opening the silver-tinted door on Duke's Whirlpool side-by-side refrigerator, Brad removed a gallon carton of Tropicana orange juice from the top shelf. After ensuring that nobody was watching, he quickly took three healthy gulps straight from the plastic container. Why get a cup dirty when you can drink from the jug with impunity? In his haste, some of the citrus fluid accidentally dribbled out of the sides of his mouth on the third swig. But, Teen Angel was nimble enough to shift his torso and spread his feet wide apart so that none of the cold liquid hit his clothes or shoes. It fell harmlessly to the kitchen floor in a couple of orange splats.

Brad then peeled an overly-ripe banana and devoured the monkey-fruit in about two swallows. Still chewing the last remnants, he tossed the bruised peel at an open trash receptacle in front of the partition leading to the breakfast nook. But Lieutenant Ackerman was no Magic Johnson that day. The banana skin hit the rim of the waste basket and fell straight to the Terrazzo tile. Next he searched for and found a large Tupperware bowl, located a carton of out-of-date skim milk then grabbed a huge box of *New and Improved* Wheaties cereal. Ackerman needed his 'Breakfast of Champions' if he was going to perform to maximum capacity today on the golf course. Several spoons fell to the floor as he fumbled around in a drawer of flatware. They made that high pitched, metallic noise as they crashed in front of the stove. Teen Angel picked up one of the fallen utensils to use with his cereal, gave it a cursory wipe on his shirtsleeve then crammed the others back into the drawer; still dirty. Ackerman left the drawer half open; he was merely going through the motions to close it. When Brad opened the box of breakfast cereal he quickly discovered nothing new and improved. It was the same old stuff.

In the master suite, Tanya Billings had finished dressing and was putting up an ironing board in the middle of the bedroom. She looked sharp in her crisp, winter blue uniform. Her rank insignia, nametag and ribbons were perfectly aligned. Duke was still in the bathroom leaning over the sink shaving in his skivvies. Tanya had noticed that the skipper's khaki shirt and pants were fairly wrinkled so she took it upon herself to iron them out. Somehow sensing that Teen Angel was about to leave Commander O' Grady came out of his bedroom, still clad only in his skivvies and carrying a face towel stained with fresh blood. He had three small pieces of toilet paper covering razor nicks on his face, and shaving cream was visible in his left ear canal. Duke invited Ackerman to join Tanya and himself for breakfast at the Camellia Grill. But Brad hastily declined because he wanted to tune up his golf swing by hitting a few practice shots at the Driving Range before his big match with CAG Sullivan.

"Oh and that reminds me Lieutenant," Duke used this formal title for Tanya's sake, not that she really cared. "The Secretary of the Navy is in town today. You're going to be paired up with SECNAV Andrews and you'll be playing against CAG and Admiral Tommy Thompson. So don't screw this up bub!" warned Commander O' Grady in a heartfelt tone of voice but meaning business just the same. Suddenly the phone call that he picked up yesterday in Duke's office flashed back into Brad's mind. Ackerman reassured the skipper that he would successfully fulfill his part in today's mini-drama. He let the screen door slam shut behind him then trotted down the front porch. Teen Angel fired up his Porsche and drove off toward the Naval Air Station. He swerved just a bit as he entered traffic, Southbound on Prytania Street.

Across the Mississippi River Bridge in the township of Harvey, Juice Mayhew had lovingly kissed his sleeping children and half-awake wife goodbye before departing the house at 0614. He headed for the NAS Medical Clinic and his annual trek for a flight physical. But first he made a short pit-stop at the neighborhood Circle K convenience store on the corner of his street and Lapalco Boulevard. Once inside the store Mayhew purchased two Hubig's fruit pies, the kind baked locally by the Simon Hubig Company. The little dessert treats had evolved into a New Orleans tradition over the past ninety years even though they contained about a million calories each. He also picked up two Yoo-Hoo chocolate drinks, one to wash down each pie, and a Louisiana Power Ball lottery ticket. The grand prize had been boosted to over 80 million smackers during the past week. Jack exchanged pleasantries with the cashier, paid with a scruffy looking ten dollar bill then punched his beige Toyota Camry back into some lighter than usual Saturday morning traffic. It would take him about twenty minutes to reach the Medical Clinic at the Naval Air Station in Belle Chasse. He had plenty of time to spare to make his 7AM appointment with the flight surgeon. Like most naval aviators, Commander Mayhew didn't trust flight surgeons, hated flight physicals and always sought to avoid hypodermic needles until the last possible moment.

Rear Admiral Tommy Thompson, a Viet Nam era F-8 Crusader driver, and currently Chief of the Naval Reserves had arranged for a limousine to pick him up at his residence in New Orleans East early that morning. From there he and his driver would rush on over to the Four Seasons Hotel to give SECNAV Hank Andrews a lift to the golf match; as well as to all the other planned activities on the base and in the Crescent City that day. When the stretch limo arrived at the Four Seasons, precisely at quarter past six, Hank Andrews was waiting with his golf bag by his side, shining up a four-iron with a dirty towel. He was wearing a bright blue *Golden Bear* golf sweater talking with a doorman at the front entranceway to the five-star hotel. The admiral himself hopped out of the black limousine to load Andrews' bag into the oversized trunk next to his own gear. As the chauffeur drove away Tommy Thompson made a comment that their arrival at the golf course should allow them plenty of time to hit a small bucket of balls at the range and still make it to the first tee by 0722. They might even have a few moments to stroke several putts on the practice green, and hone that vital skill before the friendly competition began. The always affable Hank Andrews said that would be fine but the phone call yesterday with Commander O' Grady had aroused his intense curiosity. He wanted to know a little bit more about his playing partner for the day, Lieutenant Brad Ackerman. Since Rear Admiral Thompson had played quite a few rounds of golf with Teen Angel, he proceeded to give Andrews the details as he knew them. The story went something like this.

Lieutenant Brad Ackerman was basically a *scratch* golfer who was always rather humble about his immense, God-given talent on a golf course. It was the only facet of his life where he displayed relative humility. In fact he was so modest about his golfing skills that today he really didn't take the game all that seriously; he simply played for recreation and stress reduction. But in 1980, Brad had quite an impressive sophomore season at Stanford University; earning All-American honors. In August of that year Ackerman had finished second in the United States Amateur Golf Championship held at Pinehurst Country Club. He lost the final match of the USGA sponsored event to the eventual tournament champion Hal Sutton, who fashioned a superb round of 66 in his triumph that day in North Carolina. Brad had stayed with Sutton stroke for stroke until he pumped two 300 yard tee shots out-of-bounds on the seventeenth hole, a treacherous Par 5 with water and trees lining the needle-eye fairway. He never recovered from that triple-bogey eight. Despite this uncharacteristic eruption at seventeen Brad had fired a final round of 67. But, he allowed the coveted championship to slip through his fingers on that next-to-last hole. He lost to Sutton, 1 down. Ackerman had also finished a close second in the 1980 NCAA Golf Tournament, relinquishing the individual title to Jay Don Blake of Utah State University. His demise in that tournament came at the sixteenth, a short Par 3 surrounded by ample amounts of water and alligators. Brad unraveled his game by knocking three Titleists, long into the waiting pond.

"Sounds like he could have gone pro," said Hank Andrews, scratching his right cheekbone and shifting positions in the overly posh leather bench seat in the rear of the limo. He couldn't help noticing his reflection on the picture screen of the thirteen inch TV that had been wedged into the back panel behind the driver's seat, next to a mini-bar. Hank ran a hand through his short black hair as the informative conversation continued. A little smear of Brylcream hair gel was visible in his palm.

"I think he was a lock for the PGA Tour, but for some unknown reason he chose to chase the *wings of gold* and not dimpled little golf balls for his profession," concluded Admiral Thompson while gazing out the left window at the muddy waters of the Mississippi River rushing by at 65 miles per hour. The flag officer could plainly see the steam, paddlewheel showboats tied up to the Riverwalk pier, preparing for their daily influx of tourists desiring a Cajun lunch cruise. The limousine was soon on the down slope of the GNO Bridge about to make its exit onto General De Gaulle Drive, and the surface streets leading to the Belle Chasse Naval Air Station.

"So he chose to soar with the eagles up in the wild blue yonder and not chase them down with a putter in his hand and golf tees in his pocket?" deduced Andrews.

"Something along those lines Mr. Secretary." The conversation dried up as the limousine driver accelerated and sped off Eastbound on De Gaulle Drive. Tommy Thompson nonchalantly opened the tiny refrigerator in front of him and popped open a Diet Pepsi without offering any refreshment to SECNAV.

Hank silently allowed this flagrant breach of protocol to slide. His sixth sense told him that additional, good-natured infringements would undoubtedly follow throughout the day, especially in his dealings with navy attack pilots. Since his presidential appointment and Senate conformation as Secretary of the Navy, Hank had become accustomed to receiving royal treatment, occasionally leavened by being regarded as just one of the boys. Naval aviators were fairly well-known for their occasional lack of decorum. Andrews always considered it an endearing quality, not to be a gigantic kiss-ass, especially around politicians who could easily be as phony as a three-dollar bill.

Fifteen minutes later the limousine was approaching the front gate of the Naval Air Station, when something caught the attention of Hank Andrews. It was a huge billboard off on the right side of Belle Chasse Highway, approximately one half mile from the main gate of the naval base. The billboard had a picture of two A-7 Corsair jets, in tight formation, streaking through the crystal blue sky over the Louisiana Superdome in downtown New Orleans. As the limo advanced toward the billboard, Andrews squeezed his eyeballs into a tight squint, temporarily overcoming his astigmatism, so he could begin to make out the caption. It read: 'See the jets? Hear the noise? Get used to it! It's the sound of freedom!' As the SECNAV surveyed the billboard's message, Tommy Thompson watched Andrews' face and demeanor. He knew that an explanation was probably warranted. A smile soon filled Andrews' face. With a tremendous sense of personal pride, Admiral Thompson explained that he had paid for this advertisement out of his own pocket. In fact, the billboard sign had been in place for the last six months because a citizen's group had been extremely vocal in protesting the jet aircraft noise in and around the rustic neighborhoods of Belle Chasse. Andrews completely understood the sentiment and nodded his approval for the gentle yet robust advertising campaign. His smile persisted.

As the stretch limousine turned onto Russell Drive, the main drag leading into the Naval Air Station from Belle Chasse Highway, Admiral Thompson, dressed in civilian clothes, rolled down the driver's side rear window and removed his Navy ID card from an eel skin wallet. The black tri-fold contained no credit cards, only his Navy identification, two sweat-stained twenty dollar bills, five tens, a dog-eared picture of his three daughters, and an organ-donor card. It was 0645 and the line of cars waiting to get onto the base for the start of Drill Weekend was characteristically long and slow moving. Recently, the base Commanding Officer had to institute some increased security measures due to a terrorist threat against all U.S. armed forces by some *rag head* militant group in Iraq. As they waited in the procession, Andrews and Thompson observed and admired a museum-style display of tactical aircraft. The warplanes had been erected on *sticks* as enduring monuments and the collection lined the entire length of the road feeding into the main gate. All the services were represented in the impressive array of jets. The limo inched forward with the cluster of sluggish traffic as Tommy Thompson tossed his empty soda can into a brown paper trash bag.

Just in front of the guardhouse to the main gate, a sign was visible indicating that today there was a mandatory 100% ID check in progress. Actually, since the end of the Gulf War earlier in 1991, the base had been fairly lax in its security procedures, but of course that had all changed when news of the credible threat from a Middle-East terrorist organization had been uncovered. Vehicles also had to weave around orange barricades situated about fifty feet from the guardhouse. A young Third Class sailor, dressed in his winter blue uniform, waved the Admiral's limo forward as it successfully navigated through the last set of orange barricades. This particular Petty Officer had been a last minute replacement on guard duty that Saturday morning because one of the regularly scheduled gate guards had gone to sick call at 0600 in the medical clinic.

As the limousine coasted to a stop next to the guard shack, Admiral Thompson uttered an obligatory 'good morning' to the young sailor then politely offered his ID card for a closer inspection. The sailor gazed intently at the green identification card, wrinkled up his youthful face just a bit then asked Tommy Thompson a sincere question.

"Excuse me but what does this word RADM mean on your ID card?" As the admiral's face boiled red with indignation, Secretary Andrews turned his face slightly to the right so Tommy Thompson couldn't see him chuckling at the remark. Turn about was fair play he thought, in this breach of military etiquette directed at the flag officer. Apparently, since he was a last minute replacement on guard duty, the sailor had not attended the security briefing held the night before. At that meeting the NAS Executive Officer had notified the security staff that SECNAV and Admiral Thompson would be onboard today and to expect them to come through the front gate at approximately 1200. Of course nobody except Duke O' Grady knew that SECNAV and the admiral would be playing a round of golf before the formal VA-204 activation announcement was given at the squadron, so this caught everyone by surprise at the main entrance to the base. It didn't help that the sailor had never laid eyes on Admiral Thompson before either.

As a more senior gate guard hastily approached the limousine and saluted the admiral onboard, Tommy Thompson informed the young Petty Officer that he would be happy to explain the acronym RADM to him at 1300 in the NAS Commanding Officer's office.

"Make sure both you and your skipper are wearing Dress Blue uniforms at this meeting sailor," ordered Admiral Thompson. The sailor braced up as the chauffeur accelerated on through the gate. Secretary Andrews thought the whole episode was priceless. The limo made a left turn onto Thompson Trail, the street named in honor of Admiral Thompson then continued for a short distance to the golf course parking lot where they unloaded their equipment.

CHAPTER 14

▼

A LITTLE FACE TIME

Commander Jack Mayhew was now running about nine minutes behind his precise schedule, and he wasn't at all happy about it. The leisurely drive he had planned to the NAS Medical Clinic that morning had been unexpectedly interrupted by a temporary closure of the Belle Chasse Tunnel. Due to the restriction Southbound traffic on Highway 23 had been re-routed over the draw bridge that spans the inter-coastal waterway. Unfortunately for Juice, the retractable section of the bridge was raised to the up position before he could get across. In Southeastern Louisiana working tugboats, pleasure craft and barges routinely disrupted vehicular traffic, especially in the vicinity of the huge Port of New Orleans. Somewhat incensed, Jack sat impatiently on the lower half of the bridge's roadway with his engine turned off to save fuel.

On his car radio he was listening to a sports talk program featuring local broadcaster Buddy Dillaberto discussing an upcoming football game between the hometown Saints and the reviled Bears of Chicago. Mike Ditka, the Bears' ostentatious Head Coach was the in-studio guest on the radio show. Since the Saints appeared to be heading for their first ever NFC championship that season, Juice was highly interested in hearing the gist of the conversation. Likewise, *Iron Mike* was usually good for an entertaining expletive or two whenever his feathers got ruffled, and 'Buddy D' was an expert at feather ruffling. In his peripheral vision, Juice nonchalantly monitored a flock of seagulls as they flew over his vehicle headed towards the open gulf waters, some forty miles away. Two of the birds shit on the trunk and rear window of Mayhew's Camry, although at the time he didn't realize it.

As the unsettling delay persisted, Commander Mayhew became increasingly aware that he would make it to his 0700 appointment at the clinic with only a couple of minutes to spare. When the steel grate of the bridge settled lethargically back, flush into its down position, Jack cranked up the engine of his beige Toyota. Surrounded by a pack of about forty other cars, various pick up trucks and big rigs he pressed up and over the inter-coastal canal. Most of the traffic at that early hour was traveling to the Naval Air Station for work. But several vehicles were towing boats, obviously bound for lower Plaquemines Parish and the *sportsman's paradise* fishing experience in the gulf waters of the Pelican State.

At 0655 Juice switched off the ignition and parked his Toyota in the front lot of the medical clinic in a spot reserved for O-5's and above. The VA-204 Maintenance Officer yanked up the emergency brake to further ensure his automobile's immobility then popped out of the driver's side. Before closing the car door Mayhew reached into the plastic grocery bag from his stop at the Circle K convenience store and pulled out the Hubig's fruit pies and Yoo-Hoo chocolate drinks. With a sheepish grin he tossed the two bottled beverages into a six pack cooler, half full of crushed ice. He calmly deposited the *Igloo* in the foot area of the passenger seat. Next he placed the Hubig's pies neatly on the driver's bucket seat, adjacent to a thick stack of napkins, before moving off to the Aviation Physiology Department inside the medical clinic. Jack Mayhew pre-positioned these two dessert snacks, one lemon and one apple, as his post-flight physical celebration treat. He would thoroughly enjoy this well-deserved compensation during the short ride over to the squadron. This would be his personal indulgence, after suffering through thirty days of bland tasting diet meals and barely palatable diet Cranberry juice cocktails. With his medical *up chit* in hand, Jack would devour the fruit tarts with great relish, rewarding himself for a job well done. Still smiling, he softly closed the car door, used his flight jacket sleeve to buff out an unsightly water stain on the hood of his Camry then walked across the gravel parking lot toward the medical clinic's front entrance. With his calloused right thumb, Jack pressed a button on a small black module to lock his car doors and set the burglar alarm. Commander Mayhew soon disappeared behind the double doors of the clinic.

In a secluded section of the BEQ parking facility, strategically out of sight from prying eyes, Commander O' Grady lightly kissed Tanya Billing's soft hand. Tanya expressed her gratitude for last night and especially for the Camellia Grill breakfast they shared that morning, even though it had been a rushed meal. A moment later she surreptitiously exited the skipper's '57 T-Bird in search of her own vehicle. Petty Officer Billings had lived in the Bachelor Enlisted Quarters ever since her arrival at NAS New Orleans for duty. The BEQ was substantially more than a barracks. It was similar to living in an apartment complex on a small college campus and most of the younger enlisted personnel thoroughly enjoyed the relaxed lifestyle it provided. Tanya was no exception.

Five minutes later, Duke was climbing the stairs of the VA-204 squadron spaces. His bombing hop briefed at 0745 and the squadron had *Quarters* (a muster) scheduled for 0730. He had just enough time to sip another quick cup of coffee, scan the message board, and perhaps read some personal mail left over from yesterday. Wearing a freshly pressed set of khakis, the skipper walked unruffled into the Ready Room. He secured his piss cutter cap in the left side of a taut web belt then removed his cup from the coffee mug board. He immediately noticed that the exterior of the mug had a big mouth print planted on the rim. As the cup dangled down from its hook, Duke could clearly see that the highly incriminating marks had been etched in bright red lipstick. He raised his eyes cynically hoping to spot the joker off guard; perhaps waiting in the shadows to witness the skipper's reaction to the taunt. The only officers in the Ready Room were Lieutenant Commander "Pops" Petibone and Lieutenant "Comatose" Gross. The two aviators hadn't even detected O' Grady's stealthy entrance. They were way too busy playing ace-deuce on the other side of the room. Duke decided the time was right for some early morning impertinence, and Eli Petibone was always an easy target. But Pops was already anticipating the grilling he would receive this morning from his squadron brethren. He was way ahead of the airplane of life that Saturday; prepared with his rapid retort before the skipper even asked the inevitable question.

"Hey Pops, how did your rather *mature* dates turn out last night," badgered the skipper. Awaiting a response, Duke shifted his focus to the coffee pot as he poured himself a half-cup of the steaming hot liquid.

"They worked out great skipper. One had never *given* a blow job and the other had never *seen* a blow job being given. I'm so ashamed; a *new* low!" After a brief analytical delay, Duke and Pops both laughed at the curt response, truthful or not.

"You are such a nasty boy Pops," said Comatose Gross without even raising his head from the game board. It was his turn to roll the dice and he was within striking range of a victory over the best ace-deuce player in the squadron. O' Grady stirred three lumps of sugar and a dash of non-dairy creamer into his coffee then did an about face heading for his office.

In the hallway outside of the Admin Department Duke literally bumped into Lieutenant Cline, spilling a few drops of coffee onto the waxed deck below in the process. Some of it splashed up and soiled Duke's black Corfam shoes. Today Cookie would be on the skipper's wing for a low-level bomb hop to the Camp Shelby aerial bombing range in Mississippi. Duke would lead the division of Corsairs on VR-179, a visual flight rules, low-level training route. After making an undetected ingress, the warplanes would deliver several inert 1000 pound bombs into the target's bulls-eye. Duke and Cookie were expert weapons delivery pilots.

"Did you and Teen Angel play house last night skipper with those two split tails?" inquired Cookie sarcastically, knowing he probably wouldn't get the response he was hoping for. "Did the dental hygienist become a charter member of Duke's *helmet club*?"

"Shouldn't you be downstairs preparing for morning muster Lieutenant?" Cookie got the idea and let Duke of the hook, at least for now. An airman from Admin grabbed a mop and cleaned up the skipper's mess. O' Grady found his office and hunched down behind the oak desk. Still weary from the night before, he removed his shoes then arched rearward deep into the leather swivel chair to stretch his back muscles and shoulders. He sat there motionless for awhile, blowing on his coffee to cool it down. At that moment Duke felt older than Danny Glover's character in *Lethal Weapon*.

Finally taking a healthy slurp of his java, the skipper delicately ripped open a large manila envelope that had a San Francisco postmark embossed in the upper right hand corner. It also had about thirty 5 cent stamps littered all over the front. There was no return address. Duke was a tad curious, but likewise already had a pretty good idea what to expect in the envelope's contents. His left hand reached inside and returned with an 8 x 10 color glossy of Cookie and Rocky, both with shit-eating grins plastered all over their guilty faces, standing in front of Carol Doda's strip joint in downtown San Francisco. The two wise guys were posed conspicuously in front of the club with its owner, Carol Doda, positioned in between them for a staged photograph. A neon marquee sign was clearly visible in the background. The bare-breasted stripper, a local legend in Frisco's seedier nightlife, was stretched out on the hood of a black and white sedan that had the following inscription printed on the driver's side front door: *Official Vehicle of the Commanding Officer, Naval Air Station Alameda*.

Two weeks ago, Commander O' Grady had approved a cross-country flight to NAS Alameda for Lieutenant Commander Stone and Lieutenant Cline. Naval Aviators routinely take airplanes for extended periods of time for instrument flight proficiency and airways navigation training. Stone and Cline had planned this trip to coincide with a Thanksgiving feast at the home of Rocky's Mom and Dad in Walnut Creek, a sprawling suburb of San Francisco. Prior to embarking on the little tandem excursion to the *city by the bay*, Duke had overheard Cookie on the phone speaking rather respectfully with the CO of NAS Alameda. In fact Lieutenant Cline was begging the CO to loan him a Navy car for the weekend visit. With some coaxing and charm, Cookie Cline had apparently talked the CO, an F-4 Phantom jockey, into relinquishing his own official car for the two-day stopover. Cookie had outdone himself, yet again!

When Commander O' Grady independently confirmed that his Squadron Weapons Officer had finagled the CO's official vehicle, he gave Cookie this piece of parting advice, using his best New York City accent: 'Don't let me hear of *youz* two wise *guyz* taking the Captain's car over to Carol Doda's strip club.' Of course that was the first place they went! Duke smiled, knowing he probably would have done the same thing as a junior officer, and maybe even today as the Commanding Officer. He slipped the photo into the bottom right-hand drawer of his tattered desk. There it would remain until it could be properly employed at an appropriate venue to exact a little retribution. Undoubtedly the time for reprisal would be in the not to distant future. O' Grady rubbed his socked feet together as he emptied the remaining contents of the manila envelope onto the top of his desk. It was some fluffy sawdust and an orange matchbook from Duke's favorite Italian restaurant in San Francisco, *Little Joes Baby Joes on Broadway*. Ah, the final insult, culinary envy!

Sitting tolerantly at the 'hold short' line for Runway 04, Commander Mike Morley had just received takeoff clearance from the NAS New Orleans control tower. Shroud was scheduled early that morning to fly a PMCF (Post-Maintenance Check Flight) sortie on airplane number 407. A refurbished TF-41 motor, returned from AIMD (Aircraft Intermediate Maintenance Department), had been installed into the jet's fuselage the previous afternoon by mechanics from the AD shop. Senior Chief John Esposito had personally supervised the engine change. He even had the AD techs put in some overtime to complete the job just before sundown because the night shift maintenance crew had been given the evening off by the MO, Commander Mayhew. So now an engine acceptance flight had to be successfully performed before Maintenance Control could report another 'up' aircraft to the *River Rattler* CO.

Shroud closed and locked his glass canopy then informed the tower controller he would need a few extra minutes on the runway for engine parameter data collection purposes. He likewise reminded the controller that his mission was a 'test flight' just in case the tower supervisor had missed that tidbit of information on the VA-204 flight schedule. This request undoubtedly pissed off the pair of F-15 Eagles leaving the arming area, knowing they would have to wait for Commander Morley to complete his rather extensive cockpit checks before they could jump into the air themselves. Eagle drivers hated converting precious JP-5 jet fuel into mere exhaust, and not closing velocity (V_c) on a bogey. But, Shroud could care less about inconveniencing the Air Force pukes, and they knew it. He would simply take his time while holding in position on the active duty runway, writing down what he saw on the cockpit gauges. Their squadron lost the full-contact crud game last night, so they could kiss his ass!

Mike Morley maneuvered the light gray attack jet onto the runway's centerline then stomped on the brake pedals with the rubber heels of his flight boots. The aircraft screeched to a stop in the middle of the 04 painted on the concrete. Shroud didn't believe in leaving too much concrete behind his cherished butt when he launched from a land-based airport. It could be *wasted* concrete especially if he was required to execute a high-speed abort at the other end for some reason. Morley noticed that the white color of the large numbers surrounding his A-7 was becoming obscure due to tire skid marks, leaked hydraulic fluid and hot exhaust gasses. Next he jammed the Corsair's throttle forward to the MRT (Military Rated Thrust) or 'firewall' position. The airplane shuddered under the influence of 15,000 pounds of unbridled thrust surging out of the ass end. Shroud had to slightly increase his foot pressure on the brake pedals to stop the *sluf* from creeping forward.

As the turbofan jet engine gradually spun up to its highest power setting, Morley monitored his engine instruments then jotted down several numbers in a PMCF kneeboard booklet with his reliable government pen. Turbine outlet pressure (TOP), turbine inlet temperature (T I T), revolutions per minute (RPM), fuel flow, oil pressure, hydraulic pressure and time from idle to MRT were all scanned and noted in black ink. It usually took the A-7E's powerful turbine engine a minimum of seven seconds to a maximum of 15 seconds to transition from its idle setting to its maximum thrust. At the ship, this time period could seem like an eternity, especially at night or if you were low and underpowered on the glide slope. *Pucker factor* always compelled Corsair drivers to keep at least a *handful* of power on their jet's engine. That corresponding throttle position was a survival instinct and it was ingrained into their left hand through experience. They never went near the idle stop when landing on the deck of an aircraft carrier except after successfully snagging a cross deck pendant (arresting wire) with their tail hook. Even then, it felt uncomfortable to be at idle power, taxiing around on the rolling and pitching deck of a flat top.

Shroud was now just about ready to release his brakes and start a mile long takeoff roll. He raised the head-knocker to the 'armed' position on his ejection seat then fastened the bayonet fittings of his oxygen mask tightly to both sides of his haze gray form-fit helmet. The polyurethane mask felt cool on his face as he eagerly gulped at the fresh 100% oxygen. Commander Morley spotted his Nomex flight gloves resting next to the plugged in hose of his G-suit. Then he made one last survey of his warplane's control surfaces by executing a final wipe-out of the cockpit with his stick and foot controls. The Eagle drivers were now becoming increasingly impatient with Commander Morley's delaying tactics. They didn't care for breathing in his exhaust fumes either while sitting at the hold short line. Even with their oxygen masks on snug and their canopies lowered, the fumes were sickening. Looking in the rear-view mirror, Shroud could see the giant tail of the Corsair above the canopy breaker on his ejection seat. It was cycling left and right in coordinated movement with his rudder pedal inputs. In his side-view mirrors, he also monitored the corresponding movements of his elevator slabs. Finally, Shroud focused briefly on the wings of the jet to observe and verify the synchronized movements of the ailerons. Satisfied, he released his brakes and accelerated.

The acceleration forces quickly pushed his body back into the hard ejection seat and his eyes bugged out a tad under the impressive power of the warplane. Morley grunted momentarily to accept the forces being exerted on his forty-year old frame. At the 3 board he rotated the attack jet's nose with a subtle rearward pull on the black control stick. The aircraft was accelerating through 152 knots when the nose gently leaped into the air. Shroud leveled off at 20 feet above the concrete, raised his gear and flaps then hastily accelerated to 300 knots. His intention was to fly an extremely low, low transition that Saturday morning.

"Rattler maintenance, 407 has jumped into the air," reported Commander Morley on button 20, the squadron common frequency." He had the freak tuned into his back radio on the left side of plane's cockpit.

"Roger that sir, have a safe flight," was the answer from the radio operator in Maintenance Control.

"Tower, Alpha Fox 407," said Shroud on button three. The small microphone inside of his oxygen mask rubbed up against upper lip. The bayonet clips were about one notch past their usual spot causing the mask to hug his face too closely. Several short hairs from his extra-thick moustache got tangled in the tiny holes of the microphone causing some minor irritation for Morley.

"Go ahead 407," replied the twenty-eight year old female tower controller.

"407 is airborne and switching to tactical." He was flying such a low transition that maybe the tower couldn't tell his jet was actually airborne thought Morley.

"Roger that 407. See you when you get back." Shroud flew over the gate guards standing their watch at the rear entrance to the base. He cleared their shack and the trees surrounding it by about 20 feet before he initiated a climb to fifteen thousand. *Throttle slams*, eight miles high were next on his PMCF agenda. Shroud hated throttle slams!

At 0730 the entire squadron, with a few notable exceptions, was gathered together in military formation on the extra-clean hangar bay floor for Quarters (morning muster). The deck actually shined because it was so clean and buffed. Commander O'Grady was standing out in front of the group, wearing his recently pressed khaki uniform. He never looked so smart in his *permanent press* khakis. The entire formation was surrounded by recently polished attack jets positioned in the hangar bay. First, Duke welcomed them all to December's Drill Weekend. Next he said a few inspirational words about the CAG corrosion inspection and the 'all hands' crawfish boil to pump up the troops. Then Commander O' Grady turned the formation over to Lieutenant Commander Stone, the Assistant Maintenance Officer (AMO), for final instructions. As the two men saluted each other, the skipper ordered Rocky to carry out the *plan of attack*, his personal terminology for the Plan of the Day. He made no mention of Secretary Andrews' upcoming visit or the impending squadron activation for a carrier deployment. Duke could see the Air Wing staff officers and enlisted men waiting in the wings with their note pads and inspection checklists at the ready. He walked off toward his locker to change into his zoom bag before the 0745 briefing for the bomb hop he would lead this morning to the Camp Shelby target. As he climbed the staircase he saw his name stenciled on the top step in bright orange paint. All of the VA-204 pilots had their names painted onto the stairs, in ascending order of rank. Duke still couldn't fathom that he was the Commanding Officer of an A-7 squadron, one of the finest in the Navy, active duty or reserve. The skipper disappeared into the officer's locker room.

Teen Angel had strolled into the Pro Shop of the Aviation Oaks Golf Course with about twenty-eight minutes to spare before the 0722 starting time at the first tee. As his spikes transitioned from the outside asphalt to the carpeted floor inside they dug deep into the soft yet vibrant material. Ackerman wasn't *situationally* aware or fully prepared for this transition, so he tripped but did manage to catch himself on the soft drink cold case, preventing an outright fall. The chubby, brunette cashier behind the counter witnessed his clumsiness causing Brad to blush a bit when he saw her giggle at his lumbering misfortune. Lieutenant Ackerman was the first member of the *august* foursome to arrive at the Pro Shop, although CAG Sullivan, Admiral Thompson and Secretary Andrews were already in the parking lot unloading their gear and slipping on their golf shoes.

Several middle-age men and a pair of older women were milling about smartly in the cramped little golf store. Brad recognized the two silver haired gals as the females that Pops Petibone was sharing a table with at the O' Club the previous evening. In his estimation, the elder babes looked no worse for the wear. They both sported plain white shorts with colorful matching blouses and fairly new, brown *Etonic* golf shoes. For some reason, Teen Angel wondered if they were in fact sisters. Perhaps it was their synchronized dress. He also hoped their tee time wasn't before 0722. Following women on a golf course usually made for one long, sluggish trek. In Brad's experience, women also displayed fairly poor golf etiquette. Most of them seemed to believe that if they 'waved a foursome through' due to their slow play, this was tantamount to admitting athletic inferiority on the links. Whenever he was stuck playing behind women, Ackerman almost never asked to 'play through' due to some unpleasant repercussions he had suffered in the past. He simply endured their languid play because it nurtured his self-composure.

Over near the *Ping* putter exhibit, two stout looking men were examining Karsten Solheim's latest innovations in *flat sticks*. They had removed about a half dozen putters from the display rack and were busy stroking balls into a contraption that pumped the ball right back at their feet. Amazingly, the pair was betting on each and every putt. Golfers will bet on anything that has to do with their beloved game. On the other side of the sales floor, one portly gentleman was admiring a $400 Calloway *Big Bertha* driver. He even took the liberty of a few practice swings with the club inside the shop. The metal wood barely missed a light fixture over his head that was hanging perilously low from the raised ceiling. William Waverly, the Head Golf Professional from Lockerbie, Scotland took notice when he heard the man actually sparking the club on the carpeted floor. Mr. Waverly pretended to listen intently as three chaps swapped amusing golf stories with him near the door to his office, but his mind was on the *Big Bertha*.

Brad leaned over the counter and asked Charlotte, the plump brunette with a seductive smile, for a dozen Titleist 100 compression golf balls as he placed a large bottle of *Gatorade* on the glass top. He also requested two tokens for a small bucket of range balls and informed her that he wanted to pay for one military green fee and his half of an electric cart. Ackerman handed the twenty-something woman a hundred dollar bill and waited for his four sleeves of Titleists, two gold tokens, a cart receipt and some change. Teen Angel twisted off the top of the

Gatorade bottle and sucked back a healthy swig of the chilled, green liquid. He had to keep his head hydrated so he could think straight. Charlotte placed the C-note under the drawer of the shop's cash register. After bagging his golf balls and range tokens, she removed forty-six bucks from the register as change for Brad. She counted out the currency as she placed each bill into his right palm. Brad crumbled the bills then stuffed them neatly into his shirt pocket. He put the golf cart receipt in his right front pocket.

"Your hubby is a helicopter mechanic in the 4th MAW (Marine Air Wing) and you have two kids right?" asked Teen Angel in a highly cordial manner. "One is a new-born."

"That's right. How'd you know that?" she responded while rearranging some dispersed hair strands behind her left ear.

"We spoke a couple of months ago at the base gas station. You were filling up and I was buying a quart of oil. Good memory I guess," said Brad shrugging his shoulders. He walked out with his hands full. This time he did not stumble while negotiating the harrowing doorway. The brief conversation made Charlotte feel giddy in that somebody would remember her after a chance encounter two months ago. Her self-esteem was at an all-time low. As Brad Ackerman departed Charlotte's eyes followed his movements for just a moment then she turned to the next man in line. It was the admiral's driver and he quickly paid the total tab for Tommy Thompson and Hank Andrews. Thompson had given him a blank, signed check just a few moments ago in the parking lot.

Ackerman placed a small metallic-looking bucket into the receptacle of a rusty contraption just outside the Pro Shop door underneath a wooden canopy. Oil and grease soiled the immediate area underneath the appliance. This mixture was combined with some sort of white, lime-looking substance obviously meant to soak up the petroleum products. Thin cobwebs draped lazily downward from the awning, gently swaying in the morning breeze. They were almost transparent. Teen Angel curtly reminded himself that he was *not* at Augusta National. Brad deposited the two gold-colored tokens into the slot of the machine then waited for the tired old range balls to come tumbling down into the pail. They rattled around inside the mechanism, making more noise than they deserved to. It was a hollow sound, as if the range ball apparatus would soon need refilling. Three of the golf balls bounced out of the bucket and skipped around on the dirty concrete below. At least they bounced. Ackerman didn't have the energy or desire to chase and retrieve the errant spheres. He simply headed off in the direction of the cart shack with his hands now extra full.

After securing his set of clubs onto the back of an electric golf cart, Teen Angel deposited a dozen brand new Titleists into the zippered ball compartment of his bag. He retrieved a *number two* and slid the dimpled ball along with several royal blue tees into his right front pocket next to the Porsche keys. The pocket bulged from the excess so he removed the car keys and stashed them in his bag with the remaining eleven Titleist golf balls. Then Brad plopped the empty Titleist sleeves and the basket of range balls into a large webbed container on the back of the cart and jumped into the frayed vinyl of the left seat. He steered the not so sturdy vehicle toward the driving range. The cart creaked as it moved, bouncing and jiggling along the uneven concrete path from the cart shack. As he drove, Lieutenant Ackerman spotted Commander Sullivan, all five foot seven inches of him, walking along the narrow pathway from the parking lot to the Pro Shop. CAG was wearing a serious smile and shouldering a pristine, *tour* golf bag that probably cost more than his entire collection of clubs. The obviously heavy load caused Squid Sullivan to lean just a tad to the left as he walked; as if to counterbalance the immense weight of the huge bag. This was the type of hefty golf bag that the touring pros used. Of course they didn't have to purchase these five hundred dollar behemoths, their sponsors gave them as gifts. The professionals also didn't have to carry their own clubs in them. They paid caddies to lug their sticks around in these gigantic bags. CAG obviously wanted to *look* like a golfer, but the mammoth bag proved he was trying way too hard. Ackerman diverted onto the grass and veered towards Sullivan.

"Hello CAG. How are you hitting 'em these days?" inquired Teen Angel stopping the cart next to Commander Sullivan, the commanding officer of Carrier Air Wing Reserve Twenty (CVWR-20). It had been over three months since the two aviators had played a round of golf together. That match was in August during a *Texas Scramble* tournament at Nellis AFB in Las Vegas. They didn't come close to winning but had a great time chasing down shots in the grandeur of the foothills of the Sierra Nevada Mountains. They even flew a Low level/ACM hop together around Spring Mountain and the Desert National Wildlife Range.

"Long and straight Teen Angel; straight into the water," replied Squid Sullivan after a pregnant pause for maximum effect. He knew Brad was all too familiar with his talent level on the links. With a dull thud, CAG Sullivan dropped his cumbersome bag down to the wet grass next to the cart path. He looked relieved for the momentary respite. His right shoulder still slumped from the arduous load.

"I understand we will be getting a little *face time* with SECNAV today," said Brad in a sincere tone, his eyes squinting. Ackerman took in another quick sip of

Gatorade, spilling a few drops out of the sides of his mouth and down onto his pants. "Have you met him yet?" asked Brad, wiping green beads of liquid from his face.

"Yes, and I need to tell you a few things before we start playing, and before I *shank* my first shot into the woods," chuckled Commander Sullivan. For some reason CAG took this opportunity to put on his short eyeball glasses. He slipped the empty black case back into his shirt pocket. Fashion statements were not his thing.

"Squid, don't you know you are never supposed to utter *that* word on a golf course; the *S* word. It will curse you and you'll never be able to stop doing it," chided Brad. Sullivan and Ackerman shared a brief laugh at that comment. It was nervous laughter because the old wives' tale was actually true. If you say the word shank on a golf course, you will shank several shots during your round.

CAG Sullivan then proceeded to inform Teen Angel about the real purpose of Secretary Andrews visit to NAS New Orleans that weekend. Teen Angel listened intently as the Air Wing Commander revealed the intricate details of VA-204's impending squadron activation for the upcoming carrier deployment onboard USS *Enterprise.* Even though he intuitively understood that this would mean great sacrifice, Lieutenant Ackerman was noticeably elated at the prospect of making another extended carrier deployment. Especially one that would undoubtedly be as prestigious and memorable as this one would be, being the final A-7 cruise forever. Brad even had a few old shipmates onboard CVN-65 in ship's company and in the active duty Carrier Air Wing, CAG-2.

"I have already spoken to Captain Madison, CAG-2, and he has agreed to make you one of the LSO Team Leaders for the cruise Brad," said Sullivan. Commander Sullivan knew Lieutenant Ackerman was a superbly qualified Landing Signal Officer. Brad had even kept Sullivan off the one-wire a time or two, thus preventing an embarrassing situation for the Air Wing Commander.

"*Spine Ripper* Madison?" asked Brad. His voice elevated an octave or two. "By the way, nice bag," teased Ackerman.

"Yep, the one and only," replied Sullivan already anticipating the rejoinder and ignoring the taunt.

"Spine Ripper Madison is a real dickhead, but you already know that don't you?" Ackerman placed his right hand over his mouth and chin, contemplating the future while sitting in a raggedy golf cart at seven in the morning in Belle Chasse, Louisiana. Spine Ripper's presence onboard the ship changed the whole dynamic of the carrier deployment.

"Don't worry. This is an opportunity to excel and I have every confidence that the *River Rattlers* will do just that. Even you Teen Angel! Besides, the Captain of *Enterprise*, *Long Horn* Angus, is an avid golfer; a ten handicap" reassured Commander Sullivan. "You two will get along great and you can keep Long Horn occupied and out of Spine Ripper's hair during port visits. Then that'll keep Spine Ripper off your CO's back for awhile. See, you do have some redeeming residual value." Commander Sullivan was obviously pleased with his little barb at Brad's expense. With that said CAG Sullivan hoisted his golf bag, told Brad he would see him at the practice range then walked off to the pro shop. He leaned even further to the left as he toddled away. Brad drove toward the driving range situated adjacent to the first tee and practice putting green.

SECNAV and Admiral Thompson were busy with their metal woods, punching out low line drive shots that suddenly swerved to the right after about thirty yards of travel into the crisp dawn air. Dozens of their red-striped balls were sent scalded to the bottom of the lake that lined the brown-green grass and separated the driving range from the 18th fairway. One of Tommy Thompson's shots actually skipped like a flat rock on top of the water for several seconds before succumbing to gravity and sinking to the muddy bottom. Ackerman winced as he watched each ugly shot depart the practice tee area. For a moment, Teen Angel wondered where they got those range balls since he hadn't seen them near the Pro Shop this morning. Brad parked the golf cart next to the practice green. He then yanked a wedge, a seven iron and a three-wood from his bag and walked over to the practice tee with the clubs and his small bucket of balls.

"Excuse me, but would you two mind if I made a subtle suggestion?" asked Teen Angel in a humble yet boldly confident tenor. Tommy Thompson immediately recognized the voice, smiled then removed his right hand from the metal driver as he turned to shake hands vigorously with Brad. The handshake lasted longer than it should have. Thompson then remembered his manners.

"Lieutenant Brad Ackerman let me introduce the Honorable H. Lawrence Andrews III, Secretary of the Navy," said Admiral Thompson to formally introduce the two men. Brad took Andrews' hand and looked him square in the eye as they shook. Hank Andrews was an impressive figure. He stood a shade less than six feet four inches in his golf spikes and he had the build of a semi-serious weight lifter. His neatly trimmed black hair glistened in the early sunlight, probably from the Brylcream. Ackerman quickly noticed that SECNAV gave a *manly* handshake, not one of those wimpy greetings you normally receive from a phony bologna politician who isn't really interested in making your acquaintance.

"Damn glad to meet you Mr. Secretary, said Teen Angel with appropriate deference yet without coming off as a political groupie, or as someone awed by conferred status. He almost sounded like the rush chairman, Tim Matheson's character from the movie *Animal House*.

"Please, call me Hank," requested Andrews. "Now what was that you were saying about a suggestion?" Ackerman dropped his clubs and small bucket of range balls in the practice area next to SECNAV. He knelt down behind Andrews white tee which was dug into the sod about half way. It still had a range ball resting on top, awaiting its final fate. The morning dew quickly made a large wet spot on the left knee of Brad's Chino golf slacks. Teen Angel then placed another tee, one from his pocket, about eight inches directly behind Hank's tee and shoved it down about half way into the short grass and moist, yet firm dirt. He then repeated this little trick behind the tee of Tommy Thompson only a few feet away. Teen Angel explained that he wanted them both to draw their club straight back on the next shot so that the metal head passed directly over the rear tee. He instructed them to accomplish this task *before* they began to coil their body, elevate their club, and complete their downward swing motion through the ball. This would prevent them from slicing, or at least make the left-to-right ball movement much less pronounced. Brad gave them this tip because he had discerned that both men swung at the ball using an out-to-in swing motion; a technique that ensured a slice on the ball as it departed the tee box. Golf was a simple matter of physics and intense practice. Teen Angel had just given them their first lesson on controlling ball movement; undoubtedly more instruction would be warranted as the day wore on. Admiral Thompson and Secretary Andrews could hardly believe their eyes as the next five tee shots rocketed straight out for about 200 yards before they veered lazily and softly back to the right.

"That'll be 100 bucks," joked Ackerman. Actually, curing a slice was worth a whole lot more. The two high handicap golfers were elated and stunned at the same time.

The three men continued to pound balls into the driving range grass as CAG Sullivan joined them on the practice tee. Sullivan didn't have a club in his hand; he just watched as the others continued to hit practice shots. A similar introduction scene was repeated between Commander Sullivan and Secretary Andrews. It was now about eleven minutes until their 0722 starting time on the number one hole. After a few more moments of slugging away, CAG Sullivan broke the silence by informing the foursome what the pairings would be for the match. Ackerman and Andrews would be pitted as a team against himself and Admiral Thompson. When all the handicaps were calculated, it meant that CAG Sullivan and Tommy Thompson would receive five shots per nine holes from the team of Ackerman and Andrews. Brad was a two handicap, SECNAV a seventeen. CAG carried a handicap of fourteen while the Admiral sported a *sandbagged* fifteen. That meant that Teen Angel and SECNAV had to give them five shots per nine holes. CAG was pleased by this arrangement because he believed that his team actually stood a good chance of winning some serious dough on the links. Although Squid Sullivan had never won any money *from* Brad he had received a few hundred dollars playing as his partner. The idea of winning some cash from Teen Angel and Secretary Andrews was an intoxicating prospect and CAG Sullivan was anxious to get the match started. He watched as the other three continued to casually hit range balls into the cool breeze.

"How about we play 5 dollar *Nassau* best ball, with an individual side bet of 20 bucks per man," suggested Sullivan as he walked behind the other members of his foursome, brushing away some grass and dirt from his left forearm. The long red-orange rays of the sun were beginning to rise ever higher into the dawn skyline off to the East causing CAG Sullivan to squint.

"CAG my dog's water bowl costs more than 20 dollars," responded Hank Andrews as he pumped out another 220 yard line drive shot down the right center of the driving range. His ball nearly clipped the white 200 yard sign before it eased off gently to the right. Hank made a mental note to take the time and show his true appreciation to Lieutenant Ackerman for this saving grace. If this five-minute lesson cured him of his God-awful slice, he would no longer have to suffer through the indignation of playing at Congressional Country Cub in Washington, D.C. There, Andrews routinely received painful taunts from Senators, House Members, and their array of high-priced lobbyists, about his lack of golfing skill.

"How about a hundred bucks per man as the side bet?" recommended Hank Andrews.

"Done," responded Sullivan without checking with Tommy Thompson. CAG didn't want to appear weak-kneed in front of SECNAV or the admiral.

"Are you still playing with those *ladies* clubs CAG?" ragged Teen Angel as he skillfully lobbed a wedge to within twelve feet of the flagstick on the practice green, situated a short 80 yards away on the left side of the driving range area. Brad never took his eyes off the flight of the ball as he made the comment, psychologically stirring the pot just a bit before the match.

"Very funny Mr. Ackerman," replied Commander Sullivan in his stern, embarrassed voice. Squid Sullivan's face turned beet red as the other men got a big belly laugh form the two previous comments. All four golfers then meandered over to the practice putting green. It was now 0716. Brad's father always used to teach him that golf is a unique game. If you can manage to hit one or two great shots per round, you will play for the rest of your life. It's like a drug. You crave that superb feeling of hitting the perfect shot. Brad's father was very astute for a submarine sailor. After a few minutes of practice putting the group drove their carts the remaining forty yards, parking next to the green ball washer adjacent to the first hole. Brad flipped a blue tee into the air and it pointed toward himself as it came to rest on the freshly mowed, damp grass. He would be the first to play. The green turf felt cool and refreshing under his spiked feet as he walked to the far right side of the first tee box.

Teen Angel bent down and placed his brand new #2 Titleist on top of a royal blue tee that he had pressed into the ground until only a nub of wood remained exposed above the grass. He hunched over, ever so slightly, as he addressed the ball standing about four feet from the right side *championship* tee marker. The ball was resting about six inches from that marker. Each tee marker at the Aviation Oaks Golf Club was a meticulously hand-crafted set of wood carvings portraying military aircraft. This particular set was a pair of blue A-7 Corsairs with fluorescent orange tails. Someone had actually taken the time to spray paint the tails orange, the VA-204 *River Rattlers* official squadron color. On this hole the regular men's tee was marked by a couple of white F-15 Eagles while the ladies tee box was depicted by two red A-10 Warthogs. Ackerman wondered if this hierarchical arrangement of tee markings meant anything if you read between the lines. Brad waggled the clubface on his shiny persimmon club a few times then informed his playing partner that he intended to hit the three-wood about 240 yards over the creek that ran sideways across the number one fairway. After clearing the creek by about twenty yards on the fly, the ball would then leak a bit to the right and run straight toward the hole on this dog-legged fairway. Ackerman repositioned his feet so that his left shoe was slightly *open* from a square position. This would give him a slightly outside-to-inside swing arc through the ball. The air was still and not a sound was heard as Teen Angel effortlessly coiled back then released his club head through the ball at about 110 miles per hour swing speed. He was *Jerry Pate* smooth throughout his entire swing motion. The ductile face of the persimmon wood made a soft knocking sound as it impacted the black #2 on the extra-white Titleist, launching the dimpled sphere precisely where Brad had predicted. A sly smile slowly inched across his face as the ball came to a rest about 30 yards from the front edge of the #1 green. He still could summon up his God-given talent.

"That's my partner!" shouted Hank Andrews in a truly amazed tone of voice. It was going to be a long and expensive four hours of golf thought CAG Sullivan as he plunged a tee into the grass and quickly addressed his ball without a whiff of a practice swing.

"Commander Sullivan, aren't you going to limber up with a few practice swings?" asked Hank Andrews who hadn't seen Sullivan handle a club until just now. Brad rolled his eyes because he was pretty sure what the response would be.

"Mister Secretary, have you ever seen a dog stretch before he chases a car?" said CAG in his deadpan voice. Sullivan then pulled his club back and stroked it through the ball. He shanked the orange sphere deep into a wooded area lining the right side of the first fairway.

CHAPTER 15

▼

WHAT KIND OF ASS HOLE WOULD BOMB THE KING OF MARDI GRAS

Commander Jack Mayhew closed and locked a dark brown door behind him. He was now inside the men's head, which was located on the other side of a gray wall directly behind the medical clinic's laboratory. The tiny room, which was not well lighted, provided only enough space for a single person at a time to utilize the facility. Designed for one specific purpose, the bathroom contained only a small sink and mirror, a hand towel dispenser, and a rotary receptacle situated about two feet above the porcelain urinal. With a black felt tip pen Mayhew scrawled his name, rank and social security number onto a white tag then attached the adhesive strip of paper to an empty urine sample bottle. Next he unzipped his green flight suit, rearranged the family jewels then proceeded to pee lazily into the opening of the plastic vessel. Luckily Jack had taken several healthy swigs of *Kentwood* water just before departing the house that morning, so he did indeed have some piss to share with the lab technicians.

Despite a sign requesting a full dose, Juice filled the flimsy container up to about the three quarter level before squeezing himself off and finishing the remainder of his business in the urinal water. Jack capped the bottle with a red form-fitted top then flushed before placing the warm but not wet container into the rotary receptacle just above the urinal's flush handle. It fit in nicely with about seven other sample bottles already sitting in a tray. The metal tray was positioned inside of a revolving door mechanism which the lab techs could swivel around at their leisure, to retrieve all of the day's urine samples when they were ready to begin processing them. Juice flushed a second time then departed the bathroom headed for the lab and the ordeal of his annual blood draw. Having his blood extracted was not a favorite activity for Jack Mayhew because like most naval aviators he hated needles being stuck into his body. He also detested watching precious blood slowly leak out of his veins into five empty glass tubes.

Commander Mayhew ambled languidly around the corner and got into a short line leading away from the laboratory door. Not so long ago, Jack Mayhew routinely attempted to bypass the lab portion of his annual flight physical. He had even successfully gotten away with it a couple of times in his naval career. But since he was caught and summarily reprimanded the last time for such childish behavior, he had stopped pulling the stunt. That embarrassing incident occurred just two years ago at this Medical Clinic and with the same flight surgeon on duty that day. Juice lowered and shook his head as he stood behind three men, all in green zoom bags, who were leaning up against the bulkhead standing in a staggered row. There were two Air Force pilots directly in front of him and a Coast Guard air crewman who was obviously next to get his blood drawn. As Jack settled comfortably into the back of the line, a P-3 NFO (Naval Flight Officer) emerged from the doorway and the *coastie* air crewman walked passed him into the unfriendly confines of the laboratory.

As Commander Mayhew inched forward he saw a picture hanging down from the top of the doorway to the lab. It was a cartoon image of a vampire and his ghoulishly long fangs were dripping with red ripe blood. Of course the caricature was supposed to be humorous, but Juice was certain that only the lab techs could appreciate such a macabre form of humor. Three more guys were now behind Jack in the lab procession and he grew increasingly apprehensive the closer he edged toward the door. Curiously, nobody in the line was talking. After approximately four minutes, the coast guard air crewman departed the laboratory. The puncture wound in his left arm was visibly covered with thick gauze and a single strand of medical tape. He looked none the worse for the wear even though a small smear of blood could be clearly seen seeping through, staining the gauze and white medical tape. Mayhew grimaced as he realized that several hairs would be ripped out of his own forearm tomorrow morning in the shower, when he got the courage up to remove the tape that would conceal his needle mark. He would however, be able to elicit some major sympathy from his young daughter because of the trauma he would suffer today at the hands of the lab techs. The bloody gauze would serve as his proof to Ashley and it would undoubtedly yield several well-deserved hugs and kisses. The first Air Force pilot in the line ahead of Jack replaced the *coastie* and plopped his butt down into the blood draw chair. Two burly lab techs quickly strapped the Air Force captain in. After he rolled up the left sleeve of his flight suit, the men in the white coats quickly wrapped a rubber hose around his bicep to tighten up and expose the vein in his elbow joint.

Juice had now moved forward far enough and was in such close proximity to the doorway that he could see the entire episode as it unfolded. Mayhew's vivid imagination quickly carried him far away from reality. One of the corpsman, the hairy one, lingered near the Air Force captain slapping a wooden *nun's* ruler on his vein to make it bulge even further. It was probably just a rude diversion though, similar to the way dentists used their good looking dental assistants to distract patients just before they plunged a Novocain laden needle into the soft flesh of their mouths. The other corpsman, cleverly out of sight, was busy preparing a syringe with a two inch long hypodermic needle and the five glass vials needed to suck out the blood. The lab tech stooped over like the *Hunchback of Notre Dame* as he prepared for his onslaught on the captain's arm.

The medical lab was actually a scary place. All around the cramped space were machines and gadgets that seemed to make shallow humming noises as they whirled and twirled and did whatever it is that lab equipment does. An ample variety of colorful bottles containing chemicals, potions and lotions adorned the back wall while a contraption that resembled an oscilloscope was buzzing away, resonating its eerie electrical sounds from one corner of the room. Juice imagined that he saw sparks spewing out from the top of the appliance. As Jack's eyes surveyed the fullness of the room he could see long, curled glass tubes and plastic Petri dishes were strewn everywhere, dripping their toxic contents onto the dingy countertop. Jack Mayhew immediately thought of the laboratory scene from *Young Frankenstein* and the many bells, whistles and flashing lights it contained as Gene Wilder and Terri Garr worked on Peter Boyle lying on the cold slab. The whole panorama was quite intimidating for laypeople, even more so when the portrait featured two white-coated *Igor's* tending to a hapless monster strapped uncomfortably to a chair. Slowly coming out of his self-induced catatonic state, Juice watched the ensuing action with utter amazement.

The second corpsman was now literally hovering over the young Air Force captain, openly brandishing his *foot long* hypodermic device. With one rather clumsy stab he thrust the sharp instrument deep into the captain's forearm. Blood immediately trickled from the puncture. But the lab tech apparently missed the pilot's exposed vein because he quickly removed the needle then made a second, successful jab. Next the corpsman awkwardly inserted the first of five glass tubes into the opposite end of the syringe apparatus as warm, red blood instantly began to flow. Mayhew watched as the Air Force captain's eyes rolled back in their sockets and his head slumped forward. Incredibly he had passed out. Jack had now returned to full reality but was likewise astonished by what he was witnessing. He had heard about people fainting while having their blood drawn but in his entire fifteen-year naval career he had never actually seen it happen. Commander Mayhew thought the stories were merely folk legend in the archives of Naval Aviation. The twin *Igors* didn't miss a beat. They continued to drain the required five vials of blood from the now helpless Air Force captain. Only after filling the fifth tube did *Igor number one* crack open a stick of smelling salts and wave it under the nose of his victim to revive him. Juice saw that his face was ashen and bloodless as he was pulled up and out of the chair by *Igor number two*. The captain stumbled a bit, pushed down his left sleeve then made his way through the doorway to continue his journey in the maze of the medical clinic.

"Next!" called out *Igor number two* sounding like a barber in a small Indiana town.

The Air Force pilot in front of Jack timidly walked into the lab and sat in the chair. This meant Juice was in the on deck circle, so he briefly puffed out his chest and sucked in his gut. Unconsciously, Mayhew moved to the edge of the doorway, ever more apprehensive about what had just transpired before his very eyes. Inside the lab a similar scenario was being repeated except that this Air Force pilot, an A-10 major of Hispanic ancestry, wanted the blood to be sucked out of his right arm. With his right thumb and index finger, an increasingly nervous Juice grabbed the collar of his flight suit. As he looked at the other five people standing in line behind him, he unconsciously twisted his head and neck around in Rodney Dangerfield fashion. Commander Mayhew made quick cursory eye contact with a black, female air traffic controller at the end of the line then averted his gaze as he saw the duty flight surgeon sneak past her walking toward his office. The flight surgeon had several government pens and a prescription pad stuck into the front pocket of his white smock. When Jack turned his blank stare back to the scene in the lab, the same smelling salt commotion was being repeated. Incredibly, the second Air Force pilot had passed out as well and was being brought back to consciousness by *Igor number one*. This was enough empirical evidence for Jack. In his mind, something was indeed wrong. Juice walked to the back of the line and stood behind the female air traffic controller. He wanted to wait this one out for a while.

"Tower Alpha Fox 407 is at the short initial for a carrier break," reported Commander Morley to the air traffic controller inside the control tower at Naval Air Station New Orleans. He was transmitting on button three after comfortably settling his attack jet to an altitude of 1200 feet above the ground. He was flying just under an overcast sky filled with mostly puffy clouds. The whole backdrop of the sky was white, gray and purple on that fine December morning. Shroud was on the extended centerline, half way between the eight mile bridge and the end of runway four. Glancing at the inertial navigation system (INS) with his peripheral vision he noticed that the wind had picked up in the last hour; it was now blowing at twenty-two knots out of the Northeast. From this point over the ground Shroud would accelerate to an indicated airspeed of 520 knots and dip even lower to 800 feet to prepare for the carrier break maneuver and his final landing phase. This was the culmination of a successful post-maintenance check flight (PMCF) on the new motor that had been installed into the fuselage of 407. Morley had flown to an altitude of 40,000 feet out over the Gulf of Mexico, performed all the required throttle slams and performance evaluations, and the jet's TF-41 turbine engine had passed the check hop with flying colors. As Shroud descended he quickly accelerated and lined up with the runway. Up ahead he could see a division of Corsairs taxiing out of the *River Rattler* line. Must be the skipper's bombing hop, he thought.

"407 roger, at the approach end cleared for a left carrier break, altimeter 29.93, wind is zero six zero at 15 knots, gusting to 20, you have light civil traffic on the bayou approach to Southern Seaplane airport," was the tower chief's reply.

"Tally Ho on traffic," replied Morley after locating the high-wing, single-engine aircraft skidding just above the water of the bayou running parallel to the long runway at NAS New Orleans. At 800 feet AGL and 540 knots, Morley's whole body tensed in anticipation of the 5 G *break turn* he would perform in approximately 23 seconds over the approach end of Runway 04. A tiny bead of sweat seeped out of his damp skull cap and trickled down past his right ear into the collar of his flight suit. Shroud figured, and rightly so, that his squadron buddies and numerous enlisted men would be watching so he wanted to look good in the break to pump them up as well. As he rapidly approached the runway, Morley could distinguish the bright orange of a form-fit helmet in the cockpit of the lead Corsair in the division taxiing below. This confirmed that it was Duke O' Grady leading the flight because the skipper was the only pilot in the squadron with the guts to wear a fluorescent orange helmet; everybody else settled for haze gray. Throughout his 40 year existence, John O' Grady had never been like everybody else. In Duke's mind, too much conformity robbed you of your innate individuality and he abhorred that in human beings.

"Look good or die trying," whispered Shroud to himself. Over the numbers, Commander Morley sharply pivoted the Corsair's control stick from the neutral position so that it slapped abruptly up against the inner portion of his left thigh. The left wing of the Corsair rapidly plummeted toward the ground as Shroud dumped it hard in the break turn. His head jerked a bit to the right, opposite but not equal to the force being exerted by the left break turn. Next, with his left hand, Morley slammed the throttle to the idle stop and smoothly extended the giant speed brake out from the bottom of the A-7's fuselage. The warplane was in a seventy-five degree bank angle and Shroud's G-suit quickly inflated squeezing his waist and legs as the G meter gauge registered first 3 then 4, before finally settling on 5. Shroud grunted and breathed heavily inside the tight-fitting oxygen mask as his body strained to withstand the G forces being exerted on his physique. His face briefly contorted due to the intensity of the pressure. Instantly, adrenaline kicked in and he felt a sudden rush of excitement flood over him in the cockpit as he completed the 180 degree break turn, still level at 800 feet above the airport. He had not lost a foot of altitude in the initial stages of his aggressive aerial maneuver.

But just as abruptly as the boost of adrenaline had flooded his body with sudden energy, he was subjected to a queasy, sinking feeling deep in the pit of his stomach. That ill at ease sensation you experience when your sixth sense tickles your abdomen and tells you that something is all wrong but you just aren't cognizant of the reason yet. Almost immediately, Morley felt the airplane lose thrust and begin slowly descending without any control input. Shroud's brow furled as his eyes watched the engine gauges spooling down. Simultaneously, his ears sensed that the cockpit had quickly become engulfed by an uncomfortably silence. For a moment he tried to convince himself that his eyes were lying, that this wasn't happening. But it was! Incredibly, this last throttle slam in the carrier break had shut down the jet's engine. The turbofan had survived at least ten throttle slams at various altitudes during the PMCF but on this last one in the carrier break the TF-41 had decided to flameout. Or had he inadvertently gone past the idle stop during his dynamic break maneuver? Momentarily confused, Shroud himself wasn't sure at this point. Snapping himself out of the temporary disorientation, his mind rapidly began to focus on reigniting the thrust giving fire in the Corsair's motor. He didn't have the luxury of embarrassment or humility right now. His elevated *pucker factor* precluded that!

It was a simple choice between putting some flame back into the engine's burner can or *un-ass* the aircraft by punching out over that slimy little canal that paralleled runway four to the North. But Commander Morley had a tremendous fear of both sharks and alligators. Actually he feared *anything* swimming in the water that could tear his body to shreds and eat him for supper. As a child Morley had experienced vivid nightmares of being eaten alive by a Great White or a Hammerhead shark. He actually refused to go see any of the *Jaws* movies in high school, loathed Peter Benchley, and never ever ate any kind of seafood. Rocky would always tell people that Shroud suffered from a chronic case of tuna-phobia. Of course huge belly-laughs would routinely follow this revelation causing Shroud to leave the room with a red, embarrassed face.

That creepy, uninviting canal below was probably full of ten-foot gators Commander Morley thought in an awkward moment of reflection, all wearing bibs with his picture on them. Shroud pressed a button on the throttle to bring in the giant speed brake as the time critical items (TCI's) for an engine restart now flashed lucidly through his brain. All of his emergency procedures training and those excruciating *assholes and elbows* simulator flights back at NAS Cecil Field would now pay off. Shroud scanned the cockpit as his hands began the restart process. Minimum of 300 knots airspeed, check; he had 340 knots but it was decelerating. Throttle in the idle position, check; his left hand confirmed the throttle was resting in the idle gate. Switch to the backup fuel pump, check; Morley's eyes locked in on the panel as his left hand rotated a black knob over to the alternate fuel pump side. The skullcap under his helmet was now abruptly becoming saturated with sweat droplets but he didn't have time to notice.

The warplane's altitude was 260 feet above the unpalatable, black and green waters of the canal when the turbine engine started to shoot exhaust out of the ass end once again. The A-7 passed just above the Cessna seaplane on final approach to Southern Seaplane airport. The civilian pilot never saw the Corsair whizzing by overhead with a mere 80 feet of vertical separation. Shroud's airspeed accelerated to 320 knots and he was gently climbing back up to 500 feet as he punched out his speed brake into the wind stream once again to decelerate back to landing speed. In a left bank at 220 knots Morley threw his gear and flaps down and reported that he was turning into the groove for a full stop landing.

"You're cleared to land 407. Is everything okay up there?" asked the tower controller who was slightly concerned over the aircraft's obviously low altitude on downwind.

"No problems. I had to maneuver to avoid a flock of sea gulls on the downwind," replied Commander Morley hoping this would put an end to any additional, annoying inquiries. It did, for the moment.

As Shroud plunked his main mounts down a few feet past the numbers a shard of light gray smoke puffed up from underneath the belly of the A-7. During the approach, he hadn't even paid much attention to the Fresnel lens, the landing aid lighting system used by navy carrier jocks onboard ship and at the field. Visible white vortices spiraled from the tips of both swept back wings as Commander Morley rotated the Corsair's nose up eight degrees to use an aerodynamic braking technique. This procedure would make it easier to stop the jet on the 8000 foot hunk of concrete. At 100 knots groundspeed the Corsair lost all residual lift and the snout of the warplane fell through the horizon, planting the nose wheel firmly but gently onto the deck. Morley left the active runway at the end and selected the ground controller, button two, on his front radio. Shroud had been given clearance to taxi and told to 'monitor ground' by the tower chief so he did not make any further transmissions to the control tower. Still rebounding from his traumatic experience in the break, he even forgot to call *Rattler* maintenance to inform them he was on deck taxiing in. Moving at 15 knots groundspeed past the LAANG alert hangar, Shroud quickly made it back to the throat entranceway of the VA-204 flight line.

Duke O' Grady's division of four had just rounded the corner at the other end of the field, switched to button three and called for takeoff as Shroud's jet whizzed past them holding short. The skipper had indeed witnessed 407's extra low altitude on downwind but since he was on button two with ground he hadn't heard any of the conversation between Shroud and the tower controller.

"Tower Alpha Fox 401 and flight is ready for departure," said Duke as he closed his canopy and fastened the bayonet clips of his oxygen mask to the sides of his orange helmet. One minute and thirty seconds later each of the four jets was in perfect echelon left position on the runway awaiting the skipper's hand signal for engine turn up. Upon receiving that gesture, two fingers swinging back and forth inside of Duke's cockpit, four 500 degree centigrade plumes of gray black exhaust now spewed from the division of Corsairs on the departure end of runway 04. Then, separated by approximately eight seconds, the jets thundered down the concrete quickly building up to the 147 knots airspeed required for rotation in the A-7. Each aircraft leaped off the ground and began to chase after Commander O' Grady's jet already heading toward the murky waters off the gulf coast of Mississippi and the Camp Shelby bombing range.

Standing on the 7th tee, SECNAV Andrews and his partner Teen Angel now enjoyed a comfortable 3 up lead over Admiral Thompson and CAG Sullivan, having won the last three holes in the best ball competition. Hank Andrews, Tommy Thompson and Brad Ackerman had already hit their tee shots to the 172 yard par three hole that was protected by a menacing water hazard on its right side which ran from mid-fairway to just behind the green. The hole was likewise guarded by a pair of extra-large bunkers on the left. All three men had landed their shots safely on the dance floor and were anxious to attempt their birdie putts. Now the group was patiently waiting for CAG to serve up one of his orange golf balls. A few moments earlier, Sullivan had furtively watched Brad make his club selection, a five-iron, even though this was against USGA rules to do so. After witnessing Teen Angel's shot land softly onto the manicured Bermuda grass of the 7th green and spin back to a distance of 15 feet from the pin, CAG didn't hesitate to yank a five-iron out of his huge bag.

Even though he could never hit a five-iron 172 yards into a stiff, fifteen knot crosswind breeze, pride prevented Sullivan from selecting a three-iron or four-wood that day in front of the Secretary of the Navy. So there he was, addressing his ball and waggling a club that was sure to leave him 25 yards short of the green, even if he stroked it as pure as Jack Nicklaus. After what seemed to be an inordinate amount of club waggling, CAG coiled then unleashed his shot. The orange ball stayed relatively low and straight off the tee but then made a sharp ugly turn to the right, landing well short of the green and plummeting deep into the middle of the water hazard. The orange sphere resembled a dying quail that had suddenly stopped flying in mid-flight. A small stream of water burst up about three feet into the air as the ball impacted the surface of the pond. In disgust Sullivan threw the five-iron down, thumping one of the tee box markers with the hozzle of the club. He quickly retrieved the five-iron trying to hide his embarrassment.

"Damn it Teen Angel, there's something wrong with these clubs. They're bent or twisted or something," complained Sullivan shaking his head in disgust. Golfers are notoriously superstitious; more so than even major league baseball players, who wear rally caps, who don't change their underwear on a winning streak, who have their bats blessed by a parish priest, or who step over foul lines when coming on or off the playing field. It's relatively common for golfers to concoct all sorts of lame excuses for poor performance or to adopt a variety of odd behaviors if they believe it will enhance their performance. For instance in a tournament, Brad Ackerman would only use a 100 compression, #2 black Titleist golf ball, the kind with a soft Balata cover and a liquid core. Also, one golf coach at Stanford would always harp on his protégés that 'if you think you got it, don't go to sleep because you're going to lose it.' Superstition serves as an integral component in the mental aspect of the sport because 90% of the game of golf is half mental. At least that's what Hubert Green would always argue while sharing a barley pop at the bar with his fellow tour professionals after missing the cut on a Friday afternoon.

As CAG walked head down back toward his bag, Brad quickly snatched the five-iron from his hand. Ackerman proceeded to tee up one of his brand new Titleist golf balls and let loose an aggressive but silky smooth swing through the ball. With a sort of clapping noise, steel on Balata, the Titleist bolted off the face of the five-iron sky high, traveling down the right-center of the fairway. The flight of the ball was momentarily camouflaged by the soft gray white clouds of the overcast panorama. As the four men watched and squinted, the ball quickly reappeared, shifting its path ever so slightly to the left, drawing toward the pin, which was cut approximately eighteen feet from the left edge of the green.

"Aint nothing wrong with these clubs CAG," chided Ackerman as the Titleist gently plopped down onto the firm, verdant grass of the 7th green, settling about 20 feet past then spinning back to a distance of 9 feet from the cup. Brad winked as he handed the iron back to CAG Sullivan. All four men laughed then drove off down the fairway in their golf carts.

Tommy Thompson stopped his cart near the edge of the water hazard to let CAG Sullivan out. Since he was effectively out of play on this hole, Sullivan wanted to search for golf balls in the cool water while the other three men in the foursome finished out their putts. A soaring Cypress tree stood majestically near the lake as it had for the past one hundred fifty years or so. Its massive branches were covered with hanging, dripping Spanish moss and part of its tree trunk was actually a few feet into the pond. In the near distance, CAG could make out the silent silhouette of a six-foot alligator sunning himself in the tall rye grass on the opposite bank of the small lake; maintaining a vigilant gaze over his territory. CAG gripped his five-iron a little tighter as his eyes scanned for any balls he could reach at the water's edge. All the while his peripheral vision kept the gator in semi-focus as he plucked up balls from the mud, examined them then stuffed the acceptable ones into his right front pocket. As Sullivan continued to scrutinize the water hazard for errant golf balls he was suddenly startled when a rather large Cotton mouth snake slithered by, just in front of brown and white *FootJoys*. The coal black reptile rushed out from underneath the gaping Cypress tree roots, seeking the refuge of the pond's black depths, and causing Sullivan to leap backward a few feet in a fleeting moment of shock.

"Snake," yelled CAG with an audible shriek, just as Hank Andrews was in the middle of his putting backstroke. In unison, Brad, Tommy and Hank all raised there heads in reaction to the bellowing, raised decibel scream released from CAG Sullivan's lungs. SECNAV missed the putt of course, running the ball past the cup a good twelve feet. As he walked over to mark his ball on the green he cast a disgruntled gaze in Sullivan's general direction. Hank tossed a quarter down behind his ball to mark it, and as he picked it up Andrews licked his left thumb then used the moisture to wipe clean the face of his putter.

While Tommy Thompson judiciously studied his own slippery birdie attempt, Teen Angel suddenly recalled one of his more infamous exploits with a snake on a golf course. It happened when he was a senior at Burbank High School in southern California, some fourteen years ago. Brad was playing alone, just trying to take in a few more holes before darkness ended play for the day. He was on his home course, De Bell Country Club, which is nestled deep in the rustic foothills of Burbank, California. That day Ackerman was playing behind a thirty-something woman who had miraculously managed to keep pace with his swift playing speed. He never had to even think of asking the redhead for the courtesy of playing through due to her lethargic tempo. She kept up nicely. That is until the sixth hole. On that hole, a medium length par 4, Brad noticed that the woman, stylishly dressed in a soft blue culotte, had apparently disappeared into the long ditch that spans the entire length of the fairway on the left side. She was obviously searching for a wayward shot. As Ackerman approached her position he intended to stick his head through the row of small orange trees that lined the cart path, separating the fairway from the ditch. He would politely request that she let him play through while she continued her search. Just as Teen Angel leaned through the tree branches to make cursory eye contact, the woman let out an ear-piercing screech. This alarmed Brad causing him to grip the sand-wedge in his right hand even tighter and to instinctively scan the horizon for signs of danger.

Pushing his way completely through the orange trees, using the golf club to brush aside tree limbs and spider webs, Brad immediately realized the serious dilemma the woman was facing. In looking for her ball, she had inadvertently disturbed a family of Western Diamondback rattlesnakes lodged in a dirt pit underneath a flat granite rock. The woman stood frozen, eight feet from the serpent den, unable to move a muscle due to the trauma of the situation. And, judging from the high-pitched sound of his rattling tail, papa snake was not at all pleased by her physical presence in the vicinity of his babies. Without hesitation, Teen Angel rapidly moved to her position, disregarding the blood that trickled from a scratch on his neck sustained by rough contact with a tree branch. Briefly adopting his knight in shining armor posture, he leaned over to take the woman's small hand. In her eyes Teen Angel could see the terror she was experiencing and it instantly magnified his sense of urgency to affect her rescue. He grabbed hold of her gloved, left hand and yanked her up and out of the shallow pit. As he deftly maneuvered her body around, to give her rear end a final push up the embankment, the soft ground under his left foot gave way and Brad tumbled ass over tea kettle down into the ditch. Dirt dust flew everywhere. In an instant, Ackerman had changed positions with the woman and the dilemma had been effectively reversed.

Well, this was the last straw for papa rattlesnake. 6 foot 2 inch Brad Ackerman was apparently a greater, imminent threat to his slimy little family so the cold-blooded reptile unleashed his coiled up body and lunged the remaining three feet toward Brad. With astonishing quickness the serpent sank its fangs deep into the soft flesh of Ackerman's exposed left forearm. Teen Angel could actually feel the toxic venom spreading in his body as the snake injected his forearm with the warm viscous fluid. But unlike most snake attacks, the serpent seemed unable to recoil away from Brad, his oversized victim. Incredibly, the fangs of the pit viper, one longer than the other, actually appeared to get hung up during the strike on Ackerman's arm. The snake's jaws remained attached to Brad's arm and the entire length of its scaly body writhed in the effort to become disentangled. Realizing this, Brad grabbed the snake behind its bulbous head and snapped it away from his flesh in one swift, aggressive movement. Relocating his sand-wedge in the dirt Teen Angel beat the rattlesnake in the head until it breathed its last. Unfortunately, when Ackerman squeezed the snake's neck, it pumped another healthy does of venom into his forearm.

Although somewhat dazed by the poison flowing in his body, Ackerman could still hear the redhead screaming at the top of the embankment. He motioned for her to retrieve the golf cart and in a flash she drove Brad to the pro shop where the head professional, Paul Sanchez, summoned an ambulance. Teen Angel was conscious, but showing signs of labored breathing, when the paramedic squad arrived 12 minutes later, sirens blaring. Brad had to endure a three-day stay in Saint Joseph's Medical Center and several injections of antivenin as a result of his little wrestling match with that daddy snake. But, the thirty-something redhead properly rewarded his bravery a week later in the friendly confines of her waterbed.

The smile on Teen Angel's face was just beginning to spread when the thunderous sound of four departing Corsairs broke the peaceful silence of the golf course. The skipper's division of jets could be seen rising over the tree line on their initial takeoff. The three men on the 7th green, and CAG still at the waters' edge stopped what they were doing to watch the attack jets screech across the milky horizon. Never could a more beautiful and impressive sight be seen. All four men in the foursome literally stopped in their tracks to witness the launch. The sight of warplanes flying still had a hypnotic affect over each of them despite their numerous years of close association to all the various experiences of tactical naval aviation.

After sinking the winning birdie putt on 7, Admiral Thompson was first to hit from the tee box at number 8, a long par 5 that doglegged sharply to the left. Unfortunately, Tommy pulled the ball badly with his driver and it hooked into a section of oak trees. After successfully finding the fairway with their tee shots, Teen Angel, Hank Andrews and CAG Sullivan all helped the admiral try to locate his ball in the woods. But, after the customary five minutes search time, Brad and SECNAV drove off in the cart to hit their approach shots toward the 8th green. CAG and Tommy Thompson continued looking for the ball for several minutes but to no avail.

Brushing a pair of love bugs away from his cheek, Brad turned his head back down the fairway. He could now see CAG addressing his ball on the left side of the short grass with a three-wood. After making an ugly stab at his ball, and almost losing his balance, Sullivan yelled out "Fore!" Getting the message, Ackerman and Andrews both ducked behind their cart, not sure when it was safe to reemerge. After a short delay, Sullivan's orange ball bounced around in a small grove of trees just behind Brad's right ear, finally coming to rest directly behind the largest, oldest oak tree in southern Louisiana. The ball was actually nested in between two thick roots and there was no way that any human being was going to be able to make contact with it using a golf club.

"What do you think I'll need for my next shot?" shouted Sullivan, using his gloved hand as a makeshift megaphone.

"A McCullough chain saw CAG," echoed Teen Angel in his characteristically sarcastic voice. The retort caused Hank Andrews to chuckle out loud. CAG Sullivan just bristled and hustled off to his cart, the brunt of yet another snide but good-natured remark.

"Do you have any idea why I am in New Orleans Lieutenant Ackerman?" inquired SECNAV as both men simultaneously settled into the tattered leather of the golf cart's bench seat.

"Yes sir I do, and I was wondering what made you pick VA-204 to be a part of the air wing on what I understand will be the very last A-7 carrier deployment."

As their conversation ensued Teen Angel lifted his right foot and used a tee to scrape the mud and grass out of his spikes. He noticed that one spike was missing as the residue of grass and mud fell harmlessly to the turf next to the cart. Brad kept one eye peeled to his left side, just in case Tommy Thompson's ball decided to take a bead on their position.

"Good news travels fast around here doesn't it?" responded Hank Andrews realizing his little secret cat had been effectively let out of the bag. This meant that he would lose the element of surprise for his momentous announcement, scheduled to be delivered at the All Officer's Meeting (AOM) in the *River Rattler* Ready Room today at 1300.

As the two men sat patiently awaiting Admiral Thompson to either find his lost ball in the woods or give up and drop another with two penalty strokes to continue play, Andrews recollected the story which helped him decide to give the *River Rattlers* the call to active duty in Carrier Air Wing Two. He gave Teen Angel the superficial details of the accelerated F-18 transition schedule then he provided a more intimate explanation of his selection of VA-204 to fill the void in CAG-2's air wing. As he spoke, Hank shifted positions in the leather cart seat and his New Orleans drawl became slightly more pronounced. It seems that during his brief tenure as Secretary of the Navy, the officers of VA-204 had twice, graciously requested that Hank Andrews be the keynote speaker at their annual Mardi Gras bash. Since its inception some nine years ago, the party and its festivities had grown in size and stature, evolving into one of the major highlights of the carnival season. This was especially true for the large military contingent living in the New Orleans area. And, thanks to Dana Rothschild and her influential lawyer father, the event was well represented by local dignitaries and politicians as well. The party wasn't close to the size of Endymion's *Extravaganza*, but it had grown incrementally each year since its beginning and had become an eagerly anticipated event.

Since being sworn in as the Commanding Officer of Attack Squadron 204 in January 1991, Duke O' Grady had personally sent a *River Rattler* Mardi Gras party invitation to Secretary Andrews. He had done so for the past two carnival seasons. The last invitation card had been sent just three weeks ago, in hopes of giving the Secretary and his staff adequate time to clear his schedule and accommodate the speaking request. But due to other pressing political commitments, Andrews had been unable to accept both speaking engagements. Leaning forward just a tad, Andrews adjusted his *Ben Hogan* golf visor then pulled this year's invitation from the left rear pocket of his golf slacks. He held the card out as if to display it to Brad, who of course already knew all about the invitation and its humorous contents.

The outside cover of the card showed a colorful depiction of *Rex*, the recognized *King of Carnival*. In the picture King Rex, appropriately costumed as an aging monarch, is clad entirely in whiter than white royal clothing, including a ballerina leotard, all laced with gold trim. His outfit is complete with gaudy faux jewels on his magnificent golden crown and official ruling scepter. In the overly staged drama, Rex is standing on top of a highly decorative Mardi Gras float humbly toasting his lovely teen-age Queen on *Fat Tuesday*, the culmination day of the carnival season. This event is one of the most anticipated, traditional events of the Mardi Gras social scene. The teen-ager selected for this distinctly prized honor in carnival lore, is located in the reviewing stand of the Old Boston Club on Canal Street in downtown New Orleans. She is wearing a luxurious ball gown that cost way too much money, and is ceremoniously surrounded by prominent businessmen and politicians, all hoping for a few seconds of valuable exposure on local television. Underneath this photograph, at the bottom of the front of the card, is the following inscription: '*What kind of asshole would bomb Rex, King of Carnival?*' The words evoke a rather suggestive enticement to say the least.

When you open up the card, the inside left panel has a cropped photo of an A-7 Corsair in a 60 degree dive. The warplane is taking aim at King Rex and pitching two MK-83 Snakeye bombs toward his royal float as it proceeds along the parade route on Canal Street. An oversized red bull's eye marks the king's position on the float, tongue in cheek of course. On the right side panel of the card is a group photograph of all the VA-204 officers with their hands raised high. The message portrayed is that they are all ready and willing to volunteer for the infamous mission of bombing King Rex. Underneath that photo is the following warm invitation: '*The officers of Attack Squadron 204 cordially invite you to come on down and get bombed at Mardi Gras 1992.*' Hank Andrews smiled widely as he read the inscription once again. He remembered the enthusiastic reaction his own staff gave the first time they saw the card at his office in the Pentagon.

Finally, if you were inquisitive enough to look, the back of the card depicts the familiar toasting scene at the Old Boston Club, but in the aftermath of the mock aerial bombing attack by an A-7 Corsair. The king's golden crown and scepter, float parts, leotard, doubloons, beads and the queen's ball gown are literally strewn everywhere in the large crater created by the explosion. Of course, the card is supposed to be taken in the humorous light in which it was intended, and only a few people had complained about the blatant political incorrectness of the invitation. As always, Duke O' Grady didn't give a rat's ass if people complained; he was proud of the card and would fight for its continued existence. Hank Andrews told Teen Angel that it was this card from VA-204 that convinced him to select the *River Rattler's* to make the final A-7 Corsair deployment with CVW-2 onboard USS *Enterprise*. Ackerman shook his head without uttering a word, released the foot brake on the cart then the pair drove on down the fairway to hit their next shots. Teen Angel had learned al long time ago how to manage infamy.

CHAPTER 16

▼

BURN THE EVIDENCE

Bobby Boone gave Commander Morley a 'thumbs in' signal indicating that the nose wheel of Corsair 407 had been securely chocked. An oversized set of wood blocks, connected by a piece of thick hemp rope, was planted firmly on the black tarmac of the *River Rattler* flight line. Resting underneath the sleek intake duct of the Corsair, the thick hunks of wood had been wedged in front of and behind the twin nose tires of the aircraft to prevent it from moving. The chocks, painted bright yellow, were soiled with grease, oil and hydraulic stains. Next Airman Boone made a slicing gesture across his throat with the palm of his right hand to advise Shroud that he was ready for the engine to be shut down. In one fluid motion, Morley moved the A-7's throttle inboard then quickly aft past the idle stop to secure the engine. For the second time in less than eight minutes the powerful TF-41 turbine began to wind down; this time on purpose. As the jet's internal fire was extinguished due to fuel starvation, its engine instruments slowly peeled back, decreasing until all the gauges read zero. The large artificial horizon instrument wobbled as it weakened then tumbled upside down when electrical output from the warplane's 28 volt generator was finally eliminated. 407's dying engine emitted a familiar, hollow whine while its ear-piercing noise slowly ceased. The huge turbine blades however, continued to spin vigorously because of the twenty knots of natural wind being forced down the intake duct. The nickel and steel blades made a click clack sound as their counterclockwise rotation persisted.

While Airman Boone moved closer to the left cheek of the Corsair, anticipating Commander Morley's deplaning, his eyes scanned the jet for anything unsafe or out of the ordinary, like a fire on shutdown or fluid leaks. Instinctively, the young plane captain looked to ensure that the daunting ejection seat was indeed safe. Before raising his canopy and taxiing into the flight line area, Shroud Morley had located a thin metal lever, or *head knocker*, at the top portion of the ESCAPAC ejection seat. With his ungloved right hand he had snapped the head knocker down, locking it into its safe position directly behind his gray helmet. This action prevented the ejection seat from being inadvertently actuated while Morley went about removing himself from the cockpit of the A-7. Shroud popped the four Koch fittings on his torso harness then leaned over to the right to disconnect the G-suit hose, oxygen and radio lines. He was now released from the seat pan. Gathering his kneeboard, chart bag, flight gloves and two pocket checklists Morley climbed up and out of the ejection seat. On a post-maintenance check hop, pilots carried their regular emergency procedures checklist and the PMCF checklist. Shroud then crawled over the edge of the left side canopy railing, trying to locate the square steps of the Corsair's interior boarding ladder with his boots. Bobby Boone, who was now nestled up close to the aircraft, grabbed the commander's size 9 foot and easily maneuvered the aviator's steel-toed boot into the first step of the internal ladder. A few seconds later Morley was standing next to Boone on solid ground again, with an expression of relief on his face. His green flight suit was full of sweat in the crotch and shoulders. These are the areas where a tight-fitting torso harness puts the most stress and pressure on an aviator's body. Boone paid no attention; he merely went about his normal post-flight routine.

Despite spending his entire morning closely monitoring CAG corrosion inspection activities, Senior Chief Esposito had actually watched Commander Morley in the carrier break. Strolling back to his office, he had noticed the jet's unusually low altitude on the downwind leg.

"Everything ok with 407 Commander," inquired Esposito. Before he spoke, the senior chief had removed both hands from his flight jacket pockets and was flashing a shaky 'thumbs up" signal. He was earnestly trying to make focused eye contact with the squadron Admin Officer, Mike Morley. The question was left intentionally vague to allow suitable wiggle room for Shroud, should he be in need of some. Over the past forty years in the Navy, John Esposito had learned that naval aviators were often in need of wiggle room so he wasn't in the habit of pressing them into a corner unless he was left with absolutely no other alternative.

"The jet is up and ready for the next sortie senior chief," replied Shroud as he removed his helmet and placed a damp skull cap, Nomex gloves and two checklists inside the plush confines of the form fit headgear. Held firmly, Morley dangled the helmet and its contents, along with a green chart bag, casually down his left side. In that moment, Morley had decided that the motor was fine and that he must have been overly aggressive with his throttle movements during the carrier break maneuver. Then and there, Shroud concluded that he had *accidentally* shut down the engine. The TF-41 had *not* flamed out on its own, therefore the aircraft was up and ready for the next mission.

"I couldn't help but notice that your altitude dipped somewhat in the last part of your break sir," prodded Esposito. "You're sure the jet is up?" The senior chief was still seeking Commander Morley's brown eyes, but Shroud was avoiding eye contact and trying hard not to appear intentionally evasive. Airman Boone was busy stowing the Corsair's internal ladder and preparing to perform his turn-around inspection. Neither he nor Esposito had seen the civilian seaplane and its near miss with 407. Mike Morley quickly realized he would have to put an end to the line of questioning, lest it become more invasive.

"I had to maneuver on the downwind to avoid a small flock of Canadian geese flying south for the winter. That's my story and I'm sticking to it!" answered Commander Morley. Oh and senior chief, the angle-of-attack indexer is loose. Please have it tightened up." Shroud then turned and brusquely walked off toward maintenance control, his messy *helmet hair* flapping in the breeze. Although his curiosity was unsatisfied, Esposito knew their discussion was in essence, effectively over.

Jack Mayhew sat uncomfortably in a poorly padded chair just outside the duty flight surgeon's office. His left arm had the tell-tale evidence of a lab tech's invasion of his vein with a hypodermic needle. Held in place by two strands of painfully adhesive medical tape, a double-thick chunk of gauze covered the puncture wound on the inside of Commander Mayhew's elbow joint. The white bandage material had a tiny dot of red in the center. Fortunately, Jack's blood always seemed to coagulate fairly quickly; maybe the cranberry juice had something to do with that. Mayhew had reluctantly done his annual duty by relinquishing the required five vials of blood for testing. He had completed the hearing evaluation, chest x-ray and almost all of the other tests included in a standard, navy flight physical. He was tired, bored and hungry, and wanted to be released from the medical torture chamber as soon as possible. All that remained for him now was the eye exam, weigh in and of course, the final *hands on* assault by the duty sawbones. Probing, prodding, squeezing, coughing, latex gloves and *KY Jelly* would undoubtedly be involved in that final ordeal. Juice squirmed in the chair then unconsciously squeezed his butt cheeks together. But, in less than thirty minutes his flight physical would be complete for yet another year. In less than one half of an hour the flight surgeon would sign his 'up chit' and Juice would be out of the clinic, enjoying the culinary delight of the two Hubig's pies waiting for him in the car. Like one of Pavlov's dogs, Mayhew could actually feel saliva flowing freely inside of his mouth at just the thought of wolfing down the well-earned dessert pies. The eye examination was probably the next torment in this year's ordeal he thought.

Two years ago the NAS clinic had acquired a new fangled appliance to test for glaucoma. This glaucoma assessment, of course, came after the regular vision screening and color blindness evaluation. Juice called the new device the *puffer*, because the contraption shot a stream of cold air into the patient's eye sockets to measure eyeball pressure. It was basically a big pain in the ass; something to be avoided if at all possible. Using this device, the patient had to first allow his chin to be positioned inside of an uncomfortable rubber stirrup situated at the front of the apparatus. Then you waited in agony, continually blinking, while trying to anticipate the timing of the rude puff of air that was about to invade your eyes. Then wham, it hits you when you least expect it! The only thing worse according to Juice was enduring a *manual* glaucoma test. The manual test is where a burly navy corpsman would hold you down in a recliner chair while another corpsman attempted to place a delicate metal instrument onto the surface of your eyeball; again endeavoring to measure internal eyeball pressure. Jack Mayhew had suffered through the manual glaucoma test several times in the past fourteen years and he despised it. This year he would endure the lesser of two evils during the glaucoma exam.

"Commander Mayhew," called out an enlisted man in a neatly pressed white smock.

The second class petty officer was wearing a stethoscope draped around the back of his neck and had three or four pens stuffed awkwardly in his front pocket. His curly blonde locks needed trimming thought Mayhew as he rose from the chair and raised his hand to identify himself to the fresh faced corpsman. Jack didn't recognize the corpsman because he had just transferred to NAS New Orleans from the Naval Air Station in Point Mugu, California about seven weeks ago. Holding a clipboard filled with various forms and paperwork, the petty officer directed Juice over to the clinic scale, a counterweight and balance type of device, which stood about two feet from the duty flight surgeon's office door. The weighing gadget was also positioned directly in front of a wall that featured a limited edition print of two F-8 Crusaders from VF-51 flying over top of the USS *Ticonderoga* (CV-14). Obviously the weigh in was to precede the eye assessment this year. Jack smiled when he noticed the painting had been autographed by Vice Admiral James B. Stockdale, a Viet Nam era Medal-of-Honor recipient.

After he removed his black aviator boots Juice hopped up onto the base plate of the scale, noticeably anxious to get this milestone behind him for another year. In the back portion of the scale, the corpsman located a flat metal rod and slid it up to measure Mayhew's height, which was a shade less than 5 feet 11 inches. As the corpsman repositioned the top portion of the measuring rod down onto Jack's scalp, Juice stiffened his body and pressed a tad upwards on his toes. He was attempting to get every possible quarter inch. The corpsman didn't say a word; either not noticing or not caring that Mayhew was slightly up on his tiptoes. Jack strained his neck a bit to watch as the petty officer removed one of the black government pens from his front pocket then wrote down 71 inches on a medical chart with Mayhew's name printed at the top. At 71 inches, Juice knew that his maximum weight was 203 pounds. Earlier today after drying off from his morning shower and then removing one of Ashley's *Barbie* dolls from the digital scale in the master bathroom, Jack was elated to see that he weighed in at 199 pounds in the nude. In thirty-two days this time around on the *Juice plan* diet, he had shed 21 pounds of extra padding. The weigh in would be a breeze; nothing to stress about. Jack turned his head back toward the F-8 print then let out a shallow sigh of relief.

The corpsman lifted up the top two sheets on his clipboard to take a peek at Mayhew's flight physical results from the previous year. He saw that Jack tipped the scales at 198 pounds on the 11th of December 1990, the date of his last flight physical. With this in mind, the corpsman reached back to the counterweight device on the *Detecto* scale and swiftly pushed the large measuring bar over to the right, stopping just short of the balance window. With a muffled thud he plopped the lead weight into the 150 pound grooved notch. Next, with his left index finger, the petty officer slid the smaller, precision measuring bar slowly over toward the right. A perplexed look began to fill Jack's face as the corpsman reached then went just beyond the 50 pound mark with the precision measuring piece. Inconceivably, the counterweight mechanism inside the balance window did not budge meaning that, according to the clinic scale, Jack weighed *more* than 200 pounds. Juice was speechless. Without hesitation the petty officer repositioned the large block of lead, dropping it abruptly into the 200 pound notch. It quickly locked into that position at the top of the scale. Again he gradually slid the precision piece of metal slowly to the right. As it reached the 10 pound mark, the counterweight device began to rise then it floated in the middle of the balance window. Again without vacillation or discussion, the corpsman continued to perform his job. In black ink he jotted down 210 pounds on Mayhew's chart. Unbelievably, the clinic scale had determined Commander Mayhew's weight to be 210 pounds; 7 pounds *over* his limit of 203. Instead of being 4 pounds under, Jack was 7 pounds over his targeted maximum weight for a naval aviator. Juice was now sufficiently compelled to speak.

"Is there something wrong with your scale Petty Officer Ridowski," asked Mayhew after first confirming the corpsman's identity on his blue clinic nametag. Jack's voice sounded displeased as anxiety began to creep up on him from out of nowhere. Curiously, he didn't feel the least bit anxious during his unintentional departure from controlled flight yesterday out over the Gulf of Mexico, but the thought of being told he was overweight brought out the butterflies.

"No sir, we had it calibrated this morning and it is working just fine," responded Corpsman Ridowski. Apparently the flight surgeon, Jack's old nemesis Lieutenant Ken Carrigan, had overheard the conversation as it unfolded at the scale. Tossing aside the EKG printout he was reading Lieutenant Carrigan picked up his stethoscope then quickly maneuvered around the edge of his cheap desk. He stood in his office doorway, observing the *two minute rule*, assessing the situation for a moment then he addressed Mayhew.

"What seems to be the problem Juice?" Carrigan was somewhat familiar with Jack and felt entirely comfortable using his tactical call sign to address him in public. In fact he and Mayhew had shared a ride in a TA-7, the two-seat version of the Corsair, just a couple of months ago on an ACM detachment to NAS Key West, Florida. Jack had first offered the hop to Carrigan as a means of bringing the flight surgeon into the fold so to speak, thereby taking him off the enemies list, at least temporarily. Dr. Carrigan, who Juice always called *Wrongway* because of his penchant for wearing a stethoscope backwards around his neck, approached and placed his right palm on Jack's shoulder blades to express his concern. Mayhew was still standing on the scale and still not believing that he weighed in at 210 pounds. In his left hand Dr. Carrigan held an ink pen. Annoyingly, he clicked the top four or five times.

"Wrongway I think your scale is all fouled up," exclaimed Mayhew. "Can we try it again?" As he finished that last statement Juice stepped off the grated base plate. In an instant he removed his Nomex flight suit, orange undershirt and thick tube socks. Juice chucked the clothing onto a nearby chair. *They* must be the source of the extra weight he reasoned to himself. Jack now stood in the center of the room in his white skivvies, not caring if any females were in the vicinity. His 'up chit' was at stake here and now and he knew it.

"Well now that you're nearly naked Juice, why don't you get back onto the scale," said Wrongway. Both he and Petty Officer Ridowski held their laughter in check. Dr. Carrigan then proceeded to repeat the same steps that Corpsman Ridowski had performed earlier. Wrongway inched the precision measuring bar slowly to the right. As it reached the number 7 this time, the balance window showed that the correct weight was being displayed. Without his clothes on Jack weighed 207 pounds; 4 pounds overweight. Juice was still dumbfounded. Had he somehow miscalculated his own weight? He had never done it before in his Navy career. Was he actually four pounds over his limit? Mayhew himself was utterly confused at this point.

"That just can't be doc. I weighed myself at 0530 this morning on a brand new digital scale, and I was a full 4 pounds under my maximum," exclaimed Juice in a dubious voice.

"Where did you buy that scale Commander, at K-Mart?" cracked Ridowski. Ken Carrigan gave the corpsman a crusty look to register his disgust at the insensitive comment. Commander Mayhew simply ignored the petty officer's insolence. Suddenly realizing the magnitude of his insubordination, Ridowski lowered his head then buried a blank stare into some paperwork on the clipboard.

"Perhaps it wasn't properly calibrated at the factory. Or maybe someone has tampered with it since you brought it home Jack." Ken Carrigan was trying to sound empathetic, like doctors are supposed to sound in traumatic times like this. His last suggestion brought on an increased level of anxiety in Mayhew. After all, he had two rather rambunctious children scampering around at home. Either one of them could have easily fiddled with his digital scale without Jack's knowledge. Not maliciously of course, but just being inquisitive kids and by being *button pushers* like Jack had always been himself since childhood.

"This is the only scale that counts Juice," said Wrongway Carrigan tapping the top of the counterweight appliance. "Let's go to my office for a minute," he suggested. With that said Petty Officer Ridowski nodded his head respectfully at the flight surgeon then returned to his desk to retrieve the next patient's paperwork. There were still about twenty flight physicals to complete before the day was over and before he could go to the Enlisted Club to share a cold bottle of suds with his buddies. The corpsman's mind swiftly shifted focus to his next patient seated in the waiting room.

Dr. Ken Carrigan closed his office door quietly then eased past Juice to the chair behind his desk. Medical papers and files were neatly stacked up in the 'in basket' on the right side of the particle board countertop of the desk. On top of a prescription script pad an expensive *Mount Blanc* fountain pen lay next to a pair of *Bill Blass* designer reading glasses. A medical degree from Penn State, bestowed on this kid a mere two and a half years ago, was hung in a garish frame just behind Lieutenant Carrigan's head. It was probably positioned there to hide an ugly stain on the wall thought Mayhew. Shit, Juice still had several pairs of socks older than this so-called *doctor*. Wrongway Carrigan could sense the power he held over Mayhew in this precarious situation. Despite what most pilots believed, he didn't relish the dilemma nor did he want to abuse his authority. But, at the same time, he had taken an oath to the Navy and he had to uphold his allegiance to the Naval Medical Corps. After a few more moments of uneasy reflection, Carrigan explained that he would issue Mayhew a temporary 'up chit' which would be good for a two week timeframe. In that fourteen day period he told Jack that he should be able to lose the four pounds needed to dip below his max limit. Heck it was probably just water weight anyway, and he could drop it pretty easily. However, if he didn't pass the next weigh in fourteen days from now, Dr. Carrigan would have no choice but to ground Commander Mayhew and place him on the 'fat boy' program until he lost the extra pounds.

The 'fat boy' program would mean total embarrassment and nonstop teasing from his squadron mates. It also meant that Juice would have to show up to the base gymnasium each morning at 0600 for an hour of directed calisthenics. Twenty-four year old Ensign Donna Detweiller, the NAS New Orleans Physical Fitness Officer, was lead instructor of the 'fat boy' program. The half Jordanian, half Californian exercise freak utilized a strict regimen of punishing aerobics to rebuke her victims. Word was that, as a physical trainer, Donna Detweiller was a killer who displayed absolutely no mercy. She had jet black hair, a perfectly hardened body and lifeless ebony colored eyes. Juice himself had sent several of his chubby enlisted men to her on the 'fat boy' program. After her four week course of therapy, those enlisted men had come back about 10 to 15 pounds lighter; but they were broken men. For 28 days, the five foot tall, vivacious Ensign Detweiller had exercised them harder than the drill sergeants did at boot camp. Donna loved her job and thoroughly enjoyed her well-deserved nickname: *Doomsday* Detweiller. Jack knew he had no choice but to accept this deal being offered to him by Wrongway Carrigan.

"Go do your eye exam and when you're done I'll have your temporary 'up chit' ready for you here in my office Juice," advised Lieutenant Carrigan in a soothing voice. It didn't help. Jack was still seething inside as he got up, opened the door, and walked toward the eye lab. He would still have some explaining to do at the squadron and he wasn't looking forward to the ribbing he would have to endure; good-natured or not.

At 200 feet AGL, Commander John O'Grady tuned his Tactical Navigation radio to channel 27, the TACAN frequency for the municipal airport in Gulfport, Mississippi. Duke could hear the A-7's turbofan engine humming pleasantly through the thick ear pads of his orange helmet. It was the reassuring, high-pitched sound that all *sluf* drivers had become accustomed too from their earliest days in the fleet training squadron (RAG). Shifting his head slightly to the left in the cockpit of Corsair 401, Duke could clearly see the blue green waters of the gulf pounding the seashore of Cat Island just below as he streaked by overhead. Very few sunbathers were on the white sands of the island shoreline that morning. The twenty knots of wind flurrying and gusting about that day kicked up numerous whitecaps, making the salt water and beach appear much less alluring to the teenage beachcomber crowd. The sea state was pretty rough to say the least. In fact, Duke had spotted no sailboats on this day, which was highly unusual for a Saturday. Normally, Breton Sound and the cool waters off Southern Mississippi were cluttered with sailboat traffic every weekend. There would be several doctors, lawyers, tobacco executives and casino tycoons, all pretending to be sailors, but actually just trying to avoid a collision at sea in the crowded coastal waters. A rusty white shrimp boat, nagged by about sixty squawking sea gulls, disappeared under Duke's right wing. Plodding along against the choppy whitecaps with her huge fishing nets out of the salt water, she was steaming at fifteen knots for the Mississippi River gulf outlet. Her cargo of shellfish was destined for the tables of New Orleans finest restaurants.

The skipper double-checked his Inertial Navigation System (INS) coordinates and saw that the next turn for his division of warplanes would be in 52 seconds. Duke glanced at his $10 *Casio* wristwatch to confirm that the INS was accurate in its timing. It was! In less than a minute the four A-7's, flying at 520 knots in a *battle-box* formation, would execute a 90 degree *Tac turn* and make their *coast in* over the I-10 twin-span bridge. Flying along the published VR-179 low level navigation route, the four jets would go *feet wet* about three miles west of the Pascagoula shipyards. Three US Navy vessels, all light cruisers, and a British fast frigate were dry docked in the yard for repairs and upgrades.

In the right side of 401's canopy glass Duke observed his wingman, Lieutenant Cookie Cline piloting Corsair 415, maintaining perfect position in the battle box. Cookie was a shade less than three-quarters of a mile directly abeam of Duke's aircraft and about twenty feet lower in altitude. Squinting his eyeballs behind corrective lenses, the skipper could make out the blue silhouette of three

Mk-83 practice bombs, which were loaded onto the port side triple-ejector rack (TER) of 415. For some reason Duke raised his sun visor and rotated his head to the left then back to the right, sweeping his vision throughout the cockpit and visible exterior of the warplane. He wanted to make visual contact with the six bombs he was carrying under his swept wings; dummy ordnance that he would soon deliver to the practice target at Camp Shelby bombing range. Instinctively, he checked to make sure the Master Arm Switch, just in front of his left knee on the pilot's armament panel, was locked in the 'safe' position. All appeared normal as Duke lowered his visor back down.

Just over the top of a fresh-water lake located in the middle of a tiny island 2 miles southwest of Pascagoula, Duke O' Grady added a handful of power then yanked his jet into a coordinated 45 degree angle-of-bank turn. Over in 415, Cookie Cline had been monitoring his own INS counting down the seconds to this third check point on the VR-179, visual flight rules track. Patiently waiting for the *Tac left* maneuver that he knew was about to occur, Cookie had pulled his aircraft behind the wing line of the skipper's jet a full 8 seconds prior to the turn initiated by O' Grady at the fresh-water lake checkpoint. Cline had smartly rolled 415 into a 60 degree bank, pulled three G's then rapidly accelerated into a mirror position, this time on the skipper's left side in the battle box formation. The lead section of aircraft was now heading 007 degrees, zooming toward the sawmill checkpoint some twelve miles up ahead on the route. The second section of jets, with Brain Child Bracken as the wingman in 411 and Comatose Gross as the section leader in 410, was trailing Duke and Cookie by approximately 1 mile. Over the lake, the second section performed the same *Tac left* maneuver then slid in behind Duke and Cookie for the coast in. Comatose Gross clumsily dropped his VR-179 *strip chart* to the floorboard of 410 during his 3.5 G left turn. He lost fifty feet of altitude when he reached down between his legs to pick it up with his left hand. In about twenty-two minutes the division of Corsairs would be yanking and banking over the Camp Shelby target; flinging blue bombs and spurting off live 20mm cannon shells at the practice range bull's eyes. It was indeed a great job being allowed to fly these light attack bomber jets!

T-Ben Hebert and Pops Petibone sat tolerantly in the confining cabin of a Coast Guard HH-65A helicopter. The hardback bench seats in the rear of the orange colored chopper provided little comfort to its passengers. Both aviators wore their green flight suits, survival vests and helmets, and both aviators clutched a helmet bag. Parked at the throat of the Coast Guard ramp, the Dauphine's 39 foot diameter rotor blades were spinning up at a medium range RPM while its flight crew awaited takeoff clearance from the NAS New Orleans control tower. Surrounded by corrosion-resistant composite structure material, the shrouded tail rotor of the Dauphine whined like a bee hive after being disturbed by a Louisiana Black Bear. Soon the 9000 pound rotorcraft would hover over the dull green grass on the infield section of Runway 14 then depart to the East, flying at 300 feet AGL on the Bridge Route. They would undoubtedly *buzz* their primary competition in the war-on-drugs, the Customs interdiction pilots who occupied the hangar next door. Competition is a healthy thing because it keeps you eternally young and strong by weeding out the weak. Perhaps Darwin was right!

Lieutenants Hebert and Petibone had been selected by Commander Randy Bracken, the VA-204 Safety Officer, to participate in a search-and-rescue exercise (SAREX) this morning. With the various extra curricular activity taking place this Drill Weekend, Brain Child Bracken figured to catch the squadron off guard by scheduling a surprise SAREX. As the Safety Officer, Bracken routinely tested people's reactions to stressful situations involving flight operations. In his mind, it was invaluable training that would intuitively kick in when confronted by real life trauma. Commander Bracken had coordinated last weekend with the *coasties* who were always eager to help out in search-and-rescue training for their *big brothers*, the Navy. Over a Blackened Redfish lunch at the O' Club, Brain Child and the skipper of the Coast Guard squadron had planned the intricate logistics details of today's exercise. In addition to his squadron being designated as the primary rescuers, the USCG skipper had kindly agreed to provide a pair of Corsair pilots with transportation out to a small atoll in the Chandelier Island chain, approximately fifty miles east of the NAS. The lonely and uncharted coral reef sat out in the shallow waters of Breton Sound, inhabited only by turtles, brown pelicans, and the occasional wayward sea lion. T-Ben would play the role of the 'downed aviator' in today's scenario, complete with a simulated broken back, while Pops was merely tagging along to videotape the eventual rescue operation as it developed.

The 120 knot helicopter, pride of the Aerospatiale Corporation, had been a staple of the Coast Guard fleet since the early 1980's. Today the copter crew would drop the two A-7 drivers off on the sandy isle then linger in the area for awhile, awestruck by the ominous, fifteen foot green shapes they would see slicing through the water below. The Dauphine would wait until Duke O' Grady's division of Corsairs, after their bombing evolution was completed, could first locate T-Ben then vector them back for a rescue pick up. If done properly, the entire training evolution would take less than 45 minutes from initiation of the simulated Mayday call by Lieutenant Hebert on his PRC-90, hand-held emergency radio. T-Ben fidgeted in the uncomfortable seat as the pilot-in-command gradually raised his collective and the HH-65A gently lifted up, wobbling five feet above the black tarmac then sliding out over the infield lawn of Runway 14. Rotor downwash violently whipped long fragments of the recently mowed turf as the Dauphine siphoned some of the cut green grass up through its carbon fiber blades. Thanks to Randy Bracken, in twenty-five minutes he and Pops Petibone would be standing in the middle of a small chunk of land, almost certainly being pelted by grains of sand blown at fifteen knots or more. Brown pelicans would protest loudly, trying to drive off the human invaders temporarily occupying their island retreat. Pops would have the privilege of recording the whole episode on videotape. Perhaps he could record something hilarious involving T-Ben for posterity. Pops gripped the *RCA* video camera tighter as he sensed the HH-65A was about to be cleared for takeoff.

Like most fixed-wing aviators, Pops Petibone hated everything about helicopters. 'They don't fly, they just beat the air into submission' he would always argue. Of course, he borrowed this highly philosophic quote from Teen Angel. Last year, when the Chief of Naval Operations (CNO) instituted a new rule requiring that all Navy pilots had to successfully complete helicopter dunker training, Pops had almost resigned from the Naval Reserves. But, Lieutenant Commander Rocky Stone had talked him out of it while sharing a few beers and some Buffalo wings at a casino in Fallon, Nevada. For good measure, they also shared two hookers at the *Mustang Ranch* later that same evening. Afterward, Rocky assured Pops that he would be seated next to him each time the *dunker* device hit the swimming pool water then flipped upside down to simulate a helicopter crash at sea. Pops had a slight fear of drowning but Rocky reassured him that the ordeal would be over quickly. Jim Stone's charm was mighty convincing when it needed to be, with men as well as with split tails. The next day, with Rocky close by his side, Pops made it through the dunker torment just fine. The Dauphine slowly twisted in mid-air then departed low and ever so slow over the right edge of the US Customs hangar. One of the Citation pilots jogging around the flight line below flipped the Coast Guard chopper the finger as his long hair swirled about fiercely in reaction to the rotor's downwash.

Pushing through the clinic's double doors, a temporary 'up chit' held limply in his thick-skinned right hand, Juice Mayhew moseyed unhurriedly over to his car. Eventually he would have to hand the 'up chit' to the *River Rattler* Ops Officer, Commander Steve Fitzgerald. It was part of Klutz Fitzgerald's job description to verify the medical, training and operational readiness status of each pilot in VA-204. Soon after that exchange, Jack knew his squadron mates would all learn of his failure to meet the maximum weight standards. The teasing would be unmerciful because A-7 squadrons are notorious for eating their young. Even though Jack understood that a pilot should never bleed in shark infested waters, he cringed at just the thought of the hazing he would receive, both subtle and blatant. After all, he was well acquainted with the innovative minds of his buddies and recognized that they would undoubtedly create all sorts of barbs for him to suffer through. It was then that Juice spotted the seagull shit stains on the trunk and rear window of his Toyota Camry. His shoulders slumped even further as his body language betrayed his level of disgust. Jack stuffed the 'up chit' into his left side chest pocket.

"Isn't that just swell," uttered Jack in absolute repugnance after first spitting onto the asphalt. His extremely lousy day was now almost complete. An X-ray technician with a perplexed look on her face was standing beside her *VW Beetle* in the parking lot. She momentarily stared at Commander Mayhew wondering if the comment was meant for her or if Jack was just talking to himself. Unzipping his right side chest pocket, Juice fumbled for the car keys buried amongst a handful of coins, some lint and a non-winning Power Ball lottery ticket that bulged within the small zippered compartment of his flight suit.

Back inside the medical clinic Dr. Carrigan had removed his white smock and opened the door to the brown colored locker standing off in one corner of his office. Wrongway removed a wire hanger, snaked it inside the shoulders of his coat then hung it up clumsily on the top rung. Dressed only in his khaki uniform, Lieutenant Carrigan now resembled every other naval officer, except for the medical insignia pinned on the left side of his collar. Carrigan had an 11:45 lunch date with Doomsday Detweiller and he was anxious to meet her at Christina's Empress of China Bistro to share some pleasant conversation and a big plate of *Lomi Lomi*. He also intended to hit on her pretty hard. Sitting inconspicuously at the bottom of the metal locker was a brown bag. Inside the paper sack was a bottle of *Crown Royal*. Every man has his price and Ken Carrigan's was a bottle of his favorite whiskey. Bribery was alive and well onboard the Naval Air Station.

A similar brown paper sack, concealing a bottle of *Canadian Club*, was neatly stuffed inside the middle drawer of Petty Officer Ridowski's desk. Simply stated, the two men had been successfully bribed into jury-rigging the clinic scale so that it read eight pounds heavy. Apparently the VA-204 squadron practical joker had convinced Carrigan and Ridowski to go along with his cruel little hoax played on an unsuspecting victim, Commander Jack Mayhew. And their acting performance was flawless; Jack never suspected a thing that morning in the clinic. Later that evening, the two co-conspirators would enjoy the spoils of their nefarious deed; Carrigan in front of a fireplace with Ensign Detweiller and Ridowski with several of his buddies at the BEQ.

Delicately holding the black security module that was attached to his car keys, Mayhew pressed what he thought was the 'door unlock' button. Unfortunately, Jack pushed the red 'emergency' switch on the remote control device and the Camry's horn system began to blare uncontrollably. The car's lights also blinked in harmony with the horn noise. Nobody in the parking lot even gave a second look in his direction. Great security mechanism; everybody was so desensitized to it that it had no affect. Somewhat embarrassed, Jack groped for and finally found the correct knob then quickly silenced the emergency signal. He then pressed the 'door unlock' button. That annoying, yet familiar, double-squeal sound told Jack that the doors to his Toyota were now unlocked.

Pulling open the driver's side door to his Camry, Juice immediately spotted the Hubig's fruit pies and stack of napkins he had strategically placed on the front bucket seat only a few hours before. Wearing a frown, he abruptly brushed aside the napkins, crudely tossed the two pies down to the asphalt then got in and fired up the four-cylinder engine. At first Jack forgot to release the parking brake, so the car sort of chugged forward as he let out the clutch and goosed the accelerator. Realizing his mistake, Jack pumped the E-Brake to the down position then watched in the rear view mirror as the Hubig's pies began to disappear in the distance. Two black birds had already spotted the discarded desserts and had landed next to them in the parking lot. After about two hundred yards of angrily speeding off toward the squadron building, Jack doubled back and humbly retrieved the pies from the asphalt. He could always freeze the little fruit treats for future enjoyment. He pitched the pies into the cooler.

Lieutenant Ed Cline smoothly squeezed the trigger to successfully expend his remaining 20mm canon shells into a strafing target at the Camp Shelby bombing range. Cookie was tracking his objective at 510 knots in a 20 degree dive angle. He had selected the 'gun high' position on 415's machine gun for this last pass, which meant that bullets would be forced out of the heated muzzle at a rate of 6000 rounds per minute. On the head up display (HUD), Cookie had placed the fluorescent pipper of his gun sight directly over the dilapidated turret on an old WW II tank. About 150 projectiles spewed from his gun barrel and pumped precisely into the vintage piece of heavy artillery, positioned behind and just to the left of the main circular bombing target.

Cookie must have had some extra shells loaded that day by the ordnance crew because he had to make an additional run on the tank. As the squadron Weapons

Officer he had probably struck some sort of deal with the ordnance shop supervisor that morning for the additional ammo. When he pulled off the target after his last strafe run was completed, Cookie vigorously yanked on about 6 G's then arched his head upward and to the left to search for Commander O' Grady and the other two Corsairs circling overhead. Instinctively, Cookie moved his Master Arm Switch to the 'safe' position after he jammed the throttle forward to the MRT stop, accelerated then climbed away from the tank. His altitude dipped to just under 300 feet in the strafing run.

Waiting for Lieutenant Cline to finish up, Duke had established the formation in a left hand orbit at 300 knots and 7000 feet AGL. The skipper, flying in a thirty-degree angle of bank, was closely monitoring Cookie's progress during the last strafing run. He had skillfully situated himself and the two jets on his wing at the eleven o'clock position when Cookie began his pull off target. This is where Cline expected to locate Duke and this is exactly where he was when Cookie looked up to find the skipper patiently waiting for him to re-join the formation. Outside the cockpit Duke O' Grady was notoriously sloppy. But when his butt was strapped into an ESCAPAC ejection seat he transformed into a merciless perfectionist. He always taught his colleagues that 'You fly the jet. Don't let the jet fly you! If it is not where you want it to be then put it there!' Of course, this ethic was pounded into the heads of all naval aviators, beginning in flight school.

When the entire flight was back on his wing Duke would check off target with the Camp Shelby controllers then turn the division of warplanes south for the short trek out to the 'Eagle Gulf Warning Area' to partake in some aggressive ACM tactics. Dog fighting was a suitable reward for enduring thirty minutes of bomb deliveries. Cookie pumped out the speed brake, to slow his closing velocity on the division of aircraft then neatly joined the formation on the outside of the turn radius, on Duke's right side. The brilliant sun sparkled off Duke's canopy glass causing Cookie to temporarily narrow his eyes to keep sight of the lead Corsair. Cline quickly removed his oxygen mask to scratch an itch on his nose that he'd endured for the last twenty minutes or so flying around the bombing range. The relief felt exquisite.

"Master Arm safe," advised Duke using Button 20 on the back radio.

"Two."

"Three."

Four," were the sequenced replies received from the other three Corsairs.

"Shelby, Alpha Foxtrot 401 is joined and departing your airspace," said the skipper to the target controllers. He was already established at 320 knots and accelerating to the south as he climbed up to 15,000 feet above the lush Mississippi farmlands below. The cushy cockpit of an A-7 was the only place that Duke really felt exhilarated, and truly felt alive. For an experienced tactical naval aviator, the cockpit is their nest, their sanctuary; a very cozy little bubble to forget their troubles and ply their chosen profession. At least for the two hours they were airborne; especially when flying off the ship. It had this feel in all situations, except for night time. Then you couldn't wait to be chained down, to safe the ejection seat and take your butt out of the cockpit and head below decks.

"Roger that 401, we'll see you the next time around. Nice shooting today skipper. Your CEP's (circular error probabilities) will be faxed over to you within the hour," was the response from the chief controller. CEP's were basically the bombing proficiency scores recorded by the range weapons computers during the bomb drops. They let each pilot know how he and his jet performed on that particular day's events. Of course the competition was keen amongst naval aviators in an A-7 squadron. Each pilot was striving for a 'Battle E' (E for Excellence) in all of the various disciplines and delivery techniques required of a fleet attack pilot.

On the flight out to Eagle Gulf, the division was flying in 'cruise' formation. This arrangement was fairly loose and provided some latitude for Duke's wingman to experiment on the brief trip to the coastline of Mississippi. Ten minutes into the leg Cookie discovered two yellow school buses underneath his right wing, driving westbound on Interstate 10. At this hour of the morning they were more than likely filled with students heading out on a field trip. Cookie Cline wasted no time in taking full advantage of this golden opportunity to engage in some realistic training.

"Hey, skipper, I've got two targets of opportunity, three o'clock less than a mile," reported Lieutenant Cline to his flight leader. Duke had already seen the school buses and was way ahead of Cookie, as usual.

"Cookie, you and Comatose are cleared to attack using a pop-up roll ahead maneuver. The 'hard deck' is 400 feet AGL," said Duke. "I don't want you 'little pups' tying the world's record for low altitude flight today, or scaring a bunch of innocent kids."

As soon as the skipper's radio transmission was finished, Lieutenants Cline and Gross peeled away sharply from the formation then dove swiftly for the deck. Both of their hearts were pounding deeply inside their chest cavities as adrenaline now flowed freely from their adrenal glands. On 415 and 410's instrument panels, the altimeter needles spun down rapidly; first through 9000 feet then 6000 then 2000 as the jets were descending at a rate of 8000 feet per minute. The pair maintained visual contact on each other as they prepared to execute their simulated attack on the two targets of opportunity. Just above the tree tops paralleling the freeway, level at 200 feet and flying in excess of 540 knots, Cookie's attack run came first, from the northeast side of I-10. He could see the silhouette of the Gulf Coast Coliseum off in the distance as he popped up to 2800 feet to initiate his attack. Comatose Gross followed Cookie's lead, approaching from the southeast. The two warplanes were a mere half of a mile apart.

The skipper and Brain Child Bracken calmly monitored the action from 15,000 feet, still tracking out to Eagle Gulf. Duke did momentarily alter his base course slightly, by thirty degrees, to keep his attacking pilots in sight. Separated by about six seconds, the attacking section proceeded to simulate dive bombing the school busses from two opposing ingress angles. For some reason, in his head Cookie Cline heard the deep, rich chords of a base guitar playing the notes from the Chicano rock-and-roll song *Low Riders*. These words traversed through his brain as he rolled 415 inverted, pulled the nose back down hard through the horizon then settled his bomb sight onto the lead school bus: *Low riders don't drive to fast now.* The music was as clear as if the band *War* was somehow inside of Cookie's helmet, playing their signature song. Sixty-seven fourth graders, four teachers and two school bus drivers were totally unaware of the mock aerial assault being waged against them that morning as they traveled down the highway towards the Confederate Museum in Gulfport, Mississippi.

Just as Cookie streaked overhead the bus, level at 250 feet, a red Master Warning light illuminated on his instrument panel. Lieutenant Cline automatically pulled up and away from the ground to assess his jet's condition. In an instant he was climbing through 5000 feet with his eyes glued to Duke O' Grady's airplane about three miles up ahead. Almost immediately Cline realized that 415 had experienced a PC-2 hydraulics failure. Time critical memory items for a PC-2 emergency flashed into focus and the low rider song screeched to a quick halt. He reached for his Emergency Pocket Checklist as a backup to his fine-tuned memory.

"Skipper, 415 has a PC-2 problem," reported Lieutenant Cline on the squadron frequency. Without hesitation Duke O' Grady reversed his aircraft's direction, located Lieutenant Cline in 415 then joined on his right side in close parade formation. The skipper put his oxygen mask back on and cinched it up tight to his face. Comatose Gross quickly found Randy Bracken in 411, joined up on him then the two remained in the vicinity but well out of the way at 17,000 feet. As he passed underneath 415, Duke scrutinized the underside of the jet to ascertain if there were any fluid leaks that could pose a potential fire hazard. He also checked for signs of midair collision or 20mm 'frag' damage. He didn't see anything out of the ordinary. Once snuggled up next to Cookie, the skipper passed the flight lead to him by tapping his left index finger on the front of his orange helmet then pointing back at Cookie's Corsair. This meant that Duke was now following Cookie's lead.

"I didn't see any leaks or damage on your fuselage Cookie. I think you can make it back to home plate with no problem. I'll hang with you for the RTB. You will of course have to take a field arrested landing," said O' Grady. "Brain Child, you and Comatose head on out to 'Eagle G' and complete the remainder of the mission. We'll see y'all back on deck later for our flight debrief." The skipper didn't have to say another word; all members of the flight new what to do.

"Shit Cookie, I was hoping to whip your ass today in a dogfight, complained Brain Child Bracken. Now you're running home with your tail between your legs."

"Too bad so sad Child. I guess that's the breaks of naval air," responded Cookie as he and Duke descended to 7000 feet and turned to 250 degrees, the direct course for NAS New Orleans.

Duke started calling River Rattler maintenance to advise them of the inbound jets and the downing discrepancy on 415. Fifteen minutes later, back at the field, Cookie declared an in flight emergency with the NAS control tower then made an uneventful arrested landing. Moments before his field trap, the NAS fire trucks, clinic ambulance, and base CDO were all properly positioned on the taxiway adjacent to runway 32, to provide assistance during the emergency. Cookie decided to make his arrestment on runway 32, the short runway, so his squadron mates and other jets could still utilize the 8000 foot long runway. He didn't want to bottle up runway 04 by bleeding hydraulic fluid all over the arresting cable and concrete. Even faced with an emergency situation, Naval Aviators continue to maintain situational awareness. After his trap, Cookie shut down the A-7's engine, while bleeding a small amount of red hydraulic fluid into the center of runway 32. Driving a yellow GSE tractor, ADAN Earl Hamilton leisurely towed 415 back to the *River Rattler* flight line while munching down a *Hostess* cupcake. The attack jet would be fixed and ready for its next mission in less than two hours. SC Esposito would not allow anything less. He'd have maintenance control put their best man on the job.

Five minutes after going 'feet wet' again Brain Child Bracken and Comatose Gross entered the Whiskey-453 warning area looking forward to some 'turning and burning' ACM. But they immediately received a simulated Mayday call from what sounded like T-Ben's voice on 243.0, the UHF 'guard' frequency. Bracken of course, knew all about the SAREX because he had planned the entire exercise.

T-Ben and Pops were indeed standing on an uncharted coral reef in the middle of Breton Sound. Pops Petibone was holding a video camera and T-Ben Hebert was speaking semi-intelligently into his PRC-90. T-Ben had brought along a *Popeil* pocket fishing rod and a few lures with him. He had smuggled them in his helmet bag, so he was getting in a little salt water angling during the training exercise. Even though Redfish and Speckled Trout were in season he'd only gotten a couple of nibbles on his fish bait, an unrealistic looking shrimp. Hebert cast the line out once again then initiated some friendly conversation with his temporarily marooned squadron mate. He threw in a few Mayday calls on the PRC-90 for good measure, just to keep the exercise moving along. T-Ben didn't want to remain on the island much longer because he had to get back to the squadron and boil up ten sacks of live crawfish for the annual Christmas party scheduled for 1600 today.

"Hey Pops, did you ever buy that king size, antique bedroom set from the gay couple on Bourbon Street?" inquired T-Ben. You do realize you'll have to watch out for not just one but *two* sets of pecker tracks on the mattress!" Hebert made another cast into the wind and got a bite half way through the reel in. As T-Ben tugged hard on his mini-fishing rod to set the hook, Petibone focused the camera on the Cajun pilot standing about ten feet out into the surf, fighting his fish. He, of course, disregarded the sarcastic comments. Petibone routinely ignored T-Ben Hebert. Besides, Pops had turned the mattress over and had bought a vinyl cover for it. Anyway, it was the best $4,000 he'd spent this year.

"I just want to get this SAR shit over with as quickly as possible T-Ben," said Pops as he pulled his arms out of the sleeves of his flight suit. He then tied them tight around his waste. The sun felt good on his neck and arms but the wind cut right through his orange tee shirt.

"Well, it ain't over until the fat lady picks up the fork in the road Pops," replied Hebert bending down to unhook the two-pound Redfish he had snagged on his last cast. With his left hand T-Ben gently guided the exhausted fish back out into the salt water.

"Well thanks a lot for that beautiful sentiment. Who are you, *Yogi Heberra*?" chided Petibone at the comment. Pops laid the video camera down on his helmet bag to crack his knuckles.

It only took twenty minutes of UHF triangulation for Bracken and Gross to pin point the exact position of the role-playing downed aviator and his proverbial film making buddy Cecil B. DePetibone. Bracken dispatched Comatose to make a low 'fly by' for verification of the location while he communicated all the pertinent information to the USCG Dauphine to draw the practical exercise to a close. Pops, knowing the general direction form where the rescue Corsairs would be coming from, pointed his camera to the north and set the focus feature on infinity. Peering through the 'focus finder' lens, he initially had trouble spotting Comatose as he approached the coral reef. T-Ben couldn't find him either so he kept on fishing, not wanting to be too distracted from his endeavor. But, both aviators could hear the hollow whine of the jet as it got closer to their location on the island. They both knew from experience that the A-7 was approaching at an extremely low altitude at an exceptionally high rate of speed. Pops kept on filming the northern approach corridor. Suddenly, as if out of nowhere, 410 was on top of them at about 15 feet over the water and flying in excess of 550 knots airspeed. T-Ben Hebert chucked his fishing rod and dived into the water. Pops Petibone, still holding the video camera, ducked as if to avoid a collision with 410. The Corsair was that low, and the whole episode was caught on tape!

"Shit hot," yelled T-Ben as he bobbed up from the waves and pumped his clenched fist toward the sky, watching with an envious expression on his face as 410 streaked off into the distance. "Hey Pops, we gotta burn that tape," he said quickly changing gears. Petibone agreed. Luckily Pops had a cigarette lighter in his flight suit pocket and the two pilots burned the videotape in the sand before the Coast Guard HH-65A arrived to give them a lift back home.

Inside the medical clinic laboratory, a corpsman was about to finish up the last urinalysis exam for the day's scheduled flight physicals. He had already completed his microchemistry analysis of the twenty-seven urine specimens using the paper dipstick method, and had recorded the color change results onto the medical charts of all the patients. However on one of the samples he had been compelled to perform a more complete microscopic urinalysis using the lab's light microscope. A test tube containing the suspicious specimen was just now completing its ten minute centrifuge regimen, spinning down from the required 3000 revolutions per minute speed. A soft buzzer sounded on the silver and black centrifuge appliance, alerting the corpsman that the urine sample inside was now ready to be observed under a microscope.

When he examined the urine under the light microscope the laboratory technician promptly concluded that the specimen contained abnormally elevated concentrations of oxalate (hyperoxaluria) and uric acid (hyperuricosuria) crystals. The test also revealed a greatly reduced level of citrate in the fluid. Both of these conditions could be a precursor to the formation of kidney stones. Sitting down behind a typewriter the corpsman drafted a short memorandum to the flight surgeon, Dr. Ken Carrigan. The memo informed Carrigan that the patient, Commander Jack Mayhew, should be scheduled for a repeat urinalysis just to be on the safe side. The concerned corpsman wanted to check Mayhew for proper kidney functioning and for the possibility that calcium crystals were already present inside his kidney tract. Kidney stones were a permanently grounding condition in naval aviation, so the lab tech wanted to be absolutely certain before taking any further drastic steps and possibly ending a pilot's aviation career. After signing the memo, the corpsman placed it on top of a stack of papers inside Ken Carrigan's input basket. The flight surgeon was still out to lunch at the Officer's Club. Jack Mayhew was in the VA-204 parking lot still sitting inside his Toyota Camry. He was stalling his entrance to the squadron spaces.

CHAPTER 17

▼

THE AOM

Despite the fact that it was 1220 and the annual CAG Corrosion Inspection had rounded the clubhouse turn like Secretariat in the Belmont Stakes, Senior Chief John Esposito's grimace and growl had not diminished. He was still stalking around the squadron spaces after receiving a direct order from Lieutenant Commander Jim Stone, the Assistant Maintenance Officer (AMO), to closely monitor the inspection activities and report back periodically. Even though the ambient air temperature had peaked at 60 degrees Fahrenheit, typically warm weather for a Cajun December, Esposito had not removed his leather flight jacket all morning. This was the same cherished, although weathered, flight jacket that Vice Admiral Elmo Schnaubel had gratefully awarded to him over 24 years ago. Without hesitation in July of 1967, Esposito had fearlessly jumped sixty feet into the ocean water to save a fellow sailor who had been blown off the flight deck of the USS *Forrestal* (CV-59) by an F-4 Phantom's exhaust. The gallant episode occurred in the Gulf of Tonkin, eighty miles off the coastline of North Viet Nam, in the South China Sea as jets from Carrier Air Wing 17 were conducting air strikes deep into enemy territory. Ironically on July 29, 1967, a scant three weeks after his heroic deed, Esposito and the youthful sailor he had saved from the drink both held a fire hose for the better part of 14 hours as they fought the worst carrier fire in US Navy history. In less than thirty minutes, everybody onboard the *Forrestal* became a man that day while struggling against the carnage. As a result of Esposito not taking off the brown leather flight jacket, his shaved head was laden with sweat droplets that would slide down either side of his strong face, or the back of his bulging neckline. He was literally forced to dab his bald scalp and the nape of his neck often with a handkerchief just to keep somewhat dry. The delicate white cloth was rapidly becoming extra clammy in his left hand.

Rocky Stone had chosen Esposito as his emissary mainly because the senior chief personally knew the entire CVWR-20 inspection team, having served with them on numerous occasions during his near forty year career in this man's Navy. And, more importantly, every member of the CAG inspection team knew and respected Senior Chief Esposito. As enormously competitive individuals, naval aviators always search for any advantage they could utilize to win the contest they were currently engaged in. Needless to say, tensions were running a bit hot in the maintenance spaces because the Air Wing assessment team was not there to help; they were there to criticize and reprimand. The only slight smile that had even cracked Senior Chief Esposito's face that morning was when he spotted the 'Nuke the Gay Whales' sticker on the beat up bumper of his Ford F-150 pickup truck in the parking lot.

One unexpected wrinkle had come from the NAS control tower about thirty minutes ago. The tower supervisor had called down to VA-204 and every other aviation command onboard the air base, to ask each squadron to check for inadvertent emergency beacon activation. After receiving word of the call from maintenance control, Esposito had dispatched two plane captains to check the seat pans of each Corsair on deck, both on the flight line and inside the hangar bay. None of the VA-204 beacons had been accidentally actuated; the tower would have to search elsewhere for its guilty party. Inside the line shack Senior Chief Esposito, who finally found a moment to relax, was sitting at his desk quietly listening to an old Merle Haggard tune. Two massive arms were folded over his barrel chest, just above a protruding gut. Both forearm tattoos were visible. As a testament to this moment of relaxation, Esposito's left foot was resting, perched on the edge of an open desk drawer, keeping time to the music. The song, *I'm Proud to be an Okie from Muskogee* was playing softly on the stereo receiver in the background when two enlisted men pushed through the screen door and walked into his office. John Esposito immediately noticed that their dungarees were clean and freshly pressed, although some sweat stains had just begun to weep through the faded blue, denim fabric. The pair, both from the ordnance shop, had obviously been hard at work that morning loading bombs and IR testing heat-seeking, AIM-9M missile heads. Each man held a *River Rattler* ball cap firmly in his right hand as they stood at semi-attention in the line division chief's office. To the senior chief the younger of the two men looked like a frightened bunny, anxiously parked on the other side of his desk hoping to avoid fate. Alex Forrest, the Glenn Close character from the 1987 motion picture *Fatal Attraction*, could easily force him into a pot of scalding hot water thought Esposito as he grinned.

"Petty Officer Barr and Airman Williams reporting as ordered senior chief," stated Petty Officer Second Class Josh Barr. Barr, the taller of the two ordnance men, was from Dayton, Ohio and the son of Belgian immigrants. He looked like nothing more than a tall drink of water with freckles and red hair. This proverbial red-headed step child was routinely referred to as *Opie* by his squadron mates because of his uncanny resemblance to Ron Howard, the child actor who had played Sheriff Andy Taylor's son on *The Andy Griffith Show* in the 1960's. Barr's tone and demeanor in the line shack that afternoon were appropriately deferential. Anything less would have instigated the senior chief's ire and Josh Barr didn't want to do that *again*. Esposito scanned their faces with intensity. Sensing the powerful, penetrating stare both men braced up and stood at attention in front of the metal desk, eyes focused on the dull tan wall behind the senior chief. Airman Thaddeus Williams couldn't help but notice a framed black-and-white picture of Esposito shaking hands with President Richard Nixon, in front of what looked like *Air Force One*. In the photograph, Esposito was a young sailor all decked out in dress whites. A *dixie cup* hat sat cockeyed on his prematurely bald noggin, obviously blown askew by a stiff breeze on the tarmac that morning at Andrews Air Force Base.

Briefly, Esposito thought he saw an inkling of a smile break across Williams' chubby black face then suddenly recede. The senior chief wasn't sure if Williams' insolent facial expression was due to the photo of him shaking hands with the thirty-seventh President of the United States, or if it was because just last week someone had painted his office walls a bright pink. By now almost everyone in the squadron had heard of the infamous incident and how Esposito had fumed before assigning a three-man work detail to scrape off the pink color then re-paint the walls tan. Apparently some of his more playful and bold squadron mates wanted to make John Esposito's fortieth and last year in the Navy one of his most memorable. John Esposito had a pretty good idea who the primary perpetrator was but he didn't have conclusive evidence, yet. He would, however, patiently bide his time and eventually discover the culprit's identity. You don't spend four decades in the Navy without figuring out how to uncover those persistent little secrets that proliferate during a naval career. Suitable vengeance would be his to enjoy in due time. The senior chief's eyes burned and his jaw muscles clenched momentarily at the hint of an insult, but he resisted lashing out at Airman Williams.

Casually flipping a set of keys to Petty Officer Barr to disrupt his now blank stare, Esposito explained that he wanted the two of them to drive over to the picnic grounds with the five crawfish pots, and other related party gear and food items that were sitting in the bed of his pickup truck. He ordered the sailors to prepare the picnic area for the annual 'all hands' *River Rattler* Christmas bash that would begin promptly at 1600. The senior chief instructed them to police up any trash, tap the keg of *Budweiser* beer, arrange the picnic tables, ice down the cold drinks, and set up the crawfish paraphernalia.

"Lieutenant Hebert should be on deck in about thirty minutes. He'll be picking up ten sacks of live *mudbugs* at Salvo's Seafood and doing the boiling for us this year. I want everything to be all set so he can start cooking right away. People should begin to show up just after 1600, so make sure we're ready to receive our families and honored guests," snorted Esposito. "Now about face your little butts on out of my office and make it happen!" The two enlisted men verbalized a fervent 'aye aye' then did a crisp about face maneuver to beat feet out of the line shack.

"And bring that *crazy Salvadoran* with you too," barked Esposito as the two men slipped from his office relatively unscathed this time. The senior chief immediately resumed a tranquil posture behind his desk as Hank Williams began belting out the words *Jambalaya, crawfish pie, filet gumbo* on the stereo receiver. Esposito calmly tapped a #2 pencil on his desktop, trying to enjoy the rhythm of the music. He knew his peace would only last a few more precious moments before another fire would flare up needing his special brand of water to put it out.

Two minutes later, as the Cajun tune was winding down to its conclusion, the flimsy screen door of the line shack creaked open again. This time it was Vladimir Gonzales, the half Russian, half Salvadoran airframes mechanic who had transferred into VA-204 in June of 1991. Unlike Barr and Williams, Gonzales was wearing a soiled pair of pants. Hydraulic fluid and oil stains were smeared all over the right pant leg of his blue dungarees. Grease blemishes even tarnished his otherwise highly polished work boots. Looking like a nervous civilian traveling around Nazi Germany during WW II, Gonzales approached the senior chief's desk holding some papers in his clean, outstretched right hand.

"See senior chief, I am a naturalized American citizen. I have been for five years now." His chest puffed up, Gonzales was visibly proud as he held out the papers for Esposito to peruse. The senior chief, of course, was fully aware that Gonzales had earned American citizenship. He just liked to pull his chain a little by referring to him as that *crazy Salvadoran.* Gonzales was a good man, a dedicated worker and the senior chief knew it. But everybody needs to be torqued up from time to time; it's good for the circulation thought Esposito.

"What the hell is that on your pants buster?" bristled Esposito deftly changing the subject. The senior chief unexpectedly rose out of his chair to appear even more menacing then reached over with his massive bear claw of a hand and silenced the country music with a swift twist of the volume knob.

"I've been working on 415's PC-2 failure senior chief. I must have gotten some hydraulic fluid on them," was the hasty response from Petty Officer Third Class Gonzales.

"Well go change into some fresh dungarees and get on over to the picnic grounds to help set up for the Christmas party," grumbled Esposito. "By the way, great job on 415. Way to hustle young man. Now get out of my office and make it happen." Esposito's neck muscles and carotid artery bulged, and his eyes bugged out a bit as he spoke. Even though the air conditioner was working just fine in the line shack, Esposito patted his scalp once more with the damp handkerchief. Gonzales stuffed the short stack of naturalization papers in his back pocket then headed for the clean pair of blue denims hanging inside his locker.

Climbing up the officer's staircase, Lieutenant Ackerman caught up to Commander Mayhew just as Juice was about to open the door to enter the squadron admin spaces located above the hangar bay floor. Jack Mayhew, the MO, had decided to avoid his office in the maintenance spaces for now even though he knew the CAG Corrosion Inspection was probably winding down to a successful conclusion. His AMO, Lieutenant Commander Rocky Stone, could manage without him for a few more minutes. Mayhew was moving lethargically because he was not in a hurry to enter the squadron knowing the mental anguish he would undoubtedly suffer once the news of his failed flight physical became public knowledge amongst his colleagues. Coming up from the rear, an energetic Brad Ackerman was still wearing his golfing togs and a pair of untied *Reebok* running shoes. Untied sneakers were the latest fashion rage with all the *valley girls* and *valley dudes* in Southern California, and as a member of the motion picture industry in Hollywood Teen Angel liked to keep up with the latest trends. He also enjoyed the comic effect that his phony bologna, Hollywood persona had on his conservative buddies in VA-204. Like Petty Officer Gonzales, Brad was headed for his locker in the cubbyhole adjacent to the officer's head. There he would shower up then slip into his khaki leisure suit for the remainder of this momentous first day of Drill Weekend for December 1991.

Juice stood on a metal walkway in between the door and the top step of the staircase. Reaching for the doorknob but hearing the commotion to his rear,

Commander Mayhew turned to make eye contact with Teen Angel slowly gaining on him from behind. Ackerman was climbing the stairs methodically, from memory, using his peripheral vision because he was pompously re-counting the 120 bucks he had just won from Admiral Thompson and CAG Sullivan in the golf match. Holding the wad of cash in his left hand, Brad tapped his right index finger lightly on the end of his tongue to moisten the tip then he arrogantly fingered each piece of currency as if to savor every bill.

"So nice of you to make an appearance at Drill Weekend Lieutenant Ackerman," scolded Mayhew. I guess you are here to get a little *face time* with the skipper now, huh Teen Angel?" From the tenor of his voice, Ackerman assessed fairly quickly that Juice Mayhew was in one of his fowler moods and should be actively avoided. But, a fearless Teen Angel decided to do some good-natured prying anyway.

"Hey Juice. Why the long face? Did your wife ask you to buy her some tampons at the commissary again?"

"Cute, very cute skin dick," was Juice's sarcastic reply. But, at the same time, Jack had a little tidbit of information up his sleeve that he assumed would demoralize Mister Brad Ackerman from Hollywood, California, at least temporarily.

"Oh by the way, you need to report to Chief Martin ASAP pal," said Mayhew in a sardonic tone. "I saw the list last night," he added with pleasure.

"Oh no, not another piss test," exclaimed Teen Angel in mock disbelief. Displaying artificial disgust, Brad crammed the roll of bills deep into his front left pocket. He knew he had nothing to worry about.

"Yep, you have been chosen once more to participate in the *random* drug screening. Chief Martin is taking samples in the officer's head and I'm sure he'll be delighted to see you again. Your little bunk buddy Rocky got tabbed as well," informed Jack with a somewhat contented grin on his face; his own dilemma momentarily compartmentalized on the back burner. The two aviators were now facing each other on the dimly lit walkway, a few feet from the door. Ackerman towered over Juice who was quite a bit shorter than Brad.

Beginning in 1980 under the Jimmy Carter Administration, the Department of Defense started a quarterly drug screening program in which each command in the military service would have to *arbitrarily* select some of its people to contribute a urine sample for a drug check. Of course, the *no tolerance* piss test was searching to detect the presence of illegal, controlled substances in DOD personnel. By far the most commonly used method to ensure the so-called indiscriminate nature of the selection process was to designate a number between zero and nine then compare that to either the first or last digit of the social security numbers of each member of the command. A matching numeral meant you had to make a little side trip to the head and surrender some urine in a bottle. In his entire naval career, Teen Angel had been randomly selected for the drug screening almost every quarter. Ackerman's Advanced Training Command skipper had once told him 'Brad you *look like* a drug user because you part your hair down the center. That's why you are chosen so frequently.' Ackerman had learned early on that the alleged arbitrary aspect of the drug screening program was not so capricious. Even though this treatment smacked of discrimination, over the years it had become a running gag to Teen Angel. In his whole life Brad Ackerman had never taken any drugs, not even an aspirin.

Of course Jim Stone spent a good deal of time running around with his *center-parted* hair on fire and his ass catching. So he must look like a drug user too, reasoned Brad. Since their arrival at VA-204, both Ackerman and Stone believed that the squadron Executive Officer, Commander Slug Levitan, had routinely fingered them for drug screening. After all, they both part their hair down the middle and the XO's 15 year old son began parting his the same way a week after meeting Teen Angel and Rocky at a squadron 'all hands' function last year. Suffice it to say that Commander Levitan was not happy with them due to the influence they had exerted over his normally straight-laced, teenage son.

"Nice shoes," remarked Juice as he and Teen Angel walked through the doorway into the admin spaces. "Did you buy those sneakers in South Central LA?" Commander Mayhew looked at the back of Brad's head as the young lieutenant strolled toward the officer's locker room for a well-deserved shower. As he watched his squadron mate move off down the hallway, Juice couldn't help but wonder about Teen Angel.

At 1305, thirty of the forty-five cushy, airline style seats in the *River Rattler* Ready Room were now occupied by VA-204 pilots anxiously awaiting the start of the AOM (All Officers Meeting). The aviators traded insults, wisecracks, and good-natured taunts back and forth across a room filled with various mementos depicting VA-204's rich tradition as a Navy attack squadron. About one third of the men wore green Nomex flight suits, while the other two thirds had found time to put on their polyester blend khaki uniforms. John O' Grady, in freshly ironed khakis, was already squished down in his leather chair sitting comfy and low, sipping hot coffee. A cloth sign reading 'CO' in stenciled black letters on an orange background adorned the top rear of the chair. Everyone was waiting for the Operations Officer, Commander Steve Fitzgerald, to begin the customary and somewhat monotonous AOM activities before the first training lecture could commence. These training lectures were usually an open invitation to barbs from the audience and always proved to be quite entertaining as well as informative. The seat on Duke O' Grady's right side, reserved for the Executive Officer, was of course empty. Commander Levitan, the XO, was flying for FedEx in Japan and would not return to New Orleans until the next Drill Weekend in January. He wasn't missed!

"What time does the 1300 AOM start?" moaned Lieutenant Chuck "Rifle Boy" Hayward as he stood behind a video camera mounted on top of a tripod in a secluded corner. As the ridiculing repartee registered with the crowd, nervous laughter rippled across the room like *the wave* at a New York Mets double-header. As the squadron's Aviation Safety Officer, Lieutenant Hayward's job at all AOM's was to tape the training lectures for posterity. As he spoke Rifle Boy was busy focusing the camera lens on the lectern at the front of the Ready Room. His eyes never lifted from the focus-finder window on the video camera's right side even though he knew the acerbic effect his comment would have on the group of men.

Holding a stack of rumpled papers in is left hand, to give off the appearance of self-importance and to hopefully deflect any criticism over his late arrival, Commander Fitzgerald slipped into the Ready Room through the side door. He quickly freshened his mug of lukewarm, decaffeinated coffee with a dose of hot liquid from the glass pot sitting on top of the *Bunn* coffeemaker. Six minutes behind schedule, Klutz Fitzgerald walked up to the lectern at the front of the room to begin the AOM. After tossing the stack of papers down onto the podium and then briefly adjusting his inexpensive reading glasses, Klutz threw a fleeting glance at the skipper as if to apologize for his tardiness. As usual, Duke was in a forgiving mood. The roomful of officers grew subdued and quiet, at least for the moment.

"Hey Cookie, can you go find Rocky for me, he's late," requested Klutz in a shallow voice.

"I'll get right on that sir," said Lieutenant Cline. Cookie didn't budge he merely changed positions and deepened his posture in the leather seat. You could sense the total amusement by the roomful of aviators at the teasingly disrespectful demeanor.

Fitzgerald's first announcement concerned the shipment of brown aviator shoes from the *Bates Company* that had just arrived yesterday afternoon. Forty-four boxes of brown Corfam shoes were conspicuously lined up along the back wall of the Ready Room waiting for Lieutenant T-Ben Hebert to hand them out. He would do so tomorrow morning beginning at 0700 advised Klutz. Several heads bobbed up and down at that announcement, as if to confer their fervent approval. T-Ben had ordered the shoes for all officers and chiefs after last month's drill weekend when the CNO had decided to allow aviators the privilege of wearing brown shoes again after a 20 year hiatus. Like their wings of gold, bronze-colored footwear was another distinction separating the *brown shoe Navy* (plane drivers) from the *black shoe Navy* (boat drivers). It was a simple matter of pride among naval aviators that was finally being reinstated after a far too long interruption.

Next, after first advising that Lieutenant Commander Stone would deliver the formal report on this year's CAG Corrosion Inspection just before the AOM was adjourned, Commander Fitzgerald spent about fifteen minutes discussing the squadron's current state of operational readiness, qualification by agonizing qualification. He also delved into the plans his Ops Department had already sketched for the first three Drill Weekends of 1992; preparations that included a two-week ACM detachment to NAS Key West, Florida in the latter part of February.

"Come on, Klutz, we need it faster and funnier!" teased Lieutenant Theodore *Plato* Themopolis in a perfect deadpan voice from the cheap seats at the back of the Ready Room. The officers burst out in laughter as the remark cut deep into the serious tone set by Fitzgerald. Duke grinned visibly then hunkered down further in his chair to bite his right thumbnail.

As the frivolity subsided, Klutz then went around the room to each Department Head, yielding the floor for five minutes. As was normal in an AOM he was allowing them time to discuss topics pertinent to their jurisdiction within the squadron. Even though he knew that Rocky Stone would debrief the corrosion inspection results, Klutz focused his eyes on Juice Mayhew to give him an opportunity to speak to the All Officers Meeting as the squadron's Maintenance Officer. Fitzgerald was already fully aware of Mayhew's flight physical results but decided this was not an appropriate venue to discuss the delicate situation.

"You got anything Juice?" asked Fitzgerald, not realizing he had just unwittingly set Jack up to be the brunt of a joke.

"He *did* have something but he got *rid* of it!" yelled out Cookie Cline, heckling as usual from the middle of a crowded Ready Room. "Thank God for Procaine Penicillin!" continued Cookie. Mayhew just shook his head and tried to hide a blushing red face from his squadron mates. The room swelled with laughter.

Finally, Commander Fitzgerald offered the stage to the skipper for his comments. Duke O' Grady deposited a nearly empty coffee cup into the receptacle on his chair's armrest. Slowly he rose out of his comfortable seat then clumsily maneuvered himself behind the dais to address his officers. Yes, Duke was atypically disheveled for a high-ranking military officer, but his men were well aware of what he could do once his butt was strapped into 42,000 pounds of Corsair. Inside the cockpit Commander O' Grady was simply perfection and his fellow aviators would follow his lead anywhere. Before he could begin to speak, Rifle Boy Hayward looked up from the *Samsung* video camera and yelled out a standard question for the skipper of VA-204. It was an inquiry that Duke always seemed to have a suitable response to, no matter how many times he was asked the same question over and over again.

"Hey skipper, why do women control the world?" The room bloated with anticipation the second Hayward stopped speaking. Everyone seemed to unconsciously lean in towards Duke O' Grady to hear his astute answer. The scene was similar to that TV commercial when the guy in the restaurant says, 'My broker is EF Hutton and EF Hutton says.'

"Because they got half the money and all the pussy!" replied Duke without hesitation and without changing his semi-serious facial expression behind the podium. Immediately the audience howled its approval. Some of the officers even exchanged high fives in their seats. The uproar and the fact that he had not heard Duke's witty retort caused Shroud Morley to move his jaw around in an unsuccessful attempt to clear the muffling pressure rapidly building up inside of his inner ears. His ear drums were saturated by the 100% oxygen he had apparently hyperventilated throughout his body during the distressing experience, endured just a short while ago in the break at the end of his PMCF test hop. This was, of course, a normal condition for all military aviators after breathing pure oxygen during long flights but it usually manifested itself the next morning around 3AM as they lay comfortably in bed. Perhaps the rather traumatic flame out and relight ordeal had caused Commander Morley to breath extra heavy amounts of undiluted oxygen into his system. Suddenly, after a couple of val salva maneuvers, his ears cleared and normal hearing returned. As the pandemonium generated by John O'Grady's clever comment dwindled, all eyes in the room refocused on Duke at the front of the Ready Room by the chalkboard.

Leaning over the top of the podium, as if to prop up his exhausted body, the skipper proceeded to tell the humorous story of LT junior grade Bill Pack. Duke used an appropriate amount of drama and fanfare as he recalled Bill Pack's harrowing first experience with Teen Angel at the urinal in the officer's bathroom early Friday morning. He spoke of how the new squadron Aviation Intelligence Officer (AI) had pissed on himself yesterday after spending less than 20 seconds in the enchanting company of Lieutenant Brad Ackerman.

"Those of you that know Mister Ackerman, can you really blame LTJG Pack for that initial reaction?" asked the skipper taking a quick pot shot at Brad to the delight of his listeners. Subdued chuckles proliferated throughout the room as the story unfolded, but Bill Pack wasn't savvy enough to even be embarrassed by the skipper's rather accurate and detailed account of his dousing at the urinal. Then and there Duke decided that the new AI's tactical call sign would be *Piddle*. Piddle Pack in honor of the clear plastic receptacles that aviators used to piss in during long missions.

"Lets all say Hello to LTJG Pack," instructed the skipper to the roomful of aviators. This was of course a customary, welcoming gesture extended to anybody new to the squadron. It was a Naval Aviation tradition to slightly embarrass new squadron members and even distinguished guests with some simple verbal abuse; if only to make them feel they are being treated no better or no worse than anybody else.

"Hello ass hole!" was the bellowing salutation to the junior officer. Every man in the Ready Room joined in loud and clear then waited for the second part of the welcome routine.

"Lets all say Hello to the ass hole," said the skipper.

"Hello 'Piddle' Pack!" The quasi-hazing was fulfilled at least for the moment. More would undoubtedly follow but, for now, LTJG William Pack had just become an accepted member of the VA-204 *River Rattler* family. The two pilots sitting next to him slapped Bill Pack vigorously on the back to convey their approval. Duke then made a fleeting remark about having one more important announcement but that it would have to wait until 1500 when the scheduled training lectures were completed. Removing himself from behind the podium the skipper politely turned the proceedings back over to Commander Fitzgerald, the official emcee of the All Officers Meeting. It was time for the formal training lectures to begin. Klutz instinctively eyeballed Teen Angel and Cookie as he nervously struggled at the podium to find his sheet of paper that listed the sequence of events for the training. Usually the epitome of neatness, Klutz appeared fairly uncomfortable with his shirttail almost completely pulled out and bulging from his khaki pants. From underneath a stack of papers Fitzgerald at last located his lecture line-up sheet.

CHAPTER 18

▼

DUST OFF YOUR SEA BAGS GENTS

Since the annual CAG Corrosion Inspection was finally over, and VA-204 had come through the ordeal yet again with flying colors, Senior Chief John Esposito had hitched a ride to the NAS picnic grounds with his counterpart from CVWR-20. Roland Mays, the CAG-20 maintenance chief, had forgotten a book in his room at the BEQ and was on his way to retrieve it before the C-9 flight back to Jacksonville, Florida. Senior Chief Mays, an A-6 electronics technician by trade, was re-reading *Flight of the Intruder* an old Stephen Coonts novel. In his haste to get over to the chow hall bright and early this morning, he had inadvertently left it on the night stand when he checked out at 0530. Mays had owned Coonts' action-thriller since its first publication in 1986 and didn't want to lose it even though this worn paperback version had been passed around for over five years amongst the chief petty officers at NAS Cecil Field. Apparently chief petty officers were lethargic readers.

The two 'old salts' in the automobile each drank a can of *Pepsi-Light* as they rode the short mile and a half distance to the picnic grounds. John Esposito anxiously flipped the car's air conditioner to the 'max cold' position, roughly popped the top on his soda can then sucked a healthy swig of the cool liquid down his gullet. He was still wearing his warm leather flight jacket, which caused a raised eyebrow to appear on Roland Mays' face as he drove the official Navy vehicle down Russell Avenue. After taking in another robust mouthful, Esposito shifted slightly in his seat then tugged at the crotch of his khaki pants attempting to give the family jewels some extra breathing room down there. Neither man felt particularly compelled to speak so the ride was quiet except for the noise of super-cooled air gushing out of the air conditioner vents.

Senior Chief Esposito had about thirty minutes to monitor the progress of the ongoing preparation activities at the picnic grounds before he had to be back in the Ready Room for Lieutenant Commander Stone's formal inspection debriefing. Within the isolated confines of the automobile, both senior chiefs could finally drop their guard and relax as they neared the end of another successful Navy day.

As the white sedan pulled into a gravel parking lot between the BEQ and the picnic area, Esposito could plainly see that his men had been very busy indeed preparing for the annual 'all hands' Christmas party. Wood and aluminum picnic tables had been scrubbed spotless, food and beverage supplies were appropriately arranged and the grass had been policed of all trash and debris. And Vladimir Gonzales, that *crazy Salvadoran*, had just finished setting up the last of five extra-large crawfish pots within the shade of a huge oak tree in a secluded corner of the picnic grounds. Five sets of propane tanks, black rubber hoses, burners and support apparatus were aligned three feet from the base of the tree all in a perfect row. Five wooden, stirring paddles were leaning up against each pot as if awaiting the culinary artist's imminent arrival. Fallen leaves surrounded the oak tree giving the setting a warm, rustic look as Petty Officer Gonzales was busy filling the pots with water. He was conveniently using a borrowed hose attached to a rusty faucet, protruding from the right side of the BEQ building. Gonzales filled each silver-colored tub with fresh water to exactly nine inches below the brim. This water level would effectively accommodate for the increase in total volume when baskets of live, medium-sized crawfish were inserted to begin the thirty-minute boiling process.

As soon as Roland Mays had dropped Senior Chief Esposito off, T-Ben Hebert casually slid his late-model pickup truck to a halt on the thinning grass next to the five boiling pots. In the bed of his truck lay ten sacks of live, farm-raised crawfish, purchased just fifteen minutes ago at Salvos Seafood Restaurant. They were farm-raised because the official start of Louisiana crawfish season in the Atchafalaya Basin was still a few months off. A strong fish odor permeated deep into your nostrils when you came within twenty feet of the sacks. If you looked close enough you could see hundreds of sooty, black tentacles and red, spiny claws intertwined as each live crustacean struggled in vain to find some private space inside the mesh sacks. Positioned underneath the back window of the Chevy truck were five large glass jars of *Zatarains Crab Boil*, eleven bags of small red potatoes, seventy-five pounds of Cajun sausage, three hundred cobs of corn, and ample amounts of garlic cloves and celery sticks.

Senior Chief Esposito greeted Lieutenant Hebert with a crisp salute as he exited the driver's side of his Dodge *Dakota* and slammed the green door shut. The dented door closed with an audible screech, the only remaining evidence of an accident T-Ben's wife had been involved in seven months ago in the Algiers section of New Orleans' West Bank. T-Ben's wife had gotten *T-Boned* on General De Gaulle Drive, and Glen Hebert hadn't gotten around to fixing the door; he would never get around to it. After briefly exchanging the rudimentary pleasantries with Lieutenant Hebert, Esposito quickly summoned his three-man work detail to assist with unloading of the food items. Even the senior chief helped out by lugging three extra-heavy bags of live, squirming crawfish over to the boiling pots. For all but a precious few, this would be their final destination.

When they finished unloading Hebert's Dodge *Dakota* truck and sorting the food items, T-Ben immediately turned the stereo on inside the cab of his pickup then opened both doors to expose the six inch *Bose* speakers hidden inside the door panels. Quite suddenly the quiet serenity of the picnic grounds was infiltrated by the blaring sound of T-Ben's 80 watt, *Marantz* car stereo. *Barracuda* was playing on the classic rock station and T-Ben was a huge fan of Ann and Nancy Wilson. He cranked the volume way up and strummed his *air guitar* for fifteen seconds as the crescendo guitar solo played to end the hard rock song. With a plastic *Winston* lighter in his right hand, the same butane device he had happily discovered washed up onto the beach this morning during the search and rescue exercise, T-Ben began to light the propane fires under the five crawfish pots. After opening the valve on each bulbous propane tank, he allowed the highly flammable gas to flow for about four seconds before introducing a flame into the metal burner receptacle. With a discernable whoosh, the five fires roared to life under the pots one by one. It would take about thirty minutes to bring each pot containing approximately 8 gallons of water to a proper boiling temperature before the cooking process could commence. When all the flames were going strong, Hebert dumped a half jar of the *Zatarain's Crab Boil* mixture into the water. He then gave each pot a vigorous stirring with one of the wooden paddles.

Soon Lieutenant Hebert would cook the crawfish in the same manner that his old grand pappy had taught him some twenty years ago on the Black Bayou in Cocodrie, Louisiana. To keep Cajun tradition alive, T-Ben would first select out one live crawfish from each sack. He would then save that crawfish's life by tossing the little guy into the shallow creek that ran directly behind the edge of the picnic grounds. This blatant act of superstition, inculcated into him by his Acadian grandpa, was meant to keep the crawfish population swelled and healthy for the next harvest. Next, T-Ben would slice open each sack using his surgical steel *Gerber* knife. Hebert would hear that familiar, soft squealing sound that each crawfish emits as they are dumped live into the vat of boiling water. The whining noise would cease as the tiny red bodies sank beneath the 250 degree, spicy bubbling water. All four men smiled simultaneously as Esposito finished delivering his final praise of their efforts. The senior chief then walked back to the squadron building so that he could attend the debriefing of the corrosion inspection. The leather flight jacket was slung over his right shoulder as he strolled off into the distance. He was still sweating.

Back in the *River Rattler* Ready Room, next up in the program that afternoon was Lieutenant Brad Ackerman. As Duke O' Grady eased back down into his comfy chair, and as Rocky Stone finally entered the room with formal inspection results in his hand, Klutz Fitzgerald called on Brad to take center stage at the AOM. Rocky planted his butt in the seat next to Commander Mayhew and quickly handed the inspection results paperwork over to Jack for his reading pleasure. Juice ignored the papers at first trying to appear ever calm, cool and collected. Rocky winked provocatively at Juice as if he knew something that he shouldn't causing an uneasy quiver to methodically course through Mayhew's body. Juice scratched his right temple region as he pondered the meaning of Rocky's potentially incendiary wink.

Teen Angel was now at the podium with his back to the crowd writing a few words down on the chalkboard. He purposely made a screeching sound with the tip of the new piece of chalk to ensure that all eyes and ears were focused on him. Chalk dust floated down to the floor as he rudely etched the board surface at a 45 degree angle. The miniscule white particles glimmered during their cascading effect. Brad had been scheduled last month to give a short lecture entitled 'Life Stress Points' which would feature tips on how Naval Aviators could more effectively recognize and manage stress in their daily lives. In the early 1990's, stress management had become a popular self-help industry for millions of working professionals, thanks to celebrities like Dr. Laura Schlessinger and Oprah Winfrey who frequently featured the topic on their radio and television broadcasts.

Out in California, Ackerman had consulted with Dr. Frank Dully, one of the Navy's more notorious flight surgeons, regarding the structure and mechanics of this lesson. The colorful Dr. Dully just happened to live in Encino, a bustling suburb of Los Angeles, having settled there shortly after his retirement from the Navy in 1988. The sandbagging flight surgeon, who was a frequent golf partner of Brad's at the Riviera Country Club, was more than happy to assist Teen Angel. It was the least he could do to repay Teen Angel for all the money they had won together during $10 Nassau golf betting on the Riviera course. With Dully's help, Ackerman finished preparing the text of his lecture just last weekend. He had even studied the script on the three hour flight from Los Angeles International Airport to New Orleans Thursday afternoon. Teen Angel was fully prepared not only to deliver the lecture but to expertly deflect any smart ass remarks thrown at him by his beloved squadron mates.

"So how was your little liaison with that rather rotund woman last night in the BOQ," whispered Cookie Cline stretching his neck around the side of Rocky's chair so that his face was a mere three inches from his buddy's right shoulder. Juice Mayhew maneuvered his head position slightly to hear the answer, trying not to be too obvious. Cookie hadn't gotten a real clear response to this same question at the squadron officer's party last evening at Randy Bracken's house. And like most real men, he wanted to know all the lurid details of any sexual encounter to satiate his own need for lust, even if Rocky's selection of woman last evening wasn't the queen of the hop.

"I can't believe she drank the poison!" answered Rocky in a breathy voice so that only Cookie could hear his extremely personal and somewhat demeaning answer. His tenor conveyed the blatant pride of sexual conquest that only men can truly appreciate.

"You are so nasty Rocky," replied Cline in an envious tone but attempting to register a modicum of disgust with his good friend, if only for appearance sake. Juice Mayhew was a bit disappointed at not being able to hear the whispered response.

As Brad finished jotting down notes on the chalkboard, he turned to confront his audience. A slow developing smirk came to his tanned, boyish face as he made eye contact with first Rocky Stone then Cookie Cline. Rifle Boy Hayward rechecked his settings on the video camera then steadied the tripod to record the ensuing training session. Teen Angel cleared his throat and began to speak with the type of confidence his squadron mates had come to expect from him. But he was rudely interrupted almost immediately.

"Nice shoes you were wearing after your golf match this morning Teen Angel. Did you buy them from the *hood* in South Central?" teased Commander Randy Bracken from the front row.

"Those shoes cost more than your pick-up truck Brain Child!" cracked Ackerman. The audience stirred with satisfaction at Teen Angel's disparaging retort.

"Isn't it about time to visit your barber and get those long locks coiffed," said Pops Petibone from the back row to chime in with his own brand of mock ridicule as well.

"I don't have a barber. I have a professional hair stylist from the motion picture industry do my hair bub!" responded Brad. "Now can we please get this lecture started? I have a plane to catch tomorrow afternoon."

"Why are *you* giving a lecture?" shouted Rifle Boy from behind the video camera. "In what area do *you* possess expertise?"

"Look fellas, I don't know *anything* and I can prove it!" Brad raised both hands and displayed open palms to his colleagues as if to quell their clamor. "Now, if y'all will just settle down a bit, I will get on with this here training lecture." With that said, Teen Angel began his talk on stress. The discussion covered a variety of topics related to stress recognition and successful management of anxiety. He proceeded just as he had rehearsed.

Nearing the end of his twenty minute speech, Teen Angel produced a large chart of normal and abnormal life experiences; angst producing events that routinely take place in everyone's life sooner or later. The chart had been drawn on a piece of white butcher block paper with black, blue and red felt tipped *Sharpie* pens, the red color used for accentuation purposes. Brad attached it to a not so sturdy metal stand situated on the right side of the podium. The chart depicted several different life episodes on the left side and the various 'stress point' values associated with those occurrences on the right side. The theory was that if you could locate events that had recently occurred in your personal life and add up the points, a total value of 100 or more meant you might be a good candidate to make a poor decision due to the weight of stress in your life. For instance, a divorce was worth 60 stress points, moving to a new duty station added 40 more to your total, while financial difficulties meant an additional 30.

Taking Dr. Dully's advice to heart, Lieutenant Ackerman boldly challenged his squadron mates to be honest and correctly evaluate their current stress condition. He reiterated that although professional aviators are good at *compartmentalization* (successfully putting stress aside while performing admirably in their chosen profession), 100 points or higher on the total stress points scale meant you had an elevated probability of experiencing an anxiety related event or incident in your professional occupation.

"Many of us are getting up there in years," said Brad. He made a conciliatory glance at Duke O' Grady before delivering his next line. "Sorry skipper, I meant no offense, but we're no longer bulletproof. All of us have transitioned beyond the stage of being *young and dumb and full of cum*, except of course for you Cookie," teased Ackerman. Cookie Cline simply smiled in admiration at being mentioned so prominently in a training lecture given by his buddy Brad. He didn't realize at first that Teen Angel was using him as the butt of a joke.

"And remember, the number one point-getter is death of a spouse. It's worth a grand total of 100 points right off the bat," advised Teen Angel.

"Uh, that's *without* life insurance!" chimed in Rocky without conveying any facial expression. The room erupted yet again with an appreciative laughter. Milwaukee Brewers announcer Bob Eucker couldn't have delivered the deadpan line any better. Lieutenant Ackerman decided to end his lecture on that note. Besides the punch line given so appropriately by Lieutenant Commander Stone, he could sense that the squadron's chief petty officers were gathered just outside the doorway, anxious to take a seat for the corrosion inspection debriefing.

As Brad turned the AOM proceedings back over to Klutz Fitzgerald, twelve chiefs clustered in from the hallway taking their seats as Duke O'Grady silently got up and left the *Ready Room*. Senior Chief Esposito stood at the rear of the room next to Rifle Boy Hayward and the video camera. His back was leaning up against the bulkhead next to a picture of a Corsair shooting a Sidewinder missile at a smudge pot on NAS Fallon Nevada's live-fire range. Esposito was still holding the leather flight jacket in his left hand. After about seven minutes of unnecessary formalities by Commander Fitzgerald, Rocky Stone finally walked up to the podium with his stack of corrosion inspection papers documenting this year's results. He would only speak for an uncomfortable eight minutes before being gratefully interrupted by the skipper's reappearance in the *Ready Room*.

"Attention on deck," belted out O' Grady as he thrust himself into the room from the side doorway, flanked by CAG Sullivan and Admiral Thompson. A civilian wearing a stylishly blue *Armani* suit and wingtips lagged behind the three officers. Two other civilians in blue blazers remained in the vicinity of the doorway. Everyone in the *Ready Room* leaped out of his chair and assumed a rigid posture while the four men entered. Almost immediately, several of the VA-204 aviators recognized H. Lawrence Andrews III, the Secretary of the Navy, as the civilian in the blue three-piece suit. Rather quickly the officers and chiefs standing at attention began to discern that something big must be in the offing. Duke made a lazy gesture with his hand to shoo Lieutenant Commander Stone back to his seat then stood behind the podium to address his officers. Rocky was only too happy to acquiesce to the skipper's request to vacate the podium and did so without hesitation. He tripped slightly over Bracken's big feet in the process.

"Take your seats gents," ordered Duke O' Grady with his more serious sounding voice. After a moment or two, everyone was adequately situated and the room grew suddenly calm.

"Men, the Secretary of the Navy would like to address you," blurted out Duke in his normal blunt style. "Mister Secretary," said the skipper as he departed the podium to make room for Hank Andrews. Commander O' Grady touched shoulders with Andrews as he wedged his way in between CAG Sullivan and Admiral Thompson. Duke pressed back a little too hard and got chalk all over the back of his neatly pressed khaki shirt. The three officers stood behind Andrews just in front of the left-side of the chalkboard; each with his hands hung low in the *fig leaf* position.

Behind the podium Hank Andrews felt the sting of forty or so blank stares glaring at him. He singled out one familiar face by making fleeting eye contact with Lieutenant Brad Ackerman. Andrews exchanged a cordial smile with Teen Angel, who basically was responsible for him winning $120 bucks on the golf course that very morning, not to mention giving him some expert golf swing advice along the way to improve his game. Tension was now so thick in the room you could cut it with a *Ghinsu* steak knife. As usual, Rocky Stone was the first to break through the political ice. Rocky noticed that Andrews was wearing his black *beltway wingtips*, and disgustedly surmised that the *Armani* suit he was sporting probably cost a cool 2000 bucks. Lieutenant Commander Stone simply couldn't resist this once in a lifetime opportunity for Naval Aviation infamy. Seizing upon the moment, Rocky quickly rose from his chair and gestured with his right hand as he surveyed the august audience in the Ready Room.

"Gentlemen before we begin, let's all say hello to the Secretary of the Navy," said Rocky to instigate the standard response from his squadron mates. CAG Sullivan quivered at the front of the room because he knew what was coming next. Admiral Thompson fidgeted while Commander O' Grady nervously gnawed at the hangnail on his right pinky finger.

"Hello Asshole!" shouted the pilots with obvious pleasure. Not truly knowing their place in this type of indignant display, the twelve chiefs remained subdued and quiet. Of course they had witnessed this performance many times before in their Navy careers and it was relatively tame compared to the behavioral dynamic found in a traditional chief's initiation ceremony. But the *Ready Room* was not their home turf. Senior Chief Esposito cracked a slight smirk as he eye balled the junior officers in the room to see their reactions. Of course Rocky Stone was not finished; he still had to complete the salutation with the second half of the greeting.

"Let's all say hello to the asshole wearing inside the beltway wingtips and fancy pants."

"Hello Mister Secretary," bellowed the aviators at the top of their lungs, many of them pumping their clenched fists toward the ceiling of the *Ready Room*. Rifle Boy Hayward almost knocked over the video camera tripod in his own youthful exuberance. The ice had indeed been broken; shattered is more like it. Hank Andrews was pleasantly pleased to be treated like one of the boys. He was not a politician to be caught up in unnecessary episodes of pomp and circumstance, although on occasion he enjoyed some minor ass kissing for political purposes. There was an appropriate place for ass kissing. This was not the venue and Andrews knew it. Hank was still a Cajun boy at heart and humbly honored to be accepted as just one of the clan in *Attack Squadron* 204. He simply smiled while peering down at the text of a prepared statement then ran his fingers slowly through a slightly messy hairstyle. When he completed this JFK mannerism, Hank began his quasi-speech.

For the next 10 minutes Secretary Andrews proceeded to explain the motivation and rationale behind a momentous decision he had recently made at the Pentagon; a choice that would catapult the *River Rattlers* of Attack Squadron 204 into Naval Aviation history. He briefly discussed the accelerated F-18 transition training schedule and even made a passing reference to the *Tailhook* scandal, which had plagued his office since September of 1991. As Hank Andrews continued, the various faces inside the *Ready Room* all seemed to register similar reactions as the story slowly unfolded before them. Eyes widened, jaws clenched and bodies grew more and more uncomfortable in their leather seats. Finally they were told that the squadron would be formally activated to augment Carrier Air Wing Two, filling the void left by VA-113's absence during their transition to the F-18 Hornet. As such, VA-204 would be given four months preparation time to train and be operationally ready for a six month carrier deployment onboard USS *Enterprise* (CVN-65). The *River Rattlers* would be accorded the honor of being an integral part of the carrier air wing that would make the last A-7 Corsair cruise ever. It was history in the making.

"The six month cruise will begin on April 12th." Secretary Andrews paused briefly at this juncture as if to elicit responses, even though in this case he *was* the arbiter of equity. He cleared his throat slightly and shifted his weight from the left side to his right. It was only then that Andrews realized his speech was being recorded on videotape. It made no difference; his integrity was intact. Hank looked up from the text and surveyed his spectators with the warm, caring eyes he had received from his mother's side of the family. Although retaining their professional decorum, the men in the room were suddenly no longer calm and quiet. In the audience a number of the guys began to grumble and complain under their breath. Those standing at the front by the chalkboard and lectern could not hear the grumbling, but to those seated in the middle of the room it was quite discernable. Leather chairs made those somewhat embarrassing friction noises as bodies squirmed and writhed in reaction to the initial anxiety of the historic announcement. Intuitively, Teen Angel sensed this undertone of dismay in several of his less than pleased colleagues. Cookie Cline, sitting next to Brad, felt it as well. Undoubtedly, family separation and a significant loss of income during the six-month carrier deployment fueled this preliminary consternation. Cookie could not side idly by and just bite his lip. He knew he had to act and act now. He leaped out of his seat in the middle of the room, startling Teen Angel with his sudden, brash movement.

"Quit your belly aching," harangued Lieutenant Cline. "You guys bitch and moan and complain all the time about nothing but crap. The truth is that we all love every aspect about being a naval aviator; even the sacrifice of family separation. We wouldn't have it any other way. We chose this career and we love it! Even though we left active duty we all returned as reservists to our first love, tactical naval aviation. So let's knock off the complaining and get the squadron prepared to go to sea and show those active duty pukes what we reservists are made of. Let's get out there and kick some butt for six months," scolded Lieutenant Cline. Cookie quickly dropped himself back down into his waiting chair. Brad's mouth was unconsciously gaping wide open as he scrutinized Cookie's face. For ten seconds the room wallowed in stunned silence. Then, slowly but surely, every man realized that Cookie was right. Arrogant, but right! Even Juice Mayhew, who hated going on carrier cruises, felt a stirring of deeply rooted patriotism welling up inside of him in reaction to Lieutenant Cline's rousing remarks.

"Yeah, at least we can go out there on that bird farm and fight for truth, justice and the Republican way," teased Brad Ackerman. He was gradually coming out of his semi-paralyzed state sitting next to Cookie. At the front of the room, Duke O'Grady beamed with delight. He had never felt prouder of one of his men.

"I got just two little words for you Cookie. SHUT THE FUCK UP!" said Rocky in a mildly admonishing fashion. Of course, everybody got a big belly laugh out of that comment. The AOM was effectively over at that point as everyone got up to banter and jaw about what was now in store for the squadron. The scene was reminiscent of elephants having sex on the Discovery Channel on late night TV; a lot of standing, lethargic body movements, sweating, moaning and groaning and then several months later you have the ultimate result.

CHAPTER 19

▼

MUD BUGS & SANTA CLAUS

Lieutenant Glen Hebert had extinguished all five flames on the boiling pots about thirty minutes ago to allow the crawfish, sausage and vegetables to fully soak up the *Zatarains* seasoning mixture and complete the cooking process. The sausage and vegetables mixed in with the crawfish was part of the Louisiana tradition known as *lagniappe*, meaning to get a little something extra. It's like buying a *dressed* shrimp Po-boy and getting nine or ten additional deep fried shrimp gushing out of the sides of the sandwich. *Lagniappe* is a thriving part of Louisiana folklore; always alive and well at a crawfish boil.

After watching a Cajun band set up their instruments, microphones and amplifiers near the rented *Spacewalk* (a covered jumping platform designed for children) and then shooting the shit with the female fiddle player for a spell, T-Ben had temporarily lost track of time. Peeking at the blue face on his faux *Rolex* wrist watch Hebert politely excused himself then walked back to check the crawfish to see if they were ready to eat. Popping the top on the middle boiling pot T-Ben reached in with one of the stirring paddles, juggled around a few ears of corn and hunks of sausage then pulled out a couple of the plump, red-colored crawdads. Steam rose from the two *mud bugs* as they lay on the flat surface of the wood paddle, held parallel to the ground by T-Ben's strong right hand. Hebert re-covered the pot then let the shellfish slide down off the paddle onto the top of the silver lid.

After leaning the wooden stirring device back up against the side of the middle pot, Glen picked up one of the cooked crawdads, the larger of the two, with the thumb and index finger of his left hand. It was seriously hot but, growing up on a Louisiana Bayou, Hebert had become immune to the intense heat of freshly boiled or fried seafood. He had learned to be impervious to high temperatures in order to avoid being tormented as a sissy by his old grand pappy Boudreaux; the patriarch of his mother's side of the family. In one continuous motion T-Ben deftly snapped the four-inch *mud bug* into two pieces, pinched the succulent, white tail meat into his salivating mouth then sucked out the warm, seasoned juices from the back of the crawdad's head. He had been taught this method of eating crawfish when he was only two years old so he was quite good at it now. In a flash Glen repeated the traditional ritual with the second crawfish. Hebert deposited the empty reddish remains into a *Hefty* trash bag, but tossed one of the heads to a squirrel climbing down the trunk of the oak tree. After some initial hesitation and head bobs, the grey varmint snatched up the *mud bug* shell and scampered back up the thick, uneven bark with the carcass. In the relative security of massive tree limbs the squirrel would scavenge any residual flesh from the exoskeleton of the crawfish. Apparently Louisiana squirrels are, on occasion, prone to carnivorous behavior.

Hebert then looked to ensure that two of the extra-large waste bags were tied to each picnic table. This would make garbage clean up a lot easier, four hours from now, when the Christmas party was finally concluded. Based on his initial crawfish sample and a subsequent appraisal of one red potato and a garlic clove, T-Ben abruptly decided to give the seafood and vegetables a few more minutes of soaking time for good measure. Ten minutes later he and Vladimir Gonzales would dump the five baskets of boiled shellfish, sausage and vegetables out onto three picnic tables. The banged up aluminum tables had been pushed together and were completely covered with newspapers to absorb juices and fish odor. Stacked adjacent to the metal legs of each table were two hundred or so box bottoms to be used by the party-goers for collecting crawfish and for chucking their empty carcasses after eating.

In spite of the macho demeanor, the boiled seafood had in fact burned the back of Glen's esophagus as it traveled down to his stomach, so he needed some liquid refreshment to cool the burning sensation now throbbing in his throat. About twenty yards from the row of crawfish pots sat another dog-eared aluminum table containing picnic supplies all neatly arranged for easy access. Hebert strolled over to that location and removed a large maroon cup from a transparent bag resting on one end of the table. He held the plastic container under the spigot at the end of a black rubber hose that was attached to a keg of beer sitting in a large barrel full of crushed ice; the metal keg had just been successfully tapped by Airman Thaddeus Williams only a few moments before. It was Williams' first try at tapping a keg so Petty Officer Barr had to show him the ropes. As T-Ben pressed down on the valve stem device to fill his twelve-ounce cup with some cold *Coors Light*, he plucked up a small chunk of ice. Plunking the ice through his lips, he lazily sucked on the melting droplets of cooled water then let the cube slip down past his soft palate, soothing his aching gullet. This keg of brew was one of two that had been situated under an awning, stretching out from the screen-covered, indoor section of the picnic grounds. The bulging kegs were several feet away from six over-sized coolers containing a variety of soft drinks for the non-alcohol drinkers and children who would be in attendance at this year's squadron Christmas party.

As he chugged his goblet of suds, T-Ben noticed that guests were already arriving at the party site. He hastily rushed over to his truck and switched off the stereo, abruptly silencing a Credence Clearwater Revival tune. John Fogerty's rousing rendition of *Born on the Bayou* was suppressed in mid lyric. Undoubtedly the Cajun band that Duke O' Grady had hired for this year's party would begin playing music very shortly. Looking back towards the parking lot, Hebert recognized the familiar faces of squadron dependents and friends emerging from SUV's, minivans and station wagons, all making their way over to the picnic area. Some of his trusty squadron mates were already parking their cars in the gravel lot adjoining the BEQ. T-Ben spotted Commander Mayhew walking on the grass with his wife and two young children. Juice was holding hands with Loretta Mayhew who was likewise clutching the hand of their son Trevor. Five-year old Ashley was giggling while riding on top of her daddy's broad shoulders. She held a *Beanie Baby* teddy bear in her left hand and her right forearm was wrapped tightly around Juice's thick neck. The chokehold Ashley had on her daddy was reminiscent of Hulk Hogan trying to twist off Andre the Giant's head during a cage match, but Juice didn't mind. The entire scene conveyed a loving family ready to share several hours of seasonal joy and fun times together. Glen Hebert's open-mouth smile divulged his genuinely warm feelings for the intimate portrait presented by the slowly approaching Mayhew family.

The AOM must be over surmised Hebert as he looked down and saw that his watch was showing it to be 4: 02PM. 'I probably didn't miss much' thought T-Ben. At that precise moment the six-man band, *Zydeco Scream*, began to play

Cajun square dance music, to properly greet the party guests with a dose of good ole Louisiana hospitality upon their arrival. Their first selection was titled *Momma Please Don't go to the Bingo Hall Tonight.* Surely they would play some traditional Christmas music later in the festivities, especially when Santa Claus made his grand entrance. Hearing the electric guitar, fiddle, washboard, squeeze box accordion and banjo made T-Ben feel highly nostalgic about the familiar Cajun-Creole sounds of his youth. He snapped his fingers in time with the Zydeco beat then plodded back over to the crawfish pots to cook the remaining five sacks of live mud bugs and assorted vegetables. As he re-lit the five propane burners, red, blue and white flames spread out evenly under the flat bottom of each boiling pot. It would only take eight minutes to return the water and seasoning blend back to a searing boil. Glen dumped the remaining *Zatarains* powder into each vat then languidly stirred the zesty mixture for a few seconds. He raised his head making eye contact with the female fiddle player then looked away searching for his wife's tan Pontiac *Grand Am*. He knew she would arrive soon, so his eye contact with the fiddle player was superficial.

Eli Petibone parked his off-white Chevy *Bronco* behind the picnic area then traversed a rickety walkway across the babbling brook that meandered behind the picnic grounds. In the middle of the makeshift bridge, he lazily kicked the bull frog that blocked his path down into the murky creek water. It made a small splash before the startled amphibian frog-kicked its way over to a partially submerged log to escape any additional abuse. Pops was carrying a sizeable cardboard carton that contained one hundred long stem *San Lorenzo* roses. The red flower buds had been flown to New Orleans all the way from the *left coast.* Prior to the arrival of Lieutenant Junior Grade Bill Pack, Pops was the most junior officer in VA-204, so he was charged with managing the Officer's Mess. Today it was his responsibility to ensure that each female guest at the Christmas party received a single red rose, courtesy of VA-204. The Chief's Mess had gone in halves with the Officers this year so each rosebud had a greeting card attached to its stem that read: 'Compliments of the Officers and Men of Attack Squadron Two Zero Four.' After giving his buddy T-Ben an energetic slap on the back and gulping a hunk of sausage, Pops walked over to take up a position between the BEQ parking lot and ground zero of the picnic area. From this vantage point, next to the teeter totter and swing set, he would happily distribute red roses to all the women. Petibone pursed his lips open then tried to suck and blow on the sausage piece that rested on his singed tongue. He sauntered off carrying the box of flowers, attempting to make the spicy chunk of meat just a bit cooler in his mouth before swallowing.

These initial arrivals at the Christmas party obviously had experience with crawfish boils, so they wasted no time. As children began to play around the swing set and *Spacewalk*, wives and girlfriends grabbed several sodas out of the iced-down coolers then secured their spots at a favorite picnic table. A few men were already busy trickling out some of the cold beer into cups or their personal mugs brought from home. One impatient ordnance man, who apparently couldn't wait for his refreshment, guzzled a half cup of the chilled brew before filling his plastic glass to the brim on the second try at the keg. The beer foamed over his hand and forearm as he walked away happy. His ordnance shop buddies, standing in line behind him, all laughed at his genuine although decidedly awkward eagerness for a sip of beer.

Most of the people made a beeline straight over to the three aluminum tables where the first batch of cooked crawdads was waiting to be gathered and eaten. Almost immediately a long line had formed. After first selecting a sturdy box bottom, the guests began to dish out the boiled shellfish, sausage and vegetables using a metal ladle device. Adding to his sense of culinary pride, T-Ben noticed that not too many of the box bottoms left with less than a full load of food. Soon the party guests found their way over to a table where they began to eat and socialize as if there wasn't a care in the world that required their immediate attention. Everywhere people were pinching the tails and sucking the heads of the crawfish, and gnawing on sausage or corncobs. Then, after vigorously swabbing their dripping mouths with a paper towel, the guests proceeded to chitchat about life. This was the down-home, folksy atmosphere that Duke O' Grady intended to pervade the squadron Christmas party. The intricate planning had paid off. The skipper would be most pleased by what he would see when he made his fashionably late entrance to the party.

As Juice Mayhew and his family drew nearer to him, Pops Petibone pulled out an especially long and lovely red rose from the white cardboard box that lay on the grass beside him. He didn't wait but brusquely approached Loretta Mayhew and promptly handed her the flower. Loretta, after graciously accepting the rose and skimming over the attached card, leaned in close and kissed Pops softly on his right cheek during a brief, friendly embrace. Loretta then leaned back and nimbly wiped the faint lip print off of Pops' face with her moistened right thumb. Some of the crimson *Max Factor* lipstick was actually rubbed into Petibone's skin however, giving his cheek that rouge glow. Loretta stood off to the side perusing the card and twirling her extra long, brunette hair as Jack Mayhew approached Petibone.

Juice, apparently pleased by this gesture extended to his loving wife, forcefully shook Petibone's hand after Loretta was finished depositing then partially removing her lipstick prints from the young lieutenant's stubbly cheek. Juice had to juggle a bit to keep Ashley somewhat balanced on his shoulders and this made Pops chuckle during the handshake. Petibone figured one day to have a brood of his own; but first a wife would be nice. After the brief encounter with Pops, Juice gently removed Ashley's grip from around his neck then pulled her off his shoulders plopping the five-year old tenderly down to the ground. He watched pensively as his two children ran off to join the other kids in the ongoing, trampoline-style fun at the *Spacewalk*. After twenty long seconds, Mr. and Mrs. Mayhew shuffled off toward the crawfish table, Loretta to *gorge* on mudbugs and Juice to mingle with the other guests while munching some peppery celery sticks. Loretta would *purge* in the ladies room of the BEQ shortly after consuming two pounds of the shellfish, and after hearing several comments from women who were amazed that she could eat so much yet remain so slender. Little did they know that bulimia was the secret of her success. Forty-five minutes later, Pops had eighty-eight fewer roses than he started out with and both sides of his face were well splattered with various shades and name brands of lipstick. He didn't seem to mind!

Teen Angel, Rocky and Cookie arrived together at 1700, emerging from Jim Stone's gray, squadron logo vehicle all wearing their khaki uniforms. They were followed in quick succession by Duke O' Grady, Randy Bracken, Admiral Thompson, CAG Sullivan and SECNAV Andrews. The latter five arrived in the Admiral's official black limousine. Each time Teen Angel attended a Navy picnic it always reminded him of the submarine barbeques his father would take him to as a young boy back on the sub base in New London, Connecticut. As he walked toward the gathering of people, Brad fondly recalled the barrels of corn-on-the cob and the barbeque grills with those luscious burgers, hot dogs and chicken quarters being cooked up by the submarine crewmen for all the families. He remembered enjoying the soft ball games with the crew and running around the bases as a burly submarine sailor chased him with the large white ball. He vividly recollected the warm feeling that exuded from the pristine setting of the ball field and the surrounding rolling hills, which were nestled up close to the East bank of the Thames River, near the quiet city of Groton.

This was the same glass-like river that the boomers and fast attack boats would navigate out of to reach Long Island Sound, and eventually the open waters of the Atlantic Ocean, to begin their sixty-day patrols. Brad also recalled how too many times he had watched sadly as his own father's submarine passed under the

I-95 Bridge heading south. And then how he had to endure the excruciating two months or longer wait to see his daddy again. Sometimes the 'off crew' of the submarine would make an effort to spend time with the children of the crewmen out on patrol. It was a sort of like being a *Big Brother* until their dads returned home from the sea. Brad remembered how in 1967, one of the off crewmen had actually helped him build a jet black *Pinewood Derby* car in the wood shop at the sub base, and how that little wooden racer eventually won the County championship. Fond reminiscences filled his head for a moment until the bad recollections fought them off and began to consume his thought process.

Teen Angel tried to put the next memory out of his mind but it was too strong, too emotional, and he relived this one often. Unexpectedly he began to summon up a mental picture of the last time he had watched his dad's boat leaving for a patrol. Brad and his mother stood in prophetic silence wearing their heavy coats, holding hands and gazing at the USS *Scorpion* as it departed Norfolk Naval Base on February 15, 1968. Tears swelled in their eyes then slowly rolled down their cheeks. Standing under a lamp post that chilly day and looking out at the narrow channel, a frigid gust of wind blew the light fixture above their heads until the bulb's filament gave out leaving the two in an eerie darkness. Brad Ackerman had no idea that he would never see his father again after that foggy morning at 0400. A little more than three months later his father and ninety-eight other brave crewmen would vanish into the vast depths of the Atlantic, 400 miles southwest of the Azores. Teen Angel really missed his dad right then.

The irritating, scratching noise of a washboard being strummed by the Zydeco band suddenly pierced Brad's eardrums. Snapping out of his daze, he trailed his squadron mates over to the boiling pots. He quickened his pace to catch up with Rocky and Cookie, all the while keeping an eye peeled for Danielle Le Claire who had promised to make an appearance at the party. Brad intended to consume some sausage and perhaps a few cold drinks, but he had no remote intention of eating anything that swims in a Louisiana ditch filled with muddy water. T-Ben Hebert had other ideas that afternoon for his buddy Teen Angel.

Over on the MAG-46 flight line, adjacent to VA-204's tarmac, a single-engine UH-1M was about to begin turning its rotor blades. In the right seat of the grayish colored helicopter sat a rather portly Marine Corps major just finishing up his Pre-Start Checklist. He wore a standard-issue green zoom bag, size 46R, with a yellow and black nametag. His call sign *Belush* was embossed on the Velcro nametag underneath his gold wings. Apparently his uncanny resemblance to the *Saturday Night Live* comic John Belushi was responsible for the call sign. The major's flight boots had obviously been polished to a mirror-quality shine that very morning, probably around 0415 when most normal human beings were deep in REM sleep. His hair was extra high and tight because he had just gotten his weekly hatchet job from Leilani, the plump, Polynesian *butcher* who cut hair at the Navy Exchange barber shop. The major skipped lunch that day for the trip to the barber.

"Collective down, cyclic centered, anti-torque neutral," he called out in a loud and clear voice, reading from his Pocket NATOPS Checklist. Before cranking up the Huey's T53-L engine, the major looked back at his enlisted air crewman who promptly flashed him a thumbs-up signal. Seated next to the air crewman was a stout man wearing a long white beard, an obvious phony, and a Santa suit. The garb was made of red velvet-like material. If you looked close enough you could recognize that it was none other than Senior Chief John Esposito wearing the get up and toting a huge green bag filled with chocolate Santa's for all the children at the *River Rattler* Christmas party.

Sitting in the back of the Huey Esposito shoved the floppy Saint Nick cap back on his bald scalp then hiked up the red and white, oversized sleeves of his costume. As he looked down at his wrist watch, the velvety outfit was beginning to make him itch and sweat even more than normal. Although he was most uncomfortable, the senior chief was anxious to perform his yearly duty by playing the role of Santa Claus for the squadron's offspring. He had been playing Santa for the past eighteen years in each command that he was assigned to. Esposito dabbed his brow and forehead with the left sleeve of the costume. They still had about ten minutes before the Marine Huey would take off and deliver him, as old Saint Nick, to the picnic grounds precisely at 1730.

"Let's make it happen major," shouted Esposito after inserting his ear plugs. In less than a minute the huge rotor blades slowly began to turn in a counter-clockwise direction. The helicopter initially jiggled like a top, on its last legs, about to spin out of control. In nine minutes the Huey would surrender Santa, out from the side door of the helo, to the delight of the children in attendance at the Christmas party. Esposito pushed the foam plugs further into his ear canals to deaden the increasingly painful engine noise.

Glen Hebert lowered his wooden paddle then exchanged welcoming high-fives with Rocky, Cookie and Teen Angel as the three aviators eased up next to him while he was ministering to the boiling seafood. The black wraparound apron worn by T-Ben had a huge cartoon crawfish on the front with the words 'Chef Craw Daddy' emblazed in gold, italicized lettering. The apron and its obvious connotation made Cookie smile. Klutz Fitzgerald, who was standing next to

T-Ben with a cup of beer in his right hand, leaned over and whispered something into Rocky's ear then walked off to locate the skipper.

"Today's the day Angel," advised Hebert. "Today I am gonna convince you to try this Cajun delicacy, a freshly boiled crawdad."

"Come on Angel, you can do it. Be a man for Christ's sake. They actually taste great the way T-Ben doctors em up," advised Cookie. T-Ben had already raked himself a box full of crawfish and stashed it behind the boiling pot on the far left side. He scooped up and handful then dropped them gently onto the lid of that pot. Next, in rapid succession, he proceeded to quickly knock down three medium-size tails and drain their heads of the warm, zesty juices.

"There's no way I am putting a mud bug into my mouth!" stated Brad in his best cynical tone of voice. Teen Angel scrunched up his face as he witnessed Lieutenant Hebert rudely suck out the juice from the third crawfish head then toss its somewhat empty remains back into the trash-side of his cardboard box bottom. "You know in about three hours all those spices are gonna come out of your rear end like a fire ball from Hell!" cracked Teen Angel.

For some unknown reason, Teen Angel suddenly remembered how he had once been duped into eating steamed barnacles at an Officer's Club in Portugal. A Spanish Army Colonel, who had just shared a satisfying round of golf with Midshipman Ackerman, had treated Brad to a traditional Portuguese dinner to thank him for the golf tips he had freely given during the match. The Spanish officer's statuesque wife and three sons had joined them for the feast. That evening at the O' Club the appetizer was delivered by a dumpy-looking waiter who reeked with body odor. It was shortly after the Sangria had arrived and the flamenco dancers had moved on to another table. Each time the waiter came around the children couldn't suppress their giggles to the chagrin of their father who was wearing his full mess-dress uniform for the informal occasion. On a red-and-white checkerboard tablecloth in front of Midshipman Ackerman sat a dish with a steaming pile of what looked like a rocky substance. Several small holes were distinctly visible all over the outside surface of the platter of food. The waiter also dropped a utensil next to each plate. The metal tool resembled a dentist's pick; the kind used for exploring cavities in molars.

After the smelly waiter showed Brad how to pick out the little treats that were buried deep inside the crevices with the dentist's pick, Ackerman reluctantly began to follow the lead and eat. The children continued to giggle, only this time Brad was the object of their ridicule. Soon Ackerman had wolfed down about a dozen of the warm, salty critters as a first course to the Portuguese meal. As a young, nineteen year-old midshipman on his first summer cruise, Ackerman didn't have the nerve that night to ask what he was eating. He simply dipped the hot, white-colored meat into a lukewarm cup of fresh drawn butter then sucked it off the pointy end of the dentist's pick into his mouth to chew and swallow. Brad literally gagged after being advised by the colonel's wife what the salty, so-called delicacy was. In effect, some middle-age man had been paid ten escudos to scrape the bottom of an old rust bucket floating in the harbor, and Brad had eaten the results of that effort.

At that moment SECNAV emerged from the crowd of party guests and walked up to join the ongoing conversation. Still dressed in his blue suit he settled in next to Brad Ackerman. CAG and the admiral remained close on the secretary's right flank similar to ducklings following their mother around the yard. Perhaps because he was comfortable with the situation, standing next to his golfing partner, Hank Andrews didn't even observe the *two-minute rule*; he just barged in and began talking to the group of pilots gathered near the boiling pots. He wanted to know where the chef had bought the crawfish since they were out of season.

"At Salvo's Seafood in Belle Chasse sir," replied a respectful Lieutenant Hebert, not really knowing whom it was that he was addressing. "They're farmed-raised, Belle River crawfish." Hebert recognized Rear Admiral Thompson and Commander Sullivan, but his courteous conversational demeanor was not due to their presence; he had been successfully raised by his mother to address any man as sir and any woman as ma'am. Growing up, T-Ben had always been too afraid to defy his mom, even when he reached six feet in height at the tender age of fourteen. He was afraid to disobey her because she would simply turn over all disciplinary matters to her own father, Papa Boudreaux, who would happily administer the necessary whipping using the same three-foot hickory switch he had used on her bottom so many times in the past. The switch was hung up in the outside shed which housed the lawn tractor, tools and fishing gear.

"Oh I know that place, I used to eat fried shrimp and oyster Po-Boys there when I was a youngster," remarked Secretary Andrews. Hank cleared his throat then slowly averted his eyes to look at Teen Angel, his morning golf partner. "You're not eating the crawfish Lieutenant Ackerman?" questioned Secretary Andrews. He noticed that everyone else in the group was fully enjoying the crawdads.

"No Mister Secretary, Teen Angel is one of those left-wing, Hollywood faggots who only munches on caviar and escargot," taunted Rocky, interrupting the intended flow of the SECNAV'S conversation. He was, of course, engaging in some pot-stirring of his own at his squadron mate's expense. Glen Hebert's ears perked up a bit after the term 'Mister Secretary' was used by Jim Stone. Upon hearing this comical explanation, Hank Andrews quickly slipped his left hand into T-Ben's cardboard box and removed a crawfish.

"I took your advice today on the golf course Lieutenant Ackerman. So I want you to listen to me now," said Andrews as he handed Brad the rather large crawfish. Somewhat stunned by this blunt gesture in front of his buddies, Ackerman reluctantly took the shellfish into his right hand. Hank then grabbed another crawdad and instructed Brad on the finer points of removing the head, peeling back the top two ribs of the tail and then squeezing free the meat to pop into your mouth. Teen Angel clumsily followed Andrews' instructions to the letter, but before he could shove the tail meat into his mouth T-Ben produced a can of *Tony Chachere's Original Creole Seasoning*. For his first-ever crawfish, T-Ben offered Teen Angel a little *lagniappe*. He sprinkled Ackerman's three-inch crawfish tail with a healthy dose of the *Tony Chachere's* for some additional flavor. Throwing caution to the wind, and because Hank Andrews had put him squarely on the spot, Teen Angel tentatively placed the crawfish into his mouth, gave three or four feeble chews then swallowed hard. It was simply delicious and at that moment he wondered why he had resisted eating them for so long. The entire group broke out in spontaneous applause as Teen Angel reached into T-Ben's box for a handful of crawfish.

Turning to Admiral Thompson, Hank Andrews, the native New Orleanian, explained how Cajuns could make a gumbo out of almost anything. Growing up in New Orleans Hank's maternal grandma had indeed prepared *Road-kill* Gumbo and Nutria (swamp rat) Gumbo then fed it to the family simply calling it Seafood Gumbo. But, she was also a gourmet cook and would routinely prepare Alligator Sauce Pecan, File Gumbo, Crawfish Pie, Jambalaya and Turtle Soup for the family to eat. CAG Sullivan, a former cowpoke from South Dakota, wasn't sure what to make of SECNAV'S story, but he smiled anyway throughout the long-winded rendition.

Over on the far side of the picnic grounds, near the BEQ, Duke O' Grady was busy talking to a couple of men with semi-familiar looking faces. The many voices of these two men, however, were highly familiar. The skipper was chatting up a storm with none other than New Orleans' radio personalities *Walton and Johnson*. Duke had invited the infamous duo to the Christmas party just last week and they had cleared their schedules in order to attend. The sometimes, caustic DJ's were those cheeky, self-proclaimed *radio gawds* who ruled the morning, drive-time airwaves in New Orleans and the gulf coast. Duke was happy they could be there.

"We were told this 'ed be a big 'un skipper; a great dawg and pony show," said Steve Johnson, the taller and leaner of the two men. He was using his patented, trailer-trash impression known as *Billy Ed Hatfield* from Klute, Texas. The skipper had to laugh upon hearing one of his most favorite radio voices up close and in person. O' Grady was a bigger fan of *Walton and Johnson* that he was of the notorious *Grease Man* whom he idolized as a young RAG student in VA-174 during his days at NAS Cecil Field in Jacksonville, Florida. As the three continued to talk, they could hear four or five women in the background trying to sell each other Amway cosmetic products or hand-weaved Longaberger baskets or subscriptions to the Herbal-Life weight loss system. This made all three of them chuckle as they turned to make their way over to the crawfish table. T-Ben and Teen Angel, his new helper, were just pouring the last five batches of freshly boiled crawfish out onto the newspaper-covered table. Transparent white steam spiraled up from the large pile as the enticing aroma of crawfish wafted its way throughout the picnic area attracting more hungry party guests to the table.

Rocky Stone, beer in one hand and sausage in the other, had wandered off from T-Ben and Teen Angel in pursuit of Klutz Fitzgerald. He apparently wanted to continue the discussion started earlier when Klutz had whispered something provocative into his ear. Rocky found Klutz after a brief search and the pair stood off a distance from the main crowd, deeply embroiled in conversation. Earlier in the day, Commander Fitzgerald and Lieutenant Commander Stone had bumped into each other in the makeshift store run by the VA-204 Enlisted Man's Mess. Just outside the door to that cramped space in the hangar, they had shared a brief dialogue over a cup of coffee while splitting a package of Hostess *Twinkies*. Fairly quickly, and with a suspicious tone, Klutz had told Rocky about the dirty rotten trick perpetrated on Juice Mayhew during the weigh-in for his annual flight physical that morning. Apparently Klutz had bumped into Wrongway Carrigan at *Christina's Empress of China* during his lunch break. At 1145, Commander Fitzgerald was actually leaving the Chinese restaurant as Lieutenant Carrigan and Ensign Detweiller were arriving for the buffet. In an apparent guilt trip, the flight surgeon had revealed the sordid details of the minor conspiracy hatched against Jack Mayhew in the clinic.

In the Enlisted Man's Mess store, after taking his first healthy bite of the *Twinkie*, Klutz had come right out and inquired if Rocky had been the one to set Juice up for the fall at the NAS clinic. Rocky of course denied any knowledge of the heinous but extremely humorous practical joke played on the squadron Maintenance Officer, Commander Mayhew. Klutz had carefully examined Rocky's face as he made his denial in between bites of the *Twinkie*, and judged him to be sincere. But he still wasn't totally convinced that Stone wasn't involved in some sort of melodramatic conspiracy with Jack Mayhew as the hapless victim. As the aviators talked they soon became aware of Cookie Cline taunting Juice Mayhew a few yards away from them, close to the *Spacewalk* contraption. Apparently Cookie had found Commander Mayhew and was actively teasing him about having taken a *Patton pill* earlier in the day because he had flunked his weigh-in. Not wanting the ridicule to get too far out of hand, Rocky and Klutz ambled over to Cookie and Juice. At first they just listened to the ongoing banter.

"Maybe you should make a 911 call to Jack La Lanne or something Juice, chided Cookie after guzzling some foamy beer from his plastic cup. "Or just double up on that anger management medication you've been taking for the past 6 months," suggested Cookie. "Perhaps you should check into the Betty Ford Clinic to deal with your addiction to desserts, or maybe the Betty Crocker Clinic." Jack squirmed as he ignored Lieutenant Cline's relentless and insensitive comments. He continued to watch his children bouncing on the trampoline device. Even though he could sense Rocky had gotten a big kick out of listening to Cookie rib Juice, this last comment was just too much for Klutz Fitzgerald to take. He decided it was time to step in and save Jack Mayhew from any additional, unnecessary embarrassment at the hands of the teasing Lieutenant Cline.

In slow, methodic terms, Klutz explained to Juice about the plot against him and that the medical clinic had faxed Mayhew's real 'up chit' to his office just before the start of the AOM. This was the reason that Klutz was late to show up for the AOM. He further explained that some unknown perpetrator had successfully bribed Lieutenant Wrongway Carrigan, the duty flight surgeon, and Corpsman Ridowski to alter the clinic scale so that it read several pounds higher than the actual weight.

"Jack you are really several pounds under your maximum weight. The *Juice Plan* worked like a champ, like it always does for you," informed Klutz to a visibly relieved Mayhew. His relief was only temporary however. Mayhew's forehead suddenly developed three long, distinctive wrinkles that rolled from his hairline down, causing his brow to furrow and his face to evolve into a menacing scowl.

"Is Lieutenant Carrigan here at the party Klutz?" asked Jack Mayhew, visibly huffing.

"I thought I saw him earlier over by the band," responded Fitzgerald.

"Did you two hooligans have anything to do with this prank?" asked Juice, temporarily diverting his attention to Rocky and Cookie, the two usual partners in crime.

"It wasn't us," said Cookie in a highly defensive tenor.

"I think you are lying," accused Juice.

"Why would we bald face lie to you Jack?" said Rocky.

"Because you are both liars, and that's what liars do, they lie! Not that there's anything wrong with being a liar. I actually admire a good lie every now and then because I myself am a liar," admonished Jack. Although somewhat comforted that he was in an up status and wouldn't have to join Ensign Detweiller in her *fat boy* program on Monday morning, he was still fuming.

"I'm gonna kill that guy when I catch him," muttered Juice under his breath as he stormed off searching for co-conspirators. Unfortunately, when he finally located Lieutenant Wrongway Carrigan, standing next to Donna Detweiller, the apologetic flight surgeon couldn't reveal who the practical joker was. The plan had been clandestinely concocted over the phone a few weeks ago and the bribes for him and the corpsman had mysteriously appeared in their offices two days later. Carrigan and Ridowski just went along with the gag after their bribery booty had inexplicably showed up on their desks along with a typed note detailing what was to be done and when.

Assistant District Attorney Dannielle Le Claire pulled her *Lexus* into the BEQ parking lot. She was almost an hour and a half late arriving at the Christmas party, but what an entrance she was about to make. Some people were greedily devouring the last remnants of the crawfish and vegetables at their tables, but most of the guests were standing up mingling and shooting the breeze with other party-goers. The crowd was thick and gathered in a small clearing in the middle of the picnic grounds. Kids were still playing on the teeter totter and swing set and frolicking inside the *Spacewalk*. The children were also eagerly awaiting the arrival of Santa Claus and his traditional bag of goodies. Teen Angel was munching down crawfish, anxiously awaiting the imminent arrival of his potential new girlfriend, Danielle Le Claire. And then there she was, emerging from her vehicle. The wait would be worth it!

Danielle Le Claire was wearing a pair of those designer flip flops with a delicate gold anklet on her right foot, and a toe ring on the second toe of her left foot. Her sculpted toenails were painted a bright, fire engine red. If feet could actually be attractive, hers were. Danielle was also clad in snug pair of stone washed *Guess Jeans*, without a belt, and a tight-fitting white top. The T-shirt exposed her navel in a most flirtatious manner as she walked. Looking further north her eyebrows were deep, dark and distinctive. Her eyelashes were also thick, although artificially enhanced with *Merle Norman* mascara, rendering them long and slightly furled at the ends. Cookie Cline was the first to spot Danielle as she closed the door on her Lexus SC 400 then proceeded to make her way toward the festivities.

"Hey Rocky, do chicks know about *camel toe*," inquired a wide-eyed Cookie as he tugged on Lieutenant Commander Stone's sleeve and gestured toward Danielle. Miss Le Claire's *camel toe* was straining against the fitted fabric of her denim jeans as she approached the party crowd from the parking lot.

"Of course they do dummy, they are the ones that invented it!" replied a scornful Rocky as his eyes immediately focused on the obvious object of Cookie's question, Danielle's crotch. "She is a little baby doll," said Rocky as his eyes peered at Danielle over the top of his aviator sunglasses. Instinctively, Rocky sucked in his slight gut, the small paunch that he called his *sag of success*.

As Danielle Le Claire sashayed her svelte body across the picnic grounds, the crowd of guests parted to make a pathway for her like the Red Sea before Moses' staff! Of course, she was making a beeline straight for Brad Ackerman. Every male eye was fixed on her cover girl-grade beauty. Some men, who were accompanied to the Christmas party by their wives or girlfriends, tried extra hard to avoid the overt dimension of staring behavior. They stared using their peripheral vision. But when Danielle greeted Teen Angel with a sensuous, warm, wet kiss, the stares suddenly became blatant; at least for the duration of the embrace. Brad was simultaneously humbled and arrogant when Danielle's left foot pulled up parallel to the ground as the kiss and hug lasted longer than it should. At least three sets of eyebrows, and Juice's one long eyebrow that stretches across his entire forehead, were raised up at the sight of Teen Angel embracing his newest and latest squeeze. Danielle could taste the spices from the crawfish on Brad's mouth and tongue. The assistant DA licked her own lips as she pulled away to speak with Brad. Her conversation was intimate and highly revealing, and delivered in a hushed voice.

"You are an incredibly sexy man Brad Ackerman. When we first met at the Officer's Club last night I quickly asked myself 'Am I gonna kiss this man?" Well, after thirty minutes with you I changed that question to 'Am I gonna sleep with this man?' Then after another thirty minutes I answered my own question, 'Oh yes, I will have this man in my bed soon!' Your big bedroom eyes and flirty seductive demeanor is irresistible. It makes me get all puffy down there, if you know what I mean," said Danielle in a highly candid manner.

"Gulp," Brad swallowed his own overflowing saliva hard at this comment. He was speechless as they walked toward the beer keg hand in hand. Teen Angel walked a bit awkwardly at first because his *short arm* had been stimulated somewhat by Miss Le Claire's sensuous rhetoric.

On the far side of the picnic area a Marine Corps Huey was gradually approaching at approximately 200 feet above the ground. The MAG-46 chopper's forward speed was less than ten knots. After the lead singer of *Zydeco Scream* announced ole Saint Nick's imminent arrival into a microphone that reeked of beer, the Cajun band struck up a lively rendition of *Here Comes Santa Claus*. Children soon began to leave the *Spacewalk* and swing set to scamper over to a spot adjacent to the intended landing area for the helicopter. Comatose Gross and Plato Themopolis, dressed in civilian clothes, greeted the kids with warm smiles. Actually they had both drawn the short straws at the AOM and were thus officially selected to perform wrangler duties that afternoon. It was their job to control the children and place them into a suitable waiting area where they would be safe from the downwash of the rotor blades as Santa disembarked the Huey. Naturally the kids were excited and exuberant, especially those who had witnessed Santa being delivered by helicopter at past VA-204 Christmas parties.

Trevor and Ashley Mayhew were among the first to arrive at the landing site and Comatose Gross quickly directed them into the safe area. Leaves and dried, recently-mowed grass swirled up as the Marine Major gently placed the Huey's two landing skids onto a prepared surface, the left skid first followed by the right. One wayward red rose could also be plainly seen twirling around in reaction to the tremendous wind generated by the Huey's rotor blades. The enlisted crewman hopped up and shoved the left-side door aft as the Major killed the engine and the rotor blades slowly rotated to a stop. The crewman then jumped down to the grass and grabbed the overstuffed green goody bag from Senior Chief Esposito who now had his red hat and white beard in their proper positions. Next, Santa lethargically slid his big body over the lower edge of the door, planting his tall black boots firmly onto the ground. Handing the goody bag over to Santa, the air crewman jumped back into the rear of the helo and closed the side door with one quick shove. In a minute Esposito was seated in a *Lazy-Boy* chair, the one temporarily stolen from the BOQ lobby last evening. He waved to the children and bellowed out a loud 'ho ho ho' to the throng of people. Esposito was now ready to hand out the yummy, chocolate Santa candies, most of which were still unbroken after the helicopter ride.

Plato and Comatose had successfully corralled the kids into forming a single-file line that stretched back about eighty feet. Ashley Mayhew was first to walk up to Santa and receive her gift. As she reached for her chocolate Santa with her left hand, she tugged on the white beard with her right hand.

"Is that you again Mista Spasito?" she asked. Several of the adults laughed out loud at the remark. Standing in between Randy Bracken and Dana Rothschild,

Loretta Mayhew's face got bright red because her daughter had uncannily remembered John Esposito playing the part of Santa Claus at last year's party. Yes, Ashley was intelligent, way too intelligent for a five year-old girl.

CHAPTER 20

▼

"YEP, I CAN MAKE THAT LEG"

February 9, 1992 started off as an extremely frigid and blustery day in Belle Chasse, Louisiana. An arctic cold front, straight from Canada, had passed through at about midnight and the wind was howling steadily out of the northeast at twenty-two knots with an occasional gust reaching twenty-eight. At 0540 that morning, the temperature was hovering around the forty-one degree mark but the wind chill factor made the gulf coast air feel like it was considerably less than thirty degrees on Mister Fahrenheit's scale. Undoubtedly, green flight jackets would be the order of the day, both in and out of the cockpit for the two-leg cross country flight to Nevada. Starting in less than three hours, all twelve *River Rattler* A-7E Corsairs would be flown to the Fallon Naval Air Station, approximately sixty miles east of Reno in the silver state. All the aircraft would make a short fuel stop at Buckley Air Force Base in Denver along the way before hopping over the Sierra Nevada mountain range to land on the fourteen-thousand foot hunk of concrete at Fallon. Commander Klutz Fitzgerald's 'op plan' had scheduled three flights of four to depart in 45 minute intervals, beginning at 0830 with the launch of the skipper's flight. Included in Duke's division of attack jets were wingmen and typical suspects Rocky Stone, Cookie Cline and Teen Angel Ackerman. Randy Bracken and Juice Mayhew would be the flight leads for the remaining two divisions of Corsairs.

Active-duty Carrier Air Wing Two (CAG-2), with VA-204 thrown into the mix courtesy of SECNAV Hank Andrews, would begin its three-week, pre-deployment weapons detachment at the Fallon live-fire range tomorrow morning. Commander "Spine Ripper" Madison himself, the CAG, would kick off the training detachment at 0730 by offering a few choice words of inspiration to his carrier air wing before the start of the in-briefing at the spacious base auditorium. Spine Ripper's motivational homilies, as well as his trap-bagging behavior while on cruise, were legend in the lore of Naval Aviation. CAG Madison could always be counted on to deliver a guttural, controversial quote or two while chomping on a saliva-moistened cigar. In fact he was almost never seen without an unlit stogie hanging rudely from his mouth or twisting nervously in his stubby, callused fingers. Madison's favorite brand was *Tiparillo* and he would invariably remove the plastic tip to suck directly on the pungent, rolled tobacco leaves. Commander Madison's breath routinely smelled like a tobacco curing house in Winston-Salem, making his personal tirades all the more difficult to endure if you were on the receiving end.

CAG Madison even brought an unlit cigar with him into the cockpit when he flew. During one particularly funny tailhook party skit the senior LSO from VA-25, Lieutenant "Loose Lips" Matherne, had jokingly referred to Madison's cigars as his little, queer security blanket. Lieutenant Matherne would hear an earful of shit the next morning in Spine Ripper's stateroom onboard USS *Enterprise* for that insensitive, although humorous, remark. Two months later, Madison would reconcile by naming Loose Lips his next Air Wing Landing Signal Officer. Quite frequently during motivational speaking opportunities, Commander Madison's passion overflowed into Tasmanian devil-like aggression causing his tact and diplomacy to temporarily disappear like barefoot kissin' cousins at a Kentucky backwoods family reunion. Henry Kissinger, the ultimate diplomat and pacifist, was not in danger of becoming the uncouth air wing commander's best friend. Never the less, Commander Madison's leadership skills were impeccable and he was on the fast track for flag rank.

Lieutenant Brad Ackerman had flown into town on a Southwest Airlines flight fairly late the evening before. The Boeing 737 made three stops, mostly in Texas, before finally landing at New Orleans International Airport. The last stopover at Houston Hobby was delayed by two hours while maintenance technicians repaired a cabin pressurization problem on the Boeing jet, affectionately referred to as the flying cigar by airline pilots. Teen Angel was in the process of waking up in his uncomfortably tiny bed in room 308 of the Bachelor Officer's Quarters. He had set his alarm clock for 0545 which meant that he would have logged only about four and a half hours of actual sleep the previous night in his BOQ room. Gradually stirring in the twin bed he felt a twinge of pain shooting through his left ear. Apparently Brad had slept on a folded under left ear for the past two hours, and as he was waking he suddenly began to be cognizant of the sharp pain emanating from that region. Brad repositioned his body to the right side as he rubbed some blood back into the fold of his left ear. He slowly opened his brown eyes then focused momentarily on the clock face, which was reading 5:42 AM. Sluggishly, he reached over and tried to turn the alarm function off. But Ackerman missed, stopping one detent short of the off position. Immediately his room was filled with the sounds of Mason Williams hammering out *Classical Gas* on a twelve-string, acoustic guitar. So as not to be defeated, Teen Angel casually pulled the radio's electrical cord from the wall socket behind the nightstand. Room 308 returned to peaceful silence as Brad forced himself out of the bed to head for a hot shower and cold bathroom linoleum.

Thirty-five minutes later Brad crawled out of his car in the VA-204 parking area just as Mr. and Mrs. Jack Mayhew drove their Toyota into the lot. The freshly-waxed Camry's engine sputtered just a tad, due to a missing valve, as the mid-size car slowed to a stop. Ackerman's parachute bag, full of packed belongings for the Fallon trip, was sitting behind his Porsche's dirty rear bumper on the slimy asphalt. The surface of the parking lot was still somewhat damp after an early morning drizzle. Teen Angel was wearing a winter-weight flight suit with his green fleet jacket, and his body shivered as he exhaled into the stiff breeze. Loretta Mayhew, in the driver's seat with her hands at the 'ten and two position' on the steering wheel, was the first to spot Teen Angel standing, straining against the wind behind his vehicle. Juice, his upper torso twisted around in the passenger's seat, had his head buried in the back seat pre-positioning his gear.

As Brad turned to see who was arriving, he cupped his hands to blow some warm air into them. Ackerman's breath, super-cooled by the freezing wind, was visible as it escaped from the many apertures in his cupped hands. As he stroked his palms together to generate some friction heat in them, he unexpectedly made direct eye contact with Loretta. Smiling, Teen Angel gave Loretta a sarcastic, all-knowing wink of his right eye. Even from twenty feet away Brad could sense that Loretta was not all that happy to be losing her husband for the next three weeks while he was off playing cowboy, light attack pilot in the mountains of Nevada. And, the real slap in the face for Loretta was the six month separation she and her two children would have to tolerate during the historic final Corsair cruise onboard the carrier *Enterprise*. Loretta set the parking brake with her right hand then in one continuous motion elbowed Jack in the ribs to get his attention.

Juice dropped the can of *Barbesol* shave cream he was stuffing into the parachute bag then gasped to catch a breath after his wife's well-positioned elbow stab to his defenseless ribcage. Turning around in the bucket seat Jack found himself peering straight into Brad Ackerman's cow eyes. Teen Angel simply focused his stare on their Camry.

"If Teen Angel makes one smart ass comment to me, I swear Jack, I, I, I won't be responsible for what I'll do to him," moaned Loretta to her husband. Her body slumped into the back of the driver's seat after the gut-wrenching comment came out of her anorexic frame. Her expressionless face soon turned into a sad frown, complete with a protruding, pouting bottom lip.

"What could he possible say that would piss you off any more than you already are right now babe?" asked Jack in reply. Juice averted his attention from Teen Angel by shielding his eyes with a massive right hand as he turned to face Loretta. Mayhew gently stroked his wife's forehead, pushing her long hair to the side as he spoke. The caress didn't have the soothing effect he was hoping for.

Seizing an opportunity to tease Jack's beloved wife, Ackerman clenched his fists together, bit his lower lip in a provocative manner then began to prance around the parking lot. His dance was overly dramatic and seductive in nature because he was trying to really lay it on thick for Mrs. Mayhew. Ackerman's early morning ballet was less than blatant but more than subtle teasing. Three weeks ago, over a few beers in the club, Juice had already revealed to Brad his wife's disdain for the upcoming carrier deployment. Loretta didn't understand why a Naval Reserve squadron from New Orleans, Louisiana had to be activated during peacetime, let alone go out to sea for six months. Desert Storm was over. Teen Angel twirled and slowly gyrated his body with his right hand thrust way above his head as he began approaching the Mayhew's Camry. Then Ackerman lowered his right arm and pumped his fists together, like a pair of valves pushing into twin cylinders. He was performing the classic white man's boogie as visible puffs of air flooded rhythmically out of his mouth. Stopping at the driver's side window Brad interrupted his gyrations in order to speak with Loretta.

But Mrs. Mayhew wanted no part of a sunrise conversation with Lieutenant Brad Ackerman, especially that day. She knew that his dancing demeanor and insulting body language were meant to show Jack how much fun they were going to have in Fallon for the next three weeks. Even though she had a soft spot for Teen Angel in her heart, Loretta frankly resented this being thrown into her face by VA-204's Hollywood, playboy pilot. Jack's wife just stared straight ahead, refusing to even roll down her window to say hello to Brad. Jack leaned over and kissed his wife hard on the lips, dragged his bags from the rear seat and escorted

Teen Angel to the side door of the squadron building. Loretta drove off in a huff, hurrying back home so the baby sitter could get to her high school in time for the first class.

At 1015 the last division of A-7 Corsairs was airborne with wheels in the well, talking to the New Orleans Departure controllers and rapidly climbing to 35,000 feet. This first leg of the cross-country flight would land and make a one hour pit stop at Buckley AFB, a Colorado Air National Guard facility just north of Denver. There the pilots would wolf down burgers and fries at the infamous *Tarmac Treats* café as T-Line (Transient Line) personnel refueled the aircraft. All twelve of the *slufs* had made the launch that morning without too much of a hitch, thanks primarily to the hustle of the *River Rattler* maintenance crew. Forty minutes after the last Corsair was airborne, over at the NAS New Orleans air terminal, a C-9 from the Dallas VR squadron was preparing to take on passengers at the quarterdeck. The transport aircraft was just cranking up its APU (auxiliary power unit) in order to begin the boarding process for about ninety individuals, the remainder of VA-204's personnel. The APU engine whined at a high pitch causing several people milling about smartly in front of the terminal building to insert index fingers into their ear canals as protection from the noise. The DC-9 jet was the staple of the Naval Aviation Logistics Office (NALO) and was used to move both cargo and people around the world to accommodate the Navy's commitments. The flight, scheduled to depart NAS Belle Chasse at 1115, would take three and a half hours to make the non-stop journey to Fallon, Nevada.

Senior Chief Esposito played the role of *wrangler* for the 12 plane launch and then again at the Base Ops passenger terminal for the C-9 flight to NAS Fallon. The senior chief didn't raise his voice once that day, he simply used his notorious reputation and forceful body language to *lasso* and *corral* any stray enlisted men. At the passenger terminal, he kept them in a holding pen at Base Ops then guided them up the boarding ladder into the C-9's cabin section. Twenty minutes later the sleek passenger jet was climbing northwest, bound for Nevada. Almost immediately, most of the men leaned back to take a much-deserved nap for the duration of the flight. Three hundred miles ahead, Duke O' Grady was leading his division of attack jets on their cross country flight to NAS Fallon. In a few hours his squadron aircraft would be recovered in that desert location by members of the advance detachment. Lieutenant Sugar^2 Cane, an avid gambler, was the OINC (officer-in-charge) of that advance det, and his team of twelve aviation mechanics and technicians had been in Fallon for twenty-four hours busily preparing for the *River Rattler's* arrival. In that short span of time Mark Cane had already lost four hundred fifty dollars at the craps tables. Although Sugar^2 was an ardent gambler he wasn't very good at it. Apparently he himself was not fully aware of this fact because he was an unrepentant glutton for gambling punishment. Pit bosses at several different casinos from Las Vegas to Miami Beach usually welcomed him with open arms during his layovers with United Airlines. They knew him by his first name, which is never a good sign. Lieutenant Cane's lovely, pregnant wife Trish was unaware of this aspect of her husband's personal behavior, as well as a few other skeletons he had kept strategically hidden in his private closet.

At Flight Level 350, in loose cruise formation, Duke's flight of four Corsairs had passed to the northeast of Dallas Love Field and was now just south of Wichita Falls, Texas. The snub-nosed jets were clipping along nicely at 7and 1/2 miles per minute despite being confronted by an eighty knot headwind. Thanks to the near-sighted design engineers at LTV, the A-7E Corsair climbed like a wounded duck above 10,000 feet, so it had taken the jets quite a long while to reach their cruising altitude. Seated snugly within the familiar confines of AF 401's cockpit, with an oxygen mask dangling down in front of his torso harness and resting on his lap, Commander O' Grady was actively daydreaming as he led his flight westbound. At this particular moment in his reverie Duke was thinking of how warm and cozy he had felt that morning lying next to Tanya Billings under the heavy blankets. He was briefly fantasizing about her taut, slender legs and those extra long blonde locks. He recalled how her platinum hair gently slid through his fingers as he kissed her engorged lips passionately at 0530 that morning during their final lovemaking session. How could any man not smile while reminiscing about such memories, especially when those recollections were such fresh ones? Duke was also thinking that before she had driven off to the NAS dental clinic that morning to begin her eight hour teeth cleaning shift, Tanya had probably made the bed and ironed two of his khakis shirts. She probably even swept the stale *Krispy Kreme* crumbs off the kitchen floor. Tanya was a good girl. Maybe he would marry her some day. Nah! Duke shook his head vigorously from side to side as his daydream abruptly came to a screeching halt.

"AF 401, contact Fort Worth Center on 324.77," instructed an air traffic controller. The balding middle-age man, seated at a radar screen some twenty-nine miles away in the ARTCC, was currently monitoring the progress of several different aircraft. He would alternate speaking to them in between bites of the *Mrs. Freshley's* pastry he had just ripped out of its hermetically sealed wrapper. His coffee was stale; the bear claw was not. Duke O'Grady, doodling on a kneeboard card with his black government pen, didn't respond immediately to the center's call. After a pregnant pause Teen Angel, flying on Commander O' Grady's left side, quickly assumed the skipper must be distracted. Brad figured Duke was probably visualizing some bikini-clad chick fetching him a fancy fruit drink as he lay contentedly on the sands of a beach in some tropical locale; Cancun or the Seychelles Islands perhaps.

"Delta two eleven I've lost your transponder, please recycle for me."

"Two eleven roger," replied the Delta captain after waving a finger at his copilot.

"Good morning center, Southwest seventy-seven-checking in at three nine zero with light continuous chop." Fort Worth Center's aircraft activity was heating up that morning.

"Roger Southwest seventy-seven, we've had pilot reports of some moderate clear air turbulence in your sector," replied the air traffic controller. After a few more seconds of non-response from Duke O'Grady, the controller brushed away some crumbs from the corner of his mouth then decided to give the Corsair flight leader another call.

"AF 401, contact Fort Worth Center on 324.77," repeated the air traffic controller in a more forceful tone after first swallowing down a large, half-chewed chunk of his breakfast pastry. Somewhat startled, Duke dropped his pen to the floorboard of the Corsair. The plastic pen settled in between the ruder pedals out of sight.

"Ah shit!" O' Grady muttered out loud to himself in reaction to his clumsiness. The skipper had heard this second center call but didn't quite hear who it was that he was in instructed to contact on the next frequency. Duke pulled the oxygen mask up from his lap and positioned it on his face to speak.

"Hey Teen Angel, who are we supposed to contact on 324.77?" asked Duke on the back radio frequency in a muffled tone of voice, as if this would prevent Rocky and Cookie from hearing about his slightly embarrassing predicament.

"*New York* Center skipper," replied Ackerman. After responding to the skipper's inquiry, Brad allowed his oxygen mask to dangle from the left side bayonet fitting of his helmet. He let out a snort then stretched his lips into a grin. Teen Angel was obviously pleased with himself for setting Duke up for a fall. The skipper must have been daydreaming pretty heavily in the cockpit of AF 401 because he quickly took Brad's bait without so much as a moment of hesitation or reflection.

"AF 401 switching to 324.77, adios," replied Duke. After advising Fort Worth Center that he had indeed received the last radio transmission, O' Grady casually flipped his UHF radio knobs until the numbers 324.77 could be seen in the frequency widow. In the formation of Corsairs, his three wingmen switched over to the new center frequency in their own cockpits with a bit more relish than usual. Anticipation can be a great motivator.

"New York Center AF 401, flight level 350" called out O'Grady on 324.77. His voice was clear and extremely professional, although misguided.

"Two."

"Three."

"Four."

Duke waited a moment, but there was no response from the ARTCC.

"Uh skipper I believe its Fort Worth Center in this part of Texas," advised Cookie, letting Duke off the hook he had so readily swallowed from Teen Angel's luring comment. Realizing he had been scammed a red-faced Duke O' Grady checked in with Fort Worth Center without further complications. But the joke had been played to its successful conclusion and he was the unwitting butt.

"I'll get even with you later Lieutenant Ackerman," said O' Grady. All four pilots laughed momentarily at the skipper's sophomoric mistake, induced by that masterful practical joker Brad Ackerman. Several minutes passed in silence as the jets continued to streak through the crystal blue skies of the Lone Star state. With his left hand, Duke cranked up the volume on both of his UHF radios a few more decibels.

"Hey Puke," suddenly cracked over the back radio, breaking the awkward silence between the members of Duke's division of Corsairs. Commander O' Grady's flight of four was still cruising comfortably at 35,000 feet just about 45 miles southwest of Sheppard AFB. Duke had descended his flight to that altitude from 39,000 feet just fifteen minutes ago due to moderate clear air turbulence at that higher altitude. Several pilot reports (PIREPS) given to Fort Worth Center in that sector had reported there was only minor clear air turbulence at 35,000 feet. As soon as he heard the word *puke*, the skipper of course knew whose voice was speaking the highly disrespectful expression loud and clear over the UHF airways for all to hear. Duke peered out of his left side canopy glass only to see Teen Angel's jet in the 8 o'clock position, tucked in tight at about five feet from his own aircraft. Ackerman was a lot closer than he probably should be for a cross country flight in visual meteorological flight conditions. Brad was of course screwing with the skipper a little because his oxygen mask was off and his visor was raised as he flipped Duke the bird from out of the right side of his cockpit. Brad's slightly chubby face glowed from the morning sunlight that sparkled off his canopy and danced on his cockpit instruments. Duke turned his head forward then flashed Teen Angel his left middle finger. As he gave Ackerman the universal, warm and friendly yet highly caustic hello between naval aviators, the back of

Duke's ungloved left hand touched the inside of his canopy glass. The minus eleven degree surrounding air mass made it uncomfortable, almost painful to maintain contact with the thick glass for more than a few seconds, despite the fact that it was warmed by an electric heating element on the Corsair.

Suddenly, Duke's thoughts raced uncontrollably to a vision of his ex-wife Cassandra. Perhaps it was the freezing canopy glass against his unprotected bare skin that compelled him to conjure up a mental picture of his ex-wife at that moment. He labored so hard not to think of her on a daily basis. The bitterly cold canopy and resulting full-body shiver probably reminded Duke of his ex-wife's frigid attitude toward him during the last three years of their wedded bliss. Sure, he bore most of the blame for dissolution of their nuptials. Most assuredly, he had bent a marital vow or two in their twelve years together. Over that time span, Duke had engaged in several dalliances with other women outside of his marriage to Cassandra. But, after all, that was part of the makeup and mystique of being a dashing young naval aviator. And, there was plenty of blame to be assigned in her direction for their failed relationship. Surely she could forgive him for these routine human sins and keep the marriage together. But, alas, she could not. Duke had always commented to his closest squadron mates that his wife, when she finally made up her mind to pursue a divorce, had discarded him like it was 1979 and he was a pair of purple polyester, bell-bottomed slacks! Even Barry Gibb threw his into the dumpster.

Duke's mind quickly returned to the more pleasurable thoughts of Tanya Billings and to the strong feelings he held for her. O' Grady shifted his body around in the ejection seat then scratched the inside of his right thigh just underneath the restricting edge of his sweaty G-suit. His right leg was slightly numb from the rim of the hard seat pan pressing up against his femoral artery. The four jets continued to fly on a northwest heading. Way out on the skipper's right wing, Cookie Cline inflated his G-suit by pushing the pres-to-test button on the lower left side panel of the Corsair's cockpit. He had a habit of doing this in flight when he was bored to tears during a particularly slow phase of a mission. After the conditioned bled air had slowly leaked out of his speed slacks, Cookie inflated his G-suit yet again then scanned the skies to make reassuring eye contact with the other three attack jets.

"Hey Cookie, do you remember our last cross country flight to Sheppard AFB?" asked Rocky on button twenty. Sheppard AFB is home to the notorious Officer Training School for Air Force nurses. Additionally, it was a fairly well-known fact that at an Air Force nurse's graduation party, naval aviators got more ass than a *Hertz* rental car in Las Vegas.

"Yeah, you and I went up there for that Air Force nurse's graduation shindig and related festivities the third Friday of last month," answered Cookie Cline with obvious accent on the *related festivities* terminology. That Friday afternoon, Cookie and Rocky had strolled into the Sheppard Officer's Club and plopped their butts down at the far side of the bar to drink a few beers together and share stories from the previous three weeks in their lives. At the other end of the bar, some sixty feet away, there were about fifteen Air Force pilots congregating with the latest graduates from the Air Force Nurse Officer Training School. Without being too obvious, Cookie counted twenty-two newly commissioned Air Force nurses wearing their second lieutenant uniform for the very first time. At least ten of them were semi-attractive females of various skin tones. After his second bottle of *Budweiser* had been drained, Rocky ordered a kamikaze. Within seconds of its arrival Rocky chugged it down then bit aggressively into the glass. Several of the nurses were simultaneously appalled yet curiously turned on by this display of courageous stupidity. That demeanor, combined with their wings of gold proved to be a strong attraction. Within 20 minutes every nurse had migrated to the other end of the bar with the Naval Aviators, leaving the Air Force pilots all alone, talking with their hands and reminiscing about their best landing on a 14,000 foot runway. Cookie and Rocky didn't get much actual sleep later than same evening in Wichita Falls.

One of the nurses they met that Friday night was a thirty-year old divorcee from Battle Creek, Michigan. She had that demure girl-next-door look of innocence. Rocky commented that she was 'the kind of woman you wanted to break down like a double barrel shot gun then bend her over a fur topped trash can and really go to work for about twenty minutes or so.' Once broken out of their self-imposed sexual exile women like these are without question some of the nastiest females on the planet! The formation of jets flew on into a flawlessly blue sky.

At NAS Fallon Lieutenant Mark Cane, officer-in-charge of VA-204's advance detachment, was just pushing through the big wooden door of the O' Club. He was heading back to the flight line after enjoying a short stack of hotcakes, two orders of thick sliced bacon and three cups of scalding hot coffee in the dining room. Cane liked his java strong, his pancakes drenched and his bacon extra crispy. Emerging from behind the heavy door he lost his footing momentarily on a slick patch of transparent ice covering the sidewalk. After regaining his composure, Mark stretched out his arms in much the same way a tightrope walker would use a pole to maintain balance above the circus crowd. As Sugar[2] walked gingerly on the icy sidewalk toward the parking lot, he was oblivious to the fact that a drop of maple syrup was caked in the right corner of his mouth. The Filipino cashier who took Cane's ten dollar bill that morning had seen the syrup on his lips but did not tell him about it. She just gave him that disgusted look as he walked away from the cash register, like it had never happened to her before.

Overnight about three inches of dry powdery snow had fallen, giving the air station a pleasant wintry glow. Being a native of Salt Lake City, Mark Cane was fairly acclimatized to winter weather and freezing temperatures. He actually loved blizzards and all manner of winter sports. Yesterday, just after his arrival on the base, Sugar[2] had made final arrangements for the *River Rattler* officers to take a short skiing excursion. The trip would take place on the first Saturday of the weapons detachment at Heavenly Valley on the California side of Lake Tahoe, and he was excited by the prospect of showcasing his skiing prowess. That morning outside the O' Club, Lieutenant Cane walked right up to a fresh snowdrift and began to construct a five foot high snowman in the parking lot. All naval aviators are merely big kids at heart and Mark Cane was no exception to that rule. He gently rolled and packed a three-foot diameter snowball to serve as the base of his creation and ten minutes later he was putting the finishing touches on this, his fifth snowman of the season. The other four were made with his lovely wife's help in Utah; one was even built on the grounds of the Mormon Temple in Salt Lake.

What was unusual about this latest masterpiece was that Cane not only gave the snowman the standard face, but that he decided to include other parts of the snowman's anatomy. The face was constructed out of several rocks, an old discarded cigar butt, a couple of large brown buttons, a wilted carrot and a lengthy red scarf. All of these objects were discovered either inside of, or in the vicinity of, the O' Club trashcan. Two small tree branches, ripped from a lonely tree, served as arms and a soiled, blue watch cap was placed on the snowman's head to keep it warm. For the final touch Cane inserted what appeared to be a twelve-inch dick on the lower portion of the snowman, made out of the Italian zucchini he had purchased at the base commissary this morning, specifically for that purpose. Behind him, Cane could hear a few chuckles erupt from a group of five as they approached the front door of the club and couldn't help but pass the X-rated snowman. Lieutenant Cane located his rental car then drove back to the flight line to await the imminent arrival of twelve Corsairs.

"AF-401, Denver Center, I will need you to be level at 10,000 feet in five minutes so that I can hand you off to approach," advised the sector air traffic controller. On this leg of the cross country flight Duke was purposely staying as high as possible for as long as possible to conserve every precious drop of JP-5 jet fuel.

But now he could delay no longer, it was time to descend the formation for their impeding approach into Buckley AFB.

"Watch this center. AF-401 is leaving three five zero for one zero thousand, altimeter 29.97," said Duke. "Hang on fellas," he instructed his wingmen. With that said Duke abruptly flipped his Corsair jet on its backside then pulled evenly on the stick until the G-meter gauge read exactly 4 G's. In an instant the stubby nose of his attack jet was in an inverted 60 degree dive towards mother Earth. Just as smoothly, Duke used his ailerons to put the attack aircraft right side up again. His three wingmen stayed with him throughout the aggressive, precision maneuver. It was an *E-ticket* ride! The four Corsairs were now hurtling toward the mud at over 15,000 feet per minute rate of descent. In less than two minutes the formation of jets was level at 10,000 feet, 35 miles from Buckley AFB and zipping along at 540 knots indicted airspeed above the snow-covered Colorado terrain. The landscape was pristine, as if untouched by any form of organic life.

"Very impressive AF-401, contact Buckley Approach Control on 254.9. Have a great day sir," were the final words of the ARTCC controller. Eleven minutes later the flight of four landed on runway 32 at Buckley, taxied to the transient line then shut down their engines to refuel.

Passing through the flight planning section of Base Operations, Rocky suddenly smiled but kept walking at a brisk pace towards his waiting cheeseburger and chili fries. After wolfing down his mega-calorie meal then pausing in the head to take a well-deserved piss, Rocky strolled back to the flight planning room with a glint in his eye and chili on his left sleeve. Back in flight planning, he watched in disbelief as about twelve young Air Force pilots were busy going over their flight plans in excruciatingly meticulous detail, right down to a minutia of small elements. They had kneeboard cards filled with checkpoint fuel figures and winds aloft reports, as well as weather station frequencies and notes on position reporting procedures should they haphazardly stray from a radar controlled environment. These knuckleheads weren't in the middle of the deep dark ocean, with only a boat to land on. They were in the middle of fucking Colorado. Rocky was disgusted and could take it no longer. He was going take it upon himself to teach these Air Force pukes a lesson about cross-country flying. After clearing his throat to gain their attention, Rocky whipped out his black, U.S. government issued pen then sauntered over to a high altitude navigation chart hanging on the wall. When he was sure that all twelve Air Force pilots were watching him, at least in their peripheral vision, Rocky placed one end of the pen on Buckley then measured off four times using the "200 nautical mile" pen as his calculating device.

The pen made a slapping noise as he crudely measured out an intended route of flight on the wall chart.

"200, 400, 600, 800. Yep I can make that leg!" said Rocky as he turned and proceeded towards his airplane on the T-line. That fine day in Colorado, Rocky Stone taught those Air Force boys the value of their U.S. government-issued pen when planning a cross-country flight. Each of them had two of the pens in the left-side pocket of their green flight suits. Now, thanks to Lieutenant Commander Rocky Stone, they all became aware of an alternate use for the writing instrument!

CHAPTER 21

▼

A SHOW-AND-TELL STORY

The first night of any Fallon weapons detachment was usually begun around 1900 at the infamous *Bulls-Eye Bar* inside the NAS O' Club. This meeting time was a couple of hours after all the squadron's airplanes had been recovered and bedded down. At dusk on February 9, 1992 a gloomy chill saturated the Sunday evening air. By 1715 that day all ninety-two of Carrier Air Wing Two's (CAG-2) airplanes sat on the flight line of *Strike U* in the Nevada desert. By 1830 eighty planes were in an 'UP' status, fully prepared for an ambitious flight operations schedule set to kick off at 1100 the next morning. This was the prelude to three weeks of intensive, pre-deployment weapons training designed to render the air wing operationally ready for its impending around-the-world journey. The April through October cruise was of course doubly special since it was the first instance in which a Navy Reserve squadron had been activated during peacetime for a carrier deployment. Additionally, it would be the swan song for the mighty A-7E Corsair which would be retired then sent rudely into the Davis-Monthan bone yard upon return of the USS *Enterprise*. During the next nineteen days all phases of carrier warfare would be examined and successfully completed in a cycle of rigorous training and testing.

Off in the distance the twilight sun was just disappearing behind a grove of thick pine trees that lined the Lake Tahoe resort area on the California/Nevada border. At that very moment hordes of skiers were shushing down the slippery slopes of the Squaw Valley and Heavenly ski resorts, perhaps making their final run down the mountain before congregating at the lodge to share an Irish coffee in front of a blazing fireplace. To the northeast dull gray, snow clouds loomed over the peak of a 9, 000 foot high mountain range. These rugged foothills served as one edge of the Dixie Valley Tactics Range in the northwestern portion of the GABBS MOA (Military Operating Area). The jagged topography was perfect for practicing terrain masking, an attack pilot's trick for avoiding radar detection while proceeding to a bombing target on the Fallon weapons range. Back on the flight line, three nineteen year-old airman stood a less than vigilant guard over the airplanes, each serving a four hour shift of duty before being relieved by another young enlisted man in soiled dungarees. The scene conveyed a foreboding feel even though a soothing tranquility spread evenly over the tarmac area. This was the calm that preceded tomorrow's storm of aviation activity. The muffled crackle of a walkie-talkie radio momentarily disturbed the serenity of the tarmac.

Unlike the Officers Club at NAS Miramar, where wearing a sweaty zoom bag was the secret to sexual success in the barroom on a Wednesday night in San Diego, the standard procedure for pilots on this first night at Fallon was to quickly shed their flight suits then pop into the shower stall for a hot bath in the slimy, soft water of a double occupancy BOQ room. Clad in civilian clothes, air wing officers would then scurry over to the O' Club to spend a few quality hours drinking, carousing and generally catching up on sea stories shared with old shipmates from carrier cruises past. This initial flurry of activity would undoubtedly be followed up with several hours of cheap gambling at the Fallon Casino or by some good ole fashioned whoring at the Mustang Ranch whorehouse. The dilapidated building of the world famous brothel was situated just at the outskirts of the community on a desolate patch of highway leading into Reno, Nevada. The Mustang Ranch had consistently proven to be a bustling hot spot during Fallon weapons detachments for officers and enlisted men alike. The hookers employed there always looked forward to an Air Wing coming to town because their pocket books invariably received a much-needed shot in the arm. This routine behavioral dynamic, carousing with hookers at the Mustang Ranch, had been in place for over fifty years and every tactical naval aviator had encountered it during his career. It was one of many unique, shared experiences that bonded aviators together for all eternity in the brotherhood of carrier naval aviation.

The front of the Fallon Officers Club featured a rather unique adornment; one that had become a legend in tactical naval aviation. The slanted shingle roof of the O' Club had a rather large bulls-eye painted on it. The bright red bulls-eye was perfectly aligned with the front entranceway of the O' Club. The roof had also been outfitted with a lever arm in the center of the structure. Attached to that lever arm was a hollowed-out B-61 practice bomb. Commonly referred to as the *silver bullet*, the B-61 is the bomb shape that simulates a tactical nuclear weapon. The lever arm's long chain allowed the B-61 to swing back and forth pointing directly at the center of the bulls-eye. The message was clear. Inside of this building was *ground zero*, the world famous Bulls-eye Bar.

In the bar room, situated directly above the antique brass mirror which was mounted on a wall behind the bar, that same bulls-eye scene had been taken to its logical final step. The silver B-61 was impaled half way into the center of the bulls-eye with shards of material, twisted steel and concrete flying up all around the impact spot. Scattered all around the outer ring of the bulls-eye, some enterprising individual had painted two human ass holes, four elbows and one guy running around with his hair on fire. That scene and all of its props was meant to portray the exact moment of impact and detonation of the nuclear device. But the message was part of a double entendre. *Ground zero* was also where the fun began onboard Fallon Naval Air Station, and the good times spread out from this center point. It was an impressive and most memorable display; one in which successive Commanding Officers of NAS Fallon took tremendous pride.

Clustered casually at the west end of the bar precisely at 1900 were Rocky Stone, Cookie Cline, Juice Mayhew, Comatose Gross, Pops Petibone, T-Ben Hebert, Sugar^2 Cane and Teen Angel Ackerman. All eight aviators had the smell of heavy soap and cheap after-shave lotion, except for Brad Ackerman who had splashed on the usual amount of expensive *Escada* to complement his close shave. On the wall behind this group of *River Rattler* pilots were several air wing and squadron plaques commemorating successful completion of weapons detachments past. Typically, pilots would search the plaques for their names or for the names of old shipmates, if only to experience the déjà vu phenomenon. The cramped O' Club bar was about half full and it had the distinct aroma of spilled beer around the barstools and near the video games area in the south corner of the establishment. Four E-2 pilots were already engaged in a rousing game of *fooz ball* drinking their glasses of iced tea and *Diet Pepsi*.

In the center of the group of *River Rattlers*, holding a dice cup provocatively in his left hand, was an F-14 Tomcat pilot and LSO (Landing Signals Officer) named Quentin McCracken; call sign *Big Dog*. McCracken wore a flowered Hawaiian shirt and a floppy, straw golf hat sporting the *Shark* logo unique to Greg Norman products. Teen Angel and Big Dog McCracken had gone through

Navy flight school together and had even been BOQ roomies in Pensacola, Florida at the fourteen week Aviation Indoctrination (AI) course. Nine months after completing that AI school the two student naval aviators were back together at VT-25 in Beeville, Texas for the advanced training syllabus, flying the A-4 Sky Hawk. After earning the coveted wings of gold and making it successfully into their fleet squadrons, both pilots had been selected to train as Landing Signal Officers and had studied together at the LSO School in Pensacola. That night at the *Fleet Aviator Bar*, Big Dog McCracken was trying to hold his own in deep water amongst a circling crowd of light attack aviators; a serious challenge for any F-14 interceptor pilot to be sure!

Throwing down cocktails that evening in the O' Club was a chubby, yet semi-attractive bar tender named Caroline Simpson. The forty-something Caroline had been serving drinks at the Fallon Officers Club for well over a decade, so she was extremely familiar with pilot jargon and come on lines. She was also the widow of a dead A-6 Intruder BN (Bombardier Navigator) who was lost at sea eleven years ago in a midair collision during an ACM engagement. Her ten-year old son Josh was born seven months after the fatal accident that claimed the life of his father. In the aftermath of the incident, Caroline hardly had time to grieve as she was forced to be strong and emotionally stable for her only child. Over the years as a bartender onboard Fallon Naval Air Station, Caroline had come to realize that flying successfully in the tactical aviation community, especially off aircraft carriers, tended to foster and nurture a cocky attitude in a pilot. This was the legendary manner that most Naval Aviators are notorious for possessing and displaying on a routine basis. She knew the Navy bred them that way on their first day of flight training, so they would have a better chance of surviving and thriving in a combat scenario. The bar tending job had made Caroline Simpson callous and somewhat immune to the aviators' antics, and yet she was always tolerant of Navy pilots and their arrogant barroom demeanor. She had learned to endure their egotistical conduct if only to savor it for its stress relief and obvious comic value. Strangely, it had actually helped to soothe Caroline's emotional rancor and better equipped her to cope with the tragic loss of her husband.

Carol Baby, as she was known to the naval aviators who frequented the bar, had a pixie-style haircut that was tri-colored or neapolitan because she was somewhat fickle; she couldn't make up her mind on the perfect tint for her short locks. Her puffy round eyes yearned to be blue but hadn't quite developed beyond a dull, light green stage so she wore designer contact lenses shaded baby-blue. Carol Baby also carried about ten to fifteen pounds to much weight for her 5 foot 7 inch frame but it didn't seem to detract from her subtle good looks. Instead of fad dieting and exercise, she routinely wore black for its slimming affect to offset the extra pounds. That evening however, Caroline wore a red plaid skirt, similar to the skirts worn by Catholic High School girls back in New Orleans; only hers was mid-thigh in length. The Jesuit nuns would never allow this back in Orleans Parrish. This skirt was combined with a tight-fitting, black spandex top, strategically covered by a man's unbuttoned, long sleeve white shirt. Caroline had rolled up the sleeves of the shirt to give off that Burt Reynolds look from the disco era; half masculine, half feminine. Her ensemble was completed with pink bobby socks and black and white saddle shoes. Carol Baby looked like she was 17.

That night, in between hustling beers and mixed drinks, Caroline Simpson was watching and listening intently to the ongoing and often heated discussions taking place all around the bar. Aviators were playing with dice cups, talking with their hands and slapping each other on the back; all while guzzling gallons of alcohol and consuming bar snacks from little glass dishes. Of particular interest to Caroline that evening was the VA-204 pilots and their ongoing, cynical dialogue with Big Dog McCracken. After twisting off the cap to three more bottles of *Michelob Light*, Caroline decided to break into that conversation and ask Lieutenant McCracken a question that seemed to be haunting her for some odd reason. Getting his full attention, Caroline Simpson looked Big Dog McCracken square in the eye. Her fake baby blues were radiant as she spoke without hesitation or any visible fear; always a good sign in a woman.

"So Lieutenant, how did you get that call sign Big Dog?" inquired Carol Baby as she wiped a small patch of the bar using a moist towel and a circular motion. As she leaned over some of her ample cleavage began peeking through the tight-fitting spandex, and the man's shirt she had chosen to wear that night. As soon as he heard the words come out of Caroline's mouth, Teen Angel chugged back a healthy amount of his beer then grinned modestly in anticipation. Brad Ackerman already knew Big Dog McCracken's stock comeback to this all too often asked question. Like so many others, he had heard it many times before in his career. Quentin McCracken immediately adopted his snooty facade.

"Well honey, it's a show and tell story," replied McCracken as he took in a deep, closed-mouth breath while simultaneously wrinkling up his nose. Then, bending his fingers back towards the palm, Big Dog checked the condition of the nails on his left hand in an aloof, detached manner. The entire group of *River Rattler* pilots suddenly stopped drinking their beers and cocktails. All of them subconsciously leaned in towards the bar, opened their eyes wide with expectation and drew curiously quiet. They were giving Big Dog McCracken temporary ownership of the full stage for delivery of his classic line.

"Whaddya mean, show and tell?" asked Caroline in an anxious tone. Even as the words left her lips, she knew that a clever retort was about to unfold at her expense. But her brain and hidden intellect was already gearing up to fight back. As she nervously awaited the punch line from Big Dog, Carol Baby gently bit her lower lip then made a squinting grimace with her right eye, all while continuing to scan Lieutenant McCracken's unshaven face.

"I show and then you tell!" exclaimed Big Dog without cracking a smile. As if on cue, big belly laughs erupted immediately from the group of *River Rattler* pilots and Juice Mayhew delivered a slap of approval onto Big Dog's back as reward for a job well done. Several pilots exchanged high fives in a haughty display of endorsement for the mild sexual harassment of the female bartender. But a slightly red-faced, 42 year old Caroline already knew how to shut their whole party up and she did so without much of a delay. Her coy posture suddenly changed.

"Well then, I want you to show it to me RIGHT HERE AND RIGHT NOW BIG BOY?" demanded Caroline, wiping her mouth brazenly with the damp bar towel. Reddish pink lipstick stains were visible on the towel as she tossed the white cloth down onto the bar in front of McCracken, to put emphasis on her challenge to the now blushing F-14 LSO. Caroline's bulging eyes purposely stared down at Big Dog's crotch as she played the moment for all it was worth. In a most engaging manner, she had successfully put Lieutenant McCracken and all the *River Rattlers* in their place, at least for the next several moments. As the uproarious laughter settled back down to more of a muffled tone the bar phone began to ring. Caroline turned her back to the bar room and quickly located the telephone sitting underneath the Louis XIV Cognac display, next to the cash register. She snatched the black telephone receiver off the hook and held it snugly to her left ear. Crossing her legs as she stood casually behind the bar, Caroline plugged her other ear with a long right index finger, as if to drown out all the commotion and clamor. This action allowed Big Dog to temporarily slide off the hook he had placed himself on, courtesy of the bold and semi-beautiful Caroline Simpson.

On the bar phone was Lieutenant Sugar[2] Cane's wife calling from their home in Utah. A very pregnant Mrs. Cane was desperately attempting to locate her beloved husband so she could bitch at him for awhile to pacify the restlessness and achy nerves syndrome she had been suffering through for the past several hours.

"Is there a Lieutenant Cane in the bar? It's your wife," announced Caroline as she roughly placed the telephone receiver down onto the damp towel she used to wipe up spilt beer. As an experienced bar tender at an Officers Club, Caroline was all too familiar with the next response from the O' Club patrons.

"Hooray," shouted the pilots surrounding Mark Cane. All eight men crowded even closer to the bar in between the tall blue stools to get Caroline's attention and make their drink order known.

"The drinks are on Sugar Sugar," bellowed Rocky Stone as he raised a long-neck bottle of *Budweiser* in mock tribute to his squadron mate. According to Naval Aviation tradition, any pilot whose wife calls him at the bar must buy a round of drinks for his entire party. So Lieutenant Mark Cane would be purchasing the next round of nine alcoholic beverages. This of course pleased his squadron mates not only because they would receive a free brewski, but because it would be at Mark Cane's expense. It was a double pleasure. Sugar^2 Cane grabbed the phone off the towel and began to listen to his wife's dialogue in a most disgusted manner. A small amount of beer had transferred from the wet towel to the phone's earpiece and then into Cane's right ear. He didn't even notice.

Mrs. Cane began their little, long-distance chat by vehemently complaining to her wayward husband about the painful and premature contractions she was currently enduring at that very moment. These were pains that she had to bear because she was carrying HIS CHILD in her uterus. The distressed look on Mark Cane's face made it obvious that he loathed the topic of conversation. Pulling the phone momentarily from his ear and laying it back into the moist towel Cane hastily removed two, crisp twenty dollar bills from his wallet. He made brief eye contact with Caroline Simpson then casually tossed the twenties down onto the bar to make restitution for his round of drinks. Mrs. Cane continued to fume and ramble on the other end of the line, not aware that her husband couldn't even hear her. As he hunched back over the edge of the bar with the phone re-glued into his ear, Mark Cane looked somewhat like an ostrich searching for a suitable place to bury his head deep in the sand. Nevertheless, he continued to listen patiently to the relentless ranting of his spouse.

Standing next to Sugar Sugar, drinking from a fresh bottle of *Coors Light*, Teen Angel's extra sensitive ears could plainly hear Mrs. Cane bitching and moaning about being pregnant with Mark's child. Brad abruptly and correctly discerned that she was trying to make Sugar^2 feel a little guilty about being on this squadron weapons detachment and going on a peacetime cruise while she would be bearing his first born child. Hell, Mrs. Cane was probably attempting to make the squadron and the entire naval service feel guilty as well over her plight. When he could take it no more, Mark Cane made up an excuse then respectfully hung up on his young, irate wife. Instantly, Teen Angel picked up a cold bottle of beer and handed it to a dejected looking Mark Cane. Standing at the far west end of the bar, Ackerman then proceeded to slide his right arm around Cane's thin neck in preparation for telling him a short story that his father used to share with him about childbirth. After popping a fried mozzarella cheese stick into his mouth and swallowing it down his gullet, Brad proceeded to tell the tale.

Whenever the time was appropriate, and this seemed to be quite often, Chief Ackerman would inform his adolescent son Brad about American Indian women and their unique child bearing practices. According to Chief Ackerman, Indian wives wouldn't dream of bothering their warrior husbands with something as trivial as childbirth. While today's so-called *modern women*, according to Chief Ackerman, had evolved into taking full undue advantage of birthing babies. They even receive all sorts of unnecessary benefits from childbirth in contemporary America. Benefits like too much sympathy and weeks of maternity leave from their jobs. Brad's father said it was all a bunch of bullshit contrived by the women's liberation movement, especially the NOW organization. Brad's father would tell him that in the glory days of the Old West, Native American women would not bother their men with such drivel. In fact, on the day they were to give birth, Indian women would simply go out into the woods and locate a riverbank, slide a piece of rawhide in between their teeth then give birth to their husband's baby. All this maternity activity took place in the early morning hours of the day. These same Indian wives would then use the cold river water to clean themselves and the newborn baby up after the ordeal. These resilient women would be back in the fields that very afternoon attending to the crops and completing their daily chores around the wigwam.

"According to my dad, Indian women were tough and the pain of childbirth is merely a myth perpetuated by modern-day women's libbers," concluded Teen Angel with a wink and a nod of approval at Sugar² Cane. Brad's right hand squeezed Cane's neck roughly.

Chief Ackerman would advise Brad of this little-known fact often as if he was trying to influence his juvenile son on a future ethnic choice of bride. At this point in the account, Teen Angel was not only talking to Mark Cane, but the whole west end of the bar seemed to be listening attentively to the narrative; reaping the benefit of Chief Ackerman's profound wisdom on the subject of childbirth. Caroline Simpson just shook her pretty head in amazement and continued to deliver liquid relief in the O' Club bar room, now teeming with aviators. As the small crowd at the west end of the saloon pondered this profound theory, a tiny voice of dissension was suddenly heard speaking up to Brad's immediate left.

When Teen Angel turned sharply to his left his eyes beheld a diminutive black woman wearing a khaki uniform with gold oak leaves, symbolic of the Lieutenant Commander rank in the Navy.

"Excuse me miss, but would you care to chime in on our discussion of child-birth" said Lieutenant Ackerman. A repugnant quality was evident in Brad's tone. Clad in his civilian attire and green flight jacket no rank hierarchy was apparent between them, so Brad took full advantage of the situation and threw a little bit of disrespect at the superior, although female officer. Rocky and Cookie's ears, discerning the definite change in Teen Angel's voice, also turned to face the black female officer. The blue NAVAIRPAC name tag on the right side of the woman's khaki uniform read: 'LCDR LESLIE LANCE.' She sported no warfare specialty insignia on the left side of her blouse, but she wore black *Corfam* shoes on her tiny feet. She was also dressed in tan panty-hose and a skirt. The hemline rested just above her knees.

"I'm not sure you even have a clue what the pain of childbirth is like," said Leslie Lance in a matter-of-fact fashion. Her dark eyes never flinched as she held tight to Teen Angel's downward gaze, not allowing him to avert his stare. Brad figured, although incorrectly, that she was all of 4 foot 11 inches tall as he watched her puff up a petite upper body.

"Ok slick, why don't you tell us all about it," said Lieutenant Commander Stone from just behind Teen Angel's left shoulder. Rocky held his long-neck *Bud* in an adversarial fashion as he waited for the pint-sized female to reply to his chal-lenge. Little did these men realize that Leslie Lance relished such moments and she almost never lost a confrontation. Leslie placed her half-full glass of Bloody Mary Mix softly onto the bar then stepped into the middle of the group of avia-tors. She was now effectively surrounded by pilots.

"Alright boys, if you insist then I will. First, I want all of you VA-204 pilots to grab your upper lip and pinch it in between your thumb and index finger. None of the aviators were curious enough to wonder how she knew they were all *River Rattlers*.

"Now I want you to really squeeze those lips gentlemen, and don't hold back on me," instructed Leslie Lance. If anyone else in the other parts of the O' Club had even taken the time to notice the shenanigans occurring at the west end of the bar, they would have seen twelve Corsair pilots and one Tomcat driver clutching their upper lips while a short African-American female officer directed the entire comedic episode.

"Ok that's good gentlemen," said Lance as she eyed every participant in her little charade. "Keep pinching. You're not really pinching," said Lance as she looked sternly at Cookie Cline who was merely pretending to go along with the demonstration.

"Ok, Ok, I'm pinching," said Cookie as he reapplied the pressure on his upper lip with his index finger and thumb. Even Juice Mayhew was a willing part of the show now.

"Now I want you to just pull those lips right back over your heads!" All thirteen men busted up laughing. They had been had; fools every one of them thanks to the bravado and cunning of Lieutenant Commander Lance. Behind the bar, Caroline couldn't contain her laughter. She hastily looked for the Bloody Mary Mix. Leslie Lance wouldn't have to pay for another drink that evening. Caroline was that proud of the woman for holding her own in a sea of light attack sharks.

"Boys, that's a fairly accurate equivalent to the pain of childbirth," concluded Lance as she made her way back to a full glass of spicy tomato juice. The crowd parted to allow her easy access back to the bar even as they began to wonder who this black female officer was.

Brad couldn't help but giggle to himself even as the episode faded into history. He suddenly remembered that Leslie Lance was referring to a very funny clip from *The Tonight Show with Johnny Carson*. On that specific episode, a female celebrity guest tried to give Johnny Carson a better idea of the pain involved in childbirth. That female celebrity pulled the very same trick on the 'dean of late night television' during a particularly hilarious segment of the network talk show. Of course this stunt cracked Carson up so much that he was rolling on the carpet behind his desk on *The Tonight Show* set. Carson threw his patented pencil at the camera as he fell over backward, laughing hysterically. Brad even recalled that the show's producer, Freddie De Cordova, had to break for a commercial because the segment was so highly interrupted by Carson's rolling in apparently uncontrollable laughter. Who is this woman, thought Teen Angel? He intended to find out as he snuggled up next to her at the bar, his curiosity running wild. Ackerman had a sneaking suspicion they were going to be fast friends.

Back at the Fallon BOQ, CAG Madison had summoned Duke O' Grady to his room for a 1945 meeting. This would be an initial introduction and get acquainted session since the two aviators had never met during their careers in the Navy. Duke hoped the meeting would be short and sweet since he was anxious to join his officers in the evening's festivities at the club and then later at the Fallon Casino. Although the two pilots had never met before their mutual reputations preceded them both in the mind of each man. CAG had heard that Duke possessed a somewhat lax leadership style, that he detested senior officers and that he was a gifted Naval Aviator. Duke knew all too well the renowned anecdotes associated with the highly colorful Spine Ripper Madison and his legendary temper. On the second deck of the BOQ, Duke walked down a narrow hallway toward Madison's room, number 201. The carpet was a soiled grey and the walls were a dreary off-white. Commander O' Grady's right wing tip shoe had a glob of maple syrup on the toe from the pancake breakfast he had enjoyed six days ago in New Orleans at the *Denny's* restaurant near the Oakwood Mall.

As O' Grady arrived at Commander Madison's door, he carelessly bumped into the CAG Master Chief who was just departing after a 30 minute bitching session with Spine Ripper. The chief dropped a few papers from a Plexiglas clipboard he was holding and they rained down onto the carpet. A few moments of awkwardness ensued between the senior enlisted man and the Commanding Officer of Attack Squadron 204. After the Master Chief retrieved his stray papers he straightened up and continued to walk down the hallway. Almost immediately, Duke felt a chill go down his back as Master Chief Scott's face came into full view. Right there on the second deck of the Bachelor Officer's Quarters in Fallon Nevada O' Grady had a sensation of déjà vu overtake him. He knew this enlisted man from somewhere in his naval career but just can't place him at that particular moment. The tiny unshaven hairs on the back of Duke's neck stood up a moment later as he heard the Master Chief speak to another man on down the hallway. Duke turned then scratched his forehead as he wandered over to a wooden door with the numerals 201 nailed into the center. He knocked three times on the wood before he was invited in by CAG Madison's booming voice. Duke partially sucked in his gut, cranked the brass knob to the right then pushed the door open. He walked into Madison's room and into the presence of naval aviation greatness for the first time in his career. Duke audaciously slammed the door shut behind him. Playing softly on the black and white television in the background was an episode of *Cheers*. In the scene, Woody Harrelson's character was trying to dissuade his visiting cousin, played by guest star Harry Connick Jr., from seeking a romantic relationship with his boss, bar manager Rebecca.

CAG Madison apparently wanted to have a short preliminary encounter with Commander John O'Grady before the weapons detachment kicked off tomorrow morning at 0730. In the privacy of a BOQ room, Spine Ripper Madison began to lay out his personal attitude and his active duty air wing's feelings about naval reservists. Sitting on a brown leather chair, still wearing his green flight suit, Madison fumbled for the unlit cigar he had positioned in an ash tray on a dilapidated dresser. CAG's custom-made flight boots were off and resting next to the leather chair. The boots were awaiting a fresh coat of brown polish. With no hesitation, the Air Wing Commander began speaking with the skipper of VA-204.

He did so without even exchanging a customary initial greeting. His tone was coarse and unapologetic.

"In my experience Commander O' Grady, Naval Reserve pilots are a bunch of prima donnas who just want you to flip them the keys to a jet for a couple of hours so they can have fun and pretend to be tactical naval aviators again, a few days each month. Then, before they run back to their cushy little airline pilot jobs, they want the American taxpayers to write them huge paychecks for their short amount of actual service." Madison was on a roll. Duke picked some lint off the front of his black *Calvin Klein* shirt then let it fall to the carpet. He quickly reestablished eye contact with Madison as CAG continued his tirade, all while undulating that cigar in the stubby fingers of his left hand. Duke wondered if it doubled as a security blanket for Madison.

"Reserve enlisted men are undisciplined and rapidly getting fat around the middle. Additionally, they have lost their work ethic and routinely call officers and chiefs by their first names or tactical call signs. Like all Navy Reserve outfits, your squadron is soft skipper," harangued Madison. Subconsciously, Duke took another silent breath to suck in his gut even further. At that moment, a bulb in the light fixture above the sink began to flicker.

"Active duty carrier air wings have no need for this Commander O' Grady because it jeopardizes people's lives unnecessarily. The only reason you and your men are here is because of that stupid fucking Secretary of the Navy from New Orleans who wants to prove something in the political arena so he can move up the corporate ladder in the bureaucracy. But now you and your entire squadron are on active duty and that laidback attitude will not be tolerated skipper!" O' Grady squirmed a bit at this dressing down from CAG, not because he was worried but because he knew every word coming out of Madison's mouth was false. Duke nervously picked more lint off of his shirtsleeve. Shifting his weight from the left side to the right, the skipper realized he couldn't be silent any longer.

"Throw every challenge you got in your active duty trick bag at my men CAG. They will chew it up, spit it out then ask for more. With all due respect sir, this air wing is damn lucky to have the *River Rattlers* in it for this deployment you pompous ass!" Madison was stunned but likewise proud of John O'Grady for shielding his squadron against his onslaught.

"I'll gladly by you a beer at the club tonight CAG, but if you'll excuse me I'm gonna join my officers now at the bar," advised Duke as he walked out of the room, rudely slamming the door and leaving Commander Madison speechless for only the second time in his career.

CAG Madison's mouth stayed open for a full minute as he contemplated Duke's strong rebuttal. As he closed his lips together, CAG Madison couldn't help but be impressed by the way Duke vehemently defended his men against the verbal attack delivered by the air wing commander. Part of his diatribe was real and part was facade because, unknown to Commander O' Grady, he was measuring Duke in this initial meeting. Similar to Admiral Hymen Rickover, Commander Madison tested all of his officers in this manner in order to gauge their inner fortitude. It was part of his personal leadership style and a way to pump up his men to bring out their best qualities while enduring verbal adversity. CAG also knew that Duke had another little revelation that awaited him. Duke would most likely meet this surprise tonight at the bar; it would be LCDR Leslie Lance, his newly appointed AMO (Assistant Maintenance Officer), courtesy of SEC-NAV Andrews and Congresswoman Trish Schneider of Colorado.

CHAPTER 22

▼

YOU DON'T EVER
TURN OFF THE KING

As a middle-aged, African-American woman Lieutenant Commander Leslie Lance was sneaky cute, meaning that you didn't notice her approaching from long distances. Just a shade under sixty-two inches tall, she kind of snuck up on you and could easily advance on a position without too much hoopla. But when she eased herself into your close proximity you soon discovered and could rapidly appreciate how beautiful a woman she really was. She was sneaky cute! That first night at the Fallon O 'Club bar, Brad Ackerman was duly impressed with her clear, smooth skin as well as her obvious intellect and confidence. Their initial conversation was going quite well when Brad suddenly checked his watch then briefly excused himself so that he could go make a quick, overdue phone call to his girlfriend Danielle Le Claire back in Louisiana. It was about 9:15pm (CST) in New Orleans and Teen Angel correctly figured Danielle would be home from her Sunday horseback riding lesson, probably enjoying a glass of Chardonnay in her living room while studying several legal briefs for tomorrow's docket of court cases in the *crescent city*.

Brad also correctly assumed that Leslie Lance could successfully hold her own in the Officers Club without him, at least for the next fifteen or twenty minutes. But Lieutenant Commander Lance would not be in the bar room when Teen Angel ended his phone conversation with Miss Le Claire. It seems that Leslie was somewhat appalled by Rocky Stone's behavior that night, especially from what she witnessed in the fifteen minutes of Brad Ackerman's absence. Rocky was pretty much sloppy drunk after consuming six beers in rather rapid succession. While pounding down his seventh, he was shamelessly vying for the attention of a fairly young, female bar patron. The woman, Sara Marinovich, was all of twenty-two and had joined her two girlfriends for a night out, beginning with a couple hours of cavorting around naval aviators inside the Officers Club. The first night of any Air Wing detachment was prime time and perennially good for meeting prospective husband material. All the local girls in the surrounding towns were acutely aware of this fact.

Since her graduation from UNLV in December 1991, Sara had worked as a hostess at a locally owned eatery named Crazy Lee's Diner. The 1950's retro café, owned by her father, was situated next to the Fallon Casino, a prime location in the small country town. The sign just under the marquee simply read 'Good Food' and the Lee Marinovich family had been serving up just that in Fallon, Nevada for well over forty years. By 2015 that evening, Rocky was all over Sara like a barnacle attached to the rusty keel of a worn out sailboat. At 2030, his fellow squadron mates had to literally scrape him off of the unwilling Sara, in order to get him to leave the O' Club and take the short ride with them out to the Fallon Casino.

Teen Angel was just hanging up the pay phone when he saw the group of *River Rattler* pilots leaving the bar, heading for three rental vehicles parked just outside on the slick grounds of the snow-lined parking lot. Instinctively, Brad patted the right thigh area of his jeans, to feel for the set of rental car keys just to make sure they were in his pocket. When he saw Juice Mayhew and Cookie Cline make a beeline for the men's head, Teen Angel decided he needed to take a leak himself. The bathroom was completely empty as the three men walked in; unusual because the bar was now full to its capacity with drinking aviators. Brad lined himself up squarely with the urinal on the far left side of the bathroom. Teen Angel unzipped his jeans then maneuvered his tally whacker from behind white underwear until it was in the proper position. Relief was instantaneous. Brad was soon closing up his fly, washing his hands in warm water at the sink and checking his look in the mirror. Cookie and Juice had strolled into adjoining toilet stalls, lowered their trousers then sat on the cold seats almost simultaneously.

Jack Mayhew was the kind of man who would squat down in the toilet stall next to yours to take a dump then, without provocation, strike up a casual conversation with you. It had the demoralizing effect of breaking your concentration for the task at hand while sitting on the toilet! As soon as Juice spoke, Cookie cut him off. Teen Angel just shook his head in amazement as he threw wet paper towels into a garbage bin then walked out of the bathroom to give his buddies a few moments alone.

"Please Juice, let me get this over with so we can drive out to the Casino and win some money at the craps tables," pleaded Cookie. He rolled down about five yards of toilet paper as he spoke the words to Juice. The toilet paper piled up on the bathroom floor before Cookie pulled it up to his lap.

"No sweat Cook," replied Jack. "I'll zip my lips." A loud and distinctive splash was heard emanating from Mayhew's toilet bowl. Juice grunted and squeezed his lower body to force the excrement completely out of his bowels and down into the bowl. Some of the toilet water splashed up to soak the lower portion of Mayhew's thighs. No sooner than the splash was heard, the foulest stench imaginable permeated the bathroom. Instantaneously, Cookie realized he had to get out and get out now! He fumbled with the toilet paper for several seconds, pulled his pants back up then zipped and reset his belt. Lieutenant Cline left the men's room without even washing his hands or speaking to Jack. Cookie literally leaped through the bathroom door to make his escape, brushing aside an EA-6B NFO who was trying to enter the bathroom in the process. The NFO's glasses were knocked slightly askew in the encounter. Cookie had held his breath for the last minute and a half and didn't suck in any more oxygen until he was outside in the fresh mountain air of Nevada.

The Prowler NFO straightened the *John Denver* signature, horn-rimmed glasses on his face. He took a few additional moments to collect himself after the brush with Cookie Cline then entered the men's room. Without warning, his nostrils were assaulted by the horrific odor left behind by Jack Mayhew. Juice, now busy scrubbing his hands in cold soapy water, had left a lengthy snake of a terd in the bowl amongst the toilet paper. He hadn't bothered to flush it down. The NFO had the regrettable luck of pushing open the wrong toilet stall door.

"You know you could have flushed and sprayed some bathroom deodorizer before you left this stall pal," said the Prowler NFO as if to reproach Juice. Jack Mayhew didn't answer at first he just continued to lather up his hands at the sink. The NFO's face was contorted as he endured the stink just long enough to enter the stall and push down the flush handle on Juice's toilet. The Prowler NFO tried not to look at the contents of the bowl but he couldn't help himself. Macabre inquisitiveness got the better of him at that moment. The Prowler NFO thought to himself that Mayhew's long pile of crap was what is typically referred to as a *golden knifer*, because theoretically, it needed to be hacked up with a sharp knife blade into several smaller pieces before it would actually flush successfully down the toilet hole. He was both disgusted and impressed with Juice's work all at the same time. Hearing the toilet flush for a second time Jack grabbed about ten paper towels then spoke to the Prowler NFO.

"I wanted to flush and spray but I figured that terd was way to impressive not to be shared with someone. You're that lucky someone bub!" said Juice as he quickly dried his hands then eased out the door in search of a grey *Chevy Suburban* rental vehicle. But in his haste, Jack had forgotten something. He had neglected to put his college graduation ring back on his right ring finger. Mayhew had taken it off and placed it on the back of the porcelain sink so that slimy soap would not get encrusted in the small crevices of the ring's design when he washed his hands. Unfortunately, Jack wouldn't realize that he had lost the valued piece of jewelry until three weeks later when his daughter Ashley would ask him about the missing ring. Juice chuckled as he saw the x-rated snowman that sat on the grass near the sidewalk leading from the parking lot to the O' Club. He soon spotted the *Suburban* and several of his squadron mates already climbing into the SUV. Around the lot, Juice could see more *River Rattlers* as they piled into three other rented automobiles. In two minutes the *Suburban* was pulling out of its parking spot headed first for the main gate then for the casino in downtown Fallon.

"Why are brides smiling as they walk down the aisle at their wedding?" asked Duke in a joking fashion. Lightly patting the passenger-side dashboard as he asked the question, Duke had all but forgotten about his ugly encounter with CAG Madison. The skipper was seated in the right front seat of the grey *Suburban* on charcoal-colored leather seats. Because he only drank half a beer so far that night, the designated driver was Teen Angel Ackerman. Brad's head was looking out the left window as he was in the process of backing out of a tight parking spot.

"I don't know skipper, why are brides smiling as they walk down the aisle," asked Glen Hebert sitting in the very back of the SUV, next to a drunk and obnoxious Rocky Stone.

"Because they know they have given their last blow job!" Amid raucous laughter spiraling forward from the back of the *Chevy*, Teen Angel stopped the huge SUV after fifteen feet of rearward movement then shifted from Reverse to Drive. As he inched the huge truck forward three little honeys emerged from a Jeep *Grand Cherokee*, headed for the O' Club. The girls were dressed to the nines, wearing their long cashmere coats for warmth. Even though he had just engaged in a romantic conversation with his girlfriend Danielle Le Claire back at her home in New Orleans, Brad couldn't help himself; he honked the horn twice at the women as they shuffled past the right side of the *Suburban.*

"Yeah, I wouldn't kick them out of bed for eating crackers," said Cookie from the second row of seats in the SUV. Cookie swigged his bottle of *Coors Light* after registering approval of Brad's behavior. He quickly stuffed the beer bottle back down between his legs and out of sight.

"You know you're acting like a common Negro when you beep the horn like that Teen Angel," chided a somewhat befuddled T-Ben. Growing up in the deep-south and raised under the heavy influence of his maternal grandfather, Hebert still had a few prejudiced bones in his body. Every now and then that bigotry came out in his demeanor and speech when you least expected it. It was basically harmless though. Idle chatter began to spew inside the *Suburban.*

"Hey, you know what they say about rental vehicles? Never ever buy a rental car that was driven by Daffy Drucker," advised Juice Mayhew from the second bench seat of the SUV.

"Yeah Daffy would do all sorts of terrible things to rental cars as I recall," said Rocky, slurring his words slightly. Daffy Drucker, the CAG-2 LSO, had a notorious reputation for destroying rented automobiles, but only after he had purchased the daily insurance premium on them. Daffy would routinely return cars to the rental companies with fuzed clutch plates, shattered automatic transmissions and severely damaged fenders. In fact, he had finally been blackballed nationwide. No rental car company would do business with James "Daffy" Drucker.

"I'm so hungry I could eat the asshole out of a dead rhinoceros," said T-Ben. As he maneuvered cautiously around the last row of parked cars, Teen Angel spotted Leslie Lance walking toward the BOQ. Her blue pumps were damp from the wet snow on the sidewalk. Brad rolled down the window and politely invited Lieutenant Commander Lance to join them for the short trip to the Fallon casino. Because of their conversation in the O' Club that night, Ackerman already knew that Leslie is the squadron's new Assistant Maintenance Officer. Teen Angel likewise realized that he is the *only* member of the squadron who was aware of this fact, so he figured the ride to the casino could prove to be quite an interesting one. Without delay, Leslie accepted Brad's gracious invitation. After Duke hopped out of the passenger-side door, Leslie Lance eased her butt into the car and sat in between Teen Angel and the skipper of VA-204, her new commanding officer. For the first two minutes of the ride toward the NAS Fallon front gate the *Suburban* was consumed by a stunned silence. This would soon be disrupted.

On the outskirts of town, situated along a dusty road leading towards Reno, Senior Chief John Esposito and ADAN Earl Hamilton had just sat down at the bar inside the Lazy *B*, Fallon's infamous whorehouse. Light brown desert grime, picked up while walking in the parking lot of the establishment was caked on the soles of both men's shoes. About twenty vehicles were parked on that dirt patch in the shadow of an eerie red light that hung on the outside of the building. This was about the normal amount of clientele for a Sunday night at the Lazy *B* Ranch. Once inside, Esposito had taken the liberty of ordering the first round of drinks as the youthful Hamilton scoped out the joint like a shy fox peering into an old hen house with the door jarred loose. The sly smile never left his young face. As he gazed around the darkened brothel, Hamilton soon recognized the familiar faces of several enlisted men he had become acquainted with while attending the "A" School in Florida. Their smiles were equally apparent.

Off in a dimly lit corner of the barroom, one of the nubile prostitutes was playing games with a few of Hamilton's "A" School buddies. Apparently she was waving a *two-for-the-price-of-one* voucher over her head, tantalizing the horny sailors with the prospect of redeeming its value with her and one of her shapely colleagues that evening. When she brazenly tossed the coupon down onto the dirty floor of the bar, several of the sailors lunged under a table to scramble for the prized shard of paper. Witnessing this audacious behavior, Senior Chief Esposito thought they resembled three kids chasing down a foul ball on a Saturday afternoon in the stands at Wrigley Field.

Tonight was going to be the Airman Hamilton's first experience with hookers so the senior chief had decided to take him under his wing and offer expert tutelage to his teenage protégé. If the untested airman learned fast at the Lazy *B*, maybe Esposito would escort him to the legendary Mustang Ranch near Reno the following weekend. In other words, Hamilton would have to learn to crawl before the senior chief would allow him to walk. Of course tonight's lesson would be on the fine art of whoring, a tradition shared by sailors worldwide. Precisely at 2045, a heavy-set bar maid with over-bleached blonde hair poured out two bottles of *Lowenbrau* for Hamilton and Esposito. Momentarily losing her concentration, she overfilled Esposito's frosty mug, which was not tilted to the required 45 degree slant. Sudsy beer overflowed from the top of the thick glass, eased down the sides of the mug then congregated into a small pool on the bar. Without hesitation, the fifty-year old bar maid pulled a red towel from the pocket of her dingy apron and proceeded to expertly sop up the liquid. She winked at Esposito as she rung out the spilled beer into a steel sink behind the bar. The damp towel was quickly deposited back into the soiled apron pocket then the bartender continued to wait on sailors crowded around the horseshoe-shaped bar.

After a healthy chug of the German beer, the senior chief grabbed a small booklet from behind the silver-colored napkin dispenser. Esposito clumsily knocked over a saltshaker as he handed the little pamphlet to Airman Hamilton. The brochure read: Lazy *B* Ranch Menu, but the plastic-coated document didn't contain the standard provisions of a typical menu. It was a selection list of brothel *services* and their associated prices. In his nearly forty-year career in the Navy, Senior Chief Esposito had been to NAS Fallon and the Lazy *B* house of ill repute hundreds of times, so he was quite familiar with the menu's assortment of professional services. Like a trendy bar that serves up dozens of beer brands and challenges its customers to try them all, Esposito had indulged in nearly all of the selections available on the menu at one time or another. His personal favorites included:

#1 *Krakatoa*..$45
#4 *Around-the-World in 80 Minutes*...............$80
#12 *Hell Bent for Leather*............................$85
#21 *Doublemint Twins*...............................$99
#33 *Three-Holer*......................................$99

As he perused the left side of the menu, Earl Hamilton's face turned slightly crimson in color. He squirmed nervously in the fabric-covered barstool while gently biting his lower lip on its right side. Then, after exactly two minutes of studying the menu, the airman's eager eyes focused in on the kind of services he wanted to partake of that evening in the Nevada desert. As Hamilton perused the menu Esposito spotted a Chief Petty Officer Callahan from VA-145, CAG-2'S A-6 Intruder squadron. Callahan was on the floor under a table. He was falling-down drunk and it wasn't even 2100. Esposito had seen this guy's embarrassing act many times before, all over the world. He had always thought to himself that the guy must be made up of 95% liver because his daily routine was to get sloppy drunk immediately after work.

"I'll have number twenty-one senior chief," blurted out Hamilton as he hastily reached around with his right hand for an eel skin wallet brimming with per diem money. He fumbled a bit as he pulled the wallet out of his back pocket and plopped it down onto the bar.

"Don't tell me son, tell her," said Esposito pointing his craggy left index finger toward Miss Karla, the Lazy *B* Ranch Madame on duty that night. The senior chief almost choked on a slug of beer as the over-zealous airman stumbled slightly while rising from his seat. Earl Hamilton, dirty shoes and all, proceeded to make his first prostitute deal with the Madame in short order fashion. Many more would follow throughout his Navy career.

"Looks like somebody is in for a sweet ride," exclaimed John Esposito as Hamilton walked at a rapid pace down a darkened hallway with two hookers glued to his skinny, nineteen-year old arm. Esposito finished off his first beer then made quick eye contact with the bar maid, indicating his desire for another round. He then turned to an old guy seated next to him and made a friendly request.

"Why don't you just stuff that cigarette up your butt like a suppository? You'll get the nicotine a lot faster and that way and I won't have to toss you across the room." The old geezer crushed out his unfiltered *Camel* in an ashtray then left the Lazy *B*.

At the front gate of NAS Fallon, Teen Angel punched off his headlights then slowed the Chevy Suburban down to a crawl so that he could exchange a kind word and a friendly face with the gate guard on duty. Ackerman's smiles were always warm and sincere therefore they were usually appreciated by the recipient. At 2100 that evening everyone in the automobile was singing along with the local *oldies* radio station, generally getting more boisterous as the car ride progressed; everyone except Leslie Lance. Teen Angel was apparently the only one who correctly perceived her restrained distress. This may have been because she was sitting next to Brad in the front seat or perhaps because they had shared some quality conversation in the Officer's Club a few minutes ago. Either way, Lieutenant Ackerman could feel the tension building in her petite body as he drove on. He also knew from their previous conversation at the bar that Leslie was basically an implant forced on VA-204 for this final A-7 cruise at the insistence of Congresswoman Trish Schneider. The only female Member of the House of Representatives from Colorado had used her position as Co-Chairman of the House Committee on Military Affairs to basically bully the Secretary of the Navy into this small concession. Duke O' Grady would be most displeased when Teen Angel revealed this fact to him later that night at the Blackjack table. Like almost every Navy pilot, O' Grady was a passionate male chauvinist who wanted to preserve his sacred domain of combat carrier aviation as a safe haven for men only. It wouldn't help that Duke would be down $245 dollars at the time of Brad's revelation.

Lieutenant Commander Leslie Lance was born and raised in Tupelo, Mississippi by her destitute widowed father, now a spry seventy-two year old preacher. Her father's congregation, one of three Assembly of God Churches in the small southern town, actually boasted of having had Elvis Presley's mother as a member for a spell in 1962. Even though Gladys Presley couldn't carry a tune or read a single note of music, every Sunday morning before worship service there was a shameless competition to see who would stand next to her in the choir box. Leslie Lance held a BA in electrical engineering from Ole Miss and a Masters Degree in the same discipline from MIT. She had received *summa cum laude* honors at both universities so there wasn't any doubt about her intellectual capacity. Suffice it to say that Leslie Lance had prevailed over the economic adversity that confronted her in early childhood.

At that particular moment, in the short journey to the Fallon Nugget Casino Leslie was slowly getting perturbed by the unnecessary racket emanating from inside the Suburban. It seems that her new squadron mates had a bad habit of engaging in raucous sing-alongs whenever three or more of them were trapped in a vehicle together. *Barbara Ann*, an old standard from the 60s, was the current selection piercing through the cool night air. When the SUV slowly accelerated away from the main gate seven off-key voices could be heard trying to keep up with the pitch-perfect sound of the Beach Boys, backed up by Jan and Dean. As he drove onward, and the song faded to an end, Teen Angel couldn't help but notice that the aroma of Leslie's soft hair was subtly intoxicating. He privately took in a deep lingering breath. Ackerman breathed in slowly to get the full measure of her personal scent; it was beguiling to say the least. A radio advertisement for *Playtex Mini-Pads* caused everyone in the automobile to seek other amusements and forget about singing for the moment. The Suburban was now in total darkness traveling at a good clip down a lonesome road leading to the small town of Fallon. Spirals of dust flew upwards and outwards from underneath the SUV's steel-belted radials. The twisting corkscrews of desert dirt resembled vortices flowing from a jet's wingtips at takeoff on a frozen morning in Maine.

After about twenty seconds, a slightly uncomfortable Teen Angel decided he could take no more of the feminine commercial so he started fumbling with the radio to locate something more suitable for listening in the coed car. As he punched the black buttons of the vehicle's stereo, Brad finally cut into the song *Maggie Mae* by Rod Stewart playing on 101.7 The tune was at about the mid way point of its three minute cycle. Brad momentarily returned his right hand back to the steering wheel of the SUV and listened. As if instinctively, Teen Angel reached back down for the radio knobs with the intention of switching stations and turning off the Rod Stewart classic. But, for some strange reason, Stewart's raspy voice was oddly hypnotic and Brad couldn't quite bring himself to turn the ballad off. Ackerman hesitated then rolled his eyes as if to peer at the top of the car. He wrinkled up his lower lip then sucked in a deep breath of mountain air. Teen Angel was literally hypnotized by the sound of Rod Stewart's scratchy voice. Still he wanted to turn the music off. He started to reach down with his right hand a second time but stopped short again. He didn't have the will power to do it. Ackerman couldn't turn off the Rod Stewart song because that unique, gravelly voice was just too powerful. Ackerman was effectively paralyzed, at least for the time being. Teen Angel contorted his lips, nervously scratched the right side of his neck then looked at Leslie Lance and Duke O' Grady with his peripheral vision. Thank goodness Duke and Leslie weren't paying any attention to his antics with the car radio; both of their heads were coiled to the right. Now totally embarrassed by his own wishy-washy behavior, Ackerman looked around to see if anybody at all had been watching him. To his delight, the five other car occupants in the back seats were paying even less attention as they were embroiled in deep conversations with one another. Cookie swigged at his beer bottle in between exchanging quips with Juice and Sugar[2].

Shortly after the high pitched, crescendo sound of the Balalaikas mercifully signaled the end of *Maggie Mae* the Elvis song *Return to Sender* began playing on the radio station. *We had a quarrel, a lover's spat, I'll write I'm sorry but my letter keeps coming back*, belted out Elvis over a saxophone solo in the background. Teen Angel, not enamored in the least by Elvis Presley or his waffling tenor voice, immediately changed the car radio's channel. Curiously, Brad felt a peculiar sense of relief seep into his body after he punched the button to turn off the Elvis tune. After all, in Brad's humble estimation, it was a lame-ass song that should never have sold a million copies, except maybe in the Deep South. Strangely enough, this behavior by Teen Angel did earn the undivided attention of Lieutenant Commander Lance. Maneuvering to her left in the front seat of the Suburban, Leslie's demeanor promptly took on a motherly tone with Brad. She deliberately moved her supple right hand down to the car radio then delicately placed her left palm flush on Ackerman's nearest shoulder. Without hesitation, Lance switched the Elvis song back on and cranked up the volume slightly with an abrupt twist. Leslie's whole demeanor was like that of a tolerant mother about to divulge an indelible fact of life to her young, impressionable son. She was patient and methodical in her speech and in her physical actions with Ackerman. She raised her right index finger in front of her face and slowly shook it back and forth at Teen Angel. Brad briefly looked at Leslie seated next to him in the front seat then resumed his gaze out of the windshield at the dark road ahead. He thought for a moment that Leslie was going slap him gently on the wrist.

"Uh, Uh, Uh, you never turn off the King or rock and roll!" instructed Lieutenant Commander Lance in a soft, velvety voice. But she was equally firm in her overall disposition. Even though she was visibly disgusted with Brad's disrespectful behavior, Leslie purposely maintained her composure. Otherwise this important lesson might fall on deaf ears. She was after all still a southern belle and that dictated a certain style and subtle charisma. At first Teen Angel seemed a bit stunned by Leslie's actions. With his lower jaw stuck in the open mouth position, Brad felt like a kid caught stealing quarters from his mother's hidden cup of laundry money.

"I am sorry Leslie, it won't happen again," promised Teen Angel. Brad grinned slightly on the inside and on the outside at the simple humor of the episode. Nobody in the car paid any attention to this scene unfolding in the front seat; nobody except Duke O'Grady who pretended as though he was preoccupied. In fact, the skipper had heard every precious word. The Suburban continued onward for about another five minutes before it pulled into the half-full parking lot of the Fallon Nugget Casino. An array of dazzling light bulbs flashed on then off then back on again. The bright sequence was painful to the eyes if you watched too closely. The neon lights made their characteristic electric buzzing sound as they illuminated the shadowy Nevada sky. Teen Angel's six male passengers immediately piled out of the SUV then without any delay made their way into the gaming room of the casino. Ackerman was left to bring up the rear, walking at a casual pace with Leslie Lance. This would be her first time entering a gambling establishment. Somehow Brad sensed this and took his time getting to the front door, allowing her ample opportunity to suggest an alternative venue.

The Nugget Casino and saloon was the second oldest building in downtown Fallon; the first being the Courthouse which included the city's modest-sized jail in its basement. The town's forefathers probably figured that justice must be firmly established prior to allowing the twin sins of gambling and prostitution to take up residence in their desert community. The *Lazy B* Ranch brothel was the third building constructed within the city limits of Fallon. What more suitable entertainment could a workingman hope for during the gold rush of 1849 than gambling and prostitution? Across the street from the Nugget, next to a Baskin and Robbins ice cream shop was Fallon's only Cinema. That chilly February night in 1992 the theater was featuring a twin bill on their big screen, so movie-goers could enjoy two of Hollywood's finest productions for the price of one. *Silence of the Lambs* and *City Slickers* was displayed in bold black letters on the theater's old-time marquee. Exactly eleven people were in attendance, meaning the theater had raked in a grand total of thirty-three dollars revenue that Sunday evening. Brad Ackerman couldn't help but notice the old-style marquee as he strolled toward the front entrance of the casino. At that moment he realized how much he missed his buddies back in the motion picture business. Teen Angel turned his attention from the theater and smirked as he graciously opened the door to allow Leslie Lance to enter the Nugget Casino. The demure African-American woman hadn't uttered a word in protest. At that moment, Leslie Lance thought that Lieutenant Brad Ackerman was indeed an officer and a gentleman, at least most of the time.

Just inside the front entrance already seated at a rousing Blackjack game were Duke, Juice, and T-Ben. A shapely cocktail waitress wearing a skimpy outfit was busy delivering drinks to the six men and one woman at the green felt table. The skipper had a short stack of blue, twenty-dollar chips and a large pile of green, five-dollar markers. In the rear of the undersized gaming room Cookie and Rocky were wedging their way around a craps table buying chips with several crisp, twenty-dollar bills. Sugar^2 was off to the right side methodically dropping coins into a slot machine. He held tightly to a paper cup filled with about eighty or so nickels as he repeatedly yanked on the one-armed bandit. Thirty-three nickels dropped down into the machine's payout pan after Sugar^2 pulled and got two cherry stems and the number 7 in a row. Leslie Lance shivered as she felt the inviting warmth of the air inside the Nugget surround her body. She politely excused herself to the Ladies Room. The Blackjack dealer at Duke's table had just tossed down an Ace of Spades for herself and was inquiring if anybody wanted to purchase insurance for that particular hand. There were no takers and in five seconds there were seven losers when she flipped over her hole card, a Queen of Hearts. Brad maneuvered in behind Duke to watch some of the action. His right arm brushed up against the cocktail waitresses' left breast as he squeezed in tight. Teen Angel nudged Duke with his elbow as he got close, as if to make his presence known. The skipper acknowledged him warmly despite watching the dealer's manicured hand callously sweep away three of his blue chips then scoop up all of the other player's bets. The female dealer's natural hair color looked like it desperately needed a dye job thought Brad as she deposited chips into her wooden receptacle. To break the pain of the moment at the Blackjack table T-Ben Hebert decided it was time to speak up as a man seated next to him removed an LA Dodgers baseball cap from his scalp.

"You know if I had hair I would never cut it like that!" remarked T-Ben in a sneering manner towards the Dodgers fan. The cute dealer with the dull hair scraped her pink fingernails along the green felt of the tabletop as she whisked the player's cards away, before dropping them into the back of the dealing shoe. Juice laughed at T-Ben's comment and the Dodger fan's face got red.

Finally snuggled up to the edge of a large craps table, the only one in the Fallon Nugget, Rocky and Cookie were already placing bets on the *back line* as well as the *come line*. Cookie rubbed his eyes, yawned then took a swallow from a longneck beer. Rocky never took his eyes off the table as he gulped down a healthy amount of his martini. A redheaded Texan wearing a brand new Stetson was throwing the dice and rolling just about every combination of numbers but the 'ten' he was hoping for. The shooter wearing the beaver felt cowboy hat was an E-2 Hawkeye NFO, and the Executive Officer of VAW-114. Because he was so animated in his delivery technique, his designer glasses would go askew each time he tossed the dice down the table. Hoots and hollers could be heard from several of the XO's squadron mates who had gathered around the table in support. Cookie and Rocky had made several hundred dollars on this pass of the dice alone, so they chimed in with their own boisterous voices. The croupier used a wooden stick to shove the pair of dice back to the Texan at the south corner of the craps table.

"Keep rolling numbers XO," shouted Cookie as the NFO from Waco chucked the dice down the table once more. The red plastic dice tumbled after contacting the far edge of the table, coming to rest with a 'nine' showing.

"Pay the *back line* nines," yelled Rocky with obvious gusto. The croupier in the pit of the craps table scooted several more chips over to Rocky and Cookie who had just about every number on the *back line* covered with bets at that point. Rocky had to pee like a racehorse but he choked off the inclination. Gambling money was being earned hand over fist. Pissing would have to wait. More people began to crowd around the craps table to witness the winning streak first hand.

Emerging from the Ladies Room, Leslie Lance immediately looked up to see what the commotion was at the craps table. Teen Angel intercepted her in mid-stride and suggested they head over to Crazy Lee's Diner for a cup of coffee and a hunk of cake. She agreed without hesitation and the pair exited through a side door. The 50s diner was strategically located next door to the Nugget Casino. A baby blue and white 1957 Chevy convertible could be seen rotating ever-so-slowly on a steel post, ten feet above the café's roof. Inside of Lees, 1950s memorabilia could be seen everywhere. Several movie posters from that era adorned the walls including Humphrey Bogart in *The African Queen*, Marilyn Monroe in *Gentlemen Prefer Blondes*, Grace Kelley in *The Country Girl*, James Dean in *Rebel Without a Cause* and Marlon Brando in *On the Waterfront*. Ackerman suddenly felt very nostalgic and right at home because of this tribute to Hollywood.

Runaround Sue by Dion and the Belmonts was thumping loudly out of the juke box as Teen Angel politely pulled out a chair for Leslie at a quaint table near the entrance to Lee's. On the black-and-white TV screen, an episode or *Ozzie and Harriet* was just beginning with the introduction of Ricky Nelson. As Leslie and Brad surveyed the inside of Crazy Lee's Diner they could see old-style milkshake machines behind the counter top. These were the machines that had the long mixing blades which scraped loudly at those tall silver goblets used to create the perfect chocolate milkshake. An open can of *Hershey's Malt* sat prominently between two of the machines. The diner's food service counter featured several round, mushroom-style stools that sat low to the checkerboard floor. Metal canisters with retro *Coca-Cola* advertisements painted on the outside held an ample supply of napkins for Lee Marinovich's customers. Wood ceiling fans kept the air moving in the joint so people remained cool. You could feel the heavy nostalgia in Crazy Lee's Diner, even if you hadn't been alive in the 50s. A bell clanged loudly from the kitchen area. It reminded Teen Angel of the trolley cars in uptown New Orleans. He really missed Danielle Le Claire but wouldn't admit it to anyone.

Ackerman giggled under his breath then handed Leslie Lance a menu. The menu at Crazy Lee's was cleverly designed with food and beverage selections that perfectly matched their given pseudonyms. The menu included:

> *From Here to Eternity* Cup-a-Joe
> Bill Hailey & the Comet's *Rock-Around-the-Clock* 24 Hour Breakfast Special
> Del Shannon's *Runaway* Cheese Fries
> James Dean's *Rebel Without a Cause* Cheese Burger (without the cheese)
> *Teen Angel* Food Cake
> The Marx Brother's *Duck Soup* Chili
> The *Rat Pack* Frank and Dean's Beans
> Marilyn Monroe's *Naked* Banana Split (without a cherry on top)

After an appropriate amount of time, a waitress wearing a poodle skirt took Brad and Leslie's order. Her black-and-white saddle shoes, bobby socks and Mickey Mouse Club keychain were in mint condition. The young woman, sporting a baby blue ribbon in her tight ponytail, never stopped popping her *Wrigley's Juicy Fruit* gum. She was in perfect character the whole time. Her nametag said: Annette.

Five minutes later Brad was enjoying a huge slice of cake while sucking down a thick chocolate malt through two straws. As Leslie stirred her cup of coffee, muffled moans could be heard from the Nugget's casino floor, even inside Crazy Lee's. The Texan had rolled a seven and was forced to pass the dice. His run was over after twenty-four straight rolls. Cookie and Rocky had made about four hundred bucks apiece. They each flipped the croupier a twenty-dollar chip as the next shooter prepared to come out with the dice. A short stocky man promptly rolled an eleven as the dice now shifted to a good-looking brunette on Rocky's right. She proceeded to roll a three and the dice now belonged to Rocky. He promptly threw snake eyes. After losing on three straight rolls and suddenly fed up with Rocky's advice at the craps table, Cookie spoke to his gambling partner in a decidedly unhappy fashion.

"Don't you ever get tired of being wrong? You know, even a broken watch is right twice each day!" But the night was still young and more gambling was in order.

After witnessing a disgusting display of a spoiled rotten kids seated at the table in the back of Crazy Lee's Diner, Teen Angel decided it was an appropriate time to spout off some of his philosophy of life for Leslie's amusement.

"Perpetuation of the human species is dependent upon the ignorance of youth!" Leslie Lance looked at Brad with an incredulous face.

"I get these ideas. I don't know where they come from!" quipped Brad. Ackerman plunged a wedge of *Teen Angel* Food Cake into his mouth. A small blob of caramel sauce inadvertently dropped down onto the face of his *Movado* watch. Without warning Brad recalled the scene inside of Tara Thomason's New York City hotel room. A feeling of bitterness cascaded inside of his mind. Even though he hated Tara, he had never really stopped loving her. The intense emotional pain of that humbling experience afflicted him still.

CHAPTER 23

▼

NO HUNG BOMBS IN CAG-2

At 0236 Teen Angel was wide-awake in his twin-sized BOQ bed; why he did not know. Ackerman had hit the sack just after midnight on a full stomach and with warm memories of Crazy Lee's Diner and the Fallon Nugget Casino still dancing in his head. The naked Brad had fallen asleep almost immediately but less than three hours later his eyes were full open, staring mindlessly at the ceiling fan as it whirled around at sixty revolutions per minute. Teen Angel tossed and turned from side to side to no avail. Next he wedged his body tightly around the two extra pillows he had talked the BOQ maid out of that afternoon, just after he checked into his room. Brad lay in bed with one pillow between his legs and the other snuggled deep inside the grasp of his arms; his usual routine. At that moment he looked like two fishing worms wrapped up together as they dangled on a treble hook in the cool waters of the Snake River beside *Spencer's Mountain* in Idaho. But nothing seemed to help restore Ackerman to dreamland. He glanced casually at the face of the alarm clock. It read 2:38AM in bold red letters. The invading light from the rising sun and impending sound of the clock's alarm feature loomed large in his mind. These two would combine to make any additional sleep impossible he thought. He would have to fly two bombing hops that day on less than three hours sleep; normal for most A-7 Corsair pilots in the prime of their Naval Aviation career.

Undaunted, Teen Angel tried to force his way back into some much-needed slumber. Maybe he could count sheep. Yea, that's the ticket, count some dumb-ass sheep as they jumped aimlessly about in a green field by a babbling brook in Ireland. This method always seemed to work for Rocky on an Indian Ocean cruise, why not him?

"One, two, three, four, five," counted Brad out loud as he envisioned several sheep leaping over a dilapidated rock fence near an emerald-colored cottage in Innisfree, Ireland. Perhaps next he would conjure up visions of John Wayne and Maureen O'Hara pedaling on a bike built for two, with Barry Fitzgerald in hot pursuit, riding in his horse and buggy. *The Quiet Man* was Teen Angel's favorite John Ford movie.

"Six, seven, eight, nine, ten." Shit, that old wives tale doesn't really work, he thought in disgust. Maybe it only helps old wives get back to sleep. Rocky had lied to him again. Suddenly the source of his restlessness was finally revealed, or so he thought. For some unknown reason that 'son of a preacher man' song kept playing in his mind.

"Come on Lord," pleaded Teen Angel as he sought divine intervention. The words of the 1968 classic cascaded through his mind loud and clear now.

> *Billy Ray was a preacher's son*
> *And when his daddy would visit he'd come along*
> *When they gathered around and started talkin'*
> *That's when Billy would take me walkin'*

It was almost as if Dusty Springfield herself was right there in his room, *stealing kisses from me on the sly* and singing her oldies but goodies in a nonstop onslaught. Over and over the lyrics paraded through his thought process even as he tried to flush them out and concentrate on sleeping. It was a lost cause.

To exacerbate his plight, every ten seconds or so the double white and single green strobes of the NAS Fallon rotating beacon cut through the frigid night air. The piercing light of the beacon flashed through the windowpane and onto the face of a cheap nineteen-inch television in Brad's BOQ room. On every other pass, the beacon would catch Teen Angel with one eye open. But it was so dark in Nevada that morning that the penetrating green and white light could be seen by Brad even through his closed eyelids.

"Come on Lord, work with me here" implored Teen Angel. He thrashed about once more then buried his face deep inside the foam pillow that supported his head. But the song's lyrics came back once again, louder than ever.

The only one who could ever reach me
Was the son of a preacher man
The only boy who could ever teach me
Was the son of a preacher man

Teen Angel's last look at the face of the alarm clock came at 3:43AM. Ten minutes later he was fast asleep. Dusty Springfield and her "son of a preacher man"
song had finally faded into oblivion. Brad alternated between dreaming, heavy
snoring and talking in his sleep until the alarm sounded at 0545. In his dream he
conjured up lucid and confused visions of both his ex-college girlfriend Tara
Thomason, and his current flame Danielle Le Claire.

His fuzzy final dream sequence began twenty minutes prior to the shrill sound
emanating from the plastic alarm clock. It featured a pristine setting in the wine
country of the Napa-Sonoma Valley in Northern California. In the fantasy Brad
and Tara were ambling slowly through a secluded vineyard, hand in hand taking
in the fresh, sweet aroma of ripening grapes hanging tantalizingly low on their
vines as Danielle Le Claire spied on the former couple from behind a decrepit one
room shack that had been used for rancid grape storage and removal long ago.
The tiny cottage had a brick chimney leading up from a charred fireplace where
migrant workers would burn kindling wood to warm their hands during the
frigid winter months of Sonoma County. In the dream, mutual passion was
steadily building as Tara and Brad strolled through the supple, moistened
grounds of the grape farm, plucking the bursting fruit and eating at their leisure.
In his vision, the pair of ex-lovers appeared to be carefully nurturing their growing desires by enticing one another through coy smiles, soft caresses, dripping
grape juice from pouting lips, and quick glances with over-sized bedroom eyes.
Teen Angel moaned loudly in the moistened sheets of the small bed. He darted
his eyeballs quickly back and forth under closed eyelids as the dream sequence
continued to build to its crescendo.

The improvised trail through the chateau sent the lovebirds up and over the
incline of a gentle rolling hill then down to a small pond of crystal clear water
below. Somehow the decaying old shack, with Danielle Le Claire still strategically
hidden behind it, followed along as the two walked onward in the dream. Off in
the near distance, Teen Angel could make out the silhouette of an antique row-
boat resting invitingly on a damp shoreline. The craft resembled one of those tarnished vessels you would see tied up within the lazy confines of an ancient harbor
in a cheesy advertisement peddling time-share vacations in Crete. Although her
myopic eyes couldn't see that far, Tara trusted Brad's vision skills and manly

instincts. In the dream she simply clung tightly to his grip, never once stopping their forward progress to search for her misplaced contact lenses. Simultaneously their brains meshed together, locking onto the same passionate thought, as they now trotted briskly over to the boat. After catching her breath, Tara climbed into the dinghy and Ackerman pushed the wood ship gently and silently into the glassy waters of the pond. The ripple from the plunging bow cascaded onto the surface of the tranquil water, spreading out like a harmless tsunami. At that moment the sun became slightly obscured behind one of those elongated stratus clouds that stretched elegantly across the mid-afternoon sky. The brilliant sun-rays split in every direction like they were being forced through prism in an undergraduate physics experiment at a UCLA lab session. The streams of light gently kissed the surface of the pond then glistened as the ripple of water continued to cascade outward on the peaceful lake.

Once safely inside the boat, the duo nestled deep into the fluffy foam cushions that lay across the wooden seats. Tara's frilly, flowery summer dress ruffled gently upwards, reacting to the placid force of a soft breeze that permeated over the pond. Her luxurious, bleach blonde hair flowed down draping her bare shoulders as she leaned rearward to arch her back. Tara then kicked the sandals off her pretty little bare feet to feel the warmth of the zephyr as it blew across her now writhing body. A few strands of long hair playfully nuzzled across the corners of her delicate mouth as her eyes sought out Brad's in a purposeful manner. After nimbly retrieving Tara's wayward Gucci sandal from the cool water, Brad began to casually row with the rotting oars towards a large Weeping Willow tree; its branches draped low across one side of the pond. As they approached the shade and concealment of the weakened, greenish tree limbs the wind kicked up and swirled again. Tara's dress flowed freely up and out from her playful, lithe body. Danielle and the old storage shack had now moved to a strategic spot behind the Weeping Willow tree. Ackerman's fuzzy dream was now in full, vivid swing.

While brazenly attempting to see up beyond the ruffled edges of Tara's flowing summer dress, Teen Angel clumsily dropped one of the oak oars overboard, obviously shaken because he had discovered that his former girlfriend was not wearing any panties in this dream. Sharon Stone would be proud Ackerman thought in his subconscious state of mind. As the dream continued, Brad and Tara watch as the rotting hulk of the oak oar sinks rapidly to the bottom of the serene lake, just missing a small school of Perch on the way to the sandy bottom. Brad is now forced to sit in the narrow front position of the boat, one oar in hand, with his back to Tara. From that location he takes a few strokes from each side of the love vessel in order to keep the couple traversing the waters directly inbound to the inviting seclusion provided by the canopy of Weeping Willow tree limbs. It is then that Teen Angel begins to become slightly cognizant of a rather hastily developing hard spot that is burgeoning in the front section of his lavender-colored Bermuda shorts. As the boat gently slides into position under the shade and much-needed camouflage of the droopy tree, Teen Angel notices that Tara has deftly taken out a chessboard from under one of the cushions in the back of the craft. This was truly an odd dream for a dashing young Naval Aviator to be experiencing. As the discolored dinghy comes to rest on the shaded water, Brad removes both of the white Patten leather shoes and black socks from his feet then tosses them aside in a nonchalant James Dean fashion. Attempting to display his superior intellect, all 188 IQ points, Teen Angel nimbly chooses to play the black after Tara moves her white Queen's pawn to Queen's level three. All the while he is still semi-cognizant of Danielle spying on them from behind the base of the tree. She is monitoring his surreal dream sequence from that tactical vantage point, holding a legal brief in her right hand and a glass of Chardonnay in her left. It was a strange dream to say the least.

"Tara, Tara, trust me on this one subject babe," groaned Teen Angel in his now quickly evaporating state of sleep. When he awoke a minute later and popped the snooze button on the alarm clock, his body was cold and clammy. The sheets were stuck to him like a cellophane wrapper around a plastic Tupperware bowl. He didn't even remember the dream he was having for the past twenty minutes. Brad quickly pissed, showered and shaved before heading out for the opening day activities of the weapons detachment. Like the *Werewolf of London*, his hair was perfect even after he stumbled briefly coming down the dark BOQ stairwell.

The VA-204 Plan of the Day, or as Duke O'Grady liked to refer to it *The Plan of Attack*, hung on a bulletin board in the downstairs lounge near the front entrance of the BOQ. The NAS Fallon BOQ was a rather drafty old structure with leaky pipes, soft water and a dilapidated outer facade that had served its primary purpose in the Navy for well for over forty-two years. This lengthy span of time represented a longer useful existence than most Navy aircraft or maritime vessels, surface or sub-surface. The VA-204 Plan of the Day, which had been typed up by Yeoman First Class Alex Yarborough the evening before, was tacked up on the large rectangular-shaped bulletin board. The off-white piece of paper swayed rhythmically, along with eight others from the squadrons of CAG-2, as a warm breeze flowed out of a rusty heater vent in the ceiling. There were also nine separate Squadron Flight Schedules pinned to the corkboard.

The bulletin board overlooked two beer-stained pool tables in the BOQ lounge area, which at 0615 on February 9, 1992 had been unoccupied for the past four hours or so. A blemished cue ball lay still on the tainted green felt of one pool table; the other had two pool cues resting on top with a half-empty can of *Coors* perched precariously on the table's edge. The floor of the BOQ lounge was filthy by Navy standards and the six pieces of furniture situated around the big-screen TV had the distinct stench of stale beer. The foul odor boldly wafted up from deep within the cushy material whenever anybody sat down. According to the *River Rattler* flight plan, that morning's scheduled activities would kick off at 0730 as Captain John Madison, the Air Wing Commander, would deliver his infamous 'welcome aboard' speech in the base auditorium. This inexorably colorful salutation by "Spine Ripper" Madison would immediately precede a short Flight Surgeon lecture and the usual Fallon Course Rules briefing. Individual squadron AOM meetings were scheduled for 0900. The first flight briefings of the three-week weapons detachment would begin precisely at 1030, in preparation for a 1200 takeoff. As usual, the last recovery would be at 2200 after a night ordnance delivery hop on Bravo-17, an aerial bombing target centrally located in the GABBS MOA of the Fallon Weapons Range.

At 0630 the O' Club was bustling with officers scrambling to eat a hearty breakfast prior to beginning the traditionally long first day that characterized any weapons detachment. Cookie and Rocky were already wolfing down fried eggs, French toast and several large glasses of fresh-squeezed orange juice as Brad joined them. Two minutes later they tried not to notice as Teen Angel emptied eight packets of *Equal* into his mug of coffee then stirred in about two ounces of pure cream for good measure. Ackerman, who generally detested the taste of straight java, always had to "doctor up" coffee so that he could actually get it paste his uvula and down into his stomach. Rocky just ignored Brad's coffee antics, as he bit into another wedge of cinnamon-flavored French toast. He had seen this act many times before. But Cookie on the other hand, couldn't resist getting in the morning's first jab.

"Did they teach you that little queer, coffee stunt in Hollywood Teen Angel?" Without missing a beat Ackerman responded to his squadron mate's politically incorrect insult.

"I take my 'Cup a Joe' just like I take my women Cookie boy; too sweet and lightly tanned." The three friends seated at the table laughed too hard for that time of the morning, then continued to eat their meals. Lieutenant Commander Leslie Lance, seated two tables behind Ackerman's, heard the entire un-amusing conversation. Even though she had never given birth Leslie still had the instinctual gift of *mother hearing*. Leslie spooned a dainty portion of buttery grits into her mouth, hesitated to allow for some additional cooling, then swallowed.

Duke O'Grady was seated at a large round table near the back of the room along with Spine Ripper Madison, Brain Child Bracken and Juice Mayhew. All four men were enjoying large stacks of hotcakes with five or six slices of thick-cut bacon on the side. Duke had his pancakes literally covered with fresh frozen, thawed out blueberries and *Mrs. Butterworth's* syrup. A side dish of almost burned, hash-browned potatoes sat next to Duke's plate of blueberry flapjacks. It was half eaten with a few strands of potato liberally spread out on the table cloth in front of O' Grady. Duke didn't give a rat's ass that he was kind of a slob at the breakfast table. Around the room pilots from all nine of CAG-2's tactical squadrons were busy eating their morning feast. It was hectic to say the least. At a table next to Duke and CAG Madison sat three Tomcat pilots and one Radar Intercept Officer (RIO) from the Wolfpack of VF-1. Rocky had commented earlier to Cookie that the RIO had one "lonely eye" or a "loose eye" as some people would aptly describe it. After first shifting the wire-rimmed glasses on his face for better viewing, the Wolfpack RIO started to vigorously swipe a pink packet of *Sweet and Low* back and forth in front of his face, to loosen the contents for more efficient pouring. As he swung the paper package briskly back and forth in front of his glasses, the packet slipped through his fingers, flying towards the next table, finally coming to rest in the middle of CAG Madison's half-eaten scrambled eggs. Similar to that E.F. Hutton commercial, the entire O' Club suddenly went silent but then erupted into hysterical chuckles as Duke O' Grady, without missing a beat, plucked the pink packet out of Spine Ripper's eggs with his fork. He deposited the *Sweet and Low* package into a napkin then inserted his fork back into a hunk of pancake waiting on his plate. CAG Madison, for a change, was at a loss for words. The Wolfpack RIO turned bright red. He would not live this incident down for about the next two months or so.

At Teen Angel's table, just before he and his squadron mates were about to depart the breakfast scene, Rocky suddenly got philosophical. This was unusual for 0630 on a Monday morning. Rocky usually waited until he had about six beers in his belly before he spouted off universal thoughts on life. Before disgorging some early morning rhetoric to his closest friends, Rocky held a three-inch rasher of bacon out in front of his face, surveyed its undercooked condition, then he began to speak.

"You know boys, cowboy is not *bulls and blood, dust and mud or the roar of the Sunday crowd. It's not boots and chaps and cowboy hats or spurs and latigo.* Sorry

Garth Brooks, but cowboy is much more than *that damned old rodeo*. Cowboy is a state of mind!"

"What the hell is he talking about Teen Angel," whispered Cookie with a dubious grin on his face as he leaned in close to Brad. Ackerman just shook his head in mock disbelief. He knew Rocky would continue on unabated until he had delivered his entire piece of philosophy that chilly February morning.

"Today's Tactical Naval Aviators are contemporary cowboys who ride bucking broncos named Corsair, Tomcat, Intruder and Hornet. And these modern-day, kerosene cowboys ride for the full eight seconds every time out of the chute." Rocky dropped the thick hunk of bacon back down to his plate. It splashed some syrup onto the white linen tablecloth as it landed. He was obviously very proud of the sentiment he had just shared with his two closet friends in the squadron. Rocky fancied himself as a great thinker, just to pester those around him.

"Shut up and finish your orange juice so we can get to the base auditorium you skin dick," instructed Teen Angel with a grimaced face. Ackerman picked his teeth with a half-clean, right pinky finger he spoke. He was pretending to be uncouth for Rocky's benefit. Suddenly Ackerman thought of another line of questioning for his best friend. Shifting uncomfortably in his seat Brad addressed Rocky more directly and in a lower tone of voice so nobody else in the room could hear. Cookie's ears perked up in reaction to Teen Angel's body language for the question. It was evidently going to be a sensitive subject about to be broached by Brad.

"So, did that Latino woman you met at the craps table last night get naked with you Rocky?" whispered Ackerman. Brad shifted in close to Rocky's left earlobe as he spoke in a muffled manner.

"She got naked enough," was the curt reply. LCDR Rocky Stone gulped down the last of his OJ as Brad laughed a bit nervously. Teen Angel actually knew what that comment meant because he had seen Rocky's act many times before, and his personal guilt was showing a bit. Ackerman had facilitated sexual encounters for Rocky too many times in the past.

"Do you speak any Spanish Rocky?" inquired Teen Angel.

"I speak enough to get by," answered Rocky.

"What do you mean by that comment?"

"Well when I go South of the border I simply ask the cab driver this question: Donde esta la senorita con el burro."

"You are so disgusting Rocky, but I love you anyway," chided Ackerman. Brad was feeling extremely guilty at this point in the embarrassing conversation.

Cookie was merely enthralled by the various rude and crude comments verbalized that morning at their breakfast table. After all, Lieutenant Brad "Teen Angel" Ackerman and Lieutenant Commander Jim "Rocky" Stone were his naval aviation heroes. Cookie Cline relished the time he spent with them.

Suddenly Cookie adopted an aloof posture to their semi-disgusting, although appealing dialogue. He now had his eyes glued to the new waitress who had just moseyed into the room sporting a steaming pot of fresh coffee. Cookie noticed that the young waitress assigned to duty in this section of the O' Club was busier than a one-legged woman in an ass-kicking contest. She had a slightly weathered look in her face, as if she had been ridden hard and put up wet once too often. But as a cowboy would say, the new waitress was a real looker and Cookie was definitely looking in her direction. The CAG Weapons Detachment wasn't even officially kicked off yet, but ideas were already dancing though Cookie Cline's mind like Tchaikovsky's sugar plum fairies from *The Nutcracker Suite* in D minor. That was until he looked down at her feet.

She was wearing a pair of those flippy-floppy shoes that in the Navy were known as shower-shoes. But these were platform shower-shoes, the kind a geisha girl would be wearing while giving you a warm, to die for, sponge bath in Sasebo, Japan. The problem was that the new waitress shouldn't have been wearing the flip-flops because she had incredibly ugly toes. Her toes resembled oversized, albino Brazil nuts that had all gone haywire. Each appendage on both of her feet pointed in a different direction. The uniformity of the distortion was made complete because each "little piggy" rested high up on the neighboring toe making them look like a hammer on an anvil in a medieval blacksmith shop. The new waitress also had a large gap between toe #2 and toe # 3 on her left foot. Her feet were, in a word, butt ugly! No spa pedicure treatment, expensive toe polish, European buffing wax or industrial strength foot lotion could alter the hideousness of those toes. Only a blind man could have sex with her and those feet thought Cookie. Suddenly Cookie's face contorted as he looked away in repugnance. He almost choked on his last bite of buttery French toast.

Over at CAG'S table, breakfast had just concluded as the tone and demeanor turned decidedly more serious. Unknown to everyone in VA-204 except for Duke O'Grady, the *River Rattler* XO, Slug Levitan, had quietly resigned his position in the Naval Reserves eighteen days ago. The poorly worded letter of resignation had been faxed directly to CAG Madison with a courtesy copy forwarded in snail mail to the VA-204 Commanding Officer the same day. Commander Levitan, a great paper-pusher and Full Contact Crud player, had apparently decided he would quit the squadron rather than agree to go on the six-month, around-the-world USS *Enterprise* cruise. CAG Madison, after consulting with Duke O' Grady, had selected Commander Jack "Juice" Mayhew to be field upgraded to the job of VA-204 Executive Officer. Spine Ripper and Duke were informing Juice at that very moment and Commander O' Grady was also ready that day to name Rocky as his replacement Maintenance Officer, with Lieutenant Commander Leslie Lance as the new Assistant MO. As Rocky, Cookie and Teen Angel were heading for the door, Spine Ripper Madison was busy enlightening Juice on the selection and his personal expectations for an attack squadron Executive Officer working in Carrier Air Wing Two.

Just below CAG Madison's scalp, loose skin had bunched up and folded over onto the back of his neck. This stocky sparkplug of a man was indeed menacing in his appearance as beads of sweat started to form and run down to his khaki collar. Juice Mayhew, ever confident of his own abilities, shook his head in acknowledgment, vigorously shook CAG Madison's hand then rose from his chair and walked toward the cashier to pay the breakfast check for the entire table. Before leaving, Mayhew gulped down the last of his third cup of black coffee then left a five-dollar bill on the table as a tip for the cute new waitress wearing the high-soled flip flops. Jack's "per diem belly" protruded just a bit over his khaki belt as he walked hurriedly toward the cashier. Spine Ripper's brief would commence precisely at 0730 and it was always a good idea to be in your seat about fifteen minutes before CAG Madison entered a room to speak. The O' Club breakfast room was emptied in eight minutes as 250 men wearing khaki uniforms adorned with Navy 'wings of gold' meandered toward the Base Auditorium across the street from the NAS Fallon Officer's Club.

The base auditorium was the largest and oldest structure onboard the Naval Air Station Fallon, having been built in 1941. Like all the buildings on the base it had an "off tan" look. Over the years the cement block structure had been severely weathered by an assault from the sun, wind, sand, rain and snow that were a constant feature of the desert environment in South Western Nevada. In fact, the outer facade of the base auditorium had been treated particularly harshly by the elements contained in Mother Nature's potent arsenal. It was pock marked from an almost continuous blitz of sand storms over the past 50 years. As the aviators filed into the giant auditorium, Rocky marveled at the grandeur of the spacious, great old room. Dropping rudely down into a shabby, green leather seat he once again began to prepare for his philosophical pontification. But first he slowly surveyed the full extent of the capacious room with its fifty-foot high ceiling. At the front of the auditorium was a gigantic movie screen concealed by an extra heavy, set of drapes. The cloth material of the long curtains was maroon in color and tattered from its lengthy existence and lack of proper and timely dry cleaning. The two-level auditorium featured row upon row of theater-style seats; 975 on the bottom floor and 302 in the balcony section to be exact. Half the seats were still in fairly descent condition but the other half were literally worn out from decades of weapons detachments and free-of-charge motion picture shows that played every night on the Naval Air Station. Sailors and children of sailors can be quite destructive with buttered popcorn and *Milk Duds* if given a long enough leash and an adequate amount of time to wreak their havoc.

Rocky continued to scan the room as Cookie and Teen Angel settled in next to him, ready to take notes during the Course Rules Briefing and exchange the inevitable, good-natured insults with the rest of the Air Wing pilots. Brad made cursory eye contact with Lieutenant Kimber Kennedy, the CAG-2 flight surgeon and Lieutenant Commander "Daffy" Drucker, the senior Landing Signal Officer in the Carrier Air Wing. The flooring in the auditorium appeared to be made of quality ceramic tile or some kind of marble material. It was a rich navy blue in color and each individual tile had a noticeable shine. This fact probably made the Command Master Chief of the base extremely proud of the airmen who polished the floor daily with one of those unwieldy buffing machines and a bottle of that foul-smelling liquid wax. On the sidewalls of the auditorium were over-sized and ancient-looking fixtures sculpted out of a pasty white substance. Rocky wasn't even sure what these artifacts were but their appearance gave off tell tale signs of Greek influence in the architecture. Flying raptors, galloping stallions, large busted women and overly muscled God-like men were everywhere in its structural design. Rocky then surveyed the men in the khaki-colored clothing as the room began to settle down in anticipation of CAG Madison's entrance.

"You know Teen Angel, this room is filled with America's finest men; true heroes every one of them. They are indeed modern day Roy Rogers; cowboys after my own heart," spouted Rocky. Nobody was actually listening to him at that point. After you first met Rocky Stone, it didn't take long for you to realize that he spent too much of his time vacillating between anxiety and arrogance, between paranoia and unbridled confidence. It was a very confusing, emotionally exhausting situation to be trapped in. The slightly haggard lines on Rocky's face and the premature graying hair gradually receding from his scalp betrayed his true condition to the savvy individual.

"Attention on deck," shouted the CAG Administrative Officer. As the roomful of naval aviators snapped to attention, Captain "Spine Ripper" Madison made his way up to the podium, chomping on his cigar as he walked and looking very much the sparkplug of a man that he was in life. Without any further pomp or circumstance, CAG began to address the men of Carrier Air Wing Two immediately after arriving behind the wooden platform. His oratory, as usual, would be succinct, gruff and to the point. CAG Madison's opening remarks traditionally lasted for only two or three minutes, but his words would be memorable and extremely motivating to everybody who heard them. He reminded you of General Patton, as played by George C. Scott, during his initial address to the troops at the beginning of the Academy Award winning movie about the "old blood and guts" tank commander himself. As CAG raised his head to speak, he deftly dislodged a piece of cheap meat that had become stuck in his molars on the right side of his mouth. He used his tongue to swipe the sausage remnant away from the gap in his lower jaw, off his gums and then swallowed the half-chewed piece down into his throat. As his mature eyes leveled with the room, Captain Madison was addressing a sea of Khaki uniforms, gold wings and brown aviator's shoes sitting in the audience. It was always his personal policy that he wouldn't allow his officers to put on their green zoom bags until flight ops actually began. The room waited impatiently for CAG'S crotchety eloquence to be unleashed. They didn't have to wait much longer before his gravelly voice thundered into the spacious old auditorium.

"Men," Spine Ripper purposely paused to clear his throat and to give off the appearance of attempting to impart a great piece of philosophical wisdom to his spellbound audience of Naval Aviators and Chief Petty Officers. He removed the unlit cigar from his mouth then fidgeted with it in the discolored fingers of his left hand.

"In the civilian world, there are only two reasons that human beings kill other human beings. They kill for money and they kill for sex. There is always a dick in there somewhere." Uncomfortable, muffled giggles could be heard all over the auditorium as Captain Madison continued talking without missing a beat or changing the serious expression on his face.

"Tactical Naval Aviators kill to protect the future of democracy and the posterity of our beloved nation. They kill to secure the longevity of our children and the survival of our democratic way of life. Never forget that you are a weapons system. You are a highly trained expert. Your job is to kill the enemy before he ever has an opportunity to kill you. The people of the United States of America have entrusted you warriors with this most noble of human responsibilities." And you just might have to carry out this noble responsibility because those damned rag heads are acting up again over in the Middle East. President Bush may have to call upon us to go over there on this cruise and spank 'em, so let's all be fully prepared for this possibility." At this point in his speech, Captain Madison shifted gears to conclude his remarks by addressing his squadron Commanding Officers.

"Skippers, I want you to keep your aviators busy and active over the next three weeks. Remember, there is nothing more dangerous than a bored pilot!" instructed Spine Ripper Madison, his steely blue eyes registered deepest sincerity. The men in the auditorium shifted positions in their seats, trying not to draw too much attention to themselves as CAG continued talking. Some of his words at this point were lost on deaf ears. Teen Angel, Rocky and Cookie were looking for obvious signs from each other out of their peripheral vision, all the while continuing to focus on CAG behind the lectern at the front of the room. Spine ripper kept talking and twiddling his skinny cigar.

"Enthusiasm is not threatened or diminished by discipline. Enthusiasm is bolstered and accentuated by discipline. Focus your men's enthusiasm skippers." Most of the people in the room didn't know exactly what to make of this little tidbit of philosophy. But it could be used in any context, forcing you to use the analytical part of your brain to engage in analysis of situations.

"And finally gentlemen, there are no hung bombs in CAG-2. If you have a hung bomb on your jet just pick up a heading of 270 degrees until your aircraft runs out of fuel! Gentlemen, let's all have a safe and productive weapons detachment."

"Attention on deck." bellowed the CAG Administrative officer once again. Everybody in the room braced up in the attention position for a second time as Captain Madison walked out of a side door and into his awaiting black car in the parking lot. He had a 1030 brief for an ACM hop flying an F-14 Tomcat with VF-1. He would undoubtedly kick a few butts over the next three weeks to help groom his Air Wing for their upcoming around-the-world deployment onboard USS *Enterprise*.

The room was literally buzzing after CAG left, but settled down quickly as Lieutenant Kimber Kennedy, the NAS Fallon flight surgeon, stood up and placed all six feet three inches of her lovely, 29 year-old frame behind the podium. From the very day she graduated Flight Surgeon School at the Naval Aero-Medical Institute (NAMI) in Pensacola, Lieutenant Kennedy's tactical call sign had been Timber. She was sarcastically referred to as "Timber" because she was the tallest female flight surgeon either side of the Mississippi River, and she had an exceedingly soft spot in her heart for middle-aged Naval Aviators, especially those around the same age as Duke O' Grady. In fact, if you were wearing wings of gold and had reached the advanced age of forty or higher, "Timber" Kennedy was known to go down like a rock in water at the chance to have sex with the more mature Naval Aviator. She was like a lonely, giant Sequoia in California's Redwood National Park that gets cut down by a burly lumberjack in the deafening silence of the woodland. The lumberjack yells "Timber" as the huge tree crackles slowly from the final cut of the saw's jagged edge then quickly falls to the forest floor with a huge loud thud. This was Lieutenant Kimber Kennedy's renowned reputation and propensity for sex with older Naval Aviators, and it had justly earned her the call sign Timber.

Kimber Kennedy was addressing the pilots of CAG-2, just prior to the standard NAS Fallon Course Rules Briefing, because seventeen of the men had flight physicals scheduled over the ensuing three weeks of the weapons detachment. Likewise, for twenty-three pilots there was a required Flight Physiology Course on the agenda, and Kimber Kennedy would be integrally involved with all of these evolutions. For comic affect, during her eight-minute talk Lieutenant Kennedy held up a cold, twelve inch-long metal, proctoscope. She held it provocatively in her let hand, and boldly brandished the invasive-looking device as if to playfully threaten anyone who had the audacity to challenge her authority in matters where Aviation Medicine was concerned. Based on the total number of quieted men seated in the room with their jaws dropped during her brief comments, the prop worked on most of the people in the base auditorium.

As directed by the Chief of Naval Education and Training (CNET), Kimber explained to the pilots of CAG-2 that the Aviation Physiology class would be slightly different. This year's physiology course would incorporate the standard altitude chamber flight up to 40,000 feet, featuring the customary and quite humorous hypoxia demonstration. It would also include a full half-day of ground school on a variety of pertinent subjects. But the training would also include a new requirement that had just been handed down that week from Admiral Kendrick "Needle Nose" Ramsey, CNET himself. This latest addition to the Aviation Physiology syllabus was for everyone to participate in helicopter dunker training. Prior to this year, the dunker requirement was only in effect for helicopter pilots and crewmembers. Needle Nose Ramsey had fought the Navy system long and hard to change this rule and for good reason. Seven months ago, when he was Commander of Carrier Task Force Eleven, Admiral Ramsey had watched helplessly from the Admiral's Bridge of the USS *Eisenhower* as an SH-3 helicopter crashed into the ocean while attempting to rescue an enlisted man who had been blown overboard by Tomcat exhaust during flex-deck flight operations. During that rescue mission, shortly after successfully snatching the enlisted man up and out of the cold sea, the SH-3 inadvertently hit the water. The helicopter quickly capsized then wallowed in the waves on the starboard side of the ship for over thirty minutes before mercifully sinking. The horrific action was so close to the massive carrier that you could almost reach out and snatch the men out of the drink. All five of the helicopter crewmen survived the ordeal, but the twenty-four year old ordnance man who had been blown overboard then pulled out of the ocean, tragically drowned. The young "ordie" had never been to helicopter dunker training. Ramsey was all too aware that this was actually the second tragic event that had recently plagued the carrier navy with helicopters sinking at sea. From that day forward Admiral Ramsey vowed to change the helicopter dunker rules. Two weeks ago he had finally convinced the Chief of Naval Operations (CNO) to add helicopter dunker training to the Aviation Physiology curriculum for all participants.

After concluding her remarks, Timber Kennedy sashayed back to sit in a tattered, green leather seat. Many sets of eyes were on her feminine form as she moved entirely too elegantly for a seventy-five inch tall woman. In lady-like fashion she crossed her right leg over the left. Kimber knew she was being watched closely. Tan pantyhose glistened in the indirect light as her khaki skirt barely moved across endlessly long legs. Two seconds later, the gigantic purple curtain in the front of the auditorium opened slowly to reveal the movie screen. The familiar videotape of the NAS Fallon "Course Rules Brief" began to play for its full, excruciating sixteen minutes.

CHAPTER 24

▼

SKIPPER, IT'S FOR YOU

The initial VA-204 All Officers Meeting of the 1992 CAG-2 Weapons Detachment was scheduled to commence at 0900 in space number 222 of Hangar 17. The River Rattlers had been assigned this second floor area of Hangar 17 as their squadron Ready Room for the duration of the detachment. The room was the proverbial shit hole of all the spaces available for Air Wings to utilize when visiting NAS Fallon for their weapons training. Commander Frank "Dirty Dick" Winslow, the CAG-2 Administration Officer and bespectacled F-14 RIO, had pulled a few strings to ensure that "those puke reservists from New Orleans" got this exceedingly undesirable room assignment for the entire three weeks of training. Dirty Dick, a wannabe Navy pilot from about the age of 12, literally loathed Reserve Naval Aviators, because of the prima donna factor and because of their notoriously acute arrogance. His lifelong myopia had something to do with this negative emotion toward all Navy pilots as well. It made no difference to him how much flight time and experience they possessed Dirty Dick had a chronic hatred for reservists before ever meeting them. No amount of good deeds or heroism could prove their overall worth in his prejudiced eyes.

Room 222 had only one redeeming feature; it contained a huge bay window spanning the length of the room, a distance of approximately 28 feet across. The glass had a dingy appearance to it after decades of sand storms and streaks of dull paint from errant brushes over the years. It also had perpetually darkened, sooty corners on all the windowpanes, the result of jet exhaust that had blown up that high on the outer facade of Hangar 17. But the bay window overlooked the entire flight line, so anybody could monitor aviation activities from this second story vantage point and get a bird's eye view of the action unfolding down on the tarmac. Other than that, the cavernous old room was in shambles. It desperately needed a coat or two of fresh latex paint, and the sooner the better. Additionally, all the furniture pieces were in various states of disrepair. Commander Duke O' Grady would make sure that Senior Chief Esposito had several of his Line Division men take care of the paint situation before the River Rattler pilots departed for their skiing trip to Lake Tahoe on Friday evening after the first week of weapons training. This skiing extravaganza, better known as the *officer's admin*, had been meticulously planned by Cookie Cline about four weeks ago during an extra-long layover in Reno on his American Airlines commercial pilot job.

Every aspect of the officer's admin was painstakingly designed by Cookie to yield maximum entertainment value and relaxation potential for his squadron mates to enjoy after a hard first week of strike training. For the River Rattler pilots that weekend, it would definitely be a "blow off steam" event gliding down the slopes of the Heavenly Valley Ski Resort and drinking hot alcoholic beverages in the quaint lodge located at the bottom of the expert run. As an extra benefit, that weekend the chalet would be chocked full of ski bunnies that could serve as "eye candy" and living, breathing "targets of opportunity" for his squadron mates' pleasure. Cookie knew that if all went well with the officer's admin, he would receive many well-deserved accolades from his highly esteemed, professional colleagues. The ego factor alone drove him to excellence in his planning endeavor.

To locate Hangar 17, you had to drive past the prestigious Naval Strike Air Warfare Center (NSAWC), situated on the Southwest side of NAS Fallon. If Naval Fighter Weapons School ("Top Gun") was the premier program of instruction for fighter pilots to attend then NSAWC was the foremost schooling for attack pilots to graduate from. The school is world renowned as the pinnacle institution of carrier air warfare training. Their Strike Syllabus offers the most comprehensive training for Carrier Air Wings and Strike Leaders in preparation for their upcoming at sea deployments. Also, at various times during the calendar year, squadrons would send their mid-level aviators to SLATS (Strike Leader Attack Training Syllabus) training given at the NSAWC. This is the course that trained tactical naval aviators to be designated as Strike Leaders in their Air Wing. VA-204 could boast of having 12 SLATS graduates among their twenty pilots,

Teen Angel and Rocky being the most recent to complete the course and be selected as Carrier Air Wing Strike Leaders.

Prior to the beginning of the AOM, in the back of Room 222, Duke O'Grady was having a cup of coffee and chit chatting with his Operations Officer Klutz Fitzgerald, Comatose Gross, Shroud Morley and Brain Child Bracken. The four men looked like spectators gathered around a guru, desperate to hear about the meaning of life straight from the prophet's mouth. An extra-large box of three-dozen glazed donuts lay on the tabletop next to a Joe Dimaggio 'Mister Coffee' java machine. Somehow during the informal dialogue the subject of his ex-wife came up and Duke was telling fascinating stories for all five aviators to enjoy together while consuming their Colombian coffee and *Krispy Kreme* delicacies. Breaking into the middle of the story being told, Duke's less-than-eloquent words sounded something like this to a fly on the wall.

"When I tried to be her proverbial knight in shining armor, she would always cut the legs out from underneath my proud white stallion with her razor-sharp, double-edged sword of a tongue. Her cutting comments could slice you to the bone and since her tongue was double-edged the remarks would filet your self-esteem twice, once going in and once coming out of your ears," recalled O' Grady. His makeshift audience didn't know whether to smile uncomfortably or pat the skipper vigorously on the back for successfully struggling through his Hell of a marriage and still coming out alive, with his self-confidence intact. After a brief pause Duke sipped hot coffee from a tarnished old mug, wiped some glaze flakes away from his lower lip then continued to entertain his listeners. The four aviators drew closer so as not to miss any tidbit from the commanding officer during his storytelling venture. Duke used his right pinky finger to clear out some wax from a slightly clogged ear canal. He swiped the yellowish substance on the side of his flight suit three times then continued to tell the story of marital bliss.

"At those particularly harsh moments in our failing marriage, I would tell my lovely wife a story about the Ozark Airlines pilot from Waukegan, Illinois. This guy had apparently taken all the crap he was able to absorb from his bitch of a wife. One day in the spring of '89 this distraught airline pilot killed his wife then systematically dismembered her body with a *Poulan* chain saw." Duke lowered his tone of voice just a bit for melodramatic effect.

"Next he wrapped the individual body parts in some of that white meat packing paper then stored her in his box freezer like she was a side of beef." Duke would often use this story to try and keep his wife in line. If she started to bitch too much he would simply walk over to the box freezer, stand stoically next to the white appliance then open and close the lid in a rather macabre, suggestive manner with a sneer on his unshaven face. It was just a gentle reminder to his wife of what could lay ahead if she persisted with her bitchy behavior. The little suggestive stunt had the effect of shutting Duke's wife up for about an hour or so. Klutz Fitzgerald laughed nervously then walked to the front of the Ready Room to begin the AOM. The storytelling session quickly dispersed as all the VA-204 officers found their chairs in the Ready Room.

Twenty-seven minutes into the AOM proceedings Duke stood directly in front of a large rectangular blackboard to deliver inspirational, weapons detachment words to his cadre of pilots. But before he does so it is his duty to introduce Lieutenant Commander Leslie Lance, the newly implanted Assistant Maintenance Officer, to the rest of his officer corps. Since Juice Mayhew had been fleet upgraded by CAG Madison to the position of Executive Officer, Rocky Stone was promoted by Duke to serve as the Department Head of Maintenance. Leslie Lance would be his Assistant MO. Surely this was a match made in Hades. Cookie Cline, seated behind and to the left of Leslie Lance, tapped her lightly on the shoulder then coyly handed the new AMO a simple slip of paper. Turning around to squarely face Cookie, Lieutenant Commander Lance accepted the paper but exhibited an anxious, hesitant look on her face as if she somehow knew that she was being set up for a fall. The pre-formatted piece of paper contained a fill-in-the-blanks apology note. The blanks had been filled in with a red crayon. The note read like this:

> *Dear: Admiral/Captain/Commander (select one)* <u>Leslie Lance</u> .
> *Please allow me to apologize to you now for what I/We may do to you later.*
> *My/Our behavior will be totally inexcusable, to say the least.*
> *If appropriate, please offer My/Our sincerest apology to Mr./Mrs.* <u>Lance</u> .

Leslie contorted her smooth-skinned face as she read the note then turned back toward Commander O' Grady at the front of the room.

"Come on skipper, we need it to come much faster and much funnier," chided Rocky from the back of the Ready Room. Commander O' Grady smiled for a brief moment then continued speaking. The rest of the officer's smiles lasted a few seconds longer.

Shortly after Duke finished making his initial, formal introduction of Lieutenant Commander Lance, Teen Angel decided the time was ripe to tease Leslie just a tad in front of the unforgiving AOM crowd assembled in the *River Rattler* Ready Room. The new AMO would get a healthy does of teasing on the *Enter-*

prise cruise, so she might as well learn how to deflect the attention now, reasoned Lieutenant Ackerman.

"Gee how very stylish, how fast can you run the 100 yard dash?" mimicked Ackerman in his best Clint Eastwood impersonation. *The Enforcer*, a 1976 Dirty Harry movie, was vivid in Brad's mind as he jokingly mocked Leslie in the same way that Clint Eastwood's Inspector Harry Callahan character taunted Tyne Daly's Lt Kate Moore character during the detective interview. Teen Angel was fond of using Clint Eastwood movie character lines to make a point, sarcastic or otherwise, and the room bellowed with laughter at the new AMO's obvious expense. But Leslie Lance was fully prepared for this type of reaction to her presence in a venue usually reserved for macho, heroic men only. In fact as a highly intelligent black woman, she had struggled almost her entire life for legitimacy, acceptance and credibility. Leslie was also abundantly equipped to handle the inevitable teasing onslaughts of Brad Ackerman in particular. She had received several warnings about the infamous, slightly arrogant Teen Angel from various friends in the Navy.

"I can do anything that a man can do, thank you very much *Mister Brad*," responded Lieutenant Commander Lance in her usual Southern, deferential fashion of speaking. She always displayed a respectful demeanor, even to a rude pilot who had just insulted her in front of 20 naval officers, even if it was meant to be a soft joke. Leslie's father the reverend Reginald Lance had raised her as a proper southern belle, of African-American decent, from day one. But then, unexpectedly, Leslie lashed out at Ackerman in her own progressive, independent manner. Teen Angel was not prepared, nor did he even see her gentle tirade coming.

"I can do anything a man can do Teen Angel, except maybe piss up that wall," echoed Leslie while pointing to the south side bulkhead of Room 222. This diminutive woman had just delivered a bomb and hit the target directly on its bull's eye. The Ready Room was suddenly stilled for several moments and Brad's jaw unconsciously protruded wide open.

"Touché Lieutenant Commander Lance," injected Commander O' Grady to effectively halt the verbal nonsense from developing any further, at least for now. The squadron had to get on to other more pressing business.

"Let's all say hello to Lieutenant Commander Lance," shouted Klutz Fitzgerald to initiate the traditional welcoming routine of Naval Aviators.

"Hello asshole," responded the raucous crowd in the Ready Room.

"Let's all say hello to the asshole."

"Hello Leslie." The ritual was complete and Leslie Lance was now officially a *River Rattler*. The AOM continued then was promptly dismissed 15 minutes prior to the first flight briefing of the day, set to begin at 1030.

On the East side of NAS Fallon are a group of innocuous-looking buildings that contain everything associated with Aviation Physiology Training. The training facility was caddy corner to the NAS Fallon Medical Clinic, both located on McCain Avenue. It was definitely the domain of Dr. Kimber Kennedy and she loved hanging out on this part of the Naval Air Station, wearing her long white coat and fingering the stethoscope draped around her supple neck with elongated, lithe fingers. Kimber was especially proud of her inch-long fingernails that she always had cut in a French manicure, whatever that is. For obvious reasons, her flight physical recipients who had prostate glands were less than enamored by the generous length of her narrow fingers and French cut, manicured nails. Inside the Aviation Physiology edifice there was a tall, narrow building that housed an ejection seat training device. The skinny brick structure, although not charred by flames, resembled the buildings that are commonly seen at firefighting training facilities in every major city around the country. The main structure inside the gate of the Aviation Physiology Training grounds held the altitude chamber and several classrooms where lectures and instructional videos were given to students. The vast complex also featured an Olympic-sized swimming pool that had a Dilbert Dunker on the near side and a Helicopter Dunker on the far side of the pool. At 1000 that morning fourteen CAG-2 pilots were scheduled to begin Aviation Physiology Training. The day's activities would include an altitude chamber flight to 40,000 feet combined with Helicopter Dunker Training that was now standard for all aircrew in the Navy. A half-day of formal classes would be held tomorrow morning to complete the aviation physiology course of instruction. Only then would these fourteen aviators fulfill their four-year cycle of refresher training in aviation physiology. Only then would Kimber Kennedy stamp and sign their logbooks rendering the aviators safe from having to repeat this pain-in-the-ass ordeal for about 1400 days or so.

One of the pilots scheduled for Aviation Physiology Training that day was a Tomcat guy named Lieutenant Troy "Clown" Klinger. This colorful, tactical call sign had stuck to Troy since flight school because his father was a professional clown working in the Ringling Brothers/Barnum and Bailey traveling circus, and he had been such for the past thirty years. In High School, Troy himself had worked in Abilene as a rodeo clown keeping angry Brahma bulls off downed cowboys that had just been rudely tossed to the dirt and off the bull's powerful back. Clown Klinger hated helicopters and had vowed to never set foot inside of one for the duration of his naval aviation career. He often referred to helos as 'death traps waiting for their next hapless victim to climb onboard' and constantly ridiculed those "rotor heads" that flopped around inside them. This being the case, at 1002 that morning Troy was verbosely questioning Dr. Kimber Kennedy about why he was being forced to participate in the Helicopter Dunker Training. Without missing a beat or saying a word, Kimber was prepared to deal with the grief she was receiving from young Lieutenant Klinger. With her left hand, she motioned to the Corpsman standing by the light switch at the back door of the classroom. A moment later the overhead lights dimmed and a short seven-minute videotape began to roll on the scratched up screen in the front of the training room. One of long, skinny light bulbs in the plastic ceiling apparatus flickered a bit before finally extinguishing its fluorescent light. Clown Klinger pretended to fall asleep with his stubbly face resting in the open palm of his right hand, his elbow and desk assuming the weight of an oversized head.

The recorded video was Pilot Landing Aid Television (PLAT) coverage of an "at sea" helicopter rescue recovering two downed aircrew men during a USS *Constellation* (CV-64) cruise. The grainy, black-and-white footage began by showing an SH-3 helicopter from the HS-6 Indians at 0628 on March 5, 1990. The "Sea King" was flying in the Starboard Delta position, snuggled up next to the massive aircraft carrier that was lumbering along at 18 knots through slightly choppy seas. The SH-3 chopper was hovering lazily at about ninety feet above the white-capped ocean water as a school of thirty to forty Great White sharks lurked just beneath the surface, swimming and searching with their lifeless doll's eyes. The setting was deep inside the unfriendly confines of the foreboding Indian Ocean, approximately sixty miles off the coast of a British territorial island known as Diego Garcia. This early morning flight deck activity was apparently the first aircraft launch of the day for the ship and Carrier Task Force Eight, steaming for the Straits of Hormuz and the Persian Gulf region of the Middle East.

After spending about sixty seconds getting bored watching the SH-3 raise and lower its dipping sonar array into foamy sea water, the PLAT camera operator slowly shifted his focus over to catapult #2 to record the late launch of a KA-6D. The cat shot was "late" because the KA-6D had to have a left main mount changed just prior to it's scheduled launch time of 0620. A Line Division deck crew from the VA-145 Swordsmen, Connie's Intruder Squadron, removed and replaced the balding tire in world record time of just under eight minutes. The five men scurrying around on the flight deck were reminiscent of a NASCAR crew working on Jeff Gordon's #24 racecar in a crucial pit stop during the last few laps of the Talledega 400. As the camera's lens focused precisely on the KA-6D, the airplane lined up and taxied into launch position on catapult #2. The nose wheel steering of the jet was clearly seen making minor last second adjustments during the slow, deliberate taxi down the cat track. In the foreground of the videotape footage, an E-2C Hawkeye was hooked up to a GSE tractor. The early warning aircraft was being towed across the "foul line" headed for elevator #1 and some much needed maintenance down below in the hangar bay. As he drove, the overly relaxed tug driver hauling the Hawkeye across the flight deck rested his left foot high up on a flat portion of the glare shield on the tow tractor. The safety helmet that was supposed to be strapped tightly to his head was sitting next to his foot on the glare shield. The VAW-113 Line Division Chief Petty Officer would have a few stern words with this GSE driver later in the mess decks at lunchtime. Relaxation on the flight deck was sheer insolence and could get people killed if not effectively stymied. Most chiefs knew how to thwart unwanted behavior from both officers and enlisted personnel. It was part of the basic qualifications to promote to E-7.

The gray radar dome and four vertical tail fins of the Hawkeye disappeared from the camera's view just as six black panels of the Jet Blast Deflector (JBD) on "cat two" abruptly snapped into position about eight feet behind the Intruder's tail cone. At idle, the KA-6D medium attack jet was emitting exhaust gasses in the neighborhood of 420 degrees Fahrenheit according to its cockpit instruments. In reaction to 3,000 pounds of hydraulic fluid pressure, the extra thick concrete plates of the jet blast deflector made a horrendously loud screeching noise as its joints jolted and locked the JBD into a sixty-degree upright position. Scalding fumes were now being effectively ricocheted skyward, safely away from personnel, aircraft and equipment on the flight deck of the carrier. As a "yellow-shirted" flight deck director squeezed both hands together in front of a pair of grimy goggles fastened snuggly to his smudged face, the Intruder pilot gently stomped on his brakes to comply with the "stop" signal. The underbelly of the KA-6D cockpit came to an abrupt halt just above the catapult's steel launch shuttle mechanism. The flight deck director first made eye contact with the Intruder pilot then cupped his right elbow inside his left palm. Next the flight director extended his right arm signaling the aircrew to lower the jet's launch bar. The white-colored launch bar lowered and the T-shaped end came to rest just in front of the shuttle device, perfectly aligned with the near end of the catapult track.

Cotton white steam gently snaked up from deep beneath the entire 300-foot length of the cat track on catapult #2, defying the 23 knots of wind that howled over the carrier deck. The dense steam emanating from the bowels of the ship totally engulfed the attack aircraft, momentarily obscuring the "Iron Tadpole's" cockpit from the view of flight deck personnel. It was truly an eerie sight. Even though Harold Faltermeyer's anthem was not playing in the background and Kenny Loggins wasn't singing *Danger Zone*, the PLAT TV images were highly reminiscent of the opening slow motion scene in the Tom Cruise movie *Top Gun*. The Intruder pilot pushed his throttles to their maximum rate of thrust to comply with a two-finger "turn up" signal from the "yellow shirt" standing eighteen feet to the right of his 29 million dollar jet. The yellow-shirted flight director then thrust his left arm high up over his head while simultaneously extending his right arm toward the bow of the ship. This L-shaped signal meant that the attack jet was to be taken into tension on the catapult in final preparation for the cat shot and launch. As 650 degrees of jet exhaust forcefully exited the tail cone of the Intruder, the airplane quickly hunched down and forward, as its launch bar was rudely grabbed by the catapult's shuttle apparatus. Only then did the young Lieutenant in the left seat of the Intruder begin to methodically wipe out his aircraft's flight controls with a continuous, circular motion of the stick and a vigorous pumping action on the two rudder pedals. This "control check" procedure was required for the flight deck crew monitoring the impending aircraft launch so they could give their final "thumbs up" approval for the cat shot. From his vantage point just below the Navigation Bridge, the PLAT camera operator fiddled with his focus knob just a bit as the video footage continued.

Standing confidently on the non-skid flight deck with his right boot in a small spill of hydraulic fluid was Lieutenant Commander Hubbard Wooten, all six feet five inches and 245 pounds of him. "Wookie" Wooten probably had about 40 pounds of hair on his body, twenty pounds on his back alone. An S-3A Viking pilot by trade, Wookie was one of *Connie's* four Catapult and Arresting Gear Officers. On this third line period of *Connie's* 1990 deployment Wookie was about to finish up his "ship's company" tour before transferring to the VS-37 Sawbucks for his Department Head duty. He would COD off the ship in four weeks. In the video, Lieutenant Commander Wooten was standing to the right of the yellow shirt approximately four feet up the deck toward the bow of the ship. After receiving a "thumbs up" signal from all of the fight deck observers surrounding the Intruder on cat #2, the yellow-shirted flight director looked unequivocally at Wookie Wooten. While making this positive eye contact, the flight director gently patted the palms of both his hands on his helmet-covered forehead just above the goggles protecting his eyes. Next, the yellow shirt pointed directly toward the Cat Officer in a decisive fashion. This signal meant that the Cat Officer now had complete control over the Intruder and the temporal sequence of the launch. Wookie, accepting control from the fight director, vigorously flaunted the "two-finger turn up" signal high over his head. Wooten was standing a mere fifteen feet from the KA-6D's man-eating, jet engine intakes, his eyes surveying up and down the entire length of catapult #2. Wookie scanned the cockpit for the final salute from the naval aviator occupying the left seat of the aircraft. Way up in the third story of the carrier's island Captain Tony "Angelo" Dundee sipped some lukewarm, black coffee from a cracked mug. As the Air Boss of *Connie's* Pri Fly tower, Angelo scrutinized the deck dance below as it unfolded under his watchful eye.

Shortly after smartly saluting the Cat Officer and preparing their heads and bodies to endure the powerful jolt from the steam-powered cat stroke, the aircrew was hurled down the cat track. The KA-6D literally jumped into the air at the bow of the ship, its airspeed indicator read 143 knots. The whole E-ticket ride of the cat shot took less than two seconds to complete. In the video, the jet was now in a shallow left turn climbing up to 500 feet to comply with its "Zip Lip" VFR departure procedure. At seven miles ahead of the ship the Intruder would then commence a climb up to the "low holding" position. 3,000 feet overhead the *Connie* the KA-D would perform airborne refueling duty for the next two hours. This version of the Gruman medium attack bomber was the in-flight refueling/ tanker aircraft used predominantly by carrier air wings for twenty years.

Eight seconds after its catapult launch the Intruder's left engine was seen flaming out on the PLAT videotape in a massive explosion and jet fuel fire. The pungent, orange flames almost swallowed up the pilot and BN inside the cockpit. The television camera recorded the flight crew punching off the extra fuel tanks and aerial refueling apparatus it was toting on parent racks under its wings. But this "lightening up the aircraft" technique didn't seem to help the dire situation all that much. The unnatural and pronounced left yaw of the jet's nose caused the aircraft to drift from its intended flight path as it struggled to stay airborne. Ultimately the pilot lost control of the Intruder then initiated a low-speed ejection sequence as the jet slowly sank toward its eventual demise. Without its pilot at the controls, the crippled KA-6D floundered at 30 feet or so above the water, its only operating engine now at idle power. It resembled a wounded duck filled with #4 lead pellets above a Wisconsin lake in late December. The airplane struggled valiantly to continue flying without its aircrew before crashing into the ocean about a half-mile directly in front of the enormous carrier. The tactical jet floated for about thirty seconds then suddenly sank to the bottom of the ocean floor, 1600 feet down, never to be seen again. In the darkened classroom, Kimber Kennedy observed several of her Aviation Physiology students shifting anxiously in their desk chairs, fidgeting nervously. Clown Klinger tugged at the collar on his khaki uniform shirt. A bead of sweat trickled from his right sideburn down his face and underneath his jaw before stretching diagonally across the front of his neck. The moisture settled further down to the middle part of his chest.

As the video film continued PLAT television cameras recorded a pair of successful seat separations, then followed along as two parachutes fully deployed and splashed safely into the waves on the port side of the aircraft carrier. From *Connie's* Navigation Bridge Captain Conrad Sperry, call sign Dobler, ordered the *Constellation's* engines to "all stop" then called 'left full rudder' to the helmsman in order bring the mammoth flat top ship into a hard left turn. This action effectively turned the carrier's four humongous propellers and its array of twenty, powerfully twisting blades away from the bobbing aviators. Hundreds of men working on the flight deck scampered over to the port side of the ship to watch the scene as it ensued. Horns, whistles, bells and sirens blared loudly, announcing to everyone on the aircraft carrier that something had gone wrong, horribly wrong, with the launch of the Intruder. In a flash, the SH-3 helicopter darted from "Starboard D" and repositioned to a fifteen-foot hover directly over the floating aircrew men to effect the at sea rescue. Rotor wash howled downward toward the ocean water, gusting and splashing sea spray in all directions.

The PLAT camera followed along as a wet-suited, rescue swimmer leaped from the open hatchway door on the starboard side of the Sea King. With both arms wrapped tightly around his upper torso, cleft chin tucked into the manubrim part of his sternum, the swimmer hardly made a splash as he landed about four feet from the Intruder's BN. After spitting out some excess brine, the rescue swimmer immediately began to perform his job in the choppy environment. A yellow, cushioned, horse-collar rescue wire was lowered into the seawater from the helo. This action was required to effectively remove any potentially deadly, static electric charge from the wire rescue device. The horse-collar languished in the water for a few seconds before both downed aviators took the free ride up from the menacing Indian Ocean and into the inviting comfort of the chopper. In less than three minutes everyone was out of the water, safely inside the warmth of the gyrating helicopter. But then something else went terribly awry. *Murphy* ("anything that can go wrong, will go wrong") was apparently alive and well at the crash sight. As he lifted up and away from the rescue scene, the SH-3 pilot pulled pitch right into the port side catwalk of the *Connie*. The Sea King's rotor blade splintered into a thousand fragments as the helo plummeted powerless into the ocean. In the video, the helicopter instantly capsized then disappeared from view as it sank helplessly into the drink at about two feet per second rate of descent. This at sea tragedy was unexpectedly multiplied with the crash of the SH-3 rescue helicopter. The PLAT camera now focused on the debris field scattered across the water and on the men as they emerged from the sinking helicopter, one at a time. One man didn't make it out alive.

Suddenly Kimber Kennedy flipped the projector off and the classroom lights were simultaneously and rudely switched on by the corpsman. It was as if the two of them had rehearsed this scene hundreds of times before because it was highly choreographed for dramatic result. Bright fluorescent light invaded each retina sitting in the room.

"Gentlemen, the A-6 pilot never made it out of the SH-3. He drowned on the descent to the bottom of the ocean. His lifeless body was recovered two days later," stated Lieutenant Kennedy in a matter-of-fact tone, but barely above a whisper for the fully intended theatrical affect. Pilots squirmed in their chairs even more now. Clown Klinger continued to sweat at an even greater pace. The corpsman smirked.

"The Intruder pilot had never been through helicopter dunker training. Everybody else in this incident had been. This is why CNET made the decision to send all aircrew men through the helicopter dunker training ASAP, because it saves lives. Are there any more questions or complaints before we get started?" solicited Kimber. Not a sound was heard. Everyone in the classroom was now fully onboard with the helicopter dunker training, even Clown Klinger. Lieutenant Kennedy was content; her point had been made yet again. The corpsman's smirk grew even wider.

"Gents if you would follow me, I'll take you down to the altitude chamber for today's flight," instructed the young corpsman in a semi-mocking voice. Thirty minutes later they were all at 40,000 feet inside the low-pressure chamber, playing paddy cake or scrawling their names on a white memo pad during the hypoxia demonstration.

Over in space number 222 of Hangar 17, Teen Angel was comfortably seated on a wooden chair next to the SDO desk, his right leg crossed over the left. He was trying in vain to shoot-the-shit with Cookie Cline in between annoying, business-related phone calls. Commander Duke O' Grady, settled deep down into his cushy CO's chair at the front of the Ready Room, disregarded them both as he silently prepared for his first flight briefing. At that moment Duke casually dropped a blank briefing card onto the floor next to his right foot, leaned forward then hunched over. The skipper was now sprucing up the shine on his brown-leather flight boots with a tan buffing cloth, popping the rag smartly in between buffs. Commander Juice Mayhew, the newly appointed *River Rattler*

Executive Officer, had positioned himself three chairs away from Duke in the front row of seats. Juice was holding a NATOPS Weapons Delivery Manual with his left hand while conspicuously nibbling at a pesky hangnail on his right index finger. Juice would bite then spit out nail fragments in between brushing up on AIM-9M Sidewinder launch procedures. Later in this first week of weapons training Jack Mayhew would be firing the live heat-seeking missile toward a burning "smudge pot" target as it floated harmlessly toward the ground underneath a miniature parachute. The live missile-firing event would take place in the GABBS South MOA on Friday at 0800.

Lieutenant Cookie Cline, who was the Squadron Duty Officer for the entire day, would spend much of his time in that capacity filling out mundane, statistical paperwork and answering obtuse questions posed by CAG-2 staffers over the black, dialup telephone. The SDO desk, where Cookie had planted himself about forty minutes ago, was an old piece of furniture that was made from some sort of soft, light-colored wood. The veneer was covered with tell tale scratches and pen marks from previous abusers. At that moment, as Cookie gabbed on the phone line with Senior Chief Esposito down in Maintenance Control, the desk was littered with numerous papers askew all over the top. About seven black, government-issue pens adorned the desktop with six more just inside the center drawer as backup. Pens had a habit of disappearing in a navy squadron fairly quickly. The center drawer also contained a jumbo-sized *Milky Way* candy bar that Cookie had purchased at the Navy Exchange then strategically positioned inside the desk for his pleasurable consumption later in the day. The sugar and caramel high would of course bring a contented smile to his freshly shaved face from first bite to last.

A three-hole punch and two staplers surrounded the telephone receiver, and a large brown tape dispenser sat ready to dole out any quantity of Scotch tape needed by the SDO. Cookie continued talking and actively listening as Senior Chief Esposito handed his end of the telephone line over to Lieutenant Commander Leslie Lance. Leslie had some additional maintenance-related issues she needed to clarify with the SDO as the weapons det got started that morning. Brad Ackerman, still trying to distract Cookie, didn't have a flight brief until 1430. He was, however, required to attend a CAG LSO meeting scheduled for 1330 in the conference room down the hall. In that gathering, all of the CAG-2 Landing Signal Officers would discuss the definitive details of next month's Carrier Qualification (CQ) cycle onboard USS *Enterprise*. The CQ line period was scheduled for March 29-31, 1992 and this would be the final preparation and planning meeting for the carrier qualification of Air Wing Two.

At 1045 in the paraloft downstairs, Lieutenant Commander "Rocky" Stone stood next to his locker putting on a pair of musty, green speed slacks. Right boot resting on a bench, he was tucking in his pant leg and zipping up the right side of his G-suit, all while vigorously teasing with three squadron mates. After signing and accepting their jets, the four aviators would meet their plane captains and conduct thorough preflight inspections in the crisp Fallon air. At precisely 1200, the division of attack aircraft would be wheels-in-the-well proceeding indirectly over to the Bravo-17 target for ordnance delivery training. But first the four Corsairs would fly the VR-208 low-level navigation route, attempting to "sneak into" the R-4804 restricted zone. Hopefully the division of combat planes would go undetected by simulated enemy radar, anti-aircraft-artillery, surface-to-air missile batteries, and adversary fighter jets loitering over the target area. The problem with this concept was the men who operated these weapons installations and who would be flying the adversary planes knew exactly when and where the Corsairs would arrive at Bravo-17. In fact they could actively track them by using the many detection devices and sensors that had been strategically placed all along the low-level flight routes inside the Gabbs MOA. Once the attack jets were detected leaving Walker Lake on VR-208, they would arrive overhead the Bravo-17 target a scant six minutes later. It was a set up from the get go. But it was an integral part of the "war games" type of training included in every CAG weapons det.

Rocky would lead this bombing hop that would feature Pops Petibone, Comatose Gross and Sugar^2 Cane as his trusted wingmen. In five minutes the four pilots departed Maintenance Control and walked confidently onto the frigid flight line toward their Corsairs. All the aviators carried similar equipment with them. Each man had something called a "How-to-Fly Book" that they had created specifically for Fallon and its various weapons ranges. The customized booklet included local Course Rules and restrictions, special operating procedures, Rules of Engagement, radio frequencies, divert airfield information and bingo profiles specific to the Fallon area of operation. Of course, in his personal equipment, Rocky always carried what he called an A-7 pilot's survival kit. The "survival kit" consisted of a disposable razor, a pack of *Wrigley's* spearmint chewing gum and an extra-large *Trojan* condom with a reservoir tip. Rocky always got a big belly laugh whenever he mentioned his A-7 pilot's survival kit to squadron mates. It was likewise legendary among his naval aviator colleagues throughout the world. Women didn't recognize the humor in it for some strange reason.

The preflight, start up, systems and weapons checks all came off without a hitch for this sortie. Next the four attack planes proceeded through the "final checker" position to arm their weapons, get a positive "growl tone" on their inert Sidewinder missiles, and activate their TACS Pods. The formation of Corsairs then lethargically taxied in a staggered column toward the duty runway for take-off. They looked like gray ducks moving sluggishly off to the pond for a swim.

"Did you see the windsock Rocky?" asked Pops Petibone utilizing button twenty on the back radio. Like a good naval aviator, Pops was trying to stay ahead of his airplane and the division of jets by anticipating the lineup on the runway.

"Yes I did, and it was limp as the skipper's dick!" replied Stone. All four aviators chuckled in response to Rocky's goading banter on the UHF. As they continued toward the approach end of runway 31 the division of Corsairs taxied by an FA-18 Hornet that was parked on the transient flight line. The "fourth generation" tactical aircraft gleamed in the morning sunlight as if beckoning would-be Strike-Fighter pilots to come take a ride at Mach 2.

"I hear that Hornet jet is so advanced that it comes complete with a bleed air blowjob and an accu-jack. It gives you something to do in the cockpit for those long, lonesome nights holding in marshal overhead the ship, just waiting for your push time," said Lieutenant Cane on Button #20, the *River Rattler* squadron common frequency.

"Rocky, you would probably kill yourself just taxiing an advanced jet like that," cracked Comatose Gross. Rocky, his O_2 mask dangling down over the left side of the Corsair cockpit, didn't respond to his squadron mate's mockery. He let them have their head for now. Three minutes later the flight of four was airborne, streaking at 520 knots toward the Initial Point (IP) for VR-208.

"Let the fun begin," muttered Rocky to himself as he cinched up the oxygen mask even tighter to his face. He took a cursory glance through the "heads up device" to get his bearings straight. The clear-plastic HUD sat high up on the Corsair's glare shield, under the bullet-proof windscreen. Rocky banked the attack jet forty degrees to the left, while taking one last look at his three buddies flying in Combat Spread formation all around him. The word precision came to his brain at that moment, and he was indeed proud to be wearing the wings of gold. Lieutenant Commander Rocky Stone then shifted his gaze to the four, live MK-84 bombs slung under his wings. The "Snake Eye" retarded bombs were attached to parent racks for a smoother aerodynamic feel and much less parasitic drag. Eight tons of high explosive ordnance would all find its way to the bull's eye today he arrogantly thought. Rocky wasn't wrong. Like most attack aviators, he loved pointing his jet's nose to the ground in a weapons delivery dive.

"Fallon Control, AF-407 and flight are at the IP for VR-208," reported Rocky to the Gabbs MOA air traffic controllers. The flight of four was now flying comfortably at 80 feet above the Nevada desert, zigzagging over the mountainous topography, "terrain masking" to avoid detection by radar and SAM sites. The Fallon mountain range always had a look of rugged serenity, especially on a frosty February morning. Today was no different. The familiar guitar chords and lyrics of *Taking Care of Business*, a Bachman Turner Overdrive classic, surged through Rocky's thought process as he led the flight onward. If he could just get laid tonight, all would be right with his world. Rocky took his un-gloved hands momentarily off the Corsair's trimmed flight controls and throttle. He strummed his "air guitar" rhythmically along with the recognizable BTO beat now playing relentlessly in his head.

Seventy-five minutes later, all the green MK-84's from the division of *River Rattler* Corsairs had hit in the general vicinity of Bravo-17's various targeting points that consisted of numerous jeeps, tanks, tents, SAM sites, and small metal structures. After the final dive-bombing run, all the planes in the formation reported *Winchester* (no ordnance remaining to be expended) to Rocky, all except for one. Sugar^2 Cane had a lone, live bomb stuck on the inboard parent rack under his left wing. The eight-foot long arming wire was still flailing in the wind stream, visibly attached to the bomb's nose fuse as the weapon dangled down from station #3. The piece of live ordnance had obviously misfired during the last attack run. Lieutenant Cane had the dreaded first "hung bomb" of Carrier Air Wing Two's weapons detachment. As the flight of Corsairs checked off target with range controllers and departed the R-4804 restricted area, Rocky flashed a familiar signal to Sugar^2 Cane from his cockpit. The "kiss off" hand signal effectively kicked Sugar^2 and his jet out of the formation. This meant that Cane had to independently set himself up for a "hung ordnance" approach back at NAS Fallon. The long straight-in flight procedure, prescribed by the Course Rules for a "hung ordnance" approach, would be to Runway 13. Cane knew this because the ATIS information on button #1 announced that the wind had shifted in the last hour, so that it was now gusting from the southeast at twelve knots. After his kiss off, Cane hastily descended 2500 feet to split off from the other three jets to set up his "hung ordnance" approach.

At 1255, Sugar^2 Cane was gently maneuvering his Corsair at 1200 feet AGL and 250 knots, cruising directly above Interstate 95. He was heading toward NAS Fallon. Down below was an ex-hippie couple from Berkeley, motoring lazily along at 52MPH in the fast lane of Highway 95. They drove a 1968, psychedelic VW Van. The couple was driving along fat, mega-liberal and happy in search of the next *Grateful Dead* concert or protest rally. Without warning from the # 3 parent rack, a round, six inch piece of steel thrust downward, forcibly ejecting the green 2000 pound bomb away from the left wing of Cane's A-7 Corsair. The thin arming wire stayed with his aircraft. As the armed piece of weaponry departed the matted gray on the underside of the wing it was instantly in ballistic, free-fall flight. The MK-84 bomb now angled silently toward the Nevada desert and Highway 95 below. Eighteen seconds later, the live "Snake Eye" bomb hit the sand, twenty-eight feet from the Interstate on its eastern side. It caused a massive explosion and fireball. The blast left a twenty-one foot wide and fourteen-foot deep crater in the soft soil. Sand, desert debris, burning cactus limbs, and even a few small animals instantly soared to a height of 1100 feet. The blast pattern stretched outward to approximately 400 feet in all directions from ground zero. The heat and overpressure from the detonation was actually felt by Lieutenant Cane inside his cockpit as he whisked away from the scene, accelerating to 350 knots indicated airspeed. 'Maybe nobody noticed,' he hoped while swallowing hard.

Looking down to survey the condition of his cockpit, Cane noticed the number three weapons station was still selected and that the "Master Arm" switch was in the up and "armed" position. He must have inadvertently pushed his red "pickle switch" (weapon release button) on the control stick while maneuvering the Corsair. Suddenly Cane realized he had forgotten to perform his "weapons safe" checklist after leaving the Bravo17 target area. He had mistakenly left his weapons system armed and bomb station #3 selected after the hung bomb condition had manifest itself on the last attack run. Cane's face flushed and the pit of his stomach ached as he initially contemplated the magnitude of his error and worse yet, the residual consequences. For some reason, Gus Grissom's "Mercury space capsule excuse" flickered inside his thought process.

"The bomb just blew," he rationalized, "it just blew." But that lame excuse probably wouldn't cut it with Duke O' Grady or CAG Madison, he quickly reasoned. Cane surveyed the damage in his rear-view mirror as he flew on. His whole body winced. The powerful MK-84 explosion had yielded several secondary fires all around the lonely stretch of freeway. Orange and red flames engulfed a few lonesome trees that decorated this section of the highway. The blast even hurled numerous pieces of shrapnel into the VW van, but the two UC Berkley graduates were unaware and unhurt. Cane meekly landed his Corsair on Runway 13 five minutes later. He taxied the attack jet into the flight line, shut down his turbine engine then walked humbly into Maintenance Control to fill out his yellow sheet and Incident Report Form. It would be a long afternoon for Lieutenant Cane.

Unbelievably, ninety minutes had passed since the last infuriating phone call had reached the SDO desk. Cookie and Teen Angel were still jabbering away about a variety of subjects when Cookie had to take a piss, right then and there.

"I gotta take a leak NOW Teen Angel," exclaimed Cookie. As he spoke the words, Lieutenant Cline pushed the SDO chair rearward then pranced toward the front door of the Ready Room. He pinched off his penis as he sashayed. Quicker than a bum on a bologna sandwich, Brad amiably offered to watch the SDO desk for his friend while he hit the head to relieve himself of about a pint of piss.

"No slack in light attack buddy," I'll cover the duty desk until you return, said Ackerman without hesitation.

"You sure you got it?" asked Cookie as he approached the front door. He was humbly checking the level of his squadron mate's devotion and loyalty.

"Trust me on this one subject Bub, I got it!" reassured Ackerman. Cookie Cline dashed down the hallway into the Men's Head. He arrived just in the nick of time.

Back in the VA-204 Ready Room, Brad Ackerman had plopped down into the SDO chair then promptly put his feet high up on the desktop to relax. He rested both flight boots awkwardly on his green LSO Log Book and closed his eyes pretending to be fast asleep. Ten seconds later the SDO phone rang. Teen Angel picked up the receiver after the second ring. He held the phone snugly to the right side of his baby face.

"Attack Squadron 204, Lieutenant Ackerman speaking. May I help you sir," was the standard mantra spoken by Teen Angel into the telephone. A slight bit of arrogance resonated in his tone and body language.

"Teen Angel, this is CAG Madison. One of your jets just dropped a live bomb on Highway 95. I want to know who the fuck it was and I want to know RIGHT NOW!" screamed the Air Wing Commander. Spine Ripper's neck veins were bulging to their maximum protuberance over in the CAG-2 spaces.

"Skipper it's for you!" advised Lieutenant Ackerman as he held the phone conspicuously and purposefully away from his right ear. Teen Angel was staring straight at Duke O' Grady who was still sitting in his CO's chair at the front of the Ready Room.

CHAPTER 25

▼

HANOI HILTON

After the "Cane Hung Bomb Mutiny" had gradually subsided, the remainder of week one of the weapons det unfolded normally for the *River Rattlers* and for the other squadrons in CAG-2. The Carrier Air Wing did have a hell of a first day, but nobody had died or gotten hurt and Spine Ripper Madison had actually seen some great things developing during the initial strike exercises on the Fallon weapons range. In fact, Captain Madison was so pleased with the stellar performance of his men that he gave the Air Wing a half-day off on Friday of week one. This meant that individual squadron weekend recreational activities could get kicked off earlier than originally planned. At 0915 on that first Friday morning, Brad Ackerman was down in the VA-204 paraloft unzipping his G-suit after completing his only scheduled sortie for the day. He had flown AF-411, the Corsair with his name painted on the side, and had successfully punched out a burning smudge pot for Juice Mayhew to destroy with a live AIM-9M Sidewinder, heat-seeking missile. From the moment the supersonic "heater" launched off Mayhew's left cheek mount station and tracked the parachuted smudge pot at Mach 2.5, the lethal air-to-air weapon performed perfectly. The canards and tail fins steered the $84,000 weapon directly to its intended, airborne target for the quick, hard kill. The only wrinkle in the missile fire flight was when Teen Angel patronizingly reminded Juice to 'wait until I am tucked back underneath your jet before you launch that heater Bub, or I'll kick your ass all over the Gabbs MOA.' After completing the Missile-X, Juice and Teen Angel flew three '2 v unknown' ACM engagements against a section of F-5's from the VFC-13 Saints, in the heart of the warning area. The Saints threw in an F-16 Falcon for good measure and to add an element of surprise to the air combat maneuvering dog-fights. The "fur balls" were long, arduous and hard fought by each man in his metal, or carbon fiber, flying machine. Both Jack Mayhew and Brad Ackerman soaked their green Nomex flight suits with dripping sweat during numerous sustained turns at 6G's of acceleration force.

45 minutes later following his debrief, Lieutenant Ackerman was lying naked and sprawled out on the queen-sized bed inside his BOQ room, number 212. Teen Angel made certain that his door was locked and the dead bolt was set and checked for security. He didn't want any surprises to come marching in un-announced. Surprises like Filipino maids carrying vacuum cleaners or squadron mates looking for a practical joke advantage. The adjoining door of the BOQ bathroom that Brad shared with Lieutenant Comatose Gross, who was occupying room 214, was securely locked as well. A set of baby blue window shades were drawn and tightly shut over Brad's second story window that overlooked Rick-over Street, one of NAS Fallon's main drags. The lower half of Ackerman's nude body was partially covered up by a cream-colored bedspread. His left calf and size eleven foot protruded from under the covers. The soft, black hairs that covered his left Achilles tendon tingled as they reacted to some lingering, static electricity contained in the fabric of the cotton and polyester blend bedspread.

Teen Angel had wedged three pillows tight up against the headboard to prop his cranium up for an impending phone conversation. Before jumping into the shower stall to rinse the dried sweat off his body, Lieutenant Ackerman had decided to make a quick but essential telephone call back to New Orleans. He was quietly hoping to catch Danielle Le Claire in her office and not in the court-room litigating some momentous, precedent-setting case or out to a gourmet lunch at *K-Paul's* in the central business district. In a strange way, Teen Angel actually needed to speak with his woman in the *Crescent City* to gain some mea-sure of reassurance from her. As he leaned further back against the pillows and headboard it felt like sand fleas were nipping at the middle of his back. Brad hunched slightly forward then grabbed a hairbrush from the top of the night-stand. He used the brush to scratch in between his shoulder blades, gaining some relief from the semi-hard bristles, as they raked side-to-side. Ackerman tossed the hairbrush to the foot of the bed then used a remote control device to turn on the nineteen-inch, black-and-white TV. The television was bolted down inside the entertainment hutch in the south corner of his BOQ room. He hurriedly channel surfed with the remote until locating the CNN station then muted the sound.

Teen Angel used his right middle finger to flick a red ant off the lampshade that rested on the nightstand. The annoying insect landed harmlessly on the gray carpet about seven feet away from his bed.

After he dialed Danielle's private, Assistant District Attorney number, Teen Angel toyed with the supple hairs on his chest, listened to the ring tone and waited for her to pick up the receiver on the other end. Anybody who knew Danielle immediately surmised that she had an uncanny capacity to destroy a man with a mere glance, or she could build up his self-esteem to the highest heights with a simple touch of her gentle hand. This certainly was an awesome responsibility entrusted to Miss Le Claire, or any woman for that matter. She picked up Brad's call on the fifth ring. The couple talked, giggled and exchanged both romantic and overtly sexual innuendos for the next twelve minutes. They were in fact, head-over-heels in love with one another but didn't have the emotional courage to make that admission just yet in their burgeoning relationship. Both of them had been burned badly in the past and the sting of lost love and heartbreak was still quite apparent, hovering just under the surface. In the last minute of the conversation Danielle gave Ackerman the "bum's rush" to get him off the telephone without any further delay. She had an important, working lunch meeting at *Commander's Palace* restaurant with her boss, New Orleans District Attorney Harry Connick. Teen Angel was elated that he'd gotten her on the horn for a few minutes.

After his phone conversation with Danielle Le Claire had concluded, Teen Angel rinsed dried sweat off his body for five minutes in the shower stall. The soft water droplets felt slimy to the touch as he toweled himself dry on the bathmat. He quickly shaved with a disposable razorblade then threw on a pair of *Guess* jeans and a multi-colored *Tommy Bahama* Hawaiian shirt. Brad wore no underwear. At 0500 earlier that morning, Ackerman hadn't gotten around to shaving because the bathroom light bulb had burned out, and shaving was an activity best accomplished in the light. Teen Angel slipped on a pair of tan-colored *Bass* sandals then admired his physique in the mirror as he splashed an extra helping of *Escada* cologne for men all over his neck. His 24 inch overnight bag already packed, he was now ready for a little Lake Tahoe gambling at Harrah's Casino and some snow skiing action at the Heavenly Valley Resort. Slamming the door to his room shut, Lieutenant Ackerman strolled down the hallway on the second deck of the Bachelor Officers Quarters to pick up Commander Jack Mayhew, the newly appointed squadron XO and occupant of room 201. Teen Angel and Juice would take the two-hour, minivan ride up to Lake Tahoe together, along with Rocky, Cookie, T-Ben and Leslie Lance. Halfway down the hall, Brad began to strut like a peacock over to Juice's room. He smelled delicious, to paraphrase what Danielle always said about his choice of cologne. Brad was going to knock but thought better of the idea once he arrived at 201. Teen Angel simply burst through Mayhew's door in one swift, coordinated motion. He pushed with his left hand, leading with a strong left shoulder and the meaty portion of his bicep then waltzed on in.

As the door swung wide open and into Jack's quarters, the room initially appeared to be dark and empty, with no activity inside. But almost instantaneously Teen Angel sensed in his gut that something was desperately out of place. As Brad switched on the lights, the tiny little hairs on the back of his neck stood up as he stepped further inside to probe. Ackerman's emotions were ambiguous at that point because he didn't know what he was faced with. Should he feel like a cop clearing a room during a warrant entry into a felon's lair? Or should he feel like *Inspector Clousseau* searching for Kato's latest ambush ploy in a *Pink Panther* motion picture? He moved on. Standing adjacent to the vanity sink in the small bedroom, Brad finally spotted Mayhew's feet sticking out of the bathroom area. Juice was lying down on his right side on the bathroom tile, just in front of the shower stall. At first Ackerman simply hoped that Juice was playing a practical joke on him, and a poor prank at best. But as he approached Mayhew on the floor, Teen Angel abruptly realized that this was no hoax. This was something serious and it was unfolding right before his eyes. Curled up in a fetal position, Jack's body came into full view as Brad continued to the entrance door of the bathroom and parked himself next to Mayhew's feet. Jack had one white sock on and one off. Gazing down at Juice's severely contorted face, Ackerman knew immediately that the XO was obviously experiencing acute pain. His whole body appeared to be immersed in excruciating, overwhelming agony. Jack's grimaced face resembled the look of a human victim that had just been stung several times by an Irukanji Jellyfish off the Aussie coast of northern Queensland. And the tentacles were still firing, actively injecting their lethal venom. But this wasn't one of those National Geographic specials documenting Australian aquatic life on the PBS channel. This was real life. Mayhew's breathing was rapid and shallow. His face was ashen and his eyes were tightly shut. Jack's mouth held 28 clenched teeth behind lips that were stretched and constricted. His compressed choppers were uncovered and available for full viewing. Mayhew's flight suit was excessively taut because underneath the green Nomex material his body was rigid and stiff like, a two by four plank. He was also ten to fifteen pounds overweight, as usual.

"Juice, what the fuck is going on here Bub?" asked Teen Angel with a tinge of anxiety in his voice, perhaps still hoping that this was all just a dirty trick. Instinctively reacting to Brad's familiar voice, Mayhew merely writhed and moaned further in pain as he attempted to collect himself and push his body up from the tile with both hands flat on the floor. But his maneuvering was in vain. Jack didn't have the requisite amount of strength at that moment to raise himself fully off the deck. Under the weight of his own hulking frame, his weakened wrists caved in simultaneously. As Juice began to collapse back down to the cold tile, Ackerman deftly reached downward with both hands to catch his buddy and pull him up to his feet. Ackerman's forearm muscles tensed up and strained under the heavy, awkward load. Brad positioned Mayhew's left arm around his neck, messing up the collar on the cleaned and pressed Hawaiian "surfer-boy" shirt he had just put on. He then snaked his own arm securely around Jack's waistline then walked him slowly over to the side of the bed. Juice's whole torso winced visibly as he sat down on the edge. Once there, he finally made cursory visual contact with Lieutenant Ackerman's face. Realizing that he couldn't use deceit to explain his way out of this embarrassing episode, Jack decided to level with his friend Teen Angel. Tell the truth then play on Ackerman's sympathies was his quickly hatched, master plan. Jack's eyes were not fully open as he began to speak. His face was still distorted from the intense amount of pain he was enduring. The lack of color in his exposed skin was still disturbing.

"My left kidney is trying to pass a golf ball-sized stone Brad," admitted Juice in a matter-of-fact tone. Mayhew's broken body looked like it had just taken a 15 round beating at the hands of heavyweight champion Muhammad Ali. The candid admission was quite stunning because both aviators knew that passing a kidney stone was a grounding medical condition for tactical naval aviators. Kidney stones meant that your precious naval aviation career was in grave jeopardy of being snatched away from you by a panel of white-coated flight surgeons seated behind a long, impressive-looking table. Both men understood that kidney stone waivers were nearly impossible to get approved. You had more chance of getting an eyesight waiver issued by NAMI than you were likely to receive a kidney stone waiver. The absolute vulnerability contained in Jack's truthful confession was instantly evident to the empathetic Brad Ackerman.

"I passed one about seven years ago on a fishing trip with Loretta back in Jacksonville. I actually fell out of the little boat we had rented. Loretta had to fish me out of the river with a net. This is exactly how it felt then." Mayhew's voice was weak and labored as he forced out the words. Ackerman shifted nervously standing next to Jack's bed, both hands resting on his hips as he listened intently. Teen

Angel slowly began to become cognizant of the dilemma he was being confronted with by hearing Mayhew's declaration. Brad ambled over to the vanity sink, removed the lone white sock from the basin then turned on the cold water. He dripped the stream of semi-clear fluid into a clean, plastic glass then brought it back over to Jack. Mayhew took a long, slow swig of the cool liquid. It tasted like shit, but Juice drank it down anyway. The thyroid cartilage of his Adam's Apple visibly pumped up and down as he tried to swallow easy.

"I thought the condition was corrected back then but I guess I was dead wrong," admitted Mayhew. The vision was beginning to return to his eyes as he focused on Brad's face tying to make positive eye communication with his squadron mate. Juice wanted to make an initial assessment of where he stood with Teen Angel as the young Lieutenant gathered in his sobering admission. He decided to go for broke and lay his cards out on the table. Juice's lips regained some color as he exhorted the words out of his voice box.

"Brad, you gotta help me out here. It would kill me if I couldn't fly tactical jets anymore." Jack stared Teen Angel straight in the eye, never wavering as he made his solemn appeal. Like Mayhew's truthful confession, this request was equally startling to Brad Ackerman, but not totally unexpected. Faced with a similar set of circumstances, he would make the same earnest plea to Jack, he quickly reasoned.

"Juice, don't get your panties in a wad. Your secret is safe with me Bub," confided Ackerman. "I hate them flight surgeons almost as much as you do Jack." The proclamation immediately imparted a sense of refuge and job security to Juice Mayhew. But more than the spoken words, it was the genuine sincerity of the eye contact and facial expressions between the two men that provided Jack with the positive reassurance and sanctuary he was pleading for. Mayhew's tactical naval aviation career was safe for now, and his friend was doing him a solid favor. He would undoubtedly find a way to repay Teen Angel's honorable discretion at some point in the near future. Juice also realized that Brad was now a lifelong, loyal friend. The kidney stone passed two minutes later.

After spotting Juice and Teen Angel finally emerging from the side door of the Fallon BOQ, Cookie Cline honked the horn twice while seated on the driver's side of a midnight blue *Dodge Caravan*. The minivan, parked next to the curb in the BOQ lot, was impatiently waiting for Mayhew and Ackerman with it's engine idling and the heater pumping out 78 degrees of warm, recycled air. Jack and Brad would be the last two passengers slated to take the ride up to Lake Tahoe in that vehicle. Duke O' Grady had in fact authorized the rental of four minivans for the Fallon detachment and for the Admin trip to Tahoe. At that moment the other three vehicles were well on their way, speeding northbound along US Highway 95 toward "the biggest little city in the world," Reno, Nevada. Already comfortably situated inside this last van was Leslie Lance, who sat in the front bucket seat next to Cookie. Rocky and T-Ben were occupying the middle bench seat. This meant that Juice and Teen Angel would be relegated to the "back of the bus" for the two-hour and fifteen minute trek up to the lake and the VA-204 Admin hotel. Actually, the stern position wouldn't be all that bad because it was the closest spot to a large Styrofoam cooler of beer that rested in the cargo hold at the rear of the van. Rocky and T-Ben had already helped themselves to a can containing some of Golden, Colorado's finest, iced cold brew.

"Youz guyz are 20 minutes late, so lets shake a leg," scolded Cookie Cline as he revved the 200 horsepower engine of the minivan trying to goad them on down the slushy sidewalk from the BOQ.

"We got places to go, people to see, things to do and cats to annihilate," quipped Cookie. The line was one of Lieutenant Cline's favorites. He had borrowed it from the Ken Keasey novel, later turned into a motion picture, *Sometimes a Great Notion* then changed it a little bit to fit his own personality. The line usually got a blank stare from outsiders who didn't know Cookie all that well. Leslie Lance was no exception today.

"Let's get hopping boys," said Cookie as he pounded his palm gently on the outside of the frosty, driver's side door. His breath smoked from the warm confines of the van into the frigid afternoon air. Using the right entrance hatch Juice and Teen Angel climbed into the back of the van without much fanfare, compared to what had just transpired thirty minutes earlier in room 201. T-Ben Hebert closed the cumbersome, sliding door behind Ackerman as he eased past him into the rear section of the minivan. The smell of fresh *Escada* cologne rubbed off onto Lieutenant Hebert's right shirtsleeve as Teen Angel brushed past him. T-Ben had to make two attempts to get the clumsy door latched then locked. Once all of his passengers were safely seated and securely belted in, Cookie shifted the vehicle into "drive" then headed for the NAS Fallon front gate at 30 MPH. Three minutes later Lieutenant Cline exchanged pleasantries with a nineteen year-old, female gate guard then drove off the base. She had red hair, always a weakness for Cookie. Leslie just shook her head slowly in semi-disgust. What had she gotten herself into with these womanizing, *River Rattler* pilots? She was bewildered to say the least.

As the blue van departed the front gate and headed toward the majestic mountain roads that spiral out of Fallon, Leslie Lance pulled a Trisha Yearwood cassette tape out of her purse. She would need some assistance in mitigating the objectionable, physical presence of Rocky Stone in the car for the next couple of hours. Leslie had swiftly learned to dislike Lieutenant Commander Stone, her immediate boss, during her first week in the squadron as the new AMO. The 1991 debut album of the young singer from Monticello, Georgia, entitled *She's in Love With the Boy*, was Leslie's favorite Country and Western record. Although she loved Elvis recordings more, Miss Yearwood and other country musicians were rapidly gaining favor in her mind. Leslie popped the cassette into the car stereo and turned the volume up a few decibels. Trisha's sultry southern voice soon bellowed out of the speaker system, singing something about a young girl named Katie sitting on her front porch watching chickens peck at the muddy ground. Almost immediately Rocky Stone began to complain about Leslie's choice and genre of music.

"Uhhh, do we have to listen to this honky tonk crap?" he implored. He tapped Cookie Cline on the right shoulder as he posed the rude question to all the passengers in the minivan.

"Leave Leslie alone Rock. It's her radio for the entire drive up to the Lake," advised Cookie. Cline glared at Rocky Stone's mug using the rear-view mirror. Leslie was pleasantly surprised at the support she was receiving from Lieutenant Cline. She raised her eyebrows, lightly punched Cookie on his right thigh muscle to thank him then silently mouthed along with the words of the song. She stared straight out the windshield and lip-synced in perfect unison with Trisha. T-Ben popped the tab open on another cold *Coors Light* and smiled inwardly. Temporarily thwarted, Lieutenant Commander Stone then switched gears himself. He decided to take advantage of the captive audience inside the van. Apparently the time was once again ripe for Jim Stone to tell some "Rocky Horror" stories about his primary occupation as a Boeing 727 commercial airline Captain. Rocky chugged mightily to drain the last of his beer, crushed the empty can on the floorboard under his shoe then began to chatter. The story went something like this.

On his last Delta Airlines flight, airline Captain Stone had just finished regaling the co-pilot with his infamous flight attendant joke, known worldwide.

"How do you conjugate the adjective stupid," he asked the first officer.

"I don't know sir," was the timid reply from the second-year pilot near the bottom of the Delta Airlines seniority list. The young co-pilot continued to steer the B-727 aircraft, cruising in the light chop at 35,000 feet MSL, directly over the J-42 Jet Navigation Route.

"Stupid, stupider and stewardess!" barked Rocky in a deep slow voice. He cackled loudly as he slapped the back of his co-pilot for additional dramatic effect. A few minutes after the levity had died down in the cockpit Rocky had gotten up from his Captain's chair during the middle-portion of the trip from Nashville to Dallas to use the forward lavatory. Six cups of decaffeinated coffee and two Diet Coke's had finally gotten the better of his large but normally patient bladder. As he emerged from the cockpit, the flimsy door to the forward bathroom swung open and a rather hefty, bare-footed Asian woman exited the toilet area. Rocky hastily surmised that she was wearing way too much makeup but not enough hair spray. After swinging the bathroom door closed the Asian lady lethargically waddled back to her seat in the coach section. The woman weighed in at close to 380-pounds and wore a flowery pink muumuu, probably purchased at Omar the Tentmaker's Bargain Basement Superstore in Honolulu. She also sported a floppy straw hat with an unrestrained brim. Her extra-wide hips unintentionally grazed the heads, shoulders and elbows of a few snoozing people as she inelegantly made her way down the aisle of the First Class and Coach cabins. Unknown to Rocky, who was fat, dumb and happy at the time, the rotund woman had been squatting on the toilet for the past fifteen minutes taking a good old-fashioned, country crap. The half-Korean, half-Japanese woman actually had to flush the toilet seven times to dispose of her waste.

Immediately after Captain Stone re-opened that same forward lavatory door the lingering, vile stench rushed out and hit him in the face, even as he watched the woman meander toward the rear of the airplane. The shocking assault on his nose and mouth was like receiving a sharp left-hook from the lightweight champion in the 5th round at Madison Square Garden. Rocky partially gagged up the chilidog he ate for breakfast then forced it back down his gullet. His balled-up, left fist was pressed firmly against his mouth for added protection against vomiting. None of his passengers in the First Class cabin would see him puke today. Rocky suddenly didn't have to use the toilet anymore. He simply did an about face, sauntered rapidly back into the cockpit then closed the door tightly behind him. He could breathe again. Once seated back in the command chair of the 727, Rocky called on the intercom phone to the flight attendant's station to ask a favor of the in-flight crew. In compliance with Captain Stone's demand, the lead flight attendant located the *Glade* deodorizer and proceeded to empty the entire contents of the aerosol can into the forward bathroom and First Class galley area. Back in the cockpit, Rocky's whole body tensed up as he heard a female pilot's squeaky voice over the radio, coming from a Southwest jet, speaking to air traffic controllers.

"In a disgusted tone, I said 'Go get a woman's job' over the VHF radio," admitted Rocky to his squadron mates in the car. The high-pitched voice of a woman over any airplane's radios while airborne always made Rocky scowl. He truly felt that women had no business in the cockpit of an aircraft.

Isn't that sort of a sexist, chauvinistic remark?" harangued T-Ben seated next to Rocky in the middle row of leather seats. Lieutenant Hebert smirked briefly then waited for his verbal punishment from Rocky for the obvious insubordination implied by the question. Cookie merged the van into the fast lane of Highway 95. He also eagerly awaited Rocky's terse reply.

"T-Ben, I was leading men into combat while you were still flunking college algebra exams and getting rejected by ugly chicks with bad teeth in the back seat of your cream-colored Pinto. So shut your trap and let me continue with my Rocky Horror stories," counseled Lieutenant Commander Stone. His demeanor was one of modest mockery towards Hebert. In the front seat, Leslie Lance didn't find anything about Rocky to be remotely humorous. He was a rude, arrogant, inconsiderate, sexist ass hole in her humble opinion. It didn't seem to matter to her that he was a truly gifted Naval Aviator and a heroic attack pilot. Leslie cranked up the volume on the stereo just a bit more then asked Teen Angel to hand her a Pepsi from the cooler.

For what it was worth, Rocky didn't much care what Leslie Lance thought of him. He had already given Lieutenant Commander Lance some cursory thought this past week while working closely with her in the *River Rattler* Maintenance Department. He had abruptly dismissed the notion of having any kind of sexual liaison with her, discreet or otherwise, almost immediately. He figured that having sex with Leslie Lance would be extremely "clinical!" It would be similar in dynamic to bringing a six-year old child to the pediatrician for a booster shot. You and the kid both cringe at the very thought of it. Then when the time finally arrives, you gotta go through with it, but you both don't want to. Yeah, sex with Leslie Lance would most definitely be a "clinical" activity. Nothing out of the ordinary, just a quick swab of the arm with an alcohol-soaked cotton ball, and then administer the unwanted injection to an unwilling recipient. Clinical! Besides, Rocky's mind was way ahead of the minivan anyway. He was already contemplating the snow skiing at Heavenly Valley and more importantly, the ski bunny encounters at the Broken Leg Lodge located at the bottom of the expert run. Rocky had summarily decided it was time to cut another weak woman out of the herd. He always believed in practicing good wildlife management. As a confirmed bachelor, he was a big proponent of the "tag and release program!" Tag 'em then release back into the wild. It would be another unfulfilling "sexual hit and run" this weekend for Rocky Stone on the picturesque shores of South Lake Tahoe, probably another new low for him. Three hours later, all of the

VA-204 officers had checked into their rooms at Harrah's Hotel and Casino. The fun and relaxation was about to begin.

To properly kick off the *River Rattler* Admin and to siphon off the correct amount of steam Duke had prearranged to meet at 1615 on that Friday afternoon with Juice, Teen Angel, Rocky and Cookie. They would all share a beer or two and partake in some of the gambling action at Harrah's Casino located on the bottom floor of the huge hotel complex. The five had agreed to rendezvous in the spacious hotel lobby then walk down to the casino together where they would play Craps or Blackjack at the cheapest "minimum bet" tables they could find. The evening's grand plan would feature a few hours of gambling fun followed up by a prime rib dinner at the Cactus Creek Southwestern Steakhouse. This hidden jewel of a restaurant was neatly tucked away on a remote corner of North Virginia Street, just off the main strip in South Lake Tahoe. Of course the real highlight of the evening, trolling for ski bunnies, would take place around 2100 at the Broken Leg Lodge over in the ski resort at Heavenly Valley.

At 1600 all five of the aviators had arrived in the lobby decked out in their green flight jackets, early as usual. The remainder of the squadron officers, Leslie Lance included, had made alternative initial plans but would meet up later that night at the Cactus Creek to eat red meat and reinforce their bonds with one another. After exchanging greetings Duke and his party of five began to take the leisurely stroll down to the casino floor. The pathway from the lobby to the casino area was intentionally created so that all guests had to walk past Harrah's mini shopping mall in order to get to the gaming area. Harrah's had actually hired a Behavioral Psychologist to make these types of psychological suggestions during the architectural planning phase in the initial construction of the hotel. Apparently the high-priced PhD from UCSD had earned his "mind-over-matter" consulting fee many times over because business was booming from day one in Harrah's world famous mini-mall. On the walk Duke and his ducklings happened to meander past a shop named the "Hanoi Hilton" Luxury Spa. It was a nail salon owned and operated solely by women who had immigrated to America from Saigon shortly after the Viet Nam War had concluded. The name of the establishment was simultaneously offensive and most curious for Naval Aviators familiar with the activities that had transpired at the real Hanoi Hilton prisoner-of-war camp. Apparently curiosity was the order of the day because all five pilots stopped in front of the spa's huge viewing window to peer into the Hanoi Hilton to alleviate their inquisitiveness. The sizeable, glass transom resembled the screening area of traditional whorehouses in Thailand where potential clients would congregate behind an extra-large casement and choose from a multitude of prostitutes seated on carpeted rows of stadium-style seats. The hookers in Thailand actually wore numbers, like thoroughbred racehorses, on the back and front of their skimpy clothing to make the selection process easier on the patrons who didn't speak Thai. You simply presented the house Madame with a 5 x 7 card that had your selected number or numbers written down on it then proceed to the cashier for payment in Baht. In five minutes your choice would be waiting for you in one of the tiny rooms at the rear of the establishment. In bewildered silence, the five men glared inside the spa from behind the relative security of the windowpane.

Just then a Hispanic woman brushed past Juice Mayhew who was standing fat, dumb and happy, closest to the entrance door of the spa with his mouth gaping wide open. The slender Latina quickly slid into the Hanoi Hilton for some sort of manicure or pedicure treatment. This was most likely part of her weekly ritual based on the way she was superbly adorned in designer fashion togs and expensive gold jewelry. Juice couldn't help but notice that she walked with her feet pointed outward from a straight-line path at about a 45-degree angle like Charley Chaplin's "little tramp" character. She was basically walking on the outside portion of her feet so that her sandals wore out in that area first. The inside half of her soles showed almost no sign wear and tear. Juice also observed that the Latin woman wore two hideous-looking rings on the middle toes of both feet. Toe rings were apparently the latest fashion trend sweeping through California. Without hesitation, the woman walked straight back to the "pedicure pool" area, kicked off her sandals and plopped into a comfortable-looking, massage chair. In the Hanoi Hilton Luxury Spa that evening there were about fifteen women all seated in a row, dressed to kill. Their black chairs appeared to be vibrating at full force and each woman had at least one foot dipped into a pool of bubbling blue water that smelled of Lilacs. Most of the ladies' also had one foot propped up on a wooden pedestal being vigorously rubbed and buffed by a diminutive Viet Namese pedicurist. The feet and calves being massaged were buttered up with some sort of industrial-strength foot cream. The little Viet Namese girls only knew about eleven words in English. 'You pay now, yes, no, is good' was about the extent of their English vocabulary, or so they would have their clients believe. Feigning English ignorance gave the pedicurists the shield behind which they could gossip and giggle about their clients in front of their faces with impunity as they manipulated feet, ankles and calves.

Duke noticed that after the buttered up leg was finished being rubbed and burnished with the foot lotion, cherry red nail polish was being applied to all the toes. To apply the crimson polish the women had their appendages divided by petite and puffy rubber wedges that had been stuck in between the digits to lift and separate each little piggy for better access by the spa pedicure technician. Strategically placed next to each white-coated pedicurist was a tray that held an array of odd-looking devices. It resembled the dental tray that contained all the various tools used by an oral surgeon during a root canal procedure. Most of the pedicure gadgets were made of metal but some of the utensils seemed to be made of ceramic and stone. Other paraphernalia visible on the tray were various sizes of buffing strips and even an apparatus that resembled a spray-paint gun. The gun was obviously used for shooting high-pressure polish onto ladies' nails for maximum shine. The Vietnamese spa technicians were cutting, trimming and filing fingernails and toenails with steel clippers and buffers. They were also scrubbing and scraping dead skin from calloused heels with pumice stones. Apparently the nails were being ground down to a manageable length and the feet were being softened to a supple texture. It looked like a torture session to Duke O' Grady, to say the least. He shivered as he turned and walked away. Teen Angel simply smiled as he followed close behind Duke. Brad had seen this all before in Hollywood, many times over. He had even had a manicure a time or two, but didn't let his squadron mates know this fact. Ridicule was a strong motivator.

Once on the colorful floor of Harrah's casino, Cookie and Rocky hastily sought out a craps table, to engage in their favorite gambling activity, playing the back line. The duo couldn't seem to get the money out of their wallets quick enough as they snuggled up to the south end of a long green table, surrounded by finely dressed men and women. In a matter of seconds they were both happily betting on "seven come eleven" and putting cash down to cover "triple odds" back line numbers. One raven-haired woman blew her warm, sultry breath all over the red dice cubes each time she shook them in her left hand. The pit boss was obviously getting pissed at this breach of etiquette, but allowed the woman to continue blowing on the dice because each time she bent over to toss them a low-cut dress revealed most of her 38D breasts. As luck would have it, the well-endowed babe tossed eighteen straight numbers and the table patrons were screaming with wild anticipation at each roll of the dice. Playing "triple odds" numbers on the back line allowed Rocky and Cookie to quickly win about five hundred bucks each. Their faces glowed at the good fortune. Cookie audaciously ordered a nearly naked cocktail waitress to fetch them double shots of tequila and long, fat cigars to celebrate.

Directly across the aisle from Rocky and Cookie's craps table, Duke had found a five-dollar roulette wheel to his liking. He was soon placing bets on the red square and the number 32. Next to Duke's roulette wheel, Juice and Teen

Angel sat down to play Blackjack at a ten-dollar minimum bet table. Harrah's casino was a lively place with a raucous atmosphere almost twenty-four hours a day. It featured a stunning assortment of flashing lights, bells, sirens and whistles that boldly announced the gambling winners, mostly at the "one-armed-bandit" slots. The gigantic room was brilliantly lit up to ensure that gamblers didn't get tired of the late night action before they had exhausted all of their financial resources. Harrah's casino floor contained over 500 slot machines and gaming tables and it was the largest in Lake Tahoe. At the Blackjack table Teen Angel and Juice sat in finely appointed leather chairs and watched a game of 21 already in progress as it unfolded. One lone player was challenging the dealer and he looked exhausted. The man was an athletic-looking African-American. He wore a gaudy, black Oakland Raiders T-shirt that had 'Just Win Baby' printed on the front in oversized silver letters. The muscles in the man's arms bulged as he dropped down what appeared to be his last three, one hundred dollar bills into the betting circle in front of his seat position. Sweat beads welled up inside the fine hairs that formed his thick eyebrows as he sipped the residue of a vodka martini.

"Deal," instructed the man as a skinny cocktail waitress, dressed like a French maid, conveniently retrieved his empty martini glass from the felt table. The trio of C-notes he had tossed down were clean, fresh pieces of currency, without any wrinkles. After making eye contact with a tuxedoed pit boss standing to his left and receiving a nod of approval, the aloof dealer immediately delivered four cards into position. The dealer's hand showed a king of spades up. The Raider's fan had a two of hearts on top and a ten of diamonds hidden underneath. The black man scraped the smooth, green felt of the tabletop with his right index finger, indicating he wanted another card from the seven-deck shoe. He kicked out from his chair and stood, as if he realized what was transpiring with the rest of his money. Sure enough, the dealer flopped down a jack of clubs next to the man's cards to bust his hand.

"Shit," exclaimed the player even though he had probably suspected what was coming out of the Blackjack shoe. The man watched helplessly as the dealer rudely pushed the three C-notes down into a slot at the right side of the table. The losing gambler and Raiders fan walked away in silence. Juice and Teen Angel now had the table to themselves. A meager amount of money was pulled from their wallets to start their own gambling action. More cheers were heard emanating from Rocky and Cookie's craps table, only this time it was another woman tossing the dice.

After twenty minutes of playing Blackjack and basically breaking even, a striking young woman with lengthy blonde hair approached Teen Angel from behind and tapped him softly on the left shoulder. The lady was a tall, long-legged beauty in a flowing lavender gown with a demure smile across her flawless face. She appeared to desire anonymity because perched on her nose was a pair of incognito, librarian-style glasses. Even so, this hot babe moved as if she had been taught to walk in an elegant and graceful manner from the day she had taken her first footsteps. After pushing on his current hand with the dealer, Brad turned and instantly recognized that it was Elle MacPherson, the Australian supermodel standing behind him. The spectacles didn't work. Ackerman's heart skipped a beat as he literally breathed in her stunning good looks and penetrating brown eyes. Juice Mayhew's jaw dropped yet again as the six foot tall model nicknamed "The Body" hugged Brad warmly. With her delicate red lips, she kissed Teen Angel lightly on the cheek then sat down in between the two men at the Blackjack table. Elle's lipstick left a faint imprint on Brad's right cheek. She didn't wipe it off. Suffice it to say that gambling at the Blackjack table was suspended temporarily as Elle and Brad held hands and conversed like old lovers. Even the pit boss and dealer were stunned at their overly cordial interaction. They knew who she was. But who was this man wearing a green flight jacket covered in silly-looking patches?

Brad Ackerman and Elle MacPherson had initially met at Universal Studios' back lot on the set of the 1991 movie *Hook*. This was shortly after a bitter divorce from her first husband had been finalized in court, preceded of course by ten months of media frenzy on the tabloid story. A month after their initial encounter, Teen Angel took Elle flying in one of the Hollywood stunt aircraft, a Stearman biplane. She didn't even puke during the acrobatics, so Brad let her fly the airplane for a while. A week later they shared a couple of drinks and several Maryland Blue Crab Cakes at the *Hook* "wrap party" in Stephen Spielberg's Beverly Hills home. So the two were fairly well acquainted but in a strictly platonic sense. It didn't take long for three autograph hounds in the casino to recognize the supermodel and start nipping at her heels for a signature. Brad politely but firmly sent them all away, saving Elle from having to get rude to protect her privacy. The full-length dress that Elle wore was a simply stunning, lavender creation from the *Vera Wang* collection. It took Jack Mayhew's breath away just to see how elegantly her body moved underneath the silky smooth fabric. Brad could sense Jack's anticipation so he proceeded with the formal introduction.

"Jack Mayhew, I would like to introduce you to my friend Elle MacPherson. Elle, this is my squadron mate Jack Mayhew," said Brad. Jack's eyes were as big as silver dollars as he extended his right hand to shake. He couldn't speak at first. In his defense, looking into Elle's eyes is extraordinarily unfair and exceedingly dangerous. Besides, it is hard to talk when your breath has been stolen away from your lungs.

"Hello mate," said Elle in her classic Aussie accent that caused all mortal men's hearts to flutter. The two shook hands robustly.

"Great to make your acquaintance ma'am," was all that Juice could conjure up at that point. He was still a little breathless. The Blackjack dealer cleared his throat to see if anybody wanted to gamble anymore. Elle leaned in Brad's direction and whispered something into his left ear. Teen Angel nodded in an affirmative fashion then stood up from his chair.

Juice, tell Duke I will see y'all at the steakhouse," advised Brad. With that said, Elle and Teen Angel sauntered away from the table. As they moved away Brad couldn't help but gloat just a bit for his squadron mate. It was a good experience to feel Jack Mayhew's envy hit him in the back like a dart. As they continued to walk, Teen Angel allowed Elle to proceed ahead of him about five feet. Instinctively sensing she had left Brad behind, Elle turned to see what was stalling his progress.

"I just enjoy watching you move," admitted Teen Angel. Miss MacPherson blushed then grabbed Brad by the hand to nudge him along next to her side. They shared three cups of coffee and a piece of strawberry cheesecake in Harrah's diner just around the corner from the Hanoi Hilton. They made up for lost time with two hours of gratifying conversation.

CHAPTER 26

▼

FAT, DUMB AND HAPPY

South Lake Tahoe and Heavenly Valley had never seen anything quite like it before. It happened at 0900 on Saturday morning the 15th day of February 1992, the day after Valentine's Day. Twenty-five officers from the *River Rattlers* of VA-204 simultaneously came barreling down the slippery slopes of the mountain ski resort all decked out in their green, winter flight suits. The winter weight and waterproof Nomex material combined to make the cold-weather flight suit, an exquisite piece of ski apparel. Since most of this idea was Commander Duke O'Grady's inspiration, he had pre-positioned a photographer in the middle of the intermediate-level ski run. The local photographer had been hired by Duke for two hundred and fifty bucks to snap several commemorative photos of the *River Rattlers* as the squadron mates approached him then swooshed on by. Duke planned to use one of the better snapshots as the cover photo on his next party invitation. He would host this pre-cruise party in New Orleans, after CAG-2 carrier qualifications were completed, one week prior to the USS *Enterprise* deployment.

Riding up the ski lift to begin the 0900 photo run, Rocky was seated next to Randy Bracken. Brain Child Bracken was somewhat nervous because, unlike his socialite wife Dana Rothschild, he wasn't all that talented with a pair of 210 cm snow skis strapped to his feet. In fact Brain Child was downright clumsy on packed powder. He still had a few residual knee pains from vacations he had taken with Dana to the Swiss Alps as souvenirs of his snow skiing ineptness. Bracken reached down with one of the ski poles to scratch his right foot through the thick *Nordica* boot. The *Tyrolia* bindings on that snow boot were set too tight and made his instep itch feverishly. At 0822, Rocky and Brain Child were the last two *River Rattler* officers to go up the mountain to prepare for the photo run. As the lift ascended into the crisp morning air, Rocky's demeanor was tranquil, completely at ease. His eyes beheld the majestic, rugged beauty of the Sierra Nevada Mountains and its exquisite woodlands in all of their full glory. The jagged peaks cut the skyline with meticulous precision. The thick blanket of snow covering the ground was extraordinarily white and its condition pristine. Even the snow making machines looked charming running up the side of the hill just outside of the tree lines that weaved a wooden mantle around each ski run. Down below the sound of skiers swooshing past underneath their lift chair could be heard as they raced down the slopes, edging their skis into the packed powder. The bright color of their ski clothes created a vivid contrast with the spotless, white backdrop. Up above the sky was a brilliant blue. It was the kind of blinding blue that you can only witness while climbing toward the top of a grand mountain peak. At that moment, Rocky was reminded of the John Denver tune *Annie's Song*. The breathtaking scenery of icy Lake Tahoe below and the surrounding mountains above truly "filled up his senses" as he allowed the splendor and grandeur to seep into his thirsty eyes.

Suddenly Rocky spotted the strawberry blonde chick he had made a futile pass at the night before in the Broken Leg Lodge. She was riding the ski lift down the mountain for some reason. Rocky's hot breath became even more visible as it exited his mouth and entered the frigid Lake Tahoe environment. The woman, sipping on a cup of hot cider, rode with one leg dangling in the light wind and one stretched out across the metal bench seat. Maybe she had gotten injured getting off the ski lift, or maybe she had just chickened out once she reached the top of the mountain. Rocky's attempts, the previous night, to snag the blonde for some harmless sex had been unsuccessful and it annoyed him immensely because he had taken a healthy dose of grief from his buddies over the amorous failure. 'She must be a lesbian,' he explained last evening to unsympathetic squadron mates in the lodge who had witnessed his fruitless efforts with the hot, fair-haired beauty. Luckily Brain Child Bracken was way too anxious about the impending ski run to notice Rocky's blonde babe, or to rekindle any scorn. He was also scratching furiously at his foot with the tip of a ski pole.

As Rocky watched the woman slide on by, unaccompanied in her ski lift chair, he closed his eyes to feel the chilly breeze as it gently swept across his unshaved face. With both eyes shut, Lieutenant Commander Jim Stone recalled the previous evening as if trying to analyze what went wrong with his exploits. He remembered spotting her right away upon entering the lodge after dinner. She was seated alone on a high-perched stool at the bar. The attractive, reddish hue of her soft curls immediately spoke volumes to Jim Stone. Rocky's belly was somewhat distended from the sixteen ounces of rare prime rib he had devoured at the Cactus Creek minutes before. He sucked his gut in and puffed his chest out as he made eye contact with her light-colored, strawberry locks. Rocky instantly judged that she was a synthetic blonde, probably at a cost of three hundred semolians every six to eight weeks. At first glance the green-eyed wench had a slight smile on her pursed lips as she stirred the White Lady cocktail resting in front of her on the bar. Using a straw, she toyed with the green olive that lay at the bottom of the crystal glass. Unknown to her, the friendly bartender had made the alcohol concoction with a double dose of *Tanqueray* Gin because he could tell she needed the extra kick. Rocky's eyes were riveted to this woman from the start. She turned on her bar stool to face the gathering crowd inside the Broken Leg Ski Lodge.

Underneath a black, cotton skirt that fit too loosely on her slender frame, the woman maneuvered firm thigh muscles to cross her right leg over the left in a lady-like fashion. Her pantyhose bristled in reaction to the leg movements as static electricity jumped between the nylon particles of the translucent material. The blissful expression on her petite face quickly changed as three boisterous men entered the ski lodge bar room and sat down near her to order their first round of drinks. The three men were Rocky, Juice and Cookie. All of them were suspects in her mind. From that point on the woman's shoulders slumped slightly forward and her facial features drooped considerably. She had a circumspect look on her pretty face. It was a slightly sullen, sad appearance, as if she had been severely mistreated by domineering men once too often in thirty-four years of life. She desperately wanted to believe that men were basically good human beings, but past experience blocked her from reaching that ultimate conclusion. Past reality caused this woman to be extremely cautious when dealing with the male of the species. And it showed conspicuously in the body language she displayed around men. The vulnerable woman did not want to put herself in the uncomfortable position of being emotionally hurt and taken advantage of yet again by another overbearing male. Rocky's advances were doomed from the get go. Although he didn't realize it at the time, he understood that now.

The ski lift suddenly stopped with a tremendous jolt causing all the chairs to swing and sway underneath the steel cable. Rocky opened his eyes and saw that he and Brain Child Bracken were suspended in their lift chair about thirty yards from the top of the mountain. A youngster was apparently having trouble exiting his bench seat so the lift master had halted the movement to allow the kid some extra time to get off the ski lift and move out of the way. The forward motion resumed after a brief thirty-second delay. The child was no worse for the ordeal and was soon rushing down the slopes at breakneck speed. Once they hopped off the ski lift, Rocky and Brain Child joined their squadron mates who had congregated next to an ancient-looking tree to prepare for the photo run. The massive pine was over a hundred feet tall colored in a dark, forest shade of green. Juice poked mischievously at Bracken's boots with his ski pole. He knew how Randy felt about snow skiing. Randy shirked his face and tugged at the lift ticket attached to the zipper on his winter-weight flight suit.

The local photographer was standing beside a five-foot high tripod, directly in the middle of the intermediate-level ski run waiting for the *River Rattlers* to make their triumphant appearance on the hill. He and his camera were situated in a shallow crater behind a bumpy mogul that offered some measure of protection. Even so, skiers whooshed past, narrowly averting physical contact in some instances with him and his tripod. His clothing was blemished by snow that had been sprayed on him by passing skiers who used the edges of their skis to spew the powdery substance while whisking past. Some of the skiers probably had showered the guy on purpose as an insult for his aggravating presence in the middle of the ski run. But this was what he had been hired to do, despite the hazardous and somewhat humiliating predicament it placed him in on the intermediate slope. Besides, his rent was overdue by eleven days, so he could certainly use the 250 smackers Duke had given him up front for the job. The return was worth the risk. The photo guy wore a navy blue wool cap on his head and a thick, goose-down parka to stay as warm as possible during the photography session. He cupped his hands together and blew into them for added warmth. Why couldn't I get hired to snap pictures of Elle MacPherson in her micro-bikini over at Squaw Valley, he wondered? She's probably freezing her ass off wearing only a thong and a pair of *Ugg* boots right now, he chuckled to himself. Undoubtedly, her 1993 calendar will feature a few hard nipple shots taken today at Squaw Valley. Little did he know that Elle's calendar shoot wasn't set to begin until 1600 that afternoon. The mountain sunlight had to be at a certain angle to achieve the look that the set designer and director were attempting to capture on Miss MacPherson for the calendar's January picture.

Bolted down on top of the tripod was the photo guy's $1900 35mm *Minolta*, complete with a lengthy, telephoto lens attached. He had saved his pennies for over a year to purchase this superb piece of photographic equipment last May. That morning the single-lens reflex camera was loaded with Kodak-Color 1000-speed film to capture the moving subjects as they approached. 1000-speed film is extremely sensitive to light exposure, and thus fast enough to stop any action for a still shot with splendid clarity and color quality. The frigid camera-man rubbed the crystal dial on his watch to clear the fog and check the time. Pre-cisely at 0900 he spotted a line of Nomex green sliding on the snow towards his position. Twenty-five figures had gathered together in a line-abreast formation and were advancing at approximately 10 miles per hour down the snow-covered hill. They looked like the Rockefeller Square Christmas tree tumbling lethargi-cally down an embankment. Duke had wanted a slow pace to ensure the picture captured all of his officers descending the mountain slope at Heavenly. Using a cheap pair of binoculars the photographer noticed something peculiar in the middle of the line of skiers approaching his camera. As the scene came into sharper focus, he recognized that it was an orange, Ski Patrol rescue sled being guided by two of the men in green, one in front and one in back. The two skiers guiding the sled purposely used a snowplow technique with the tips of their skis to keep their pace under control. The rescue sled appeared to be occupied by a female but the cameraman couldn't be certain because the distance was still too great. Dropping the binoculars to his chest, he started snapping preliminary shots using the maximum power on his telephoto lens. The green procession continued toward him at a leisurely tempo. Owing to the sheer novelty of this event, other skiers on the mountain moved out of the way to allow the *River Rattler* officers free passage down the slick incline. Most of the skiers were uncertain as to what it was that they were witnessing.

Last night over their cup of coffee at Harrah's diner, Brad talked Elle MacPherson into skiing with his squadron mates the next day for a few hours, before her modeling gig commenced over at Squaw Valley. She had likewise gra-ciously agreed to appear in Duke's party invitation photo. Then a thought just sort of materialized in Ackerman's head as they conversed over their coffee and gourmet dessert. Wiping away graham-cracker crust crumbs from his mouth Teen Angel explained his innovative idea to Elle. The supermodel would be riding down the mountain in a Ski Patrol sled, as if she had been saved by squad-ron pilots from some sort of peril on the treacherous slopes of Heavenly Valley. She would have her leg trussed up in a makeshift brace for comic and dramatic effect. Elle thought the idea was terrific and was only too happy to accommodate

her Hollywood stunt pilot friend's request. In order to secure her modeling services, all Brad had to do was pay for the coffee and cheesecake at Harrah's diner.
Small price to pay, he thought. The deal was sealed.

As the squadron officers neared his position the photographer suddenly recognized Miss MacPherson to be the woman riding in the rescue sled. Peering
through the camera's viewfinder the photo guy bit his tongue, breaking the skin
slightly and almost causing blood to flow. A small blood-blister formed at the site
of his teeth marks. The photographer's heart skipped two beats because Elle
looked simply divine in her designer ski apparel and because he had never captured such a famous model on film before. Being expert skiers, Shroud Morley
and Comatose Gross were acting as the Ski Patrol stand-ins, guiding Elle slowly
and safely down in the rescue sled. The line of green stopped about eight feet
from the tripod with several interested onlookers now gathered around the
squadron officers, and Elle MacPherson in the rescue sled. The cameraman
inserted a fresh roll of film into the *Minolta* and continued snapping photos.

Firmly planting their ski poles deep into the packed powder, directly in front
and behind the Ski Patrol sled, Shroud Morley and Comatose Gross grabbed
hold of Miss MacPherson's arms. She delicately but awkwardly rose to her feet
and exited the rescue sled, pretending to limp on an injured right ankle. After
first stepping out of his skis, Teen Angel walked up to Elle and handed her a pair
of crutches. Brad had spoken with the Heavenly Valley manager earlier that
morning, pre-arranging for the crutches to be waiting near the tripod. The pristine venue and novel conception made for a great set of pictures with all the
VA-204 officers gathered around Elle, standing on crutches near the rescue sled.
The local photographer got his wish come true that day thanks to Teen Angel,
Duke and the *River Rattlers* of Attack Squadron 204. Elle amiably signed a
"model release form" twenty minutes later for the photo guy. He would be able
to make a few extra bucks with some of the shots and his rent would never be late
again. Suddenly an Intruder pilot from the VA-145 *Swordsmen* swooshed up to
see what all the commotion was about. He nearly slipped and fell into the crowd
of VA-204 onlookers.

"Say isn't that Christie Brinkley," he exclaimed while tapping Cookie Cline
on his shoulder. Cookie turned around and recognized the A-6 pilot to be Bob
Gallagher, call sign "Clueless." Gallagher and Cline had flown several formation
hops together back in Beeville, Texas during the advanced jet training phase of
flight school.

"You know your call sign should be changed to "Scarecrow" because just like
the straw man in *The Wizard of Oz* you apparently have no brain! That's Rachel

Hunter you knucklehead," said Cookie with a grin. More evidence to corroborate Cookie's diagnosis of Lieutenant Gallagher would be provided eleven days later during the Weapons Det.

A running barb between Corsair and Intruder pilots holds that of all the ordnance loaded onto the parent stations or ejector racks of an A-6, *most* of the bombs successfully depart the aircraft and collide with the earth. Of those bombs that impact the ground, *most* of them hit in the general vicinity of the intended target that the "double-ugly jet was gunning for. This affable antagonism between the light attack and medium attack communities in Naval Aviation was always good for a laugh or two in any Air Wing setting. The third and final week of the CAG-2 Weapons Detachment fueled this congenial, competitive rivalry even more. Week three was progressing along without a hitch until Thursday evening, the night before the final Air Wing Graduation Strike of the Weapons Detachment. That evening on the last sortie of the day, two A-6 Intruders from the VA-145 Swordsmen were pitching a load of inert MK-82 bombs at the Nevada desert from an altitude of about 8,000 feet AGL. The section of Intruders was practicing their over-the-shoulder bombing technique, and for some reason both cockpit weapons system computers weren't being all that helpful. To the amazement of the two Bombardier Navigators (BN's) along for the ride on this ordnance delivery hop, most of the five hundred pound practice bombs landed close to the bull's eye on the target designated as Bravo-20. This aerial bombing range was located in the middle of the R-4813 restricted area on a dried out lakebed. The target was notoriously difficult to spot in the dark with the naked, middle-aged eye. Thursday evening of week three was extremely dark, which didn't help with target recognition. There wasn't a *Commander's Moon* to be found anywhere in Nevada. That night on his eighth attack run the pilot of NH-513, Lieutenant Robert "Clueless" Gallagher, couldn't punch off his last MK-82. He even made two additional 45-degree dive-bombing runs but they were to no avail as well. Lieutenant Gallagher had "hung ordnance" clinging to his medium-attack jet, the second such embarrassing event of the weapons detachment.

"Gee swell," muttered Lieutenant Gallagher to himself inside of his sweaty oxygen mask. Gallagher's eyes were focused at the MK-82 bomb hanging on the triple ejector rack under his left wing. The BN seated on the right side of the Intruder's gloomy cockpit didn't hear or sense his pilot's level of frustration. Pulling his head up and out of the weapons sighting device, the BN tugged at the crotch of his damp flight suit to rearrange his nut sack. He also lifted his butt cheeks slightly, to reposition the cushy "donut ring" contraption he was sitting on. The hard ejection seat pan of the A-6 Intruder had always been abnormally uncomfortable for this NFO, Lieutenant Commander. In fact, he dreaded sitting in the A-6 cockpit for more than an hour at a time, and had so ever since completing BN School at Whidbey Island Naval Air Station nine years ago. It was a gigantic pain-in-the-ass for this BN. He was also afflicted with a scorching case of hemorrhoids since the age of twenty-two, another pain-in-the-ass predicament. Needless to say, this BN hated pulling G's in an A-6. He stuffed a gum wrapper inside the flap pocket on the left shoulder of his flight suit then popped a fresh piece of spearmint-flavored *Trident* into his dehydrated mouth. The Naval Flight Officer chewed vigorously, with lips wide open, like a conceited teenage girl in a Manhattan Prep School. The BN then raised his left butt cheek and silently farted in Gallagher's direction for good measure. But Clueless Gallagher couldn't smell his BN's foul addition to the cockpit environment because his oxygen mask was cinched up fairly tight to his face. Woody on the other hand, with his mask dangling down in front of his SV-2 vest immediately got a whiff of the putrid odor that was engulfing the Intruder's shadowy confines. A devious smile of appreciation spread so hastily across his face that he bit the inside of his cheek while gnawing on the gum.

After rendezvousing at 10,000 feet overhead Bravo-20 with the other Intruder in the hop, Clueless informed his wingman that he had a hung bomb and that he would proceed back to NAS Fallon individually. The wingman acknowledged this on the squadron frequency, flashed his wing lights a few times then smartly broke away from Clueless and his jet by pulling a four-G break turn. The wingman performed an aileron roll as he departed and rapidly accelerated to 425 knots while descending to 2500 feet AGL. Gallagher's hazel eyes followed his wingman's position and formation lights until he was sure his own aircraft was in the clear by several thousand feet. In the subdued red light of the Intruder's cockpit, Clueless verbally checked his flight off target with the Bravo-20 controllers. Three minutes later, he licked his lips several times to moisten them inside the rubbery oxygen mask. Clueless unconsciously felt for his water bottle, but there was no time to hydrate his head now. Gallagher's left hand retarded the Intruder's two throttles back to 70 percent power to slowly begin decelerating his jet. The Pratt and Whitney J-52 engines reacted immediately to the power reduction, the high-pitch whine of their powerful turbines lost a few decibels. Lieutenant Gallagher then shifted focus and studied the CG-18 World Aeronautical Chart on his kneeboard to confirm their bearings in the Restricted Area. He flipped the clear visor shield on his helmet to the up position, readjusted his oxygen mask then proceeded to set up for a long, lazy straight-in approach to runway 25 at NAS Fallon.

"Woody would you dial in the Fallon TACAN freak for me and take us out of the 'air-to-air' mode," Gallagher asked his BN, Lieutenant Commander Tom "Woody" Carlson. Clueless was now busily rearranging his kneeboard that contained the CG-18 aerial navigation chart, a personalized "How to Fly" book, NAS Fallon bingo figures, a yellow notepad and a Volume Five approach plate. Woody Carlson adjusted his glasses then rotated the numbers on the TACAN receiver box from channel 29 until it read 88 in the little viewing window. The NFO likewise switched the navigational instrument from the 'air-to-air' position over to the 'transmit and receive' mode. The fat, TACAN indicator needle unlocked itself for a moment and rotated around the HSI instrument for a couple of turns. Abruptly the head of the thick #2 needle locked and pointed directly toward the Fallon/Hazen VORTAC. The needle briefly quivered on the instrument gauge in a high frequency vibration then was motionless.

"210 degrees right off the nose Rob," said Carlson. Woody knew that Gallagher hated to be called Clueless. In fact, Gallagher loathed hearing the name Clueless and had ever since being given the unflattering call sign in flight school at VT-25 in Beeville, Texas. When they were alone Woody respected Gallagher's wishes. But when Clueless was out of ear range, Woody would often make jokes about Gallagher while drinking at the bar with his fellow NFO's. Woody would regale them with the story of how Ensign Gallagher had earned his call sign "Clueless" at VT-25. It seems that during a 'hot seat' event on an FCLP training hop, young Ensign Gallagher had forgotten an extremely important rule regarding the Angle-of-Attack probe on the A-4 Sky Hawk. The rule was 'DO NOT TOUCH' if the jet's turbine engine was running and the probe was still hot. After grabbing the 300-degree AOA probe during a short preflight inspection of the A-4, several layers of his skin were burned off. The epidermis and dermis layers of skin on his left palm actually peeled right off his ungloved hand. Very little of his blood was spilled onto the tarmac that day because the extreme heat of the Angle-of-Attack probe actually cauterized the opening wound in his palm. To teach him a valuable lesson, Gallagher received a 'DOWN' from his LSO for the foolish mistake. He was also delayed in receiving his Navy wings of gold because Clueless was medically unfit to fly for eight weeks after the incident. He had never even looked at an AOA probe for more than a few seconds ever since that fateful day in Beeville, Texas. Lieutenant Gallagher was also one of the only Tactical Naval Aviators who actually wore his green Nomex flight gloves religiously. He wore them because he was slightly self-conscious of the scared skin tissue and because residual pain in his left palm would nip at him occasionally as a cruel reminder of his blunder.

Clueless expertly flew the A-6 down to 1500 feet above the surface of the desert as he precisely lined up the all-weather, medium attack aircraft with the runway off in the distance. The Runway End Identifier Lights (REIL) lights were approximately 12 miles away and the center-mounted, in-flight refueling probe on the A-6 was pointing straight at them. Looking down to his right in the cockpit, Gallagher dialed 340.2 into his primary radio receiver. This was the main NAS Fallon control tower frequency. As the Intruder continued, Clueless apparently didn't perceive that his heading was 210 and that the duty runway at NAS Fallon was 25, according to ATIS information being broadcast over the secondary radio. He also didn't recognize that Woody Carlson had somehow dialed in the wrong TACAN freak. Woody had put 88 into the TACAN receiver instead of 82. Channel 88 was the TACAN frequency for Fallon Municipal Airport not Naval Air Station Fallon. And so it was that Clueless was now gradually decelerating from 320 knots, flying toward runway 21, a 5700-foot stretch of concrete at Fallon Muni. Flying fat, dumb and happy Lieutenant Gallagher maneuvered his jet for the ten-mile "hung ordnance" straight-in approach to what he thought was runway 25 at NAS Fallon. But that airport was five miles further southeast than Clueless realized. Nevertheless, his eyes were fixated on runway 21 at Fallon Municipal. Woody Carlson had lost situational awareness as well.

"Navy Tower, NH-513 is just inside of ten miles on a "hung ordnance" straight in for runway 25," reported Clueless as he bumped his boards out into the wind stream with a quick tug on the throttle's speed brake switch. Instantly, both aircrew men sensed the Intruder's change of configuration and quickened rate of deceleration. In his peripheral vision, Gallagher could see the speed brakes as they opened up on his wingtips. The Intruder's anti-collision light flashed and reflected red light off the metal speed brakes back into the murky cockpit. Clueless motioned to Woody with his right hand, gently reminding him to strap his oxygen mask back onto his mug. Lieutenant Commander Carlson spit the spearmint gum into his left hand and wadded it up into a piece of yellow notebook paper from his own kneeboard. Carlson inserted the butterfly bayonet fittings of his oxygen mask into the sides of his helmet, cinched the breathing device up snug then locked his inertia reel for the impending full stop landing.

"November Hotel 513 the pattern is empty. Your playmate is at the initial for the break. You're cleared for landing. Check all lights on bright and steady," advised the tower chief at NAS Fallon. Clueless momentarily contorted his face and brow as if somewhat confused by the tower chief's final comment. He eyed the 'Master Light Switch' and his individual selections on the cockpit panel. He reconfirmed that all of his aircraft lights were selected to bright and steady and the Master Switch was ON. Can't that guy in the tower see ten miles thought Gallagher? The Intruder continued straight ahead, steadily descending at 100 feet per minute rate of descent. At five miles from the end of the runway, flying at 150 knots, Gallagher threw his gear handle to the "down" position and lowered the landing flaps to full. Silently, he finished the "Landing Checklist" and with a nod of approval from Woody, Clueless prepared to bring the Intruder in for a safe touchdown. As the angle-of-attack indexer revealed an amber ball, meaning the airplane was flying at the proper airspeed for landing, Woody grabbed onto a handhold above the glare shield on the right side of the A-6 cockpit. The BN was now fully prepared for the landing jolt of the 36,000-pound attack jet.

As Clueless touched down and brought his throttles back to the idle stops, the tiny hairs on the back of his neck immediately began to stand up like lead shavings being drawn to a powerful magnet. When his jet's groundspeed had decelerated back to eighty knots Lieutenant Gallagher spotted a ramp full of Cessna 172's and a lone fuel pump situated on the near side of the General Aviation tarmac. Only then did he comprehend that he had unintentionally landed his A-6 at the wrong airport. Clueless hastily flipped off his exterior lights then jammed the throttles to their MRT stops. He simultaneously and instinctively pushed the speed brake knob on the throttle quadrant to suck in his boards. The Intruder picked up fifty knots of groundspeed in a heartbeat. Clueless pulled the control stick rearward into his lap and the medium-attack jet rotated back into the sky. Lieutenant Gallagher was now hoping against hope that no one had witnessed his major-league blunder. But it was too late, of course. The tower controller at Fallon Municipal was already on the landline to the tower supervisor at NAS Fallon. Intuitively, Gallagher's heart sank and the tickling hairs dropped down on the back of his neck. Butterflies of anxiety immediately attacked the pit of his stomach. He knew the indignation that lay ahead for him at both the squadron and Air Wing level.

"We got your boy over here and he is just now completing a touch and go. You should have him over there in a few minutes," said the chief controller at Fallon Muni. "And he still has that hung bomb with him!" Fifteen minutes later, while filling out their yellow sheets in the Maintenance Control office, gentle humiliation was being heaped onto Clueless by his wingman. CAG Madison had already left word with the VA-145 skipper to have Lieutenant Gallagher and Lieutenant Commander Carlson report to the Air Wing Commander's BOQ room thirty minutes after their flight debrief was complete.

An hour later, decked out in his rugged *Marlboro Man* civilian clothes and *Lucchese* eel-skin boots, Duke O'Grady swaggered down the hallway on the first deck of the NAS Fallon BOQ toward CAG Madison's room. He was wearing his beloved *Wrangler* cowboy shirt, the one that had George Strait's signature stamped on the inside of the collar. The shirt was a brilliant shade of red. It was designed with the 'cowboy cut' in it's tailoring, meaning that it left ample room for a beer belly or spare tire around the waist. John O' Grady had neither condition of course. Duke had bought the shirt at a place called The Boot Barn in Wichita, Kansas during a layover on a cross-country hop to McConnell Air Force Base last summer. He had purchased the shirt because it was extra-comfortable and because his favorite Country-Western song was *Amarillo by Morning*, a George Strait classic. Duke was also wearing his oversized silver belt buckle, the type that rodeo cowboys earn for staying on the Brahma Bull for the full 8 seconds. The freshly shined buckle was oval-shaped and featured the silhouette of a bucking bronco stamped deep into the reflective metal just above his call sign "Duke" imprinted with italicized lettering.

That Thursday evening, Commander O'Grady had also been summoned to meet with Commander Madison. According to the hand-written note that had been slipped under Duke's door by a CAG-2 Yeoman, the meeting with the Air Wing Commander was on a matter of grave importance. O'Grady didn't receive the note until 2155 because he had been playing shuffleboard with a few of his squadron mates at the Officer's Club Bar. Duke had also been nibbling from several plates of fried chicken wings, generously dipped in *Cattleman's* Barbeque Sauce or *Hidden Valley* Ranch Dressing for the past hour and a half. Some of the viscous barbeque sauce had dripped down onto his jeans leaving an unsightly brown stain on the right thigh area of the denims.

As Duke O'Grady arrived at Commander Madison's door, Lieutenant Gallagher and Lieutenant Commander Carlson were standing at attention just outside of CAG's room. The pair was basically braced up against the wall sweaty and stinking, wearing khaki uniforms in preparation for their inevitable, formal dressing down at the hands of the Air Wing Commander. They had been more or less at attention for the past twenty minutes waiting for their turn on the hot seat with "Spine Ripper" Madison.

"Hey guys, how you doing?" asked Duke as he scratched the back of his hairline with an index finger and eased past them in the passageway. O'Grady used his best New York accent attempting to lighten up the sullen moment for both of them. Duke perceived from their contrite body language that the Intruder crew was not making a social call on Spine Ripper Madison. The gossiping, good news of the A-6 landing at the wrong airfield had also spread like a wild fire into the O' Club just minutes after it had occurred. Remember, the Third Law of Thermodynamics: If the heat is on somebody else it can't be on you! Gallagher simply nodded his head modestly to acknowledge Duke's presence. Clueless had seen John O'Grady from time-to-time during the past three weeks and recognized him as the flamboyant VA-204 Commanding Officer. Just as Duke was about to knock, CAG's door flung open and a Senior Chief Petty Officer exited in a rushed, slightly flustered manner. The six foot two inch chief brushed up against Commander O'Grady before making fleeting eye contact with Duke. He offered a desultory admission of guilt for accidentally bumping into the *River Rattler* skipper then ambled on down the corridor at a lively pace. The Senior Chief was headed to the base Communications Center to retrieve an important, 'priority' message that had been sitting inside the CAG-2 mail slot since 1148 MST that morning. Apparently someone on the Senior Chief's Admin staff had neglected to make a mail run that afternoon, and CAG Madison was pretty pissed off. The Senior Chief had been directed to fetch the message, bring it straight back to the Air Wing Commander himself, and to be damn quick about it. As Duke O'Grady watched the Senior Chief walk away, he wrinkled up his lips over to the right side of his face, as if trying to coerce more analytical brainpower into the situation. This was the same man that O'Grady had stumbled across earlier in the Weapons Detachment. Once again Duke experienced a déjà vu sensation surround him at the mere sight of the enlisted man. He had served with this guy somewhere before in his Navy career but still couldn't make the connection. Duke rubbed his forehead then entered into CAG Madison's dimly lit room.

CAG was seated on a swivel chair in front of a metal desk facing the entrance door. He was holding a thin, unlit cigar characteristically fumbling with it between his stubby fingers. Behind him, papers and file folders were stacked neatly on the right and left side of the desk leaving the middle section empty. A cheap lamp provided 40 watts of light to the desktop. In the far corner of the room, inside the 'bargain basement' entertainment hutch, a 20-inch television was showing the introduction footage to the *Jetson's* cartoon. The sound had been muted and George Jetson had just begun walking Astro on the futuristic, doggie treadmill. Duke grinned as the black cat made its grand appearance in the promo and was chased by Astro. The mad dash by the dog caused George Jetson to slip and fall then get stuck on the rotating, runaway treadmill track. At that moment Duke realized that Spine Ripper Madison reminded him a lot of the Mr. Spacely character. Commander Madison was dressed only in a white t-shirt and boxer shorts, sporting bare feet that stretched out across a lavender throw rug. He was obviously ready to turn in for the night, but had a few items that needed to be cleaned up before his head could hit the pillow in peace. This visual of CAG Madison in his underwear provoked Duke to reach around and pull his own skivvies down and out of his butt crack through the thick denim jeans. O'Grady pushed the door closed behind him as he moved deeper into the room to stand adjacent to the vanity sink facing the Air Wing Commander. CAG Madison had a disheartened look about him. The craggy wrinkles on his aging face became more profound as he began to speak in a forlorn fashion with Duke O'Grady. It seems that about two hours ago, CAG Madison had received a telephone call from Vice Admiral Thompson. Tommy Thompson, the Chief of the Naval Reserve, had called Spine Ripper to personally deliver some dreadful news to him and to pass along a solemn request from a grieving widow. Yesterday morning the recently sworn in skipper of VA-203, Commander Ken "Judy" Grant, had crashed in an A-7 during a Post Maintenance Check Flight (PMCF). The accident happened in the vicinity of NAS Cecil Field in Jacksonville, Florida. The Corsair had impacted the ground about five hundred feet from a residential area known as Orange Park. The attack jet had smashed into a grove of Dogwood Trees causing a fuel fire that raged for over an hour. Just prior to the impact, Judy Grant had successfully ejected from the crippled Corsair but tragically he did not survive the accident. The aircraft crash had occurred at 1114 EST and the news hadn't made its way onto all of the 'message boards' around the Navy just yet, for various reasons. The crash had been covered on CNN, but nobody in CAG-2 had any spare time to watch television on the Weapons Detachment, least of all news stories.

Vice Admiral Thompson offered only sketchy reports to CAG Madison on the telephone call then segued to another aspect of the tragedy in their conversation. In speaking with the VA-203 Casualty Assistance Officer, Judy's bereaved widow Sherry had requested to have a memorial service for her husband onboard the USS *Eisenhower* on Sunday afternoon. She likewise expressed her sincere desire to have Duke O'Grady, her husband's college roommate and Navy flight school partner, deliver the eulogy. The Secretary of the Navy, the Honorable H. Lawrence Andrews III, had approved both requests about four hours ago from his office at the Pentagon. Although initially stunned by the news Duke composed his emotions then quickly agreed to Sherry's request. He left CAG's room still in a daze. As Commander O'Grady departed, he could plainly hear CAG Madison ripping the Intruder crew a new ass hole. Duke thought he heard Commander Madison scream something about Lieutenant Gallagher being close to receiving a FNAB Board, and that this was the worst blunder by a professional man since Bill Buckner's error in Game Six of the 1986 World Series. Madison's call sign of "Spine Ripper" was well deserved. Duke O'Grady was heading for Teen Angel's room to share a brief chat before hitting the sack for the night. The two of them now had an early morning briefing for their cross-country flight to NAS Cecil Field. Duke would need Brad Ackerman for moral support that weekend in Florida.

CHAPTER 27

▼

EULOGY FOR A HYBRID PILOT

Commander John O'Grady clenched his teeth while pumping out seventy-five sit-ups and fifty push-ups before hitting the sack precisely at 2300 on Thursday evening. On the TV a re-run episode of *Gilligan's Island* was just finishing up. The lame but annoyingly memorable theme song of the syndicated show pierced through the still night air of Duke's BOQ room as he exercised. After his late night meeting with CAG Madison had concluded, Duke had knocked on Teen Angel's door to inform him of their cross-country flight to NAS Cecil Field. He determined that they would takeoff in section at 0615 the next morning and thus both aviators would miss the Graduation Alpha Strike, the final sortie of the CAG-2 Weapons Detachment. The grand finale mission would have to use VA-204's manned, turning spare aircraft to ensure that the *River Rattlers* successfully launched eight Corsairs in the strike package. Duke had stayed and chatted with Lieutenant Ackerman for the better part of thirty minutes before realizing they both needed to get some rest in preparation for their 0400 wake up call on Friday. At 0350 the next morning, a severely restless John O'Grady had been tossing and turning since transitioning into deep REM sleep around 0145.

Duke was lying flat on his back quietly snoring, with his left foot hanging uncovered over the edge of the bed. The big toe on that foot was partially infected due to an in-grown toenail attacking the inside portion of the appendage. Those push-ups a few hours earlier had conspired to exacerbate the infection. The spike-tipped nail had started to rudely press up against the soft interior flesh of his toe a month after O'Grady had yanked out a jagged hang nail last Christmas eve. Duke hadn't sought to remedy the situation except for soaking the foot in warm salt water and sleeping with it outside of the constraining sheet and comforter of his bed. The cool night air always seemed to relax the pulsing, painful sensation caused by the pointed edge of the sharp nail, as opposed to his foot being wedged tightly under the covers. Sooner or later O'Grady would have to seek medical attention because the inflamed toe had caused him to walk with a barely perceptible limp ever since the end of the Lake Tahoe ski trip eleven day ago. He decided to seek the assistance of a civilian sawbones, instead of going to a Navy flight surgeon, later in the month. Some sort of 'procedure' would most likely be involved.

Just then a black Jumping Spider emerged from under the white top sheet. It crawled menacingly up and over Duke's exposed left foot. Duke's muffled snore and occasional sleep apnea continued unabated. The eight-legged creature cleverly attached some silk to the edge of the cotton flat sheet then rappelled down to the carpet in search of its next meal. A tasty fly, ant or moth would do just fine. The spider burrowed into the thick rug under the television stand to ambush any delicious morsel that unwittingly passed by its lair. Duke gasped for his breath then turned over in the twin bed to continue the nightmare he was suffering through. He unconsciously threw off all the covers and repositioned his entire body so that the infected toe was now perched, hanging down off the other side of the bed. Despite all the commotion, he stayed sound asleep.

For some reason, Duke was dreaming about his experience at SERE School of all things. The repressed, twelve year old memories were flashing across his mind quite vividly at that point in the dream. In a sweat, Duke suddenly remembered where he had seen that 6 foot 2 inch, déjà vu Senior Chief he kept bumping into on the Weapons Det. He was the tanned and buffed role player who took great pleasure in tormenting Duke at Warner Springs, the west coast SERE School complex. During the Survival, Evasion, Resistance and Escape training, students jokingly referred to the guy as Moon Doggie, the Surf Nazi of Coronado. Back in 1980 Duke O'Grady was a junior grade Lieutenant freshly graduated from VA-122, the Corsair Replacement Air Group (RAG) squadron at NAS Lemoore. SERE School represented the last formal training for Duke prior to entering the active Navy fleet with the *Shrikes* of VA-94, who were on deployment in the Indian Ocean onboard USS *Ranger* at the time. SERE School was designed to simulate being shot down behind enemy lines. It taught aviators how to survive in the foreign location, how to avoid getting captured by the enemy, how to resist torture and finally how to escape from a POW camp environment. The training was incredibly valuable for prospective POW'S. It was also quite a humbling experience for arrogant aviators.

Back in 1980, the déjà vu Senior Chief was a 2nd Class Petty Officer serving at NAS North Island in Coronado with FASOTRAGRUPAC. Duke recalled that the guy was a Navy SEAL who had volunteered to play the role of one of the Soviet Union prison guards during the extremely realistic POW camp phase of the SERE training program. The guy was a stud who probably could have been a linebacker for the Oakland Raiders in his spare time. He was likewise a really gifted actor who had a natural Russian accent to boot. Jack Nicholson couldn't have played the part any better. Duke also recollected that the Surf Nazi of Coronado had a particular fondness for making his life a living Hell for the 5 days of the simulated POW camp. O'Grady would never forget him, ever!

In his dream Duke was re-living some of the more heinous events that took place in Warner Springs. First, the Surf Nazi tortured Lieutenant O'Grady by strapping him completely naked onto the 'water board' device. With his head and upper body tilted backward at a thirty-degree angle, cup after cup of water was repeatedly poured down into Duke's forced open mouth. The diabolical Surf Nazi cackled with Communist glee then threatened to kill O'Grady by drowning him right then and there unless he would agree to sign a war criminal confession letter. Duke gagged incessantly but was allowed to puke up the excess fluid just in time to take a breath and replicate the tortuous onslaught once again. Unknown to any of the SERE School students at the time, the torture training was highly scripted and closely monitored. On the water board, the trainee was never in danger of drowning because the liquid could not run up hill into the prisoner's lungs. But the sensation of drowning was amazingly real and extraordinarily efficient in breaking POW inmates without actually injuring them in the process.

Next, the Surf Nazi would beat Duke for several minutes and throw him up against a thin metal restraining wall that bent and made a crackling noise for maximum psychological effect on the POW trainee's mind. The physical assault didn't hurt all that much but the sights and sounds worked effectively to trick your mind into believing your body was being brutally punished. Finally the Surf Nazi shackled Duke naked into the wooden stocks then poured ice cold water over him without warning numerous times during the frigid night. Needless to say, sleep deprivation was also an integral component of the odious plan to break Duke as a POW in the mock, torture-training program. O'Grady woke two minutes before his alarm was set to go off. He was sweating profusely. Duke skipped his morning push-ups and headed straight for the shower stall. It was going to be a long, hard weekend in Jacksonville, Florida.

At 0545 that Friday morning, about eighty CAG-2 aviators were streaming out of the Fallon base auditorium. A definite sense of accomplishment and elation permeated the cool desert air because it was the last day of the Weapons Detachment and because the graduation Alpha Strike was always a grand event to participate in. The final Alpha Strike flight brief had just concluded and the men were now headed for their individual squadrons to suit up and to sign for their aircraft in Maintenance Control. As testament to their relaxed, confident demeanor several of the men stopped to play in the freshly fallen layer of snow that covered the ground. The Air Wing would launch thirty-six airplanes beginning at 0715 for the major assault on the Bravo-17 target. Eighteen jets from various aggressor squadrons and the Strike Warfare Center would defend the target area against the Alpha Strike Group. CAG Madison had selected Commander Russ Tory to lead the final strike. Tory whose tactical call sign was "Rhino" served as Commanding Officer of the VF-1 *Wolfpack*. He was an unusually talented Naval Aviator. As a young Lieutenant, Rhino was the 'Opposing Solo' for two years while a member of the *Blue Angels* Flight Demonstration Team. Most everyone in Carrier Air Wing Two knew that his next tour of duty would be a triumphant return to the *Blues* as their CO. Duke always called Russ Tory "Shorty" because he was only 5 feet 7 inches tall.

Rocky, Cookie and Juice rode to the squadron building together in one of the rented sport utility vehicles. Cookie complained the whole way because he didn't get any flapjacks that morning due to the early flight brief for the Alpha Strike. Juice and Rocky would each lead a division of VA-204 Corsairs in this final strike hop. Rocky Stone's division would be the 'Iron Hand' HARM shooters. Their mission would be to suppress all the surface-to-air missile sites along the intended route of flight, and in the target area. The four Corsairs in Rocky's group would shoot for hard or soft kills against the enemy. Either tactic was fine. Their goal was to make sure the SAM sites didn't light up any CAG-2 airplanes with acquisition radar, or launch any of their missiles at the strike package. Juice's flight would pound the target with four MK-84 bombs apiece. Two members of Juice's division of Corsairs, Comatose Gross and Shroud Morley were to knock out some of the various pieces of military hardware that were spread out all around Bravo 17. Mangled tanks, worn out troop trucks and retired yellow school busses were their personal favorite targets of opportunity. There would be plenty to choose from on Bravo-17 that day because a fresh batch had been delivered the night before. Juice and his wingman, Lieutenant T-Ben Hebert, were to bomb the simulated arms factory that was nestled up next to the mountain range on the target. The industrial facility was heavily fortified with SA-11 Gadfly and SA-14 Gauntlet SAM sites in addition to standard Anti-Aircraft Artillery (AAA) batteries. The entire area would be guarded by aggressor aircraft like F-5 Tigers, F-16 Falcons and F-18 Hornets. The aggressor pilots were eager to engage CAG-2 jets in air combat maneuvering then brag about their conquests at the debrief or the O' Club Bar. If the aggressors could achieve a guns solution on any of the CAG-2 jets their egos would inflate to even greater heights.

Cookie Cline's job in the Alpha Strike was to stay awake, bore holes in the sky and try to overcome the boredom or arcing around at 15,000 feet. He was going to be manning one of the four airborne tanker aircraft in the training hop. Cookie would be pumping out gas to F-14's while flying an A-7 equipped with an aerial refueling package. He would meet four VF-2 Tomcats in 'high holding' overhead the rendezvous point inside the R-4813 Restricted Area. Cookie's jet would have approximately 8,000 pounds of JP-5 to offer up to the Tomcats. In the airborne exchange each "turkey" would receive 300 gallons, approximately 2000 pounds of jet propellant. This would give the "flying tennis courts" about 23 minutes worth of extra fuel if they didn't use their gas-guzzling, Zone-5 afterburner. Juice Mayhew pulled the SUV into the front lot of Building 222 and parked in the VA-204 Executive Officer's space. The three aviators piled out and marched straight to the parachute loft to throw on their flight gear for the hop. A fresh mound of steaming dog shit was waiting for Juice in the bottom of his locker. A piddle pack filled with lukewarm urine had likewise been slipped into Mayhew's helmet bag, hidden strategically underneath his kneeboard. Just because he had fleeted up to XO didn't mean that Juice Mayhew was off limits to the squadron practical joker.

By 0615 Rocky had reviewed all the Maintenance Action Forms (MAF) in the aircraft book for AF-415. This A-7E was one of the last few VA-204 Corsairs that hadn't been converted to the NH markings of Carrier Air Wing Two. When the CQ detachment rolled around at the end of March, all the *River Rattler* planes would be painted up with NH and CVW-2 on their tails. The transformation from a reserve squadron to an active duty outfit would be complete. Lieutenant Commander Stone signed for his jet and was now meandering out toward the airplane sitting on the tarmac. The Corsair was loaded with a TACS POD, a HARM Anti-Radiation Missile and a Sidewinder. Senior Chief Esposito was striding next to Rocky as he made his way to AF-415. The brilliant morning sun was just now making its grand entrance by peaking over the mountains off to the East. The yellow-orange sunlight cast a long, lazy shadow from Building 222 out over the snow-covered flight line. As Rocky and Esposito arrived at 415, two Corsairs lifted off Runway 25 in a section takeoff. Their jet engines roared mightily in the near distance as they flew in close formation, sucking up their gear and flaps in perfect unison. The pair of Corsairs made a low transition at about twenty-five feet above the snow-swept concrete. When they reached the end of Runway 25 the section of attack jets initiated a gradual climb. Their turbine noise echoed and ricocheted off the large squadron building. It was indeed a beautiful sight to behold against the pristine backdrop of snow-covered mountains and the burgeoning first light of day. Every eye was on the two planes that were now in a climbing left turn. So close and precise in their formation, they looked like they were bolted together.

"Ah, the sweet sights and sounds of freedom," commented Rocky in Senior Chief Esposito's direction. Rocky's plane captain, Carlos Lopez, a Salvadoran-American, giggled then continued to prepare the A-7 for its impending launch.

"Say, who are those guys Senior Chief and where are they going," asked Rocky. He hadn't noticed any sorties on the flight schedule with takeoff times before 0715.

"That's the skipper and Lieutenant Ackerman," responded Esposito. "They're flying on some sort of last minute mission that CAG Madison assigned to them late last night. That's all I know about the flight." Rocky suddenly realized that he hadn't seen Duke or Teen Angel at the Alpha Strike flight brief that morning. It had somehow escaped his attention. Rocky scratched his rear end and continued the pre-flight inspection of AF-415. Senior Chief Esposito hollered for that 'Crazy Salvadoran' to come to him at once over by the tail cone of AF-415. 'You're not a real American citizen until you can show me your *Sam's Club* card' Esposito would always tell the young Salvadoran just to taunt him.

Twenty minutes later as the young plane captain strapped Rocky into the ESCAPAC ejection seat of the A-7 Corsair, Teen Angel and Duke were already leveling off at 37,000 feet heading for McConnell Air Force Base in Wichita, Kansas. This would be the mid-point fuel stop on their cross-country journey to NAS Cecil Field in Jacksonville, Florida. Duke had given flight leader responsibilities for this hop to Teen Angel because he wanted to work on the text of his eulogy speech during the trip to Cecil Field. Commander O'Grady's Corsair was on autopilot and his throttle was locked at a 92% power setting. Flying in a loose tactical formation Duke monitored Lieutenant Ackerman's aircraft out of his peripheral vision and with occasional looks up out of the cockpit. He also casually listened for FAA controller calls on the UHF radio. O'Grady was physically in the A-7 cockpit but he was spiritually elsewhere.

Duke and Teen Angel both had copies of the 'ALL NAVY' message regarding the fatal A-7 crash that Judy was involved in earlier in the week. The message had been retrieved from the Communications Center at 2215 the night before by Duke's SERE school nemesis, and CAG-2 Senior Chief. The 'Surf Nazi of Coronado' had graciously made copies for each squadron CO. The report contained more initial details of the lethal accident. At that moment Duke was busy reading the 'priority' message, fondly remembering his longtime friend Ken Grant. There was no time for mourning right then. The message stated that Commander Ken Grant was undoubtedly a hero who would most-assuredly be recommended for the Navy's Distinguished Flying Cross due to his gallant actions that day. Duke read on with a renewed sense of pride. According to radio transmissions, Commander Grant's A-7E had experienced a catastrophic engine failure just after takeoff from NAS Cecil Field. The flameout occurred in the vicinity of Orange Park, a densely populated area in northeast Florida. Judy had bravely and unselfishly steered his crippled jet away from the Orange Park Mall and crashed into a relatively secluded stand of trees near the far end of the shopping center's giant parking lot. Consequently no body was injured on the ground and no property was damaged, other than Dogwood and Cabbage Palmetto trees, by the impact of the jet or the ensuing fuel fire. Judy had apparently delayed initiating his ejection until the last possible moment, approximately 10 feet above the ground. This heroic action by Commander Grant ensured that his aircraft would not hit the mall or a residential neighborhood that was in close proximity to the shopping facility. Judy had saved the lives of dozens of innocent people on the ground, who were shopping or just enjoying their families at home. But his ejection was out of the envelope for the A-7's zero-zero ESCAPAC ejection seat. It was out of the envelope because the ballistic, free-falling Corsair was still in a thirty degree angle-of-bank with a ten degrees nose down attitude, descending at 1000 feet per minute when Judy punched out. According to the report, Commander Grant was killed instantly upon impact because the ESCAPAC did not have enough time in the ejection sequence to initiate seat/man separation. Judy's lifeless body remained in the ejection seat until removed by accident investigators from VA-203 eleven hours later. O'Grady pulled the O$_2$ mask up to his face and took a big swig of fresh, 100% oxygen to clear his mind. He also made a quick peak at Teen Angel's jet.

Duke and Judy had been the best of friends at Clemson University and had suffered through ROTC and Navy flight school together. Judy Grant had routinely given credit to his friend Duke O'Grady for inspiring him to succeed at whatever his goal was in life. Whether it was passing a calculus exam or earning his Navy wings of gold, Duke O'Grady always gave Judy Grant gentle kicks of encouragement in the ass to keep him motivated. During the first few hectic weeks of flight school in Pensacola, while sharing a couple of beers at McGuire's Irish Pub to de-stress, Duke actually shared an inspirational letter with Judy. O'Grady's Dad had written the piece of correspondence on the day his son graduated from college. Duke's father, a career electrician by trade, wanted to motivate his oldest boy as he headed off to Pensacola for flight training. Duke's Dad had given him the letter fifteen years ago on May 18, 1977 right after the Commencement Ceremony at Clemson University had wrapped up. From that day forward, John O'Grady kept that letter in his wallet. He referred to it every now and then for moral support and encouragement. It had provided extra incentive to O'Grady on numerous occasions throughout his adult life. Each time he read his father's letter the poignant words buoyed his spirits and instilled feelings of strength and tenacity into Duke. The letter always helped O'Grady to overcome any adversity he was confronted with in life.

"River 401 switch to Los Angeles Center on 312.5," barked an air traffic controller to Teen Angel. Duke heard the transmission in his peripheral hearing.

"River 401 switching to 312.5, so long" replied Ackerman. Duke dialed the numbers 312.5 into his front radio then listened for Ackerman to talk.

"Teen Angel," said Brad to see if Duke was up the correct frequency with him.

"Two," responded Duke to reassure Lieutenant Ackerman that his head was still in the game somewhat. O'Grady stopped listening to the radio for the next five minutes after acknowledging that he was on the proper frequency to his flight leader. At that moment, Duke pulled his Dad's letter out from the back of his leather, duo-fold wallet and read it in the cockpit. O'Grady carefully unfolded the fifteen-year old piece of paper. The extraordinarily wrinkled letter read like this:

My Beloved Son,

I wanted to take some time to write you a letter on the occasion of your graduation from college. You must be incredibly pleased and enormously energized by what is unfolding at this stage in your life. Undoubtedly, windows of professional opportunity are opening wider for you with each passing day. I urge you to continue setting lofty, personal goals for yourself because I believe that you have a destiny and an unquestioned capacity to achieve great things. You will most certainly serve as a leader and mentor for your brothers and sisters, encouraging and guiding them to follow in your triumphant footsteps.

Despite the obstacles that have been thrown into your path these past several years, you have persevered through hard work and dedication, both in your private life and in your studies at Clemson University. The initial fruits of your labor are only now becoming a reality and your entire family is tremendously happy to witness your scholastic achievement. I have never been more honored to be your Dad.

In the past year, I have spoken with my own Father on numerous occasions during your forward progress and have relayed to him how overjoyed I was with his first grandson. About a month ago, I asked him this rhetorical question as tears filled my eyes: "Dad, do you have any idea how gratifying it is when your children are victorious in their life's endeavors?" He of course understood this sentiment and what it is that I am feeling for you at this moment in our lives. As your self-assurance and competence are nurtured, always remember to maintain an element of humility as an integral component of your basic character. This dynamic will keep you on a healthy, even keel with each new success that you achieve. I am confident this is merely the beginning and that you will realize many grand accomplishments in the course of your lifetime son.

I am so very proud of you John. You are an amazing young man who will indeed mature into a remarkable and talented gentleman. Never forget your roots and where you came from. You are a child of God. Never abandon the Lord. Always seek the wisdom and guidance contained in His Holy Word and in the example provided by the life of our Savior Jesus Christ. Unfortunately, I went through a period when I forgot that God and His Will are what we should strive to align our personal lives with. Don't make the same mistakes that I have made. Be a better man than me John. I am paying for my blunders, but I have also learned valuable lessons about the critical aspects that characterize a good Christian man.

Go out now into the world and seek your individual destiny, fame and fortune. Never forget your family, and always be available to assist them whenever they may need you. I love you John, and have never been more proud of you my son.

Your Dad

Tears filled Duke's eyes as he folded the letter up and stuffed it back into the bowels of his brown wallet. He and Teen Angel would land at McConnell Air

Force Base in an hour and thirty minutes for refueling and a late breakfast in the Ops cafeteria. O'Grady pulled out a yellow legal pad and began to jot down some initial ideas for the eulogy text. He looked up and saw Teen Angel's jet about 1000 feet from him in the ten o'clock position. Duke scanned his instrument panel and found everything was normal.

Juice Mayhew had just crossed the initial point for his division's final bombing run at the industrial plant target. Rocky's HARM division had apparently performed their mission well that day. Even though several CAG-2 jets had been lit up by enemy acquisition radar, not a single 'blue' aircraft had been successfully fired upon by enemy SAM sites. Mayhew's four Corsairs accelerated to 520 knots and methodically completed their weapons checklist. The only thing left to do was to flip on their Master Arm Switch, pop up and roll ahead, then precisely deliver their load of Snakeye retarded, MK-84 bombs square into the target. Of course after dropping their ordnance they would have to fight their way out of the target area, defending themselves against aggressor fighters that would engage them in a fierce dogfight all along the egress route. The final CAG-2 Strike Package that morning included eight F-14 Tomcats (4 strike escort, 3 fighter sweep, and 1 battle damage assessment TARPS jet); fourteen A-7E Corsairs (4 HARM Shooters, 8 bombers and 2 tankers); six A-6 Intruders (2 tankers and 4 Bombers); two Prowlers (Jamming); two Hawk Eyes (AEW and Fighter Control); and four S-3A Vikings (2 over the horizon targeting and 2 Samson decoy birds). The Defense Package integrated six F-5's, six F-16's and six F-18's, plus the SAM sites and AAA batteries. In thirty seconds, the raging fight would be on. It would look like a huge, metal fur ball or a stirred up hornet's nest overhead Bravo-17 in a few minutes.

Juice Mayhew would be the first attack aircraft to bomb the target. He and T-Ben Hebert were flying at 40 feet coming in from the northwest part of the restricted area. As Juice pulled the Corsair's stick back to initiate his 'pop up' bombing maneuver, he felt his G-suit inflate and squeeze both calves and his flabby abdomen with compressed bleed air. The G Meter registered five and a half G's of acceleration force in the pop up. Juice quickly reached his planned pinnacle altitude of about 1500 feet. He then flipped the attack jet inverted and jerked the nose back down so that the weapons system pipper could acquire the appropriate aim point on the factory target. Commander Mayhew could plainly see T-Ben Hebert's aircraft mirror his own jet's maneuvers and positioning. The two Corsairs were a quarter of a mile apart and were now rapidly converging on the industrial plant. Juice pressed his pickle switch first and all four bombs departed his wings and fell toward the target. Mayhew saw the Snakeye devices extend to retard the bombs downward fall. His jet got an instant infusion of lift because 8,000 pounds of ordnance drag had suddenly been pickled off. Five seconds later T-Ben Hebert delivered his four MK-84 bombs toward the buildings. The explosions rocked the ground and the massive fire plumes and rising smoke filled the air, partially blocking a portion of the sunlight momentarily. The tremendous heat and blast concussion from the detonations could actually be felt in the Corsair cockpits as the two jets now sought the safety of a protected egress.

On his pullout from the target, Juice wrenched the control stick deep into his lap. The G-meter read 7.5 G's. Juice had aggressively overstressed his jet and for about 1 and ¾ seconds he blacked out in the cockpit. He was the temporary victim of G Loss of Consciousness or G-LOC. 1 and ¾ seconds at 520 knots airspeed is an extremely long period of time especially when you are in close proximity to other aircraft, the mountains and desert terrain. Unconsciously relaxing the pressure control stick, Juice recovered his senses as his Corsair was heading straight for a small hill. He instinctively shook his head and tightened his stomach muscles to bring some blood back into his brain then searched the Nevada skies for his wingman.

"T-Ben, how do you read this transmitter?" asked Juice on button 20, his eyes still scanning the skies for Lieutenant Hebert's aircraft.

"You're coming in weak and stupid, now break left Juice and look up," advised Hebert in an anxious, heated voice. Mayhew pulled his Corsair into a steep right hand turn and focused his eyes on the sky above Bravo-17.

"Your *other* left dummy!" Get up here into this fight," admonished Lieutenant Hebert. Juice reversed his jet's path and instantly spotted T-Ben about five thousand feet above him, tangled up in a dogfight with two F-5s. Mayhew advanced his throttle to MRT then pulled up and into the engagement. He quickly called 'snap shot' firing solution on one of the F-5's flying on the outside of T-Ben's turn radius. The four of them spent the next fifteen minutes dog fighting to their heart's delight. God it felt good to be in an air combat maneuvering engagement. How lucky could any man be to get paid to do that stuff for a living.

A key lesson that all A-7 pilots learn by going to the *Top Gun* DACM (Defensive Air Combat Maneuvering) Course is this: It really doesn't matter how perfectly you fly your own "hunk of metal" in order to maneuver behind your adversary flying in his "hunk of metal." Even if you achieve a guns solution at 1200-1800 feet behind the bogey and with the appropriate lead angle, there will inevitably be 3 or 4 other jets lined up behind you with a guns solution on your airplane. You become too predicable in a protracted ACM engagement. For a Corsair pilot the moral of the story is this: 'Get in quick, get your load off, get out quicker,' the VA-204 Squadron motto. If you have to fight your way out of a target environment, take a quick shot with your heater missile or 20mm guns then get out by diving for the deck. Apparently Juice and T-Ben forgot those life-saving adages taught by the Miramar instructors. They were having too much fun fighting and killing aggressor F-5s in a fur ball of metal and exhaust fumes.

All the Alpha Strike airplanes landed 45 minutes later at NAS Fallon without incident. The final debrief was held at 1200 in the Air Combat Debriefing Facility at the Naval Strike Warfare Center. The entire strike had been recorded using TACS PODS and was played back on the huge digital screens for analysis by all the players involved. It was a state of the art learning center. The aircraft departed back to their respective home Naval Air Stations starting at 1500. The CAG-2 Weapons Detachment had come to an end. Carrier Air Wing Two was certified by the Commanding Officer of NSWC to wage war against any enemy of the United States of America. The only other requirement prior to deployment on the Big E would be to complete day and night carrier qualifications next month. Despite a couple of screw-ups, CAG Madison was extremely proud of his Air Wing and of all the hard work they had expended during the Weapons Detachment.

Two days later at 1345 on Sunday, Commander O'Grady and Lieutenant Ackerman stood underneath a crystal clear, blue sky on the spotless flight deck of the USS *Eisenhower* (CVN-69). Enlisted men from the ship's company had scrubbed the flat top's deck with wire brushes and bleach, especially the area around catapults 2, 3 and 4, for seven hours on Saturday morning. Their CO wanted to render the non-skid deck as immaculate as was humanly possible for Ken Grant's Memorial Service. Not a cloud was to be found in the sky and the sun shined brilliantly as it provided a perfect 72 degrees to Jacksonville, Florida. Odd weather for February in northeast Florida, but a welcome meteorological condition nonetheless. Duke and Teen Angel were decked out in heavily starched, royal blue flight suits and highly polished black boots. Even their khaki piss-cutter caps looked crisp and sharp on their heads that day. It was Teen Angel's idea to borrow blue flight suits from the *Dolphins* of VA-203 to give them both an extra appearance of professionalism and decorum for the funeral service. Ken Grant's widow Sherry had specifically requested that Commander O'Grady wear a flight suit when he delivered Judy's eulogy. Ever since marrying Ken, Sherry had derived a particularly heightened sense of comfort and security around men in flight suits. Today Sherry Grant would need all the consolation she could muster up to endure her husband's Memorial Service and burial with dignity and grace. Everyone else onboard the IKE that afternoon was wearing a dress blue uniform, business suit or an appropriately demure, funeral dress.

When the memorial service kicked off at 1400, Commander O'Grady would be seated up front in a special VIP section of chairs, facing the crowd of mourners. His name was actually printed in black letters on a white index card and taped to the back of the last seat in the row. The VIP section was situated directly behind and to the right of the speaker's podium. The row of cushy seats was just in front of the crotch of the mighty ship, in between the JBD of catapult 2 and the far end of the cat track on catapult 3. On cats 1 and 2 the ship's handler had parked two VA-203 Corsairs, AF-300 and AF-301, in tribute to the *Dolphins* fallen skipper. The Corsair jets had been craned aboard Saturday evening especially for the event. Commander O'Grady indicated to Lieutenant Ackerman that he had a few butterflies of nervousness but felt he was prepared to eulogize his friend. He had practiced the eulogy numerous times on Saturday with Teen Angel as his only discriminating critic. The speech was perfect according to Ackerman. Judy would be proud to have the words spoken on his behalf advised Brad. Duke drew in a deep breath. He detected the slight aroma of jet fuel and hydraulic fluid. It was a very nostalgic odor for any carrier aviator and had the ability to elicit both good and not so good memories. Duke rubbed his left eye with an index finger. It made a squeaking noise as he massaged the eyeball in its socket.

The VIP's seated with Duke would include both Senators and the 4th District Congressman from the State of Florida, the Secretary of the Navy, the CNO, and Judy's own minister, the man who had baptized him twenty-two years ago. The Baptist preacher would officiate the memorial service and subsequent burial at the National Cemetery just up the road in Fernandina Beach, Florida, Ken's boyhood home. To say the least this was an august group of individuals for Duke O'Grady to be included in. Each VIP would have a few minutes of microphone time and television camera exposure before Duke would present his carefully scripted eulogy speech for Commander Ken Grant. O'Grady would follow Sherry Grant at the podium. Sherry would read her husband's favorite poem entitled *High Flight* by Gillespie Magee and try not to cry in the process.

Duke and Teen Angel stopped their conversation to more fully survey the scene on the flight deck. About four hundred chairs had been set out for the audience partitioned into two segments, in rows of twenty each, ten deep. The roped off chairs were spread out all over the aircraft landing area of the ship, facing the bow on the angle deck. Already seated in the audience were numerous Admirals and Marine Corps Generals, various squadron members, plus civilian friends and local business tycoons. Because Ken was a selected reservist in the Navy who's primary occupation was interceptor pilot for U. S. Customs in Jacksonville, the Assistant Commissioner of Customs Air Operations and every one the Customs pilots from his home branch were in attendance. All the Customs personnel were dressed in their 'police blue' flight suits, wearing shoulder holsters and 9mm pistols. Again this was at Sherry Grant's request. Up front and off to the left side was a special group of seats reserved for the family members. Those family member seats were completely surrounded by a vast array of flowers. It was more flowers than Duke had ever seen assembled at one time. The standing arrangements were huge and thick with the colorful flora and ribbons of condolence. A guest book station with several action photographs of Judy Grant was positioned at the entrance to the audience seating area. It was likewise deluged by a gorgeous display of flowers.

The IKE looked magnificent that day. All of her signal flags were stretched out over the island, flapping in the mild breeze. Enlisted men donning their dress blues manned the rail along the catwalks in tribute to Commander Grant. GSA equipment was perfectly lined up in the six-pack area. Eight men wearing Scottish kilts stood by the tailpipe of AF-300 playing *Amazing Grace* on their bagpipes in a somber tone. At that moment the ship's senior Boatswains Mate began blowing his pipe over the 1-MC to announce the arrival of all the high-ranking dignitaries who had just begun to make their way up the gangway and across IKE's Quarter Deck. The Memorial Service was just about to begin. Duke shook hands robustly with Brad Ackerman then took his seat. Teen Angel found an empty chair in the rear of the audience behind the group of Customs pilots. Fifteen minutes later everyone was seated. Eight pilots, four from VA-203 and four from U.S. Customs, slowly and methodically carried Judy's flag-draped coffin through the aisle separating the audience seats. They carefully placed the casket on a table just in front of the podium then walked over to stand by the nose of AF-300. A color guard was next in the procession. With the utmost precision, they presented the American and Navy flags and a local Marine Corps band played the National Anthem. Everyone either saluted or placed their right hand over their hearts in humble respect. Then a trio of church people strummed their acoustic guitars and sang a medley of well-known gospel tunes. The lone female singer was off key when she sang *I Surrender All*.

After each of the dignitaries had their five minutes at the microphone, Sherry Grant stood behind the podium and read Ken's favorite poem. Dressed in black, Sherry looked worn out from the emotional roller coaster she had been riding for the past several days. But her demeanor was calm and confident as she read the words. Her voice never wavered. Out in the audience several women could be heard sobbing, not at the text of the poem but at the tribulation Sherry was suffering through just to be able to speak to a crowd of people that soon after her beloved husband's death. When she finished Duke O'Grady rose from his chair then walked up to the podium. He exchanged a warm hug with his friend's widow. Duke wasn't the first to let loose of the hug. Sherry squeezed O'Grady hard and didn't seem to want to let him go. She finally relented and returned to her seat. Duke gathered himself, placed his stapled eulogy text down on the angled top of the podium then faced the audience. He had taken a fair amount of time deciding exactly how he should remember Ken Grant before such a distinguished crowd of people. On Friday during the second leg of the cross-country flight to NAS Cecil, Duke had decided to incorporate the fact that Judy Grant was an aviator for both the Navy and U.S. Customs into the concept of the eulogy. His idea was to refer to Ken Grant as a 'hybrid pilot' because he was truly a mixture of both aviation communities. Commander O'Grady took one last look at Sherry then winked reassuringly at SECNAV before clearing his throat and beginning his speech. In front of him, the eulogy paper read like this:

Eulogy for a "Hybrid" Pilot
Commander Kenneth Oliver Grant, USNR
by Commander John Patrick O'Grady, USN

We have gathered here today to celebrate the remarkable and storied life of Kenneth Oliver Grant, who was simply called "Judy" early on in his life that began almost 38 years ago in Fernandina Beach, Florida

Although this day is filled with sorrow, we can take great comfort in knowing that Judy lived a wonderful life

Always at full throttle

Sometimes running around as if his hair was on fire and his ass was catching

Judy didn't seem to know what temperance or mediocrity were or where you would go to find them

As such, Ken Grant's self-esteem was absolutely indisputable

But Judy wasn't pompous or arrogant, his was a gentle self-confidence, and it was one of his most endearing qualities

My remarks here today are intended to paint a snapshot of Judy Grant's professional experience

The words have been choreographed so that all of us can derive a sense of what it was like to live the kind of life that Judy was privileged to lead

Judy Grant was a modern-day Kerosene Cowboy, riding a bucking bronco in the rodeo of his two chosen professions

But his bronc wasn't made of hair and hoof

It was made of metal and wires, carbon fiber and glass, bombs and bullets

And Judy always rode for the full 8 seconds, every time out of the chute, strapped to his saddle inside the cockpit

From the first day you met Judy, you knew you were in the presence of greatness

You quickly realized that his contagious smile could immediately light up any room, rendering even the most stubborn people helpless to defend against his cheerful demeanor and positive attitude

Judy loved being a Navy Light Attack Pilot and he cherished being a Customs Interceptor Pilot

And he was exceptionally gifted at both

Because of this we should refer to him as a "Hybrid" Pilot

He was a truly a unique mixture of the "best of the best" from both these aviation careers

Let's take a moment to compare his two professions

First off there are some subtle language differences between the two communities

Light Attack pilots say strange things like:

Fox Two, Night Carrier Landing, Rules of Engagement, HARM, Beyond Visual Range, Initial for the Break

Customs pilots use odd term such as:

HALCON, Human Smuggling, Chopped Asset, Duty Weapon, The End Game, Prone Cuffing Technique

Light Attack pilots say things like "Nice shot skipper"

Customs pilots talk of "Air intercepts in the drug transit zone"

Light Attack pilots have Tactical Call Signs like:

Beast, Ratso, Balls, Big Dog, and Teen Angel

Customs Pilots have nicknames such as:

Montana, Butch, G-Money, Rock, and Winthorpe

Light Attack pilots use the HF radio to make phone patches to their wives back home, while flying 8000 miles away

Customs pilots use their SATCOM radio to inform ground controllers where the suspect aircraft is landing

Light Attack pilots tell stories of delivering cluster bombs on target, and finally getting a tone for their Sidewinder shot in an ACM engagement

Customs pilots tell tales of taking ground fire while flying over an ongoing drug smuggling operation, filming the scene for evidence purposes and the President's morning briefing

If they couldn't fly jets, Customs pilots would be trial lawyers, successfully prosecuting heinous criminals

Light Attack pilots would be rock stars, strumming their electric guitar on stage, the apple of every woman's eye

Customs pilots think they are bullet proof

Light Attack pilots know they are bullet proof

Navy Light Attack pilots have anxieties about not looking good around the ship

Customs pilots have anxieties about performing undercover operations

Friends of Light Attack pilots fondly recall when the two of them combined to score the winning touchdown in a high school football game

Friends of Customs pilots brag about the bottle of pure vanilla brought back to them from Puerto Vallarta, or the fresh Colombian coffee all the way from Bogotá

Colleagues of Light Attack pilots tell tales of the time the two of them conspired to get their Commanding Officer thrown in jail on trumped up charges

Colleagues of Customs pilots remember when they teamed up to almost burn down the church camp at age twelve

Children of Light Attack pilots boast of the time Daddy put them into the cockpit of a jet, let them wear his helmet, and allowed them to push all the buttons, even the red ones

Children of Customs pilots are proud to know that their Daddy rescued 40 people the night after a big storm blew through the Florida Keys

Wives of Light Attack pilots gloat to their girlfriends about the matching China dolls he bought for her and their two daughters in Hong Kong

Wives of Customs boldly pilots speak of the time their husband flew five Secret Service Agents to augment the President's security force, 30 minutes after an assassination attempt

Parents of Light Attack pilots proudly tell their church friends that their son flies a 40 million dollar jet

Parents of Customs pilots proudly tell their church friends that their son just helped seize 40 million dollars of laundered drug cartel money

Both types of pilots appear to be fearless on the outside because they tend to shield the rest of us from sensitivities they hold on the inside

Both types of pilots detest flight surgeons because it's their job to take our job away

Both types of pilots believe that needles are something you find on a Christmas tree, not a device used to draw blood from their veins

Both types of pilots respect and admire their parents

Adore their wives

Cherish their children

Laugh and tease with close friends

Vigorously compete with professional colleagues

I want to reiterate, Judy was a "Hybrid" pilot because he represented the best of both

He wished everyone could be just like him

Every morning you would see him emerge from his silver truck, a strapping, flight-jacketed, matinee idol

His wit was stunning

His intellect impressive

His humor infectious

His heart massive

Judy was a man's man

I would bet that he hadn't spent more than a couple thousand dollars in his whole life on a personal wardrobe

With the possible exception of a closet full of cowboy boots and corduroy pants

Judy lived a great life, always doing what he loved to do

Flying a variety of aircraft

Spending quality time with family

Joking with friends and coworkers

Every one of us should be so lucky

Commander Ken Grant died on February 26, 1992 displaying his exemplary courage and genuine heroism to the very end

Eyewitness accounts confirm that Judy was maneuvering his A-7 aircraft until the last possible moment, attempting to steer it away from populated areas on the ground, before finally initiating ejection at tree top level

Kenneth "Judy" Grant is a true American hero, who served his country with honor and great distinction

His life was filled with the kind or things that screen writers extol in their scripts

But movie directors can never adequately capture on the big screen, precisely because it was reality not fantasy

Sherry, we all love you and we all love Ken.

We will all miss him

We are all better people for having him touch our lives

And, we all look forward to being reunited with him in Heaven

Until we meet again, Good bye my friend

Out in the audience people were simultaneously crying and chuckling as they listened intently to the eulogy. Duke O'Grady removed his speech from the podium, took one last look at the flag-draped coffin then turned around just in time to salute as four Corsairs from VA-205 did a low fly by of the USS *Eisenhower*. The number three man in the formation initiated an aggressive pull up to remove himself form the division of attack jets. The missing man formation flew by the bow of the ship at about 250 knots then disappeared out over the ocean. Ken Grant was buried to the sound of taps blowing on the bugle three hours later.

CHAPTER 28

▼

STICKY VICKY

On Tuesday March 31, 1992 Lieutenant Commander Jim Stone and Lieutenant Brad Ackerman were winging their way west in a pair of haze-gray Corsairs. Their destination was Naval Air Station Miramar in sunny San Diego, California, America's finest city. *Fighter Town USA* and all of the legendary, hedonistic pleasures therein were only a few short hours away for Rocky and Teen Angel. The two *River Rattler* Landing Signal Officers would be among a group of distinguished LSO's from around the nation who would wave the CQ deck to qualify all CAG-2 pilots in both day and night shipboard landings. This carrier qualification line period would be the final training phase for Air Wing Two just prior to the April 30th deployment date of USS *Enterprise*. The training evolution would begin on Thursday April 2 at 1000 when the "Air Boss" would bark out his first 'Signal Charlie, ready to land aircraft' over the Big E's UHF tower frequency. The CQ would last four full days and nights with a fifth set aside for any stragglers or pilots experiencing difficulty with getting safely back aboard the ship.

At 0845 Rocky and Teen Angel had just crossed from Louisiana into Texas, cruising comfortably along at Flight Level 350 and at an indicated airspeed of .92 Mach. Lieutenant Commander Stone was the flight leader for this leg of the journey that was headed for an interim fuel stop at Cannon Air Force Base in Clovis, New Mexico. Rocky's wingman Teen Angel was flying NH-411, the A-7E with Ackerman's name and tactical call sign printed on the side in bold black letters, just below the canopy rail. After breaking one jet that morning, due to a bleed air leak in the turbine section of the engine, Rocky had finally planted his butt into the cockpit of NH-402. All of the River Rattler jets were now painted up with NH and CAG-2 Carrier Air Wing markings. The transformation from a Naval Reserve to an active duty squadron was almost complete.

After the last, inquisitive radio transmission from Houston Center, Rocky was checking his aircraft's position and flight plan waypoints on the Inertial Navigation System. He was also fumbling awkwardly with an "IFR Enroute High Altitude" chart for that area of the country. The section of Corsairs was navigating along the J-58 jet route just northwest of the Turnn Intersection. Both Teen Angel and Rocky had their autopilots engaged to allow hands free flying. Based on the INS coordinates and TACAN azimuth correlation, it appeared that the section of A-7E's was about three miles left of the high altitude airway's centerline. Lieutenant Commander Stone made a note of this navigational error on his kneeboard so he wouldn't forget to write up the discrepancy, or gripe, after the hop was completed. He then planned to perform a "flyover update" overhead the Dallas VORTAC to correct the drifting INS system. Even as he made his mental notes, Rocky continued to fiddle with the H-5/H-6 chart. In the cramped confines of the A-7E, folding and unfolding aviation maps in flight was a gigantic nuisance.

Rocky was about to lose his temper with the cumbersome chart when Teen Angel spoke to him on the squadron tactical frequency. Ackerman's resonant baritone voice always had a calming affect for anybody who heard it. As an extremely talented LSO, Teen Angel had the capacity to talk any pilot safely back aboard the ship during inclement weather or on their personal night in the bolter barrel. He could also talk anyone down if they were screwed into the ceiling over some personal dilemma. Effective, persuasive communication was Brad's God-given talent. As a Tactical Naval Aviator and Landing Signal Officer he was often called upon to use this skill to save lives or to salvage bruised egos.

"You were late again this morning Rock," chided Teen Angel over the UHF radio. Brad's tone was more noble than demeaning. As he waited for Rocky's reply Ackerman allowed the oxygen mask to fall from his smooth, boyish face back into his lap. Teen Angel made sure that the hard rubber mask and attached oxygen regulator fell back down gently. He certainly didn't want to pop himself in the balls because at that particular moment in the ejection seat, his nut sack was being severely squeezed by the tight-fitting harness of his flight gear. Doubly exposed as they were, his testicles were extra vulnerable to any kind of trauma, however slight. Brad checked his own INS coordinates against their position on the jet route then quickly monitored his aircraft's fuel state. The fuel gauge needles indicated 7200 pounds of JP-5 remaining in the tanks. Burning 3200 pounds of gas per hour meant Teen Angel had two hours and fifteen minutes until engine flameout. Cannon AFB was sixty-two minutes off in the distance according to the INS. Plenty of reserve fuel in case of emergency.

"You're fucking lucky I showed up at all partner!" snapped Rocky after about a ten second delay to think of a proper response. Stone moved his head a little to the right in the Corsair cockpit as if to gaze over at Brad who was flying in close combat spread on the starboard side of the formation. Rocky couldn't see his wingman's head too well because of the glare emanating from NH-411's canopy glass due to the angle of the rising sun off to the East. Rocky's own oxygen mask dangled down from his form-fit helmet. He only had the left-side bayonet fitting of the rubbery mask attached to his helmet. His visor was up so Rocky adjusted it to the down position. The shaded, plastic shield gave him only a partially improved view or Teen Angel's head 1200 feet away.

"Why did you pick Cannon? That place is a dump out in the middle of Nowhere, New Mexico," reasoned Teen Angel. His tone had a twinge of sarcasm hidden just beneath the words, but present nonetheless. Canon AFB was certainly not direct routing for a flight from New Orleans to San Diego. The typical fuel stop for a Corsair would be El Paso or Albuquerque. Brad laughed after releasing the microphone switch on his throttle quadrant. Ackerman already knew the answer to his probing, rhetorical question. Cookie Cline had regaled him with the story shortly after it had happened last summer, as the two aviators shared a Daiquiri and some juicy gossip on Bourbon Street.

"I got a blow job from one of the T-Line girls at Canon about eight months ago. It made the time pass by fairly quickly as they refueled Cookie and me on a cross-country hop. You know how boring it can be to wait for an Air Force Refueling Squadron to pump gas into your jet on the Transient Flight Line," answered Rocky in a forthright tone. Stone briefly monitored his oil pressure and engine temperature gauges then pulled out a fingernail clipper to remove some loose skin from his left thumbnail. As he clipped off the tiny patch of skin he dug the sharp edge of the clipper too deeply into his flesh and immediately drew a trickle of blood.

"The blow job made at least thirty-eight seconds of that refueling time enjoyable," Rocky added with relish. He wiped his thumb several times on the left pant leg of his G-suit until coagulation finally stopped the bleeding. The bloodstain quickly blended in with the salty sweat stains embedded deeply into Rocky's speed slacks. Stone folded the fingernail clipper then slipped it back into the right breast pocket of his flight suit.

"United 838 heavy, traffic at eleven o'clock and ten miles. It's a flight of two Navy Corsairs level at 350," reported the air traffic controller from the Houston Air Route Traffic Control Center.

"838 heavy is looking, no joy" was the reply from the United Airlines co-pilot. The thirty-year old co-pilot munched on a piece of his baked chicken, in flight meal after making the radio transmission. He clumsily spilled some *Diet Pepsi* onto the floorboard of the DC-10.

"We are requesting Flight Level 410 to get out of this light chop," added the United Captain with a deep authoritative voice. He was apparently still looking to find an altitude that offered a smooth ride for his passengers. The United captain sliced off another hunk of his New York Steak and stuffed it into his mouth with a silverware fork.

"United 838 heavy I'll have to check with the next sector, break NH-402 you've got DC-10 traffic at eleven o'clock and eight miles. He is at flight level 370, opposite direction. Switch to Fort Worth Center on 278.4," advised the controller.

"402 tallyho on the big iron flying the friendly skies. Switching to Fort Worth on 278.4. Catch y'all later," replied Rocky. Stone and Ackerman both reached down to the UHF transceiver on the left side of the Corsair's cockpit and dialed in the new radio frequency. Stone paused for a few seconds to make sure the center frequency was clear before he checked his flight in with the new sector controller.

"Rocky," said Lieutenant Commander Stone on 278.4. He was checking to see if his wingman had successfully made the transition to the new frequency.

"Two," responded Teen Angel. Rocky was now clear to speak with air traffic controllers at the Fort Worth Center. Ackerman was up on the right freak with him.

"Fort Worth Center NH-402, flight level 350. We have a visual on the jumbo jet at ten o' clock and six miles, converging."

"Roger that Navy NH-402, Forth Worth Center, good morning."

"Top of the morning to you sir." Rocky used a heavy Irish accent in his greeting to the air traffic controller. He sounded like a young Barry Fitzgerald, straight out of a Dublin pub. It caused a chuckle on the ground at the Fort Worth ARTCC. Teen Angel just sneered over in NH-411. He'd heard this act before.

Since it was a good bet that center controllers wouldn't be talking to their flight for a while, Rocky and Teen Angel unconsciously relaxed and began to daydream a bit inside the familiar nest of their beloved A-7E Corsair. After making a perfunctory glance at the instrument panel, and scribbling some figures down on his kneeboard pad, Ackerman began to nostalgically reminisce about his real job back in Hollywood. Being recalled to active duty several times over the past three months, to prepare for the *Enterprise* cruise, had caused him to miss a lot of action and job opportunities in the motion picture industry. This was a genuine loss for Brad because he loved being a stunt pilot working and flying on location among the stars and starlets. It was a sincere pleasure for him to bring daredevil, aviation exploits to life and to have them recorded for posterity on film. Teen Angel was also paid quite handsomely in *Tinsel Town* for his superb piloting skills. During the second and third weeks of March, Brad had actually flown several missions while toiling away on a new Stephen Spielberg movie about dinosaurs brought back to life on a secluded Central American island called Isla Nubar.

The screenplay, based on a Michael Crichton science fiction novel, placed the giant beasts in an amusement park setting, which was sort of ironic to Teen Angel's way of thinking. The regeneration process of the dinosaurs, a 20th Century variation of what Dr. Frankenstein had attempted in Mary Shelley's book, used semi-complete DNA strands extracted from dinosaur blood as the starting point. In the story, the dinosaur blood had been drawn from the stomachs of fossilized mosquitoes with a miniscule hypodermic needle. According to the storyline, these special insects had died millions of years ago shortly after biting and sucking out the bodily fluids of various pre-historic creatures. Like an Egyptian mummy, the little pests had been perfectly preserved in tree sap and were just waiting for the right enterprising scientist to come along and discover their true potential, under girding the foundation for a theme park. The film was entitled *Jurassic Park*. There weren't a whole bunch of flying scenes included in the script, but Brad had been contracted by the world-renowned motion picture director to perform the few that were required. In fifteen days of aerial filming and stunt flying, Ackerman had pulled in a cool $15,000 thanks to the generosity of his friend Spielberg. Ackerman had also made two new acquaintances and golfing buddies on the production, Jeff Goldblum and Laura Dern. Brad mailed 3500 bucks to his Mom in Connecticut the same day he cashed Spielberg's check.

Danielle Le Claire, the fiery New Orleans Assistant District Attorney, was also on Teen Angel's mind that morning. It was becoming quite apparent to Brad that Danielle was his new found, true love. Conceivably, she was the woman he had been subconsciously searching for during the past decade. Perhaps she could wipe away any remnants of the powerful passion he felt for Tara Thomason so long ago at Stanford University. Maybe Miss Le Claire could erase the intense and still plaguing, emotional pain Tara had inflicted on him that dreadful afternoon in New York City. At that moment the poignant song lyrics written by Brian Wilson in 1965 flooded into his thought process as the pair of attack jets continued zooming westbound deeper into Texas.

> *She was gonna be my wife*
> *And I was gonna be her man,*
> *But she let another guy come between us*
> *And it ruined our plan,*
> *Well Rhonda you caught my eye,*
> *And I could give you lotsa reasons why,*
> *You gotta help me Rhonda,*
> *Help me get her out of my heart.*

Over the past few weeks, Teen Angel had slowly come to the realization that he didn't enjoy life as much when he was away from Danielle Le Claire for long periods of time. Unwittingly, Brad was becoming a hopeless romantic despite every inclination as a rough and tumble Naval Aviator to resist that metamorphosis. Ackerman recognized that Danielle was his match in almost every respect and that he had fallen in love with her on several different levels that help determine and bolster that amorous sentiment. She was stunningly beautiful, incredibly intelligent and professionally successful. She possessed a great sense of humor, exceptional conversational skills, was fun loving and had ferocious tenacity, both in and out of the courtroom. Danielle also maintained an extremely strong spiritual compass that made up for Brad's minor deficiency in the religious arena. Over the weekend, during some sleepless early mornings, Ackerman had been tinkering with a poem that he was composing for Danielle. Imagine that, a Tactical Naval Aviator writing a poem. Teen Angel had to conceal this dalliance into the realm of poetry at all costs, lest he suffer severe indignation at the unmerciful hands of his squadron mates. Corsair squadrons had the notorious reputation of "eating their young" and spitting out the mutilated, masticated carcasses of worthless hacks with great ease. Duke O'Grady, a warrior-poet himself, would probably cut Ackerman some major slack, but Rocky would not understand this romantic, quixotic streak that was slowly seeping into Teen Angel's character. Rocky Stone was not that forgiving of perceived weakness.

Despite the insomnia writing dynamic, Brad wanted the rhymed verses to be perfect before he gave them to Danielle, accompanied by a beautiful arrangement of three-dozen *San Lorenzo* roses, red of course. Inside the *Sluf* cockpit, Ackerman pulled a folded piece of legal-sized paper out from his black, eel skin wallet. He carefully unfolded the sweaty, yellow paper and read the poem out loud in the cockpit. It read like this:

A "Brief" Poem for Danielle (cause I gotta get some sleep)

She can own the heart of any man with her luscious lips
And steal their souls with her captivating style

She can rob men of their virtue with her intoxicating voice
And make them blush with her contagious smile

Her infectious intellect stirs the male mind
And hypnotic eyes cause their knees to go weak

Her mere touch makes the masculine heart skip three beats
And perpetual youth stimulates them to perform at their peak

Danielle, Danielle, Danielle, Danielle,
The name cascades through a man's brain
Helpless and hoping all the while
And praying not to go insane

Will he marry her or will they just shack up together? That was the real question haunting Teen Angel. Would she have him as her lawfully wedded husband? Over and over in his brain Ackerman had analyzed the situation using Rocky's infamous "love market" theory. After sucking back a few beers at the bar, Rocky always pontificated that when you look at a couple you can quickly tell which one of the two was in control of that relationship. It would always be the partner who possessed the most intrinsic value if they were both single and available on the open love market. Brad knew that Danielle was in control of their romance at this point. She was more valuable than he would be if thrown back onto the singles meat market scene. He stuffed the poem away into a hidden compartment deep inside his wallet. Teen Angel then began to think about the upcoming vacation he and Danielle would share with Juice Mayhew, his wife Loretta and their two great kids, Ashley and Travis. The two-week Los Angeles escape would precede the *Enterprise* cruise by eight days. Ackerman was still finalizing the last minute details of the excursion but he knew it would include Disneyland, Knott's Berry Farm, Universal Studios, the LA Dodgers, Hollywood and the beach. He also knew that he would do everything in his power, like calling in favors from friends and professional acquaintances, to ensure that those fourteen days would be a wonderful, relaxing time for everyone involved. Brad was pondering and juggling so many different thoughts simultaneously at that moment while flying the Corsair, the impending CQ deck was the furthest thing from his mind. Teen Angel shifted his position in the ejection seat to relieve some of the pressure on his balls and to release a little blood flow back into the numb section of his butt cheeks. He quickly sucked in three healthy swigs of pure oxygen through his mask then checked his altimeter.

Over in Lieutenant Commander Stone's cockpit, Rocky was daydreaming as well. Most of his thoughts however, were somewhat more graphic and explicit than those of Teen Angel. His newest nemesis Leslie Lance crossed his mind a few times, as did that dumb ass, progressive congresswoman from Colorado. For purely aesthetic reasons Trish Schneider, that idiot Democrat from Denver, was directly responsible for forcing Lieutenant Commander Lance onto VA-204 in the first place. In Rocky's mind, Schneider had abused her "inside the beltway" political clout to pry open the inner sanctum of the *River Rattler* "boys only flying club" in order to inject a female into the mix. And Rocky hated it! What holy territory would this "congress person" armed with a feminist agenda strike next? Submarines? The SEALS? Perhaps the cockpits of carrier-based aviation chuckled Lieutenant Commander Stone to himself. But in all reality he realized that no part of Tactical Naval Aviation or the Naval service was safe now. The "pussification" of the Navy was well underway, and it was being engineered by a female; a female holding the House Armed Services Committee hostage to her mega-liberal political philosophy. Based upon this argument and on her abysmal performance to date, Rocky was going to have to teach Lieutenant Commander Leslie Lance a valuable lesson sooner or later, one that would keep her professionally alive in the demanding environment of a Navy A-7E squadron. He had resigned himself toward not embarrassing Leslie too much in front of the *River Rattler* officers because he actually liked her a little. But teach her a lesson he would nonetheless.

Wednesday night at the Miramar O' Club, complete with all of those lovely ladies from San Diego, and the many self-indulgent diversions of that venue loomed large in Rocky's thought pattern as well. Surely he would get laid Wednesday night after tripping the light fantastic for a spell on the hard wood dance floor of the Miramar Officers Club. The *Body Shop*, a world famous strip club in San Diego, might also be part of their Wednesday night activities, probably around midnight after the rollicking O' Club scene had died down. The young and well-endowed enlisted girl at Canon AFB, who always wore a tight-fitting white T-shirt while working the flight line, was likewise nagging at Rocky's thoughts. Ah, the possibilities that lay ahead were simply awesome. Rocky scratched his right cheek then peered out of his canopy glass at a "cattle car" railroad train leaving from the Forth Worth stockyards down below. The trainload of beef was moving in a southeasterly direction, probably headed toward the slaughterhouses of Lafayette, Louisiana. Of course the ultimate destination of the cows was the dining room tables of private homes and fancy steakhouses in and around New Orleans and Baton Rouge. Lieutenant Commander Stone brought his eyes back into the cockpit then briefly monitored his hydraulic pressure and fuel flow gauges. Everything appeared normal.

The Forth Worth stockyards elicited some unforgettable memories for Rocky and he recalled a few of them at that moment. In early November of 1991, Rocky had taken a Corsair jet on a cross-country flight to NAS Dallas. He had flown to Hensley Field in Grand Prairie, Texas that weekend because he had been invited by a stewardess to watch a college football game between the SMU Mustangs and the Houston Cougars. The stew, a petite twenty-four year old Asian-American chick from Arlington, Texas had flown with Rocky on a few commercial airline trips just prior to the invitation. She could have been Bob Seger's "black-haired beauty with big dark eyes" except for the pair of slightly crooked incisor teeth in her lower jaw. The youthful flight attendant had actually taken a liking to Rocky because she enjoyed his straightforward manner with women as well as their considerable age difference. The Asian babe was also a proud alumnus of Southern Methodist University, having graduated in June of 1989. The college game turned out to be a terrific gridiron event because the SMU Mustangs beat the Houston team 41-16, thus avenging a 95-21 shellacking they had suffered at the hands of the Cougars two years earlier. In that 1989 game, Houston's future Heisman trophy winning quarterback Andre Ware had pummeled the Mustangs by tossing and running the football for over 600 yards of total offense in just three quarters of play. Ware had even rubbed the defeat into their faces during post-game interviews that were featured the next morning in local Dallas newspapers. The November 1991 revenge game was suitable vengeance for the Mustang football squad, and all the SMU students and alumni who remembered the pigskin embarrassment of 1989.

But it was the Friday evening before the college football game that conjured up the most vivid recollections of Dallas and those Fort Worth stockyards for

Rocky Stone. On that November weekend in 1991, the Asian stew wasn't going to pick Rocky up for the SMU football game until Saturday morning at 0800. Mainly because her airline trip returning from London's Heathrow airport didn't get her back home until around midnight Friday. Since he was basically on his own until the next morning, Rocky had borrowed a VF-201 Tomcat pilot's car to drive out to a place in the Fort Worth Stockyards called *Billy Bob's Texas*. The country western nightclub touted itself as the largest honky tonk on the planet. Rocky remembered that he experienced everything under the sun in Texas that evening. He started off by eating a belt-busting dinner in the Buckaroo Café. The Buckaroo is a barbeque joint located in the southeast corner of Billy Bob's massive complex. The place was quaint, only about fifteen hundred square feet in size, but it had a distinct Texas flare in its ambiance. Above the entrance was a bronzed statue of a huge ten-gallon cowboy hat with a pair of spurs dangling down on the right side. All the waitresses wore long, navy blue sundresses with red roper-style cowgirl boots. And they spoke with that characteristic Texas twang. Each of the picnic-style tables in the Buckaroo had red and white checkerboard tablecloths as their primary adornment and the serving size portions of the meals could make a lumberjack blush. Rocky filled his belly by feasting on a sumptuous dinner of tender, "cut-with-a-fork" BBQ brisket, extra-thick Texas toast, plump red beans and fresh wedge-cut home fries. The ever-so-slowly cooked brisket melted in his mouth shortly after it passed his lips and hit his palate. The fleshy red beans gave Rocky a tremendous case of gas fairly rapidly after digestion began inside his distended stomach. Of course, this culinary artistry was all washed down his gullet with a couple of *Shiner Bock* brewskies, the beer brewed locally, deep in the heart of the lone star state. Rocky recalled that he had to loosen his belt one notch just to walk normally after consuming that BBQ meal.

After supper Rocky had paid the meager, five-dollar admission fee to get a choice seat up close and personal to the Brahma bulls performing in the bull riding corral at Billy Bob's. It was well worth parting with the *fin* to watch as ten, courageous bovine-riding cowboys braved the backs of ten, two-ton, pissed-off Brahma bulls. All the rodeo enthusiasts that night were completely entertained by the bravery of the cowboys, some of whom were merely nineteen-years old. Those fans who were seated closest to the railing inside the arena, had the extra special treat of having viscous bull snot slung all over their dude hats, colorful cowboy shirts and *Wrangler* jeans. They were so close to the action on the railing that these patrons could actually see the anger in the animals' bulging eyes. The foul stench of the bulls literally attacked the nostrils of those paying customers lucky enough to be in the first two or three rows of the small rodeo arena. Rocky Stone was ecstatic to say the least, because as a modern day kerosene cowboy, he had the privilege of watching his closest cousins ply their trade that evening at Billy Bob's. He realized that cowpunchers are a dying breed. To Rocky's dismay, these cowboys were relics, slowly disappearing from the landscape of contemporary America. Rocky chugged the last of his third beer and placed the empty bottle underneath the rusty bench seat. He then stood and smartly saluted the young cowboys as he departed the rodeo grounds, heading off to find Billy Bob's concert hall and dance floor.

Rocky fondly recollected that he watched a country western concert that night, featuring a new cowboy singer named Toby Keith as the lead act followed by Martina McBride and her band of pickers. After Toby stole all of the young girl's hearts with his simple yet poignant cowpoke tunes, Martina McBride strolled onto the country and western stage. As little Martina sang, Rocky pranced around the dance floor doing the Texas two-step with several of the hot local ladies. All around Billy Bob's people were buying turquoise jewelry, playing punching bag games, and engaging in mechanical bull riding competitions. Rocky even got his picture taken while sitting proudly on top of a stuffed Brahma bull, wearing a Stetson cowboy hat. He also bought a pair of *Tony Lama* cowboy boots, on sale in the gift shop, to wear at the SMU game the next day. The shit kickers were made of taupe-colored Anaconda snakeskin. Just prior to leaving Billy Bob's that evening, Rocky helped one of the bouncers break up a fight between three drunks. He felt like James Dalton, head bouncer of the *Double Deuce Club* in the Patrick Swayze movie *Road House*. What a night it was back on November 6, 1991. Shaking off the daydream Rocky performed a "flyover update" as the Corsairs flew over the top of Dallas and its VORTAC navigation station. Lieutenant Commander Stone noticed that his INS was almost 5 miles off before he entered the correction factor into the black box to correct the drifty system. He jotted down the error calculations on his kneeboard pad so he could inform the VA-204 avionics mechanics when he landed the jet at NAS Miramar in a few hours. This would help them successfully troubleshoot and repair the Inertial Navigation System. Rocky raised the glare shield on his helmet, yawned broadly then stared at the UHF radio. He hadn't heard much out of Fort Worth Center or Lieutenant Ackerman for the past several minutes. Ackerman's silence was normal for Tactical Naval Aviator's who routinely practice "zip lip" procedures while aviating. Center's silence was not.

"Fort Worth, NH-402, you still down there?" inquired Rocky.

"Navy NH-402, Fort Worth Center, rest assured, we are still here sir. Break, Delta 191 heavy, descend and maintain Flight Level 210," was the retort from the controllers. Teen Angel nodded his head. He knew that uncomfortable feeling all too well. Positive two-way communication while airborne had a way of soothing anxiety.

"Delta 191 heavy, roger. We're leaving Flight Level 370 for 210."

Ten minutes later the section of Corsairs was just northwest of Dallas, about to cross overhead the Batik Intersection on J-58, when suddenly Rocky Stone's Master Caution panel illuminated with flashing red and yellow lights. His instrument panel was lit up like a small Christmas tree complete with sequenced, blinking lights. Calmly, Lieutenant Commander Stone's eyes focused on his instruments and Master Caution Panel as he began to assess his jet's condition. Almost immediately, Rocky realized that NH-402 was rapidly losing pressure in its PC-2 lines, the most critical of all the hydraulic systems in the A-7E. Stone already knew the emergency procedures associated with this predicament. He had regurgitated them from memory about a thousand times since he began flying the Corsair. However, he pulled out his Pocket NATOPS Checklist anyway, to augment his knowledge of the "time critical" memory items. Rocky's hands were slow and deliberate as he performed the emergency procedure steps contained in the checklist. But the damage to the PC-2 system had already been done. He could feel it in his control stick shortly after disengaging the A-7's autopilot. Stone's Corsair maneuvered like a lethargic, diesel truck. He needed to get the Corsair on the ground pretty quick to fix the problem before it degenerated any further.

Surveying his aviation chart, Rocky started to search for suitable "bingo field" alternatives for himself and Teen Angel to divert into. He hastily narrowed his choices down to two locations, Naval Air Station Dallas which was behind them and Sheppard Air Force Base which lay ahead of them. According to his calculations, both hunks of concrete were almost equidistant from their present location on J-58. Sheppard was approximately 14 miles further away. Lieutenant Commander Stone also surmised that wherever they landed, he and Teen Angel would probably have to spend at least one night on the ground while the PC-2 system on NH-402 was being repaired. It might take until the next day just to find the appropriate parts and have them delivered counter-to-counter by UPS or FedEx. These facts started his tactical thought process swirling at an even faster pace. Landing at Sheppard AFB in Wichita Falls, Texas had distinct advantages, despite the fact that Air Force technicians would be working on his jet. While the hydraulics system was being patched-up, he and Teen Angel could share a few alcoholic beverages with some of the female students attending the famed Air Force Nurse School onboard Sheppard AFB. Rocky's last trip to a Friday night nurse graduation in Wichita Falls was indeed a memorable one. In the Officer's Club that evening, he and Cookie Cline had stolen away the attention of all the just-graduated and ready-to-party nurses from a group of Air Force pilots. Much to the utter dismay of the F-111 pukes, every nurse had incrementally moved from their end of the bar to the opposite end, where Rocky and Cookie were casually playing "ship, captain, crew" with a raggedy dice cup. This all happened within twenty minutes of Cookie and Rocky's strategically timed arrival into the O' Club that Friday. The "Flying Edsel" pilots were left with nothing to cherish and brag about other than the cute little ascots draped around their necks and the lead wings on their chests. They also told tall stories about the night they were allowed to take amphetamines to stay awake on an 18-hour flight around the borders of France en route to the Gulf of Sidra so they could drop a load of bombs one thousand yards short of Moammar Gadhafi's house.

On the other hand, landing at NAS Dallas meant another shot at Billy Bob's while actual Navy mechanics from CVWR-20 worked on his airplane. After about thirty seconds of tactical contemplation, Rocky settled on NAS Dallas as the divert location. Hensley Field in Grand Prairie, Texas had finally won out in the decision-making process because of the combustible hydraulic fluid that could be spraying all over the fuselage of his aircraft and because of the very real fire hazard posed by a PC-2 failure. The fourteen miles shorter distance to cover meant he would be airborne for about three or four minutes less time in this emergency situation. Conceivably, that trivial amount of time could mean the difference between his jet catching on fire and not. It could represent the difference between life and death. Stone punched the latitude and longitude coordinates for NAS Dallas into the Inertial Navigation System then hit "Direct" on the INS keypad. The INS needle on the Horizontal Situation Indicator (HSI) spun around to a 128-degree heading as the DME window settled on 38 miles to the selected destination. It was now time to let Lieutenant Ackerman in on his dilemma.

"Hey Teen Angel, you got a minute?" asked Rocky Stone in a deadpan voice. The transmission was sent out on the "squadron tactical" frequency, button 20 on the back (#2) UHF radio. It didn't take Ackerman long to respond. Even though he gave Rocky a sassy response, somehow Brad speculated that his flight leader wasn't fooling around with the question or the tone of voice.

"For you Rock, I got two minutes," replied Ackerman. Brad glanced out of his cockpit to peek at Rocky flying about 1500 feet from his attack jet. The pair of

Corsairs was still level at 35,000 feet streaking across a cloudless, baby blue Texas sky.

"Could you snuggle up underneath me for a second and see if I have any hydraulic fluid leaking on my belly?" asked Lieutenant Commander Stone. Rocky tucked his Pocket NATOPS Checklist away in a cubbyhole on the right side of the Corsair cockpit then focused his eyes on Lieutenant Ackerman's aircraft. Teen Angel was already maneuvering into a close formation position even before he replied to Rocky's request. Teen Angel's closing rate on Rocky's aircraft was slow but steady.

"I'll be there faster than you can say Ticonderoga bub!" replied Ackerman. Brad had pumped his throttle up about 10 percent and initiated a shallow crossing angle into Stone's Corsair using moderate aileron input. As Teen Angel slid into position underneath his flight leader, he immediately spotted several lines of red hydraulic fluid streaming everywhere on the underside of Rocky's jet. The crimson-colored liquid appeared to be seeping out from the front of the speed brake assembly but Ackerman couldn't be certain of its origin. Despite the fact that the Corsairs were flying at .92 Mach, hydraulic fluid adhered to Rocky's airplane due to the surface friction of the flowing substance. Tiny droplets of the hydraulic fluid actually hit Ackerman's bulletproof glass on the front of his canopy, slightly blurring his view out of the HUD. As if sensing what Brad's inspection would discover, Rocky had begun a gradual left turn back toward NAS Dallas. Even though he didn't sense the angle-of-bank initiated by Rocky, Teen Angel clung to his flight leader's jet as if they were riveted together. He was a mere three feet from the bottom of NH-402's fuselage and continued to survey the belly area for any additional signs of damage. When Rocky had completed his reversal turn, Brad dropped down then steered his Corsair back out to a close parade position on NH-402's right wing.

"You are covered in hydraulic fluid Rock. It appears to be spewing out of your speed brake," reported Ackerman. Brad waited for his flight leader's acknowledgment and any further instructions.

"I thought so," said Rocky on button 20. Jim Stone then switched his transmitter over to the front UHF radio. "Fort Worth Center, NH-402 is declaring an emergency. I need vectors to NAS Dallas," said Stone to the air traffic controllers down below.

"Navy NH-402 roger sir, your vector to NAS Dallas is 127 degrees, its 37 miles from your present location. We'll let 'em know you are coming. Say souls onboard and fuel state please." The air traffic controller pressed a guarded red button on the control console to place an identifying mark over the blip on his radar screen that represented NH-402 and his flight of two A-7's.

"Center, one soul is all I could jam into my ejection seat. I have two hours of fuel remaining and I am rapidly losing hydraulic fluid," responded Rocky to the ATC request.

"Okay 402, descend at pilot's discretion and maintain 10,000 feet. Dallas altimeter is 29.97," advised the controller.

"PD down to 10 K, we're leaving 350," said Rocky as he pulled his throttle back to 70% and lowered the nose of the A-7 to about 8 degrees below the horizon. Teen Angel stayed tight with him in echelon formation as the pair of attack jets descended. Because of the fire hazard, Rocky fished the Nomex flight gloves out of his G-suit pocket and put them on his hands. Since earning his wings of gold, this was just the third time he had actually worn flight gloves in the cockpit of a Corsair. Lieutenant Commander Stone inserted the right side bayonet fitting of the oxygen mask into his form-fit helmet then cinched it tight up against his face. Eight minutes later at 0920, Rocky and Teen Angel both made uneventful landings at NAS Dallas. Rocky took the short-field arresting gear because he didn't have any brakes due to the massive loss of hydraulic fluid. Teen Angel landed on the off-duty runway shortly after Lieutenant Commander Stone had come to a full stop with the arresting cable firmly wedged into his tail hook. Rocky left his crippled jet bleeding hydraulic fluid all over the duty runway. A tug removed it from the runway a few moments after Rocky had crawled out of the cockpit then towed it to the VF-202 *Superheats* flight line.

Thirty minutes afterward, in the Maintenance Control shop of VF-202, one of the Tomcat Chief Petty Officers was taking good care of Stone and Ackerman. He was only too happy to oblige a fellow CAG-20 flight crewman, even though VA-204 was in the final stages of transferring over to CAG-2 and the active duty side of the Navy. When Rocky casually mentioned the possibility of borrowing a squadron car for the next twenty-four hours or so, the Chief quickly dispatched a 3rd Class Avionics Technician to fetch the keys to the duty pickup truck. While shooting the shit and waiting for the set of keys to arrive, the Maintenance Chief happened to suggest that Stone and Ackerman might want to check out a new strip club that had just opened up in downtown Dallas. It was called *The All American Bush Company* and it was all the rage for the past month and a half in the Big D. The colossal new Gentlemen's Club, over thirty thousand square feet in size, had rapidly become the top strip joint in Dallas because of the high quality of women willing to take their clothes off on eight, multicolored dance stages. It also offered a free buffet-style, gourmet meal to every patron willing to purchase at least three ten-dollar drinks from their scantily clad cocktail waitresses. Based upon the Chief's enthusiastic recommendation, Rocky quickly forgot all about Billy Bob's Texas. The evening's festivities had been set then and there. He and Teen Angel would hang around the VF-202 spaces for a few hours to "hob knob" with some of the Tomcat pilots then check into the BOQ. At around 1700, they would mosey on down to the new strip club and enjoy a relaxing evening of adult entertainment together. Sensing he was trapped by Rocky's obvious enthusiasm, Ackerman realized he had no choice in the matter. Forty minutes after checking into his BOQ room and taking a brief, rinse-and-go shower, Brad met Jim Stone in the parking lot. He would be Rocky's noble companion and trusted guardian for their night of strip clubbing.

The All American Bush Company, situated in the heart of the Big D, was just under a half hour ride from Naval Air Station Dallas. Rocky insisted that Teen Angel drive the VF-202 duty pickup truck since he knew Brad would only drink one, maybe two beers all night long no matter how much fun they were having. Even though Rocky incessantly teased him about being a gigantic wuss, Teen Angel's feeble drinking habits came in handy from time-to-time. For those squadron mates who wanted to tie one on and get really liquored up, Ackerman was a perfectly responsible, designated driver. Rocky also needed some time to de-stress from his PC-2 ordeal. The twenty-eight minute ride into downtown Dallas would be the ideal opportunity. About half way into their journey to the strip joint Teen Angel slowly approached a Jeep Grand Cherokee. The black SUV was driving at exactly 55MPH in the middle lane of I-30 heading eastbound. As Teen Angel and Rocky began to pass the Jeep, Ackerman noticed an older, grey-haired lady was driving the vehicle and that she was alone. The woman, probably 67 or 68 years old, was driving the Jeep with both hands off the steering wheel. Unbelievably, she was polishing her fingernails with an emery board, buffing strip and steering the automobile with her left knee. Intrigued by this sight, Teen Angel decided to back off just a bit and monitor the woman's behavior for its comic effect. As soon as the woman got the desired amount of shine on her fake nails she began to apply mascara to her thin eyelashes. Her eyeballs were now focused on her withered lashes in the driver-side, vanity mirror. All the while she nimbly kept steering the Grand Cherokee with that talented left knee, using her peripheral vision to maintain the Jeep's position in the middle lane. Ackerman couldn't believe what he was seeing. Rocky on the other hand, wasn't paying any attention. The woman was also gabbing away on her hands free cellular phone while driving at precisely 55 MPH on the I-30, the Tom Landry Freeway. Teen Angel figured she was setting up her next ladies Bridge game at the country club. Brad changed lanes, accelerated to 80MPH, then scooted quickly past the Grand Cherokee. Ackerman just shook his head in total amazement.

An hour later, Rocky and Teen Angel stood with their backs up against the center of the main bar inside *The All American Bush Company*. This vantage point allowed them to see the entire club and its abundant activities. And what an extraordinary venue it was to observe. The lighting and décor was exquisite all around the huge room with special emphasis around the various dance stages, bars and food tables. Of course the lighting was subdued in the lap dance forum that was furnished with the finest leather sofas and easy chairs money could buy. Standing next to Teen Angel was a young guy, probably about nineteen years of age and undoubtedly equipped with a phony ID card. The kid's eyes were as wide as a major league clean-up hitter poised in the batter's box, watching a hanging curve ball floating like a ripe grapefruit toward home plate. As the kid stared at gorgeous strippers prancing and removing all their clothing, the smirk on his boyish mug was similar to the grin that young children have on their faces after Daddy lets go of the bicycle and they continue riding down the street without falling off the bike. It was a sly, innocent smile but it conveyed a wealth of information.

Jim Stone had bought the first round of expensive beers by flipping the delicious-looking bartender a 20-dollar bill and telling her to keep the change. When the bartender reminded Rocky that the two beers cost twenty bucks, he pulled out a five from his wallet and blushed as he handed her the crinkled bill as gratuity. As they stood leaning back against the edge of the bar, Brad held a nearly full *Michelob Light* in his left hand and Rocky was fondling a half-empty Heineken in his right. Ackerman and Stone also had two plates full of various food items from the buffet line sitting on the bar behind them. The gigantic club was indeed an impressive sight to behold. The place was jam packed with older men wearing thousand dollar business suits and younger guys sporting jeans and long-sleeved cowboy shirts. The bustling activity appeared to be non-stop with seven secondary dance platforms and one primary stage with dancers performing simultaneously. At that moment Rocky was making small talk with a red headed cocktail waitress. Basically, he was badgering her with his crude comments because the twenty-something babe wore a provocative French maid outfit complete with a pushup bra, fishnet stockings, a red garter belt and three-inch high heel shoes. The black heels were the quintessential example of "catch me fuck me" pumps especially for this waitress because her costume was extra tight in all the strategic locations. Rocky noticed that she playfully stuffed tip money into her bra strap for enticement and just plain fun.

"Hey babe, you are in luck tonight because you are standing at ground zero. This is where it is all going to happen for you honey. Your wildest fantasies and dreams will come true this evening," boasted Rocky to the cocktail waitress in the French maid suit. As he spoke, Rocky pointed to the floor space where he and Brad were casually standing. The waitress giggled, she understood the innocuous nature of Rocky's humorous comment. Ackerman turned his hearing up a notch to listen in on their conversation.

"How would you like to fly for free the rest of your life on an airline, non-rev spouse pass sweetie? All it would take is for me to make one phone call to get rid of that woman who is living in my house right now to make room for you babe."

"Oh are you referring to your wife Rocky?" chimed in Brad Ackerman. He of course knew that Rocky wasn't married but he was playing along with the charade.

"Yeah the psycho-bitch from hell!" said Rocky Stone. The young cocktail waitress laughed nervously, blushed then politely declined Rocky's generous offer before moving on to the next thirsty customer. Teen Angel gently grabbed the waitress by the arm to offer some good fatherly advice. He whispered softly into her ear so Rocky couldn't hear what he was saying to her.

"For your own sanity, if I were you, I would take my shoes and socks off and run away from this place as fast as I could so you can avoid a tremendous problem sweetheart," suggested Ackerman. "He is an insane lunatic!" The woman nodded her head and walked over to a table full of businessmen. Her rebuff left Rocky frustrated yet again.

"You know Teen Angel there are three Cardinal Rules regarding women. Rule number one: All women are fucked up! Rule number two: Some women are more fucked up than others!! And rule number three: There are no exceptions to rules 1 and 2!!!

"Can I buy you a beer Rocky?" asked Ackerman.

"Absolutely partner, I'm as dry as a summer bone in Tucson," cracked Jim Stone. At that moment the disc jockey broadcast a message over the public address system that hushed the massive crowd. There was no applause just stunned silence.

"Ladies and gentlemen put your hands together for Sticky Vicky now appearing live on the main stage." The disc jockey made this announcement in a tantalizingly slow manner, accentuating each syllable as he spoke. This particular stripper was known as "Sticky Vicky" because in her routine she would throw a beach towel down on the dance floor then strip off all her clothes fairly rapidly. When she was completely nude, the stripper would then spread and drip a liberal coat of pure bees honey all over her naked body using a small, delicate paintbrush. The writhing dance routine was extraordinarily seductive. The large crowd was mostly muted, overcome with anticipation. Only a few sporadic conversations continued unabated.

As Sticky Vicky, a tall slender brunette, walked to the elevated dance platform of the main stage, every eye in the club was literally captivated by her supple movements. Even the other strippers and club employees were awestruck by her mere presence. An eerie silence began to spread through the club as she laid out a large beach towel then began her erotic dance. She was indeed the most amazingly beautiful woman Teen Angel had ever seen in his entire lifetime. As she danced and slowly, provocatively removed her clothing, even the women couldn't look away from her. Her beauty was that hypnotic. She blatantly stole your breath away. All eyes were on the brunette stripper. The men's stare was overt and wide-eyed while the women were subtle using their peripheral stare as she began to remove each article of clothing piece by tantalizing piece. Teen Angel and Rocky wanted desperately to get nearer to the stage but the crush of people prevented their movement. So Rocky and Teen Angel stood grasping and fondling their beer bottles. They were not able to tear their attention away long enough to drink the brew. The two aviators were leaning up against the bar, straining and staring in Sticky Vicky's direction, hoping for any fleeting glimpse of her naked body.

"Oooo, giddy up baby," uttered Rocky. The sheer, radiant exquisiteness of this stripper hit Rocky like a bee sting into the left ventricle of his heart chamber. After her ten-minute dance was completed it felt as though the oxygen had been allowed to flow back into the club as people began to talk and socialize once more.

Turning their backs to the dance floor, Rocky and Teen Angel tilted toward one another, each with stunned looks on their faces. After the 10 minutes of sheer hypnotic ecstasy they began to drink once more from their lukewarm bottles of beer. Not more than fifteen minutes passed before the Stone and Ackerman felt a warm presence slide in between them attempting to reach the bar. Amazingly, it was Sticky Vicky standing right there next to Teen Angel and Rocky. All of the honey had been removed from her skin and her close proximity was simply mesmerizing. From this close vantage point, Angel could see that she was *natural* perfection. None of her assets had been *store bought*. God had shined down on her.

Reaching into the front pocket of his jeans, Teen Angel pulled out a twenty-dollar bill. He then humbly placed the cash into Sticky Vicky's soft velvety hand.

"I wanted to give this to you ten minutes ago but I couldn't get near the stage babe," said Teen Angel. Sticky Vicky's face flushed at the innocence of Brad's honest gesture. She then giggled in humble embarrassment combined with a heady sense of her own tremendous beauty.

"Thank you sweetie" replied Sticky Vicky as she stuffed the paper money into the waistband of her thong panties. "Would you like me to do a lap dance for you big boy?"

"Is this a trick question? Has anybody ever turned you down?"

CHAPTER 29

▼

CQ

At 0728 on April 2, 1992 Lieutenant Brad Ackerman was sound asleep and actively dreaming in the upper rack of a bunk bed positioned in the far corner of the Junior Officer's (JO) stateroom. The billeting space, located amidships on the O-3 level onboard USS *Enterprise* (CVN-65), was large enough to comfortably accommodate twenty officers at the same time. Teen Angel had stumbled up the gangway at 0230 that Thursday morning after actually consuming two full beers and one tequila shooter during the gala festivities at NAS Miramar's Officers Club the night before. Ackerman was so exhausted from those infamous Wednesday night O' Club shenanigans that he wasn't even aware the mighty aircraft carrier had pulled its anchor and gotten underway precisely at 0700 as the *Enterprise* Plan-of-the-Day had specified. At that moment *Big E* was sailing at four knots past the Point Loma Naval Base, home of Commander Third Fleet, Submarine Squadron Eleven and numerous tenant commands that dealt with submarine operations and maintenance. CVN-65's eleven hundred and twenty three feet of grandiose steel, superstructure and flight deck eased through the water like a swan on a September lake in Minnesota. Two SH-3 helicopters from HS-11 tailed and bird-dogged the huge ship as it moved slowly along in the narrow channel. The *Sea King* choppers acted like airborne tugboats assisting the carrier's movement through a limited navigation area.

The nuclear-powered ship was steaming southbound out of San Diego Harbor headed into the open waters of the Pacific Ocean to begin four days of pre-deployment, Carrier Qualifications for the pilots of Air Wing Two. Even though its homeport was Naval Air Station Alameda in Oakland, *Enterprise* had been tied up at NAS North Island's carrier pier for the past five days. The ship's Commanding Officer, Captain Buford "Long Horn" Angus, had decided to give his crew a few days of well-deserved liberty in San Diego and Southern California just prior to the start of their six-month deployment, slated to begin on April 30, 1992. Fifty-one hundred men and a few women from the ship's company had spent hundreds of thousands of dollars while relaxing and enjoying the many entertainment venues, amusement parks and "hot spots" that Southern California had to offer. Buford Angus had dedicated most of his personal leisure time to hitting and chasing golf balls around the links at the La Costa Resort and at Torrey Pines Golf Club, overlooking Black's Beach. He never broke ninety during his five-day hiatus from the ship. He did lose his fair share of golf balls in the water hazards however.

As the massive carrier leisurely navigated out of the mouth of San Diego Bay the beautiful, rugged tip of Point Loma Peninsula could be seen just to the right of the ship as it emerged from a dissipating fog bank several hundred yards away. The dense, ragged mist was typical weather for this time of year in Dego. It was a rapidly moving, climate phenomenon associated with Southern California's notorious marine layer. As the bow of the 90, 000 ton carrier approached the deep channel next to a slightly-submerged, rocky breakwater, Captain Buford Angus directed an enlisted man on the bridge to blow the ship's thunderous whistle three times. The ensuing shrill noise was deafening to unprotected ears. Several *Enterprise* crewmembers meandering about on the flight deck stopped in their tracks to place index fingers into vulnerable ear canals. Two men in a small fishing boat that was gliding on the water in close proximity to the carrier repeated the protective behavior as well. The piercing clamor even scattered about fifteen Bottlenose Dolphins that were swimming in formation on the starboard side, jousting playfully with the bow of the ship as it cut a path through the water. Buford grinned as he shifted his butt around in the brown, leather-upholstered Captain's chair situated on the left side of *Enterprise's* navigation bridge. The crease on his khaki uniform pants and shirt was so crisp and neat it was as though the folded lines had been embedded into the fabric with a laser beam rather than a hot iron. Buford also wore a brilliantly shined pair of 24 karat gold wings above the six rows of 'fruit salad' medals and decorations he had earned over the past twenty-five years as a naval officer. Captain Buford Angus was one squared-away Naval Aviator. It was good to be Captain.

Long Horn's whistle blowing mischief was intended as a sign of respect to USS *Houston* (SSN-713) a majestic-looking, nuclear-powered attack submarine of the Los Angeles class. The sleek sub was tied up next to a tender getting some much-needed repairs and a few groceries at the Point Loma Naval Facility. USS *Houston* had been a Navy and a Hollywood celebrity ever since starring in the motion picture *The Hunt For Red October* back in 1989. She would accompany CVN-65 as her defensive carrier escort when cruise began at the end of April. *Houston* would defend Buford's ship against all enemy submarine threats and he wanted to honor the role she would play in the upcoming deployment. "Long Horn" Angus was in effect tooting his horn at the shadowy grey vessel, floating silently low in the water. Once Buford and his colossal "bird farm" made it past the protective jetty, and safely around the tip of Point Loma, he would direct the helmsman to steer a 260-degree heading, the direct course that would take his ship straight into Warning Area-291. Approximately twenty miles West of San Clemente Island, and in the heart of W-291, Captain Angus would begin to search for favorable winds, and prepare for the first CAG-2 aircraft to arrive over-head his boat. CQ would begin promptly at 1000, provided the fog cooperated and lifted. Buford sipped heartily from the unsweetened java inside his coffee mug. He winked at the Officer-of-the-Deck.

Back in the JO Bunkroom, Lieutenant Ackerman moaned loudly then turned over to his right side. He wedged his left hand snugly up under the chicken-feather pillow that his head was resting on. Since he was onboard the ship and sleeping with several other men in the same stateroom, Teen Angel was not adhering to his usual boudoir routine. He was not sleeping in the nude. Brad was wearing a pair of white *Calvin Klein* underwear. Unconsciously, Ackerman threw the sheet and wool blanket off his body then shuffled around a little more as if trying to find the perfect position in the rack to continue his slumber. During that last movement, his "tighty-whitey" under shorts had pulled themselves half way off his ass cheeks so that his "plumber's crack" was plainly visible to anyone brave enough to look. Burying his head deeper into the pillow, Brad started to softly snore like a puppy. As it slipped smoothly through the water, the gentle rolling motion of the enormous flat top boat was extraordinarily soothing. This movement was similar to a cradle that gently rocks a baby into an intense, relaxing snooze. Unexpectedly, Brad was awakened by the now audible sound of three additional, high-pitched whistle blows. Slightly stirring as he was, the blaring whistle was now perceptible to Teen Angel down on the O-3 level. Buford was apparently feeling pretty frisky that morning on the bridge as he sailed out to sea leaving the city of San Diego and seventeen *Titleist* golf balls behind in his rear-view mirror.

Ackerman yawned deeply then stretched the entire length of his body out on the twin-sized bed. His size eleven feet bumped into a sheet metal bulkhead as he extended his legs several inches beyond the end of the bunk. This intense stretching regimen was Brad's preliminary morning activity designed to prepare his brawny frame to face the rigors of the day, and to loosen up his muscles. Ackerman forced open his large, brown eyes then instinctively searched for the watch on his left arm. The tight-fitting timepiece made deep groove marks into the soft flesh on Brad's wrist. It had also restricted the blood flow to such a degree that his left hand was partially numb. The silver-colored, tungsten steel *Movado* wristwatch showed the time as being 0732. Brad pulled his underwear up above the top of his butt cheeks then threw both legs over the side of the upper bunk. He sat upright with his bare feet dangling down over the edge of the top rack for a few minutes, still trying to completely wake up. Teen Angel scratched at the right side of his "bed head" scalp then realized he needed to get moving because CQ would begin soon. The first Charlie Time was scheduled for 1000, and the C-2 Greyhound would be the initial trap of the day. The *Providers* of VRC-30 would provide logistics support for the entire CQ evolution using their Greyhound, carrier-onboard-delivery (COD) aircraft.

Teen Angel stretched his back and arms out once more. He heard a few bones and joints shudder in the elongated process. 'I am getting old' he thought. As he jumped down to the cold deck below, Teen Angel noticed that Rocky's bottom bunk was still made and had obviously not been slept in. Neither had Cookie's bed on the other side of the large room. Brad didn't have to think long before he came to the conclusion that Rocky and Cookie had obviously gotten lucky. They had gone home with those two hot babes they were hitting on so desperately in the O' Club last night. Teen Angel was sure to hear about their sexual exploits later in the day on the LSO platform and elsewhere on the ship. Ackerman recalled that the two middle-aged chicks were hair stylists who co-owned a coiffure shop in Escondido called *The Hair Team*. Brad likewise remembered the pair of women seemed extra-eager to engage in romantic behavior with a flight-suited Naval Aviator or two, or three for that matter. Ackerman shook his head as if trying to shift his thinking away from the previous evening's antics, but his mind stayed on that subject a while longer. Teen Angel wondered if his squadron mates had noticed when he chucked three shots of tequila over his right shoulder and into a thick Bougainvillea Bush, while half-heartedly participating in "shooter" toasts on the patio of the Officers Club. Ackerman's wayward tequila had probably wilted several of the vibrant Fuchsia flowers growing out of the colorful plant. Again, Brad tried to shake off all reminders of last night. That characteristic, high frequency humming noise of the ship operating at sea rang in his ears as Teen Angel maneuvered around inside the stateroom.

That first C-2 COD would probably have Rocky and Cookie among its list of passengers as well as other CAG-2 LSO's who had stayed in town last night, thought Ackerman. Moving toward one of the sinks, Teen Angel reached up and flipped on the 27 inch TV that was mounted just above a row of lockers in the JO Bunkroom. Brad grabbed his towel and black toiletries bag from one of the lockers as he waited for the TV to come on. After an eight second delay to warm up the high voltage power transformer, the television picture came into focus. To Ackerman's obvious delight, a familiar episode of *The Three Stooges* was playing on the ship's television station, commonly referred to as *Climax TV*. Comedy antics were just what Teen Angel needed to get moving after last night's drinking binge. Brad cranked the volume up just a tad. In the familiar, black-and-white scene Curly Howard was standing in a courtroom being sworn in by a Bible-holding bailiff, so the stooge could take the witness chair and testify in a heinous, chicken theft caper. He was wearing a derby-style hat made of black beaver felt and a suit that fit way too tight on his bulky frame. Curly's right hand was raised high into the air and his left palm was firmly placed on the bailiff's Bible.

"Do you swear....," Curly cut the bailiff's question off in mid-sentence, deliberately interrupting his familiar judicial mantra. The emaciated-looking bailiff dropped the Bible and almost lost his shoddy hairpiece due to the blatant rudeness.

"COITENLY NOT, but I know all the woids judgey wudgey, nyuk! nyuk! nyuk!" replied Curly with a huge grin on his face, all the while staring intently into the judge's eyes. The most popular of the stooges used his renowned Bensonhurst, New York accent as he spoke in the scene. Even though he hadn't gotten enough restful sleep the night before, Brad couldn't contain himself. He belly-laughed out loud at Curly Howard's amusing comments and slapstick demeanor inside the mock, television courtroom. Teen Angel flung the white towel around the back of his neck. He then walked through a side door and down the passageway towards the Officers Head to take a rejuvenating morning shower. The VA-204 LSO was sporting blue, flip-flop shower shoes. He had purchased the thongs at the Navy Exchange for two bucks yesterday afternoon. The last thing Brad needed was to contract an acute case of athlete's foot during this short CQ detachment. The microscopic fungus that causes *tinea pedis* always seemed to be lurking in the floor areas of showers onboard aircraft carriers. The rubbery shower shoes would prevent the bacteria from reaching his toes. Ackerman was the last officer to wake in the JO Stateroom that Thursday morning.

Bathing areas aboard modern-day aircraft carriers are a fairly interesting place. The bathroom that Teen Angel had selected was larger than most, being located next to the huge JO Stateroom in *Officers Country* on the O-3 level of the ship. Everything in the head, even the toilets, was made of pewter-colored metal, and it was always cold to the touch no matter what time of day you were in there. The ceilings and bulkheads of this particular bathroom had numerous valves, pipes and ducts crisscrossing in every direction. The various conduits transported steam, water, jet fuel, conditioned air and human waste throughout the boat to their final destination. Eight toilet stalls and ten urinals were lined up in neat rows on opposite sides of the bathroom. Teen Angel noticed that two of the urinals had warning signs posted on them advising not to flush because water pressure had been reversed in the plumbing lines for maintenance purposes. Those warning signs were hung on small chains from the top of the urinal's pipe fixtures down into the basin. Another larger poster was strategically placed on the bulkhead just above each urinal. The placard offered a suggested technique for urinating. The signs read: *If you have short stacks or low manifold pressure, please taxi up closer to the urinal to complete your business.* Teen Angel chuckled as he read those words.

For some unknown reason, the not-so-private shower stalls were positioned directly in between the toilets and urinals in this particular Officers Head. And these shower stalls were equipped with cut-rate, *lowest-bidder* showerheads that featured an "ON-OFF" button to control water flow. That annoying pushbutton was exceedingly difficult to keep pressed in the down or "ON" position. The engineering design was intended to conserve fresh water, a crucial resource on any vessel at sea. Navy brass didn't relish the idea of sailors standing in showers letting warm water cascade over their bodies for fifteen or twenty minutes at a time, depleting the ship's vital reservoir of fresh water. Thus the showerhead device was intentionally created to force sailors into releasing the knob to stop the stream of free flowing water after only a few seconds. Brad hated having to use those showerhead devices when he was onboard the ship. But he soon discovered a few tricks from senior aviators. Many years ago, after spending only a few days onboard his first aircraft carrier for a CQ detachment, Ackerman had learned to bring a large and powerful rubber band with him into the shower. The rubber band was wrapped around the showerhead appliance to keep the switch continuously pressed in the down or "ON" position for maximum water delivery. Juice Mayhew had actually taught Brad that little technique way back at Cecil Field.

But Lieutenant Ackerman had forgotten his rubber band this time out to sea. He was out of practice and his shower that morning was less than invigorating as a result.

As he twisted both water knobs off and suspended the showerhead apparatus back on its pedestal, Teen Angel stepped carefully out of the shower stall. Brad moved cautiously because he didn't want to stub his toe on the raised metal edge that lined the bottom of the cramped booth. His thong, shower shoes made their distinctive squeaking sound as he moved his feet on the wet surface of the deck. As Ackerman was drying himself off with a thirsty towel, he bellowed out his signature "Indian Yell" into the large but confined bathroom space. This frightening, three-second scream apparently had a profound affect on a man taking a dump in one of the toilet cubicles. Still perched on the toilet seat, trying to complete his business, the guy spoke to Brad from behind a metal door.

"What the fuck was that? You scared the crap out of me you skin dick," said a recognizable voice to Brad. The common sound of toilet paper being unraveled from a squeaky contraption could be heard emanating from the toilet area.

"Well then, considering what it is you are trying to accomplish in there, I helped you out Bub!" Brad continued to dry off his various body parts with the bulky towel. "Say, that queer and exceedingly feminine voice sounds very familiar to me. Is that "Daffy" Drucker, the notorious CAG-2 Landing Signal Officer?" asked Teen Angel. Ackerman's question was obviously rhetorical.

"Tis I, in the flesh Teen Angel," replied Lieutenant Commander James Drucker. The sound of highly pressurized water flushing down a toilet could be heard immediately after Daffy Drucker stopped talking. Daffy reeled off another forty inches of toilet paper. The bottom eight inches or so hit the floor and spread out under the toilet base. Drucker then pulled the single-ply TP up off the deck and folded it neatly to prepare for his next successful wipe.

"I'll see you in the *dirty shirt* wardroom for breakfast Daffy," said Ackerman as he ambled out of the bathroom and into the poorly lighted passageway. The extra-long towel was strategically draped around Brad's 36-inch torso, firmly tied off at the waist.

Twelve minutes later Teen Angel stood alone in the ordering line at the entrance to the dirty shirt wardroom. This officer's wardroom, one of two onboard the aircraft carrier, was located on the starboard side of the ship underneath Catapult One. The informal dining facility was referred to as a dirty shirt wardroom because Air Wing personnel were the usual patrons, and they normally wore stinky flight suits to eat their meals, talk with their hands, and engage in lively conversations about life. There was always more of a rushed feel in the dirty shirt wardroom because Naval Aviators and Naval Flight Officers were usually attempting to grab a bite in between briefs, de-briefs, flight missions, AOM's and combat naps. Flight deck personnel from ship's company like the Air Boss, Mini-Boss, Catapult and Arresting Gear Officers, Hangar Deck Officer and the Handler also frequented the dirty shirt wardroom. Ackerman, in his green zoom bag and white LSO float coat, had made it that morning with three minutes to spare before the mandatory 0800 closing time for the breakfast line. Brad slid a food tray down a set of metal guide rails past a plastic dispenser that housed various pieces of silverware. He grabbed two forks, one spoon, and a butter knife then pitched them onto his green tray making sure the mess crew heard the intentionally elevated racket. When one of the mess cooks glanced up in Ackerman's direction Teen Angel politely requested three eggs sunny side up, with two pancakes and one sausage link on the side.

"You got it Lieutenant," responded the cook who was decked out in a somewhat soiled apron that was wrapped loosely around his body. "But its not sausage today sir. We call it *minute steak* cause it only takes about sixty seconds to prepare once you slap it on the grill." Brad nodded his head in an approving manner then wiped some grease residue off of his palm and onto the right side of his float coat. The grease scum had transferred onto Teen Angel's hand from one of the metal guide rails.

This young Hispanic chef also wore a white cap as part of his mess cook attire, similar to those that adorn the heads of donut makers at *Krispy Kreme* shops all across America. That hat was plopped down onto the kid's bald scalp at a rather sharp angle. It was definitely askew, sort of like how LA gang bangers wear their ball caps, at an odd angle on their heads as if trying to bring additional attention to themselves from a disapproving public. The white bonnet was constructed of thick paper and it displayed the sailor's last name 'Gonzales' scribbled on the side with a black grease pencil. The grease pencil was probably borrowed from one of his buddies who worked on the flight deck. The light blue apron, wrapped insecurely around the kid's waist, featured a large CVN-65 emblem sewn into the front of all cotton material. Ackerman observed that the *Enterprise* insignia was blemished by an over-abundance of food stains. Most likely a year or more old, the ship's laundry had apparently been unable to completely wash out all the food discolorations. Teen Angel grabbed a stack of napkins and continued making small talk as the nineteen-year old cracked three jumbo eggs onto a large, rectangular griddle.

"Say Gonzales, how about throwing down a few of those mushrooms onto the griddle for me," said Teen Angel. Ackerman shifted his weight, scratched at the right side of his nose then glanced into the wardroom to see if he recognized anybody inside.

"No problemo sir, but you do realize that mushrooms have absolutely no nutritional value whatsoever," advised the kid cook. Gonzales squirted a generous amount of liquid butter onto the scorching grill then pitched several of the over-sized mushrooms into sizzling liquid. Teen Angel allowed the dietary comments to penetrate into his left ear then depart out of the right.

Brad spotted Daffy Drucker near the milk dispenser pouring out a tall glass of fresh chocolate milk into a paper cup. He also saw that Daffy had about ten saltine crackers, generously covered in peanut butter and strawberry jam, laid out on his food tray. Milk in hand Daffy took a seat in the wardroom. Ackerman turned his attention back to the mess cook just as the teenager scooped out some viscous hotcake mixture and dripped it down every so slowly from his plastic ladle. Two circles of thick batter gradually spread out next to the now sizzling cackle fruit. On the grill, one of the yolks had busted open so the young mess cook scraped that egg into a scupper drain and quickly replaced it on the searing surface with an intact yolk. In a flash, Teen Angel was seated at a long table, next to Lieutenant Commander Drucker, sharing breakfast and reminiscing conversation with six fellow LSO's from CAG-2. As the seven men ate and discussed a variety of topics from women to politics to religion and back to women again, Catapults 1 and 2 were being fired in rapid succession to test them for the Carrier Qualifications that were set to begin in less than two hours. The muffled noises and sharp vibrations of the catapult's shuttle mechanism were evident to everyone seated in the dirty shirt wardroom.

After about ten minutes of discussion, one of the Tomcat LSO's excused himself from the table. He was going to fetch a small box of *Frosted Flakes*, to enjoy later as an in-between-meal snack.

"Can I bring anybody back something while I am up," said the F-14 pilot. This courteous gesture was standard behavior in the wardroom among officers onboard any Navy vessel.

"Yeah, can you bring me some chocolate milk," answered Daffy. He had already consumed three full glasses and apparently needed a fourth to make it to lunchtime.

"No sweat Daffy." The fighter pilot walked away towards the frigid, silver-colored milk machine. A wicker basket filled with small boxes of breakfast cereal was next to the milk dispenser. The conversation was about to wind down at the table.

"Trust me on this one subject," said Ackerman as Cat One's shuttle fired forcefully then slammed two seconds later into a water brake at the bow of the ship. "This 'minute steak' is of the same superior quality as the low-grade shoe leather on a *Thom McAn* loafer." The other Landing Signal Officers laughed out loud at Brad's statement, as did a Filipino steward who was brushing crumbs off of a nearby table in the dirty shirt wardroom. Teen Angel continued to consume the mystery meat anyway. He used an overly exaggerated, open-mouth chewing style to further accentuate the disdain he was feeling for the leathery-substance that was invading his mouth and insulting his taste buds.

Fifty-five minutes later, Lieutenant Brad Ackerman pushed through a water-tight door near the fantail on the port side of the ship. The bulky hatch was next to the LSO Shack, directly underneath the LSO platform. Brad lowered his head, stepped over a 'knee knocker' then emerged out onto a narrow catwalk on the port side. After sealing the watertight door behind him Teen Angel eased past the safety net and climbed up a ladder to gain access to CVN-65's flight deck and it's very familiar LSO platform area. As he moved up the ladder he could hear the seawater bristling below and smell the distinctive salt spray filling the air. As Lieutenant Ackerman made his triumphant return to the flight deck of USS *Enterprise*, after a three year hiatus from *Big E*, the characteristic whine of C-2 Greyhound propeller noise could be heard emanating from close by. The turbo-prop aircraft was stationed overhead in the 'low holding' position about 1,000 feet above the ship. Walking leisurely, close to the protective steel scupper that guards the edge of the flight deck, Brad intuitively looked up into a light gray, overcast sky as the Greyhound continued its left-hand orbit around the boat. The COD crew must be anxious to get aboard, thought Brad as he snuck a peek at his wristwatch. They were at least 45 minutes early for their scheduled *Charlie Time*. Brad stole a fleeting glance at the LSO platform then made eye contact with a few enlisted men who were busy lathering some heavy-duty grease onto the port side turnbuckle of *Big E's* number one arresting cable. One man held a dirty-looking bucket while the other used an over-sized, barbeque brush to dig out a healthy dose of the gooey grease from that pail. He then slathered and spread the lubricating substance liberally all over the metal fitting at the end of the cumbersome arresting wire, otherwise known as a 'cross-deck pendant' in the vernacular of Naval Carrier Aviation.

Standing flatfooted on the non-skid surface of the flight deck, adjacent to the platform, Teen Angel picked up the LSO pickle switch from a large console positioned at the very front of this vital workstation. The grayish console contained knobs, phones, speakers, wind gauges, deck angle indicators, closed-circuit TV monitors and a variety of other useful LSO gadgets. Brad clutched the pickle switch mechanism firmly in his right hand and maneuvered its long, snake-like electric cable with his flight boots. The 'pickle' felt good and holding it immediately gave Brad a relaxing sense of déjà vu. While he was on active duty in the fleet, and when he wasn't flying a mission off the carrier, Teen Angel had spent thousands of hours on the LSO platform as the 'controlling' or 'back-up' Landing Signal Officer. He also would routinely stand in the background as an interested observer when not actually serving as a duty LSO. Ackerman pressed a few buttons on the pickle switch to test the 'wave off' and 'cut lights' on the Fresnel lens. Commonly referred to in Naval Aviation jargon as the 'meatball' this optical landing aid system rested several hundred feet behind the LSO platform on the port side of the aircraft carrier. The Fresnel lens, an odd-looking array of lights and lenses, was the apparatus used by Naval Aviators to maintain proper glide slope when landing on the ship both day and night. At that moment a red telephone buzzed twice on the LSO console. It was Captain Buford Angus' direct line to his Landing Signal Officers. Ackerman, still grasping the pickle switch, picked up the phone receiver to answer the Captain's call.

"Paddles here, what can I do for you skipper?" said Teen Angel in his authoritative, yet soothing LSO voice. Those simple words resonated throughout Ackerman's body immediately as he spoke them. As a proud fleet LSO, Teen Angel was privileged to be included among a super-elite group of men. This small cadre of cream-of-the-crop Naval Aviators, this LSO club in the Navy, was more exclusive than being included among the cluster of doctors who specialized in neurosurgery. Brad felt intense pride at that moment as he chatted with Captain Angus from the LSO platform of USS *Enterprise*. Lieutenant Ackerman stood confident and alone on the LSO stage with the red phone in his left hand. Teen Angel dropped the pickle back into its metal holder as he pressed the telephone receiver tightly up against his left ear. He then inserted an index finger into his right ear canal for improved hearing. Brad turned and stared up at the navigation bridge in the middle of the ship, as if he could actually see "Long Horn" Angus talking to him from his padded, Captain's chair. 'Paddles' of course, was the colloquial name given to all Landing Signal Officers. The nickname had been used ever since LSO's had utilized two oversized, ping pong-looking paddles to wave airplanes back aboard the carrier in the early days of Naval Aviation. Buford was apparently distracted up on the bridge, because he wasn't responding to Teen Angel on his hotline phone system.

"Heel to port," hollered the Air Boss over the 1MC loudspeaker system from way up in his primary flight control tower. The ship's control tower sat above "vulture's row" on the third story of the island, or superstructure of the aircraft carrier. As soon as the words of *Big E's* Air Boss came through the speaker, the massive ship abruptly swayed into a right turn. This sharp, tumultuous motion brought the port side of the ship up about 5 degrees or so above the horizon. Teen Angel, still holding the red phone and waiting for the Captain to speak to him, unconsciously dug the heels of his flight boots in against the raised port side of the flat top boat. Buford Angus was now ready to speak to Ackerman way down on the LSO platform.

"Paddles, can you trap this COD right now?" asked Captain Angus after that ten-second delay. "She's got an electrical problem with one of her generators and I want her onboard now so we can fix it." Buford had already ordered the helmsman to turn his steering wheel starboard in a 'right standard rudder' configuration. The final course of the enormous warship would be 290-degrees. That heading would put the relative wind precisely down the center of the ship's angled flight deck, upon which all CAG-2 aircraft would make their trap landings.

"No sweat Captain, tell the Greyhound girl to come on down and we'll catch her," answered Teen Angel. As Ackerman placed the red phone back down into its receptacle on the LSO console, he automatically searched for a black box appliance that sat at the rear of the ship on the left side. This simple, black box contraption, known as the 'foul deck' indicator, had two colored lights in it. When lit up, its red light indicated that the flight deck was 'foul' and thus not ready to bring aircraft aboard for a landing. Its green light meant the flight deck was 'clear' and ready to accept landings. Ackerman saw that the red light was brightly illuminated as he picked up the LSO control phone to conduct a radio check with the Air Boss in the flight control tower. He likewise snatched up the pickle switch from the console with his right hand. Because the deck was foul, Teen Angel held the pickle switch up over his head, to alert the Air Boss that the LSO acknowledged a foul deck situation. Just as soon as the green light illuminated in that black box, Ackerman would lower the pickle switch to his right side to indicate that he recognized the clear deck condition.

"Tower, paddles, radio check," said Teen Angel into the LSO phone. The wind bristled across the telephone receiver as Brad spoke. His dark blonde hair furled.

"Paddles, tower, loud and clear. How me?" replied the Air Boss.

"Got you loud and clear Boss. I am ready to wave this guy aboard sir." Ackerman was still the only Landing Signal Officer on the platform, mainly because CQ wasn't even scheduled to begin for another forty-one minutes. Teen Angel gripped the LSO phone in between his thighs as he put on his Naval Aviator sunglasses. He was looking oh so cool that morning and he knew it.

With only another 10 degrees to go in its starboard turn, the ship was almost on its intended 290-degree heading. She was sailing in relatively calm Southern California seas, directly in the heart of the Whiskey-291 Warning Area. As the aircraft carrier began to ease out of its turn, Lieutenant Ackerman could sense a vigorous wind pushing at his back. He crouched slightly to protect his body against the dynamic wind pressure. Feeling a tremendous sense of individual pride, Brad strolled confidently out onto the flight deck and away from the LSO platform. Teen Angel's personal technique as a fleet Landing Signal Officer was to actually position his body on the flight deck, several feet away from the LSO platform area. From this vantage point Ackerman would take control of aircraft making their touch-and-go or arrested landings on the carrier. It was daring to say the least, to any dilettantes that might be observing the CQ activity from vulture's row or elsewhere on the warship.

"Make a ready deck. Stand by to land aircraft," barked out the Air Boss over the 1MC. His voice was deep in pitch and imposing in tenor. Men wearing a variety of different colored float coats scurried with a little quicker gate as they left the landing area and made it across the yellow 'foul line' of the flight deck. As the ship finally steadied on its 290-degree heading Buford Angus increased the speed of the aircraft carrier to 15 knots. This meant the relative wind down the angle deck was a healthy 23 knots. Teen Angel pressed the LSO phone tighter into his left ear and toyed with the still elevated pickle switch in his right hand as if he was somewhat anxious. He took another step out onto the flight deck then gazed off in the distance behind *Big E's* fantail. Because of its semi-emergency situation, Teen Angel instinctively knew the C-2 would most likely be making a long, lazy straight-in approach to landing. Ackerman raised the pickle an inch higher above his head as he continued to focus his brown eyes behind the ship at about six to eight miles. In his peripheral vision Brad spotted a shapely looking female sailor as she walked from the Jet Blast Deflector of catapult #4 then positioned herself behind and well to the right of Ackerman. The twenty-year old Japanese-American girl, wearing clean dungarees and a dirty blue float coat, stood on the right side of the LSO platform. She was perched just above the safety net that rested several feet below. Her tiny back and tight rear end were pressed up against the LSO platform's wind deflector. This position would protect her diminutive 5-foot frame against the onslaught of the wind stream howling across the flight deck. In the grand choreography of carrier flight operations, this woman was known as the 'hook spotter' and she immediately began to spout off about the condition of the flight deck's landing area.

"Foul deck, foul deck, foul deck," said the young woman over and over again in a calm yet assertive manner. Her voice had a slightly southern, slightly Japanese accent as its undertone and it was immediately attractive to Ackerman's ears. Teen Angel made ephemeral eye contact with the hook spotter and was instantly captivated by her breathtaking beauty; even if she was wearing a sailor outfit. He thought to himself she must be 'the queen of the hop' on this boat. The hook spotter's mascara-laden lashes blinked rapidly as her black eyes were glued to the foul deck indicator near the end of the ship, its red light flashing continuously. As the hook spotter, her job was to continue this verbal harangue until the green light replaced the red in the black box mechanism. When the flight deck finally became clear, her task was to spot the next aircraft getting ready to land on the ship and report whether it's tail hook was in the up or down position. Rocket science it was not. Calculus training was not a job requirement, even though the venue for her meager profession was in the heart of the most dangerous workplace on earth, the deck of an aircraft carrier during flight operations at sea.

Leveling its wings from a shallow left hand angle of bank, the fat-looking C-2 turboprop aircraft lined up for a straight in approach to the *Big E*. The Greyhound, flying at 102 knots indicated airspeed, was approximately five miles behind the ship's stern when Teen Angel finally saw it. Flying at 600 feet over the water, the COD passed slightly to the left of USS *Truett* (FF-1095), a Knox Class fast frigate that was serving as plane guard for *Enterprise*. At 0922, none of the SH-3 helicopters were airborne and hovering in starboard delta yet; they were still being refueled over in the 'six pack' area of the ship, just below the Air Boss up in pri-fly. Lieutenant Ackerman could smell the fuel's pungent aroma being wafted about by 23 knots of wind, as several purple-shirted "grapes" pumped the volatile fluid into both SH-3's simultaneously. Even as he began to settle into his "LSO zone" Teen Angel could still vividly hear the hook spotter's continuous 'foul deck' diatribe and distinctive voice tone. On this first attempt to land aboard the carrier by the gun-shy C-2 pilot, she never descended below 500 feet. She just stayed level at that altitude and made a clearing pass over the flight deck. Teen Angel watched in utter disbelief as the Greyhound flew over the top of his position with her tail hook in the up position. The red phone on the LSO console buzzed three times before Ackerman could walk back over and pick it up to answer Captain Angus. The hook spotter couldn't hear what Buford Angus was saying from the navigation bridge, but she had a fairly good idea when she heard Lieutenant Ackerman's clever response.

"Maybe we'll have to break out a 12 gauge shotgun and shoot her out of the sky like a Mallard duck skipper," joked Teen Angel. Brad dropped the red phone back into its console receptacle and readied himself for her next try.

"Foul deck, foul deck, foul deck," yapped the hook spotter. Three minutes later, the female C-2 pilot was once again making a stab at landing on the ship. She was level at 600 feet approaching at 4 miles as a green light illuminated inside the foul deck indicator. Peering through a pair of cheap binoculars, the hook spotter informed Brad he had a 'clear deck' and that she saw a tail hook in the down position on a Greyhound aircraft. Teen Angel lowered the pickle switch in his right hand, to acknowledge a 'clear deck' to the Air Boss then concentrated even harder on the approaching COD. Ackerman kicked away the black electric cord on his pickle then once again took several steps out into the landing area, further away from the LSO platform than the last time. The hook spotter was somewhat impressed by Brad's extremely fearless LSO style. She smiled modestly as she watched him work. A slight shiver of desire rose up her spine as she inched a few steps toward Ackerman. The C-2 scooted past the 3-mile point, still at 600 feet and closing fast.

"FOUL DECK, FOUL DECK, FOUL DECK," screamed the hook spotter in rapid succession, and with many more decibels than before. Her raised voice and quickness of those repeated lines indicated the nearness of the next plane in the groove. For some unknown reason the red light was again flashing inside the black box, foul deck indicator. Teen Angel was obviously annoyed as he lifted the pickle switch above his head once more. 'What the heck can be fouling the flight deck now' he wondered. Brad's eyes never left the C-2 Greyhound. Little did he know it was just the Air Boss showing off up in the tower. He was playing with the LSO to impress his newly arrived Mini-Boss, an S-3 NFO, and to demonstrate the power he possessed as the demigod of flight operations. After several seconds, the Air Boss pressed a green button near his right knee to indicate a clear deck to Ackerman. The COD was inside of 2 miles, still flying at 600 feet, and rapidly approaching the ramp. Teen Angel could plainly make out the COD's external airspeed indexer lights as he lowered the pickle to his right side. The steady, green circle of light meant the C-2 was flying in an "on-speed" condition, thus providing the perfect angle-of-attack and aircraft attitude to make an arrested landing in the Greyhound. Thirty seconds later, the C-2 had descended to 400 feet above the surface of the ocean, at three quarters of a mile from the ass end of the aircraft carrier. The airplane was descending at 710 feet per minute, too much rate of descent for that particular approach airspeed. But at least she was descending.

"604 Greyhound ball 5.5," reported the C-2 pilot-in-command to the controlling LSO on button #3. It was indeed a female pilot's voice. This routine statement gave the side number of the plane and its current fuel state to everybody listening up on the tower frequency. The 'Greyhound ball' comment meant that the C-2 pilot was following the amber-colored, glide slope meatball on the Fresnel lens.

"Roger ball Greyhound, I've got 22 knots right down the angle deck," responded Lieutenant Ackerman. Brad had made one last check of the wind speed indicator on the LSO console before giving out that information to the pilot. Teen Angel was completely in his LSO zone, focused on controlling the C-2 until it made a successful arrested landing on the ship, or bolted and skipped over the wires altogether.

"Tower 201," said an F-14 pilot leading a flight of four fighter aircraft. The Tomcat interceptors were approaching from the East at ten miles. These eager beaver *Bounty Hunters* from VF-2, flying out of NAS Miramar, were the first CAG-2 jets to arrive at the ship for their CQ evolution. The "turkeys" were zipping along at 450 knots and 8,000 feet above the surface of the water. The *Hunter* skipper was lead pilot for this division of jets.

"On the ball," pronounced Teen Angel with a slight growl in his voice. This LSO phrase was meant to inform anybody up on button #3, the tower frequency, that a pilot was 'in the groove' or close to the ship, and flying the meatball during the final stages of a shipboard landing. Absolute silence was required in this phase of carrier flight operations. Only the Landing Signal Officer could speak, everybody else was to shut up and listen for the next break in the action. The C-2 was now in the middle position of its approach, at about ½ mile from touchdown. The lethargic Greyhound's external airspeed indexer was now showing a red circle of light, meaning its airspeed was too slow by a few precious knots. The aircraft was likewise flying below the proper glide slope and Brad sensed it immediately. Without hesitation, Teen Angel pressed the transmit button on his LSO telephone to speak to the Greyhound girl.

"A little power, you're low and slow," advised Ackerman in his soothing yet commanding voice. Instantly the female COD pilot shoved both of her throttles forward about a handful. She left the power levers in that position for approximately three seconds then pulled them back, to far back yet again. The red light on the C-2's airspeed indexer transitioned down to an amber color as the Greyhound aircraft temporarily picked up about four knots of airspeed due to the power increase. In the cockpit, the C-2 pilot watched as the meatball on the Fresnel lens dipped about two cells below the optimal center point location then rose up when the power and airspeed increase began to momentarily take effect. But as the Greyhound girl approached the ramp area of USS *Enterprise*, she transitioned through the 'burble' without making any significant increase in her throttle settings. This burble is a disturbed portion of airflow that was created due to the odd shape of *Big E's* extra-large superstructure. It had the notorious effect of pulling all aircraft down as they attempted to land on the warship, especially as they got to the 'in close' point. Suddenly, the C-2's wings tilted sharply to the left and it sank quickly toward the number one wire as it crossed over the end of the ship. The COD was now flying over the steel flight deck but it was coming down much to rapidly. And its nose was pointed to the left of the landing area's centerline. The C-2's chubby gray nose was pointed directly at Lieutenant Ackerman. The tilted posture of the Greyhound's nosecone caused the hook spotter to inch away from the flight deck and over toward the LSO safety net. 'I may have to jump in' she thought briefly. Her right work boot was suspended over the edge of the LSO platform, directly above the safety net. Swelling with apprehension, the young woman's gorgeous black eyes were as large as saucers. Her heart pounded away with an increased tempo as she dropped a pair of binoculars to the deck of the LSO platform.

"POWER. POWER. RIGHT FOR LINEUP," commanded Teen Angel. Lieutenant Ackerman's own initial anxiety had long since subsided. He was totally focused on getting this airplane aboard the carrier in a safe, expeditious manner. Inside of her cockpit, the COD pilot complied right away with the LSO's orders by adding two handfuls of power and moving her control yoke hard right. Instantaneously the C-2 aircraft stopped its rapid rate of descent and its nose straightened out to align the fuselage parallel with, but to the left of centerline. The left wing of the C-2 swooshed past Teen Angel with only eleven feet of separation between its red wingtip light and Ackerman's head. Brad could feel the wind shift and sensed the deafening propeller noise as the Greyhound flew on by. Lieutenant Ackerman was indeed a fearless LSO. Teen Angel watched as the Greyhound's tail hook hopped over the first cross-deck pendant then snatched the second. It was a 'no-grade' two wire for the female COD pilot. She had landed six and a half feet left of centerline. The landing resembled an overweight, St. Bernard dog jumping into the back of a pickup truck thought Ackerman. Teen Angel made his way back over to the LSO platform and placed the black phone in between his legs. Brad pulled a green LSO logbook out from a leg pocket on the left side of his zoom bag. He immediately began scribbling down several letters on the first page with a #2 pencil. The letters were pretty much like LSO shorthand, each symbol representing something that the aircraft did or did not do on its approach to the ship. In the margins he wrote: *This pass was similar to 'Mister Toad's Wild Ride' at Disneyland!* Teen Angel would debrief the Greyhound girl on her wild arrested landing later that day in the squadron's ready room. Maybe he would suggest that her call sign be changed to Mrs. Toad!

Brad turned again to watch the Greyhound just as the plane was being hauled back. Using a long metal tool, an enlisted man pried the arresting cable out from the point of the C-2's tail hook. Yellow-shirted 'flight directors' then directed the COD into its parking spot in the 'six pack' area of the boat. The Greyhound taxied into a spot vacated by one of the SH-3 helicopters that had completed it's refueling and was being towed by a GSE tractor up to the bow for liftoff. Once securely connected to the flight deck pad eyes with heavy-duty chains the COD shut down both engines. The annoying propeller commotion ceased just as the Greyhound's rear cargo hatch opened. Filled with immense satisfaction, Teen Angel winked at the cute hook spotter then put the LSO phone back into his left ear just in time to hear the Mini-Boss speaking on the tower frequency. This former VS-37 Commanding Officer and NFO, had a voice that was rather squeaky when compared to the Air Boss who had an A-7 pedigree as his legacy.

"201 your signal is *Dump Charlie*," chirped out the Mini-Boss. Apparently Captain Buford Angus had instructed the flight control tower to begin CQ early since his boat was already sailing into the wind.

"Roger that Boss," answered the Tomcat's flight leader. This division of F-14's was already orbiting overhead the ship at 2,000 feet in low holding. "We'll be in the break in 60 seconds sir." As the fighters maneuvered down and behind *Enterprise*, all four jets began to dump fuel to reduce their landing weights to 52,000 pounds.

While the F-14's sped toward the initial position for their carrier break, Daffy Drucker appeared on the LSO platform, rising up from the port catwalk. He gave Teen Angel a passing nod of approval then picked up his LSO equipment from the console. Five more CAG-2 Landing Signal Officers likewise made their way to the platform. All five stood in the background, cozy and near the hook spotter. From that venue they would observe the CQ action, laugh and scratch, and patiently wait their turn to be controlling LSO. One of the officers, the A-6 LSO from VA-145, offered to be the scribe and handle the logbook. Daffy gratefully handed him the official CAG-2 LSO log.

"Angel, why don't you go ahead and wave these first four 'turkeys' and I'll back you up. The *Hunter* LSO's are still on that COD," advised Drucker. Ackerman shook his head in an affirmative fashion then patted Drucker vigorously on the shoulder. Once again Teen Angel ventured out onto the flight deck to wave shipboard landings just as the hot young hook spotter resumed her 'foul deck' invective. In less than a minute four Tomcats streaked into the carrier break at 550 knots, 600 feet overhead the ship. The lead fighter, flown by VF-2's commanding officer, executed his carrier break at the bow of *Enterprise*. It was a magnificent, 'air show quality' maneuver. Both Teen Angel and Daffy noticed that the fourth Tomcat was still dumping fuel out of the dump mast between his vertical fins at the tail end of the jet. He apparently needed more time to reduce his aircraft weight to maximum carrier landing specifications. The JP-5 fuel streaming out of the turkey's dump mast quickly vaporized and dissipated as it hit the atmosphere. Five miles ahead of the ship the number four man in the fighter formation turned the dump switch to its off position then executed his own carrier break to follow his three playmates in the CQ pattern.

"201 Tomcat ball, 6.8," called out the first F-14 on tower frequency. The tactical jet was flying at 420 feet over the water, just outside of ¾ of a mile from the ship's stern. It's external airspeed indexer showed a steady, amber circle of light. The tactical jet was perfectly on speed and smack dab on optimal glide slope to start its approach.

"Roger ball Tomcat, 23 knots," responded Lieutenant Ackerman. Both Daffy and Teen Angel simultaneously lowered their pickle switches in response to a clear deck call from the hook spotter. As the controlling LSO on this pass, Teen Angel didn't need to say another word to this CQ pilot. The *Hunter* skipper's approach and arrested landing were pretty much flawless. He even correctly anticipated the extra burst of power his Tomcat would need to make it successfully through *Enterprise's* burble without too much of a deviation in the jet's airspeed and glide slope. Ackerman noticed that the huge *flying tennis court*, as he referred to it, had its turkey feathers moving and gyrating all the way down to the flight deck. The nose tire of the Tomcat touched down precisely on the white centerline in CVN-65's landing area, with just a touch of DLC (Direct Lift Control) as he snagged an OK three wire in the spaghetti. As he engaged the #3 arresting cable with his tail hook, the VF-2 commanding officer pushed his throttles to the maximum rate of thrust position. The jet engine sound was earsplitting. The F-14 skipper kept his throttles at MRT until certain his aircraft was successfully trapped onboard the carrier. Ackerman and Drucker turned to momentarily watch the Tomcat's trap then abruptly shifted their bodies back toward the fantail. The F-14's noise and jet blast were devastatingly powerful, and the pair of Landing Signal Officers braced themselves for its arrival at their position on the LSO platform. As if on cue in a choreography routine, the next 'turkey' pilot was about to complete a thirty-degree angle-of-bank left turn to begin his first landing approach to the ship. He was likewise on speed and on glide slope out of the approach turn.

In less than two minutes all four Tomcats had trapped and were being taxied to the bow catapults for their cat shots back into the CQ pattern. While Teen Angel was giving his pass comments and landing grades to the logbook scribe, he spotted four Corsairs circling above the ship at 3,000 feet. Ackerman also recognized Cookie, Rocky and several other men who were moving hastily toward the LSO platform down in the portside catwalk.

"River 410, Climax Tower, Signal Charlie," said the Air Boss on button #3.

"Four One Zero Charlie," replied Duke O'Grady in the lead Corsair. The *River Rattler* A-7 Corsairs would be the next CAG-2 jets to enter CVN-65's CQ pattern. They would mix in nicely with the turkeys. Knowing he would be greeting Rocky and Cookie, Ackerman offered his LSO telephone and pickle switch to the logbook writer. The A-6 LSO eagerly accepted the items, flipped Teen Angel his logbook then positioned himself to serve as backup Landing Signal Officer to Daffy Drucker. Up on the bow, a Tomcat suddenly went into 'zone five' afterburner on cat one. The JBD deflected the F-14's exceptionally hot exhaust gases upward at a sixty-degree angle, safely away from personnel and equipment on the flight deck. The bright orange, blast flames shooting forcefully out of the twin exhaust stacks of the fighter, produced an incredible amount of uproar and additional light, even though it was daytime. Directly behind that JBD the pilot of the next F-14 in line for a cat shot was angrily trying to get a weight board holder to lower his weight figures for launch. He soon lost his patience with the young kid holding the weight board.

"Boss, 204 is at 50,000 pounds," advised his RIO from the rear seat of the Tomcat's cockpit.

"204 will get a 50,000 pound shot," said the Mini Boss in a reassuring voice. Without much further delay, the nineteen year-old fiddled with the scroll device to lower the numbers on his weight board from 52,000 to 50,000. The Tomcat pilot finally gave him a thumb's up signal to acknowledge the corrected launch weight. The enlisted man enthusiastically returned that thumb's up signal then displayed the weight board numbers to his catapult officer. Those gross weight calculations would be entered into the steam catapult mechanism for the next F-14 cat shot. Less than five seconds later catapult #1 fired, aggressively slinging the first Tomcat back into the air for another trap landing. The entire boat shook due to the force of the catapult's rapidly moving shuttle mechanism slamming into the water break at the bow.

Fresh off the COD, Cookie and Rocky enthusiastically shook hands with Teen Angel just before they exchanged semi-flirtatious pleasantries with the female hook spotter. Both tried not to look too overly interested in front of the other officers, but they couldn't help themselves.

"Oh my, she is yummy looking," Cookie whispered into Teen Angel's ear as he continued to greet him. The stunning hook spotter just rolled her black eyes at the sly but overt behavior being displayed by both Rocky and Cookie. She still had a critical job to perform for the next four hours and didn't need male distractions clouding her mind. Standing in the back of the LSO platform as observers, it didn't take long for Cookie and Rocky to regale Teen Angel with their Miramar O' Club stories from the previous evening. In a boasting fashion, and in between the immense racket generated by F-14 and A-7 traps and cat shots, Cookie proudly gave Brad his personal impression on the members of the *Hair Team*, Candace and Olivia. As it turns out, they were actually 36 year-old twin sisters who had legally immigrated to the USA from Perth, Australia. They had arrived in California about 14 years ago to marry the two USMC AV-8 aviators they had met on the beach in Perth. One of the Harrier pilots, Olivia's hubby, had died two years into their marriage of extremely suspicious circumstances. Some of the guy's close friends and family members actually suspected thallium sulfate poisoning, but it was never proved because his body was cremated before an autopsy could be performed that could successfully detect the exceptionally lethal substance. The other woman, Candace, had divorced her Marine Corps aviator husband three years after their wedding, but not before draining him of over half his assets during the divorce proceedings. The girl's maiden name was Goolagong and they had purchased their hairstyling shop (*The Hair Team*) with proceeds from a life insurance policy and from Candace's community property settlement. Despite several Miramar pilots telling them about these suspicious sisters, Cookie and Rocky went home with the twins. They had willingly taken part in a foursome inside of a large Jacuzzi that continued on a billiard table. The various handguns and long rifles hanging on the walls of the billiard room, combined with the mounted, taxidermy-processed heads of numerous wild animals, didn't seem to bother Rocky and Cookie last night. Little did Cookie realize at the time, but he may have actually escaped a potentially perilous predicament. The woman Cookie was with, Olivia Goolagong, was like a Black Widow spider. She was cleverly lurking within the shadows, waiting until it was time to pounce upon her next helpless prey then viciously inject a dose of deadly, immobilizing secretions into the flesh of that intended victim. Teen Angel was abruptly relieved that he had left the O' Club alone the previous evening.

Four days later, every pilot in Air Wing Two was carrier qualified in both day and night shipboard landings. CAG-2 was now fully ready for its six-month, around-the-world deployment onboard USS *Enterprise*. The last aviator to complete CQ was Lieutenant Brad Ackerman, and Daffy Drucker had stayed behind to finish up Teen Angel's final night trap, an OK 3 wire. After that qualifying night trap the flight directors taxied Brad's jet up close to the island for some refueling prior to a cat shot back to the beach. Teen Angel made certain that his ejection seat remained armed as he sat in the 'six pack' area of the flight deck. He did not lower the 'head knocker' of his ESCAPAC ejection seat. Sitting alone on the flight deck getting a few thousand pounds of fuel from the *grapes*, Teen Angel pulled out a business card from *The Hair Team*. He quickly began to chuckle. He was remembering Rocky's comment about the $100 price tag of a man's haircut that the girls charged in their swanky coiffure shop.

"It was worth the high price Teen Angel, because during the haircut they would have one girl cutting and one girl blowing!" Ackerman stuffed the card back into his flight suit pocket then looked up toward pri-fly just in time to see the Air Boss eating ice cream from a paper cup. Even though it was dark and the interior of the tower was lit up with red lights, Brad could see the action clearly from his parked Corsair. He surmised that the Air Boss was really enjoying his fresh ice cream treat so he decided to tease him just a little.

"Boss 401," said Teen Angel. The response from pri-fly was delayed for some reason.

"Go ahead 401." The Air Boss, Captain Carmine "Nick" Lincoln, had to wait until he swallowed his last gulp of the cold treat before answering Ackerman.

"How's that auto-dog working out for you?" Auto-dog was the nickname all Navy men had given to ice cream that is dispensed onboard ship, because the frozen substance resembled dog crap spiraling down and out of the metal ice cream dispenser. Less than one minute after this teasing comment to the Air Boss all the flight directors around Brad's jet informed him that his aircraft was securely chained down. Next they gave him a secure engine signal. Ackerman vigorously shook his head 'NO' and gave them the catapult signal with his hands. But it was to no avail.

"401 tower, you've got a PC-1 hydraulic leak. You'll have to spend the night onboard so we can fix it. Come see me in the dirty shirt wardroom in an hour, and we'll share some auto-dog," said the Air Boss with a measure of glee in his voice. He was of course lying about the hydraulic leak.

"Roger that Boss, I'll see you in an hour sir." Brad knew he had been had, but he really didn't seem to care. The Air Boss would win this round. But at 0700 the next morning Nick Lincoln launched Teen Angel and his A-7 Corsair off the ship for a short flight to the beach. As Teen Angel raised his landing gear, two seconds after that cat shot, he marveled at how the ocean water glistened in the morning sunlight.

CHAPTER 30

▼

A STUDENT OF THE
GAME

CAG-2 Carrier Qualifications officially ended on April 5, 1992, one full day earlier than anticipated by Air Wing LSO's and Ops planners. Basically the entire training evolution progressed smoother than the sweep motion of a second hand on a *Rolex* timepiece. At 0742 Teen Angel parked the Corsair he had flown off of *Enterprise* earlier that morning, over on the west side of Naval Air Station North Island's transient aircraft line. Cookie Cline was scheduled to fly the jet home to New Orleans later in the day after he made it off the ship in a C-2 COD. Brad left all of his personal flight gear in the A-7's small baggage compartment, where the Vulcan 20mm canon was normally housed, so Cookie could transport the equipment back to the squadron in southeast Louisiana. After securing the baggage panel's Zeus fittings with a cowling tool, Ackerman buttoned up the rest of the Corsair for security purposes. He then hitched a ride with a teenaged T-Line airman down to the lot where his beloved cherry red Porsche, the one he kept in California, was parked. Teen Angel had pre-positioned the vehicle there seven days earlier, before he rode a C-9 airlift out to NAS New Orleans.

Teen Angel casually tossed his green parachute bag, filled with dirty clothes, into the small rear seating area of the sports car then anxiously jumped into the plush leather seat and fired that mother up. Because he was pretty much exhausted from the carrier qualifications, Brad drove the vintage 911S at a leisurely pace all the way back to his modest home in the hills of beautiful Burbank, California. He nonchalantly listened to three separate Garth Brooks CD's, from San Diego until he reached his driveway. But Brad didn't stay home for very long, nor did he have sufficient time to accomplish very much on the domestic front. He only had enough time to wash a load of mixed dirty laundry from his parachute bag, in cold water of course, then repack it and get prepared to hit the road once again. The next morning he hopped on a United Airlines McDonnell Douglas DC-10 commercial flight out of LAX and flew nonstop to Chicago O'Hare Airport. Ackerman had been contracted for two weeks worth of flying, working for Warner Brothers Studios on a film project called *The Fugitive*, a big screen remake of the classic television series from the mid-1960's. The exorbitant initial membership fees and monthly dues Brad shelled out to the Screen Actors Guild (SAG) and Motion Picture Pilots Association (MPPA) were well worth the expense because both unions kept him routinely employed at a hefty salary in the film industry. Union membership also allowed him to easily manipulate his stunt pilot work schedule in Hollywood to accommodate his vigorous participation in the Naval Reserves. For Teen Angel, it was a win-win situation and he realized how blessed he was to be such an integral part of these two top-notch professions.

The shooting dates in "the windy city" and Ackerman's personal "call times" were between April 7-17 for the particular scenes in the motion picture that included airborne operations and aerial cinematography. Brad's actual flying responsibilities for the next two weeks didn't involve any aerial stunt performances on the production. His job was to perform the duties of helicopter safety observer during airborne scenes filmed in the very busy, extremely congested locations in downtown Chicago and in a few of the surrounding rural venues. Brad would spend the bulk of his time clearing the Warner Brothers' Hughes 500 helicopter of any conflicting traffic or high-rise obstacles, and chit chatting with Chicago Approach controllers while the rotary-wing pilot maneuvered the aircraft for scenes. But being a "Type A" personality, Teen Angel wasn't at all content to merely fulfill this meager role on the film project; as always he yearned for more. That being the case after the first full day of shooting, Ackerman was able to weasel out one additional task from Michael Chapman, the production team's Academy Award winning cinematographer. After some deferential cajoling while sharing a bottle of *Montrachet* 1980 Chardonnay, a medium-rare Filet Mignon and a pile of steamed asparagus at *The Palm* steakhouse in Chicago, Chapman begrudgingly authorized Teen Angel to carry one of the production company's expensive video cameras with him onboard the helicopter. A gentle recommendation from Sela Ward, the former "Crimson Tide" cheerleader and female lead in the motion picture, most likely sealed the deal for Teen Angel with Chapman. Miss Ward and her fiancé Howard Sherman, had taken an immediate liking to Brad Ackerman during their initial introduction and subsequent conversations that very night, while they were all seated at the bar waiting for a table to open up in the overcrowded steakhouse.

Over the ensuing ten days with that video camera, Teen Angel was able to film several strategic scenes from the Hughes 500 cockpit as the dramatic action unfolded down below the hovering rotorcraft. And it was fun to boot, even though the fourteen-hour days in the shooting schedule were rather long and laborious at times. When his participation on the film project ended and he flew back home to southern California, Brad wasn't sure if the director, Andrew Davis, would end up cutting the video footage or include some of his shots in the final edited version of the movie when it came out in 1993. Either way, Ackerman was only too happy to expand his personal knowledge and experience base in yet another aspect of the motion picture industry. For the slightly arrogant Brad Ackerman, assimilating new and exciting things always induced humility into his demeanor, at least temporarily. Learning was always a good thing for Teen Angel and he continuously strived for it in his daily life. His "submarine sailor" father and "homecoming queen" mother had instilled this yearning desire into Brad's heart from the early days of his infancy and he never ceased to honor this inheritance. Teen Angel's mom would surely kick his butt if he ever did.

At 0930 on April 18, 1992 Teen Angel stood near the American Airlines counter at gate 32 of Terminal C in the Dallas Fort Worth Airport. He had just arrived into DFW from Chicago about 40 minutes earlier. Ackerman was now anxiously waiting for Danielle Le Claire's airplane to land in Dallas after a short hop from New Orleans. Three weeks ago Brad and Danielle had planned to meet in Texas so they could fly out to Los Angeles together to begin a ten-day, pre-cruise vacation in sunny southern California. It took some subtle wrangling by Miss Le Claire, but New Orleans District Attorney Harry Connick had rearranged his busy court docket and lawyer assignments in the *Crescent City* to accommodate Danielle's leave request. He had finally agreed let loose of his prized prosecutor so she could enjoy the ten-day excursion with her "lover boy Naval Aviator," Brad Ackerman. Teen Angel and "Angel Eyes" Le Claire would have three full days and nights alone after which they would meet up with Juice Mayhew and his family to share the remaining seven days together having loads of fun in the LA area. Jack and Loretta would of course be bringing their two wonderful children, Trevor and Ashley, along for the pre-cruise vacation festivities. The couple could hardly wait to spend quality time with the Mayhew's and their children, engaging in all sorts of family activities. Perhaps on a subconscious level, Brad and Danielle both surmised that this family-style vacation was the precursor to their own budding domestic future, lurking somewhere out there on the horizon of life.

Inching closer to the passenger waiting area of Gate 32 Brad spotted a bald gentleman who must have been suffering from a substantial amount of sleep loss. The guy had a huge melon for a cranium, propped up by an extra-thick neck. It truly resembled a hog's head and Teen Angel thought that he had seen this chap somewhere before but he couldn't be sure. The portly fellow was wearing wrinkled Army fatigues with a pair of tattered and un-shined combat boots, probably from his National Guard unit in Arkansas. His eyes were partially opened but glazed over in a semi-conscious stupor. The guy's shaved noggin rested on his clenched fist but bobbed freely around, even though it was fully supported by a locked elbow on the left knee. Teen Angel also noticed that the gentleman was sucking on his teeth, rudely maneuvering saliva and minute food particles in between the gaps of his choppers. This action created a high-pitched, constant frequency noise that could be heard throughout the passenger lounge. To put it bluntly, the guy was as fucked up as Hogan's goat. Brad wondered if the hairless Army man had spent the entire evening in Terminal C waiting on the "standby list" to catch an American Airlines fight back to Little Rock. Ackerman had never been to Arkansas, but he had flown over it several times in the past. If you called the *razorback state* your home, you lost 50 IQ points in Teen Angel's estimation. Bill Clinton, the "boy governor" and current front-runner for the Democratic Party's presidential nomination, had a lot to do with influencing Ackerman's pejorative opinion about people from Arkansas. Clinton's incredibly annoying wife Hillary only added to his disdain for Arkansas.

Just then the gate agent, an older woman with graying hair and brown skin, picked up a microphone and announced the arrival of American Airlines flight # 890 from New Orleans. Even though she was trying to disguise it, the woman spoke with a slight Hispanic drawl that overshadowed her Texas twang. She was a first generation Mexican-American born and raised in Laredo after her fourteen-year old mother had illegally crossed the Rio Grande River 54 years ago to give birth to her, the first of eleven offspring. As the woman spoke, a roll of fat bulged over her pudgy waistline, stretching against the cheap material of her blue, gate agent uniform coat. When she opened the outer door of the passenger entranceway into the lobby of the terminal, Ackerman could plainly hear the familiar sound of GE high-bypass, turbofan engines winding down as a Boeing 737 came to rest at gate 32. Almost immediately, the far end of the jet way methodically extended toward the cabin door of the aircraft, at its usual snail's pace, to make a departure path for arriving passengers. Ackerman's breathing accelerated a bit as he focused his eyes past the terminal entrance and down into the dark, elongated corridor. He subconsciously raised himself up on his tiptoes as if that would give him a longer field of view and lessen his transitory anxiety. On the terminal's closed circuit television system Carly Simon's sacred anthem *Anticipation* began playing just as some *Hunt's* ketchup dribbled slowly down out of a red bottle onto a waiting hamburger patty in the familiar TV commercial.

Brad pulled both hands out from his green flight jacket pockets and placed the tip of the left index finger into his mouth. He nipped at the soft flesh under the nail for a moment. Teen Angel dropped that hand rapidly to his side, as if he abruptly realized what his body language was conveying to anyone curious enough to be watching his demeanor. Arrogance and anxiety coursed through his veins in tandem. It was as if the two feelings were waging war against each other inside Brad's body. Suddenly Danielle appeared at the far end of the passageway. Every time Ackerman saw his woman, after being apart for a good long while, it was like seeing her fresh for the first time. From the moment he first spotted her in the Jack Black Officer's Club at NAS New Orleans, Danielle Le Claire always took his breath away. She must have been the first passenger off the airplane because she strolled alone in the jet way for about thirty seconds. It was as if Danielle had been given the stage all to herself to make a grand entrance just for Brad Ackerman's distinct, personal pleasure. Most likely the other passengers in the First Class cabin were still busy wrestling their carry-on bags out from the overhead compartment or politely commenting to the captain on his fine landing that day.

As he watched her gracefully promenade toward him, Teen Angel noticed that Danielle was wearing a deep-red, straight-line skirt that wiggled just about two inches above her knees as she walked. The size-6 dress moved in a tantalizing fashion as Miss Le Claire sashayed forward. It just naturally caught and mesmer-ized a man's stare, somewhat similar to a hungry Big Mouth Bass eyeing a plastic purple worm as it squirmed on the end of a #8 hook in a Tennessee mountain pond. It was not a miniskirt by any stretch of the imagination, but it was short enough to make her lithe, toned legs exceedingly attractive. Danielle also wore a sheer, soft white blouse. The pallid fabric was woven out of the finest silk, direct from the textile factories in Hong Kong. Its delicate material subtly revealed the outline of her bra in silhouette fashion while simultaneously complimenting the curvature of her ample, firm breasts. As she continued to move smoothly onward, Teen Angel surveyed Danielle's elegant, near six foot, form top to bottom. She wore three-inch, black high-heels and flesh-colored nylons that served to further accentuate her long, athletic legs. Her calves flexed tightly as she strode along in the heels. Offhandedly thrown over her right shoulder, Danielle was toting a blue-red leather handbag by *Gucci* with an extended, silver-colored strap. She was likewise lugging one of those very swanky *Henk* drag-along pieces of luggage, personally selected from the most expensive designer suitcase line in the world. Finally, Brad watched as Danielle's red hair was flowing carelessly across her shoulders then downward into the small of her supple back. But most striking of all her physical attributes were those mammoth, brown eyes. They were indeed *angel eyes*, powerful and soft all at the same time. No high-fashion model traipsing up and down the runways of Paris, New York or Milan had anything to offer that was more enticing that Danielle Le Claire's physical attributes.

As he made eye contact with Angel Eyes' warm engaging smile, Brad's heart skipped a few beats because she immediately gave him *that look* with her beautiful face that only a woman deeply in love can give to her man. It was a heartening expression to reassure Ackerman that she was his woman and his alone! This female, facial articulation is actually quite difficult to adequately describe. It's hard to accurately put into mere words. Many authors during the last millennium have tried but their attempts were futile. Bill Shakespeare was the closest, but he only depicted Juliet's rare beauty not *that look* which bolsters and restores a man's emotional confidence. The look has everything to do with the woman's eyes and how they react to the sight of the man they love with all their heart. The coquettishness in the woman's eyes is simultaneously shy but obvious, and it is intended for only one individual. This look proudly displays a sense of pure confidence, radiating the fact that their man can likewise see no other woman but them in his heart, mind and soul. A man must continuously earn this look from his woman. If they are successful, then it's "full steam ahead" in their romantic relationship, in the positive sense of that colloquialism. Behind closed doors, it will be similar to Susan Sarandon's torrid love scene with Jack Nicholson in *The Witches of Eastwick*. Teen Angel swept Danielle Le Claire up off her feet and deftly into his arms with one powerful motion. She let loose of the drag bag, its long metal handle instantly plopped down to the thin carpet. The stylish high-heel on her right foot likewise dropped to the floor. People inside the terminal stopped watching the ketchup commercial to stare at Brad and Danielle, smiling at the pleasing sight of two happy lovers reunited after a long separation.

When the pair finally embraced in the lobby by Gate 32 it was a deep, strong hug. Brad squeezed Danielle's torso forcefully and held onto her for a full fifteen seconds, which is an eternity for an embrace. As always, she smelled delicious, wearing a perfume from the *Clive Christian 1872* collection, the only line of fragrances that has proudly displayed Queen Victoria's royal seal for one hundred and twenty years. As he clung to her lanky frame, Teen Angel breathed in her scent and it filled up his senses completely. Danielle was a woman and a half. She was indeed a *20th Century Fox*, to use *Jim Morrison and the Doors* 1970's jargon. Danielle Le Claire was the best thing that had ever happened to Brad Ackerman, and they both knew it. Teen Angel burrowed his right hand into Danielle's luxurious red hair then moved her luscious locks away from the left ear. A ticklish chill ran up his spine as he began to speak to her. Monarch butterflies filled his abdomen. At least his hair was perfect!

"I want you," whispered Brad into that dainty ear. His voice was breathy and baritone low, like a male heartthrob in an afternoon soap episode. Ackerman's lips pressed close to the nape of Danielle's neck as he waited impatiently for the response that he anticipated from her. The response he so desperately needed to hear right then and there at DFW, in the lobby of Terminal C, Gate 32.

"You have me," replied Danielle. Brad's temporary anxiety was now completely dissipated. His body relaxed. After about eleven seconds Danielle released from their mutual embrace, well before Teen Angel did. Finally Brad let loose of his firm grip on her slender body and lowered her gently back down to the carpeted floor.

"Oooo, I really liked that," exclaimed Danielle. "You hugged me longer than I hugged you." They exchanged a slow, wet kiss right there in the terminal for all to see, even though the passengers now pretended not to notice. Some of Danielle's lipstick transferred onto Brad's lips. When the kiss was finally over, she wiped away the red smear with her left thumb. Brad retrieved Danielle's pricey piece of luggage from the carpet and after she put her shoe back on they headed toward Gate 44 and the airplane that would fly them to Los Angeles. They had 38 minutes until boarding time.

As the couple passed by Gate 40, Teen Angel abruptly ushered Danielle into one of the three *Brighton* shops that are located inside the various terminals at DFW. Like all women Miss Le Claire just loved jewelry. Gold or silver, real or costume it didn't matter and Brad Ackerman was fully aware of this. As they browsed through the tiny store Danielle quickly became intrigued by a silver bracelet that rested inside the lighted jewelry case of the shop. The sterling silver trinket was delicately designed and featured miniature hearts in its unpretentious pattern along with semi-precious gemstones.

"How much is this gorgeous bracelet?" Danielle inquired. The female salesclerk standing behind the counter smirked then informed Danielle that unfortunately she had just sold the last one about 30 minutes ago to a good-looking, baby-faced guy.

"Can I purchase that one in the case?" asked Danielle. Her voice had a slightly pathetic, pleading quality to it. Miss Le Claire's words ended in a vaguely higher pitch than when she began the question. Danielle transferred her weight to the right foot as she leaned over the jewelry counter. Her focus shifted back and forth between the bracelet and the sales clerk's face.

"I'm so sorry Ma'am, but my boss won't let me sell the jewelry in our display case, they are for showing only," answered the sales girl. The disillusioned expression on Angel Eyes' face and her corroborative body language revealed the level of her disappointment. Teen Angel, pretending to be surveying the vast array of silver buckles and leather cowboy belts offered by *Brighton*, promptly came to Danielle's rescue at the lighted jewelry counter. Her obvious distress triggered the "knight-in-shining-armor" component of his basic character. Now standing adjacent to the display case, Ackerman pulled out a decorative, heart-shaped tin from his flight jacket pocket and handed it over to Danielle in a coy but satisfying manner. The swift grin that spread across her smooth face was an anticipatory smile, because Danielle somehow already knew what was inside the ornate tin box. Indeed it was that very same bracelet she had been admiring, and Ackerman was the handsome baby-faced man who had purchased the last one only a short time ago. The much-appreciated gift was definitely a pleasant surprise to Danielle. Perhaps Teen Angel was "trainable" after all she thought. Danielle immediately removed the bracelet from its container and placed it onto her elegant right wrist. The simple but stylish ornament complimented her outfit quite nicely. On the flight out to LAX the twosome slept, hand-in-hand, for the entire 2 and ½ hour journey. They didn't even wake up to enjoy the sumptuous in-flight meal that American offered to all its First Class passengers that morning. Teen Angel and Angel Eyes were totally comfortable with each other and they both needed the forty winks. Danielle snored softly, like a newborn puppy lazily sleeping next to several siblings after receiving a belly full of warm milk from its mother. Brad drooled a bit onto the patterned fabric of his airline seat backrest. What an attractive couple they made.

At 1225 PST, forty-five minutes after landing at LAX, the two lovebirds sat patiently in Ackerman's red, 1988 Porsche. Huddled up next to an off-white parking booth they were waiting tolerantly for the kiosk attendant, a short Pakistani male, to issue a receipt for the $120 fee Brad had just paid to him with one *C-note* and a *Jackson*. Teen Angel tapped his right index finger on the mahogany, wood-grain steering wheel and snuck a glance or two at Danielle's nylon-clad legs as she sat in the passenger-side bucket seat of the 911S. That deep-red skirt rode high up on her thigh in the cushy confines of the sports car. The plush black leather of the interior made for a nice contrast with her tan pantyhose. Even though *Brandy, You're a Fine Girl* by Looking Glass was playing softly at *K-Earth 101* on the stereo, for some reason Teen Angel began to recall a ZZ-Top concert he had attended in Austin three years ago. Or maybe it was the *She's Got Legs* music video that was flashing through his thought process at that moment. Either way, Ackerman was enjoying the exquisite visual of Danielle's extra-long legs stretched out in his automobile, with her pretty little feet kicked out of those high heels. Just then the red and white parking arm of the lot's gate system lifted up about eight feet in front of the vehicle. Teen Angel took a paper receipt from the attendant then pulled his Porsche out of the parking lot and into outbound airport traffic. He maneuvered the red coupé hastily onto World Way then headed for the Pacific Coast Highway and their intended, initial destination Malibu.

For the next ten days Teen Angel and Danielle, plus the Mayhew family when they arrived on April 21, would be spending their vacation anchored out of the Malibu Beach home owned by Brad's golfing buddy Tom Selleck, the well-known television actor. Ackerman's thirteen-hundred square foot, two-bedroom dwelling in Burbank was way too small to comfortably accommodate six people for any length of time, so he had made alternative arrangements. Tom Selleck and his two brothers Bob and Dan had been part of Teen Angel's regular, weekend foursome pretty much since his arrival into southern California when he began pursuing a career in the motion picture industry as a stunt pilot. The first time Ackerman had performed professional aviation stunts for pay was when he worked for Universal Studios in Hawaii during the final season of the TV series *Magnum PI*. He later followed his new acquaintance Tom Selleck, working as a safety pilot on the silver screen flop *Her Alibi* in the summer of 1988. After that production wrapped, Selleck had graciously introduced Brad to the world renowned film director Stephen Spielberg at the wrap party thrown at the very same beach front property he was now driving to. Based on that burgeoning, professional relationship with Spielberg, Ackerman was always able to find plenty of work as a pilot in Hollywood. He was likewise blessed with an abundance of opportunities to make the acquaintance of numerous female starlets in *tinsel town*, not that this mattered much now, since he had found Danielle Le Claire.

Ackerman's other golf buddies, Tom Selleck's brothers Bob and Dan, were real estate moguls specializing in the San Fernando Valley section of Los Angeles County. The siblings had quickly become Teen Angel's friends after helping him successfully locate and finance a cheap house in the city of Burbank, California.

The fairly inexpensive domicile, situated in the rolling foothills of the LA suburb, was close to De Bell Municipal Golf Club. This links course, nestled in the lowland valleys of the pristine San Gabriel Mountains, overlooking Burbank, was where Brad's infamous rattlesnake episode had occurred when he was a younger man. All four of the golfing partners were likewise members of the Men's Association at the prestigious Valencia Golf Club Resort in Santa Clarita. About a month ago, Ackerman had broached the subject of borrowing Selleck's huge residence on Malibu Beach for a couple of weeks. Brad had made his humble request in the Valencia Clubhouse bar just minutes after sinking a twelve-foot putt on the 18th green, ensuring that he and Tom had won $5000 dollars in a Texas Scramble, partner's match play tournament. Selleck who was scheduled to be in Tokyo, Japan promoting his latest film *Mr. Baseball* during the timeframe in question, acquiesced to Teen Angel's adamant yet placid plea without much hesitation. He decided shortly after receiving his certified check for 2500 bucks, half of the golf tournament prize money. Selleck cordially agreed to allow Brad and his friends to use his Malibu estate for the 10 day vacation. A hearty handshake and three tequila shooters sealed the deal that evening. As usual, Teen Angel chucked the last two shooters into the clubhouse fireplace without anybody in the bar noticing. To Brad, tequila tasted pretty much like turpentine, or moose piss! One was actually over his personal limit of zero.

On the scenic drive up historic Pacific Coast Highway, Brad enthusiastically contemplated the various activities that would unfold over the next two weeks, while Danielle Le Claire listened to an *Air Supply Greatest Hits* compact disc. He was putting his brain to work, rehashing all the intricate details of his strategic plan. She was nonchalantly tapping her toes and moving her torso rhythmically to the music blasting out of the premium *Becker Silverstone 980 CD* car stereo system. Danielle and Teen Angel both had their arms hanging out of the window, flapping freely in the cool beach breeze, as the sporty vehicle zipped along at 77 MPH. The moderate centrifugal forces they experienced during the many sharp curves that are a prominent feature of PCH, pushed each of them back into the leather bucket seats and slightly toward the outside of Porsche's turn radius. Teen Angel had already planned out the entire vacation, day-by-day and minute-by-minute. He was that meticulous in his organizational skills. A small flock of seagulls flew low overhead, making their characteristic and highly annoying squawking noise as they searched for the coastline and perhaps a sand crab lunch or a discarded tuna fish sandwich in a brown bag. Up ahead in the distance Teen Angel recognized the majestic, wheat-colored bluffs on the east side of PCH. This steep knoll overlooked the Pacific Ocean, providing a breathtaking setting for the Malibu campus of Pepperdine University. The couple was now only minutes from the seashore and Tom Selleck's ocean view address. Today, day one of their vacation, Brad and Danielle would unpack their luggage at the beach house then spend an hour or two walking along the shoreline, basking in the warm sunlight and relishing each other's pleasurable company. At 1530, after taking a relaxing hot shower, the pair would make the forty-five minute trek over to La Cienega Boulevard and the Beverly Hills location of *Lawry's the Prime Rib*. There they would enjoy a hand carved hunk of prime beef and share a bottle of fine wine before heading off to Chavez Ravine and the Dodgers versus Braves baseball game. Teen Angel was especially excited about the Dodger ball game because Angel Eyes Le Claire, a $500 per hour attorney, had never been to a major league baseball contest in her life. Danielle switched the CD changer over to *The Best of Chicago* album. *If You Leave Me Now* was the first song to play. Teen Angel was far too busy thinking to notice the music switch.

Day two would find these two satisfied sweethearts wolfing down a gourmet breakfast of Eggs Benedict, Crab Mornay and Blueberry crepes at *Bob Morris' Paradise Cove Beach Café*, an upscale dive in Malibu. Seated on the palm-covered veranda, Brad and Danielle would watch in amazement as flamboyant surfer dudes, riding their multicolored surfboards, would "hang ten" and skillfully dip their blonde heads back underneath the curl of a seven-foot wave. The contented couple would read the morning scandal sheet, otherwise know as the *Los Angeles Times*, and leisurely sip Colombian coffee from chipped, fine china cups. Crisp morning air would swirl as ocean swells gently pounded the sand, washing over the shoreline. Occasionally Teen Angel and Danielle would tear themselves away from the food, drink and newspaper articles to wipe their lips and chins with soft, extra-white linen napkins. Yes, the relaxing atmosphere provided by the pristine surroundings of Paradise Cove would be overwhelming.

Afterwards Brad and Danielle would again make the short jaunt over to Beverly Hills to engage in some trendy shopping activity along famed Rodeo Drive. Haggling with shopkeepers would not be part of that dynamic. Later that afternoon on day two, they would most assuredly munch on a chocolate chip cookie or two at the original *Famous Amos* food stand on Hollywood Boulevard. As usual, these legendary cookies would contain far too many chocolate chips and fresh walnuts to keep track. A pepper-steak, submarine sandwich from *Santoro's* in Burbank would serve as an early dinner. Of course the sub would be chocked full of onions, pickles, peppers, tomatoes and a secret blend of seasonings to compliment the velvety soft white bread and slow-simmered flat-iron steak. Finally, the blissful paramours would attend a Neil Diamond concert at the Hollywood

Bowl to culminate the second day of their escape from the hectic pace of the work environment.

Their last day alone together, before the Mayhew's showed up, would include a full day at the *Universal Studios Tour* riding the various attractions and visiting the studio's celebrated "back lot" area. Teen Angel would make sure that Danielle was seated on the right side of their tour bus and pressed up close to the safety railing during the "back lot" tour. That way, Bruce the mechanical shark from *Jaws*, could scare the living shit out of this over-priced, but adorable lawyer from New Orleans. As they wandered freely around the grounds of the studio, they would participate in the numerous side shows offered by the unique amusement park. Most certainly, one of those nasty, messy chiliburgers from *Tommy's* would be consumed as a noontime meal. Paper napkins would not be in short supply for this redneck feast. Their day at Universal would be followed by dinner at *The Castaway Bistro*, perched atop the hills of Burbank overlooking the entire San Fernando Valley. A cultured evening of high-class entertainment provided by the *Ahmanson Theater* would culminate the evening on day three of their vacation. At the Ahmanson they would watch a live performance of the Andrew Lloyd Weber Broadway play *Phantom of the Opera*. As usual, the crystal chandelier would be truly spectacular as it plunged down toward the audience near the end of Act Two in the musical.

When Jack, Loretta, Trevor and Ashley Mayhew finally made their way to LAX, Ackerman had plans to escort them to Disneyland, Knott's Berry Farm, Magic Mountain, Universal Studios, the Hollywood Walk of Fame, Grauman's Chinese Theater and Santa Anita Racetrack. All of these venues were a prominent part of the overall vacation strategy that Teen Angel had developed. Brad was proud to have come up with this flawless design because he knew Danielle and the Mayhew's would enjoy every second. It featured culture, amusement, stimulation and relaxation as well as local treats that only natives from southern California were cognizant of. Ackerman scratched the right side of his neck and turned his head to gaze at Angel Eyes. Her left hand rested in the middle of Brad's right thigh. Teen Angel down-shifted into second gear then turned the corner onto a private cul-de-sac. The fourth house on the left belonged to Tom Selleck. Ackerman slowly steered the Porsche into a circular driveway that adorned the front yard of the 4,000 square foot home. Brad pushed the clutch all the way to the floorboard, moved the stick shift into neutral and switched the car's engine off. The flashy, red car coasted the remaining eight feet, stopping directly adjacent to the front door and two massive statues of male lions that seemed to be guarding the walkway. The property was impressive to say the least.

Danielle exited the Porsche and ambled up the brick pathway. Ackerman was not far behind, dragging her luggage and toting his parachute bag over the right shoulder. He fumbled with Selleck's keys a bit before unlocking the front door.

About four hours later, Teen Angel and Angel Eyes were about to be seated in the dining room of the plushy confines at *Lawry's the Prime Rib* restaurant. As was always the case on a Saturday night, the mega-expensive beef joint was over-crowded and buzzing with an abundance of jet setters from the "city of angels" and the myriad of adjoining neighborhoods in Los Angeles and Orange Counties. In attendance that evening, were Hollywood moguls, high ranking politicians, real estate barons, business professionals, popular sports figures, a few drunks, a call girl or two, motion picture and television stars, singers, songwriters and entertainers of all sorts. Eight bartenders were slinging drinks at a record clip over at the mammoth bar that was situated in the far west corner of the posh eatery. Inside the on-site meat locker, butchers were extra-busy carving up specially-ordered cuts of meat for the regal patrons, most of whom were sporting designer suits by *Giorgio Armani, Luciano Carreli* and *Hugo Boss*, or dresses by *Sergio Valenti, Vera Wang* and *Valentino Garavani*. In the gourmet kitchen, a dozen chefs and pastry-cooks were clad in their characteristic white hats, actively engaged in creative, culinary artistry of all kinds. Surely this was a place to see and be seen.

Brad Ackerman was dressed in a pair of khaki slacks and a white button-down shirt he purchased on sale at *Nordstrom's Rack* ten months ago. His outfit was highlighted by a stylish, Navy blue tie from *Salvatore Ferragamo*. He wore the silk tie with a loose knot and the top button of his shirt was unfettered to flaunt a relaxed attitude. Suffice it to say that Teen Angel turned a few heads that night, both male and female. Danielle turned many more. She looked heavenly in her basic, little black dress, with a slit up the left side of the garment that revealed the better part of her toned thigh. The *Brighton* bracelet hadn't left her wrist since DFW. To Danielle's complete gratification two dozen long-stem, red roses were waiting for her at the secluded table when a hostess seated them, then pitched a menu down on their plates.

"Would you care to try our featured appetizer tonight? It's garlic encrusted escargot direct from the streets of Paris, France," asked the nubile woman with a straight face. Apparently she had not been turned down too often that evening by the opulent clientele.

"No thanks, I just ate a bar of soap. We'll take two jumbo shrimp cocktails instead if you don't mind," answered Teen Angel. A twinge of cynicism was etched in his voice. The little blonde hostess wrinkled up her cute, button nose then turned and walked away. She wasn't intelligent enough to discern what Ackerman's slightly uncouth comment was really meant to convey. Perhaps she would need six more years at the University of Southern California to augment the two she already had under her belt. As he plunked his fanny into the chair, Brad couldn't help but notice that there were more forks, spoons and knives spread out on the tablecloth than he had in his kitchen drawer back at home. The lights dimmed even further to give the establishment added ambiance, and to hide any irregularities in the cuisine. Miss Le Claire stuck her nose tenderly into the bouquet of roses and breathed in their delightful aroma. The rose petals were smooth and silky soft. They arrangement of roses smelled like, well, like expensive roses. Maybe Teen Angel was trainable after all she once again thought.

Brad and Danielle had just finished ordering two slabs of medium-rare prime rib for dinner, bone in of course, when their shrimp cocktails were delivered by a female waitress. Next the maître d'pulled the cork on a bottle of twelve-year old Chardonnay by Kendal Jackson and offered a taste to Teen Angel. Brad swirled the liquid in his glass for about ten seconds as if he were a wine connoisseur surveying the color and consistency of the aged, alcoholic beverage. He sniffed the rim of the crystal goblet before swallowing the small sample down in one swift gulp. Brad shook his head in an affirmative manner giving the maître d' a vigorous thumbs up signal.

"Pour," advised Ackerman. He placed his wineglass back down onto the tablecloth, winked at Danielle then scrutinized the customers in *Lawry's* once more. It was difficult to see the whole restaurant due to the secluded nature of their table. Brad stuffed a jumbo shrimp, slathered with cocktail sauce, into his mouth.

"My compliments sir, a very good selection," said the Cuban maître d' as he carefully filled both Danielle's and Brad's wine glasses. He shoved the bottle deep down into a metal wine holder filled with ice cubes and frigid water then walked away from the table.

Danielle dipped one of her shrimps into the chalice of red sauce, raised it to her lips and took a small bite of the crustacean. While gracefully chewing the succulent shellfish meat she examined the dining room for herself. Underneath the table she had removed her flat shoe and was softly rubbing Brad's left leg with her bare foot in a demure yet brazen fashion. Just then three guitarists approached their table and began to play. One of the musicians handed a karaoke microphone to Teen Angel who promptly stood and began to serenade Miss Le Claire. He sang the Bobby Darin tune *Dream Lover* to her in his rich baritone voice.

Every night I hope and pray,
For dream lover to come my way
A girl to hold in my arms,
And know the magic of her charms
Cause I want, a girl, to call, my own,
I want a dream lover,
So I don't have to dream alone

A blushing Danielle, as well as several patrons in the restaurant seemed quite impressed with Ackerman's resonate, crooning and stylistic prowess behind the microphone. He stood and sang for a full 2 minutes, never taking his eyes off Danielle's face. Brad worked his way around the table as he sang, so that he was positioned directly behind Miss Le Claire at the crescendo. When the 50's ballad concluded, Ackerman received a standing ovation from the surrounding clients and waiters in this cozy little section of the chic bistro. Two Caesar salads were delivered to their table just as Teen Angel lobbed the microphone back to the lead guitar player. Brad placed both of his hands on Danielle's soft shoulders in a caressing manner then lightly kissed her on the cheek. When Ackerman sat back down he began to gobble up the remainder of his jumbo shrimp, liberally drenching each bite in the spicy sauce. The evening was off to a great start.

At 1825 Brad and Danielle sat in a "field level box" along the third base foul line at *Dodger Stadium*. Their seats were in "row one" just beyond the bag at third base, directly behind the short perimeter fence that prevented fans from spilling out onto the manicured playing surface. The home team *Dodgers* were about to wrap up their pre-game batting practice and head into the clubhouse for a last minute strategy session with fiery manager Tommy Lasorda. The baseball game against their hated National League rivals, the *Atlanta Braves*, was set to begin at five minutes past seven. Brad sipped *A&W* root beer from a large paper cup and hurled tasty kernels of *Crackerjack* into his mouth at a fairly rapid pace. These two treats mixed the best with prime rib, shrimp and chardonnay. Perhaps in the later innings, when they were both hungry, he would introduce Danielle to a renowned *Dodger-Dog*. This being Danielle's first dalliance with major league baseball she seemed content to watch and analyze the action. Every now and again she would ask Teen Angel a question for clarification. Danielle was snuggled warmly inside the very blue Dodgers team jacket she had purchased from the souvenir shop twenty minutes ago. Apparently she was "thinking blue" to quote Tommy Lasorda.

As they watched those pre-game activities in the tranquil 64 degree tempera-ture of Chavez Ravine, Brett Butler, the former Atlanta Braves outfielder, jumped into the batting cage to take the last few swings of the Dodgers batting practice. On his second pitch, Butler looped a Texas-League fly ball down the left field line. It looked more like a dying quail than a baseball fresh off the bat of a major league all-star. The ball floated for a while then landed just inside the foul line coming to rest straight across from Brad and Danielle's seat location. Brad popped more of the caramel corn and peanuts into his mouth. In the process he clumsily dropped several of the kernels of corn down onto the grubby concrete around his seat. The caramel-covered corn quickly mixed in with the residue of spilt beer and soda, the faint remains mustard and ketchup from dropped hot dogs, and a few empty peanut shells left over from previous fans. When Acker-man turned his attention back toward the batting cage, he noticed that a small child appeared to be playing hide-and-seek in the stands with his young mother. The kid was no more than 18 months of age and was shuffling ever closer to Ack-erman's box seat with his head ducked for concealment in the hide-and-seek rou-tine. The mother, totally decked out in Atlanta Braves clothing, knew where her infant son was, so she wasn't panicky. From her seat four rows behind and to the right of Brad, she just kept a close watch on the developing situation, allowing her toddler to have some liberty inside the ballpark.

At that moment Orel Hershiser, the Dodger's starting pitcher for the evening's competition, just happened to be strolling casually along the left field foul line from the dugout. Orel was walking towards the bullpen to begin warm-ing up for the game. Sensing an opportunity to excel, Teen Angel raised his body up and out of the hardback chair. He then made determined eye contact with the Dodgers star hurler. Brad pointed to the baseball that Brett Butler had hit earlier, the one that was still laying just inside the foul line in short left field. Ackerman also pointed his index finger at the infant child who was now standing next to his right leg, head down still pretending to be hiding from his mom. Not a word was spoken between the two men, but the body language conveyed clear meaning. Brad's gestures indicated to Hershiser that he wanted the superstar pitcher to toss him that baseball so he could then give it to the kid at his feet as a souvenir. Her-shiser smiled briefly then shook his head yes. After a few more steps, he bent down, picked up the ball and chucked it over to Brad. Teen Angel made a nice one-handed grab of the stinging baseball then handed it to the kid. Holding the ball in his right hand, the infant wasn't exactly sure what had just transpired. But he somehow sensed it was a great thing that had just occurred. The kid's mom knew precisely what had just happened and she rushed down to personally express her gratitude. As she gave Brad a friendly hug, the young mother yelled back to her husband to see what this good-looking man just did for our son. As the mom bent over to retrieve her wayward boy, Teen Angel noticed that the kid was holding the baseball in one hand and an ample supply of dirty *Crackerjack* caramel corn in the other. The youngster had apparently picked the plump, but soiled kernels up off the mucky concrete near Brad's seat. As his mother toted him off to their seats, the infant was stuffing the filthy popcorn into his mouth just as fast as he could.

"Brad Ackerman, you are a true gentleman," remarked Danielle after witnessing the selfless act. She was indeed paying close attention to her surroundings.

"Don't spread that around to far Danielle," responded Brad. "It might ruin my reputation." Teen Angel sat back down and slapped Danielle lightly on her right leg. It was more of a love tap than an actual slap. "Let's have some fun tonight Babe."

Although she was an incredibly intelligent lawyer with superb reasoning capacity, before this night at Dodger Stadium, Danielle knew absolutely nothing about baseball. But as the Dodger game progressed that evening she began to use her brilliant analytical dexterity, applying that skill to the baseball battle as it unfolded before her. So much so that on April 18, 1992 at Dodger Stadium she became a quick study of the American Pastime. That night in the sixth inning, Danielle was so intense about learning the various strategies and tactics that envelop the game of baseball she quickly became a student of the game and the intricacies of the strategic game within the game. However, she was just about to reveal her level of naiveté to Teen Angel. With two outs in the bottom of the sixth, after Braves' shortstop Ozzie Smith had fouled off eleven straight pitches from Orel Hershiser into the stands, Danielle decided to ask Brad a question that had been puzzling her the whole evening. With a serious look on her gorgeous face she posed the perplexing question to Ackerman.

"Brad, does the catcher have extra balls?" Danielle gazed at Ackerman's big eyes as he calmly answered her question.

"I don't know. Let's go check him out in the showers after the game!"

"It must be rough being you," suggested Danielle while patting Brad's left thigh. The Dodgers beat the Braves 7-3.

CHAPTER 31

▼

THE GULAG

Senior Chief John Esposito's shaved head was already sweating profusely even though he had only been working pier side of USS *Enterprise* for a mere hour and a half. The twin cheeks of his generous, brawny behind squeezed tightly together as he marched around on the wharf roaring out commands and fulfilling his duties as outlined in the VA-204 Plan-of-the-Day. Esposito's boxer shorts, probably older than some of the kids he was working with that morning, bunched up uncomfortably in the crack of his butt as he toiled away. From time to time he had to pick at his underwear just to find some measure of relief and to keep a clean line on the back of his uniform pants. As usual, the fifty-three year olds' rock-solid gut protruded well past his beltline, generating about thirty pounds of torque on the buttons of his khaki work shirt. Even though he was wearing an over-sized, green flight jacket for warmth, this extra-pressure on the khaki garment allowed his white undershirt to be visible through the gaps in the button line of his uniform top. After thirty-nine and a half years of Naval service, Esposito didn't care that he was fifty pounds overweight. Neither did the Navy, this close to his retirement from active duty.

At 0900 on April 29, 1992 the Senior Chief was ramrodding twenty enlisted men from Attack Squadron Two Zero Four during the final phase of their "pack out" of the mighty aircraft carrier. Half the enlisted men were on the dock unloading trucks and stacking pallets while the other half were onboard the ship accepting and packing away gear into the appropriate spaces. But Esposito was not only giving orders, he was engaging in manual labor himself as well, which would help explain the cranial perspiration. A fluffy handkerchief was strategically positioned in the left rear pocket of Esposito's work trousers for wiping away beads of sweat every now and then. The taupe-colored hankie was extremely busy that day and would be until the job was finally completed, about ten hours later. Today would be especially hectic for *Big E* because it was CAG-2's final opportunity to load equipment, supplies, baggage and whatever else the Air Wing would need onboard before the warship got underway the next morning at 0800 to begin its around-the-world excursion.

Weather at NAS Alameda's carrier pier was chilly for the pack out activity, with a howling wind gusting about at fourteen knots. The stiff breeze swirled leaves, cups and paper wrappers all around, causing the carrier berth to have a distinctly littered, unmilitary appearance. The gusty wind likewise blew the morning fog away. This blustery climate phenomenon also had the effect of lowering the ambient air temperature to 46 degrees due to the wind chill factor and close proximity of the ocean water. All the news channels were reporting that San Francisco's entire bay area could expect inclement conditions soon after the sun went down. Apparently a lingering cold front was hovering just off the coastline, gradually approaching from the west bringing the associated rain and low ceilings with it. In fact it would not be CAVU for several days in Frisco.

"Airman Boone, what the fuck are you doing by that mooring line? Git yer little fanny over here and help me unload these cruise boxes so the forklift can stack 'em for final loading," Esposito barked out. Airman Bobby Boone, the kid from Tulsa, tossed another shiny penny into the seawater near the keel of CVN-65 for good luck then rapidly shuffled back from the pier's edge. Boone's dungarees were still fairly clean, letting the Senior Chief know that the Oklahoma native hadn't been working all that hard during the past ninety minutes. Once by Esposito's side, Boone immediately started yanking metal cruise boxes off the back end of a duty truck, stacking them in two not so neat rows on one of the small transfer pallets. This would give the forklift driver easy access so he could transport them to one of the larger, loading platforms at the dock's edge. As Boone worked semi-feverishly Lieutenant Commander Leslie Lance snuck up behind Esposito, or so she thought. The intuitive Senior Chief had already felt her presence even as he was snatching one of the heavier boxes, loaded with jet engine repair tools, off the bed of the pickup truck. John Esposito was like Walter "Radar" O'Reilly on *MASH*, he had an uncanny ability to sense things before they occurred. And he was almost never wrong or taken by surprise. Airman Boone dropped one of the lighter cruise boxes down onto the concrete putting a major dent in its left side panel. The crashing metal package, filled with admin paperwork and office supplies, just missed smashing into the steel-toed, work boot on Boone's right foot. Three other enlisted men in the vicinity just shook their heads and giggled at the clumsy, teenaged Okie as he recovered and arranged the rectangular box onto the wood pallet. The veins in Chief Esposito's neck bulged even more than usual. Surely this youngster would test his patience for the remainder of the work detail, probably the entire carrier deployment.

"Senior Chief, do you have any idea what is in that large, light blue container over by the brow? It has Lieutenant Brad Ackerman's name written on it with big bold letters," inquired LCDR Lance. Leslie, wearing dark blue coveralls and a *River Rattler* ball cap, had been selected by Rocky Stone, the Maintenance Officer to serve as the Officer-in-Charge of VA-204's pack out detail during the last seven days before cruise commenced. The selection got her out of New Orleans and out of Rocky's hair, at least temporarily. It likewise gave her some additionally authority to wield and an opportunity to excel or fall flat on her face in disgrace. Lieutenant Commander Stone was not predisposed to either alternative; he was neutral and willing to cut her some slack.

"No Ma'am, I haven't got a clue, but if you look over your right shoulder Lieutenant Ackerman is coming toward us," replied John Esposito. He must have had eyes in the back of his head because Esposito was facing the opposite direction from both Lance and Ackerman when he made this pronouncement. After delivering yet another cruise box to an uneven pile, he made a quick swipe and a few slow dabs at his bald noggin with the cotton handkerchief. Esposito never made eye contact with Lance; he just kept right on working. This treatment pretty much annoyed Leslie. The Senior Chief didn't really have much respect for Lieutenant Commander Lance and she was fully aware of this fact. In his way of thinking, she hadn't earned any reverence, even though she was his superior officer in theory. Esposito stuffed the damp cloth back into his rear pocket before shifting another cruise box into position for the forklift driver, on the pallet he was working with.

AD-3 Earl Hamilton, Esposito's favorite young protégé from Aurora, Illinois was driving the forklift. Hamilton maneuvered the heavy-duty steel tongs of the apparatus underneath one of the laden, wood platforms then lifted it slowly up and away from the deck. He then backed the machine away and headed toward the designated staging area for loading of the warship. A cleanly shaven AD-3 Hamilton, recently promoted to Petty Officer Third Class, drove the forklift perilously close to the edge of the pier then deposited that smaller pallet he was toting on top of a much larger one for final transfer onto *Enterprise*. All the pallets and boxes were awaiting their crane ride up to elevator number two which was lowered to the hangar deck level for the pack out activities. Since his arrival at VA-204, Esposito had pretty much taken Hamilton under his wing and protected him from harm and from himself on occasion. But the Senior Chief had likewise pushed Hamilton to go well beyond his own personnel limitations and any reduced expectations he had for his nascent career in the Navy. Esposito had always motivated Hamilton to attend any and all available training courses or perform extra duties to gain valuable experience. The kid had responded well to Esposito's rough nurturing, making the jump to E-4 a full year ahead of schedule. This demoralized many of Hamilton's contemporaries who viewed Esposito's treatment as preferential toward the Illinois native. These pessimists seemed to conveniently ignore Earl Hamilton's hard work and tireless dedication. Hamilton dropped another pallet down with a thud then steered the forklift back toward the Senior Chief to retrieve the next one in line.

Despite the frantic pace of men scampering all about the massive carrier, she almost looked docile that morning. Similar to the calm before a Category Five hurricane finally makes its grand landfall onshore to inflict havoc and destructive power on helpless victims. The majestic *Enterprise* was nuzzled up close to the dock with about a dozen taut mooring lines keeping her immense hull perfectly still in the choppy, wind-tossed water. A gigantic 65, designed by using a series of rectangular light modules, was the most prominent feature that adorned the side of the ship's superstructure. An 'E' and an 'S' signifying combat excellence and a stellar safety record were hung caddy corner to the ship's number. Numerous, over-sized military decorations, commonly known as fruit salad to service members, were positioned in three neat rows just aft of the Captain's bridge. These jumbo ribbons depicted the various achievement awards and campaign medals the aircraft carrier had earned. Gray-white steam spiraled up then quickly dissipated as it escaped from various exhaust vents and hose lines onboard CVN-65. Water poured over the side of the boat in a steady stream, emanating from several locations on the lower hull. The radar array, positioned on the mast just above the navigation bridge, was twisting slowly around and around as if conducting a self-test, preparing itself for the long journey that lay ahead. On L-2 (elevator number two) the muscles and gaudy tattoos on enlisted men's arms flexed and strained as they carried supplies and cargo every which way; all under the watchful eyes of khaki-clad Chief Petty Officers. Inside the hangar deck, beyond the enormous reinforced fireproof doors, various pieces of GSA equipment were crisscrossing at a constant rate. On both sides of the gangway two colossal cranes with their heavy wenches and mammoth grappling hooks were extra-busy transferring pallets from the dock up to the decks of the lowered elevators. Their inter-twined steel cables, designed for heavy-duty hauling, were four inches in diameter.

At the stern of the ship the United States flag, commonly referred to as the ensign in maritime vernacular, was flapping in the stiff breeze making that distinctive popping sound. Old glory seemed to be in her element that morning, humbly guarded by a Vulcan canon turret situated underneath the catwalk on both sides of the flight deck. Up on the bow the union jack, displaying its characteristic 'Don't tread on me' motto waved proudly. Other flags plainly visible were the Admiral's two-star pennant and the many signal streamers that stretched out diagonally from the top of the mast down toward the roof of the bridge. The discerning eye would readily notice that the *Enterprise* was floating low in the water due to all the cargo, supplies, equipment and fuel that was already loaded onboard for the start of cruise. Its draft would sink even lower into the seawater after the air wing flew its 100 warplanes onboard tomorrow at 1000. What a glorious site she was to behold. In about nine hours, CVN-65 would be ready to sail in defense of the American way of life, democracy, courage, and honor.

Lieutenant Brad Ackerman, now only about fifteen feet away from Leslie Lance and Senior Chief Esposito, was proudly wearing his green flight jacket. Of course, this "fleet aviator" coat was liberally decked out with a multitude of "Been-There-Done-That" and "I-Love-Me" patches sewn on the front, back and sides of the garment. Head held high, chest out, and stomach sucked appropriately in, Teen Angel sauntered with an arrogant swagger behind a small luggage cart. The smile on his baby-face was unusually glowing that morning. Ackerman's khaki, piss-cutter hat was somewhat askew on his head but his brown shoes were gleaming with a fresh spit-shine. The baggage handcart that Brad was pushing was laden with an over-stuffed duffle, a parachute bag, a 27" color television and a cruise refrigerator. He carried a fresh store receipt from *Costco* for the TV and mini-refrigerator in the left pocket of his flight jacket. Brad would collect half of the $700 price tag for the two appliances from Lieutenant Cookie Cline tomorrow night at supper. Cookie, his stateroom mate for the *Enterprise* deployment, would begrudgingly cough up the cash at the evening meal in the dirty shirt wardroom after Air Wing Two's "fly on" was concluded. Ackerman would expect the whole $350 smackers. He would not allow Cookie to piecemeal the cash back to him over time on a convenient amortization schedule. After all, Brad Ackerman wasn't a credit union. Teen Angel put the brakes on the luggage cart then walked up to Lance and Esposito.

"Top of the morning to you Senior," quipped Brad as he stopped in between his squadron mates. "Leslie, how's it hangin?" Both comments were delivered jester-style, emblematic of Teen Angel's habitual repartee. Although Ackerman's last remark was somewhat rude and insensitive, Lieutenant Commander Lance took no offense to his political incorrectness. She gave him a free pass at least for a while.

"Morning Mister Brad," answered Lance. As she spoke the three words Leslie raised her right eyebrow slightly then lowered her head to seek positive visual contact with Mister Ackerman's brown eyeballs. Senior Chief Esposito grunted then gave Teen Angel one of those nods of acknowledgment as he continued to shove boxes around and direct traffic for the duty trucks as they arrived and departed.

"Senior, do you have a minute?" Brad's tone was serious, conveying a sense of urgency and privacy all in the same short sentence. Esposito dropped the box he was lugging and gave Lieutenant Ackerman his undivided attention in the VA-204 unloading area.

"What can I do for you Lieutenant?" Esposito rubbed his hands together as if trying to remove any excess grime or dust. His eyes were riveted on Ackerman's mug. Teen Angel was coolly checking out the fingernails on his left hand, squinting his eyes as if trying to focus extra hard on the sublime condition of his latest manicure.

"Walk with me Chief," stated Brad as he motioned toward the *Enterprise* gangway with his right index finger. With that said, the two men ambled over to that large, light blue container sitting underneath the brow; the one with Ackerman's name written on the top with big bold letters. When the two of them arrived, Teen Angel patted the cumbersome-looking parcel then leaned on it for support as he began to fill the Senior Chief in on his latest venture. It would turn out to be a "cash cow" in the valuable "at-sea currency" of culinary delights, preferred beverages, and favor trading during the six-month deployment.

"Chief, let me clue you in on the contents of this package," advised Ackerman. At that moment the Senior Chief was uncharacteristically long on ears and short on mouth. Over the next few minutes Teen Angel informed Esposito that the large carton contained about a thousand videos. They were tapes of major motion pictures and prime-time television shows direct from the personal film libraries of his Hollywood buddies Stephen Spielberg, Ron Howard and George Roy Hill. The famed director George Roy Hill, now a Yale professor, sent copies of his entire film collection to Ackerman. Some of the more celebrated titles included: *Slap Shot, The Great Waldo Pepper, The Sting, Slaughterhouse Five, Butch Cassidy and the Sundance Kid*, and *The World According to Garp*. Ronnie Howard, the child star turned director, provided over four hundred videotapes including the entire series of episodes from *The Andy Griffith Show*, and *Happy Days*. Also in Opie's endowment were *American Graffiti, Cocoon, Splash, Night Shift, Grand Theft Auto, Backdraft,* and every John Wayne movie ever produced. From Stephen Spielberg and his new bride Kate Capshaw the blue box contained films like *Jaws, Raiders of the Lost Ark, Cape Fear, Indiana Jones and the Temple of Doom, Back to the Future, Always, Innerspace, Poltergeist, Twilight Zone, ET The Extra-Terrestrial, Used Cars, Hook, Close Encounters of the Third Kind* and *The Sugarland Express*, plus every television episode from all the various television productions Spielberg had directed for the small screen. All three directors had graciously donated these films to their good friend Brad Ackerman to share with the fine men of USS *Enterprise*. Teen Angel watched closely for the body language he was receiving from the Senior Chief while he was talking. He wasn't at all sure of how Esposito would react.

"Think of the possibilities Senior." Brad scratched furiously at his rear end because it felt like an insect had crawled into his underwear and bit him on the left cheek. After Esposito heard about all the movies and TV shows in the pallet, sent especially for Teen Angel from those Hollywood moguls, he finally made his comment.

"This is quite a little life you've carved out for yourself isn't it Lieutenant Teen Angel?" Esposito dug a pinky finger deep into his right ear to remove some unsightly wax that was tickling his inner canal. He wiped it onto the pants leg of his work uniform.

Brad took no offense to the cutting remark because he and Duke O' Grady had already decided to use Senior Chief Esposito to manage the TV and movie video "business" on the *Enterprise* cruise. Edging closer to Esposito, Teen Angel threw his left arm around the senior chief's bulky shoulders then walked him over to the back of the pallet, underneath the gangway. He did this so nobody would hear the remainder of the private conversation.

"John, John, John, I am not leaving you out of this modest endeavor. I want you to be in control of this stash of entertainment and get whatever you can get in the way of favors or trades, for both the squadron and for yourself. I know you'll make the right decisions. The skipper and I are counting on you." John Esposito raised his eyebrows in reaction to the familiarity with which Lieutenant Ackerman was addressing him. But he agreed to the proposition, shaking his head in the affirmative. Off in the near distance, Airman Boone fumbled yet another cruise box. Its contents spilled out onto the concrete as it crashed down with a loud bang. Although Boone was a talented plane captain, he was apparently an incompetent cargo handler. Senior Chief Esposito's breathing accelerated and his rugged face transitioned to a nice shade of magenta. He didn't even have to turn and look, he knew instinctively who was the cause of all the commotion. His extra-sensory reception was that well tuned. With a sly grin on his face, Teen Angel decided to come to Esposito's rescue. After waiting an appropriate amount of delay time for comic effect, Brad spoke.

"Senior Chief, you mind if I borrow Airman Boone for about an hour or so?" asked Ackerman. "I need his help to move a shit load of gear into my stateroom." Brad knew the question was rhetorical in nature.

"Take him for as long as you need him L T," answered the Senior Chief. John Esposito's body relaxed. His little problem child was now somebody else's quandary, at least for a while. The veins on Esposito's bulbous neck started to turn back to their normal bulge as the extra blood in his face began to gradually drain back down into the rest of his body. The two men vigorously shook hands to seal their deal then Teen Angel sauntered back over to Airman Boone. Esposito proceeded in the opposite direction. He marched toward the crane operator to make arrangements for the light blue pallet, loaded with videotapes, to be carefully hoisted up to L-2. The Senior Chief was now vested in the scheme. Sixty minutes later, Ackerman and Boone moved Teen Angel's duffle, parachute bag, color television and cruise refrigerator into Brad's tiny stateroom. Lieutenant Ackerman then released Airman Boone in the mess decks for an hour so he could go eat a hearty lunch before reporting back to Senior Chief Esposito and the pack out duties on the carrier pier.

At eight minutes after seven that evening the pack out was finally, officially completed. The USS *Enterprise* was now absolutely ready to sail in defense of American freedom and to proudly wave "old glory" around the world. The Air Wing might even have to spank a few "rag heads" before it was all said and done in early November 1992. Teen Angel and Leslie Lance met on the quarterdeck of the colossal warship at 1915. Dressed in casual civilian clothes, they were headed off to share a laid-back supper in downtown San Francisco. This would actually be the last opportunity to eat a high-quality meal until the flat top pulled into Pearl Harbor Hawaii on May 28, 1992. Although she still harbored some residual mistrust of all the *River Rattler* officers, Lieutenant Ackerman included, Lieutenant Commander Lance had agreed to Brad's friendly dinner invitation earlier in the day. Leslie's acceptance was contingent upon her being allowed to choose the restaurant and that she alone would pick up the tab for the food. How could Teen Angel say no to an offer like that? As Brad and Leslie stepped off the last non-skid stair of the gangway they walked about three hundred feet over to a dingy-looking taxi. The cab was waiting for them by a long row of open-air, connected telephone booths. About twelve enlisted men, three ensigns, two Lieutenant junior grades and one Master Chief were busy dropping quarters into the phone's coin slots. Seeking some degree of emotional support they were making last minute calls, mostly with the charges reversed, back home to their wives, girlfriends and parents. These men and boys called places like Pigeon Forge, Tennessee, Lynchburg, Virginia, Caldwell, Idaho, Shawnee, Oklahoma, Waukegan, Illinois and Woonsocket, Rhode Island. One seventeen-year old sailor, dressed in sweaty dungarees from the pack out activity, held the phone tightly in the palm of his hand and shoved snugly into his right ear. The kid tightened his grip even further on the black receiver as he bent down and stretched out a grimy left hand to the concrete underneath those phone booths. He was trying to retrieve about seven quarters that he had dropped from his pocket. It was a humorous sight because the youthful sailor desperately wanted those coins to pay for the extra minutes he was using up, but he didn't want to miss any of the conversation as it transpired over the phone. Young love has such great potential to be both comical and misguided.

According to the *Big E's* Plan-of-the-Day, liberty expired onboard the carrier tomorrow morning at 0700. This meant that all crewmen had to be back aboard by that time because the brow was going to be pulled away from the boat's quarterdeck at exactly 0715. Captain Buford "Long Horn" Angus, the ship's commanding officer, was known throughout the Navy for his extreme attention to detail when it came to keeping strict timetables. *Enterprise* was scheduled to get underway at 0800 sharp and you could bet your ass that Buford would ensure that all her mooring lines were disconnected so he could shift the colors, signifying that his aircraft carrier was at sea, at precisely 0800. In a gentlemanly fashion, Brad opened the taxi's left rear door for Leslie then they both piled in and sat down on the discolored backseat of the cab. The driver drove off in a rush, before he was even told the intended destination.

Lieutenant Ackerman had telephoned the Yellow Cab Company about an hour ago to arrange for transportation from NAS Alameda to the closest Bay Area Rapid Transit (BART) station in Oakland, California. He had also cleared it with the front gate security folks to allow his cab driver to pick them up pier side of USS *Enterprise*. It would be an eight-dollar, eleven-minute drive to Oakland's 'City Center' station. Then Ackerman and Lance would catch a BART subway train for a fifteen-minute trek under the frigid waters of San Francisco Bay over to the Powell Street exit. From there Brad and Leslie would experience a short cable car ride on the Powell-Hyde line ending up at the Vallejo Street stop. On the corner of Leavenworth and Vallejo the pair would dine at an establishment called *Stalin's Gulag*. Conveniently located in the "Russian Hill" section of downtown San Francisco *Stalin's* was home to the fattest, meatiest, juiciest, messiest three-quarter pound cheeseburgers in all of the bay area. Gorgeous waitresses and waitresses only, deliver the mega-burgers to your table using a wheelbarrow to cart the heavy culinary delight straight from the kitchen's sizzling grill. The scantily clad, serving girls are all decked out in dilapidated prison garb as part of the macabre charm and ambiance that is unique to *Stalin's Gulag*. The ladies also wear ghoulish makeup that gives them an emaciated appearance, as if they had been stuck in the infamous Siberian prison system for several years without relief.

At *Stalin's* the mammoth burgers are rudely slung down in front of you in an oversized plastic basket, resting on top of a huge hunk of fresh, wedge-cut fries or doubly thick, deep-fried onion rings. While tolerantly waiting for your rations to arrive, you will listen to overly loud symphony music from Russia's legendary composers. The compositions are masterpieces from men like Rachmaninoff, Borodin, Tchaikovsky, Korsakov, and Shostakovich. And the classical tunes reverberate through *Bose* 901 direct reflecting stereo speakers, strategically positioned all over the walls and ceiling of the eatery. While waiting you will most assuredly leer uncontrollably at others seated around you who are already enjoying their food. The yummy smell emanating from the searing, jumbo patties of prime Angus beef will waft throughout the café, causing your nostrils to take several satisfying whiffs of the aromatic surroundings. Soon your brain will commence playing those terrible tricks on you. Like one of Pavlov's dogs, your mind will begin to visualize dribbling ketchup, oozing mayo, slithering mustard, and squishy red meat juices just by contemplating the experience of biting into one of *Stalin's* cheeseburger creations. The salivating reaction is unstoppable and your mouth quickly becomes sopping wet at the mere thought. Leslie Lance had never actually eaten at *Stalin's*, but she remembered seeing enticing pictures and reading an alluring article about the one-of-a-kind establishment in one of those airline magazines during a flight from Memphis to Nashville. Thirty-two minutes later, Brad and Leslie hopped off their BART subway train at the Powell Street station. They took a long, lethargic escalator ride up to historic Powell Street. There they stood in the chilly, storm-threatening weather on the busy San Francisco avenue patiently awaiting the arrival of the next cable car that would take them to the themed restaurant selected by Leslie Lance. Brad rubbed his runny nose with the bulky sleeve of his green flight jacket. The secretions quickly disappeared into the Nomex fabric.

Cable cars have a long and illustrious history in the Golden Gate City. In the United States, San Francisco was the first and last town to feature cable cars as part of its transportation system. In fact it is the last municipality in the world to have an operating cable car line. Of course, ever since its creation in 1873 by a Scottish mining engineer named Andrew Hallidie, the cable car has been a part of the lore that is a distinctive aspect of shaky town. Almost every tourist who visits San Francisco wants to ride a cable car at least once so they can brag about the experience to their friends back home. Up and down the hilly streets they go at a constant 9 and ½ miles per hour with a brakeman in front and a conductor in the rear, communicating to each other using a series of bells. Teen Angel stood on the curb with his right foot perched just above the ten-inch drop off. He bounced the sole of his Adidas athletic shoe up and down in the gutter, as if trying to let loose of some nervous tension. Watching his antics, Leslie Lance thought that Brad Ackerman reminded her of a teenager filled with sexual angst. Just then a cable car rang its highly distinctive bell off in the near distance.

"Ding, ding, sounded the bell. The colorful cable car would be at their location in less than a minute.

"Rice-a-Roni, the San Francisco treat," sang Ackerman in his best baritone voice. Teen Angel was offering his humble rendition of the famous commercial jingle for the rice and pasta product first created by Vince Dedomenico and the Golden Grain Macaroni Company way back in 1958. The food product was now a staple in many American households and it always reminded people of San Francisco.

"I think you may be mentally disturbed Mister Brad," suggested Lance with mock disgust in her tone. She wasn't at all sure what Brad's semi-embarrassing public behavior was intended to convey. In Mississippi the grocery stores didn't sell all that many boxes of Rice-a-Roni. In fact, Leslie had never even heard the product's name before. The brakeman screeched the cable car to a halt. Six or seven people exited from the car's interior as four or five jumped onboard. Brad stumbled slightly over his own feet as he hopped up on the running board with some obvious spring in his step. He grabbed hold of a handrail, then turned and assisted Leslie Lance as she boarded a San Francisco cable car for the very first time. She smiled broadly then sat down on a wooden bench, close but not too close to Teen Angel.

Cable cars are unique because they are the only rail system where the vehicles do not operate on self-generated power. The multicolored coaches are propelled forward when they latch onto a continuously moving steel cable line that runs inside a conduit just underneath a slot between the rails. This heavy metal wire is

kept in continuous motion by an engine placed inside of a centrally located pow-
erhouse. This particular cable car on the Powell-Hyde line was jam-packed full of
patrons that evening. Numerous riders were standing on the running board holding onto the handrails, as if planning to make a quick getaway at the next stop.
One brave man, or stupid if you prefer that description, stood casually on the
running board, not bracing his body by grasping a handrail. He just leaned back
against the center section of the cable car with his hands inside of his jeans pockets. One sudden, unexpected jolt and this guy would surely fly ass-over-tea-kettle
down to the cold pavement in total embarrassment. As the car lurched forward at
just under ten miles per hour, Leslie's exposed neck got even more chilled due to
the extra wind swirling around inside the cable car's semi-enclosed, interior seating area. Goose bumps suddenly appeared on her smooth, clear skin. Seated at a
comfortable distance from Leslie, Teen Angel's mind was far away and active,
even though there were plenty of familiar sights to see along the short journey
over to Vallejo Street. He was thinking about Danielle Le Claire and the various
seaports that *Enterprise* was scheduled to visit during its around-the-world carrier
deployment. Lieutenant Ackerman was mulling over a trip to Sydney, Australia
for Danielle in August 1992 when the ship would pull into the Aussie city for a
full eight days of liberty. Thoughts of the Sydney Opera House and a sunset sail
on an expensive yacht raced through his mind. But for some strange reason the
famous Tony Bennett song about The City by The Bay was likewise whirling
around inside his cranium as well. He subconsciously mouthed the words in a
subdued voice as he watched the distinctive buildings of Chinatown ease slowly
by their little cable car.

> *I let my heart in San Francisco*
> *High on a hill it calls to me*
> *To be where little cable cars*
> *Climb half way to the stars*
> *The morning fog may chill the air*
> *I don't care ...*
> *My love waits there in San Francisco*
> *Among the blue and windy sea*
> *When I come home to you San Francisco*
> *Your golden sun will shine for me*

Brad's voice wasn't anywhere near the tenor or quality of Antonio Dominic Benedetto (aka Tony Bennett) but he began to sing out the words anyway in a slightly muffled manner. The legendary lyrics and musical notes written by Douglas Cross and George Cory in 1962, were still as fresh and poignant as ever. Leslie furrowed her brow slightly then shivered in reaction to another gust of wind that churned through the quaint but crowded seating area. A few minutes later the cable car dropped Lance and Ackerman off right at the front entrance to *Stalin's Gulag*. The place was packed with tourists and locals alike. Sensing some measure of hunger anxiety in Leslie, Brad tipped the hostess with a flirtatious wink and a crisp twenty-dollar bill. She seated them immediately at a table near a bronze bust of Joseph Stalin, the infamous Soviet dictator of Georgian ancestry. Shostakovich's Fifth Symphony in D minor was playing loudly throughout the bustling, 3000 square foot restaurant. Almost immediately, a gaunt-looking waitress handed Brad and Leslie two menus, opened up to the beverage selections page. The nametag that was sloppily attached to her ramshackle uniform read SVETLANA ROMANOV. A young woman named OLGA TOURISHEVA, obviously engaged in waitress training, stood right next to Svetlana, carrying a #2 pencil and a green notepad. Both women wore decrepit-looking skirts that were nice and short, showing plenty of firm calf and thigh muscles. Burly, overfed men wearing prison guard uniforms were always nearby inside *Stalin's*, listening attentively and closely watching each of the waitresses and their activity. Wearing a red Soviet, hammer and cycle emblem on their black Russian hats, these beefy guy's ensured that all the girls practiced good Communist work ethic, and that none of them were able to make a break for asylum. It was all part of the charm that was exclusive to an evening of fine dining and entertainment at *Stalin's Gulag* restaurant. It was just plain fun and good acting by the employees.

"Good evening my comrades. Peace be with you and our beloved father, Joseph Stalin. What I bring you, for to drink?" asked Svetlana in contrived, broken English. Svetlana's eyeballs were steely blue and on fire that night. Her Russian accent sounded artificial but did indeed add to the café's overall atmosphere. As he surveyed the beverage bill of fare, Teen Angel's eyes quickly focused on one particular selection that was somewhat familiar to him. He lowered his menu to the table then concentrated on Svetlana's tomboyish face that was coated with a light dusting of semi-morbid makeup. The artistic effect didn't detract all that much from her basic good looks.

"Well dear, you can throw a bottle of *Baltika* beer down in front of me," said Brad. Ackerman raised his eyebrows twice in a provocative manner then slowly winked to see what affect this enticing demeanor might have on the two girls all decked out in prison garb. At the time, it appeared to have none. Brad's heart sank just a bit, being consciously ignored by the young women. He nipped at the index finger of his right hand as his elevated ego took a hit.

"I'll have a chilled glass of Merlot," added Leslie. Olga used long, thin fingers to scribble the cocktail orders onto her pad of paper using waitress shorthand. Both serving girls then broke character for a brief moment. Each woman gave Ackerman a double take and a coy smile before heading off toward the bartender to fetch the drink order. Brad didn't notice the waitresses' second glance and grin, but Leslie and one brawny prison guard did. The guard gave Teen Angel a disapproving face before continuing to monitor behavior around the large, dimly lit room.

About twenty-five minutes later, Teen Angel and Leslie Lance were munching away heartily at their food, washing it all down with healthy swigs of cool beverages. Ackerman was also enjoying the morosely dressed eye candy, harmlessly bird-dogging a waitress or two in the process. Without warning the delicate sound of Shostakovich's Fifth Symphony was rudely interrupted by the music of Khachaturian's *Sabre Dance*, the final movement from his famous ballet *Gayane*. The vivacious Cossack tune was now blaring out of the *Bose* speakers throughout the restaurant. Almost immediately, four of the waitresses and two of the prison guards leaped up onto the elongated bar to begin their traditional Russian Cossack dance. Bartenders hurriedly cleared away bottles, cans, trays of munchies, and other paraphernalia to make room for the dancers. This lively performance occurs every hour on the hour at *Stalin's* each night of the week. Along with the great food and entertaining surroundings, the rowdy choreography was one of the highlights of *Stalin's Gulag* that had become legendary over time. All six members of the dance team had changed into multihued Cossack outfits for their routine. Cameras flashed from several tables as tourists collected an array of photographic souvenirs to share with relatives and friends back home in Iowa, Kentucky, Missouri and Ohio.

In the middle of the number, one guard actually hurdled from the bar onto the top of an empty dining table. The white tablecloth must have been nailed into the tabletop because it didn't move an inch on the impact. The silverware, hard-plastic glasses and a vase of silk flowers however, plummeted down to the floor. *Stalin's* patrons went wild as the nubile girls and muscular men pranced about in the rough and tumble composition. Still chewing and with his mouth partially opened, Brad raised both hands high over his head to applaud the raucous distraction. Leslie Lance stopped eating. She was enthralled by the dance activity that lasted all of five minutes. Almost as quickly as it had begun, the *Sabre*

Dance song suddenly ended. The somber tones of Tchaikovsky's *Waltz of the Flowers* from *The Nutcracker Suite* began to play, and the gulag motif returned. Strict Communist order and discipline was restored.

Teen Angel returned to chomping on some fat onion rings, generously dipped in blue-cheese dressing. Also in his basket of food was a Black Angus hamburger creation called the *Yuri Gagarin*. The *Yuri* was a full 16 ounces of prime, corn-fed beef straight from the grazing fields and stockyards of Omaha, Nebraska. *Stalin's* café always added four extra ounces of meat to the *Yuri*, to allow for shrinkage during the cooking process. *Stalin's Gulag* wanted to make certain that each customer received a full ¾ pound hamburger or more, with each *Yuri* order. This particular burger was given the name *Yuri Gagarin* because, as the menu explained, it was the first, the best and the biggest hamburger in the entire world. It was also adorned with every conceivable condiment, like badges of honor on a hero's military uniform. The sandwich was of course named after the famous cosmonaut who was the first human being launched into space way back on April 12, 1962. Brad took another vigorous bite as he made eye contact with Leslie. Miss Lance had selected a *Karl Marx* and sweet potato fries as her meal of choice. The *Karl* was simply a poppy-seed bun wrapped around a plain chunk of beef. According to the menu, it was the preferred hamburger of the proletariat, those downtrodden members of Russian society that Marx had stirred into rebellion with his philosophical ramblings. Warm meat juices ran down Leslie's right arm as her incisors tore off another portion of the burger. Brad tossed a stack of napkins to Leslie from his side of the table. Two of the napkins flew out from the stack and ended up on the floor. They both giggled at the messes they were making. Ackerman and Lance didn't care at that point because etiquette had taken a backseat to sheer gastronomic fun. The prison guard near their table remained unmoved by their antics. He never lost the stoic expression on his face.

To properly finish off the evening of culinary artistry and amusement, Brad and Leslie decided to share a gigantic hot fudge sundae named the *Gorbachev Surprise*. It was called this because the ice cream sundae actually glowed in the dark like Chernobyl, the nuclear power plant catastrophe that occurred during Gorbachev's brief tenure at the top of the Communist Party of the Soviet Union. When the waitress delivered a *Gorbie* to your table the lights were purposely dimmed so the entire restaurant could see the sundae glowing in the darkened room. At the bottom of the hot fudge sundae, underneath the ice cream, almonds, whipped cream and cherries, the frosty dish was filled with soft gooey marshmallow. After all, that "ole softy" Mikhail Gorbachev proved to be the not-so-hard-nosed Premier who presided over the demise of the Soviet Union.

The lights dimmed inside *Stalin's* quite frequently because the *Gorbie* was their hottest selling dessert item at ten bucks a pop. Teen Angel and Leslie tossed their silver spoons into an empty glass dish after consuming the entire sundae at a leisurely pace.

Two hours later, after a short tourist trip through San Francisco's Fisherman's Wharf to buy a *Giants* baseball cap and Ghirardelli Square to pick up a pound of milk chocolate, Brad gave Lieutenant Commander Lance a friendly hug on the quarterdeck of USS *Enterprise*. It was almost 2330 and Leslie was definitely bushed from the long arduous day so she decided it was time for her to turn in. Following the affable embrace, Lance toddled off to her stateroom for the evening. Before she left, Ackerman graciously thanked her for paying the dinner tab and for being a perfect dinner companion.

"See you in the morning Mister Brad. Maybe you can take me up to the LSO platform so I can observe the jets during their fly-on tomorrow afternoon. I just love you flyboys," said Lance with a slight twinge of sarcasm in her last comment. With a slow grin on his mug and nodding his head in the affirmative, Ackerman assured Leslie that she was welcome on the platform anytime. With that assurance, Lance turned and walked off the quarterdeck into the bowels of the hangar bay. She mad a beeline for the hatchway and ladder that would lead to her tiny officer's stateroom on the O-3 level of the ship. Little did she realize that events had already been placed into motion that would make her the unwitting target of a diabolically funny, yet highly insensitive prank, perpetrated by the squadron practical joker. Tomorrow morning when USS *Enterprise* sailed underneath the beautiful Oakland Bay Bridge and set her sights on the open waters of the Pacific Ocean, Leslie Lance would not be leaving her "heart" in San Francisco, she would be leaving something else. And this would affect her tenuous status within the male-dominated, VA-204 *River Rattler* community.

Teen Angel, still a bit restless from the spirited activity at *Stalin's* and from the heavy meal he had consumed, decided to walk alone on *Big E's* flight deck. Although the temperature was somewhat frigid and the air excessively breezy, it appeared as though the heavy rainsqualls that were forecast to invade San Francisco's bay area remained stalled just off the coastline. Brad slowly ascended up three ladders until he emerged out onto the flat top of the warship through the Aircraft Handler's private hatch. For nostalgia's sake, Lieutenant Ackerman wandered aimlessly around taking in the familiar sights, sounds and smells that are unique to a carrier flight deck without its usual aviation activity occurring. Basically, Brad was reminiscing just prior to making his planned late-night phone call to Danielle Le Claire back in New Orleans. Teen Angel pawed nervously at the roll of quarters in the left pocket of his flight jacket just to make sure he would have enough change for about an hour of conversation. This phone chat would be his last telephonic communication with Danielle for approximately thirty days, while the ship made the Trans Pac journey from California to Hawaii.

Ackerman first strolled toward the fantail, affectionately referred to as "the ramp" by Tactical Naval Aviators. From that perilous position on the ship Teen Angel bent forward and leaned over the end of the carrier to examine the dark waters sixty feet below. The black sea water swirled as the wind kicked up in another quick, powerful gust. Several fish must have been congregating near the screws of the boat that evening because Brad could make out their eerie luminescence just under the hull. The fish were probably nibbling away at trash particles that had been chucked carelessly into the drink from the spud locker, located thirty feet below the ramp area. Concentrating extra hard on the sound of the silence, Brad could finally make out the blasé chatter from four sailors sharing a cigarette down in the spud locker. All four kids were under the age of twenty and about to embark on their first carrier deployment. They really had no idea what they had gotten themselves into by enlisting in the carrier Navy.

Next Teen Angel stood silently in the landing area, in between wires number two and three. He gazed into the parking lot of the pier then up at the Air Control Tower, or Pri-Fly. From this central location, everything was eerily quiet. Not even the sound of a car's engine could be heard as it maneuvered on the streets of NAS Alameda. As Ackerman raised his head, he observed that only a smattering of red light was emanating from the Air Boss's lair up in the control tower of the island. And over in the parking lot adjacent to the carrier pier, just a few unmanned vehicles remained. Tomorrow morning before the sun came up, that same parking lot would be packed to the gills with families and friends wishing their sailors a bon voyage. Tears would fill many eyes and the warm liquid would stream down the cheeks and pouting faces of children, parents, wives and girlfriends.

Finally Ackerman walked over to the fabled LSO platform on *Enterprise*. He picked up the pickle switch and clutched it in his hands with sincere affection and forthright reverence. Numerous Naval Aviation memories flooded his brain like a thick, cascading swarm of flies hovering over a dead animal. Ackerman wasn't sure if he should fight them off or embrace them. He was certain of how fortunate and extremely privileged he was to be able to serve his country as a Tactical Naval Aviator. In less than nines hours, after the *Enterprise* cast off her mooring lines and departed the NAS Alameda carrier wharf, those same sentiments and recollections would all come rushing back yet again only with increased vigor. It would almost seem like Teen Angel had not gotten off active duty and never left carrier flying for a second career in Hollywood. Brad placed the pickle switch back into its receptacle on the LSO console. In a flash, Teen Angel suddenly remembered some curious guidance his father used to impart to him on women and love. Odd advice seeing as how Brad was prepubescent when his Dad had his little man-to-man talk with him on the subject of the birds and the bees. 'Women are like trolley cars,' Ackerman's father would preach. 'They'll be another one along in fifteen minutes. All you gotta do is wait son. And if you can't get laid by the stroke of midnight, then go to bed Bub!' But in the silence of the night, Lieutenant Brad Ackerman brushed that fatherly advice aside and set his sights on that row of phone booths down on the pier. Once again he toyed with the roll of quarters in his flight jacket pocket. Although she was 1800 miles away, Danielle Le Claire's sweet, soothing voice and slow Southern charm were now just minutes away. Teen Angel needed to hear that familiar N'awlins accent and allow Danielle's adorable charm to alleviate his temporary anxiety. Even though it had taken him decades of living to understand the fairer sex, Brad now fully realized what a woman can do to a man's heart, mind and soul.

ABOUT THE AUTHOR

Randy Arrington is a retired Tactical Naval Aviator who was privileged to fly several carrier-based jets during his tenure on active and reserve duty in the United States Navy. He is currently serving as a Supervisory Air Interdiction Agent with the Department of Homeland Security, Customs and Border Protection, Air and Marine Operations Branch in San Diego, California. Randy earned his PhD in Political Science from the University of New Orleans in 1998 and has taught graduate and undergraduate courses at UCLA, UCSD, LSU, Tulane, USD and UNO. He has five beautiful children who reside in New Orleans, Louisiana.

CITATIONS FOR OTHER SOURCES USED

1. *Eulogy for a Fighter Pilot* written by Pat Conroy for his father's (Colonel Don *The Great Santini* Conroy) memorial service was used as the basic model for writing my *Eulogy for a Hybrid Pilot* in Chapter 27.

978-0-595-87701-0
0-595-87701-X

Printed in the United States
80612LV00007B/4-9

9 780595 877010